Children of Eld

~ A Book of Stories ~

By Jordan Mackay

GOBLIN PRESS

Goblin Press, an imprint of Eco-Justice Press, L.L.C.
Goblin Press
P.O. Box 5409 Eugene, OR 97405
www.ecojusticepress.com

Children of Eld
By Jordan Mackay

Library of Congress Control Number: 2024936112
ISBN 978-1-945432-64-4

The Potentially Unnecessary Introduction to the Book Reviews

Here are the reviews of the first six people who have read this book all the way through so far.

These reviewers are the extraordinary type of people who are willing to beta-read a book during the messy phase when it is being written, and then are kind enough to write a last-minute review for it. They did me a great favor by doing so, and now I ask you to do them a favor in return: please accept their honest critique with the same gravitas as you would have accepted the paid critique of some nameless reviewer at a national company, or some highly paid celebrity. *(The few celebrities I happen to be acquainted with would have been unusually weird choices for book reviews.)*

So, without further ado:

The Book Reviews of the First Six Readers

"*Children of Eld* ranks in the top five fantasy books I've ever read. The characters are intriguing and relatable, with gifts to discover and flaws to overcome. The world is rich with imagery, engaging all the senses while leaving proper room for the reader's imagination to fill in the gaps. Fans of Patrick Rothfuss in particular will enjoy the thoughtful and inspired storytelling, which draws the reader deep into a lucid dream-like narrative. *Children of Eld* is a strong start to what will certainly become a beloved fantasy series."
Jeffrey Behrends, *General Contractor*

"Mackay breathes raw and real life into his characters to create a tale as heart-wrenching as it is bolstering, as playful as it is profound. In lush and visceral detail, he crafts an intricate world full of mystery, all interwoven with a coming-of-age tale that reminds me of how much adventure is still out there, and how important loving friendship can be."
Thea Abbatoy, *Naturalist*

"Jordan Mackay is my favorite storyteller. Every sentence of this book is beautifully and poetically written, and the characters of this novel will stay with me forever. I recommend *Children of Eld* to everyone!"
Nokomis Baze, *Head Tavern Wench*

"Mourn the loss of childhood and cheer the persistence of bravery; this beautiful novel examines how experience, emotion and sacrifice can shape an individual and forge a family. Mr. Mackay has created a lush world saturated with magic and riveting adventure!"
Jennifer Tang, *Homemaker*

"*Children of Eld* is a rare gem amongst fantasy novels! An ensemble of erstwhile heroes driven not by lofty ideals or worn-out tropes, but rather, drawn into the action of their very real and complicated humanity. It is a coming-of-age story, a true hero's journey where the young protagonists face overwhelming odds and malevolent supernatural forces, but also their own fears and flaws. *Children of Eld* reminds us that no matter how fragile we feel, we are made stronger by standing together."
Noah McLain, *Dragon Wrangler*

"In the beginning there was darkness, as there always is."
"Thus begins the *Children of Eld,* a remarkable book of intertwined stories. From the magical birth of Rahyn to the bone-crushing accident that nearly takes Melvin's life, [Jordan Mackay] weaves an enchanting tale of six unlikely heroes which Fate has brought together. The resulting book does not disappoint! According to the acknowledgements, some of these characters were thirty years in the making. As in all truly great fiction, it shows.
David Peyerwold, *retired Attorney Editor, C.E.B.*

This book is dedicated to Zyla, who finished the journey with me —
and to Frances, who began it.
Without the loving support and patience from both of you, this work
would not exist.

It is also dedicated to my dear old friend Katrina, whose first comment
on the story
was a gut punch that I have been laughing about ever since.
"Clearly brevity is not what you were going for."

No, Kat. It was not.

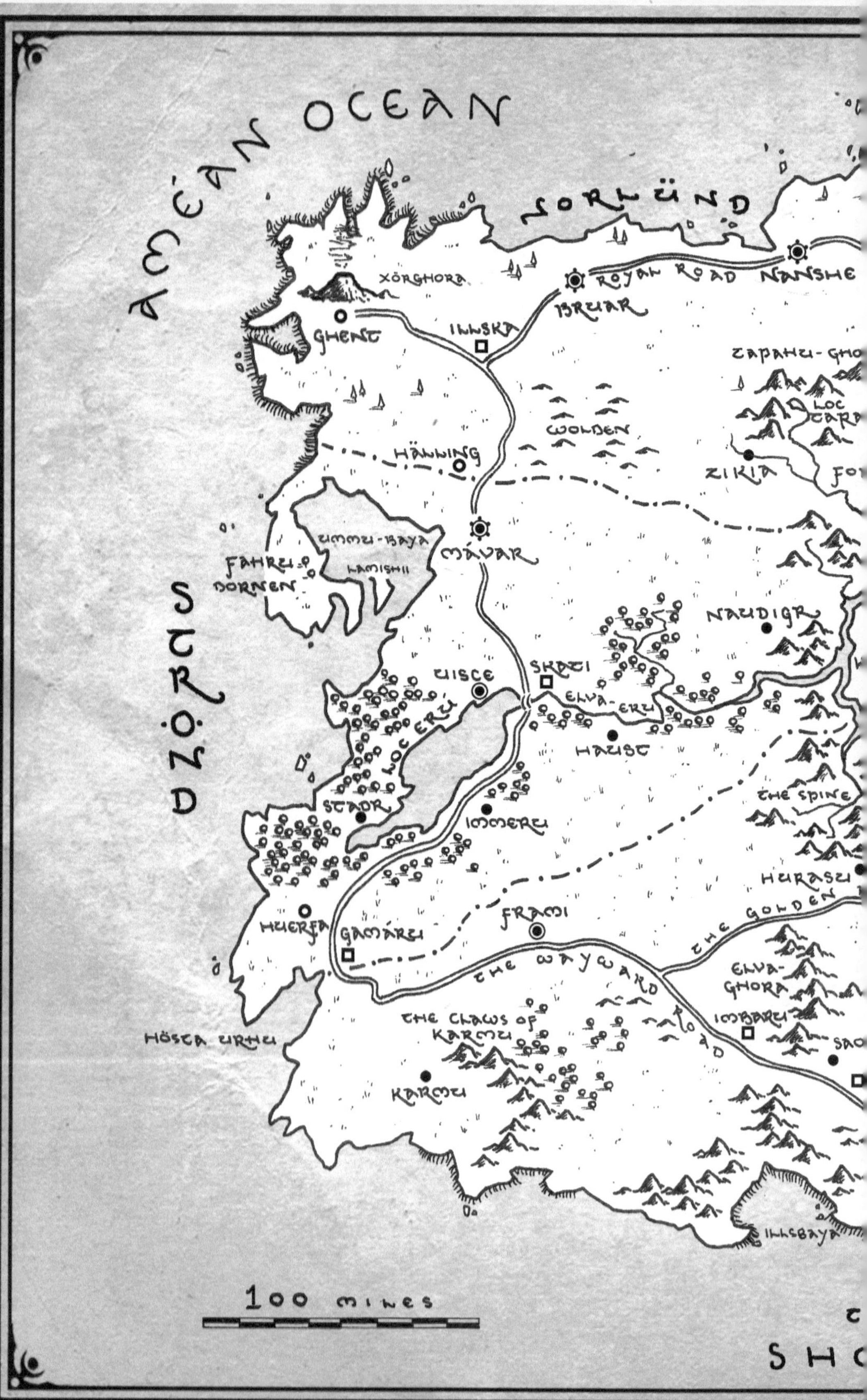

ÆMÉAN OCEAN
NORLÜND
XÖRGHORA
ROYAL ROAD
NANSHE
BRUAR
ILLSKA
GHENT
ZAPATU-GHO
LOC CARA
WOLDEN
ZIKLA
FO
HÄNNING
ZIMMU-BAYA
MÁVAR
FAHRU-DORNEN
LAMISHII
NAUDIGR
SJÖRD
UISCE
SKATI
ELVA-ERU
LOC ERU
HAUSE
THE SPINE
STADR
IMMERU
HURASU
HUERFA
GAMÁRU
FRAMI
THE GOLDEN
ELVA-GHORA
IMBARU
SAO
THE WAYWARD ROAD
THE CLAWS OF KARMU
KARMU
HÖSTA URTU
ILLSBAYA
SHO
100 MILES

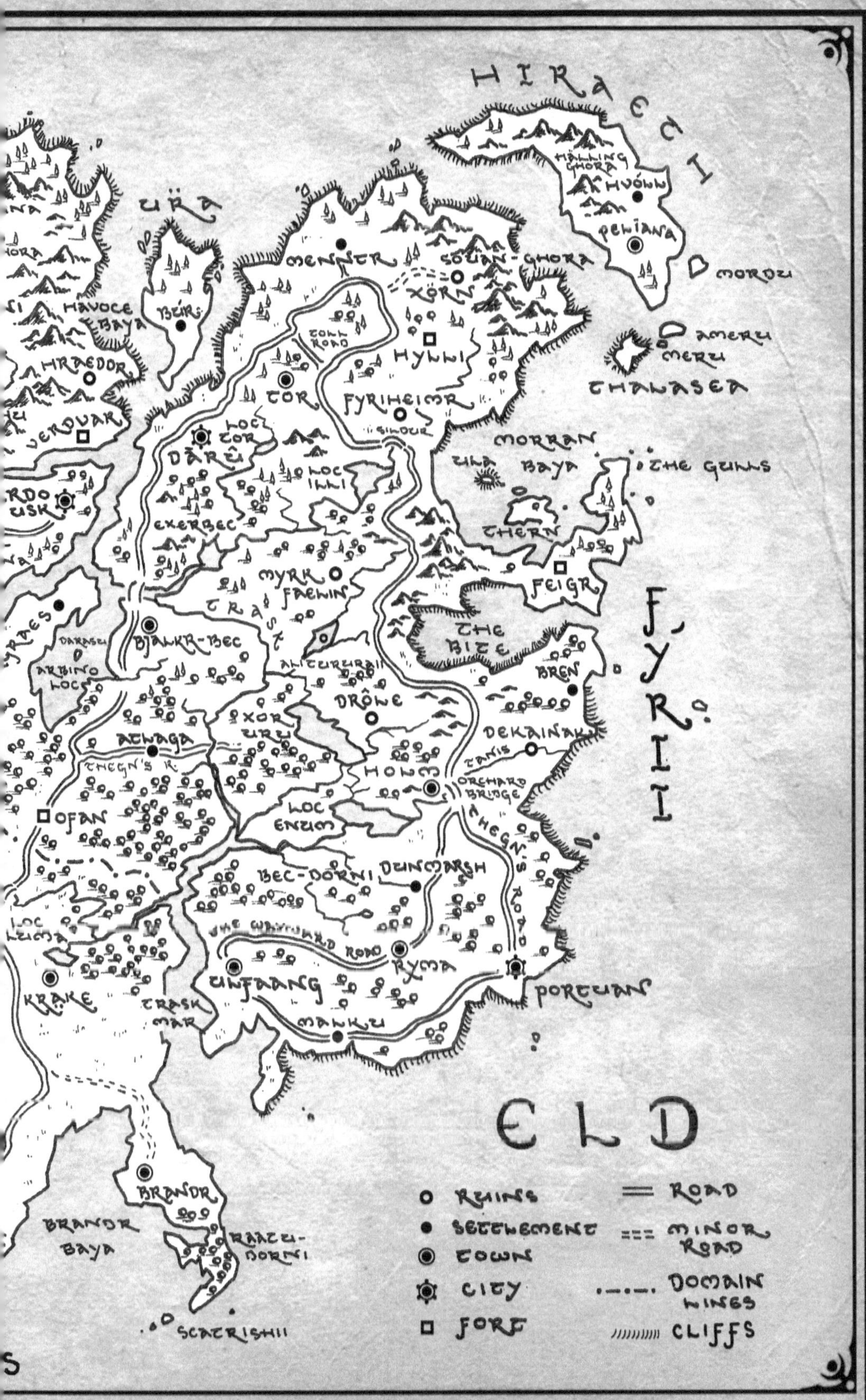

HIRAECI
CÜRA
MENNIR
SOUAN-GHORA
XORN
HYLNI
FYRIHEIMR
TOLL ROAD
COR
LOC COR
DÄREI
LOC INNI
EXERBEC
MYRK FAENIN
TRASK
BJALKR-BEC
DARASEI
ARBINO LOCE
ALICUREIBII
DRÔNE
AEWAGA
THEGN'S R.
EXOR UREI
HOLM
OFAN
LOC ENUM
LOC LEICHI
KRAKE
TRASK MAR
BEC-DORNI
DUNMARSH
THE WAYWARD ROAD
UNFAANG
RYMA
MANKU
BRANDR
BRANDR BAYA
RAATEI-DORNI
SCATRISHII
MORRAN BAYA
THE GULLS
CULA
THERN
FEIGR
THE BILE
BREN
DEKAINAK
TANIS
ORCHARD BRIDGE
A THEGN'S ROAD
PORTUAN
FYRII
HALLING GHORA
HVÓNN
PEWIANA
MORDI
AMERU
MERU
THALASEA
ELD
RUINS — ROAD
SETTLEMENT === MINOR ROAD
TOWN
CITY ·—·—· DOMAIN LINES
FORT ///////// CLIFFS
HAVOCE BAYA
HRAEDOR
VERDUAR
RDO USK
YPAES
S

Table of Contents

Introduction

"With no heart, the monstrous creature would not be animated by purpose. It must never learn its true purpose, for such a creature was surely made to devour the world that birthed it."

INTRODUCTION

In the beginning there was darkness, as there always is. A vast ocean of emptiness with waves of dark matter rolling along unimpeded through the void. They were colorless ripples of vacuous nothing, unimaginably deep and unendingly wide.

Then came the first Celestials. They came into being with a great rending of light and heat and energy. In the instance of their spontaneous birth, they created the very first force the universe had ever known: causality. The relationship between something and something else. The idea of *something,* at all. In the ripping instance of their birth, they wrote the only laws that nature has ever bothered to adhere to. Everything became anything, and anything became possible.

These Celestials were imbued with the purest reason — an intellect beyond the boundaries of comprehension. They smoldered with radiant plasma and lit the infinite sea with light. Each of them traveled on secret paths through the deep, and wherever they went, perfect destruction rippled before them, and perfect creation followed in their wake. Some were content to dance alone, spinning in celebration as an island of light. Many birthed smaller celestials, which cooled in the chilly ether and or bited around them. We will never know why they did; perhaps they were lonely, if such emotion is possible to a being so grand. But every single planet and every single moon was a miracle of creative energy from the moment of its birth. Each was a wonder of structure and opportunity. Some throbbed with molten heat, and some were swept barren by the roaring of solar winds. Some were dense and tightly formed, while others churned in colorful ripples of gases, miming a shape of solidarity as a ghost mimics the life it once led. Each of these celestial progenies were completely unique, and staggeringly beautiful.

One of these great glowing Celestials had an offspring that carried within it a rare gift: the Hum of Creation. This vibration is the cosmic milk on which that rarest possibility — organic life — can feed. A lesser

Celestial with music like that vibrating inside of it can awaken beings of clever potential, and this one did. This was the planet called Homm. That was its True Name, though there was no one yet to speak it but its parent star. This star, which was called Uros, whispered the name of *Homm* in loving oscillation, over and over in an unending mantra. Thusly did Homm fill itself with the power of that Hum of Creation until liquid heat shone up from underground, and slow rivers of gold and iron flowed in superheated magma inside its heart. Uros loved its planet Homm with the bright heat of a devoted star.

On the surface of the planet, all was the primordial chaos of creation — striations of carbon and crystal venting superheated gases. Boiling helium clouds mingled with exhalations of hydrogen and phosphorous from the planet's surface and formed tornados that glowed like foxfire and were visible from deep space. Over time, its Hum of Creation brought hydrogen and oxygen together, and its deepest crevices filled with water. The fits of infancy stilled, and the hot volatility that had been everything it knew matured into cooler layers, warmed from within by the secret heat of its True Name.

Uros gave Homm what attention it could, but it had other children and the insistence of its own divine purpose to attend to. To shine, as Uros shone, was a great effort indeed. A planet that carries the Hum of Creation inside it is a child with special needs. It cannot be bathed in careless radiation, or it would sterilize that hum. The temperature on the planet's surface cannot flux overmuch, or nothing will ever root and evolve. Uros let Homm drift further and further away from the comforting embrace of gravity to help it grow up, but the separation was hard on them both. With the drifting of the parent star, Homm was left ever more alone to explore itself. The expanding universe spun around it, and it turned inward to delve the inner mysteries of its own miasmatic depths, losing interest in the void that surrounded it. And that is why Homm never saw the hurtling approach of a bright stranger.

....

A ribbon of trailing flame erupted from behind the stranger as it streaked towards the planet. When it collided with Homm, the impact rocked the planet to its core. Hot magma oozed out of hundreds of wounds cracked across the planet's surface, and a cloud of superheated particles lifted and spun in such force that they blanketed the atmosphere.

Homm could no longer see Uros at all, and without the light of its star, the planet's surface grew cold to the touch for the very first time. Homm had never felt such violation of self, and when the stranger arose from where it had fallen to look around, Homm gathered its essence into an entity of equal size and stood up to meet it. Never before had the planet given birth to anything. It had always been occupied with the endlessness of self-perfection. But in that moment, it gave over the permission of will to its own creation and set it loose to deal with the stranger from space that had incited evolution through violent impact.

At its full height, the stranger was so tall that its feet sunk into the ground and its head almost crested the dust-choked atmosphere. Much of its original form had burned away in its descent to the planet, and the body that remained whirled with gases and flames.

The Giant that had been birthed out of the ground of Homm arose to stand face to face with this being from space. This giant's body was made of the solid rock and proto-soil of the planet itself, and the purest water filled its veins. It had been made in response to this threat from the void, and it would destroy it if it must. The two great beings observed each other for the age of a moment, and then in one erupting motion they set to grappling. They smashed and tore at each other, and the surface of the young world was trampled beneath them.

....

For Celestials, there is no need for duality. Everything is multiplic-itous, as creation is infinite, and destruction is just creation recycling itself to prepare for more creation. Duality is therefore brutishly simple, but in such simplicity is the secret to something that Uros could have never taught to Homm. Because hidden in this staggering simplicity is the fundamental recipe for organic life. It is the component combination that turns the Hum of Creation into a full-throated song.

They changed as they grappled, those two giants. The burning one, whose skin was a tornado of flames surrounding a molten heart, took on an aspect that wished to delve inside of things, to rearrange and break and build up again. It was churning wind and leveling fire. It was restless, and it was angry. But it found itself dizzy with longing for an aspect other than its own nature.

The earthen one, whose heart was a ruby suspended in the rushing of an underground river, took on an aspect that wished to flow into everything — to absorb, to perfect, to challenge and protect. It was fertile earth that contained the womb of a hidden lake. It was restless, and it was angry. But it found itself dizzy with longing for an aspect other than its own nature.

The fight between those two giants changed the nature of the surface of Homm. Where they strode, their feet kicked up mountains and depressed concavities that filled with water and formed lakes. Where they fell upon each other and grappled, oceans deepened and shelves of land were thrust up into the light, with great waterfalls of seawater pouring over them. Sometimes they tore up massive juts of rock and simply hurled them at each other. They fought for an age without meaning. But even as they fought, they could not help but grow excited at one another. After all, they were each the only other being that either of them had ever met. Their prolonged struggle had choked the atmosphere with dust, and the light of Uros barely reached them at all anymore. With such little sunlight available, the temperature plummeted until the surface of Homm became encased by glaciers of ice as tall as mountains. The winds that had been stirred up by their mighty quarrel gusted across the world with such force that snow blinded what dust did not, and they could scarcely see one another anymore. And at last, they stilled, for each grew afraid that the other would be lost to them entirely. They groped blindly through the howling dusty darkness and the driving snow and despaired of ever seeing each other again. Then a touch of earthen fingers, and a wrapping arm of flame, and they sunk to their knees in the frozen cataclysm their fighting had created of the world, and simply held each other.

I assume you can guess what happened next. If you can't, I'm sorry for you. It was great.

....

The storm blew out at last, and the wind abated, and while they lay there and got to know each other better, the dust settled enough for the light of Uros to reach the planet's surface. Homm, feeling the comforting warmth again on its skin, relaxed and returned to the contemplation of its own nature. The giants curled up together and enjoyed one another for their interesting differences, and appreciated the ways in which they were very much the same. And while they did so, they barely noticed the change their blooming love had brought to the land around them.

Life. It formed in the soil their struggles had carried so far across the planet. It formed first underneath where they lay together, in the dampness of her pleasure. It grew as a web of mycelium that spread and spread until it wove a dense tapestry underground. Through this web, nutrients flowed everywhere. Where his pleasure spilled to the earth, it became helpful worms that moved through the rich clay and worked with the mycelium net to further fertilize the soil. Though the surface of the planet was still scarred from their fighting, underground the world was beginning to proliferate with life. And, in the due course of things, so was she.

....

The Giant of Earth and Water swelled in great proportion, for it was twins that grew inside of her. When at last she gave birth, it was to two spheres of perfect proportion. They were rich with the elements of their parents, but the proud Celestial lineage of Homm was obvious as well. The first born was a beautiful dusky red and glowed with a warm light. The second born was very pale, and held within it no radiance at all. When the giants looked at what they had made, they were well pleased. They named the red sphere Ember and the white sphere Ash, as it was born without an inner fire of its own. The twins looked at each other and knew how similar they were, and how different. They nodded in shared understanding. The giants scooped their children up proudly and held them as high as they could above their heads, releasing them into the sky, where they became two moons.

Then the Giant of Earth and Water cried out in pain, for she was not done with her birthing labors after all. A third child was coming forth. And this one looked nothing like the other two and brought with it such pain in delivery that both parents feared that the giantess would die of it. The third child tore from its mother in a shudder of spines and claws, and the two giants held each other and marveled at its ferocity. It was a creature born of the last of their anger for one another. It was the first monster, and it was terrifying to behold. The body was formed of stone flesh, with a skeleton of platinum and arsenic. Bones of raw ore pushed up from its back in rows of spikes, peaking into two great horns growing out of its head. It had a mouth as wide as a river, with rows of obsidian teeth. It immediately ate the sack of earthen fluid it was born in and

would have started in on the mother herself if the Giant of Fire and Air
had not swept it up quickly and hurled it away, far across the mountains.
Both giants simply stared at each other for a long while, wondering what
they had done.

Then they looked down and saw a strange sight — the creature had
been born with its heart outside of its body. A pulsing iron ore laced with
veins of fire; it lay there at their feet with the fluids of birth still sizzling on
it. The Giant of Earth and Water wrapped it up in a cocoon of stone, and
buried it deep underground, filling the wide valley around it with a new
ocean. With no heart, the monstrous creature would not be animated
by purpose. It must never learn its true purpose, for such a creature was
surely made to devour the world that birthed it.

The Giants named their monstrous offspring *Terrasque* — which was
the first Word to describe a hunger that cannot be satisfied — and tried
to think no more about the wicked thing that their anger had birthed. But
guilt is not so easily buried as an iron heart.

....

And yet, the heart itself did not remain buried forever. Uncountable
ages after the Giantess drew an ocean up around it, the heart of the Terrasque was forced out of the deep by the eruption of a submerged volcano.
It rose towards the surface, sweeping ever further out to sea on boiling
currents of lava. As the molten stone cooled, it surrounded the iron heart
in spiny layers of igneous rock, until a mighty island was formed.

Eventually plants got a foothold on the barren landscape, and animals followed. Layers of dirt built up from cycles of growth and decay,
softening the face of the new island from a jagged stonescape to a place of
rarified beauty. The island crested into a mountainous spine, descending
from those lofted peaks into plains of dunes and grasses on one side, and
a vast primeval forest on the other, split almost in twain by the branching
path of a mighty river.

Much later — so much later that time itself had finally been loosed
on the world — the Children of Water sailed away from the distant mainland and settled there, claiming the island for themselves through force.
For they were not the first people to inhabit the island, and they would
not be the last. Conquest was to shape the destiny of that island; a legacy

of violence and war that was perhaps stirred by the secret pulsing of a monster's buried heart.

This island came to be known as Eld, and Eld is where our story begins.

There were two young people who loved each other very much, and one of them died for it. But the child their love created survived, and that child and her friends would grow up to change the fate of their entire island.

PROLOGUE
A Burning Road

It was a midsummer scorcher of a day: brutal to be working in such heat. The stones of the road were like loaves baking under an oven sky. Thralls who toiled to set and kerb them had to wrap the stones in cloth, for they were too hot to carry bare-handed. The air shimmered; water seemed to evaporate from thirsty tongues that could never get enough of it. Already three thralls were unconscious from heat-stroke, left to recover or die with the sun still cooking them. They sprawled in the gutter ditch or lay on the underlayment of hard-packed sand and broken tile. Those thralls who were still on their feet stepped over them to keep working. To pause their labors and try to help the fallen would invite nine strokes from the stinging lash. The threat of sunburn on fresh wounds discouraged all who thought to try.

Just ahead lay the inviting shade of the mighty forest known as the Eldwood. Its cooling shadows teased like a tantalizing mirage a scant hundred paces further ahead from where they labored in the heat. They had worked for eight months, through rain and snow and punishing heat, to get from where the Orchard Bridge crossed the river Tanis to where they were now: cresting the top of High Hill. The Thegn's Road was now about three miles longer for their labors. Eighteen had died so far — eighteen in eight months. It was a better year than last. Some had frozen, and some had tried to run. Two were crushed by tumbling stone at the quarry; worse still, a company mason had broken his foot. One thrall had lain down in a flooded culvert on a rainy night and let the rushing water carry the last of her breath away. And now they toiled in this heat: this terrible heat made worse by the reflective gravel and the glittering shards of pottery that crunched sharply underfoot as they hauled the heavy paving stones into their set rows. The gloom of the forest beckoned, of course — but it would be days before they made it to the edge of the tree line. Some of the thralls would not live that long.

....

Many of us will die by nightfall.

Ehlon was sure of it — as sure as a slave can be of anything — for that night, he would try to run. He toiled at the front, digging the trench that would soon be filled with sand and gravel. Wrapped around the shovel handle, his hands felt hot and dusty: hands that permanently ached and didn't legally belong to him anymore. In another life Ehlon had been a farmer — another life that had ended some years ago when he was imprisoned for land debts he could not afford to pay. *A year in a cell and two years a thrall on the Thegn's Road.* Nobody had expected him to live through it. He had already been recorded as lawfully deceased, and his lands thusly forfeit to the aristocracy. The hangman's dance was considered more merciful — but only by the people who had suffered building roads in the summertime.

Ehlon trenched his way through the midday heat, digging the road uphill towards the forest by labored inches. When the bread and water-skin were finally passed around, he rested in the shadow of a gravel barrel and watched the sky darken with gathering clouds. *A good omen.* It was a drought year, the fourth in a row, and the understory of the forest edge was dry and thirsty, *just like me. We are the same, the plants and I — all we can hope for is a little rain.*

Ehlon stared down into the valley below. There spread the patchwork fields and thatched houses of Holm: a farming town, spread out in the fertile valley beneath the forested rise on which they labored. His gaze followed the pale line of the road he had helped to build. The road descended out of sight around the curve of the hill, then reappeared down below on the valley floor. It passed by the small crofts of poorer farmers at the edge of town. It passed the larger fields of landed families and the grape and fruit orchards of the merchants who had made deals with invaders generations ago to keep their land while others went away to war. The road passed the public tannery and the wainright's yard. It passed the forge, the scaffold of the old gallows, and the grassy commons where the weekly market was held.

In front of the Welcome Holm tavern the Thegn's Road abruptly butted into the much older Wayward Road. Where they intersected, the differences in the roads were stark. The Thegn's Road looked efficiently modern. It was properly crowned to shed rain. Rows of paving stones were uniform in shape and color, like rows of gray soldiers in a ready line. There were efficient drainage ditches with kerb stones nestled like eggs into crushed gravel. It was a beautiful, terrible road. Ehlon was proud of every inch of it and hated it profoundly. By comparison, the Wayward was a cautionary tale of countless centuries of use. Its surface was a mess of weeds and cobbles. What stones still remained in the road were the gathered colors of chance and might have travelled here all the way from the sea. The majority of the road was patterns of ruts over ground that had been compressed to stony hardness. In summer, the road danced with dust; in winter, it was slick with icy mud. It looked *ancient*, because it was.

Away to the west, Ehlon heard the first growl of summer thunder. It was soft and far away, as though the sinking sun was grumbling on its way to bed. Deepening layers of cloud purpled the horizon. A bright column of lightning flashed: once, twice. *A bad omen, if no rain follows. Please rain, I beg your mercy in just this one thing. For Áine.* Slick ground and reduced visibility from a summer downpour might give Áine and he a chance. The chance to make sure that she and the baby would live through the night.

....

Áine was no Erdin thrall, nor was she free. She was the daughter of the family that cooked to feed the fifty or so women and men who slaved to build the road and the soldiers that guarded them. Her family was well-off, by local standards, for they had orchards of pears and walnuts that were generations old. She had plenty of local suitors; her parents had vaguely promised her in marriage a couple of times already on drunken evenings, and she knew they meant to strike a sober bargain soon enough. Her time as herself was almost over. Soon she would belong to someone else, as completely as the thralls who toiled before her day after day while she fed them bread and horsemeat and occasionally snuck them jam. But she knew that wedding day could never come, for she was in love with a thrall named Ehlon, and that was unthinkable. She had fed him for months and loved him for almost as long. Thrice she had joined him in pleasure when he was awake at watch, and his chain leash was long enough to seek some measure of privacy behind a canvas lean-to. One of those stolen evenings had grown inside her, and now she was heavy with child.

She hid it as carefully as a clever woman can, for loose clothing was in fashion, and a woven cloak is a good preserver of false modesty. She was often away from home cooking at the laborer's camp, and she carefully avoided visits from her parents. But after months of ripening she was now too rounded even for a draped cloak, and no layers of cloth would hide an infant's wail. If her love for Ehlon was discovered, it would mean his death and her disgrace. So she must run, and he must go with her. It was tonight. It had to be tonight. She cradled her swollen belly protectively beneath her cloak and felt the kicking of tiny feet inside her. She stared longingly at the deepening shadows of the Eldwood, and imagined never seeing her home again. Behind her, clouds as dark and tall as mountains were drifting across the valley. The sunlight of late afternoon was strangled into patches, and then vanished entirely. Thunder rolled, and a dry wind gusted up the hill.

....

As the road project had neared the edge of the Eldwood, the thegn decided to push the forest itself out of the way. This plan, it turned out, was easier envisioned than completed. The dry underbrush and giant ferns were hacked back quickly enough, but even at the edge of the Eldwood, the fortress oaks that grew in this part of the forest were many hundreds of feet tall from root to crown, with a canopy that spread even further side to side. The measure of those tree trunks was so wide that all the thralls standing shoulder to shoulder could not have encircled one. It took weeks for the blacksmith in Holm to design a saw of such cumbersome length and width that it could stretch the diameter of one trunk, with seven people pulling on each side. The blade of that saw was a nightmare of forge-welded sections and was almost as wide as a wagon cart. Now it had been in use for two months. Nine of the colossal trees had been felled so far: their corpses had smashed the understory to either side of the road. The severed stumps that remained where they had once stood were like empty stages with jagged splinters as big as spears. One dying tree was nearly felled: a heavy wedge already removed from one side, and the enormous saw buried halfway deep. Its dry branches creaked with ominous strain in the ripple of rising wind.

....

The captain called the work crew off unusually early that afternoon. The cooks at the feed wagon grumbled and hurried at prepping for early dinner. The thralls were gathered into their usual rows to be leashed to their five-line before the evening meal. It was in clusters of five that they were expected to attend to their personal needs; a stout leather leash running neck to neck through iron collars with six feet of space between them. If one person needed to use the latrine, then their other four leash partners were forced to tag along and did the best they could to look away. They ate and slept in that same arrangement. Bathing was a rare and complicated feat. Groups of women were leashed together, men likewise, and the separation between them was enforced by different feeding times. The men slept in simple canvas lean-to tents, five in a row. The women slept on the opposite side of the camp, near the soldiers. There was much atrocity that occurred on dark nights that was not spoken of in daylight hours.

The evening settled in, and the wind arose. Dinner was brief and artless, for the cooks were anxious to get home before the storm broke. An hour before twilight, the thralls were ordered into the shelter of their lean-tos. Only Áine remained behind at the cook wagon, carefully scrubbing every pot and pan far past the point of clean. The soldiers that weren't on a rotation of watch settled into their tents or played bones around a campfire. Normal evening noises were muffled by the rising boom of thunder, crackling across the valley in rolling waves of sound, chased by flashes of searing ozone.

In his tent, Ehlon sawed furiously at the cording of his leash with the hidden knife that Áine had slipped him at dinner. The leather was as thick as rope, and the knife was dull. Ehlon was propped on one elbow, and in the wan firelight, he could see the eyes of his fellow thralls shining in the dark. Not a word was spoken out loud, but the oldest of them squeezed his hand roughly and shook his head in the gloom. It was known that if one slave broke the line and tried to run, all five of them would be hung for it as a punitive example. The fate of one was the fate of all. If they wished to save themselves, each of the other men had only to call out to a guard before the leash broke, and Ehlon alone would dangle at the hangman's gibbet. Ehlon felt the men beside him tensing as he sawed through their last moments of slavery; he heard the fearful hitch of their breathing. There in the dark of the tent, their silence was all the support they could offer, but it rang in Ehlons' ears as loudly as singing. Gratitude filled him with such force that his hands began to shake, and he could no longer see them through the blurring of sudden tears.

Then the rope parted from his neck, and the five men launched out of their tent in a dusty stumbling run, pulling the leash apart between them. Four of them sprinted for the equipment cart, where picks and shovels were stored. The fifth ran to Áine. A surprised guardsman was gagged and throttled to death at that cart by eight hands; the drumming of his kicking legs was overrolled by thunder. Into the cart the desperate thralls burrowed, grasping in the dark for anything with a hickory handle. Someone shouted from across the camp. Then everyone was shouting.

Áine folded Ehlon in her arms for one breathless hug. Then she grasped up a boning knife, and together they ran towards the deepest green of the Eldwood. They did not make it fifty steps before their escape into darkness was torn apart by light.

With a sizzling pop, lightning struck the half-felled oak that towered above the camp. It tore through branch and trunk, arcing with radiance across the long saw blade lodged in its gut. Instantly the water inside the tree boiled, and the lowest center of the massive tree exploded into sinuous wedges of flame, hurling chunks of superheated bark. The booming of thunder overlapped the explosion, and a terrible rending groan began that was itself so loud that the lovers tumbled to their knees, concussed by the roar and blinded by the glare. Fire erupted up the tree in a wound that split all the way towards the highest branches. Immediately the fortress oak kindled into a flaming torch four hundred feet tall.

The flare of heat-cooked skin and sizzled hair pressed the lovers back and apart, each fleeing in desperate instinct. Áine called out to Ehlon, but the crackling noise of the burning giant was everything that could be heard over the hot rushing of wind. In the awful light of this sudden evening sun, she saw moments severed from meaning. A woman she had fed for months stood over a fallen soldier, hacking at his throat with a shovel. A tumbling rain of burning bark as large as horses smashed tents with people huddled inside them. Half-naked men tore at each other with their bare hands or gaped in wordless awe at the burning behemoth that towered above them like a wrathful god. Then a sudden thrust of wind caught the tree head-on, and it swayed, intact, for the very last time. Foundations tore: cambium from sapwood, sapwood from heartwood, and the sound of all of it separating was like screaming — the howl of a thousand-year life ending in fire. Then the tree began to topple, twisting in a burning spiral as it fell onto the road, the camp, and everyone.

....

Áine and her unborn child fled deeper into the forest, weeping as she ran. She had imagined this moment for months. She and Ehlon would have escaped, hand in hand, and although the soldiers might pursue them with cunning, they would have prevailed. It could have taken days to outpace them, of course. But she was young enough to assume that all would be well: Ehlon would help her raise their child in peace, deep in the forest, in a house they would build for themselves.

Yet life is everything unpredictable that happens between daydreams. She never imagined she would be alone, fleeing from the gaining tide of a forest fire. She did not know that flames could move as fast as wind. She had not imagined that she would see, in the minds-eye moment that she could never forget, the sight of Ehlon holding his hands up to the sky in reverent surrender as the giant tree bore down upon him. Long after the memories of her old life drifted away from her, that image would remain: the terrible beauty of his surrender.

All around her, the storm tore at the forest. The air was lit by flashes of leaping lightning and shook with the percussion of thunder. Eventually, she outran the screaming of the slaves and soldiers, though drafts of hot wind continued to be haunted by it. Flaming cinders rattled through the canopy, pattering down all around her like hellish rain. The litter of dry branches underfoot caught and ignited.

Exhausted beyond bearing, at the ridge of a low hill, Áine finally rested. There she lay for a long while, heaving lungfuls of breath. She may have slept, for she closed her eyes on a dark hillside, and when she opened them again, she was gagging on updrafts of smoke. She came staggering to her feet, one hand covering her stinging eyes and the other holding her swollen belly, and fled.

She was a stranger to these woods and had no craft or lore to guide her. It would have done her little good either way, for sight was obscured by billowing smoke and everything distorted by the leaping of sudden firelight. Tangled underbrush tripped her and tore at her cruelly. She could not breathe but in smoky gasps and was forced to crawl as often as not, with her child-heavy belly dragging beneath her. Twice she stumbled to her knees and vomited until there was nothing left inside but char and bile and the raw taste of her own throat. That second time she fell, she felt her ankle twist brutally, and shards of gasping pain pierced her mind. She lay there for a while, dazed with pain, listening to the roar of popping sap and the hungry crackling of dry branches all around her.

There was no more fear left in her for her own life — only the deepest kind of exhaustion, the sort that forgives death as it approaches when all the toil of running must surely be done. Yet she did not give up, limping through the heat and haze although the pain was awful. Mothers are fearsome beings when their cubs are threatened, capable of miraculous fortitude. Áine outran a forest fire in the dark on a twisted ankle, and her unborn daughter would survive to thank her for it.

....

At last, Áine came to a place that felt different. The dry understory had been replaced by giant ferns. They towered above her, and the moss underfoot was as thick as a blanket. She lay down on the forest floor for a while, her breath hitching rapidly in her throat. She did not have long to rest, for the smoke was thickening in the air around her, and hot light danced behind it. Her foot had now become so swollen that she could no longer hobble on it. So she crawled forward through the moss, towards a place where moonslight could be seen between the trees.

The canopy thinned above her as she crawled until she found herself at the edge of a large clearing. In the center of it lay a massive stone, so like a dead tree in appearance that one side of it even seemed to flare and branch like roots. It lay mostly buried, with only the topmost side visible above ground, tipped at a slight angle upward from the roots. The light of two moons poured across it, red and yellow, and from where she lay, Áine could see the likeness of a massive boar carved into the stone tree. Lichen grew in the carving, making the lines appear to glow greenly in the shifting layers of moonslight. The trees around the clearing bent inward towards where the petrified tree lay, as though doing reverence to it. Anywhere else in the forest, those trees would have grown above the clearing and closed it in, reaching for access to sunlight. But when that ancient tree had fallen, so long ago that time had turned its stump into stone; nothing had grown up to replace its place in the light.

Another strange thing about the clearing was the air. It was clean!

Above her, the night sparkled with stars. Around the ring of the clearing, the creeping smoke was drunk down into the ground between the roots of the trees. It looked like a waterfall pouring slowly over invisible rocks, as though the tree roots were drinking the smoke in. For anyone who had not spent the entire night running for their lives, it would have been an eerie sight. For Áine, she felt so deeply tired that she was willing to look a miracle straight in the face and call it luck. She crawled into the center of the grove, dragging herself right between the spread of the stone roots, where she lay down on the thick moss that grew there and fell asleep.

....

Áine awoke so long thereafter that twilight was spreading in the eastern sky. She had dreamed of Ehlon, but in the dream, she could not quite remember his face. She was powerfully thirsty, and her nose and throat were thick with ashes and the caustic residue of bile. Her arms were still asleep — they lay slack and tingling on the curve of her belly. She vaguely wondered if she had the strength to find water, or even if she cared to bother. The moss was so thick and soft, and the evening dark was closing in. She rolled carefully over and lay down again in a new position, favoring the darkest patch of undisturbed moss she could see. As she stretched her arms out, but a few moments from a second sleep, her fingers felt dampness in the soil. With her ear pressed so to the ground, she could hear the faintest burbling of running water.

Lifting herself into a half squat, Áine slowly peeled up the moss and leaf cover with her hands, too weak to be properly frantic. Under the living carpet, a little rivulet of clean water was trickling. The little spring was so shallow she could not cup her hands into it, so she laid her cheek to the soil and slurped at the water through the side of her mouth. She swallowed a considerable amount of mud with each gulping mouthful, but she didn't mind that at all.

....

It is worth wondering whether these muddy mouthfuls of that particular water were partly responsible for what became of her later. Taking soil that has touched both sides of the sunrise into your body is even more transformative than drinking the water, for flowing water wanders from place to place between worlds and does not linger overlong on one side or the other. Had Áine simply fallen back to sleep after drinking deeply of that spring, her life and the life of her future daughter would have turned out quite differently.

She did not fall asleep again, and that is what matters. She stayed awake and dug the moss away with her hands to get a better look at the flow of the rivulet spring. We often underestimate the importance of small decisions.

....

Áine drank from the muddy trickle for a long time and felt greatly revived by doing so. Although twilight was drawing in, sunlight still warmed the surface of the moss under the petrified tree's stone roots. She could now see that the moss grew so thickly there because much of the area was wet with moisture. Therefore, because she was curious and because she was human and didn't know better, she dug a bunch of it up with her hands.

Moss soon piled up all around her; the small trickle of water could be seen clearly now — only a handspan wide and two knuckles deep. The water looked so good that she leaned in to drink from it again, instinctively putting the crown of her head towards the petrified tree. The ground sloped away gently downhill from the tree; the spring must therefore source from under the fallen tree, and water is always cleanest at the source. However, when Áine leaned down to drink, she got a nose full of flowing water and sat back up again, leaking and coughing. When she had sneezed the last of it out, she wiped her face and stared at the water in confusion. The colors of twilight played across the surface in a thousand sparkles of rolling light. *Yet the light was moving towards the tree.* She gaped in amazement and watched the impossible working steadily against the certainty of gravity. Without a doubt, the little rivulet spring was flowing uphill.

She followed its progress with her eyes and noted where it vanished beneath the moss at the branching base of the fallen tree roots. The moss there was slick with moisture, and the tiniest burbling could be heard above the evening sounds of birdsong.

Curiosity is the cousin to obsession, and Áine now felt the thrill of it building. She knelt amongst the stone roots, which splayed out over her head like enormous, petrified tentacles. Here she dug with her hands, right against the base of the tree, at the spot where water darkened the soil. She dug straight down into the rich red mud, piling it beside her in ever-growing mounds. After some time, it became apparent that the petrified tree trunk was much thicker than she at first supposed, for she kept digging and found yet more of it buried belowground. She marveled at how little of it could be seen from the surface. She dug deeper. The ground was quite soft — layer upon layer of perfect topsoil, with loam below and a soft clay even further down. Her hole became a burrow, as wide as her kneeling body and a few feet deep, and still the work of digging consumed her.

One might also imagine that such a hole would quickly fill with the water that she was digging after. Yet the little stream poured politely down one side of her hole and continued just as amiably underground. The floor of the hole on which she knelt felt almost dry. After a long while of digging her fingernails were ragged, her hands were cramped with effort, and her twisted ankle throbbed. Sunset had quieted the singing of birds, and now the only sound she could hear was the tiny burbling of flowing water, the scraping of her hands in the soil, and her own labored breathing.

One more handful, and suddenly she felt her fingers break through into a pocket of empty space. She stopped digging immediately, retracting her hand by instinct, as fearful imaginings of a nest of biting ground spiders leapt to mind. But as she pulled her hand away, an earthen smell that was richer and sweeter than any she had ever known perfumed the air around her, and she gasped out loud for the sight of light glowing faintly from the fist-sized opening in the dirt floor of her hole. It was towards that light the little stream was flowing, and into the empty pocket of space that it now poured.

A minute of silent deliberation — and a bit more digging to widen the cavity — passed before she found the courage to press her eye to the lighted hole. At first, she could see nothing but an open chasm she had almost dug herself down into: a shaft twice as wide as her dig, sloping deeply downward. As her eyes adjusted, she could see the sinuous roots of the petrified tree coiled around and through this hole like great stone snakes, and she marveled that perhaps some plunging taproot had formed this cavity of space so long ago that the root itself had been digested by the gnawing of time. Yet what illumination could be blooming underground in such a secret hollow? Soft light seemed to emanate from the dirt walls themselves. By any measure of sense, she should not widen her dig to open up that shaft into the earth. Dirt should not be glowing, and sensible people should turn away from the lure of such preternatural mysteries.

If she stopped now, she could rest her tired body in the natural darkness, under a sky lit with familiar stars. The mystery of the softly glowing hole could be left for tomorrow to solve, or perhaps never. Why should she care about hidden hollows under petrified trees or where impossible streams choose to flow? It was better to leave such wonders behind. She had a child to think about, after all. She was no longer a girl that could afford to play with secrets. She would be a mother very soon.

But why wasn't she hungry? She had not eaten in what seemed like days. She looked at the trickling stream running down the curved wall of her dig and noted with excitement that it seemed wider at the base than it did at the top of the hole — as though more water was gathering from below ground as it flowed downward. She leaned over her belly and drank from it for a third time.

....

Now two things occurred simultaneously. The first was that her pain and exhaustion vanished. It did not ease out of her slowly, as though relaxing a tensed muscle. It simply lifted away from her like a heavy jacket shed suddenly on a warm day.

The second wonder was what tipped the scales between caution and continuation. She finished drinking and wiped her mouth on her sleeve. As she watched in amazement, those droplets of water that fell from her chin never reached the floor of the hole she was digging. They floated off the front of her mouth and landed softly upon the wall on which the spring was flowing. In awe, she dipped her fingers into the trickle and lifted them towards her face. Little drops of water swelled on her fingertips and floated back slowly against the wall. She laughed out loud, and her child squirmed excitedly inside her.

"The adventure really starts when you are in over your head," Áine whispered to herself. Then she proceeded to keep digging until she widened the hole she had started to the width of the rift below. Into that void, she carefully lowered herself, bracing against the steep slope with her feet and elbows and scooting deeper underground on her backside like a child on an earthen slide.

She did not know if she was digging into her own grave, and she no longer cared. Such is the alluring pull of the Twilight Lands when the wall between worlds has been breached.

....

Quite a bit of effort later, but no time at all, the shaft she had been carefully lowering herself down leveled out, becoming a tunnel which now extended before her. On both sides and above, the earthen tunnel was vertically punctuated by such prodigious roots that, at first, she thought the tunnel itself was hollowed out of branching wood. No longer did the roots appear stony at all, but were so vibrantly wooden and alive that she could almost feel them flexing in the earth. They glowed with a pale phosphorescence, and their loamy fragrance was richly pungent. Breathing it deeply in, Áine began to feel somewhat lightheaded. Ahead of her, the tunnel seemed to flex and contract as though it too was breathing, and she could not help but imagine that she was moving through a prodigious throat illuminated by glowing veins. She felt her heart beating slower and slower as she crawled. Yet no panic arose inside her. Only a curious feeling of being completely still — absolutely still inside, even as she continued to move forward on hands and knees. She could still hear the burbling flow of water, and a vibration deeper than the bottom of what she thought of as sound could be felt in the air all around her. But the quiet in her head was total. Stilled were the soft bellows of her breathing, and silenced was the steady cadence of her heart.

Ahead — too soon and at last — the tunnel mouth could be seen, lit with the pinkish aurora of what might be dawn. The little rivulet of water she had chased underground now flowed right beside her, widening and deepening as it went. By the time she wriggled her way to where the tunnel ended, and the open sky began, she was belly-deep in water and was floating as much as she crawled. Yet it was only when she saw what lay beyond the circle of lighted air at the tunnel entrance that she truly understood how far she had come from her home.

She crawled out into the Twilight Lands, blinking and gasping. The water that had carried her this far flowed on without her, down a slope of tumbled rock and wild blooming heather, where it eventually joined into the current of a much larger river. At her back arose the ponderous immensity of a single oak tree, so wide of trunk that she would have had to spend an afternoon circumnavigating it. The above-ground roots reared up all around her, sinuous and looping like long necks. It was from between two of these monumental roots that the little stream, and she, had emerged into this world. Above her spread the canopy of oak leaves — oh so fantastically, dramatically overhead! The oak was so tall that clouds intertwined amongst the upper branches. The canopy was wide to the edge of vision and so deeply shadowed with dancing green dusklight that she fancied at first that the sky was entirely lush with leaves. A sublime and sacred feeling stirred in her heart as she stood in that green-dappled gloaming. She pressed her cheek to one of the exposed roots and felt it pressing back. She knew with a wondrous certainty that she was standing at the base of the living tree, whose barest petrified remains lay prone in her own world. Somehow, tunneling down from that fallen stone monument, she had emerged sideways into a time long before, in a world where the tree still lived. She did not know how much time would have had to pass before a tree stump might turn to stone. It was probably a lot of time. *A whole lot.*

Far ahead of her, at the edge of the shading canopy of leaves, she could see the open sky where it tucked down behind a distant range of hills. The evening — *(morning?)* — was colored a soft palette of twilight: dusky magentas bruised with purple, honey leaking into lilac with pale blue spreading out behind it. The air was gently brisk, but warmth radiated from the ground underfoot. Áine could not tell if the sun had just set or was about to rise. She was never to find that out, for in all the time she spent in the Twilight Lands, there was no time at all, and the sun never appeared. Only one moon was visible when she finally hiked the long miles to the edge of the river and out from under the sky-wide canopy of oak leaves. The moon could be seen just beginning to peek up from behind the distant hills, as fat as a harvest pumpkin. It never rose a single moment higher but sat there, as it always had, like a glowing red crown on the mountaintop. The other moon, if there was another one in this world, had never risen in view and never would.

Áine made her way to the bank of the wide river, kicked off her shoes, and watched the water flow as slowly as syrup. Although fish swam in it as quickly as any fish might, the water itself rolled unhurriedly around them. There were clouds drifting overhead, but they moved so slowly that they may as well have been painted on the empyrean. And yet birds flew from tree to tree, as swiftly as any bird might. The violet flowering heather rippled in languid waves from a breeze that crept overland. There were no people or houses to be seen. All these things Áine observed as she sat on the riverbank, dipping her feet in the soft chill of the water while tiny fish nibbled fondly at her toes. She closed her eyes and breathed in the smells of the heath and wild lavender and the moist scent of river mud. *I can breathe if I choose to. But why bother, unless I choose to? It doesn't seem to matter in this place, but for the pleasure of smelling things.*

She had never felt so perfectly empty before. This world belonged to nobody; not even time had a claim here. Perhaps she might learn to belong to this world. She kept her eyes closed and dug her toes into the soft clay at the river's edge. She had never really *felt* the soil like that before. She could sense the ground beneath her was drifting and rolling even more slowly than the water. But it was actually *moving*. And so were the roots of the Great Tree and the fungus that held everything together underground. All stretching and blooming and claiming space. Everything was brightly alive or perfectly still. She kept her eyes closed for as long as a moment that stretched out forever. And when she opened them again, she could see that her brown skin was beginning to gray, and her toes were elongating like roots.

....

More of a silver than gray. She thought to herself, and the thought was pleasing. It was the first time she had thought of herself in longer than she knew. *A silvery white, with darker gray striping. I like that. It is a good color for my bark...for my skin? For my skin. It is a good color for my skin.* A sudden image of a giant oak tree wreathed in flame crossed her mind. The thought smeared like watercolor painted over the crude sketch of someone else's life. *Did I see that, once? Was that me?* The word *Ehlon* wandered through her heart, and she felt a flush of loss but couldn't remember why. Like trying to recall the name of someone important she had met a long time ago.

She could feel her toes beginning to taste the water hidden under the river mud. These long and clever toes would eventually draw that water up all the way through her, allowing her arms to grow their own beautiful canopy of leaves. That would be a wonderful way to experience the riverbank. *I think I have not always been here? But I am glad I am here now. I could stay here all day and be perfectly happy.* She noted, with pride, the small buds that were beginning to grow at her wrists and between her fingers. They would flower beautifully.

Then she felt her daughter kicking impatiently inside her. She knew with certainty that it was a girl child, and she felt the child's True Name nestle inside her heart like a nesting bird. *My daughter reminds me she is not ready to sit so still. I will get up and explore a while, at least for her sake.*

She sighed in a way that only a pregnant woman can who is trying to stand up after sitting still for a long time. Then she hoisted herself to her feet and began to follow the river in the direction that the water was flowing. She kept pace with the slowly rolling current. Each step she took was as deliberate as a kiss. Her toes dug into the soil, and the soil flowed responsively underfoot to support her.

....

I shall not share with you everything Áine saw, although she remembered each moment with the vivid clarity of a mind emptied of all other concerns. She traveled far enough to learn something of the nature of that place, and to know that the land was not limitless. It was an enormous island, as big as Eld and hauntingly familiar — for in a sense, it *was* Eld, at the very moment before time had torn through the energy of timelessness. When time was loosed, the world itself had doubled and split almost apart, like twins conjoined at the hip. One world spun in the dark cradle of space, galloping around its own axis. Time wore at it and seasons rushed by; civilizations rose and fell as everyone fought to preserve their fleeting legacies and prevent their own death.

The other world was like the afterglow you see when a candle you were staring at is suddenly blown out. It was the world as it had been at the exact moment before time changed everything. A picture painted with light and stone and living earth. A world suspended in the moment of leaning over the precipice of time. This world did not spin on its axis. Perhaps, somewhere else, the sun had risen and was perpetually shining. But here, on the island, it was either sunset of a day which had almost passed, or sunrise on a morning that would never come.

These two worlds sit so closely side by side that they barely overlap. Only a thin ribbon of energy holds them together at all. This ribbon is a door propped open between them. But while one planet stays still, the other is constantly spinning, so that the doorway vanishes and reappears all over the place. It might open for one evening as a hole in the ground under a petrified tree and the next morning be found in an old wine barrel in the cellar of a tavern, or a sudden vortex in the sea. The doorway between worlds might open into a closet in the room of an old house. Or a cavern. Or a large empty tortoise shell on some distant stretch of beach. It might be a rip in the foggy air that you can barely see, or a tornado, or the blazing heart of a bonfire. Inside the sleeves of an old jacket, or within the pages of a particular book on a particular shelf. It is many places, but not for long. One world turns, and the portal is dragged along with it.

This knowledge Áine gleaned from the people she met as she traveled, and each was as unique in appearance as the mind can imagine — no two ever alike, although there certainly seemed to be *species* of similarity. There were tree folk, bird-lizards, and near-humanoids that were growing into the landscape, and parts of the landscape that looked almost human. Some had wings, and many didn't. Some looked like familiar nightmares she could no longer remember to be afraid of. She pieced the story of the Twilight Lands together from gossip, and from poetry: ballads as winding as rivers, set to music that shimmered across the sky like the swaying aurora of lights that bloomed in winter above Norlünd. By the blue light of twilit bonfires Áine danced to music that lit the forest canopy — notes that physically lingered in the air, lit like fireflies.

....

Áine walked on and on, and as she did, she mulled over what she could remember of the fading story of her life *before*, in the place she had almost forgotten: some other place in which she was somebody's daughter, who was born to follow a path that led to being somebody's wife. In that some-other-place life, she had never really known how she felt about things without someone else telling her what to think about them. *I was told my purpose in life was something that could be found by doing what was expected of me. I think perhaps I was afraid of the responsibility of being myself.*

Sometimes she vaguely recalled the man who was her lover, but the memory of him began to be confused with the memory of a toppling tree, split and burning. In those moments, the word *Ehlon* tolled like a melancholy bell in her mind. Yet she no longer remembered why. She never slept, for she never grew more tired than she had been when she first arrived. She never ate; she was wise enough not to, in that timeless place where digestion is as impossible as death. And all the while, she carried her unborn daughter: kicking in the entrapment of her womb.

....

Áine walked for a long time and for no time at all. And while she wandered through the timeless gloaming, the world she had left behind continued on without her.

Years passed on Homm: a lifetime for many. The thrall revolution flared and guttered, until it appeared to be extinguished entirely. The section of road that Ehlon helped to build and died on was abandoned before it was completed. Most of the bodies of the soldiers and thralls that perished in that summer fire were never recovered from beneath the burnt tree. The thegn that had funded that construction passed away, and the thegn that replaced him had little interest in continuing where he left off.

Now seventy years of vegetation heave up through the fitted stones, and discarded tools lay rusted beneath the swallowing bracken. The long-ago summer fire which scorched that part of the forest has become an overgrown memory; only the charred trunks of ancient oaks remain to remind how hungry flames can be. For there is nothing in nature that can consume the living world as utterly and as pitilessly as a forest fire.

Nothing, that is, but the ambitions of wealthy men.

PART 1
A Company of Six

It is hard to remember sometimes that there was a time when we didn't know each other. There was a time before the friendships that held our world together, before we razed one kingdom and raised another. Before we were famous, before the road that led to war, before any of us had died. Before our children — when we were children ourselves, and, until we met, could not have felt lonelier or more lost inside the narrowing tunnels of our own lives.

Thankfully, we were still young when we found each other.

I have known the White Crow since the day I was born.
I still do not know him well.

WOOD

~ The First Story ~

*I*was born of the fox, with the fox already inside me.

There was something that was *me* before that — some other me that I would have become if the fox had not found my mother in the Twilight Lands. Without the fox, that other me might still be trapped in that other place, unable to ever be born. Or I might have somehow been born and grown up in the world beneath the tree, where the stream flows backwards through a crack underground, and time cannot follow. I do not know what that other me would have been like or what she might have become. But I do know that she would have lived her forever-life trapped in there, for there is no escaping that place if you are born inside it, with it inside of you.

The fox stole me away from the Twilight Lands, and so I was born at the edge of this world, on this island of Eld. I will tell you all I know of how this came to be. I shall try to tell it as my mother told me, when she was still able to walk and talk as you and I do. Now she has grown graceful and still, and her memories have changed into stories, and her stories are no longer about me.

....

To begin with, as everyone knows, foxes and crows are the only two animals that have dealings with the Twilight Lands. However, only foxes are able to cross through the veil between worlds. Crows are adept at finding the doorways but cannot cross over. The poor crow is like a child stuck forever indoors, watching other kids play through the window. So they loiter around the portals obsessively, observing the comings and goings of Fae, grackling and gossiping. In fact, it is often the determining presence of a murder of crows that betrays the location of an opening doorway into Twilight. They know more random tidbits of information about the Twilight Lands than any other creature alive, but they may never cross the veil to see it for themselves. When I asked Djaro why that was, he replied that crows are too closely tied to the spirit of death and resurrection to be welcome in timelessness. Yet, foxes can come and go with ease, for Karnonou bade them to carry messages across the veil between worlds long ago. This prejudicial phenomenon is why crows are often so openly hostile towards foxes.

Well, that and the egg-stealing. It's hard not to hold a grudge against someone who keeps eating your chance to have children.

....

The fox was dying. She knew it was true. She had been chasing a chubby little wood mouse through the last slashes of afternoon light — more a game than a meal, for she had been awoken by the rotund rodent as it wandered carelessly past her burrow. So she chased it through the bracken just to be sporting, but was still half asleep when something hit her in the flank, hard enough to knock her backwards. She screamed and tumbled face-over-tail downhill. There was a terrible heat at first, from a long shaft protruding all the way into her ribs — she could feel the sharp edge of it sawing around inside her. The tip of the shaft was feathered, and it tangled painfully with the underbrush as she ran. Bloody warmth spilled across the white fur of her belly, and the forest blurred around her. She could hear herself whimpering, and the sound of it scared her. So, she ran in fear through the fading sunlight until she could run no more. There was nothing else to do.

Twilight was sharpening the darkness around her, and she was a long way from her burrow. The cold of night was beginning to gather inside her chest, right in the center of where she had always felt the warm strength of being herself. She stumbled pitifully, with one foot dragging behind her, and when the sky opened above her in a sudden clearing, she knew that her running was done. It was time to find a dark place, someplace she could close her eyes and let the pain fade away for good. Ahead lay a massive fallen tree that looked like wood and smelled like stone. She made her tottering way towards the base of it, where the roots spread like a welcoming paw, and a thick softness of moss was growing. Here, by unexpected good fortune, she found a large tunnel that had been excavated by some animal so long ago that moss grew all over its interior walls. A little trickle of water overflowed the edge and crept down one wall. The vixen felt the cold water soothe the heat of her torn flesh. She wriggled deeper into the large burrow, dragging the embedded feathered arrow shaft as she went.

....

Having walked across much of the island and experienced many wonders therein, my mother had returned at last to that soft patch of earth by the slow-rolling river where she first dug her toes into twilit soil. Her arms had grown beautiful and branchy, with long graceful fingers. Fresh green leaves were visible here and there in the thick fullness of her hair, and her skin had hardened noticeably in a handsome way that thickened her legs and sharpened her features.

She was busy tickling a little silver fish with her toes when she saw something coming towards her from between the roots of the Great Tree. Gray fur brightening into orange at the chest and ears, the poor creature dragged its own death behind it. My mother could see it was a fox, for even in such a sorry state, the creature moved with that languid grace that is so particular to foxes. And yet, its fur was matted with dirt and blood, and the arrow it dragged snaked a dark rambling gouge across the leaf mulch. It hurt my mother's heart to see the vixen in such obvious pain. So she lifted her feet out of the shallow water with a sigh and started up the hill to meet the fox, holding her swollen belly before her. I kicked impatiently inside her womb, and my mother realized with some guilt that she had almost forgotten I was in there.

The vixen could go no further, and she sprawled on her side with her chest heaving, disappearing from my mother's view under the fern fronds. My mother despaired of losing track of the fox entirely until she saw the bloody fletching bobbing between the ferns like a brutal flag. She knelt at the fox's side, whispering the soothing spell that every mother knows and before the vixen could startle, she wrapped her branchy fingers around the arrow shaft and yanked it out. There was a great shudder of pain and relief from the fox, and then she laid her head upon my mother's lap and closed her eyes to die.

Which, of course, she did not. She could not. The wound would not bleed another drop, and the throbbing pain of it did not diminish in the slightest. They sat together for a countless while, while my mother stroked the fox's sodden fur and hummed tuneless notes of calming, and the fox kept perfectly still, knowing that her life must surely be spent and that stillness was appropriate. The arrow lay on the foliage nearby, slick with blood that would never dry.

. . . .

When it became obvious that no amount of surrendering is possible to a foe who cannot find you, the vixen opened her amber eyes and gazed into my mother's face. She licked my mother once on the tip of her nose and said: "I am Syrahana-yerall-aneh. Forgive me for not getting up out of your lap sooner, but the pain is terrible, and my legs are forgetting themselves. Your petting of my belly fur is very soothing."

My mother replied with some surprise: "You speak to me in my own tongue? How came you to speak?"

"I have always been able to speak. You have just now learned how to listen."

My mother laughed. "Yes, of course. It is my pleasure to understand you. I am... I was once called Áine, but I think I am much more than that now. I no longer know what my name should be. I'm glad my petting of your fur is a comfort to you."

The vixen considered for a quiet moment, shifting uncomfortably with pain. "Everything wishes to have a True Name, above all other needs. You are *Ariabeithe*, which is the word for when this Áine began to become a silver birch by drinking twilit water. But your heartbeat is echoed by another: a girl-child who is longing to be born. She is *Rahyn*. And she is trapped inside you, Ariabeithe, with your organs hardening into cambium all around her. Can you not feel the pounding of her desire to be free as she kicks inside your womb?"

My mother hid her face in shame, aware of how distant I had become in her thoughts. Standing in the shallows of the river, her head had filled with dreams of sunlight and the stretching urge to grow tall enough to brush the clouds with her fingers. As if in reminder, I began to thrash inside the fullness of her belly, pushing against the thickening uterine cocoon. She wept then, the first tears she could ever remember weeping. Those tears were as glossy as sap, coating waxen where they pattered against the vixen's pitiful wounds. My mother wept with the frustration of her fading memory, how she had changed and grown as a woman, yet stayed in the heavy fullness of pregnancy. She realized how much she longed for her pregnancy to end, to have her body back to herself again.

All the while, as she wept cloudy tears, the fox lay in her lap and watched her with quiet intensity, for a plan was forming inside of her. She pressed her ear against my mother's swollen belly and whispered secret questions to me. It was a plan that would not work unless a difficult bargain could be struck, and I was the only person who had the right to make the compromise. So she asked, and I answered, and her snuffling whiskers tickled my mother's belly until Ariabeithe couldn't help but laugh. There is, after all, little in this world or any other that tickles more than the delicate brushing of whiskers.

When my mother had spent all the moments of her crying and laughing in that shaded place under the limbs of the Great Tree, Syrahana-yer-all-aneh crawled painfully out of my mother's lap, so the two women could face each other properly. Then she looked deep into my mother's eyes and said:

"Ariabeithe. My time in this body must soon end, for I cannot live in this land with such pain burning my joy away. Your journey in your new body is just beginning; I can hear the river calling you back even now, beckoning you to sink your feet into the soft mud and learn more of what it means to be a growing part of this world — a world that is filling all the space up inside of you already. And yet, Rahyn must be born. She *must* be. But if you left this timeless world through the door between the roots, you might not live long enough to ever see it open again. And if that were so, I believe you would die with longing for your place in this land, where your feet fit so perfectly in the river mud, and you have grown into your True Name."

My mother simply nodded. She could not speak, for tears began to swim in her eyes again as she thought of never knowing all that she was meant to learn.

"But perhaps our triad of needs can be met. I have looked for the blessings of Rahyn, and she has offered them."

My mother raised an eyebrow. "My unborn baby has offered you her blessings? As though she would have the slightest idea what is best for her?"

Syrahana-yerall-aneh grinned in the smugly satisfied way that foxes do so well. "I've never heard of a human who has the slightest idea what is best for them. To be alive is all a process of guesses and luck, and aging only provides a narrowing framework of opinions and prejudices. Although she is, of course, too young to know better than to share prom-ises with foxes, she will only be given the time to learn that for herself if you accept my bargain. Please understand, it is a bargain that terrifies me to make. I have only ever been myself until now. It is all I know. If I had a hope of being healed in these lands, I would bear the pain and drag myself towards that hope. But there is nothing and nobody here that can knit a wound like mine together. Only time can do that, and there is none here."

My mother nodded and said, "Yes. I would do what I could to help comfort your body, but the pain you feel in this place will never go away. I have seen what awful madness grows in those who are living with pain such as yours in this land with no endings. I would not wish that on any creature, good fox. You should not stay here for long."

The vixen reflectively licked the wound on her flank and grimaced. "Agreed. I cannot linger here. Even now, the door may be closing behind me. I wish to be recycled into the world that gave me so many days of playing under two beautiful moons. I wish to return to the stone tree and rest in the soft moss. You cannot leave, and I cannot stay, and yet your child must still be born. Let us three make what deals we can, and let us make them quickly."

My mother ran her long fingers across her belly, and a great shudder of loss went through her. Ariabeithe hugged her knees to her chest and shook her head. The fox felt what hope had begun to rise in her draining away, and a lifetime of instinct told her to run — to fend only for herself, no matter the cost. But she was tired, so mortally tired. Her leg hurt. Her belly hurt. She did not have time to spare for soft-hearted humans. She did not have time here at all. So she spoke again.

"Ariabeithe, hear me. You cannot prevent Rahyn from the chance to be born, and live on with a child encased in wood inside you. If you try, that grief will remain forever, eating away at your core until you are as hollow as standing deadwood. Let me carry her across to the other side. She will become my own kit for as long as I have the breath to know her, and when I pass away, she will make a space inside her spirit for me. Please, Ariabeithe — please. *You cannot prevent me from dying, but you can save me.* Rahyn can save me. But only if you let her go."

....

So, my mother made the hardest choice of her life and gave me up to inhabit the womb of the fox. How this was accomplished, I cannot tell you, for I do not understand it fully myself. But I exist as you do, and that transformation is how I came to exist, so it is better if you just accept that the divide between possible and impossible is thinner than it seems.

When all was done, and her body was her own again, my mother gently carried the fox into the tunnel between the tree roots and crawled with her all the way back to where the floor shifted and became the walls of a deep hole again. As she crawled, the vixen in her arms rapidly began to swell with child.

They came at last to the end of the tunnel, where the glow of twilight still radiated out of the dirt walls themselves. My mother, who was now truly named Ariabeithe, lifted the very pregnant fox up over the lip of the hole and laid her down to birth me and die peacefully on the moss that grows so thick and soft beneath the splayed stone roots of the petrified tree.

That is where I was born and where the vixen died shortly thereafter, and began her new life as a spirit inside of me. My mother remained in the hole, reaching up from time to time to comfort her tiny crying baby daughter and pet the fur of the stiffening fox. She sang for both of us, those songs that every mother knows for saying goodbye. Just before the morning aurora was banished by the rising sun, she returned to grow at the edge of her beloved river, and the door into the Twilight Lands closed again behind her.

....

I am Rahyn, and I was able to be born because of the resourcefulness of Syrahana-yerall-aneh, whose spirit still watches over me. And because of my mother, who carried me through fire and out of my own world, and then had the courage to carry me back again

....

The White Crow watched all this take place from a branch overhead. When a door is opened into Twilight, there is always a crow somewhere nearby. Yet this was no ordinary crow, but a Bone-dancer   a skin shifting Fýrii who kept a vigilant eye on this grove, for the petrified tree was a particularly special door. And that is how I met Djaro the Crow, who was to raise me in the manner of a father and train me towards the purpose of the ancient practices of Fýrii: to protect the forest against the spreading blight of humanity. I have known him since the day I was born. I still do not know him well.

Plans of Vice and Thegn

It is desirable to begin a story at an auspicious moment, but that is not truly where it begins. Our story about a special foxgirl began with her mother and father, before she was born — as her mother's story began with her own parents, and so on, all the way back to the real beginning: form erupting from formlessness, and light from void. But ours is a story of six children, and we have only yet met one. So now we must hurry forward a number of years to give baby Rahyn a chance to grow up a bit and introduce our next child, for he will have an important part to play in what is to come.

But before we move on, let us pause for a moment and step out onto a stone balcony to observe the man who will cast a long shadow over all their childhoods, and never even know it. He is the sort of man who — by right of birth, not by merit of virtue — holds dominion over the lives of many. Such a man is the source of much grief, and his ambitions will stain the picture of all of their future lives.

....

Thegn Rory stood with his hands lightly resting on the stone railing of his private balcony and watched three of his slavers displaying their latest offerings in the courtyard below. There were eleven thralls lashed together in the chain-line, all Dekai — golden brown skin and hair that was so black it was almost blue. Eight of them were male, three were female. Even from balcony height Rory knew they were slaves by their wounds and the public display of their nudity. The naked thralls shivered in the snow, turning their faces up towards the thegn's balcony as they had been commanded. Like most thralls, their stares were heavy with resignation, their faces lean and empty. The three slavers also stared up at the balcony expectantly. They were Erdin: as pale as snow and bundled in layers of leather and fur so that they appeared to be almost twice the size of their captives. Rory nodded to them and waved them out of his courtyard with a bored gesture of his hand.

Probably dredged up from some provincial prison. Rory mused to himself. He craned his neck to get a better look. *Not a comely face amongst them. How difficult is it to import attractive thralls? I bet those skabde muli slavers are keeping the pick of the crop for themselves.*

"Remind me to bleed someone for this." He mumbled. Then he

chuckled. *Not a good sign when I start talking to myself out loud. Better ring for some company.*

The thegn reached out and pulled a silken cord that hung from a hook on the stone wall. Three floors below, he knew that a bell would chime and a servant would come running to attend him. Sometimes he liked to ring the bell just to see how fast they could make it up the stairs. There were lots of stairs.

While he waited, he looked out over his city. The snows of winter blanketed the descending circles of Portuan. From where his castle was built at the top of a hill between two promontories of land, he could see all the way down the terraced hillside of the wealthy part of town. Beyond were the great gate and imposing stone walls that ringed the landward side. His gaze traveled those descending streets, with each row of manor houses becoming less grand as it approached the bottom of the hill. In every major city, aristocrats and minor nobles always crowd towards the peak of power, striving to build as close to the castle as opportunity allowed. The families that owned those stately manor houses often shuffled when the shifting fortunes of murder and politics allowed for upward momentum. On such a winter day, the architectural details of those grand and timeless manors were indistinguishable under layers of snow, with only the number of smoking chimneys to attest to their prestige.

His musing was interrupted by the patter of gaining steps and a tentative knock on his chamber door.

"Enter."

The door opened, but the servant remained ducked out of sight. "Great Thegn: I await your pleasure." The voice quaked.

Drat. An elderly one. "Has Captain Dané returned from Drôle?"

"Yes, my Thegn. The captain and a few other of the Iron Guard were sighted at the barracks late last night."

"Then go away, grandfather. Fetch Captain Dané and a scullery maid to attend on me immediately. Tell her to bring me breakfast. Send the captain and the food in, and leave the thrall in the hallway until I'm ready for her."

"Yes, my Thegn." The old voice mumbled. Rory heard the departing shuffle of his sandals on the staircase, and sighed. Almost unwillingly, his eyes drifted towards the other balcony across his bedroom.

On the southern side of his expansive bedchamber and through a set of iron doors paneled with colored glass, there was another balcony which faced the gray vastness of the Améan Ocean. He did not like to stand upon that balcony and stare at the ocean or at the poorer side of Portuan which descended down the promontories on both sides of him to the harbor below. The sheer cliffs beneath that balcony plunged to a fearful height and he did not enjoy the look of such a vast horizon of ocean beyond. There was nothing to see in the water that truly belonged to him, and he did not like to look on things that he could not own. Rory hoped to one day turn all of the island of Eld into his dominion, but the ocean would never be ruled. So he shut out the sight of it with velvet curtains, and gazed out to the north instead, across the predictable grandeur of his city of Portuan, and the distant green of the Eldwood beyond.

....

When too much time had already passed, the clatter of metal spurs could be heard on the stairs. The door rattled under three raps of an iron gauntlet. Rory, already annoyed with waiting, took the time to belt the elaborate layers of his lounging robes before answering.

The door opened to two figures in the stone hallway. One was in skirts and huddled back out of sight in the hallway. The other, in plate armor, strode in past her, and closed the door. Removing the fearsome helmet of the Iron Guard, Captain Dané eyed Thegn Rory out of ice-blue eyes. In her other hand, she held a silver platter with the thegn's breakfast arrayed on it. There was a moment of silence, then the captain crossed the room and set the food down on a table. She saluted her thegn with a fist knocked against the armor that encased her heart.

"My Thegn. I would ask you what your pleasure is, but I can see you already have her waiting in the hallway. So instead, I will enquire: what can I do for you so early this morning?"

Rory smiled sourly. "Perhaps it was my wish that you bring me breakfast."

The armored woman sneered. "If that was your wish, then I will bid you enjoy your meal and your scullery maid and take my leave."

"You will do no such thing, captain. Linger while I eat, and guard me against the dangers of boredom and indigestion."

"It is my pleasure to serve my Great Thegn." Captain Dané tightly replied.

Rory nodded and turned away, sitting to breakfast with his back facing his captain. Only the sounds of his chewing could be heard for many minutes. The armored woman stared at his back, and thought her own thoughts. From out in the hallway, quiet weeping could be heard.

When Rory was finished, he swiveled in his seat back towards the Iron Guard and wiped his mouth on a napkin.

"Don't ever keep me waiting that long again. When I summon you, you come quickly. Do you understand?"
"Yes, Great Thegn."
"Good. Now: any progress to report on your efforts at Drôle?"
Captain Dané sighed and ran one hand through her crest of hair, scratching at the shorn hair around it. "Nothing to report that is worthy of your attention. On the first of Nöeth my soldiers stormed the fortress ruin expecting a fight, yet it was empty of all but withered scat and scattered bones. No other signs of troll occupation, and what we saw was dusty with age. We set ourselves up in the barracks, lit a fire, and fortified against incursion, but there was none. After a sennight of waiting for trolls to attack, the troops grew restless. I bade them to fell a few trees and construct cages in which we could capture whatever trolls might eventually be lured back to the fortress by our smoking chimneys. But-"
"So far, none to be found." Rory interrupted.
"Aye, Thegn: none. Perhaps they are creatures that hibernate in winter, buried in river mud like turtles. Or perhaps they are watching from a distance and biding their time. After a fortnight of searching the river banks for traces of them and baiting our cages with wasted meat, I grew weary of waiting and have returned to Portuan to make this report: the ruined fortress of Drôle seems as abandoned as we hoped it would be. Only when spring warms the river mud will we be sure if the trolls are truly gone from that place. In the meantime, I have set my soldiers to the task of repairing what damage they can within the castle itself. Time has done more harm to the old fortress than the trolls ever did; it is my hope that replacing rotting doors and reinforcing wooded bridge-walks will keep morale up."
"Morale?" Rory raised an eyebrow.
Captain Dané shifted her weight and sighed. "Wintering in that haunted ruin is... difficult. It saps the spirit in a way that is unsoldierly."

For a brief moment, Rory imagined what it might be like to spend his winter months in a ruined castle full of the bones of long-dead soldiers that had been torn apart by trolls, living every day with the constant fear that those trolls might return in force to add to their collection of corpses. Rory opened his mouth to reply sarcastically, and then closed it again.

"I see. Keep me informed if you manage to catch one alive. As you well know, we still have no idea how to kill one so that it stays properly dead, and a living one to experiment on is the only way to find out. Yet perhaps Lady Luck is on our side, and that infestation of trolls have moved on downriver. A lot can change in a hundred years."

"Yes, Thegn."

"It would help my road building project enormously if they were gone. I have no wish to repeat my ancestor Revis' folly and waste a bunch of money on dead soldiers and half-built castles. If we can retake and refurbish that fortress, then the whole stretch of the Thegn's Road that leads right past it will be usable again. Why rebuild thirty miles of abandoned road when I can just reclaim it? Saves enormous costs in materials and labor."

"Yes, Thegn."

Rory stood up and stretched, yawning. Then he remembered the naked thralls shivering out in the cold, and grumbled to himself.

"Speaking of that: when we are done here, go inform the slavers that wait for my word in the courtyard that I will buy the lot of thralls at half asking price, and to make sure that their next batch are either pleasing to look at, healthy, or both. This lot was shriveled and shabby. Barely worth clothing."

"They have seasoned in jail at Dàrŭ and traveled days on the Wayward Road in winter, Great Thegn. They are lucky to be alive at all. In times of peace, the slavers take whatever they can get."

Rory sneered. "Prisoners of Dàrŭ are available for purchase these days? Thegn Elond must have more thralls than he needs, and I am forced to pay for his leftovers. That northern *moros-queine* and his godsdamned 'justice'. He keeps the bridgewalks of Dàrŭ Above clean enough to eat off of, by jailing his Dekai from Dàrŭ-Below down to the slightest litterer and curfew-breaker. It is no wonder his jails are overflowing."

Dané shrugged. "Perhaps we could learn from his example? Our lowtown is full of sailors, and there is knavery enough to punish at the dockside taverns and night market when the drink gets flowing. Our enforcers could tighten their grip and fill your jails here, and then you would have more thralls. Saves you the trouble of importing."

Rory shook his head and stood up brusquely. "No. Ship captains are enticed into port by our brothels and taverns, and our coffers are kept full from the tariffs we impose on their cargo at the night market. If we begin to jail their crew, they will take their business elsewhere. Besides, sailors make terrible thralls. They are too willful."

"As you say, Great Thegn. You know best."

Rory narrowed his eyes at his captain, but her face remained impassive. "Indeed, I do. But the point remains that our stock of thralls is low. I have need of a considerable number at present. My road construction requires as many laborers as can be found. And yet, those idiots in the courtyard are the only slavers I have seen all winter."

"There is always the possibility the slavers are taking their stock elsewhere. It is rumored there are illegal fleshmarkets in Dunmarsh and even Ulfaang that still exist — despite your edicts."

"Nonsense. I have ordered all slavers in my thegndom to bring their wares to me. It is the law."

The Iron Guard shrugged. "Your laws do not reach as far as you imagine, Great Thegn. The swamp around Dunmarsh is a haven for outlaws, and patrolling the hundred cliffs of Ulfaang for thrall poachers is a task for a larger force than ours."

"But why would a slaver go to all that trouble to sell thralls somewhere else?"

"The private market pays better, Great Thegn. Your noble personage is somewhat well known as a purse-pinch."

Rory stared at his captain. A flush of anger reddened his pale face.

"Dare you insult me?"

Captain Dané shifted on her heels. "To report an insult is not the same as repeating one, Great Thegn. Slavers are not above gossip, and I have regrettably heard it rumored that a thrall sold at private fleshmarkets earns more for a slaver than a thrall sold to you."

Thegn Rory cracked his knuckles and turned on his heel, once again gazing out over the stone balcony. Snow had begun to fall again; the courtyard was empty. Slavers and thralls alike had left to await their pay or their fate somewhere out of the weather. A minute of silence passed as Rory struggled to regain his temper. When he spoke again, it was to himself. Captain Dané had to lean in to hear him.

"In times of peace, let all live as though free."

"Pardon, Thegn?"

"The Rule of Eld: the godsdamn Queen's Law. My royal aunt in her supposed wisdom. I was just repeating the most annoying part of it. 'In times of peace, let all live as though free.' And though she did not mean to imply that all might live as though *truly* free, for obviously that is laughable, it certainly makes gathering up an army of able-bodied thralls a damned difficult proposition. We would need a war to gather legal slaves, and an army of slaves to start a legal war. The queen's peace interrupts the progress of my ambitions most unfairly."

The Iron Guard smiled dryly. "I believe that was the very measure of her intent, Great Thegn. To prevent your honored person and the other Thegns of Eld from disrupting her majesty's peace with schemes and infighting. War on Eld is the sole concern of Her Majesty, and she intends to keep it that way. Only local uprisings are within the scope of your jurisdiction."

Rory blanched. "My jurisdiction is total dominion over my thegndom! Do not impose upon my pleasure by intoning the queen's command as though you understand it."

"I am an agent of Her Majesty's will, Thegn Rory, and I serve as her agent in the capacity she has instructed me. Although I am at your service as well, I am blood-bonded to her command. And it is not her intention to let you further your ambitions by ignoring her edicts as it pleases you. It appears that I understand the function of imperial law a good deal better than you do."

With a growl, Rory clenched his fists and lunged towards his captain, who drew her sword halfway out of the scabbard before she had a chance to think about what she was doing. Both abruptly froze where they were: he with his hands up to strike, and she in martial readiness. An ugly flush purpled his face, and he panted with the effort of restraint.

"You are a whore in armor that the queen promoted out of pity. Never speak to me in such dismissive tones again, or I will have your tongue torn from your head with hot pinschers, and take my pleasure with your scalded throat. You are mine to command and to correct, just as much as that simpering girl crouched out in the hallway. If I wanted to, I could invite her in to watch as I discipline you."

"You can try." Captain Dané replied without removing her hand from her sword handle. "But I do not think that would turn out well for either of us. Besides, *Great* Thegn — you are not my type. I, like you, prefer the scullery maid. But unlike you, I would not demean myself with rape to satisfy my urges."

Rory looked confused. "What do you mean, 'rape?' I am no rapist. That scullery girl is a thrall — she belongs to me as much as my breakfast does, or that bed over there. Property has no rights. A bed is made for use, and so are thralls."

Dané raised an eyebrow. Her hand remained on her sword hilt.

Rory sneered. "A breakfast, a slave, or a captain who forgets her place: all of these can be devoured. Your longevity only extends as far as your worth to me."

"I do not believe your threats, though I am sure you believe yourself capable of following through on them. But I am in service to Her Majesty directly, and only on loan to your court. I doubt she would appreciate your abuse of her servant."

Rory laughed dryly. "She is not here to interfere, Captain. Your position in the Iron Guard does not protect you from me."

"Nor does your position as thegn protect you from me. But so long as Her Majesty requires it of me, I will do the best I can to assist and counsel you. Do not be hasty to waste such an ally."

Rory stared at her for a moment, and then chuckled to himself. He adjusted the ties on his robes and dabbed the drool from his face at the edges of his gold-capped incisors. Like many pure-blooded Erdin, sudden anger or excitement incited a tendency to drool. It was an embarrassment for a race that prided themselves on control.

"Very well. Remember which side of the leash you are on, the next time you wish to insult me, or keep me waiting for my breakfast."

"I shall not forget, Great Thegn. Allow me to repair my lax courtesy with a suggestion that may be of some service to you."

Rory raised an eyebrow. "Proceed."

"The queen's law only applies to Eld, for her command ends where the land ends. If you have need of thralls, might I suggest that you simply take them from other islands? Although it is difficult sailing in winter, it is not impossible. There are ships docked in your harbor whose captains would be amenable to bribes if you are willing to pay enough gold to make it worth their while to risk dangerous sailing. The ocean is vast — perhaps even vast enough for your ambitions, Great Thegn."

Rory stared at his captain thoughtfully for a long moment. Then he turned and slowly walked towards the southern balcony and pulled back the heavy curtains. Pale sunlight sparkled across the water, and far below his gaze, the harbor was full of wintering ships. He imagined the captains of those ships, growing fat and restless in the taverns of low-town, and his lips curled in a satisfied smile.

"Captain Dané, I believe you might have redeemed yourself for making me late to break my fast. I command you, therefore, to take news of my plan to the captains of those ships I see languishing at harbor. Offer a generous but unspecified amount of gold for thralls, and promise punishment most dire for any captain that would dare to barter their thralls for sale at any port but mine. My generosity and my wrath are close cousins, dear captain. You will have plenty of time to ruminate on that during the remaining winter months of your post in that drafty ruin of Drôle. Perhaps you will find yourself better behaved when you are allowed to return again to Portuan. Now, get out of my sight, and send in the scullery maid. Your insolence has inflamed my appetite."

The Iron Guard gritted her teeth and bowed formally. "As you say, Great Thegn. I will leave you to your sport. I'm sure she'll be to your liking: she is a weeper."

The bonfire was so bright and hot that the windows of nearby houses were melting like wax.

FIRE

~ The Second Story ~

In my dreams, I have always imagined myself far away from the smallness of here, in a great land. The encompassing cage that is the narrow shoreline of my island melts away behind me, and I take huge steps across the measure of that new land. I will be a giant; I will fill the length of that foreign sky with the long shade of my someday legend. In a land that never could be real, I will be king over men, and I will rule them justly. In the vast space behind my eyes, I paint this land with tottering empires and the tyrants who fell them: ennobled families of elite merchants that carve golden opportunities for themselves out of flesh and timber. It is peopled by water gypsies who pole the evening rivers by the shine of dangling lanterns hung on houseboats of timber and stretched skin; bloodied myrmidon daughters breaking each other with chain and trident in pits of mud before the clamoring crowd; by ebony sailors, by Fae whose bodies are branchy and wild, and by wicked magicians that rend and unravel the loom of time itself. This is a place of beasts and heroes.

I was twelve summers old, and in my dreams, I was already one of them.

....

There was a boy who sat on the edge of a cliff by the sea, on an island that barely mattered to anyone. Well, it is more truthful to say that it mattered to his small village very much (for they were the only people who lived there) and that it mattered to anyone who wished to purchase exceptional sailcloth that was made of shimmering grass-weave the color of dusty copper. But as there are few people even amongst the drifting sea folk who have regular need of an entire sailcloth, few visitors ever made it to that island.

The boy came to the cliff edge often, for that was the best spot on the island to watch the vast movement of the sea. Every day he would walk

from the village to the cliff, even when the weather was iron winter winds
and slashes of tattering clouds. He would walk as near as he dared to
the crumbling edge where the green carpet of sand verbena clung. Then,
when his knees became watery, he would crawl further forward on hands
and knees until he could hang his head over and look down far below,
to where the white combers smashed, and the crying cormorants dove
for fish. Here was life at its brashest and most fluid — a slipstream of
primordial chaos. Here the roar and sway of the ocean stirred the boy's
daydreams. Heavy seals baying on the low rocks; the sharp darkness of
meandering sharks; the diving birds in their countless numbers. Sometimes he spotted sea turtles, or large swimming lizards, and every now and
again the breathy spout of a breaching whale. Unheeding of the boy who
perched on the cliff above them, the animals mated and fought and fed
on each other. They took sun-warm naps on the rocks, sprawled across
the mess of bird scat that carpeted everything. And all of the animals
on the shore that he could see, the boy included, stared for many long
hours out at the distant horizon, caught up in the rocking perpetuity of
the waves and wind. This spectacle played out below was the boy's daily
comfort. He would come to the cliffs to be quiet in his own head and
watch in wonder as the world churned below him.

As a younger boy, he had explored the island foot by foot. He had
tunneled a near mile of secret corridors in the dune grasses, leaving clues
and childhood treasures in flattened burrows for him and his friends to
discover days later by candlelight. The great old daganwood grove was
the verdant crown of the island and the cathedral of generations of island
children. Under the dense canopy, it was always gloaming. Everywhere
were strung faded ribbons and strings of shells that rippled and rattled in
the ceaseless wind. This was the work of generations of islanders looping
tokens of hopeful wishes up in the branches for the gods to see them
better, and perhaps take an interest in them. The place was too sacred
and eerie for casual conversation, but when nobody else was around,
the boy and his brave companions would sometimes climb up into
the highest branches. Bulwarked in a green cocoon of sweet pitch and
dancing shadows, they would pour their irreverent laughter out over the
sanctum below. Alone or in pairs, they built forts of rope and driftwood,
combed through the tangle of seaweed at the churning shoreline looking
for shipwreck debris, or scoured the deepest tide pools to catch scuttling
carbuncles and steal their wishes. Just a year ago, there was nowhere else
as perfect as his island, and nothing worth being that was better than an

adventurous boy with grass stains on his knees and elbows.

But all children must grow up. The boy had never been small in his own mind, yet lately, his shadow had lengthened confusingly. The shadow of a large boy ran behind him as he played seek and harry in the low dunes with the other children of the village, but what was that young man's shadow that darted after his throwing arm as he harpooned the biting eels in the tide pool? His woven sandals ended an inch before his heel did now, and his lengthening legs and thickening arms were no longer as "his" as they once had seemed. Everything inside him was hot and hammering. His voice dipped and sometimes broke, particularly when he was speaking to his father or trying to talk about anything around girls.

Lately, his sleep was troubled by the slow creaking of his stretching bones and the sharp ache of new muscles blooming. The moon was terribly bright on those nights. The landscape of his dreams had shifted into mountains as ample as breasts and rivers of life that flowed from the soft gathering of thighs that stretched for leggy miles to a horizon of toes. He no longer felt an easy indifference to the time that passed as he lay on his belly at the cliff's edge. He no longer felt the soft certainty of selfhood. On the day that the ships arrived and everything in his world changed, Tarquin leaned on his elbows on the edge of that cliff for the last time and daydreamed about a world that would become all too real, all too soon.

....

Tarquin had awoken late on an almost-spring morning and washed his face and hands by breaking through the thin crust of ice on the well, shivering and sneezing as he splashed himself. He ate wild oats stewed in hot goat's milk, and through the round window, eddies of sunlit mist drifted by. As he ate, he could hear the usual shuffle and jokes of the men working together on the weaving outside in the village square. Today was the first day in months that the men had gathered to practice the community trade — weaving great swaths of sailcloth is tricky enough work without sleet and numb fingers. The morning brume still lay thick on the village square, where men huddled side by side and worked near enough to see each other. Some mornings, the men would sing, or just pass a low hum back and forth. That day was too brisk for singing, and so they each were bundled into a pile of heavy cloaks and knit hats, and their breath made small chimney plumes when they yawned.

The village commons were centered around a wooden structure that was the pride of generations: the Great Loom. This loom was crafted of prodigious beams of daganwood, harvested generations ago. The boy and his friends had measured it once; lain head to foot, the Great Loom was six Tarquins wide and almost ten Tarquins long! Its wide body was a platform of tightly interlocking planks, with a ridged heddle support dividing the center. The heddle itself was big enough to climb, construct-ed of log framing and timber with pass-through gaps. Thinly braided warp ropes more than fifty feet long were properly stretched to accept the wefting of the island heather the men interwove by hand. Framing the outside edges of the great loom were time-worn dips in the wood where generations of men had knelt in their fathers' indent to continue the tradition of their inherited craft.

Tarquin stared through the window at their backs. It was nearly spring, and he was already twelve summers old. He knew he was past old enough to take his place kneeling at the loom by his father's side. Tarquin already knew how to weave the grasses into tight layers of fabric and how to boil the binding glue out of resin and charcoal. With small hands and rare patience, he had knelt with the diving women at their grinding stones and crushed the blue camate shells into a fine powder. This was the last ingredient that would seal the many woven layers of grass and glue into the flexible cloth that allowed his village to trade for imports the island could not provide. This sailcloth was tough and rot-resistant, and shimmered when the wind blew into it as though it was rippling underwater.

Tarquin knew what being a man meant — he had often tagged along with the older men as they gathered resin from the daganwood grove, harvesting it into collecting cups from little axe wounds in the tree bark. About three feet up from the base of each of the great old trees ran a circle of fading scars from generations of sap gathering. The sap harvest was always held in silence, the men peeling strips of bark back with reverent precision. Their care was crucial — the trees in that daganwood grove were the only trees ever to grow on the island. These men with their lean faces and collecting buckets had been children here too. Nobody forgets that green cathedral once they have spent time sitting under its shelter of branches on a hot day and listened to the wind rattling hundreds of gathered shells, clicking together on their reverent ribbons.

....

The doorway of his house filled with his father, and the chill winter air poured around him as he stepped inside. Tarquin hastened to gather up his bowl and horn spoon; he wiped them dry with sudden involvement. He felt his father's eyes on his back, and a soft weight filled his heart. It was too soon. It was too soon to be called to join the men at the loom; the first day he knelt was the last day of his youth. It had always been too soon; there had never, never been enough time to be young. Tarquin gritted his teeth and scrubbed his plate fiercely. Some people grow up casually: the turning over of weeks and years is nothing but turning pages in a book they read indifferently. Some people lose years to sickness or grief and stumble into adulthood cursing the time they lost. For Tarquin, he had always been aware of the time slipping away from him each day. He went to bed as late as possible and was greedy for every sunrise. He was convinced he knew the death of joy that being an adult would bring. There were no more games to play in the bracken, no more long afternoons spent gazing at the sea. Adulthood was measured one predictable day at a time, and you paid for it with your aching shoulders and the small pieces of your youthful dreams you fed to your future children.

In the doorway, Tarquin's father watched him for a long time, not saying anything. With nothing else to clean, Tarquin hunched his shoulders and stared ahead out the window. Down at the harbor, the water was gray velvet edged with white lace. Pale clouds scudded overhead. Behind the boy, the door closed quietly. His father passed by the window in front of him, carefully not looking in. After long moments, Tarquin released a ragged breath he had not known he'd been holding. He watched his father return to his place at the loom and kneel to his work.

Minutes later, Tarquin bounded through the wet heather up towards the center of the island. He could not believe his good luck — *not yet, not today!* He followed the path he had made for himself from so much regular use: up the long rise of jutting rock and creeping sand verbena that would lead to his cliff seat. But after a while, his feet slowed. Soon he was standing still, staring back behind him. The drifting mist swallowed his vaporous breath, and the air hung heavy around him. Behind and below, the snug houses of his village clustered. They looked like beehives of mud and thatch. They were the center of everything. Each of them housed people that he had known all his life. The mist washed over it all like weightless waves crashing in slow motion, revealing and obscuring in ripples as they passed. The calls of cormorants echoed off the sea.

Today is a gift. Today is borrowed time my father loaned me from tomorrow. I have to. I want to do today right. I can be helpful without kneeling. I know I can. Tarquin's feet turned towards Diver's Cove, and the rest of him followed.

....

The sea in winter is wet violence. It is winds like grasping fingers uprooting trees and viciously rattling windows. It is frigid geysers of ocean spray erupting above the tops of crumbling bluffs and ancient leviathans rising up from flooded deeps. From the first chill of Frostgate to the storms of Mantling, the goddess Thalassa grasps the islands in her cold hand and squeezes.

The island known as Aethys is a small island. It crouches like a lean beast above the waterline, its head low to the water where the village was built just up the beach from its only real harbor and rising westerly on its haunches to form a jutting cliff wall and the soft spine of a long-dormant volcano. In the spent volcano's shallow caldera, the daganwood trees grow. The island is just a few miles long and less than a mile wide. All over this rocky beast has grown a rippling pelt of wild grasses. On the far side of the island, there are a set of coves that are dotted with wind-worn arches and pillars of rock. No boats can land here, for everywhere are submerged stone teeth with a churning surf washing across them.

Since time immemorial, the women of that island have come there to dive with the hunting seals. Starting in their youth, girls are taught to swim deeply on great lungfuls of breath while keeping watchful for the movement of large swimming shadows. It is an evolving contest amongst them to see who can hold their breath longest or best judge the path of a darting harpoon through the shifting dimension of light underwater. In warmer weather, the island women would dive naked, then lay on the rocks to warm bare gooseflesh in the sun.

Now in a colder season they wrapped themselves in tight seal skins and clustered in knots around small fires. Now was not the time for deep diving; winter sharks are restless, and the leviathans come up to hunt them. Now was the season of storms, and churning tides pulled up deep tangles of seaweed and scattered small crabs and mussel clusters all over the beach. The village women took turns venturing into the shallows to drag armloads of kelp, sea cucumber and drifting plana up above the tide line to sort through. As Tarquin picked his way down the stony path towards them, he watched shyly as a group of older girls stripped to the waist and sparred with carved wooden spears. They danced through lunges and blocks, practicing the quick flick of the wrist that meant all the difference when hunting eels and blackfish. Their skin was darkly tanned, and belts of jute and braided shell jogged across their hips above the seal-pelt lacing of their diving furs.

Tarquin could hear the clattering of their short spears rebounding through the fog like the crackle of wood splitting and popping as it burns. He watched them for a lingering while, as nothing quickens a young man's blood like the brash beauty of such combatants. Then one of the sparring girls spotted him and beckoned him to come down the cliff. Tarquin galloped down to the beach, where a more casual saunter was made possible by slogging through deep sand.

"Ho Tarquin. Do you have any fruit or bread to share?" Her name was Noquomis. She was fifteen summers old and had thin shoulders and a crooked smile. Her back was a perfect tapestry of lean muscle and the blue knotwork tattoos that women wore after they had shed the first blood of maturity. To Tarquin, she was as beautiful as any tide pool with all its secret life and blooming colors. He blushed and shook his head. In that moment, he would have given any childhood treasure for a bag full of warm flatbread to share with her. He spoke quickly to distract from her look of disappointment.

"I'm here on business from my father. More camate is needed for the weavers. I think we are boiling a batch of pitch this afternoon. I would have brought you some bread if I'd known you were here. Well... I assumed you were here, but I wish I had thought it through better. Uh... because I would have loved to share bread with-" Tarquin bit off his last sentence mid-mouth. His voice had started to crack alarmingly, and Noquomis grinned coyly at him. Her teeth looked like abalone against the darkness of her tan, and like most of the other women, she wore her brown hair shoulder-length, spiked at the tips by dripping salt water.

"Well, if it is business that brings you, then don't let me hold you up. I'd send you to your mother normally, but..." She scanned the group of women warming themselves. "...I don't see her at the fires. She must be diving with Baeya." Noquomis sighed elaborately and took Tarquin by the hand. He flinched a little — her hand was cold and strong. "The camate shells are in a pile by the pestle stone. I'm not sure if we have as many collected as you'd like, but I don't mind grinding them up for you if you'd fetch them to me."

She walked with Tarquin away from her friends and back up towards the cliff face, where a pile of blue shells was stacked against a great smooth rock with many grinding holes worn into it. While Tarquin stooped and gathered the loose shells, Noquomis straddled the rock and used a rounded mortar to crush the blue shells to powder as soon as Tarquin could dump them into the hole. When the hole was half filled, she would scoop the powder into a cloth carrying bag. Over the course of an hour, they worked together, filling the bag as the sun slowly brightened the clouds and scattered spears of light across the shore.

While they worked, Noquomis asked Tarquin playful questions about the things he had seen in his island wanderings. Tarquin did his best to polish up and elaborate on his favorite tales. He was the first to find the torn tentacle of a giant squid that washed up last winter. He swore to seeing drifting lights on the high bluffs, wandering lost like lanterns held aloft upon the wind. He and his friends had once found an ornate railing from a shipwreck, and in his version of the story, he carried the large thing home almost single-handedly. She was an attentive audience, and every time she laughed and shook her head, he flushed with a secret heat and felt his bones buzzing.

Before heading off, he stopped by the main fire where his mother was chatting with his aunt, both of them with their heads tipped towards the fire while they squeezed sea water out of their hair. They were water-flecked and bare to the waist, and Tarquin could see the half-moon tracery of puckered scars that crested his mother's hip and disappeared down under her diving skins, visible like a pale constellation on her freckled skin. It was a years-ago testament to the violence of sharks that she bore with pain but wore with pride. Ellah had been a great spear hunter in her younger days: one of the finest the island had known in generations. Indeed, she would have bled out in the jaws of that summer shark if her aim had not been quick and her thrust less well practiced. But even so, the shark had died with its teeth in her hip, their mingling blood painting the low tide red, and she never again recovered the full quickness of both her legs. Ellah had lived, and healed. She made diving leathers of the shark's skin, and wove herself a belt of its teeth, and relearned how to walk until only a faint limp remained to remind her.

This had happened when Tarquin was quite young, but now she dove again as deep as any, and her harpoon arm proved to have lost none of its ambition. She had pale green eyes and hair like honey — unusual coloring for an islander. She also had a sailor's crude humor and laughed as abruptly as any barking fox, and Tarquin admired her above all others. He was glad he stopped to hug her, for her praise at his full bag of camate nourished his resolve to be more helpful, almost as much as the steaming crab meat that she carefully ladled into his hands out of their cooking pot.

Tarquin trudged back up the bluff, blowing steam off his tasty handful of crab. His mind was crowded with Noquomis — her strong legs had dangled so near to where he had knelt gathering shells that he'd sometimes brushed up against them! His thoughts were spiced with that hour of her company, and the warmth they provided bloomed in him and made him sweaty in his winter woolens. He wolfed down the crab as he neared the upper slopes of the island and tugged his hooded mantle off, wrapping it around the heavy bag of crushed shells he carried. Up at the heights, the wind swooped in from both sides of the island and the mist tore by rapidly. Tarquin wandered in a pleasant daze vaguely in the direction of home. He followed his feet haphazardly, his mind far away. *Did she feel it too? There was something there, something we shared.*

Drifting through a miasma of fantasies, it was the loud luck of a cawing seabird that alerted Tarquin to the edge of his cliff before he accidentally walked right off of it. His eyes snapped open, and he drew a startled breath. *Idiot! What good are such reveries if I'm all smashed up on the rocks far below?* Tarquin let his suddenly shaking knees give way and sank down onto the softness of damp plants. *Best to always look carefully where you are going in a heavy fog. Who knows what is just out of sight?*

His heart was racing, so he stared out to sea to calm his nerves. He could see the fog pouring across the water where it funneled into the mouth of the harbor. Here and there, patches of light drifted piecemeal over the ocean. And suddenly, something lit up, away out on the sea — something out of place. Purpled at the hazy edge of vision, sunlight caught the red and white striping of a far-off sail and the sheen of oiled wood for just a moment as a long ship cut between lufts of cloud that lay low to the water. Tarquin sharpened his eyes to it carefully, and breathless minutes passed. But it was not to be seen again — the winter brume was just too thick. The boy arose and hurried back towards the village.

....

"Father, I saw a ship! I saw one from the cliff!" Tarquin panted. He had burst in on his father drinking soup in their kitchen with a few of the older weavers. Their faces were ruddy from cold.

"Are you sure? What did it look like?"

"Umm... I just saw it for a moment, but I think it was a merchant ship? It was long, and the sail looked reddish."

"Reddish?"

"Striped with white, though."

The men glanced at each other mutely, eyebrows raising. The eldest of them leaned forward with his beard in his soup.

"Tarquin lad — that is most unlikely. Winter is no time for sailing in our waters. Thalassa forbids it, and common sense warns it off. Are you certain of what you saw?"

Tarquin's father folded his arms across his chest and leaned back in his seat. "Jerem, if the boy said he saw a ship out there, he surely did. He spends more of his time staring out to sea than any man on the island."

Tarquin's heart rose and sank rapidly at this. Was it pride or criticism coloring his father's voice?

The old man clucked his tongue. "True, I do not doubt his eyes so much as his words. If a bored boy set us to arms in a hurry, much of the afternoon will be lost. That lateen sail is not going to weave itself." The other men murmured agreement.

Tarquin's father scowled. "And what if the ship is Captain Reece and his crew, nosing in early with a cargo load to trade and expecting the sail they requested to be finished by now? We should at least quicken our pace at the loom. If that daft *ithnek* is in such a state that he would risk winter sailing, it will be his displeasure if we are without his lateen finished, and our loss. All our larder supplies are low enough — it is a boon to our island if trade opens early this year."

The men all nodded at this, and one or two rose up to wash their soup bowls in a hurry. Tarquin's father continued. "I say we assume the boy has eyes in his head and knows a ship from a sea swell. If Reece is heading into harbor, let's have the lateen coated and drying by then. And if not, if the boy is somehow mistaken, then we are none the worse for a bit of hurry." Tarquin's father winked at him across the row of balding heads, and his heart thrilled.

"And what if they aren't come to trade at all?"

"Then we'll light the night lanterns and keep an iron-shod stave near at hand."

The old man sighed and turned to look at Tarquin shrewdly. "Before I resign to this pointless haste, let's test your sailing sight, m'boy. What manner of ship do you think it was? Squat and square of sail like an oaken cog? Or was the sail lateen, flying over dhow as your father suspects?" The old man grinned, his teeth sparse and small against generous gums.

Tarquin did not hesitate. "It was surely a proper dhow, Uncle, and its sail was a triangle of striped cloth. The boat was too long and low to be a cog and too sleek to be blustering under square sail!"

The elder nodded approval and stood up with a grunt to rejoin the weavers outside. As he tottered past, he clapped Tarquin's father on the shoulder and said, "It's sure to be Reece then, and no other. That bastard is impatient for spring, so our hands will be cold to the last knuckle if we are to finish that sail tonight. Let us get back to it then. Thanks for the soup, Martin."

The men shuffled outside, and Tarquin's father walked over to him and gave the boy a rare hug. "Sharp eyes, lad. That's a good thing. Runs in the family. I, for one, have noticed that your satchel is overfull of camate, which is spilling blue dust on our floor over there." Tarquin blushed and swept at the mess with the hasty toe of his shoe.

His father continued, "Having the camate handy will save time and lessen hurry. So that's two good things you've done today. Deeds like that add up, and help make a boy into a man. Before he knows it, he has grown up to be the kind of fellow any woman would be proud to call a husband." Martin squeezed Tarquin's shoulders fondly.

"Now go keep an eye on that ship. If it is indeed headed into harbor, run and tell your mother so the women can get home in time to do some proper bartering when the cargo unloads. I, for one, am dearly hoping they have brought some loquats. I've always had a fondness for fresh fruit." He smiled down at Tarquin, and Tarquin grinned back up at him.

"Me too, father. Save me a few if they have them! I'll keep that ship well in sight."

And so, Tarquin went back to the cliff and sat through all that morning and watched the fog roll across the sea.

....

For a long time, he was bolt upright in his vigilance, the importance of his task keeping his back straight and his eyes chasing every little break in the fog. He watched while the wind blew itself around to the south, and the drifting mist began to stream away from the island. His young attention pounced on each shifting curl of vapors where the horizon leaked its clouds upon the ocean. Often, he started up nearly to his feet — was that a mast cleaving out of a suspicious bulge in the cloud bank? But always, it was something disappointing: a set of deepwater swells, a dip in air pressure, once even an entire pod of narwhals cresting the surface together and making tattered ribbons of the waves with their long horns. That was actually pretty exciting to watch. Tarquin would have never seen them if he had not been so keen to the horizon. His eyes began to ache with the strain of keeping such a wide focus.

He roused around midday to stretch his back and drain his bladder. The morning hours had passed as slowly as you might imagine — the kind of slow that means staring intently at an empty white horizon. As the afternoon eased on, sunlight broke through the island fog at last and baked the dewy wetness out of his hair and clothes. The shy smells of an early bloom wafted up from the earth: the small purple lathyrus flowers in their pea pods, the pulpy green carpet of sandwort and succulents, with little peeking yellow verbena blossoms reaching up through all of it towards the sun.

Now Tarquin leaned on his elbows, and as the warmth of growing things spread through him, a cold doubt began to grip his heart. What if he had been wrong? Hours had passed, and nothing. No ship to see anywhere — shouldn't it be halfway to harbor by now? What if he had conjured sail stripes out of prodigious imagination or addled thoughts ionized with Noquomis and adrenaline from almost walking off the cliff?

Down in the village, the men were rushing through their tasks with hurried concern, and it was all his fault. By sundown, he would be a scorned boy. His father's sudden pride would be salted with embarrassment, and Tarquin would never be thought of again as someone who can do things right. He scrubbed his sleeve across his watering eyes as he thought this and swallowed a lump of childhood grief. He must not be wrong! He could not be! He pulled his knees up to his chest and wrapped his arms around them, laying his chin on his forearms. Tarquin glared sullenly out to sea, daring a single slash of red to show itself from that offending winter pother. His head ached from ill humor. An occasional breeze blew through the tangles of his hair. The sun cooked the cliff. Time stretched slowly by.

....

The boy awoke in the gloaming to the smell of his burning village.

The light of those fires writhed on the waves of the harbor, staining the purple twilight like flaming blood. It flickered grotesquely across striated sails of red and white. Not one, but five ships lay at shallow anchor, low and long and bristled for war.

Tarquin stared at them blankly, numb with sleep and shock. A cold wave was rising in him, a wave that would break soon and sweep before it every trace of that boy he had been when he accidentally fell asleep on a warm day a lifetime ago. He felt like he was sinking down through the drowning deep, and the sounds of the distant screams in the valley below him were muffled by the pressure of his heart, thumping loudly in his throat. Everything was a frozen, roaring silence. *What have I done? What have I done to us?* Slowly, endlessly, he drew himself up to his feet. *What is left when the world has ended, what is left of anyone?*

Step by leaden step, he walked downhill through the wild sea oats, the tall stems leaning away from him in ripples. Under his senseless fingers, their panicles broke, and their seeds scattered. Smoke drifted up the valley, dragging cries of violence behind it. Overhead the two moons seemed like leering skulls set on shelves of air. Tarquin walked slowly beneath them, down towards the village to die. He made it all the way to the smoking doorway of his house. And that was where they got him.

....

Even now, so many years later, I come choking awake in the middle of the night, my eyes burning with shame and my chest heaving. It is not the memories that wake me up, for precious little of that night remains with me. I did not even register that I was in chains until many hours after we sailed from Aethys, so thorough was my shock.

Staring back out to sea as the only land I had ever known receded behind us, I finally began to recall myself. It was like being reassembled one piece at a time, but each of those pieces was something jagged and unwelcome. I would glance torpidly down at the shackles on my hands and suddenly become aware that last night I'd seen the body of my mother crumpled on the kitchen floor, her organs blossoming profanely from the cavity of her chest. I would close my eyes as the wind brattled across the sloping deck and see my father face down with a broken spear protruding from his ribs.

They were unthinkable memories, and so they crept into my mind only in flattened pieces. How awful is the intimacy of seeing someone so totally vulnerable, with the private organs beneath their skin exposed to hungry firelight? They had made me together, and in my weakness, I fell asleep and unmade them both.

Of the fate of that island, I am ashamed to say I cannot tell you more. I did not make memories in images that night because I was underwater inside, and everything was a ripple of color and noise around me. I do not know how many houses were burned because the bonfire that had been the Great Loom was so bright and hot that the windows of nearby houses were melting like wax. The bodies were collapsed bundles casting shadows, and they were everywhere. Some near the inferno at the village square had begun to cook and cremate. The smell was an indescribable fetor of baked clay and burning bowels. But beyond those staggering moments and the smell of death — nothing. Nothing. Even after hours at sea, I could not recall a single other thing.

The island grew smaller and smaller behind us. The cold wind stung my scorched cheeks, and I tried not to think about Noquomis. Had she dived deeply enough to escape the slaver's rope? Or was her body one of many dark silhouettes around that fire that would be burning forever in the back of my mind? Did my failure kill her too? I have never known the answers to those questions, for I have never found that singular courage to return to the island of my birth. I could not bear to see its ruins, nor could I ever look someone in the eyes who survived the night and had to face the devastation of that smoking sunrise and somehow rebuild and carry on. I have killed dragons that I feared less than the remains of my island village.

Please understand me when I say that much of who I have grown up to be is like a tree growing around a deep axe wound — all my reckless bravado, my fierce protectiveness of my friends — all this is because when I wake up sweating in the middle of the night, it is from dreams of the trees of my childhood, and their strings of shells that I can still hear rattling when I sleep. They are dreams of my mother, smiling as she combs my hair, and dreams of a girl whose name I will always remember but whose face I can no longer recall.

I died on an island in my youth and was reborn as a slave in chains.

....

The dhow that carried Tarquin was one of five, each loaded low to the water with cargo and thralls. The walls of the ship were tall and hollow, with benches for rowing oars and a mess of humans and cargo barrels crowded into the middle. It was an Erdin ship, but crewed mostly with Dekai — native islanders, like Tarquin. Their tanned bodies and dark hair contrasted sharply with the few Erdin on board. The Erdin are a fearsome sight to a twelve-year-old, and Tarquin avoided them carefully. The Erdin sailors were broadly muscled; thick pale skin and wide-set jaws, with a set of thick lower canines. But most alarming to Tarquin was their foam white hair, and frost-pale eyes. Their language sounded like stones rolling downhill and creaking ice.

There were twenty-eight chained thralls that had been taken from the island, Tarquin amongst them. They were lashed to heavy water barrels and forbidden to speak to each other. A few tried, and they bled for it. The rest, like Tarquin, could not have spoken if they had wished to. They were mothers of missing children, and they were orphans of war. Surviving families had been rounded up and scattered onto different ships to impose isolation. Their eyes were empty lakes, and they wept hopelessly. There was no roof overhead and precious little to keep dry under when the sky opened up and stormed.

Thalassa had warned sailors when the world was still young that winter was hers. To Tarquin's people, it was foolish blasphemy to cross the winter ocean when the Sea Queen stirred restlessly in her sleep. It was nine luckless days they sailed, and each seemed longer than the last. The day after they left Aethys behind, a storm settled in and stayed. Day and night, the sky was a mass of dark clouds with never a star to be seen. The waves were canyons they plunged through, and the winds were slick with sleet.

One night the storm winds howled obscenely, and the sail almost tore from its rigging. The wind rose and fell in a thousand voices blown up from some underworld. The Erdin held to the ropes and listened to the voices carried across the sea, laughing amongst themselves. Two of the ships were swept away from sight, scattered amongst the shifting peaks of water. The Dekai sailors and slaves huddled together in the stern, crouched in sloshing ice melt and rubbing each other's limbs to keep from freezing.

It was the longest night of Tarquin's life, but he stayed awake through it. Nobody who fell asleep that night woke up the next morning. There were twelve who died that way, and their bodies were chapped purple and glittered with such frost that it was hard at first to tell the sailors and the islanders apart. But Tarquin knew them. A baker who had loved his mother in their youth. A young girl that had played with Tarquin in the dunes. A man that used to drink with his father until they were both drunk enough to sing old songs to their wives. A woman who had shown Tarquin how to make a bird snare of woven twine. He prayed to Thalassa for each of them as he helped to lift them over the railing one by one and heard their bodies splash into the sea. *Lady draw them down to where it's warm. Lady keep them safe from further harm.*

After five days at sea, Tarquin woke up from the stupor of shock at last and began screaming.

....

Like a stone eroded by the waters of my grief, I had finally worn down the layers of torpor and found, beneath it, unbearable rage. I lashed against my chains like a wild animal, roaring inhumanly. I hadn't yet known such purpose of strength or such a clamor for vengeance. I thrashed and bit, red-blind with the shattering truth that I would never see my family or home again; they were so fundamentally destroyed that only featureless char would remain where everything that mattered to me once stood. I had not imagined that such oblivion was even possible, and my innocence burned up inside of me like a fever. I kicked out with enough force to break the aft railing, and the sailors gave me mercy when they cudgeled me senseless with a wooden oar and heaped sackcloth over my unconscious sprawl.

When I awoke, my head was swollen and pounding, but I had control of my anger again. There, under the privacy of that pile of cloth, I grieved with the choking honesty that I needed so badly. I wept until my throat burned and my eyes were swollen shut and I vomited up the worst of my disbelief. That, in a way, was my favorite part of the voyage. It was the only time I was left entirely to myself.

....

On the sixth day, the ocean was suddenly calmed. From one hour to the next, the waves dwindled from rolling hills down to lapping furrows, and the wind dropped off entirely. A warm fog drifted up from the water around them, and soon they were in the thick of it.

By midmorning, the sailors roused Tarquin and a few of the stronger slaves to join them at the oars, and the ship pulled slowly forward again. All was muffled and quiet, but the slapping of the oars on the water and the muttering of sailors. The Erdin, in particular, seemed ill at ease. They shook their heads and swore fearfully as the fog grew so thick that breathing became a wet labor. Now strange noises drifted out of the fog and echoed unnaturally around them: trees creaking, grasses rustling, the grackle of otherworldly birds. Somewhere far away, a woman laughed in a voice like falling water. The scent of apple blossoms perfumed the air. Tarquin found himself strangely comforted by the disquiet of the sailors, and as he pulled at the oar, he closed his eyes and breathed in deeply the aroma of blossoms. He had never smelled anything so sweet, and it made him light-headed. For the first time in days, he smiled to himself, cupping his hand over it to keep it hidden.

Just as suddenly as it began, the fog melted away behind them, and the ocean waves once again rose and dipped. A cold westerly lifted the sail, and the sailors let out a ragged cheer. Behind them, the fog closed again like a vaporous wall. The other two ships had apparently been swallowed within it, for they were not to be seen by us again. Tarquin stared behind them for a long time as the dark clouds of evening rolled back in. Something had been looming somewhere in that fog, he was sure of it. Something they weren't meant to find.

On the morning of the eighth day, the sun cleaved through the cloud rack at last, and the horizon was suddenly belted by a dark sash of green. This land stretched entirely across the sky before them: an island so vast to Tarquin's eyes that it looked like the ocean simply ended in front of it. The Dekai sailors were so cheered by the sight of it that Tarquin risked asking one what the place was called.

"It is Eld. Greatest of the Eastern Islands." The sailor replied, with a grin splitting his weathered face. "And we live to see it! A curse on Captain Reece and his devilish bounty, wherever he may have drifted. May the fog have swallowed him whole!"

The sailor looked at Tarquin for a moment, then ruffled his hair with a leathery hand. "Don't worry, lad — you are one of the lucky ones going upriver. We'll find someone to buy you in Dunmarsh, you just wait and see. Your journey is almost over."

By nightfall, they lay at anchor a scant mile out from the enormity of Eld. The Erdin lit three large lanterns and hung them on the side of the boat. They bobbed on the dark water for a long time, leashed to the anchor chain. Sometime after high moons, another Erdin ship drifted towards them, also bearing three lit lamps. When they had come up broadside, a plank was laid across the two ships, and two Erdin cloaked in red fur and heavy leather strode aboard. The Erdin spoke in hushed and heated tones amongst themselves. Then an arrangement was reached, and the two newcomers prodded the exhausted slaves awake.

Of the twenty-eight islanders that had left Aethys, nineteen had survived their wounds and the terrible cold. The Erdin selected all the women, pulling them roughly to their feet one by one and marching them across the gangplank and onto the other ship. Tarquin and the few other boys remained chained to their water barrels. They watched in stunned silence as the other boat drifted off into the darkness, the lapping waves almost hiding the sounds of the women weeping. That night, one of the younger boys slipped loose from his cuff and cast himself overboard to drown. And so there were seven of them left.

The next morning their ship turned in towards shore and ran north-easterly until they came to the mouth of an enormous river that rolled into the sea. This was the river Trask, and at its sea mouth, it was so wide that the opposite shore looked like another island miles away. By skillful tacking, they breached the churning river mouth and began to pull upriver by oar. A cold sun lit the day with pale ghostlight, and by afternoon it began to gently snow.

They rowed for all the hours in the day, taking turns at the oar while the great river split and divided, fed to whitewater by rushing tributaries. They rowed on to sunset as the snow continued to flurry lightly around them. The trees by the river's edge were covered in a dusting of white. Their branches were winter-black and leaned towards the water like fingers of grasping bone. Tarquin shuddered at the thought and hunched further into his cloak. He felt the ancient weight of those trees; they looked like crouched beasts ready to spring up and claw at the sky. Every time a branch split and popped in the cold, he started up in his seat.

Finally, they came to a wide tributary where the current flowed more slowly, and they dropped anchor for the night a few oar lengths from shore. That evening, the sailors shared rum with the island boys. Tarquin drank, reveling in the heat that bloomed in his chest as snowflakes melted on his hair and shoulders. He stared out at the darkened forest, feeling dizzy with drink and daydreams. The reflection of the boat's lit torches stretched like flowing carpets of light across the water. The trees closest to the water's edge were a tangle of purple shadows that the light barely touched — shadows that seemed alive. In fact, he could swear that they were staring back at him, or at least that *something* was. A shape slowly substantiated before his piercing gaze: a figure crouched behind a curtain of snow-laden branches. It was the eyes that gave it away, this crouching thing, for they glittered in the thin torchlight that reached the river's edge. The thing looked vaguely human and uncomfortably not: there was fur, as purple-gray as shadows, but the faintest blush of skin peeked through it. Ropes of reddish hair, fur-tufted ears. *Is it a girl?* Surely some fanciful flight of a rum-stumbling mind, for maidens are not often to be found crouching under evening trees in the middle of the wintery wilds!

The longer he stared at her, the more he was sure she was there but unsure of what he was seeing. Her eyes glowed with the feral intensity of something that hunts in the dark. The crouching shape looked less human by the moment, until it went loping suddenly off into the dark woods with the flick of a fox's tail. Tarquin's shoulders slumped in disappointment. He must have imagined it, and more's the pity too! She was the most interesting sight he had ever imagined crouching under a winter tree. Yet still, to share a lengthy gaze with a large fox is a wonder in itself, and he shrugged his shoulders amiably. Motes of reflected torchlight lapped across the water; the boat rocked peacefully. His chin drooped to his chest at last, and he fell asleep where he sat, feeling the tugging of the river on the anchor chain. He dreamed that a greedy purple fox ate both the moons, two cookies of red and yellow, and the stars got sucked through black teeth marks in the sky. His dream ended with a rush of shooting stars, until all light vanished. In the blackness of void, the river swept their boat back out to sea.

He awoke in the chill vapor of winter sunrise with the first hangover of his life, and vomited rum and regrets over the side of the ship. *Drinking liquor is dumb. Why do adults do this?* Tarquin thought to himself, wiping his mouth on his sleeve. His stomach lurched, and his temples throbbed evilly. *I'm certainly never doing that again!*

Solemnly made are the vows of childhood.

....

Upriver they paddled, further and further. Now the banks of the tributary were drawing in nearer as it thinned and grew shallower. The further they traveled, the slacker the tide became. The river began to redden with peat moss, and where the oars splashed the water, it would churn up golden mud. Soon the river broadened out past its banks and flooded into a standing marsh. The trees dwindled in size and thickened with climbing bracken. Beard mosses draped from most of the branches. Onward they rowed until the sky was smudged with snow clouds and the sunset gathered in. Just as their oars began to drag the river bottom, they rounded a bend in the fen and saw the shining of lanterns lit up in the trees like guttering stars.

Up ahead, an old splintering dock jutted out into the river, and men waited for them with lanterns burning in hand and pale puffs of breath obscuring their features. Further on past it, the river was spanned by a bridge of weathered stone too low to the water to sail beneath. As the boat drifted into dock, Tarquin peered out over tumbledown buildings of thatch and wood, all partially overgrown by spreading lichen. It was a small town if sparsely lit windows were any indication, built on wooden bridge walks that spanned the sinking treachery of the swamp. The buildings that Tarquin could see in the gloom were shabby and artless, walls of boards tacked together so carelessly that they seemed to lean into each other for support. The cold smell of a winter swamp painted the air. An oily smear of chimney smoke hung between the ramshackle buildings like a charcoal fog, and as he smelled it a shudder ripped through Tarquin and left him gasping, squeezing his eyes shut against burning memories.

They had come to the town of Dunmarsh, deep in the fens.

The boys were chained together and marched along the dock until it reached the shore and became a boardwalk. Planks rattled underfoot; the night hummed with the croaking of frogs. Ahead loomed the largest building Tarquin had ever seen: a three-story sprawl with a wraparound porch that leaked light from many windows. A simple sign of a cracked beer mug hung by chains above the door. Lit torches sputtered as snow drifted onto them.

Two stories above their heads, a young girl with dark hair and curious eyes drew the curtain back and watched the boys as they were led towards the building. Tarquin glanced up at her, and their eyes locked for a long moment. She gazed down at him solemnly through the dirty window. She was lovely in her own way — thin face and bright eyes, dark of skin and hair, even for an islander. And she would be the only witness to the moment Tarquin knew was coming: that unthinkable moment when he would no longer belong to himself, but become a living piece of property that could be sold or given away as easily as sailcloth.

She alone would see that he had begun this voyage as human as anyone else, that he had been trapped and caged but would never stop remembering what freedom was. So he smiled up at her gratefully, although his eyes stung with shame. She ducked her head quickly behind the curtain as he did, but he knew she was still watching him; one thin brown hand betrayed her presence at the curtain's edge.

The men who had met them at the dock stepped inside for a long minute while the boys waited in the snow with the sailors, stamping their feet to keep warm and trying to ignore their insistent hunger. The music of an accordion pushed out into the night from within, and as the front door swung back open, the acrid smell of sweat and tobacco wafted through the cold currents of air. A line of people shuffled out, so cloaked and hooded and bundled in scarves that their faces were hidden, and even their gender was lost in layers of cloth. Alone or in pairs, they drifted out, wraith-like amongst the line of chained boys. In muffled silence, they moved from boy to boy: inspecting, opening their mouths with gloved fingers, checking their eyes for pink lash and their teeth for malnutrition. When there was particular interest in a boy, he would be released from the chain line and trotted up and down the tavern yard to assure the buyer he wasn't lame of gait or clumsy.

One by one, the bundled strangers would engage the Erdin captain in hushed bartering, the barrier of mixed language see-sawing back and forth until the proper price was met. Then that boy was released from the line and led away by dark strangers. His last surviving friend, Jory, was taken by the arm and dragged off into the night. He glanced over his shoulder once, his frightened eyes resting on Tarquin for the last time before he was pushed through the doorway of a horse-drawn carriage gathering snow on the roof. Tarquin felt tears begin to run down his face as one of the strangers pushed their hand into his mouth to inspect his tongue. Then the *(woman?)* turned away and a larger figure leaned in close to Tarquin's face, blotting out his view and basting his face with a powerful reek of rye whisky breath.

"Are you a brave boy? Are you strong?" The man spoke in a rolling slur, his accent distorted by drink. "Are you worth your godsdamned golden price?"

Tarquin stared into the man's wan blue eyes. He saw hard lines, feral cunning, and the unmistakable glint of some complicated kind of shame. Tarquin suddenly felt his fear leak away, and it unhinged his mouth. "You are drunk. Why are you so drunk? You smell disgusting."

The bundled man laughed darkly, and his smaller companion shifted further away from him nervously. "I have to be drunk, little pissant, to buy a human tonight. You'll understand when you get old like me, and you need some little boy you never whelped yo'self to grow up and do your damn work for you."

The man spat in the snow and suddenly lunged forward and shoved Tarquin's shoulders roughly. Tarquin pin-wheeled his arms and slid backward on the slick ground, but he did not fall. A hot rage bubbled up his back. He lunged forward and drove his manacled fist into the man's gut, and an explosion of expelled air and wet vomit came rushing out as the stranger dropped to his knees. The Dekai sailors cursed and yanked at the chain line, and one raised a short club to knock some sense into Tarquin's skull. But the man on his knees lifted a shaking hand, palm out, and the blow never fell.

"Don't need to... that was... just what I wanted to see." The man spat a mouthful of bile and rose to his feet. He unwound the soggy scarf and wiped his face with the crook of his elbow, and Tarquin saw a pale Dekai man with a thick neck, a sparse and careless growth of beard, and cruel eyes. But his smile was unexpectedly playful as he wiped his arm across it. He turned to the Erdin captain and said, "I won't pay good gold for some skin with no spirit left in it. The little *kefe* has the speed and strength I'm looking for, and a sharp shit-stain of anger besides. I'll take him with me back to Holm if the price is gentle, and I'll kill him on principle and walk off if you try to dicker me slantwise. He's no good for anyone who doesn't have the will to hammer out that hate into something more useful. Look at him, man — the boy is steaming with it."

The Erdin's icy eyes gazed at them both: sweeping languidly from the swarthy man standing in his own vomit to the young boy with the balled-up fists, puffing hot breath and shaking with anger on the chain line. The captain slowly nodded, and his lips stretched back into a sharpened, tusky smile.

....

In my dreams, I imagined monsters that had come boiling out from their far-away land to chase the north wind. They rushed to my island with their gnashing fangs and their rending claws, and many of us were slain.

But in those dreams, my courage made me strong, and I killed them all, one by one.

The North Wind

The problem with being young is that most things in your life never happen *at* you directly; they happen around you, like a gale blowing suddenly by. All the soft things you take for granted and hadn't yet learned to tie down get lifted and spun and scattered all over the place, and sometimes you are too thin or too small, and the wind is as strong as shoving hands, and you go sprawling. Lying there on the ground, you can pretend the storm was blowing at you — that you were important enough to stir the ire of Pelios and his North Winds and he came howling down from the ice to knock you over.

But he didn't. You were just young and in the way.

So sure, at thirteen years old, you observe the world around you and narrate adventures in your head. You dream vividly. You rattle the bars in the window of stars and scream at the jailors who feed you, keep you prisoner, and maybe even love you. You scratch your name over and over again onto walls of empty air. You play out the details of escape plans in your mind, the many places you will go when you are free. Boredom is the enemy of being young because your brain is so fast and your imagination is so reckless that you must gild your world with golden fantasies, or you will go mad. If you do not daydream, or you cannot do so with vivid abandon, then your mind will starve for invention, growing ever more banal with stale self-comparisons and categorical list-making until all creative flow is dammed and dry.

At thirteen, a story begins as it must: with boredom and fantasies, and then one day, a prison bar bends, or your jailors get drunk and leave the keys to the kingdom in a pile on the floor.

Your story always begins with the bars coming down, on purpose or by accident. A jailbreak. Suddenly you are running. Suddenly, the world outside your head notices you directly for the first time. Then you learn what real danger is: the true danger of being exposed to the sky on an open road and, for the first time, catching the attention of the North Wind.

I am Talara, and I was named after a macabre old song.
I can walk on my hands, write poetry in nine languages,
and tell a tale so long that it casts its own shadow.

WIND

~ The Third Story ~

Come to my window, Talara my own —
Come watch the climbing roses grow over my home.
And when the wind howls in from the briny sea
Remember I loved you, remember my bones.

I'm under the earth now, under the loam
Where the sky is roots and the clouds are stone
I am where I always intended to be
Yet I never intended to be alone.

....

From the soot-blackened window of The Room Upstairs, Talara looked on as the island boys were sold downriver. She had seen this happen before, two winters ago, but the sight then had gutted her natural curiosity, and she had turned away from such broken lives and hidden her face. She had not been able to stand their hollow eyes or the useless shuffle of their feet as they set their humanity down and surrendered into ownership like an object. Years had passed since then; she was twelve years old now — almost an adult, to her thinking. Her blood had come on her nearly a year ago, and she'd be damned if she didn't have the courage to look this time. So she gazed frankly down at the tall boy with a tousle of brown hair and eyes as blue as winter shadows. Then he smiled sadly up at her like an old friend whose heart had been recently broken, and Talara's careful strength collapsed in a choking rush. She ducked back behind the curtain and wept for them all in little wheezing sobs. *They are children, just like me. We are the same.*

She watched them be claimed and distributed from the edge of the curtain, wiping her eyes with her non-sooty hand. She gasped in shocked delight as her boy drove his fist into one of the men who drank downstairs. However, instead of beating the boy, the man seemed encouraged to barter his price.

The pale moon was hidden by heavy snow clouds. The red moon rode above it in the sky, lighting the slushy ground with a sanguine blush. Talara disliked when only the red moon could be seen; its light was like a spreading bruise, like blood pooling in the bracken. She often imagined hidden thorn tendrils curling up everywhere in that rosy gloom.

The man loaded the boy onto an oxen cart and climbed up onto the driver's bench. The ox pulled them across the old stone bridge that the town had been built around, and they set off where the Wayward Road began: towards the next town, long miles to Holm. Talara did not know how far away it was, as she had never been much for maps and had never been there herself. In her fancies, Holm was a good place — a better place than this. She watched them set out on the rutted road. The trees around it were a swaying curtain of shadows. Draping lichen hung so heavy on the lowest branches that it almost touched the cobbles. The boy stared back towards Dunmarsh as they rolled away. His face was turned up towards her in the red light; the bruises around his forehead and the grim set of his mouth made him look much older. She moved forward into view, pressed her forehead against the glass and waved at him, never mind the soot on the window. If he could be brave while he was carried away, she could damn well be brave enough to wave him off. *Better late to courage than never to find it at all.* She felt ashamed and waved even harder until the ox cart was swallowed up by shadows and the road passed out of sight.

Talara sank down onto her knees on the clean side of the floor, moving carefully as the beams creaked with her weight. She was always cautious in that room; a fire had licked through it long ago, and nobody bothered to fix the damage. It was the room above the kitchen, and the noise and heat had always made it the last to be rented out to any but the drunkest patron. When the chimney flu had backed up many winters ago from burning years of wet greenwood, the owners of the Leaking Mug had neglected common sense and lit the kitchen with torches instead. One unfortunate thing led to another, and the drafting from the back door fanned a torch against the ceiling lath until the plaster bubbled and spat, and flames turned the ceiling into a rippling curtain of regrets.

The owners of The Mug had been lucky that the room over the kitchen was unoccupied at the time and that the daytime patrons were less tossed in the cups than they would become by nightfall, for a few of them had the sense to rally a bucket line to extinguish the fire and save the rest of the Inn. Talara's mother had been sober enough back then to fill a few buckets from the river herself.

And so, room nine at the end of the upper hallway became The Room Upstairs. Nobody ever fixed it, and nobody really cared. The kitchen was cooler for the additional airflow that vented summer heat up through the burned hole in the ceiling, and when the old owners had passed The Leaking Mug on to the current ones, the new owners had simply shrugged the damage off as a character quirk and set about with a will to abuse their inherited stock of alcohol. The only person who bothered to use that room anymore was Talara, who did so with a light foot on the charred floor joists. It always smelled like cinder chalk, and dancing dust mites mingled dourly with soot in the oily air.

....

Okay, here is the trouble — and here, an inappropriate aside to describe it. I, as in, myself, Talara, have so far written about myself in the third person perspective. Just as I attempted to do for everyone else in this book. Traditionally, thematically, this is the appropriate lens of perspective through which to communicate distance: between you and us, between ourselves and the children we once were. Oh, how disconcerting it feels to try to speak of my own life from such an informal distance! Also: tense aspect, of course, and the danger of rambling on.

So how about yes, Talara, get to the godsdamned point! I can tell you right now, when I finally got away from that place, I never went back again, not once. I don't think you need to know any more about how the room smelled — it smelled charred. Use your imagination.

....

As the last of the boys were sold and the pale strangers headed back inside to drink, Talara listened through the keyhole—

....

Nope, I just can't: this isn't working out.

So, here's what I'm thinking: let us polish up this little second-person postulation. I, as in Current First-Person Talara, writing now about us back then, am taking a moment to gripe at you. I'd like to pretend I am breaking the narrative wall to introduce some linguistic revelation that will leave you, the startled reader, agog. In actuality, it's just a cranky aside because I am frustrated about writing this book.

I had to; it had to be me. For starters, Caetal and Rahyn can't read or write. Well, they won't, anyway. They refuse to, which to my mind is the worst kind of self-imposed ignorance, but whatever. Melvin cares for each little detail yet somehow has no sense for dramatic story structure, so he's out. Tarquin could probably have done a decent enough job of it if he had the patience to finish what he started, but he rarely does. Actually, if I'm being totally honest, he did pretty good on the asides I let him narrate on, so: a few points there. As for Mathias ... well, I beat him to it, and I, therefore, had to promise to include his portentous poem tidbit, which I did. You'll read it later when you get to his story. It's a bit creepy.

Wading through Tarquin's constant asides, Caetal's forceful demands to rewrite what actually happened — and don't even get me started on how tricky it was to make any linear sense out of Rahyn's story at all. I'm just saying, I think I deserve what descriptive licenses I choose to get. And I am bloody well choosing to speak in the first person about the details of my own story from here on out! Sorry in advance to all of you linguistic purists. In future chapters, any asides of mine will likely be more traditionally footnoted and entirely optional to read. Or not. This is my first novel attempt, so it might be a bit all over the place. Just pretend this is some sort of helpful literary exercise and that I'm doing it for your own good.

....

To begin with, I was raised in a tavern. Yes, the very same shitty one you read about above, and I spent more time in that half-burned room than you can possibly know. Oh, I can TELL you all about it. I can give you a length in hours to sum up in your head: ten to twenty-six hours a day. I can say that went on for almost eight years. If you want to tally that up, and I hope you don't, it is going to add up to more than fifty thousand hours. If it doesn't add up to that, then your sums are wrong. It was, to speak plainly, forever. Especially for a child. I was in there longer than your longest notions of too long.

The circumstances that led my family to the Leaking Mug in Dunmarsh are what I would describe as a "bottoming out" of my mother's options. It was not always so: we are descended from a great people. I am blooded of the Rhymir through my mother's side. This is the only way that ancient heritage can be tracked: back through the matron Rhymira to the elder days when our world turned under different stars, and the Immortals built vaster and grander empires than this island of farmers could ever dream. The wisest and most cultured of such kingdoms was Rhymir, and our ancestors were the progenitors of poetry and the first instruments for music. The Rhymira were women of stunning athletic prowess; our performers twined and twisted their bodies into fantastic shapes. The best of them, it is told, could sing birds out of the highest branches and dance like fire blooming. In fabled times we traveled to the limits of land and over deep waters and brought our stories to any who strove to be civilized.

Alas, ruin came to Rhymir and all the empires of that gilded age. The Immortals were overthrown and imprisoned in the Great Tree, and the world they had built quickly shook itself apart. Into the wasteland that followed came such things as were called gods. I do not know if we created them, or invited them in, or whether they have been here all along, waiting in the walls like rats for someone to douse the lights. Either way, the empires of old withered in their separate miseries, wild grasses grew through their roads, and my people wandered across all of it, trying desperately to hold on to once-mighty dreams. We dwindled, but we did not forget. We drank, and we despaired. Some became sly, and many learned unscrupulous tricks to survive. Famine was everywhere during that time of shattered mountains and clouded seas. Still, we were not *unmade*; we did not forget Rhymir and the world that was.

....

Unfortunately, my mother is an idiot about men, and I am the eldest of six siblings born of five wretched fathers. I don't know what makes a smart person so very dumb, but whatever it is, my poor mother has a lot of it. When she was young, she fell in love with a landed man who traveled with her family for a while. He was a fool who wanted things that weren't meant for him and stole my grandmother's dowry chest. My mother lost her wits and the tips of both her thumbs when she spoke out in his defense and followed him into exile.

For my people, family is everything: it is the last tile left in the shattered mosaic of our race. My mother choosing my future father over her own people was unthinkable. So they were bloodied and lashed to a pole raft side by side with nothing except my grandmother's looted chest of heirlooms, which would have passed peacefully to my mother in time, anyway. Then my grandparents wept for them, and cursed them, and pushed them out into the river. This exile is called *Drift* — if the raft is swept out to sea, the banished parties are meant to die. If the boat washes up somewhere on shore and they manage to free themselves, they can lead out their diminished lives in exile... so long as they never claim the blood of Rhymir again.

The Drift. It is a word that means a hole has been opened in your chest and the wind is blowing through you. It is also a word that magi invoke to describe the encroaching madness of magic. Two years after they were Drifted, my father drifted further along without my mother. He stole most of the remaining valuables from that chest and left only baby Talara in trade. I'm sorry to admit that the exchange was not a lucky one. I will never know what happened to those cultural treasures of my family, but I do know what happened to my father. His body was found swinging from a gibbet on a castle wall in Portuan, and I'm glad of it.

My mother was no longer Rhymira. Forbidden to perform feats or music before an audience or to tell any of the Thousand Stories. She was a lost woman, stunted and cut off. And where her blood once flowed strong with the thousand stories of our people, she packed up the holes in her heart by allowing strange men into her body and pickled her stricken wits with drinking. After two children, she no longer sang to the rising sun. By four children, she could not be bothered to travel, even in spring. When my youngest sister was born (the only other girl-child, her and I bookending four brothers), my mother was so drunk and slipped out on blackroot that she forgot to name her. None of us knew who the father was, and nobody cared.

I was her last treasure: the firstborn daughter, born in freedom on the open road. I was not to be swept along in shame by my mother's Drift. I was Rhymira through my grandmother's line. I would walk with my head held high in the traditions of my people, and my mother made damn sure I would do her proud or die learning how. Therefore, when I was quite young, and she still remembered the lessons of her mother, she began to train me with everything she knew about what our people were capable of.

....

When I was two summers old, my mother taught me how to touch things: to discern between the violence of sharpened steel and the softness of old skin. She taught me to do so in silence — I communicated by learning to gesture my needs with my hands and was otherwise encouraged to not make a sound. I ceased crying early on, or I was pinched repeatedly and food was withheld. *Only by being silent can we hear the wind talking.* An infant of Rhymir learns to be as quiet as a mouse, speaking only in gestures. I was a silent shadow, touching everything and everyone with the tips of my fingers until I was old enough to earn the right to my voice.

For a normal human, this enforced silence at such a young age would be crippling. You learned to speak by aping the words of the world around you, after all. Without these elementary sounds to build patterns out of, your lips and vocal cords would never form the strength to speak at all, and in later years, you would be reduced to tonal grunts. However, the bloodline of Rhymira runs through channels that are dug deep by time. The span of our lives is unusually long, though we do not look it. We take years that others do not have to learn to do important things carefully.

After three summers, I was constantly talking, and my movement training began. Mobility in Rhymir culture does not conclude with walking upright as others do — we are taught to walk on our hands as well, to get comfortable with inversion. *Only when we are upside down do we see that the earth is a sky for the air.* Since birth, my mother had held me upside down often: when telling me stories, when playing with me, even sometimes just to help me fall asleep. I got so used to the hot pressure in my head that I sometimes felt dizzy when I was standing upright. The Rhymir believe that blood in the brain is what collects hidden insights and carries them to the heart. It is told that every man, woman and child of ancient Rhymir began their day inverted in complicated hand and head stands that moved slowly through postures meant to strengthen the muscles and rejuvenate thoughts from sluggish sleep. Once I could stand on my head and hands for half an hour, she helped me to take my first hand-steps. I will always remember how nervous I was and how my palms sweated! After a year of daily training, I was able to stand on one hand and sign with the other, hand-walking around the room as merrily as any waddling duckling.

By my fourth summer, it was time to learn to really use my body. Mother first taught me to roll around all tucked up like a driftweed, and it amused me greatly. I would laugh and laugh, rolling head over tail and colliding with everything just to see what it felt like. *Only when we are in motion do we discover the gravity of stillness.* My mother took me down to the ocean's edge each dawn, and there I learned to really sprint. Running was easy compared to walking on my hands. She taught me to tuck and flip in the air and land without hurting myself. She tied a rope between two pines, and, after a wobbling while, I learned to walk on balance across it. I even managed to walk the rope inverted, but that took a few more years and a lot of bruising tumbles. Yet tumbling itself came to me with an ease that made my mother proud; I was Rhymira through and through, she said, and damn her family for being so short-sighted about love.

By then, my father had been crow-food for more than a turn of seasons, and my mother was full of regret and beginning the drunkard's path. She rounded out with my first little brother sometime that year. Although I don't remember his father, I was fascinated by my baby brother from the moment he was born. I spent many hours carefully touching his ruddy face and tiny hands while he slept. Unlike me, he was so loud! My mother did not have the motivation to teach him to be properly silent, for he was a boy and would never be considered Rhymir unless he married into it.

Another year followed, and another brother. By then, we had drifted with the wind so far from the place of my birth that my mother barely knew what island we were on anymore. Her second son was a difficult birth, and the father was a fisherman who drowned shortly thereafter. Weeks passed with no word of his fate. When she finally got word that his pale corpse had washed up at the cove of Malku, she plunged into a grief that left her despondent for days at a time. It was not but a month later that we drifted into The Leaking Mug in Dunmarsh, and she paid for our room and meals by pawning the last of the trinkets she had stolen from her family. Once we had settled in, my mother decided it was time for me to learn to sing. She never spoke to me that year, not one normal sentence. All her words vibrated across the scale, tuning each flutter to a tonal sound. *Only by singing will we ever discover the edges of our own voice.* A hundred songs, and then a thousand, were broken up into pieces that became my organ of communication.

My mother and I staggered arpeggio across the scale — her with a son feeding from each breast, me clapping and laughing as we unknit those ancient songs and purled them together again in silly sentences that taught me new ways to voice my thoughts out loud. The *Lay of Ar-*

wald unfolded into verses that I could play with like toys. In amongst my requests for food and drink were woven the mysteries of love and loss that would come to haunt my imagination. *The Ballad of Barbarous Men* contained many colorful phrases for excusing oneself to the toilet. *Land o' Long Shadows* was full of the lessons of etiquette when dealing with strangers, and nobody learns to cuss like those that can sing *Blow-Tary-Blow* all the way through and not get cuffed for it. Because I wanted so badly to earn the right to speak freely to my mother, I was tricked into learning to sing. It was the kindest thing she ever did for me.

By my sixth year, our money had run out, and Dunmarsh had entangled us like a weed. Mother moved into a room out back with the (previous) owner slipping her food, and drink, and so much more, while his marriage fell apart and my third brother swelled up like a secret in her belly. I lived in room nine on my own now and was almost never allowed to leave it except in the early mornings while the drunk men slumbered under heavy dreams, and only the fishermen stirred. I became known as a local myth — a sunrise child that wandered barefoot through the cold taproom and vanished into thin air after breakfast.

....

You may be wondering the same thing I was: why did my mother insist on imprisoning me in room nine? For a prison it was, though I was able to let myself out whenever I wanted. Heavy drinking and a fatalistic streak had transformed her natural curiosity into cynicism; her flashing temper had morphed from a dancing baton that guided the orchestra of her emotions into a flailing rod with sharpened edges. All these years later, I cannot truly speak to her motivations for keeping me penned up in that room, for she never shared them with me. If I had to guess, I would say that she wished to keep me entirely separated from her life, or rather the life of the person that she was becoming. As time passed, it became an awful, almost unendurable kindness.

....

Shortly after the innkeeper's wife discovered the truth about her husband's straying affection and almost stabbed him and my mother to death with a pair of roasting forks, my mother determined that it was time for me to learn how to get out of trouble. So she taught me the proper ways to lie and how to get away with it. *Only by flattering someone can you discover how they view themselves. Therefore, honesty must sometimes be counted as the enemy of truth.* It turns out there is a lot to being a good liar, and much of it was harder for me to learn than you might expect, particularly at such a young age. Until that point, I had been encouraged to be attuned through my senses to my environment, to be inverted, to be playful, to be fluid, and finally, to speak my desires through song. I had never been taught to hold back or deceive. My mother made me practice the art of deception on her and her suitors. I was taught to lie about almost everything, to twist even my most inconsequential needs and observations into an opportunity for duplicity. If she caught me in a lie, I would get slapped. If I got away with it, I didn't. My face was purpled and puffy for months as I took my lessons to heart. Almost nothing teaches faster than pain. The lessons of love are longer-lasting, but pain brings you up to speed in a stinging hurry.

Some of good lying is in breath control and some of it is in gestures. A lot of lying is being able to think quickly while not letting your tells of sweat or stutter make themselves obvious. Speak plainly; have excellent details prepared, yet don't offer them up easily. Keep shivering muscles still and make steady eye contact. Disrupt their line of questioning with questions of your own, but never with a contrary air, because a liar caught in lies becomes overtly defensive. To lie convincingly, you must know your audience and their hidden blinders: vanity, complacency, desire. It is an intimate violation and a dangerous game to play with anyone. The best lies are built around truth or magnificent self-deception. The best liars are, of course, those who believe they are not lying.

Now, the complexity of lying that I am describing is based on many years of practiced social interactions, which, at six years old, I had almost no experience with. But children can learn to be good liars too, and the fundamentals of fabrication that my mother taught me at that age were the tools that I crafted my deceptions with for all the years that came thereafter. Unfortunately for me, I was a slow learner, and I paid for it painfully. I was bad at lying for long enough that I began to forget what life was like before my mother beat me all the time. Eventually, I learned to deceive convincingly, and the beatings slowed. Yet by the time they stopped entirely, a rift had opened between my mother and me that never closed. I didn't share the truth of that with her, of course. She had taught me to lie to her about everything, after all.

....

Spring became a tantalizing torture in room nine, and summer was hot and claustrophobic. I was old enough to need more room to play than just twelve feet of walls on all sides and more fresh air than cold gulps of early morning. When my seventh spring blew apple blossoms into the room through the open window, I fell to my knees and wept like a toddler. Something wild and wishful was growing inside me. I could not stop staring at the curve in the road that slipped under the trees at the edge of vision on the far side of the river. Every gentle breeze whispered to me in the language of the world outside, and I was feverish with not knowing what it all meant. Smells of earth and swamp; waves of cooling air rippling through the gloaming just after the sunset; the tight splash of the cormorants diving the river for fish.

I would sleep curled up below the window, pressed against the wall just to feel the last heat of the day bleed through the plaster. One night, I awoke suddenly with tears on my face and a wild pounding in my heart. Without thinking of the danger, I clambered out onto the sill for the first time, crouched and swaying with sleep and not even caring about the hard-packed earth far below. I climbed the sloping pitch of thatch as quietly as I could, hand over foot, along the chord beams. Moonslight was everywhere, and the swamp stretched out all around me, its hidden creeks and pools glittering amongst dark clusters of cattails. I still remember the sight of it from the rooftop so clearly.

I spent much of that summer clambering all over the buildings in town — only ever at night and only when the weather was fair. I learned much about climbing and balance, and how to judge distance in leaps and keep my weight on the balls of my feet. Sometimes, when I was feeling brazen, I would invert and walk the roof ridges hand over hand. In the early mornings, as the wicked town still slept its collective hangovers off, I would often creep down to the rickety boardwalks. I would shimmy from there down below the streets to the thick and rotting pilings that held Dunmarsh aloft above the swamp. The smell of the wetlands mingled putridly with discarded waste, and I often had to wrap my nose and mouth in cloth, for the wind that blew off the river did little to dispel the stink. Everywhere was the throaty sawing of bullfrogs, sudden fluttering of waterfowl taking wing, and the sinuous gliding menace of giant water snakes, who would chatter their tails against the pilings to distract prey from what their heads were planning.

But the fear was a thrill that drew me back often, for in the soft gloom of sunrise I could swing and clamber across a seemingly endless playground of pillars and beams that stretched as far as sight. It was delightfully creepy down there: misty as often as not, with thin morning light sifting down through the boardwalks overhead and the pilings of all those intertwined docks looking like a thousand giant fingers gripping the swamp below. I would giggle quietly to myself when those few folks that were up so early clattered across the boardwalks overhead because they were so close and never knew that at any moment, I could reach up and grab them like a bridge troll.

A loss of grip or judgment would result in a fifteen-foot drop into water or deep mud, and I admit that more than a few mornings ended with a dunking and me washing mud out of my clothing in secret. My mother was drinking so heavily by then that she probably wouldn't have noticed my muddy pants or swampy smell anyway, but I could not bear the thought of losing my stolen freedom if discovered I was sneaking out.

....

That was the winter room nine caught fire one morning and became The Room Upstairs. The patrons rallied, The Leaking Mug was spared, and in all the confusion, nobody noticed how the innkeeper died. Some say he was passed out in his cups and died of smoke inhalation, and some say it was something in the cup that killed him. Either way, the innkeeper's widow handed the tavern over to a distant cousin for coppers on the gold and was gone from Dunmarsh before her late husband was settled in his grave.

That winter was a brutal one. Snow piled in heavy layers that soaked into the peat bog and caused a lazy flooding of Dunmarsh that took weeks to ebb. All the underground larders filled with water and their contents molted with moldy bracken, and when the weather started to warm at last, a line of green lichen spread along the foot of every building in town. The Room Upstairs was too fire-gutted and drafty to winter in, so I bunked with my mother for the first time in years. It was a small space, stuffy with the stinking warmth of pleasure and the bed-wetting of young boys. After having my own room for so long, I could not bear to share a sleeping mat with siblings. Their ear-splitting wails woke me up regularly; squalling for milk or shaking from night terrors. Their very noises made them seem barbaric — strangers in familiar skin, who had never been raised to be clever about their needs, who cried out in anger and sharp laughter like savages. All the while, my pregnant mother and her men came and went throughout the night on a straw pallet that never got changed. The reeking, groaning shadows were more disquieting to me than any fear of the dark. One night my mother woke me up with a croaking howl of grief and anger that began as a violent argument between her and a lover and ended with him losing teeth and her going into labor.

She wept and raged until the midwife arrived; wet clumps of blood stained the straw around her. Her face was purpled and gasping, her legs up wide, and my stomach churned so that I couldn't bear to look at her. I had never directly witnessed her give birth before, and it made me feel queasy in a deep-down way, as though ants were crawling inside my belly. So I wandered around peering into her private things as gawkers clustered and whispered by the door.

Under a low table and an old pile of furs at the back of the room, I found something that gleamed with hammered silver. It was crafted to look like a horse: a long flat body and two pillars rising from shoulder and flank, with a plated bar half the length of my body suspended between them. Strung betwixt that bar and the body of the flat horse were eleven strings of gut wrapped in gilded wire. Later I was to learn it is an ancient instrument called a silver lyre, but on that night of screaming labor, it looked like a glittering secret that would lift me away from the pain-stained atmosphere of that stuffy room.

I cradled myself around it and drifted my fingers, feather-light, across the strings. It made a noise like water kissing wind that was so beautifully out of place that the sound of it quieted the room immediately, and my mother raised up on her elbows to watch me play. Her eyes were as dull as stones, yet she still smiled crookedly as my fingers wandered experimentally across that silver landscape of sound.

It was, to this day, one of the greatest moments of my life. I closed my eyes and shuddered with the hugeness of everything, of a world that could contain such an opportunity as this: to hear a waterfall indoors, to call up rippling faerie fire on a winter night. For those moments I was Pelios, and the winds were mine to command. I knew nothing yet of the art of making music with my hands, but I was never again going to live stunted without it. I played. All night, I played with those sounds. My fingers wove questions in the air to which I had no answers. Muscles cramped that I didn't even know I had. I played on. Curious gawkers came in and stayed, and I played on. Just before dawn my third brother was born, and my mother was watching me as he passed into this world. His cries of new breath were the first sounds in that room for hours besides her labor pains and that shivering lyre. With those cries, the spell I had accidentally woven broke, and I slumped forward in exhaustion and slept.

I woke up tucked under the crook of her arm with my face pressed against her neck. Our sweat smelled the same, as though we were one person, and I clung to her and wept as quietly as I could. Her hand reached up and tangled in my hair.

"Shah, Talara. Shah. The world is always turning. All will be well again." Her eyelids fluttered with dreams, and her voice was sleepwalking. I wept against her breast as though my heart was breaking, and although she slept through it, her fingers slowly wove my hair into knots. I think it is the last time I can remember holding her like that.

Life rips through us all, and we can do nothing but sort through the wreckage and try to describe how it felt.

....

Another year passed, and another. Another son followed from another father, and in the meantime, much had changed between my mother and me. My formal training on the lyre began in earnest. Almost as soon as she had woken from that recuperative unconsciousness that follows birthing, my mother began to instruct me on how to call the wind into those silver strings. I had passed through some childhood veil that had been unknown to me, and after that long birthing night, she never hit me again. Neither did she hug again; our relationship was encased from then on in the solemn formality of teacher and student. She instructed me with patience and an exacting control that was astonishing. I did not know what drove her at such a pace or what was running to catch up behind her. She had me at it for all the hours in a day that sleep and simple needs left empty.

When I had mastered the basics of tempo and scale, we moved on to weaving my singing in between the notes of the instrument. It became everything to me. *Music created love. Before music, there was only fondness and duty.* I would sit against the burnt walls in the Room Upstairs, cradling the silver body of this ancient relic. Using only my fingers, I could draw the seasons in through the open window like mist rising off the river. In the vibration of the strings, I found my first conception of perfection: it was something real that could be measured and touched.

A properly tuned lyre plays a shade of melancholy that no minstrel's pompous lute can mimic — it carries with it the sounds of sand falling in the hourglass. It is age, time, and a vanished empire with flowers growing up through where roads used to wander. If you have never heard the sound for yourself, I highly recommend that you do so. The silver lyre was not a common instrument even in its day; it is a great expense to craft one, and there are no artisans living who remember how it was once done. The instrument is bulky, unwieldy to an artless hand, and does not travel well. In the years that followed, I was to learn the playing of other instruments as well: the five-string rebec, which sounds like a party of droning crickets and cuts across taproom chatter better than shouting; the charmer's shawm, which turns breath into beautiful grief and can make even the most rigid men wilt with dreams of home; and, of course, the fluttering fury of the castanets.

Each instrument I trained on filled my chest with such joy, such vastness of air and light that I could scarcely breathe with excitement. I would fall asleep on most nights, clutching my thin blanket up under my throat and hugging myself to keep the vibration that welled up between my aching fingers from rattling my bones apart. Since learning to sing, I had never found something else that really meant *me*. Something that spoke with the colors that had been blooming inside my mind, something that spoke for me at all.

Each day now had a voice all its own — if I woke with a cramping gut, then the music I made was crouched and scale-deep. When morning radiance split through the low gray, my glad melodies climbed the beams of sunlight and chased the clouds apart. The Room Upstairs no longer felt like a prison; it was a proud tower with an open window from which I poured my fantasies down onto the boardwalk below. That spring, many travelers who stopped and stayed at The Leaking Mug did so because they were drawn to my music leaking like mystery through the walls. They would call up to me at the window, and I would sing them lies about my life until my mother came out and shooed them away.

....

It was inevitable that the proprietors demanded of my mother that I play the taproom at night. As we were financially destitute and at the mercy of their good graces anyway, my mother agreed. She could no longer support us through the thin coins that her pleasures commanded: something had torn inside her from birthing so many sons, and she was too tender for rough embraces ever after.

For weeks before I was allowed to play in public, she pushed me through a rigor of training that bloodied my fingers and frayed my temper. She taught me breathing tricks to make my chest lift and tilt evocatively. The indulgence of silence between pauses and how to float your voice across the room in a way that makes it sound like you are barely speaking, or that yours is the only voice worth hearing. She drove me through the tunes, faster and faster. She filled me with secrets worth knowing: how to adjust the tempo of a song to please the feet of dancers; how to roll a vibration around in the back of your throat to make it sound like the music is coming from underwater or from a long way off; how to pitch your gut voice so low that it is simply a deep hum, and let your instrument talk for you; where to interject music into a spoken story to enhance a mood; how to beg for tips without it looking like begging. Her eyes were glassy with blackroot all the time, and she rarely ate.

And then one evening, there I was: a girl of nine summers wrapped around the silver treasure of that lyre in plain view of all those rough drinking men. My mother needn't have worried. After so many hours of practice, I played their hearts as easily as they drained their cups. I sang them all away to deep glens and glad days, walking arm in arm with the women they each missed. My fingers upon the strings were the winds that fill the sails of a ship departing from home, never to return. I had them, and I held them, and I squeezed them hard. There was rarely a night where eyes were dry til midnight, and the Leaking Mug experienced a strange season of calm from the brawls and damaged furniture that had made the place infamous. My tip cup filled with coppers as my local reputation grew. I was a small brown girl with a very big instrument; a calm boat on a rocking ocean, and I had everything I wanted.

••••••••••••••••••••••••••••••••••••

It was during that time while I was learning the musician's craft that I asked my mother a very important question, and heard a very important answer.

Like most of life's moments, I was unaware at the time of the significance of the question. Nor was I aware that the answer she gave me was to influence the fate of my life, and the lives of future friends and strangers that I had not met yet. Pivotal moments happen in such ways. We rarely recognize them for what they are until much later on, if at all. But it is important to note here that in some very roundabout manner, my mother ended up having as much effect on the future of the island of Eld as had any conquering king. After all, empires are only threatened by the actions that succeed conversations. It is words, not swords, that are the first draft of destiny.

....

A short conversation, yet I remember it clearly still. It was one of those rare times when she invited me to come down from the Room Upstairs and take a walk together through Dunmarsh. The evening was lengthening towards the bloody sunset colors of autumn. Chill drafts of air tickled across our skin as we walked. My mother had a loaf of fresh bread tucked under one arm, and we were holding hands like we sometimes did when I was very young. The twilight was alive with the drone of insects eating each other, the chirrup of frogs eating those insects, and the fleshy flutter of shadow bats eating the frogs and insects alike. The air was humid and loamy.

We made it to the old bridge that is considered the edge of town, and sat down to rest on a decaying wood piling that lay by the path. We had been chatting animatedly, as we often did, *(we both enjoyed talking, though neither of us were good listeners, so we often talked at the same time,)* when I ventured a question that had been on my mind for a while.

"Why is it that the Rhymir and the Erdin people feel so *real*, but the Dekai don't? Or I guess, like... clear? Important? I don't know how to ask this."

"Not like that. Try again."

"Well, I noticed that the Dekai almost never show up in the tales I've heard of the history of the island. I mean — they are *there*. They just don't seem to have much *presence*."

"Like some haunting spirit? They take up space, do they not? Speak sense, child."

"It's just that — well, okay... I have heard so many stories about the Rhymir from you. The great performance contests of old; dances that lasted for days at a time; colorful clothing, passionate affairs — rich in lore and customs, pride and ruin that played out over generations of families. Traditions worth passing down through the ages. Our people created such important things, like music and the epic forms of the *haruta*."

My mother nodded and smiled. "Indeed. We are women of a great people."

"And then there are the Erdin, who are so powerful. Innovators and warriors alike. *'The Children of Iron that came from a doomed and distant island, conquering whatever they wished to conquer.'* Another important people. They brought civilization to Eld."

My mother frowned. "They brought war. War is not civilization."

"But then they *made* civilization. After the war. Because they are as clever as they are strong — all the tales agree. They built cities, and made roads and plumbing and... castles and... they dress nicely."

"The rich ones do. The poor of any race all tend to dress in similar rags."

"Well, yes. But the Erdin *created* those styles — you know what I mean? Layers of silken robes, armored plating, golden teeth caps. Blacks, reds, grey and gold, patterns of cloth. Complex patterns. You can tell an Erdin from a long way off, because they have *style*."

My mother nodded. "Ah. I see."

"And before they got here, what was here? Groups of Dekai living in fish-skin tents? Nobody ever talks about them, because it doesn't seem like there is much to talk about. It's like for so long they were just *here*. Existing, but not achieving much. What were they doing? Sailing around and fishing? Collecting seashells? I know they are called the *Water People*, but it doesn't seem to mean anything special. They all just look like peasants to me. Even the rich ones dress like peasants, but with cleaner clothes. I guess my question is-"

"So what you are actually trying to ask is: 'Who were the Dekai, and were they always like what they are now?'"

"I suppose so. Yes. And if there is more to them as a people. I've heard an Erdin sailor say the Dekai were born to serve the Erdin, as water serves to strengthen forged iron through quenching. But the same guy also went on to say that women were likewise born to serve men."

My mother snorted. "Obviously a cretin. Who ever heard of such nonsense? There has never been born a people who were *meant* for servitude. Only Fate demands such cruel bondage."

"So, if they were not born to serve the Erdin, then why do they? Why put up with such a life? The Dekai still outnumber the Erdin by a lot."

"Around here they do."

"Then why not take their island back?"

"Fear. And habit."

"Fear of death?"

"Amongst other fears."

"That still doesn't answer my question though. What are the Dekai? *Who were they as a people, before the Erdin came?*"

My mother turned away and broke the bread into two pieces, handing one to me. Then she took a few bites and chewed quietly. I was surprised by her silence; at her best, my mother was quite glib, and she rarely needed the time to think before answering a question cleverly. I chewed the warm pumpernickel, enjoying the flavors of harvest. Clouds of pale moths drifted about like tattered wisps of fog.

"You know, there was a time when stories of the Water People were almost as famous as the stories of the Daughters of Joy. We Rhymira trace our heritage back so far ago that time itself had barely been loosed on the world when the tales of the first daughters and sons of Rhymir began to be told. But even in our oldest recollections, there are mention of the Dekai. It is said they were a fierce and beautiful people, with bodies that were like canvases upon which they tattooed their legends of traveling across all the oceans of Homm. It is said their fingers were webbed like Merlings, and their singing was such that they could calm tempest winds and change the tumbling motion of waves. They dressed in the shimmering skins of sea snakes and armored themselves in the tough hide of the manta ray. Every winter they hibernated in vast sea caves, while ocean waves were like cold mountains, and their goddess Thalassa raged in the deep."

"Wow!"

"Indeed. Sadly, it is known in those few stories that are still told about the Dekai that it was this very habit of sleeping through the worst of winter that was to be their undoing. For it was during such a winter a few hundred years ago when the Children of Iron dared Thalassa's wrath and sailed to Eld from their far-away island of Verkön. The Erdin attacked the Dekai in great numbers while they slept, purposefully slaughtering all adult males, and any women who were not actively nursing a child at the breast. It was brutality on a scale that not even legends would attempt to recount. Such is the lasting shame of the Erdin — that race which tells so many tales of their own greatness, and yet excises the very mention of the genocide that is their most lasting legacy on this island."

I felt my throat constricting, and the prickle of tears forming as I listened to my mother's words. "I... I had no idea..."

"Of course you didn't. You are young still. Such tales are not meant for children."

"Why... why did they-"

"Why indeed? The answer to your question is far worse than the death of all those long-ago Dekai. It is the worst thing that one people can ever inflict on another people. They had not come to those sleeping caves to try and exterminate the Dekai entirely, for the Erdin had every intention of ruling the Dekai and remaking them into a servant caste. And they did not all die in their sleep in those caves. Some of the Children of Water escaped, and fought the Erdin for many years to try to avenge themselves and reclaim their home. The descendants of those resistance fighters still live. The unforgivable reason the Erdin killed every adult Dekai that they could was to try to *end their story*. To wipe out the unifying story of what it meant to be Dekai.

"With almost all of the adult Dekai gone from the island, the Erdin were able to suppress the telling of those tales that explained to the young Dekai the beauty of who they were in the world, and who they always had been. They forbid all things Dekai — clothing and songs, ritual tattoos, tales of foolish or victorious ancestors that would inspire or remind them of the people they had once belonged to. Even the language those tales were originally told in has been silenced. They burned the holy sites, stole or buried all statues and effigies of their gods. The triad of Erdin gods replaced them, and the history of the culture of this island began to be taught as the history of Erdin liberators who freed the Dekai from their primitive practices and backwater thinking. They raised those surviving children to be grateful for their own submission and to never ask too many questions about what else their lives were meant for.

"And in the end, when the majority of the slaughter of those first decades of rule were done, they created the Iron Ban to keep the Dekai from having the right to effectively arm themselves. As a final cruelty, they stole that great stone from Dekainak which was known as the Heart of Eld, turning it into a throne for the queens and kings of Erdo Usk to rest their asses on.

"*That* is why there are no stories told about the Dekai on Eld. Because they have been purposefully forgotten, and those who are unwise enough to share in the telling of those old tales find themselves dangling from the hangman's rope."

By that point I was weeping freely. I had never heard of such horrors before. The idea of wiping out the story of an entire people on purpose was the saddest thing I had ever heard. For me, a daughter of a culture for whom the shared preserving of tales is considered a sacred duty, it was as though I had just learned that a soul was something that could be eaten.

"See? This is why that story is no longer told. Even the Erdin no longer remember this tale, for they were just as thorough in teaching their own children the same lies. Nobody wants to imagine their ancestors were capable of such brutality. Hush now, Talara: hear me child. We shall not speak of this again — it is not safe. Best you put such thoughts out of your mind as well."

My mother showed unusual patience, letting me cry for the better part of five minutes before she took my hand and squeezed it hard, pulling me up to my feet. Then she towed me back towards the tavern, stumbling on unsteady feet behind her and weeping all the while.

....

More years passed. Happy years for me, mostly. I look back now and must admit they were selfish years, colored by my pride at my growing skill and all the attention I began to receive from strangers. After I finished my set at night, I would hang around and listen intently to any stories those travelers would share. I heard of the skin changers of Delos, and the ever-burning cay of Vahreen, where molten stone rivers reshape the island into striated tunnels of smooth black glass. I heard of the sail-weavers of Aethys and the fearless women who dive amongst sharks. Tales were told of The Three Keys further to the southwest: Cuiri with its impassible cliffs, little Illuro covered in chest-high grasses and swarming with wild rabbits, and the dark jungles of Duam where ape-men were said to kill and eat any sailor desperate enough to harbor there. I marveled at stories of the barrier reef that ran like a wall, horizon to horizon across the deep, and rumors of what lay somewhere beyond: that mysterious island called Verkön, from which the Children of Iron first sailed when they set out long ago to conquer the sea. Stories of that island told of wicked magi building pyramids of glass and using stolen magic to tear into the very fabric of time. Beyond that island, it is said, there is nothing but open water all the way to the Iron Tower, and the world's end.

Although I enjoyed hearing about those stories very much, I still felt a tender hollow place inside me when I thought of those Erdin of long ago, and what terrible things they had done to the Dekai of Eld. I listened to those tales of Verkön, but I never told them myself. Not until I was quite a bit older, anyway.

Of the Mainland, that great island to the east that is so big that it encompasses all sight until the very memory of the ocean is lost: of that, I heard very little. Only the underport city of Silt — a sea cave full of pirates where dark waters swept far underground into a subterranean lake — seemed to interest the men that drank at The Leaking Mug. Island people are a proud people; any land so large that a man might never walk across the breadth of it and know its secrets well is a land to be suspicious of, like a stranger on the road that refuses food and company. I collected these stories and committed them all to memory. I would retell them myself, sometimes chopping them up into little pieces and remaking them for my own amusement. Nobody minded that the stories weren't mine. I was practicing, and I was young.

....

My music, songs, and stories grew in me so much that they pushed my body to grow along with it. My legs lengthened, my chest swelled, and, soon enough, my red moon rose inside me and I knew a woman's cares, and began to sense their dangers. Within me there grew a restlessness that felt like the road outside my door began in my chest and ended somewhere far out of reach. I would wake up flushed and shaking from dreams that filled me with heat and made me want to run into the night and quench myself in the river. These yearnings, this private heat, all this made its way into my music, of course. And now, at night, my playing in the taproom was subtly changed.

There had been a sense of relative peace for three years at the Leaking Mug. The new owners were no longer new, and they had settled into a high-functioning drunken stupor that suited their patrons just fine. My music had made them well off, in a swampy kind of way, and the patrons had been mollified by my youth and the nostalgia of my lyrical dreams. But now, I blushed when a note was dropped or at a stuttering stanza. The locals I had known for years suddenly treated me differently. I gave off warmth like I was standing near a fire all the time, and everywhere at the edges of the room, a wolfish spirit prowled. I could sense the change in my audience as clearly as though they were speaking their desires out loud to me. I could feel it in the creak of their leathers as they shifted in place, in the bouncing of their legs and the drumming of their fingers against the old plank tables as I moved from songs to stories and back again. An audience is foolish if they think they are mere spectators. Nobody who sits and watches ever knows how much of a performance they are putting on for the person on stage.

....

Sometimes, empires burn suddenly. Sometimes, they fold in on themselves and drop as slowly as any dying flower. Years pass and nobody even notices how bad things have gotten until they are beyond reach: a precious kite borne aloft to the edge of sight and swept off by a strong draft you couldn't see from the ground. Families are like that too. They are little empires of people brought together by common circumstances to survive intact against uncommon odds.

My mother, no longer able to make a living as a quean, helped in the kitchens for the midday meal and drank her meager wages by nightfall. Her latest efforts to teach me anything had ended in her shouting drunken nonsense. To make matters worse, she fell into the spell of love with another man who was already drowning under his love for blackroot. When my little sister was born, stunted and early, my mother was so slipped out on his stash of blackroot that she barely knew what came out of her body. I cared for the baby girl as best I could for days until my mother returned to her senses enough to feed her. I named her Adaline. I never got to know her, but I still remember her little red face and the tiny seeking softness of her fingers.

....

A few weeks after Adaine was born, I was weeping upstairs as the island boys were sold to strangers outside, and now we are caught up with where my story began.

After the last of those children were bought and distributed, there were many men and women who had traveled to Dunmarsh for the purchase of slaves and were still empty-handed. The cargo of slaves available to buy had been many bodies fewer than promised, apparently, for I heard grumbling about it as voices passed beneath my window. Those with no slaves to take home gathered in the tavern common room with the crew that had come in on the slaver's ship. What followed was a night that could easily be heard from upstairs: the kind of angry drinking crowd that a sensible tavern-owner dreads. It was like a high-pitched note of music held for far too long. The fighting that broke out was almost inevitable.

I heard the splintering of furniture breaking, the familiar sounds of drunken violence. And, as I had many times before, I heard my mother shouting loudly amongst the angry voices of men. She was right there in the middle of it, of course. *What a waste. What a stupid, wasteful woman. She is so full of talent, and she creates nothing but sons she cannot afford to care for and daughters she cannot relive her life through.* I lay quietly in my bed, and I discovered that I hated her. I hated them all. Those awful men and my wretched mother, shouting obscenities and crashing into the street. I hated their drunken drama and their prideful stories of their colorful failures.

Outside by the docks, something was burning. I could see the flickers of light reflecting on my wall from the window, and I lay there and ignored it. The shouting poured out in a climax from the bar and drifted towards the river. Threats were screamed and silenced. I didn't care. I was done with them all. Those men, who I had sung to for so many nights — they were slavers, or buyers, or just acquiescent. That was almost as bad. And my mother really *was* the pitiful drunken whore that they all believed her to be. The light of her life was dimmed so low that I was embarrassed to share her blood. I had never felt that way before. Always pity, always duty. Never rage. I gritted my teeth and tasted my tears as they slid between them, and I wished her devils and grief with every sobbing breath. It was one of the longest nights of my life, the night I left my mother behind. It was our final fight with each other, and it all took place in my mind.

....

The next morning, she was gone. Vanished. Her room was as cold and empty as her place in my heart. She had been everything to me, and the sudden lack of her was indescribable. She was gone, and so were my siblings and the man who loved my mother almost enough, and the ship that brought the slaves to sell. Outside, snow was falling. I stood at the edge of the porch, feeling the winter sky pull the heat up out of me. I watched for their return all evening, with an empty weight growing in my chest that felt like hunger and had no name.

I waited for days, watching the river from my window. I understood that they had somehow forgotten me or left me behind on purpose, and I felt in my bones that they weren't coming back. Whatever had taken her so suddenly had traveled further away than I could follow. I wept bitterly for siblings I might never see again and all the attention I hadn't bothered to give them. They felt like strangers when they were around, but now that they were gone, I knew they were everyone in the world I could have called family. Out my window, the wind played across the river's surface in ripples that I imagined sounded like music underwater.

....

Around sunrise, the bodies of two *Orlŭks* floated by with ribbons of blood spreading in the water behind them. I watched them swept downstream by the tide, as helpless of their fate as I was. That day passed, then another. The moons rose, and set, and rose again. I could no longer be the *me* I had always been. I would not go downstairs and play for those men again. Without my mother's watchful eye, the wolves that had been prowling around the edges of the room would come bounding in, and they would tear me open. And inside my own warm guts, I might find my mother waiting, ready to be born again.

More days passed, and I became weak with hunger. Without an income, I could no longer pay for food, and when I told the tavern proprietors that I would not play anymore, they darkened to me like the hungry strangers they had always been. I was cursed now — I had become my mother's daughter at last, just another lonely woman without a plan or somewhere to be. I watched the road and the river, and the sun rose and set. The Room Upstairs ceased to be my lofty tower and became the cold place with burnt walls that it had always been. Nothing of my life remained for me except the instruments I had grown up with. Yet, the beautiful silver lyre looked tarnished and dull to my eyes. It had so often spoken my heart out loud for me. All I felt inside me now was an emptiness that seemed to go on forever. The room was airless and still, and I was drowning in it.

....

One night, I woke up with bright moonslight flooding the room. The tap room was quiet below: an early night without music, and all had gone to bed. I was dizzy with hunger, and I knew the moment I opened my eyes that I was leaving. I crept carefully over to the edge of the room, to the burned hole in the wood where the floorboards sagged under my weight. Into the space between the ceiling and floor below, I carefully slid the bulk of the silver lyre. I was lucky; it is a thin instrument, though it is wide. I shoved it back under the floor as far as it would go, and it felt like I was burying it. Such beauty hidden underfoot in soot and blackness. I wrapped the rebec and my pair of castanets up in my only change of clothes and slung it up around my shoulder in a carrying bag. The shawm I bore under my arm like a staff. There was nothing more precious to me than these instruments — I would have gladly left my shoes and clothing behind first. That said, the beautiful lyre was too heavy to carry and held too much of my mother in it.

In the warm dark of the taproom, I drew in a deep breath — *even a stink becomes nostalgic if it is familiar for long enough* — and I held that lungful of stale beer and pipe tobacco and old stories for as long as I could. By the time I exhaled it, I was already stealing from the larder as much bread, cheese, and sad, dried-up apples as I could carry. I slipped outside like the burglar I had become, stuffing a hunk of bread into my watering mouth, and shut the door softly behind me. Overhead, the yellow moon that locals call the Ash Moon hung in the sky. It was as bright and sharply crescent as I had ever seen it, and, where there were still patches of snow, the reflection gleamed. Low in the sky, the Ember Moon looked bloody and bright, like a star with a bite taken out of it. The night was mine alone, and the road ran off ahead of me. The north wind blew coldly across my face. I had nowhere to go and all the rest of my life to get there.

So I set my feet walking in the direction of the old bridge that the island boy had crossed in his wagon. From there, I followed the rutted path until it finally brought me to the ancient road known as the Wayward.

On the Wayward Road

The Wayward Road is older than memory. It was cut out of the wilderness of Eld so long ago that it is said no living islander can recall a time without it, and no stories tell the history of people on the island before the Wayward was there. The lean townships of Eld grew up around it like children clutching at their mother's skirts. Most roads are created for war or commerce; they are lines of transport that are drawn up to unite separate settlement dots into the shape of civilization. Not the Wayward — not this road. It flows as amicably and as inexorably as any river: looping and doubling back as it pleases, shallow and swift with an ancient pattern of cobbles in some places and so deeply rutted and wild in others that smaller tributary roads have been scabbed in to bypass around it. It transmutes into rope bridges where it bottoms out between the coastal scarps at Ulfaang-by-the-Sea and is buried under ruins at the felled city of Ghent, where the Erdin first landed in conquest long ago. Along the western shore, it branches into rutted paths that all lead to the ocean, and where the storms have eaten the edge of the island away, the Wayward is pocked with tide pools. Here in the east, it wanders through the vast forest of towering trees and shifting green shadows known as the Eldwood.

I didn't know any of this then, of course. I had never even set foot on the road except to stand at the edge of where it bridged across the river and headed north into the wild. Now it stretched before me like a moonlit ribbon winding between walls of gloomy bracken, and all was cold and silent but for the creaking of restless trees.

....

I had never known *real* cold — not like the cold of that road. There is no chill like the last hours before a winter sunrise: the sun is gone from the sky for so long that the shadows on the ground freeze in place. Just a few hours of travel, and I could barely remember what warmth felt like. I had already walked further than I had imagined the road even ran and encountered nothing but still more road meandering ever onward. I jogged along, hopped in place, and slapped my arms against my side to keep warm. After a while, I considered lying down to sleep, when the cold crept so deeply inside of me that everything became numb and heavy, and the frost-crusted dirt felt as soft as bed linens beneath the leather soles of my shoes. Pools of standing water glittered like secrets away under the trees. In one spot, the snowmelt flooded a low dip in the road, extending out for as far as I could see off into the dark. I wandered the edges of that unexpected pond for a long time, trying to figure a way around it, and in the end, I had to shed my boots and breeches to ford it. It felt like being scraped raw by winter wind from the waist down. The crossing only took a few thrashing minutes, but by the time I waded up on the far side, I was so breathless with cold that I lay doubled over on the ground, gasping like a fish as I scrambled back into my woolens and boots.

Often during that long night, I was startled off the road by the popping sounds of branches snapping under snow-load. Once, just as the sky was beginning to pale with dawn, something large and lanky bounded across the road right in front of me, and I huddled in stiff silence until my feet started aching with cold, straining my eyes after where it had vanished into the underbrush. Thankfully whatever it was did not return, and at last, the sun crept up behind the trees and I knew for sure that the night and all its terrors were behind me.

An hour after sunup, I felt so tired with sustained fear and weak with hunger that I sank right down in the middle of the road and ate all the food I had brought with me. It wasn't as much as it had seemed when I stole it, and I hadn't intended to eat all of it at once. I have always been bad at rationing food; I will admit that. The sun topped the tree line at last, and the road began to steam as it warmed.

As I rested, I looked around me and noted the changes that a night of travel had brought me through. The trees here were dense and larger than any I had seen growing up in Dunmarsh: giant oaks with spreading canopy as wide as eighty strides, with many other smaller trees and bushes that I had no names for growing up beneath their crown of branches. The flat lands I had always known had swollen into rises and rounds, and rivulets of meltwater flowed between them and dug little channels into the earth. Here and there, red berries clustered under saw-leaf thickets, and blushes of small flowers purpled the banks of the road. I leaned against my travel bag and let the sun draw the cold out of my legs. While I digested and watched the leather of my boots steaming, I fell asleep right there on the road.

That was stupid; I know that now. Stupid, stupid. Luckily a sleep that takes you while you are sitting upright with your head lolling backward over your own neck is not the deep sleep from which noises will not rouse you. The creaking of cart wheels rasped into my dreams from a long way off, and by the time the merchant and his bondsman rolled into view, I had scrambled off the road and hidden from sight.

I pressed myself low into the loam, and I watched them pass along the way I was going towards Holm. I wondered how the wagon had made it across the flooded dip in the road; perhaps it was built to float? The older man was driving the ox cart, huddled so deeply in his cloak and furs that he looked like a bedroll with a beard. The younger one paced beside the cart with the loping grace of a shadowcat; his leather armor creaking with cold, a crossbow ready in hand. He was barely older than a boy, yet quite large for his age: shaggy black braided hair and heavy with muscle. His dark eyes looked tired, but they darted ceaselessly amongst the trees. I held my steaming breath as they rumbled past, returning to the road only when I was sure they were well ahead of me.

....

The day trudged on, and so did I. I walked through patches of mist that obscured sections of the road. My feet were swollen and aching, and every now and then, I would walk on my hands to give my feet a rest. Cold hands on winter dirt and cobblestones are about as fun as you can imagine they would be, so I ceased that effort quickly enough. Twice more, I left the road in a hurry and hid behind a fallen log or under the spreading arms of dead ferns. Once was for a man who galloped by on a horse, leaning low against the saddle and passing my hiding spot at such speed that all I saw was the sweaty foam on the horses' flanks and a ripple of red cloak fluttering back over plate armor. The horse kicked up clods of dark mud as it tore past me, riding southwards towards Portuan. I stayed hidden until the drumming of its hooves faded from hearing between the low hills.

The second time I hid seemed more shameful: an old woman astride the shoulders of an ancient donkey plodded into view, moving about as slowly as the mist they were riding through. Yet the closer they got, the odder they seemed. The donkey's head was entirely hidden under a pile of blankets, and the woman seemed to be riding so high on the body that she was straddling the mane and upper shoulders. I imagined a centaur from the stories I had heard: so huge and proud and dangerous. In my imaginings, I substituted the old donkey woman, all slumpy and swaying like an accordion being squeezed. *A Donketaur.* I whispered to myself in mock awe. *My first sighting!* I laughed out loud; I couldn't help it. I burrowed down lower behind the hiding log, wheezing with laughter. *Fear the Donketaur!* Then the fog thinned, and the old woman turned and looked in my direction. Her eyes were huge and ice-blue, and they had elongated oval pupils. What I had mistaken for the donkey's swaddled head was actually a bundle of blankets and a heavy scarf. The woman was not remotely human. I got up and ran like a panicked idiot deeper into the woods, and it was the better part of an hour before I summoned up the courage to return to the road again. The donkey-woman was long gone.

"*The Donketaur is real,*" I whispered to myself. "*I guess anything is possible.*"

....

The last of the sunlight was bleeding out behind the hills, and my hunger had gotten quite troubling. I had easily slaked every thirst throughout the day at the small brooks that twined across the landscape, but my morning gluttony had left me without so much as a wrinkled apple. I had thought to reach Holm much sooner than this and began to wonder just how far I had come from Dunmarsh. I found a lucky hollow off the side of the road an hour before dark: a natural dip between three large trees, with the scattered char of a ring of campfire stones in the middle of it. I spread out my sleeping furs and lit a small fire on the bed of cold ashes. The sky was beautiful as the sun set, clear as glass with the shards of stars studding up everywhere. A thin mist puddled out from between the roots of the trees, and the evening chill throbbed with the last cries of songbirds. My stomach growled piteously. I had watched birds eating the red berries that grew on the side of the road all day, and before night fell, I decided to join them in their harvest. I knew well enough to stay clear of wild mushrooms, yet if birds are able to eat bugs and berries, then so must I. Carefully, I plucked and bit into a few of them. Their skins were a bright red, their insides were veined pink and white, and they had an acrid sweetness to them that was almost unpleasant. I was not so rash as to gorge myself, of course, but I certainly ate a large handful before the terrible cramping began.

....

There are thankful gaps in my memory of this evening. What I do remember is embarrassing to recall. It was... messy. Everything I had eaten came back out again from both ends of me. For hours. I vomited and expelled warm fluids until my muscles shook, and I lay as close to the heat of the fire as I dared and knew I was going to die. Stupid. Killed by berries: stupid, stupid.

Everything turned around me — a slow spinning of tree roots that bled like watercolor and throbbed with firelight. Above me, the canopy of branches looked like black cracks spreading across the sky, and all of it rolling on and on; a revolving wheel with my shivering body strapped to the hub. My throat was bitter and aching, and when I breathed, it sounded like stones clattering underwater. Muscles seized in painful ripples that rolled across my body, and when they passed, everything was warm and wet, and I cried out my mother's name in the dark. "Omella, I am here — I am alone, mother, and I am dying — Omella, I am dying! Please, please..." I sobbed out these words over and over again, something that sounded like prayer, but wasn't meant for gods. Only my mother.

It seemed like snow was falling, and it probably actually was, for the fire had banked down into hissing coals. The warmth was fading from the hollow I lay curled up in — I could sense the trees drawing it away underground, yet when I touched their roots, they felt as cold as my own bones. Maybe we were already the same thing, the trees and me? However, the trees would live to see the sunrise again, and I had begun to accept that I would not.

·······································

A ghost floated down towards me from the higher branches. Its eyes were huge and gold and terrible.

The ghost alighted nearby with a flutter of wings, and my eyes reminded my head to name it "owl." It was no ghost at all, but a pilgrim of winter alighted on a low branch to watch me pass my final breaths. I was serene then — far away from the meaning of warmth and cold. The night tunneled in my eyes. There was red, sullen coal-light, drifting snow, and the white otherness of the snow owl. I closed my eyes as the golden gaze of the owl bored into me, and I was sure in that moment it was somehow my mother, and she had heard me crying and come back to me in a body that flies over winter. She had become the music we sang together.

A spasm ripped through me, and what tears came then was all the water I had left inside.

"I am ready to go, mother, I am ready. Take me away across the deep, and when we get back to old Rhymir at last, you may eat my flesh as you always wanted to. Then I will return to your body, and you can reabsorb me and regain what I took from you when I was born. You will be Rhymira again, and I will be a bad dream you finally wake up from."

With my eyes closed, I did not see where the fox came from. Neither did the owl, I imagine. She bounded out of the night like rapids flowing over rocks, and I opened my eyes to the screeching of the owl as its neck was broken. The fox was as large as a loping dog and so beautiful it should not have existed at all. Her fur was the shifting grayish-purple of winter shadows, and when she turned and looked at me with my spirit mother hanging slackly in her jaws, I felt what can only be described as sacramental horror wash over me — an abomination on four paws, with a mouth full of bloody feathers.

My head ached savagely, and I leaned back on my elbows as everything blurred around the edges. Across the clearing, I felt the pitiful thump of the owl as it hit the ground. Then a warmth passed over me. I looked up and everything in sight was that lavender-smoke fur, with the slightest iridescence shimmering across it. I felt a tongue lick my chest, and her bloody muzzle pushed into my mouth. I tasted salt and copper and began to gag. Her paws pressed my shoulders down against the earth. The fox stood on me fully, so heavy on my chest. I could not breathe; beneath the weight of her body, I could not catch my breath. Her white breast was matted with blood. She pressed her forehead against mine and I stared into her eyes for the first time. They were honey and amber that drowned out the sight of every other color. The stars dimmed and darkened behind her, until all that was left was the shining of her eyes and the black howling in my head.

Then there was nothing.

....

Sunrise found me, and I was not dead. I lay there for a long time, patching my spirit back into my body. My head ached like the devils that haunt heavy drinking. I felt shrunken and dry, my mouth was inexplicably full of charcoal residue, and I stank with sickness. Somehow, I was alive. Even more confusing, my campfire was lit and burning cheerfully. Across the clearing, someone else's full waterskin rested against my knapsack, propped up next to a small wooden bowl that was half-full of something dark green and gross looking. I crawled right over there and drank from the skin until my stomach was tight. With my mouth moistened, I spit the last of the charcoal out in black goopy wads. Then I spooned that green glop straight into my face. It tasted like dandelion pulp and squashed worms, and my body loved it. I didn't know who had left it for me or why I had awoken with a mouth full of my own campfire charcoal. I was too worn out to make sense of any of it.

I fell asleep again curled up around that wooden bowl, and when I awoke, it was gone, and the wineskin with it. I would have thought I dreamed it but for my full bladder and the green taste still in my mouth. Rolling carefully to my feet, I hobbled to a nearby stream and stripped to rinse the stink out of my clothes. The flowing water barely felt cold at all — nothing did. I was warmed from inside, and when I looked down, I saw my naked reflection dancing on the water. Dried blood made a stripe from my chest to my chin. My hair was flecked with white feathers.

....

I felt myself in half a dream — dizzy and stumbling, one step at a time on legs as wobbly as any newborn faun. I clutched at the shawm in my arms, taking comfort from the smooth familiarity of the wooden pipe, although I could no longer remember why I was still carrying it. Currents of cold air mingled with the warmth of the sun. Beneath my feet, the road was a ripple of cobblestones as smooth as skin. I walked until I reached the slope of a great stone arch that forded a wide river. The bridge was obviously ancient; its warm russet stones pocked by weather and its proud pillars gnawed by time. On the other side of the river, with the bridge just behind me, I passed under the canopy of a grove of apple trees: some old orchard gone to wild seed. Their branches twined around each other, and their trunks were thick and dark and knobby. They formed a span of arches that grew right over the road — in some places, through it entirely. The ground around them was littered with withered brown apple husks.

I passed beneath their twisting branches in a near trance. They were almost all bare and stripped by winter, yet one held a sly secret: new green budded in the crown. Soon the snow on the roadside would melt and be replaced by the pink carpet of fallen blossoms. I imagined the scent of those rare buds, and as I breathed deeply, I became aware of the smell of baking bread carrying on the wind.

It was Holm, somewhere ahead, and it was the most wonderful thing I had ever smelled. I stumbled on, dizzy and nearly mad with longing. Away between the trees, there was a flinty flash of fur. When I peered off into the green, I saw the fox, and she was watching me. She was as large as any jackwolf, and when she grinned at me, I saw her muzzle was clean and white again. There was a flick of tail and a waterfall of motion: purple shadows and bounding muscle. And then she was gone.

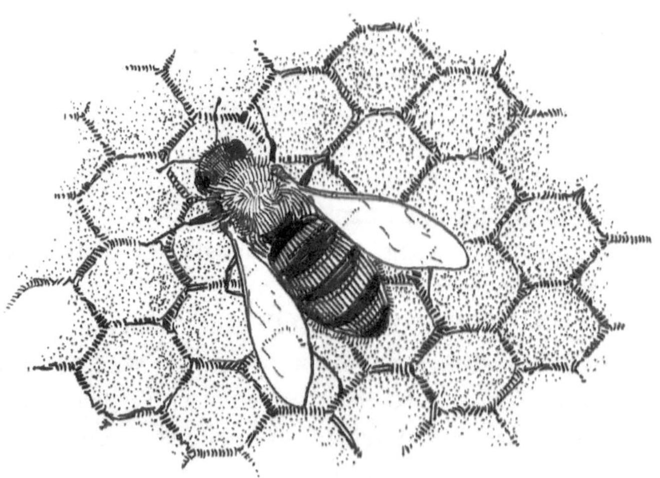

The Girl from Nearby

Honeybees are active all winter, unlike many insects whose lives are only as long as there is warmth in the world. They do not hibernate, for they are cold-blooded creatures, and the torpor of sitting so still as the world freezes around them would surely kill them, queen and all. So, when the temperature drops in autumn, they cluster together all around her, fluttering their wings and shivering in pulses like the vibrating strings of an instrument. All this kinetic energy directed towards her keeps the queen at the balmy temperature of a midsummer morning, and everyone else does what they can to get by. Bees on the outer layers of the cluster slowly crawl inward, and inner bees eat honey to replenish their energy before rotating out to the outer edges. Thusly the majority of the colony survives the winter by working together wisely. If you could see them with astral eyes, where the body is gone from view and only the energy of their efforts remains, you might perceive them as an endlessly renewing circular hourglass. Instead of the energy coming to a stop at the bottom, it flows up the rounded sides and pours itself back down again, heating everything up as it goes, with the warmest center of the queen at its heart.

Would that we humans were so industrious with our efforts!

....

Mathias the Ordanian mused over this very thought that winter afternoon, while the sunlight lit the snow drifts on the ground and set the world to sparkling. His daydreams were pleasantly jostled by the steps of the pungent gray donkey upon which he rode, and the cold air around him tinkled with the sound of the ceramic jars of honey knocking together in his saddlebag. It was summer honey, harvested while the hive was still busy making more, and it was his only means of earning money that was meant just for him. He was, on this afternoon, plodding towards the Welcome Holm tavern to sell honey to its proprietor. That honey would be spread on freshly baked bread that could be smelled from half a mile up the road. It perfumed the afternoon air so temptingly that Mathias grinned as he breathed it deeply in. The honey would be mixed with yeast and a few other secret herbal ingredients and sit fermenting in cellar barrels until it was decanted, months later, as an infamous golden mead. It was the innkeeper's pride and sold under that label. Mathias was too young to try it, of course, but the silver spriggans that Yrsa the innkeeper would pay him for his honey would make the young cleric feel just as drunk as though he had tipped a cup himself. Mathias saved his coins very carefully. So thriftily, in fact, that in all of the eleven years of his life he had never spent a single one. He didn't honestly know what value they had or why they were so prized. He just had a sense that saving money is the proper thing to do, and so he hoarded the few coins that ever made it across his hand with the zeal of a properly practiced miser.

The stinky donkey with Mathias on her back plodded down the Thegn's Road from the abbey on High Hill, and as the road leveled out, the crossroads came into sight. Here was where the two orderly troughs of packed stone that made up the Thegn's Road intersected with the ancient sparsely cobbled highway called the Wayward. Around a bend and past the edge of the overgrown grove that used to be an apple orchard, the Welcome Holm tavern would soon come into view.

But something else caught Mathias' sight first. It was little more than a flash of color under the trees that overhung the Wayward Road: the form of a large fox bounding through the branchy shadows. He saw it so briefly at first that he mistook it for a gust of dry leaves, but even so, he reined in his fusty mount and peered intently. He was looking for further movement, and for a handful of breathless moments, he saw none. And yet the feeling of being watched was suddenly keen.

The tangled gloom of low-hanging branches was impenetrable from this distance. Mathias sat for a long moment, biting his lip and swinging his fur-wrapped feet in little thoughtful circles. The large fox was still there, and it was watching him. He could *feel* it, and more curiously still, he could feel something else too. A gentle tugging, like invisible strings, tickled the hairs on his neck and made him shiver all over, all at once. And then the nameless donkey, who was known only for the miasma of its mulish effluvium, plodded without beckoning towards the ancient apple thicket and left the Thegn's Road behind. As though compelled, the flatulent beast directed herself towards the very spot that Mathias had noted, and when she arrived there, she stopped with such abrupt finality that Mathias almost tumbled off. He gripped with his knees and made dry little disapproving clucking sounds between his teeth, but his eyes scanned the apple grove eagerly.

There is a sensation that exists in all of us: a special thrill when we observe an animal in the wild. It is perhaps a nameless but compelling sense of voyeurism or the blooming of our oldest instincts that direct the difference between fleeing and following. But that thrill cannot compare to the shock of truly catching ourselves in *their* gaze. To be stared at unexpectedly when we believed ourselves to be the observer: that is electric and alarming, like the piercing gaze of a caged carnivore that suddenly makes us wonder which side of the bars we are actually on. This was the shock that befell Mathias as his eyes met the amber shining of the fox's eyes, and realized that he had not seen her fleeing movement because she had sat still under the trees and *waited* for him.

Up close, she was as big as a hunting dog and as beautiful as the twilight in autumn. He stared with superstitious awe into her eyes for the eternity of a moment. Then she vanished from sight so quickly that it was difficult to tell where she had gone but for the slow settling of disturbed leaves on the forest floor. When the burning honey of her eyes no longer dominated his attention, he noticed the crumpled body of a girl that had been hidden from view behind her. She had a flaking streak of dried blood smeared across her shirt and a few white feathers snagged in her dark hair.

In one eye of Mathias' peculiar gaze, the girl lay as one who is dead, dusted with the thin glaze of an early evening frost. For a breathless moment, he mistook that world for his. But then she hoisted herself up on wobbling elbows, brushed crushed leaves from the woolen leg of one high sock with her dirty palms and said, "Do you have an apple, please? Even a wrinkly one will do."

Then she swayed as though caught in a breeze that only she could feel. Her eyes fluttered to white, and she slumped into an unconscious heap with her head on her backpack and her arms cradled tightly around the flaring bell of a piper's shawm.

···

The difficulty by which Mathias got the girl from the forest floor up onto the back of the mephitic jack mule was an embarrassment of thin arms, blushing handholds, and much-wasted effort. Ten minutes later, and just in time for her to wake up on her own, Mathias had the prostrate girl slung over the back of the donkey. It was the ungainly angle of her head and unfortunate lungfuls of stink that finally woke her, and she glared at Mathias in a vaguely affronted way as he led her towards the tavern, himself walking awkwardly through the snow in fur-wrapped bare feet. At one point, she waved them to a stop and threw up weakly onto the side of the donkey, which did nothing helpful for the animal's smell. When she had recovered enough, Mathias dug out a large spoonful of honey and fed it to her carefully, and she took three more like that, lapping at them with the greedy enthusiasm of a baby bear.

By the time they got to the tavern stables, she had regained some color in her face and began to chatter at Mathias. She told him a very engaging story of who she was and how she came to be unconscious under the apple trees. He listened politely enough and nodded agreeably as he was meant to, and somehow knew that every bit of it was a lie. But it seemed to brighten her spirits in the telling of it, and he enjoyed the sound of her voice very much.

....

Yrsa was a self-made woman who lived alone, and the Welcome Holm tavern was hers. The building itself was more than a hundred and sixty summers old; she had taken over the care of it as a young woman. She had worked her way up from stable hand to bartender and had purchased the tavern fairly from the previous owners by never spending a single copper more than she had to in all of her working years. She was as heavy-jawed and pale in complexion as any Erdin woman could hope to be, with long flaxen hair that she kept tightly braided and finely tusked canines that peeked just over her bottom lip. Yet her stern countenance was betrayed by smiling lines around her eyes, and she possessed a great galloping laugh that carried over a crowded room as warmly as firelight.

Kindness to those in need is the mark of a truly great Innkeeper. When Mathias led Talara into the bar, Yrsa immediately noticed her unsteady steps and the hunch of hunger that had her almost doubled over and shooed them both towards a corner table as quick as the flick of a bar rag. Within minutes there were steaming bowls of mutton and barley set before them, and she sat and watched and didn't ask a word until Talara had eaten the best of both of them. While she gulped the stew bowl down, Yrsa glanced knowingly at the way her other hand never left the wooden shawm nestled in her lap. When the bowls were cleared away and Mathias' honey was accounted for and sold, the broad innkeep leaned backward in her chair until it creaked on two legs and said:

"A single meal is an easy gift for an innkeeper to make. As simple, I imagine, as a girl with a full belly might find it to play an after-dinner song? For I surely do love a spot of music in a tavern as quiet as this."

The tavern was not so quiet, truly; a late afternoon in winter is a grand time for a slowly sipped cider and a table game amongst friends. There were many tables full of farmers talking softly over games of Morris and Mancala. Afternoon snow-light lit the room coldly, but the crackling fire and the click of glass marbles warmed the ears and made the taproom drowsy. So was Talara, of course, as drowsy as exhaustion and a heavy meal. But she knew better than to pass a moment like this by. Talara was more familiar with the subtle tugging strings of the weave of destiny than Mathias was, and she could feel the air around her shivering with opportunity. She gazed deeply into Yrsa's pale eyes and saw the tracery of lines around them that she had earned by living kindly.

So Talara smiled and said, "Of course. It would be my pleasure to entertain you." She stood up from the table and took her place beside the fireplace on a stool facing the common room.

Even before she had settled onto her seat and raised the shawm to her lips, every eye was on her, as she knew it would be. She had taken the moments that a true performer always knows to take: placing her legs just so, and her arms just so, and sitting up in a way that perched her body into the poise of one who is conducting the feelings of those around them.

Then she said: "I am Talara, a daughter of old Rhymir, and I have striven through winter and journeyed many weary miles to play for you tonight."

And then she played. *And oh, how well she played* — as though the future of her life might very well depend on it.

....

At last Mathias returned to the abbey, many hours after moonsrise. He was alone, but for the whirl of his thoughts drifting up towards the twinkling stars and the slushy plodding of the reeking jennet. He was broke, and he was humming, and he had never felt happier. The four silver spriggans he had earned from the honey sale had all made their glad way into Talara's tipping hat, and he had left a bit of his heart in there too.

Stone

"Here, in the unfinished section of the wall, the strangest
feature of the abbey construction was clearly visible."

STONE

~ The Fourth Story ~

"*Splenius... trapezius... deltoid.*" Melvinari muttered to himself as he spread the muscles of the splayed rabbit apart with two thin sticks. "*Latissiumus dorsi... lungs... a punctured rectus abdominis... yuck.*" The thin young man set the sticks down and pushed his nimble fingers gently between the layers of muscle as the rabbit's organs steamed in the chilly air. "*Peel through a webbing of abdominal fascia and we find... ah yes. Here is the thing that killed you.*" An arrowhead of knapped obsidian and half an inch of a broken wood shaft were buried in the rabbit's belly. Blackened blood clotted around it thickly, and Melvinari took mental note of that too. "*Time of death within a few hours, perhaps shortly after sunrise. Not long before I got here.*"

He had found the rabbit staked to a post in the ground with a wheel of woven wicker reeds hung behind it. He had been relieving his bladder at the edge of his father's limestone quarry, and he almost tripped right over it. The concy's guts had been slit open, and its belly was tacked wide in a grim display. Melvin had come to the quarry that morning, as he often had this last year, to process limestone into quicklime. This was an arduous task that required care in measurement and mixing, and he was proud to know that his father trusted only him to get the process just right. Let other larger (*okay, maybe stronger*) men load and transport the heavy stones from the quarry at South Hill all the way over to the building site at the Abbey of Cuthain — it was to Melvinari, and he alone, to whom the task of preparing the mortar for the stone walls fell.

Every morning, once he'd tied off his horse to graze, he would begin by stoking the fire up in the carved stone behemoth of the limning kiln — this was a process that could take more than an hour to get just right. He would start with a carefully built pyramid of tinder and dried peat moss and set it alight with flint. When the small fire was built up to blazing — *a pot of dandelion root tea boiled, cold hands warmed in the meanwhile, and why not?* — Melvin would add soft brown lignite to the ember bed. The lignite had been dug up from the peat bogs around Dunmarsh, which was an awful little swamp town about eight leagues from Holm. It did not burn nearly as hot as true alchemical coal, but it burned a whole lot hotter than pine logs. Quickly, the heat of the fire would become nearly unbearable, and Melvin would move his tea kettle and himself far enough back to breathe. After all these months, he had it timed just right so that after a breakfast of buttered bread and honey and thin little slices of roast mutton, the lignite would be hot enough to put the alchemical coal straight on. This coal had also originated from the bog around Dunmarsh and was gently ensorcelled to burn even longer and hotter than normal coal. It ignited with a roaring green flame, and when it was finally spent, it would leave behind a melted slag of clinker on the kiln floor that was hard as glass and shimmered like a splash of wrought mercury.

Melvin had collected and stockpiled a sizable hoard of those clinker slabs. He meant to one day polish it up and sell it to gullible rubes as calcified dragon's blood at the great market in Portuan. But at thirteen years old, he had yet to ever see that market, so for now, he simply hoarded and schemed. He also collected rows of ceramic jars full of coal ash that had been carefully scraped from the bottom of the limning kiln. He had read that such ash was a veritable trove of rare alchemical components — lead, mercury, selenium, aluminum, even chlorine and arsenic could be distilled from coal ash with the right equipment and a patient hand. He did not yet know what he would do with such dangerous components, but he daydreamed of shelves of colorful bottles full of the deadliest concoctions.

Once the fire was stoked and bellowed up to blazing, Melvin could begin his important task of making quicklime. His father had once told him he was the youngest man in the guild of Able Masons who had ever been tasked with quicklime, and it filled him with pride. It was not that the work was particularly difficult, (he admitted to himself in private moments), it was that it was so crucial to do it correctly. In a great stone wall or a lofting buttress, untold thousands of pounds of cut stones were skillfully stacked, but it was lime mortar that bound them to one purpose and held them in their symmetry. He was musing on this very thought when he wandered over to the edge of the quarry to 'water the trees' and found the gruesome remains of the rabbit.

That morning he had been more addled with sleep than usual — up late reading, as always — and his tired mind prodded the symbolic rabbit crucifixion obsessively. As he powdered limestone in the heavy wooden crusher, the careful arrangement of the open stomach with the circle of woven wicker behind it reshaped itself in his head with every form of written symbolism he knew. Was it runic? Uisen? In Orlŭk pictography, a circle with a line straight through it was a warning, but it usually referred to dangerous terrain or the strength of a particular tribe. The ebony skinned Ramani who lived across the great sea had symbols in their language that condensed a whole poem into a single pattern, but he could not imagine they would make one so morbid. All this he had read in books, but that was as far as his knowledge extended. As he moved the trays of crushed lime into the hot kiln for calcining, he felt a shiver go down his back. It was a hostile gesture, no question about that. Someone placed it there as a direct threat.

Suddenly, the winter sunshine did not warm him anymore, and the warble of the chitteries in the canopy overhead seemed off tone. He hurried through the final cooling process, and once he had made enough of the quicklime, he bagged it and slung it over his horses' cantle without even bothering to hydrate the powder properly. He heaved himself onto the saddle and peered around warily at the light that stabbed through the gloom of the tall pine trees. Somewhere nearby, a branch broke with a loud snap. Melvin wheeled his horse around and fled the quarry glade, too spooked to look back.

....

"Father — a question?" There was a protocol well in place to interrupt his father while he was reading, and proper timing was the only way to do it. His father, Daedrim, nodded absently. A quiet minute passed as he skimmed to the end of his page. Evening firelight danced across his hawkish features; Melvin shared his sharp eyes, dark brown hair and high cheekbones but had been spared the worst of his angular nose.

Melvin watched his father read with the same detached affection he had grown up feeling. Daedrim had always been a private man with a placid disposition, but the fever that took his wife eight winters ago had also taken his sense of humor. Melvin could hardly remember his mother Abella, except as fragmented memories of warm hugs and bouncing curly blonde hair with which she would tickle his face to make him laugh. While she had lived, the house was scented with the aromatic pungency of countless bundles of drying herbs, and her legacy to her son included a whole shelf of rare books on alchemical botany and herb lore. She had mixed poultices that helped to cure the sick, banish foul vapors, and restore vigor. And in a brutal winter Melvin could barely remember, when a quarter of the townsfolk were burning up with white fever, she had been by every bedside doing a true medica's service — and had died for it. She was entombed under an elaborate cairn of rock that his father had built for her in the village graveyard. He still weeded it and kept it meticulously clean.

"Father?"

"Yes?" His father replied without looking up.

"I found something this morning at the quarry: something quite out of place. A dead rabbit with its belly tacked open."

Daedrim's eyes flicked up, then returned to his page. "There is nothing out of place about a deceased animal in the wilderness."

"It was not the fact of its death that I wanted to discuss, but rather the display of its remains. The rabbit's limbs were splayed like a book opened over-wide, and it was nailed to a wooden post driven into the ground. Behind that post, a woven circle of reeds was mounted at the height of the rabbit's chest. It was a signal of some kind, I'm sure of it. But I cannot puzzle out its meaning."

At this, his father's focus finally shifted. He stared at Melvinari for a long moment, his eyes flickering slightly as he scanned through the library of his mind. His frown deepened into a scowl. "I would guess it's Bergrem."

"What?"

"Bergrem, the woodcutter. Or one of his nativist cronies. They are as fanatical of maintaining the 'old ways' as that weathered crackpot Djaro. Zealotry is the gonfalon of the ignorant, son."

Daedrim sighed and stared into the carved stone mouth of the fireplace, and the firelight reflected double in the lenses of his reading glasses. Around them, the common room was the same as it had always been. There was a deep red rug of woven wool, a few high-backed chairs and a wall made entirely of the literal wealth of knowledge — a humble fortune in books and scrolls on a bookcase of polished marble. It was a place of learned peace: a master mason's house, where everything was sparse and functional.

They had spent the evening reading in this room together every night that Melvin could remember. His father in his chair and Melvin sprawled out on the rug with a book open in front of him. He had been raised by these books in the comfortable luxury of that house of stone. But that night, the house seemed chilled by an unusual draft, and Melvin shivered and drew closer to the warmth of the granite hearth.

"Father... isn't Bergrem your friend? I've known his son, Caetal, for as long as I can remember. And it was you who introduced us."

Daedrim closed his book. This was a rare event, and Melvin leaned forward eagerly.

"Bergrem... was not so much a friend as a long-standing colleague. 'Friends' are for children, Melvinari. Adults have no need to cultivate such frivolities. During the many years we have lived here in Holm, Bergrem worked with me on every masonic project I was contracted for, and why wouldn't he? His skill as a carpenter is matchless, and a house of stone is always supported by wooden beams."

He paused and took a sip of tepid tea, gone cold with neglect.

"Bergrem was always around and so, naturally, his son Caetal was always around — that is why you two grew up well acquainted. It is foolish to let children run loose on a construction site, so we encouraged you to play together nearby for our convenience. But I have no wish for you to count Caetal amongst your friends. He is a brutal boy, and his father is raising him to be another Bergrem: an anti-Erdin fanatic who calls himself a revolutionary.

"This island was conquered by the Erdin a long time ago. An age of cultural blending and interbreeding has passed since then, and we have no excuse to pretend that overthrowing their governance will return the island to a pure Dekai kingdom again. And why bother? Your mother was Erdin, and I am Dekai, and the mixture of those two races has done you no harm. Many are the children of Eld with mixed blood — a fair complexion is more and more common these days, and you can find blue eyes on a brown-haired child from Norlünd to the Shoals. The first call to revolution caused widespread racial slaughter and achieved nothing. There is no logic in such bloody ideology."

"I don't quite understand what this has to do with the rabbit, father. Why would Bergrem stake a dead rabbit up at the quarry? I've been reading about possible symbolic connotations all night, but I haven't gotten close to making sense of it."

"That is because you won't find that information in books, Melvinari. In younger days of the island, as you well know, our people lived in a state of savagery. In those days, there were no real roads — except perhaps the

Wayward — and so there were no great cities. Instead of organized religion, there was animism: a primitive instinct to imbue the rocks and trees with spiritual inhabitation. Back then, the most powerful leaders were the Fýrii, and they were said to commune with plants and assume the aspect of animals through ritual skin-changing. They also espoused the silly idea that it was a crime against the world of spirit to record information as a written language — that words held all power, and nothing must be written down, or the power of those words could be stolen and misused. So, they passed their learning on through rote memorization, and when they needed to communicate things that could not be simply spoken, they devised symbols to hint at greater meanings without compromising the supposed power of words. These they would sketch into mud or flesh, or in long strings of leaves that could be read like books to the familiar eye and looked like a seasonal ornament to everyone else. The true meaning of the dead rabbit is unfamiliar to me, but its message is otherwise clear."

Melvin sighed. Although his father was very learned, and it was a conversational indulgence to be able to get him to close his books long enough to talk, he did tend to speak obliquely. Melvin was not without pride, and asking endless questions like a dutiful pupil was not his ideal evening. However, the subject was a relevant one, so he pressed on.

"What was the message, father?"

"To pick a side. To remember that we are building the walls of an abbey that espouses a foreign god: an Erdin god. To warn us of the consequences of having a different point of view from theirs."

Melvin was stunned. "You think Bergrem would wish *us* harm for simply constructing stone walls? That is madness! We are not disciples of their faith, or any faith — the god Cuthain means as much to me as believing a rock in the forest has a soul. I have no use for any of it, and neither do you. He knows that! Why would he threaten us?"

"Bergrem quit my company and refused to complete a very lucrative carpenter's contract because he would no longer work on the abbey. He has likewise bullied and intimidated all carpenters from here to Portuan who have been called in to finish the job. And that is why I had to redesign the chancel out of self-supporting stone arches. As long as Bergrem and his Rangers can bring enough pressure to bear, the eastern chapel won't have so much as a wooden door, let alone joists. This is why the project is taking so long and why your help this year has been so valuable to me. It's an ideological boycott, son. A senseless crusade to turn back the clock and pretend that the Erdin never happened to this island. But they did. They happened everywhere. And so did their gods."

Daedrim took another sip of tea and snorted. Mumbling regrets to himself, he spat out a mouthful of errant tea leaves that had escaped their brewing pouch.

"Blech ... what was I... ah yes: as well as that road project and all its bloody history. The Thegn's Road ends at the abbey, but it was not meant to terminate there, as you well know. I must admit that it has crossed my mind often since we started work on this abbey that it is not just the ministry of Cuthain that is financing the project. Thegn Rory is contributing funding for its construction as well. Private deals have been struck between religion and the authority of rule, and that can be dangerous for the rest of us. Perhaps Bergrem is right to be concerned. I believe his forbearers were some of the unfortunates who died constructing that road."

Daedrim sighed and stared for a moment into the regretful emptiness of his teacup. Then he hoisted himself out of the deep imprint in his armchair and went outside to refill the kettle.

When he returned, steaming and stamping with cold, Melvin enquired:

"I know a little about the construction of the Thegn's Road, but not much. I have heard that it was worked on for many years; I have been to the place on High Hill where the old fallen tree blocks the unfinished section of the road, and I have wondered about the bodies that still lay crushed beneath it, unclaimed and unburied. But all that was long ago, right?"

Daedrim shook his head ruefully. "Not very long ago to an older man like me, and certainly not long in the memory of the thwarted thegns of Portuan."

"Which thegn ordered the road built in the first place?"

"Not one thegn, but generations of them. That road has been in process for a hundred and twenty years or more, and the work continues still. But for more than eighty years, the work has taken place far from Holm. Melvin, have you not read Davith's treatise *Progress of Power*? I thought I recommended that already."

Melvin looked indignant. "Father, I was, like, five years old when you recommended that book. It bored me senseless. I never finished it."

Daedrim's eyebrows contracted, and he very nearly smiled. "A pity.

Never too young to take an interest in politics, son. I'll summarize a few paragraphs about the Thegn's Road project if you like, but you really should read the whole book for yourself sometime."

"Yes, father." Melvin dutifully replied. And he very nearly meant it.

Daedrim retrieved a thick book with a dark blue cover off the shelf. He was as fastidious about the organization of his books as he was about the organization of the rest of his life. It did not take him long to locate the section he sought within it, for he had read the book multiple times. He recited a brief section to Melvin out loud, paraphrasing for clarity.

"It begins thusly: *the thegn of the southern territory of Fýrii planned to build a road through the vast Eldwood. The plan to construct this road was already generations old, for his great-grandfather had first envisioned a direct route from the seat of his power in Portuan to the fortress of Ofan near the western border of his thegndom. This road would be very advantageous to the ideal exercise of his ambitions, for he knew that his thegndom was not nearly wealthy enough.* —This is an instance of rather risqué humorous commentary, Melvinari; that's one of the things I appreciate about Davith as a writer. He's very funny."

"Yes father. I gathered that. Please go on."

"Very well. Let's see here... *The construction would also be very troublesome, having to be cut through a forest as large as dreaming, thick with the dangers of the primordial wilderness. The road would need to be built by slaves and prisoners, for dangerous labor demands expendable laborers. Once completed, hundreds of miles of tedious travel on the existing Wayward Road could be circumvented. As well, the financial burden of multiple tolls from the thegndom of Norlünd he would no longer have to pay and a snub on the thegn of that rich territory was enough to flavor his daydream with haughty excitement.*

"*He intended to name the road after himself, of course. But he barely lived to see the project begin: surveyors were just a few months in the field before the Red Pox swept through and ended him and his elder two sons. When his youngest son — who survived the pox by bathing regularly and having no friends — became the new thegn, he decided the road should be renamed. For nobody delighted in calling it Revis the Elder Road, not even the old thegn's mother.* ...See what I mean? Funny."

"Yes."

Daedrim eyed his son for a moment over thick eyebrows. But Melvin just stared at him placidly, so he continued to read.

"But the road was not completed by the new thegn either, although he spent a tidy fortune on digging out a stone quarry near Holm-"

"That's our quarry!" Melvin interjected.

"Yes, the very one. I lease it from the thegndom treasury in Portuan. Don't interrupt."

"Sorry."

Daedrim cleared his throat and continued. "Let's see... ah: *quarry near Holm, and constructing what was to be the first garrison fortress on the route the surveyors had planned for him. His efforts collapsed when the partially constructed castle was overwhelmed by a sudden infestation of river trolls, and all the surveyors and stone masons were gobbled up. That thegn, who was called Revis the Younger, spent the rest of his life and the best of his dignity sending groups of hired soldiers to their death attempting to expunge the trolls and regain the fortress. He never succeeded, and after he himself died leading the last of those raids, the Revis Keep was renamed Drôle — the name for 'troll' in the Uisen language."*

Melvin was trying very hard not to yawn, but even with his jaw clenched, his eyes were still watering. He tapped his fingers against the rug.

"The next thegn in line was Revis' nephew Baltha, who abandoned the idea of reclaiming Drôle from the trolls and began the sensible work of starting the road in Portuan and running the building effort north, paving over an existing wagon path. He managed to fund the project all the way to the southern bank of the river Tanis, linking his partial road to the ancient Orchard Bridge. The many years of construction efforts were slowed by boggy marshlands, hurried by organized banditry, and cost thrice the predicted expense. Baltha died an embittered man, who dwelt with the stooped hunch of poverty in his wealthy halls, always worrying about taxation and funding for the road.

"The road came to be known as the Thegn's Road. Baltha had not been well-liked, and 'Baltha Road' was liked even less. Yet some public acknowledgement of his effort was ordered by the king at Erdo-Usk, and the local lords were forced to oblige him.

"Baltha had no children of his own, but the line of thegns continued again through his sister. She birthed a nephew named Eckhart, who was reared to inherit his uncle's title and progressive vision. Eckhart was determined to succeed where his forefathers had failed, and he was ruthless enough to make the attempt at any human cost. Brutal treatment of con-

scripted road builders and an unusually high mortality rate led to a thrall revolt. A summer lightning storm further interrupting the progress of the thegn's road building ambitions, causing a wildfire that scorched High Hill and the forest bordering the town of Holm and killing most of the soldiers and thralls that survived the initial revolt. Thegn Eckhart abandoned the effort to expand the road further, convinced by his mother that the project was cursed by the gods."

Melvin stifled a yawn, pretending to rub his elbow while hiding his mouth. Daedrim glanced at him.

"That is how the road made it through Holm, son. The book goes on at further length to describe another two generations of thegns up to the present, but I can see you yawning."

"I'm sorry, father — I must be tired. Thank you for reading to me. I'm still trying to grasp what the rabbit corpse and the Thegn's Road have in common."

Daedrim looked exasperated. "Think it through, Melvinari. It is as obvious as politics. After eighty years of his family burying the bloody mess of the thrall revolt at High Hill and bearing the resultant social pressure of yet another failed attempt to connect the disparate pieces of the Thegn's Road, Thegn Rory has brought road building ambitions back to our valley. He intends to continue the work where his Great Grandfather Echkart left off. It is the very project you and I have been paid to work on, for the abbey is surely a subtle step in a larger plan. It is no mere exercise of religious fervor that imported Cuthain's clergy to our village. He is a god of enterprise, after all, and his clerics are well-funded by Thegn Rory and his family's connections. That is why Bergrem and his rangers are upset, for what benefits empire does not benefit the Eldwood. Thusly: the warning of the vivisected rabbit corpse this morning. Further proof that you should stay clear of Bergrem, and no longer waste your time at play with his son. You are too old for such games, anyway."

And with that, Daedrim turned back to his book.

Melvin flushed a little and looked away, musing on what his father had said. If his theory was correct, the situation was more complicated than goblin glyphs or clashing politics. It was not just Bergrem and his xenophobe ranger patriots, but the simple fact that Caetal's friendship was important to Melvin, no matter what his father forbade he should feel about it. They had played together for most of their lives. Although

Caetal had always been a huge boy with rough hands and a short temper, he was also keenly aware of the forests around Holm and had shown Melvin many childhood adventures.

They had built a special fort-cave in the attic of his house and then rigged the crawl-in doorway with warning bells and careful tripwires that only they knew about. Armloads of old blankets and stubs of candle, even a barrel of dried apples and a few sly skins of wine had been shared up there over many summers. He had shown Melvin how to fish, and whittle, and which berries were best to eat. They were quite different by nature: Caetal could be hard-headed, and thick-witted, and sometimes even a bit violent in that way that boys who want to spar but only have a thinner, smaller friend to torment can be. But he was a true friend. He was Melvin's only friend.

....

Over the next week, it began to snow. It was late in the season for a real dousing, but Holm would get a few inches of snowfall intermittently through to the end of Newgreen. Melvin did not enjoy the snow and did not trust anyone who did. It was one thing to go plank sledding or make a snow fort with Caetal; that was just plain fun, and only a lackwit wouldn't want to be out on a nice day careening down the side of High Hill at terrific speeds. But it was another thing entirely to have to be outside working in the snow.

His father had not asked him to return to the quarry again, which was just as well. The memory of the vivisected rabbit under those tall and creaking trees was still disquieting. Daedrim would soon be making the long trip to Portuan to personally seek out a carpenter that would be willing to carve the beams that were meant to span the nearly finished chancel. The project could not be completed without it and after more than nine years of construction, Daedrim and Melvin were eager to move on to a different venture.

At the doorway to his house, Melvin wrapped his blue knit scarf around his throat and bundled up in long layers of gray wool, with a heavy jacket buttoned up over everything. He set off at a slogging trot, lifting the trailing hem of his overcoat so it didn't drag in the snow.

It was not a long walk from his house to the abbey site: ten minutes along the Thegn's Road to the Wayward crossroad, traveling between farm fields of winter brown. Then, past the Welcome Holm tavern and the small general goods store — the former lit up cheerfully with wafting chimney smoke that smelled like roasting duck, and the latter dark and shuttered. From there, it was another ten minutes winding uphill toward the dense oak forests and the clearing where Cuthain's Abbey was being built.

The Thegn's Road ended just past the abbey in a lush barricade of massive old logs overgrown by prickly berry vines. It used to extend further, but the Eldwood beyond had been heathen lands since before the coming of the Erdin, and it was known that the Fýrii dwelt there still.

In older days, travelers had gone missing with unaccountable regularity — their packs and sometimes even their boots left abandoned by gutted campfires. Mushrooms grew in brazen rings even on the footpaths, and rangers hunted animals and demi-men under twining green twilight. There were patches of moss that grew as deep as autumn grass that could swallow a grown man to the waist. Over the years, the abandoned section of road had overgrown with unnatural vigor, and now the only remaining traces of it past the abbey could be seen as sun-dappled glimpses through enormous ferns and creeping underbrush.

Melvinari slogged through the snow, and his neighbors stared at him out their windows as he passed. He pulled the hood of his coat up to his forehead and pretended not to notice their hard looks. There was an undercurrent of tension that had lately become palpable in the air, one that Melvin could never remember feeling before. Like bad weather blowing in from a long way off, storm clouds of discontent were growing in Holm at a rate commensurate with the construction of the abbey. The abbey site could be seen for miles around: palatial in comparison to a farmer's wattle hut and imbued with the inherent authority of stone.

Up till now, there had only been three stone buildings in Holm — the tavern that stood at the crossing between the Wayward and the Thegn's Road, the mayor's home, with his large gathering room serving as the council chamber, and Melvin's own house. The tavern was expected to be grand and was the cultural pride of Holm. The mayor's house had the elected prestige of governance associated with it, so that was all right. And the rich mason and his son could be forgiven for their ornate house of stone because they could afford to build it, and the mason made it by proper hand just like the rest of the town had built theirs.

But now, a fourth stone building was taking shape at the top of High Hill — funded by foreign coins and housing a foreign god. Here in Holm, the darker native Dekai population crowded out the rarer light-skinned Erdin twenty to one. It was much the same across the whole island, except in the larger port cities where the blending of pale and tan had become more widespread as generations of sailors frequented brothels.

Melvin walked on. The road passed the wide grassy commons field and city gallows, where markets occurred frequently, and hangings far less often. In warmer months the grassy field was lush and green, but winter had browned the grass to brittle stalks, and foraging sheep had churned mud up everywhere. The road then marched purposely past the gallows on its wending way uphill, although Melvin always walked wide to keep some distance from it, unconsciously hurrying as he passed. Across that long gallows scaffold, the frayed ends of ancient ropes still swayed as grim reminders of what it meant to break the Queen's Law. Although there had never been a hanging in Melvin's lifetime, he still avoided looking at the creepy old thing. It was a macabre relic of a less civilized time.

In Holm, peace had been the custom for many years. Though there was little blending of cultures, the small population of Erdin that had settled here lived as others had in this valley since the island was born from the sea — by threshing wheat, and baking bread, and minding their own business. *Holm* is not a word that means home, though the town of Holm is inhabited by the descended generations of more than a hundred farming families (and a few dozen bachelors and widows) that proudly call it so. It is an old word descended from an even older one, and it means *flat fertile valley that was once a lake.*

Holm was not a place where revolutions were born. It was a place for marrying the first person you kissed and raising your children to tend the land that your parents had tended before you. But lately, neighbors glared at each other across their fields, and old friends of different shades avoided one another at the weekly market and sat apart in the tavern at night. Many praised the construction of the abbey; it meant some schooling for their children, proper proselytizing on holidays and perhaps somewhere safe to gather in crisis. But the few who had always opposed it had loud voices in the community, and their vehemence grew as support for their views slowly spread. For what is an education worth if it offends ancestral spirits? How sweet is the singing of sacrament when children are beguiled by invaders to believe in their conquering gods?

....

The cloister of Cuthain was a yawning arcade mouth around a courtyard of white, where only the bright red berries of the holly bushes bloomed. They peeked through the snow everywhere like drops of blood. All else in the yard was the creeping black tendrils of winter-dormant rose bushes overhung by a grey sky scudded with clouds. Melvinari listened to the steady clatter of hammer and chisel echoing down the cloister hallway. His father and two bondsmen were working in the apse at the rear of the building, engraving a wavering ocean pattern into the stone lintel above the sanctuary doorway. It was a reminder of the ocean that Cuthain had crossed to bring his message to his people, and Melvin instinctively disliked the sight of it. Not as a work of craftsmanship; there was something about the sea that always made him uneasy, and he did not like to be reminded of it. Walking under the lintel, with the carved waves rising above it, felt oppressive to him — an ecclesial threat to surrender or drown.

He had not trained in stone carving yet and had the weather been warmer, he would have been mixing mortar or assembling segmented stone mullions in the arched windows. As wet and cold as it was, his father had declared that the mortar might not cure correctly; lime migration could cause friability and enfeeble the bonding process with frost. So, Melvin found himself stuck with his least favorite task: splitting stones into span-thicknesses to prep for renewed building in the spring.

It was a tedious task that involved inspecting each of the large granite slabs carefully, looking for sedimentary layer lines where the stone was weakest. Then he would hand-crank a star drill the size of his thumb into the top of the rock until he had aching shoulders and a row of holes at a depth that could hold water, each a handspan apart. These he would fill from a water flask and wait overnight in hopes of a freeze that would expand the water plugs enough to crack the granite into layers. Or, if that didn't work, he would begin the even more laborious task of slabbing the rock by hand with a mallet and metal wedge. Either way, it meant aching muscles and sweat that stung his eyes as he worked by flickering torchlight to keep warm.

The only thing that stayed the monotony of the task from strangling his quick mind was the puzzle of the stone itself. He had to consider each section of the granite very carefully before beginning a slab.

Rock flows like everything flows — like water, like fire, like the wind. It is always moving and reforming itself, but so slowly that all the history of the island people took place between the formation of individual layers. But the sedimentary seams that rippled through the rock like a network of veins were always its weakest point — that same weakness that invited a chisel could also crack on its own in a bad cold snap, and whole sections of stone walls have collapsed under the weight of careless quarrying. A stone mason's nightmares often began with a sound like a cracking iceberg and ended with tumbling death for those working below.

Melvin was hunched over a thick slab, tracing its veins by torchlight flicker, when a stranger's voice snuck up on him from behind.

"I've heard that limestone dissolves in the rain over time. Is that so?"

Melvin swiveled up and was out of his seat before his chisel hit the ground, his heart beating like a rabbit's. In the shadow between two cloister archways stood a man dressed in dark traveler's robes. He appeared so at ease that it seemed as though he had always been standing there — that the building had been built up around *him*. He was a man of plain looks: a nondescript face on a midsized frame, commonplace in every way but for the reddish tint to his hair and the unsettling green of his eyes. They shone like fireflies caught in his skull, even in the dim light of the hallway, and they twinkled mischievously as he smiled at Melvinari.

"So, in your broad experience, would you say that a humble tower built of limestone would someday wash away in a hard rain? Because if so, why bother?"

Melvin collected himself quickly. At the root of his personal philosophy were two contradicting facts: that everything is possible and that most things are highly unlikely. It was possible that the man in front of him simply stepped out of thin air, but it was highly unlikely to have happened that way. Melvin flicked his eyes over the stranger rapidly, gathering information about him. *Fine clothing, but not well kept. No visible weapon. Pale for a Dekai, but not Erdin. He can probably move very quietly. He snuck up on me, that's all; why would I expect someone to try? There's no shame in being surprised.* He felt his assurances tighten the flush out of his cheeks, so that when he answered, his voice was flatter and calmer than his racing heart.

"It is both true and untrue that limestone dissolves in the rain. Impurities in the stone can be swept away over time by rain that is heavy with the taint of smoke, but it takes many lifetimes to show. It certainly will not crumble around you from rainy weather, if that is your concern. Marble is the same, however, and granite contains feldspar, which is also water soluble. No stone is immune to moving water, given enough time. So take a lesson and build with limestone if it pleases you."

The stranger's smile flickered, and he chuckled to himself, low in his chest. He stepped further forward out of the shadow of the archway, and the winter light painted his robe a dark blue. *Oh gods, a magus. Have a care!* The thought whirled through Melvin with excitement, and he felt his feet readjust into a more stable stance. Weirdly, his hands began to itch. Too far away for help, the tinking rhythm of his father's work crew and their chisels continued unbroken.

"I am Drinn, young master. It is my pleasure to meet a mason so puerile in this remote part of the world. I have heard of your family's masonic reputation, and I see firsthand the fine stonework that you both make. Might I enquire after your father, to discuss a project I had in mind?"

Melvin flinched and stood up taller. *Puerile?!*

"You can find my father by following the sound of the hammering, but I should warn you that folk around here are.... somewhat wary of a person like yourself. Actually, I'd say superstitious, strongly bordering on hostile. Though my father doesn't espouse these views personally, he does have to live peacefully near neighbors that do. He may not be interested in assisting you."

Drinn stared at him for a long moment, small flickers of thoughts chasing around his face. "I am... surprised. Is it that obvious what I am?"

"To me. Firstly, you wear robes dyed with *indigofera* — a plant that grows nowhere near this island, and a color of dye with portentous associations. Secondly, the air literally shimmers around you like heat; it's quite chilly today, otherwise I might not have noticed. And thirdly-"

— deep breath, careful, careful —

"-thirdly, I believe that you stepped out of the rock itself. I don't believe that you just snuck up on me, even if you'd like me to think so. I may have been distracted by my work, but I have excellent hearing. You were simply not there a moment ago, and now you are."

Melvin surprised himself with his bluntness. He had not known that he saw, or felt, any of that. He had not dreamed he would ever meet a magus and would never have flattered himself even in such fantasies that a magus would seek him out directly. If he was correct, the man before him had trapped a living flame inside his own heart, and it seared him endlessly. If legends were to be believed, he could kill Melvin by calling out the names of his unborn enemies. He was more dangerous than a violent temper and a good memory combined, and he was standing just a few feet in front of Melvin, laughing at him.

The man rocked back onto his heels, chortling so quietly to himself that only the faintest sound of wheezing could be heard. He leaned back against the column behind him and sighed, wiping a blithe tear out of one eye and watching the snow as it drifted against the walls.

"Alright. *Well then.* This is... a different conversation than I expected to be having with you, and I'm glad of it. Let us speak now of true things and leave the niceties for common folk. Can we do that now?"

Melvin nodded. His hands were suddenly prickling like he'd run them through nettles. He clutched them together behind his back to keep from scratching them.

"Good. As I said, I am called Drinn. I have traveled to this area from a long way off, and rather unintentionally. There are *things* that are seeking after me that are unlucky to speak of aloud, and I have a strong desire to not be anywhere near where they saw me last. I have never lived so far from a proper city, and I have never wanted to. But here I am now. I surmise that my presence in town will be anything but encouraged, so I must take up residence a few miles out of sight. However, I cannot live in some wattle farmer's hut — there is a safety in stone that is both real and imagined, and a third safety that is beyond your understanding, and I must live shielded within it to be at my ease.

"I'd like to hire you and your father to build me a simple tower — nothing fancy, just three stories tall, but of the finest stone you can quarry. I am willing to pay you both double or even triple your regular rates, but the construction must occur in social silence. Nobody uninvolved in the project can know where or why the tower is being constructed. There are few towers ever built in the wilderness without grave purpose; they draw attention to eyes that are looking for them, and I intend to remain anonymous for as long as I can. Now: I believe I have taken up enough of the pulpit! It is your turn to speak."

His eyes were bright, so very bright, that they were hard to look at for more than a few moments.

"I... I'm not sure what to say. I would help you if I could. But you look like a magus, and the folks of this town jump at shadows and burn wicker-men with the harvest to ward off people like you. I'm sorry, but I don't think you will find a friend here at the abbey."

The man blinked thoughtfully for a moment. His hands traced across the veins in the rock slab that Melvin had been forming, and he muttered to himself low in the back of his throat. Then he spoke.

"It is in our nature, fundamentally, to look at something a hundred times and never really see it. In fact, the more often we look, the less likely we are to notice anything out of place. We collect a thousand petty words for love but most of us never find the courage to risk invoking its True Name. I fell under the spell of affection with a woman many years ago: someone I had grown up beside as a child. I saw her almost every day, but I didn't *see* her until we were in our early twenties, and too late by then for the *me and her* that could have been. That kind of blindness is such a pity. It is a failing that robs vitality out of life's possibilities as surely as color-blindness diminishes a sunrise."

Melvin stared at him hard while he spoke, wondering what he was leading up to.

"There are countless words for almost everything, do you know that? A student of my art can get buried in words. It is like studying twenty languages all at once, but most of them have irreconcilable contradictions in translation, and the student must learn to understand that and yet simultaneously convince themselves that they don't. But more perplexing and powerful still is this: behind all that scholarly chatter, there exists a language that is, to normal speech, as a campfire is to a candlestick. Those are the Names that, if intoned through the right mouth and in the right moment, will vibrate creation in all of its deepest aspects, and across time itself. They are the elder words — the True Names that evoked form out of formlessness before time was loosed and perpetuity was extinguished beneath it. To speak these words out loud is blasphemy, for what fool would ever address the Immortals in their own tongue, as though on equal footing? Here, I have an idea: let me borrow your coat."

"Pardon me?"

"Your gray woolen walkabout, Melvinari. Your coat. Here, it's all right — we shall exchange coats. That is an even trade, isn't it?"

Melvin stared at him open-mouthed as the magus shrugged his elaborate coat off and handed it over to Melvin. It was unexpectedly heavy. There was a subtlety of silver knotwork traced around the edge of the sleeves, and the inside of the coat was lined in black silk. The blue of the dye was tremendously dark and shimmered like oil on the surface of a lake at night. Melvin did not notice himself shrugging out of his gray coat, and he certainly didn't notice himself slipping Drinn's coat on until his fingertips slid out of the soft sleeves. It hung around his shoulders like it had been tailor-fit. The great coat smelled a bit pungent; crushed thyme and powdered earth and a waft of something dead and bleached by sunlight. If a whole handful of spider webs and the plants they were clinging to were gathered up and burned, the smell was akin to that. Melvin watched Drinn as he cheerfully donned the gray wool coat and noted that he looked much thinner than he at first seemed — almost emaciated. Drinn continued on as if this was a totally normal thing that strangers did, to exchange their clothing in the steaming chill of winter.

"There are... fourteen words that I know of for stone, Melvinari, and that does not even take into account what type of stone it is. It is *Rabish* in old Dyleet, and *Mera* under-mountain in the mouths of the Delvin, who tear it apart with loving it, as Delvin are wont to do. To the Erdin it is *Acha,* or *Achavalla,* when the size is grand enough to warrant extra pomp. The Rhymir call it *Vos* and speak of it carefully, as they have become a wandering people and are somewhat suspicious of unmoving things."

He whisked Melvin's scarf off from around Melvin's neck and chuckled to himself when he held it up, noting its blue color. "So here is a root for your knowledge of *indigofera* dye — well done. All knowledge comes from somewhere humble. Somebody paid a small fortune to get you this scarf — interesting that you own it, very interesting. I will keep it safe, and you are certain you will get it back."

Melvin did, indeed, feel certain. Drinn wrapped the scarf around his neck and tucked it into his shirt so that it made him look like he had a bit of a round belly. He slouched as he continued speaking, diminishing himself subtly. Even his eyes seemed to dim to a green that was only the brightness of spring, no longer the gleam of an emerald with firelight held behind it. *Something is happening here. Why is my head buzzing so much? Why did I give him my clothes?*

"Yes, there are many words for stone, and all of them are powerful in their own way — they reveal so much about the culture that named them, its prejudices and predilections. It is fascinating to learn these words, and empowering to speak them fluently, for what person is more respected than one who speaks with a natural command of language? Yet these words are *mortal.* They were birthed by human cultures, and they will drift out of knowing when the last people pass on and even their words to describe themselves become extinct. Such a loss!

"But there is a Name that means *stone* in every language; a Word for stone that is so fundamentally true that the stones refer to *themselves* by that name. Do you think you would recognize that word if you saw it?"

Melvin blinked. "Um... what? I guess?"

Drinn nodded in satisfaction and, reaching his hand out, traced a symbol into the dust on the stone Melvin had been chiseling. Melvin leaned forward and stared at it curiously. He had never seen the symbol before, but something about it seemed familiar in a way that made no sense. The symbol was squat and rounded; tall and flaring. It seemed to shift and... *(settle?)* in Melvin's view, firming up and widening out, claiming space in the powdered rock dust — and suddenly there was a sound blooming inside Melvin's mind. It pushed forward into his mouth, and, without thinking, he whispered the Word aloud. The sound of it swelled, thickening the air in the courtyard like soup. The stones all around him shivered and shifted in yearning, groaning on such a low register that Melvin could barely hear it.

Inside the apse where his father was working, the pinging of the hammer and chisel stopped immediately and was replaced by the sound of booted feet running towards them. The word he had spoken aloud sounded like *EBEN,* but it was not a word at all — it was a hum that came up through his skull from underground. Melvin somehow knew the word — he felt like he had known it since before he was born. It meant *Homm's Bones;* it meant the bones of a celestial; it meant they were walking around on a celestial's body; building an abbey out of those bones, to worship the name of a god.

Melvin staggered beneath a sense of his own insignificance; buried under the weight of humility before the vastness of all that he suddenly realized he did not yet know. The mason's son sank to his knees. Drinn stepped blithely over him like he was not even there. The magus raised a friendly hand in greeting to Daedrim and his assistants as they ran up, casting about with their hands and eyes to see what damage had been done when the whole building groaned.

....

Melvin did not remember much else from that day.

His father conversed with Drinn politely enough once he had satisfactorily surveyed the courtyard for damage. Daedrim spoke of building options casually, as though his son was not lying stunned nearby on the floor, dressed in the dark robes of a magus, while a stranger dressed in his borrowed clothes stood nearby. It was surreal; the cold afternoon around them twisted and warped subtly as Melvin's head buzzed with the profundity of the sound of *EBEN*. His father seemed reluctant, even so. The tone of his words dipped and whined in Melvin's ears, but there was no strength in his rebuttal. By the end of the conversation, he spoke thickly and slowly, as though his mouth was full of cotton batting.

Whatever resistance Daedrim had towards helping this strange man began to die before he even started speaking. My father is no match for a magus and his magic. Drinn's words were summer pollen; they covered them all in sticky assurances, and the reverberation of *EBEN* in the stones all around them hummed like bees.

....

Somehow Melvin made it to his feet and made it home, and somehow he slept. How any of this happened, he was not to recall; there was a smashing of time and a smear of colors, and then he was in his own bed with hours behind him.

In the early morning, he awoke to the sound of his father leaving the stable on horseback, plodding slowly towards Portuan. Memories of the previous afternoon were vague shapes that darted underwater in his mind. He would have woken entirely in disbelief, but there was a dark blue coat with a hooded mantle hung on his bed post that was crawling with reflected starlight.

....

The day was strangely quiet and still. Winter muffled everything, and Melvin found it hard to leave the comfort of his bed. He read books he liked to read and snacked all day without once making a proper meal. He dozed, but awoke sweat-damp from a dream where the ground was a mouth with mountainous teeth, and it was swallowing him whole.

By then, it was nearly dusk, and the sky had purpled like a spreading bruise. Clouds that gathered throughout the day had dumped more snow, and by nightfall, a rising wind tore at the shingles on the roof and shrieked obscenely down the chimney. Melvin lit the largest fire that the fireplace could hold. He drew a blanket up around him and drank hot tea while lightning flickered at the window casement and thunder boomed away behind it. The house felt crowded, though he sat alone.

He could not help wondering if the gods themselves were angry at Melvin, for speaking of their bones so profanely; it was a fantasy that gnawed excitedly at his thoughts. *Magic was real. He had spoken it. He had felt it in the buzzing of his skin. Let the lightning boil the rain, and let the thunder tear the clouds apart. Nature could complain all it wanted; nothing would change his knowing the True Name for stone.*

Then there was a roaring concussion of light and sound, and in the blinding corona of a lightning flash, something struck hard against the front door. In the silence that follows thunder, his heart hammered loudly in his ears. *What in the hells was that?* He held his breath for as long as his lungs could bear and let it out in a slow wheeze. The sound did not come again. Into that silence drifted the pattering of rain, and from one minute to the next, the drizzle opened up into a clattering downpour.

He'd like to remember striding to the door and throwing it open to confront the terrors of the night. But Melvin didn't do that at all. He waited a full quarter hour, then wrapped himself in the dark blue of Drinn's coat and snuck out a low back window, dragging a fire-poker behind him through the tall grass and trying not to breathe too loudly. The rain pummeled his face, and his bare feet stung with cold. To the edge of the house he crept, burglar-sly, and peeked around the corner when the moon was doused behind clouds. His doorway stood thankfully empty. But when moonslight finally split the clouds again, he saw the handle of a bronze dagger buried deeply in the door.

Pinned between the quillions and the wet wood was a severed rabbit head. Its eyes stared wide at nothing; its mouth was contorted into a snarl. Blood streaked down in a spreading stain beneath it, and around the dagger handle hung a woven circle of stinging nettle.

Melvin huddled back into the shadow of the sill with his heart hammering and his eyes searching everywhere. All around him, rain fell on empty fields. Thunder grumbled softly, away to the south. He slid his hand up around the handle of the thin dagger, never taking his eyes off the road. He felt the electric prickle of the nettle sting and rubbed his hand with a mumbled curse. *Why a ring of nettles this time, when last it was wicker reeds? Is a threat of harm implicit?*

He pulled the sleeve of the jacket over his hand and yanked the dagger free. The coney head fell to the porch with a bouncing crunch, and bile licked up his throat. In an angry flash, he kicked it away into the low bushes and hurled the ring of nettles after it.

Melvin wondered if the rain would wash the blood from the door. It was a very stately door — black oak and copper hinges. It had been made by Bergrem for his father many years ago. Now there was a knife wound in it, and it could not be sanded out; it would always be there. He slid the thin dagger up into his sleeve and thought about how friendships die. Sometimes they decompose naturally. Sometimes they are stabbed with a dagger. A sullen animosity that Melvin had never felt before began to heat up his heart, and his head throbbed as he imagined Bergrem and Caetal, out there skulking somewhere in the dark.

Come for me if you dare, you keţe bastards. Melvin gritted his teeth and clutched the dagger handle so hard he felt the pommel bite into the palm of his hand. *Now I'm ready for you.*

....

The next day, sunlight was everywhere. The sky was clear indigofera, with not a cloud to be seen. Spring warmth swept snow from the town as though hurrying to tidy up after a fit of temper until thin drifts were only to be seen hiding under the shadow of the trees. Melvinari woke like a man reborn to good humor — even the bees wandering around under the garden window hummed with pleasure in the surprising warmth of the sun. Melvin packed a meal and set out for the abbey, lingering for a moment at the front door while his fingertips softly traced the wound in the wood.

He would not remember doing it, but there would never again be a time when he stepped through the door without unconsciously touching that cleft. Over time it became so much a part of the character of the door that he no longer thought about it. But he never forgot how it got there.

The abbey grounds were peopled with priests when Melvin arrived. Like bears waking from hibernation, the clear day brought them out from their barracks to drift amongst the garden patches with the peaceful disorientation of the barely awake. They were dressed mostly in the earthen tan and white robes of initiates, with the sun-lit Eye of Cuthain and its lightning tears emblazoned on their chest. Melvin chuckled to himself as he watched them bumbling about, raking at dead rose bushes and peering around at the ongoing construction. They chattered amongst themselves and wandered in and out of rooms of empty stone. He could hear their sandals shuffling against the granite floors.

All priests tended to look so similar to him that he could not tell them apart. Oh sure, there were thin priests and fat ones; dry-mouthed elders and rebellious youth barely broken in under the yoke of their god... but each was just a wide-eyed fool to Melvin, a sect of people so careless about their time walking the world that they lost the meaning of the ground by staring too long at the sky.

All the pleasures of life are wasted on those that can't wait to depart it. Melvin mused, shaking his head disgustedly. *I wonder what they think we were put here for, but to be sheep forever gnawing on the wood fence in the garden wall? There is nothing greener on the other side — I'm sure of it.* His hand traced the rough contours of the chapel wall, and *EBEN* shuddered through his mind. *Bones. Now they feel like bones. I wonder how long I will remember this feeling?*

Across the arcade of arches, a young cleric waved from the garden, and Melvin waved back at him politely. The cleric was not yet a man grown — no older than ten or eleven summers. Here was a rebuttal of Melvin's flippant prejudice, for the boy was surely as easy to spot amongst the older priests as a pigeon is in a thicket of thrushes. He was small, and seemed almost fragile; tiptoeing unsteadily through the dead garden with the tentative caution of a guest. His head seemed a little big on his thin shoulders. His hair was silver-white, so blond that sunlight reflecting off his head dappled the features of his face with a secondary glow. Melvin had seen him before but not close enough to notice the snowy pallor of his skin. *Erdin-blooded. Look at that heavy jaw.*

The boy waved again and began to wander towards him. So Melvin turned away, walking swiftly to the south side of the arcade where the walls were unfinished and peering importantly at a portico column until he was sure the boy wasn't behind him. This was the last part of the abbey's outdoor grounds to be completed — one expanse of garden wall, the cloister roof, and a lofty arch that spanned the absence where an iron gate would hang. A cobblestone path led towards the archway.

Here, in the unfinished section of the wall, the strangest feature of the abbey construction was clearly visible. A row of wrought iron bars, hammered into spikes, protruded from the top of the wall like fangs on a jaw. These bars had been buried everywhere — every three handspan, all the way around the outer enclosure. They must have cost the small half of a fortune, and nine-tenths of their length was buried from sight in the mortar of the wall! It was an absurd waste of precious iron, and his father had railed against it mightily. *How about just the spikes, mortared to ten inches deep? More than enough to detour someone trying to get over the top,* Daedrim had reasoned. But the clerics insisted on the full lengths, and they apparently had enough money to squander. So, each and every iron bar was beaten into shape onsite by the clerics themselves, blessed and entombed between the stones. Melvin stared at them now, poking up out of the unfinished wall, and shook his head in disgust. *God-addled idiots. Like prisoners paying me to mortar them in with bars that they forged themselves.*

The arch he stood near was the most recent project his father and he had completed. That was nearly a week ago, while the snow was drifting in. The rise of the arch was still curved around support scaffolding, and for a good reason — the stone arch was huge and ornate; the keystone itself must weigh a quarter ton. But it was striking workmanship, some of the finest that Melvin had ever chipped and limed. He had built it almost entirely on his own, even carving Cuthain's Eye into the keystone, with his father really only assembling the wooden scaffold and the large curve of the wood form that the arch had straddled to learn its own shape while it cured.

It had taken too long to finish, of course — Melvin had worked with the caution of someone who intends to impress but is uncertain of their task. His father had therefore hurried him through the quicklime with snow in their hair, and they had hoisted the keystone in place on winch and pulley as the sky darkened all around them and sleet gathered on the garden walls. Daedrim chided him afterwards for his slow pace and the risk of saturation in the mortar, but Melvin knew the stern hollows of his father's face as well as anyone and could tell the difference between exasperation and pride. Just to be safe, however, Melvin had left the struts and wooden form in place the whole of last week to give the arch extra time to cure.

After two hours of chisel and hammer and then breakfast, Melvin licked honey off his fingers and decided to unveil the archway. Afternoon sunlight had dried the ground until snow was a winter memory, and the air shimmered with crickets. The arch had cured under an oilskin tarp for a week in the wet and through the sunlit heat of morning. Melvin knew well enough that the mortar was cured. He set to the scaffolding with a mallet and hammered each piece apart through the slide-lock of clever wooden pegs. All remained well, and he stacked the pieces as he set them down. The sun was beginning to pink his neck, and the spring crickets were so loud in the tall grasses that he wanted to remind them to shut up and be polite. He worked steadily.

His mind was drifting into a reverie of stewed barley and roasted chicken when he raised his head at last and saw Caetal staring at him from a long way off. The large boy was crouched near the tree line, with his head and shoulders sticking up out of the grass. Their eyes met, and Caetal waved his arms twice above his head and beckoned towards the woods, shouting something that the wind carried off. Melvin scowled and looked away, his fingers unconsciously brushing against the shaft of the dagger at his belt. He wrenched the board he was working on out of the way and continued working, his eyes blurring with unexpected tears. Across the field, Caetal gestured again more frantically, and Melvin turned a shoulder to it. He was angry with himself for ever letting that rough bully into the private chambers of his heart. He had grown lonely after his mother passed, and friendship with the woodcutter's son had blinded him to Caetal's many character faults. Melvin roughly pushed the wooden form out of the way, and it landed with a heavy thud on the cobblestones below.

The archway was freestanding for the first time, and Melvin couldn't help but admire it. The keystone was a proper wedge, carefully chipped and polished, and the slabs of the span were as even and precise as a young hand could hope to make them. *It is what it should have been.* Melvin grinned and hugged himself, sweeping his gaze across the mortar lines. A snowdrift wind gusted through the arch, and Melvin shivered and shrugged Drinn's jacket back on, still carefully keeping his back averted from the direction he had spotted Caetal. Discreetly, he glanced sideways towards the tree line, but could no longer see his friend. The chirping of crickets that had been sawing loudly all around him suddenly stilled, and Melvin thought he heard his name being called from a long way off. Through that quiet moment wafted the faint scent of something green and burning.

....

It was the smell that he noticed first. It was not the red-brown smear on the cobblestone path below the arch that moving the scaffolding revealed, nor was it the careful circle of stones that surrounded it. Though he cocked his head and stared at it, the buzzing of the crickets and the heat shimmering off the cobblestones dulled his thinking. It was something else — something that the scaffolding had hidden from sight, something bubbling overhead: a greenish-white pulp that had been smeared on the mortar of the keystone above him. It stank, and he blankly stared at it. It stank like burning calcium.

Melvin had smelled this smell so often — a thousand faint fireplace memories, a hundred times kilning the quicklime — that he could not bring its unique significance to mind. He stared at the daub of plant paste while it bubbled and sizzled, and he smelled the stone burning, and all the words that meant *something is wrong* scattered across a second of slow breath that was as silent as the moment before a cave-in. Somewhere, too far away, an old friend rushed towards him through the winter wheat. Somewhere that friend cried out in warning. But words are only as powerful as the person speaking them, and young legs can only run so fast.

Gravity is faster, and stone weighs a ton.

With a grinding crackle, the stones above Melvin split along the corrupted mortar and slid apart. Melvin threw his hands up and shrieked as the keystone and half the arch plummeted down on top of him. His spine folded, and the great stone smashed him to the ground. His legs splintered like twigs, and his pelvis was crushed, and some idiot part of the last smear of his waking mind whispered *illium, sacrum, femur* and then there was pain like a fire lit inside his bones and he screamed with a part of his throat that he had never used before. It was the scream of the suddenly dying, and it tore out the last of his childhood and wrapped it around a single sound, and that sound deepened and widened into a roaring Word, and the Word reverberated *EBEN*.

The stone he was buried under splintered like glass and exploded outwards into shards as big as swords. The pressure of that weight lifted off of him suddenly, just long enough to glance down at the ruin that was once his legs and to feel the bloody warmth spreading out from his split skin. Then his vision tunneled, and his head rolled back, and before the darkness dragged him away from pain, the last thing he saw was the flushed face of a young priest kneeling over him: his mismatched eyes wide with panic, his blond hair lit by sunlight.

....

"The bodies would go where I had never been: churning down the snow-swollen Trask, back to the endless dancing of the sea. I will join them there someday. But today, I am still alive."

WATER
~ The Fifth Story ~

By the time I killed a boar-man, I had already hunted and shared the meat of more than two hundred animals. I could count each one in the blue tally markings tattooed up my arm. Seen from afar, it looks like the spreading branches of a tree that is growing just beneath my skin. But up close, each line segments into the measure of lives I have eaten and absorbed into myself. Thusly do my people keep track of what we take from the world, and what we owe for it.

....

The Orlŭk knelt and drank from the river like any animal, and the three rangers drew down on him from downwind, crouched beneath the spreading cover of ferns. There were two of the beasts at the river's edge; the second one waist deep in the water with a forked fishing trident in hand. It is possible to mistake an Orlŭk for a man from a great enough distance; up close, the smell alone will tell. Up close, they are as grayish-pink as a conch shell, and their teeth tusk out to points and little thin rivulets of drool paint ribbons down the fur on their face. They are ugly in a way that seems almost careless — like a human and a boar made a baby that neither would claim. Brutal but cunning, heavy limbed and an appetite for almost everything. They stoop when they stand, but they can run on all fours as fast as fear.

The morning was barely born, just cold slices of light between the bleached limbs of winter trees, and as Cactal drew the bowstring back, he felt a prickle of jealousy for their thick pelt of fur. His breath was a cold cloud and his frozen fingers shook on the string. The Orlŭks would be dead soon, but at least they were warm now. He sighted on the beast that fished, held the feather fletching against his cheek and waited for the flick of his father's finger. Bergrem, looking every inch a bear in layers of brown fur, crouched to the left of him. Old Tom was likewise, and to the right. Caetal concentrated on slowing his breath. Even the long braid of his hair wrapped around his neck like a scarf barely warmed him. He felt the winter prickle of exposed skin: the subtle shifts in the air, and in his mind, he imagined what it must be like to be an Orlŭk fishing in the river. He looked through the eyes of the boar man, sharing a moment of concentration with him as aquatic shadows swam below the water's surface. In the seconds before he loosed the shaft, Caetal knew the Orlŭk was hungry and wanted nothing more than fish; to get out of the river, to enjoy what cold sunlight a winter morning offered before sleeping through the rest of the day.

Then: the silent command of his father's fingers closing into a fist, and all three arrows became a blur of wooden lightning and the quiet thunder of three humming bowstrings.

....

We took what we could from the bodies: a crude dirk, a necklace of shell and bone on a leather thong, the wooden trident. I had shot the fishing Orlŭk in the neck, and he bled his surprise out into the river. When I waded into the water to retrieve his body, I found his fishing trident by its dip and wiggle and held it aloft with a fish speared on the tines. My father and Old Tom laughed fit to burst — the poor bastard had gotten lucky with breakfast just before he died! I grinned at them, but my heart felt like it was drifting downstream with the pull of the bloody current.

I was almost a man now, I suppose. Killing my first Orlŭk was something I had often hoped for, but now the only thing I felt was the rushing of the river and this bone-deep sense of being pulled along with it. I guess I stood there for a while, because my father called for the fish before I even noticed they had built a fire to cook it over. In my hand, the arrow shaft I had pulled out of its neck was slick with blood. My hand shook as I stared at it. Little drops of blood, as rich and dark as chokeberries, slid down the chipped stone of the arrowhead and were swept away by the water.

On the shore, Old Tom pushed the naked body of the kneeling Orlŭk into the river to let it drift. I looked down at my other hand and noticed it was clenched around the wrist of the one I had killed. My knuckles were white with chill, and the stiffening corpse bumped against my legs underwater. I could see its eyes staring up at me, as dull as stones. Its teeth were pulled back in a snarl of surprise, and they would be fixed in cold death that way until the fish and freshwater crabs picked his face apart.

With careful effort, I relaxed my hand and let the Orlŭk go. He drifted downriver after his friend, following where the water flowed around the bend towards Dunmarsh. The bodies would go where I had never been: churning down the snow-swollen Trask, back to the endless dancing of the sea. I will join them there someday. But today, I am still alive, and my father is calling me to breakfast. I have earned my tattoo today. I will eat what was meant for the Orlŭk, and walk the woods where he used to walk. I will take his trident as my own, for I have taken his place on the turning wheel.

··

"We got lucky them creatures were distracted, lad." Old Tom stated from across the breakfast fire, gesturing vaguely at Caetal with a handful of hot fish. His beard was littered with fish scales, but his eyes were shrewd.

"I don' want ya gettin' a pride on because yer kill was easy. You are almost a man now, and it won't help ya to assume that the gifts life offers come clean. Sometimes the wind shifts quickly against you. Sometimes them brutes are the ones huntin' you. It's not often you catch them unawares with their eyes on the water."

He picked his teeth thoughtfully with a splinter of dogwood and grunted to himself. The wide scar on his neck was almost buried between canyons of wrinkles, but when he cleared his throat, it jumped and flashed a hint of pale puckering.

"I know it, g-g-gramps. I've hunted often enough to feel where the wuh... where the w-wind is blowing." Caetal jabbed sullenly at the fire with his roasting stick. The film of fish grease sputtered and hissed.

Old Tom shrugged elaborately. "No need to be pert, pup. It's in m' nature to point out the obvious. That's why your dad has kept me around so long: he likes it when I remind him an hour after dawn breaks that the sun is comin' up."

Bergrem listened silently, chewing his fish and nodding slowly. He was not a man who wasted words.

When the fish was finished and the fire was doused and buried, the men unrolled their needle kits from their leather satchels. They were points of obsidian, as thin and fine as could be knapped by hand, with handles of twisted copper wire. They dipped these into an inkwell filled with the pulp of glastum woad, ash, and blue river clay. Bergrem worked on Old Tom, and he on him. They hummed deep in their throats while they carved a record of the Orlŭk hunt onto each other. Their humming was as old as memory — wordless droning ululations passed through generations. It was the deep rocking of the sea and the powerful rumble of a tumbling avalanche. As always, it made Caetal shiver with gooseflesh. It was a sound he could not yet produce himself, although he quietly tried to mimic it. His voice cracked, and his face flushed. He silently watched them work.

The arms and back of both men were a twisting knotwork of their kills: tiny blue remembrances that formed nautilus spirals, a honeycomb of hexagons, or the thicket likeness of blue bracken. His father's back, as muscled as the bulbs of an oak, bore the picture of a rearing bear, the blue tattoo outlining the scarred likeness of the bear's form. The blue linework on Old Tom's back radiated out from puckered scarring in the shape of a turtle, carved there in his youth when he had first joined the Rangers of Eldwood. Their skin was tanned dark and brown, and they wore their forest of shade-blue ink like a geometric spider web.

When they finished bleeding each other, they turned to work on Caetal. The fish they'd shared became a small cut that joined the march of lines heading slowly up his arm. The Orlŭk was recorded as a thin circle that Bergrem carved into his son's back — his first full shape, and it hurt like hell. When he was finished, Bergrem squeezed Caetal's shoulder hard for a long moment, and they sat in silence together for a while and watched the river flow between the trees as the ink-blued blood trickled from the fresh carving on his back.

•••••••••••••••••••••••••••••••••••

"Beaver is old. He does not move as easily as he once did. See how he drags his tail through the mud?" Bergrem pointed: *there*, and *there*. The story written on the riverbank was easy to read. "He would not drag his tail if he could avoid it. It hits the ground on his back step. He was injured once and never recovered from it. How do I know this?"

Caetal peered at the tracks. Small front paws, five toes with claws. A raccoon at first glance, perhaps, but the large back paw prints were more than twice the length of the front. They were depressed with a faint webbing mark and about the size of a human handprint. A river creature, of course, but he already knew that. But look — one back print was not as deep as the other and gently smudged by the quick dragline of a tail with every second step. Caetal grinned and pointed.

"Beaver has pain in his joints, and so he wuh — he w-waddles on a sore leg and favors the other. It might have been a w-wound perhaps, but there is no blood."

Bergrem nodded approvingly. "Yes, and his steps are close together. It pains him to walk at all, and so he places his feet with care. The walk of an old man." He winked at Old Tom, who shook his head and grumbled good-naturedly.

"Yes, perhaps he's as wizened as he seems. But his age will no' help us to make him into supper. Th' tracks must be fresh enough to matter. How do we know when Beaver walked here?" Old Tom asked, folding his arms.

This was an easy question. Caetal replied: "Beaver is hungry: he is shaking off the chill of his wuh.. his w-winter burrow, probably tired of old sticks he stored away to eat last fall. He comes to the shore looking for new g-green shoots and tender leaves because the ice has broken up and drifted, and he can feel spring is almost here. Beaver likes to feed at dusk, but he has w-wandered a fair distance from his lodge if he came out of the river this far upstream. That means he has... w-w-*widened* his circle all night long, looking for food. It rained a bit last night, yet the track is free of drip marks and mostly dry. I'd g-guess it was early this morning that he wuh..w- that he passed here."

The two rangers nodded to themselves, deep in their furs.

"Shall w-we hunt him?" Caetal asked, fingering his bow.

The two older men glanced at each other. Bergrem shrugged, but Old Tom shook his head.

"Not today, lad. I don't have th' heart to shoot at an old fellow today. We well-aged animals oughta stick together sometimes, an' spring is comin' soon enough. It would be a shame ta end his life after he waited so patiently for tha green ta return. We'll travel along further; we have ta make time. The moot is gatherin' on the morrow. We need to be there by two moons tonight — your father is set ta be speakin' before the council at sunup."

Bergrem nodded, winter puffing out of his black beard in steaming breaths. The two men, and the heavyset boy, continued along through the primeval majesty of the Eldwood.

Pale sunlight filtered down in shifting layers through the green canopy. They walked beneath trees as large as dreams, and the air was so richly heavy and the light so diluted that Caetal imagined himself, as he often did, to be floating underwater at the bottom of a lake. Looking up, the green foliage at the topmost branches swayed hundreds feet of above him, rippling in airy currents he couldn't see from the ground. Even the sound of the wind was muted down here. Decaying ferns and layers of hornwort and mood moss made a soft carpet underfoot.

As they travelled through the day, the trees diminished in grandeur, and the ground grew ever damper and spongier. They walked single file in relative silence, each of them unconsciously rolling their steps from the outside ball of their feet as quietly as any stalking fox. They walked in each other's footprints; Old Tom first (who was the smallest and fleetest-footed), followed by Caetal (whose feet were already nearly as big as his father's), and lastly, Bergrem, who was a bear of a man with feet as wide as bread loaves. To any that followed, their tracks would tell the tale of one large man walking with a heavy gait and not bothering to conceal his progress.

They intended to travel straight into the night, but as twilight gathered, they found themselves slowing down almost unconsciously. A draft of warmer air lifted the smells of the loam up to their noses. Old Tom stopped first; his hand raised in a fist. They waited in the gathering gloom of half-light as the warblers trilled in the alder thickets and listened to the lonesome crying of the loon. Caetal loved the sound; it colored the evening air with perfect melancholy. Wolves can split a midnight heart wide open with their moon song, but nothing captures the sadness of the bright colors of day bleeding away into night's uncertain shadows like one loon calling out alone. It was the time for hunting things that stirred in the dark.

Caetal's reveries dissolved as Old Tom's fist spread into an open palm, and the rangers began the hunt. He could feel in his quickening blood that Tom was right — the moment was right. All around them, the nightwalkers were waking up; the winged ones stretched and preened, the ground runners prepared to feed on the world, and on each other.

Each of the three of them silently moved into their roles. Bergrem melted away into the forest in front of them — he was the Sweep; he would disturb the prey with his presence and the smell of his bear fur and drive them towards the waiting hunters. Old Tom stretched out his body, preparing to run after any creature that came within bowshot. Unlike hunting on the plains, a forest Runner could never expect to tire out an animal by exhausting it with endurance running. Every creature they hoped to pursue was faster and more agile than any of them. So, they must take them by surprise, and only run them down when they are injured. But man-smell is strong, and all animals know it well.

Caetal went to ground and began anointing himself with the smells of the clearing. Streaks of mud, of course, and a handful of moss he scrubbed over his skin and clothing. He dug into a black ash with his bronze dagger and rubbed the bark and sap onto his hands. He crushed dried lichens and sprinkled them into his hair. Old Tom was doing likewise, and the two of them prepared themselves in companionable silence. There would be no talking until the hunt finished; there never was. A language of gestures, as old as memory, was all that was ever used. Small flicks of a finger or the dimensions of an open palm could speak as loudly as any words. ::*Wait. Look here. Do you see? Run ahead. Follow after. The prey is close. The prey is almost on us::*

When Caetal finished, he knelt at the base of the ash and strung his bow. Old Tom moved far enough away to be barely in sight with wide vision. They waited in silence for a half hour, shifting their weight subtly to stretch out muscle cramps. Caetal wished, as he had many times since they left Holm four nights ago, that Dubby had come with them. Dubby was his jackwolf, and he was Dubby's boy. It was as simple as that. Caetal had found him as a mewling pup, left to die a runt's death in the cold shallow made by two tree roots. A litter had been whelped there, and when the pack had moved on, it had apparently done so without the bother of a slower, last-teat pup.

Caetal had been just a boy of seven summers, but when he scooped up that jack pup into his arms and felt the tiny tenderness of its tongue against his cheek, he knew for the first time what love does to a young heart. He would not let this puppy die; he could not bear to live in the world without him. So, he had made a body sling for the pup under his shirt and carried it all the way back home while it mewed and wiggled blindly and tried to chew on his nipple. Caetal's mother Nura had shown him how to bladder-feed a small animal on goat's milk and, when he was old enough, the tender stewed parts of fowl and rabbit.

A jackwolf is nobody's idea of good breeding. They are a long-ago lovechild of a wolf and a coastal jackal, with the heft of the wolf but little of its dignity. They are patchy-furred, bandy-legged, and tend to slobber when excited. The little pup grew up as lanky as a beanvine and never developed the weight of a wolf at all. Dubby was now belly-tall and playful tempered, and he loved Caetal like the boy was made of sunlight and sausages. And that was alright because Caetal looked into his eager searching eyes and watched the wagging of his silly, shaggy tail and knew that he would never love anything or anybody in his whole life the way he loved that jackwolf.

He named the beast "Dubh" after a word in the Old Tongue that meant, simply, "dark brown." He wanted to give him a name with some pomp to it, but when his mother asked how Caetal would best describe the jackwolf, Caetal replied: "He's brown. He's ... dark brown."

Caetal was not very comfortable with his own imagination. He just didn't put much trust in fanciful thinking.

When they had left home, his father had forbidden him to bring Dubby along on this hunt. He was a fine hunting dog, actually — trained from birth to chase and carry, and that was all and good when flushing rabbits out of their burrows or sending up flocks of waterfowl. But the hunting of Orlŭk was the solemn work of Man. Bergrem told his sulking son that he must earn the Orlŭk on his own, not rely on the powerful nose of a tracking dog to sniff him out. Privately, Bergrem also worried that any Orlŭk would make a swift and bloody end of a dog as thin and worthless as Dubby, and he did not wish to break his son's heart. *Let the dog chase rabbits; they are harmless enough.*

Dubby was left behind for the first time since his birth and howled blue sadness from his lashing rope until they were far out of sight down the Wayward Road. Caetal, miserable without him, imagined he must be crying there still. It had been a somber four days without his leaping, wagging, drooly company.

Thoughts of Dubby were interrupted as the foliage overhead burred and rattled. Caetal whirled around in surprise. A bird of considerable size landed on a branch just above him. It was bone white, and its wings were as wide as his arms outstretched. The branch swung and creaked beneath its talons. Reflexively, the boy brought his bow arcing around with an arrow on the string when he heard Old Tom cry out a warning. He was so surprised that Tom had broken the silence of the hunt that the arrow dropped off the string, and the bird cocked his head and cackled at him. Then it launched from the branch with a rush of wings and flapped off away to the south. Both men were silent for a moment, watching it go. Then Caetal signed ::*Bad Taste? Diseased?*::

Old Tom shook his head; braided hair swung like a rope. His fingers flicked in agitation against his palm.

::*Danger. Forbidden.*::

A half-hour later, Bergrem returned with a hart trussed up and slung over his shoulder. In the dark, the antlers looked like wild branches growing out of his back. He shrugged at Caetal and Old Tom apologetically.

"Must have been moon-mad. Hart didn't even run when I drew down on him. I would have driven him back your way, but the shot was as clean as I could have hoped for, so I took it. Sorry to keep you waiting here."

He dumped the hart onto the ground, and while he lit a fire and prepared to gut it, Caetal wandered over to Old Tom.

"W-why did you say 'forbidden'? You've never stopped me from shooting at birds before."

Bergrem was striking his flint: once, twice. Sparks showered a small nest of tinder cloth. Caetal could see Old Tom's eyes shining in the spark flash.

"Did you see that bird, boy? That was no gull or kingfisher. It was a crow."

Caetal scoffed. "You are night-blind, old man. That bird was wuh... w-*white*; it was no crow."

Old Tom spat. "It was a crow, pup. It was a crow as white as driftwood and as big as a human child. You must not ever, ever shoot a crow like that."

Caetal was silent for a moment. "I've never heard of a w-white crow."

"Nor will you. Or a night-black buck, perhaps, or a great fish as red as yew berries. They are not as they appear, lad. Bone-dancers, they surely are. If the animal is too big or too bright, or th' color is just *wrong* — leave it be. You mark my word on that. It might very well be a *Fýrii* wearing the living skin of a beast as simple as you or I put on winter furs. But underneath is cunning and power. An' if you kill one of them in that state, the body deflates like a bullfrog pouch, and the spirit comes ripping out, plenty mad."

He nodded to himself and spat between his fingers to warn off wickedness. Nearby, Bergrem stopped building the fire to listen. But there wasn't much more to be said. Caetal stared off into the darkness, his mind whirling over this new information. *Bone-dancers.* The notion was unsettling.

At the base of the ash lay a broad white feather. It was larger than the pinion of a kingfisher or a gull. It shone like snow. Caetal stared at it for a while, lost in thought. Then he scooped it up with a guilty swiftness and hid it in the hem-pocket of his cloak.

....

The rest of the trip was easy enough. Bergrem led them onto the Wayward, and they walked further along for a few hours, sharing the burden of shouldering the dead hart between them. The road looked like a pale channel that crept along underfoot, barely lit by starlight. Their breath frosted around them.

They came at last to a place where everything forward was flooded by standing water. Bergrem lit the beacon lantern and led the way into the woods around it. Both moons were crescent — one waxing, one waning, but neither lighting up the evening so much as sharpening shadows. The lantern light splintered and danced across the lake that had submerged the road. But the rangers knew their way in the dark well enough. They were the ones who had diverted the course of the creek to flood here, after all.

They walked a path that was well-hidden to any eyes but theirs, more subtle than a deer trail. It followed the flooded curve of the new lake for the better part of two miles until it ended at the base of three low hills that arose like a head and shoulders out of the submergence of the surrounding swamp. The creek that had fed the flooding of the road sourced here, bubbling out from a spring at the base of the hills.

A great rampart of earth had been ringed around those hills, rammed and pocked with stones. Out of the earth, a thicket of sharpened pole stakes bloomed. Inside the rampart circle, a row of torches was smoking in the wisps of fog that curled out of the swamp on winter evenings. It was a *Muinaislinna* — an ancient hillfort: a gathering place for rangers in the wild. It promised safety and supplies for those that had sworn the Oath of Oak and death to their enemies.

Caetal had been here a few times before, but never at night. It looked foreboding in the dark, almost eerie. The leaping torchlight made the shadows of the spear thicket gnash like teeth, and Caetal shuddered.

Old Tom drew a small ram horn from his pack and blew three quavering notes on it, and a fourth that was drawn out and deep. From behind the spear thicket, the notes were answered. Two men materialized before them. Both wore furs that were sewn in striping patches of alternating color, brown and black. When standing still, their bodies blended almost perfectly with the wooden thicket of stakes. Both were armed with bows as tall as a grown man and arrows like thin javelins. Had the horn not been sounded, Caetal was sure they would have drawn down on them where they stood. Old Tom led the way into the Muinaislinna, picking his way carefully through the deadly thicket, and Caetal and his father followed with the dead hart held overhead between them.

The central hill was hollow, of course. It had been dug out with rooms and passageways long ago for reasons that have passed out of knowing. The passageways were narrow and claustrophobic, and the rooms were not much better. As they followed the torch-bearers, Caetal wondered if the place had been meant for humans at all — certainly not ones as large as the rangers, who tended towards broad shoulders. People who traveled long distances bearing the weight of dead animals earned their strength the hard way.

Caetal could easily touch the walls of each passageway with both hands as he walked. The walls were carved of stone that sparkled with veins of quartz and mica. Their breath was heavy in the still air, and their boots brattled gracelessly against the echoing stone of the floor. The hart was received in gratitude by guards at the inner chamber, and the rangers were led to a simple room where they could spread their furs out and pass the night in rest. There were no furnishings, just a large washing bowl with water in it and an empty chamber pot.

They slept a fitful night. With the lantern extinguished, the darkness underground was absolute. Old Tom had never been comfortable in enclosed spaces, and after an hour of shifting and grumbling to himself, he quietly got up and left the room to go sleep outside. Bergrem and Caetal didn't mind being underground — the spirit of Bear was a strong presence in their family. But they were woken often throughout the night by the hollow trapping of boots moving through the dark tunnels of the Muinaislinna as other rangers came and went. It was a disquieting sound, and Caetal passed the night uneasily.

....

Caetal awoke with the dark swimming around him. His head was thick with too much sleep, and he wondered idly at the hour. As a habit so deeply set it might as well be a rule, rangers never slept past sunrise. Without the regulation of the sun, Caetal felt profoundly disoriented and lost. The darkness and his sleep-muddled dizziness filled him with a sudden panic, and his hands swept around him in the dark. There was nothing there but his own furs and further on, his shaking fingers felt the edge of his leather pack. From echoing elsewhere, he could hear the reverberations of distant conversation. Even sound carried weirdly in this place — swelling and receding as though the stones themselves were breathing. After listening for a few moments, he recognized his father's voice, thrumming with passion, perhaps with anger.

Speaking before the council. By the gods, it must be half-toward midday! Shame and relief washed over him in turns. Although he was not allowed at council until his rite of manhood was confirmed, he could not bear the shame of the rangers knowing he had slept so late. He fumbled through his pack until he found the stub of a beeswax candle and lit it carefully with a wooden match. The warm light brought immediate comfort, and he refreshed himself and dressed in a hurry. Before the council dispersed, Caetal made his way up through the winding corridors towards freshening air until the afternoon sunlight breeched the mouth of the entrance chamber. The boy felt the peaceful reassurance of the sky overhead and took a few deep breaths until his spirits settled within him. Then he relieved himself of nightwater over the edge of the hill and sat on a split log bench to repair the fletching on a stripped arrow shaft.

Finally, an echo chorus of bootfalls brattled up from the underground hallway, and the Rangers of the Eldwood spilled out of the arch, each taking deep breaths of winter sunlight and shaking themselves like animals coming out of hibernation. All were clearly relieved to be out of the hill and back under the trees again. There were sixty-two of them trickling out, at Caetal's count: eighteen women, forty-one men, and three rangers that were so wrapped in cloth that their sex was difficult to guess at. *The*

Mŭrian. Caetal stared in wonder. *Are they as old as my father says? I wonder what they actually look like?*

As though overhearing his thoughts, one of those rangers turned and approached him. Caetal felt his body tense superstitiously. This ranger was tall, quite tall — a half-head over his father, and that was a lot. This ranger moved like rippling water, and its body was wrapped in layers of long cloth that overlapped like bandages. Each layer was dyed the subtle colors of the wilderness; earthen brown, fading autumn leaves, the gray-green of woodland shadows. There was a scarf wound all the way up around the face and the hood of a stalking cloak that draped down to meet it. The cloak was drawn together with an iron clasp, wrought like a sprig of holly berries. But the hands were bare to the elbow, and Caetal saw dark skin that was banded with hunter's woad tattoos in the striping of a wildcat.

The ranger bore an object bundled in leather and handed it to Caetal without a word. The object was wide and heavy. As Caetal held it in mute surprise, Bergrem strode up. He tipped his head to the tall ranger with casual, almost grudging, deference.

"This is Hel'hannah, our Warden. ...Hel'hannah, this is my son Caetal."

The tall figure peered at Caetal through their facial scarf. In a sudden drift of sunlight, their golden eyes glowed like tree sap, large and inhuman. Caetal felt a shiver go through him, and he sensed a similar discomfort from his father. Hel'hannah stretched a hand out and lifted Caetal's chin further up until they could see his eyes. Their fingernails were as sharp as talons, and Caetal felt them nip at his flesh as surely as a shaving razor. Dark brown eyes met golden ones, and Caetal was proud to remember later that he held their gaze until they looked away first.

They nodded, satisfied by something he would never understand. When they spoke, the voice was low and quiet — a tone beyond feminine and masculine. It stretched and rolled: each word drawn out with languid warmth.

"Caetal means *Little Bear* in the old tongue, as you well know. But in the language of my people, there is another meaning that is older still. It translates into *Tree Eater*. Perhaps the bear was once called an *eater of trees*, and perhaps not. So much is hidden; so much is lost. Time devours everything, even the sacred meaning behind things."

They withdrew their hand from under Caetal's throat, and he felt profoundly relieved. Hopefully, his neck wasn't as sweaty as his back was. He would have given much to appear strong in front of this Mŭrian. He had not met one of their race before; there were few living on the island who had, and almost none who knew what they looked like under the many-layered wraps of their garments. They were an ancient people, scattered to scarcity by misfortune and time. The sight of Hel'hannah unnerved him badly.

"Your father is a brave man, Caetal. But the patriots' blood runs hot in your family. He wants us to risk much, perhaps too much, to force the world back into an older shape again. I sense his fight will carry on with you. A *pity*. It is a heavy thing for a son to carry the weight of his father's ambitions." Hel'hannah's gaze hardened; father and son shifted uncomfortably before them.

Bergrem's face flushed an angry red, and he looked away. The tall Mŭrian continued speaking softly.

"Bergrem says you are grown to nearly a man." Caetal flushed with heat and nodded. Hel'hannah's gaze took on an almost pitying look. For a moment, they seemed about to say something and then checked themselves with a sigh. Overlong moments passed in silence. Then they continued.

"We can never go back to what we were, no matter what our dreams demand. Perhaps this is no longer a good time for children. Perhaps we will drag everything forward towards the end of peace, however fragile it was. If the events began here build to their intended climax, then spring will bleed all too quickly into the punishing heat of summer. The people of Eld will learn that games of war do not stay games for long. The choices of your father and those like him will become the regrets you grow up paying for."

Bergrem growled deeply in his chest. "Hel'hannah, you go too far. It is not your place to speak like this to my son. This war was brought to our shores hundreds of years ago on Erdin ships, and it never left. Your talk of peace is the thin broth that cowards feed to the fearful. Do not serve it to my son, or you will weaken him too."

Hel'hannah's eyes narrowed to slits, and they bared their teeth at Bergrem. "*Foolish Man-child.* Your kind is born sick with killing-hunger.

You speak of ancient days as though you were actually there to see them. *I was.* I remember it true. The Erdin brought themselves to the island, not war. War predated them by a long time, and your people excelled at it already. Yes, the Erdin claimed territory, and yes, they killed for it. You Dekai were the same when you first landed here so long ago. You conquered, and you killed. In the end, what is native? That which got here first? All that live under Uros takes up space for themselves. All kill. The web of life expands and makes room for everyone. But only the sick-spirited make war that lasts. It solves nothing. It saves no one."

Caetal watched in shock while Bergrem stepped up to Hel'hannah, eye to eye. Though the Mŭrian was much taller, he dwarfed them by an easy ten stone in width and muscle weight. Standing so close together, everyone could feel the tension rippling off of the two rangers. Nearby conversations were silenced by the impact of those soundless waves.

"While you wear the holly, I must honor you as warden. And we must heed your voice in council, above all others. But you cannot stop what is coming. I will do what should be done to restore Eld to better days. I will, and my son will, and our people will. You and your kind are like the setting sun. Your time here is almost gone. Remember that when you speak to me. Remember this moment, Hel'hannah. I want you to remember that I saw your end coming."

Hel'hannah stared at him in sanguine silence while rage and ruin flickered across what could be seen of their face. The only thing that moved in the stillness was the agitated flexing of their fingers. But their eyes no longer glowed quite as brightly. They had darkened like doused coals, and all that remained of the fire between Hel'hannah and Bergrem was the low crackling of banked ambitions. A long minute of silence passed, a silence in which he seemed to expand and they to contract. When the Mŭrian finally spoke again, it was to Caetal, and it was as though nothing at all had happened between his father and them.

"Young Bear, so it is that Bergrem and his companions will head south by riverboat to Kräke to rally support for their movement, as he came here intending to do. You and Tom will return to Holm, pulling a cart of supplies and posing as merchants on the road. Tom has further instructions and further to travel from there. He will be in disguise as an old man-"

(Here Bergrem snorted and rolled his eyes)

"—and you, Caetal, will pose as his hired bodyguard. If anyone asks, your cargo is herder's cheese and spun wool, headed for market. The package you hold in your hands is payment for your task. It is yours to keep until it is otherwise needed. May it always be fired only in defense. Good fortune, and stay downwind. Farewell to you both."

Hel'hannah turned on their heel and headed back underground without another word. The sun dipped behind a massing of clouds as they left, and the heat quickly bled out of the morning air. Caetal shivered unconsciously. He barely noticed himself unwrapping the package he held until the leather wrap fell to his feet and his hands felt the smooth weight of wood.

He looked down and childish wonder flushed through him. A heavy crossbow, meant for war or the hunting of giants. It was old, perhaps even older than the Iron Ban. It was shaped from black ironwood — rare and highly prized. The tiller was carved into the effigy of some beast, but so worn away by the grip of countless hands that its true likeness was obscured. The string cording was as thick as his finger. And, rarest of all, a bow beam of real blackened steel crossed the stock. Caetal's breath hitched sharply, and he glanced at his father uncertainly. Bergrem only nodded, clapped him across the back, and walked away.

A weapon of iron in Dekai hands was a death sentence if an Iron Guard caught you. Just owning one branded you a revolutionary under Erdin law. Caetal hugged it fiercely to his chest. It felt so heavy, so suddenly heavy. Old Tom, who had been standing nearby, stepped forward and wordlessly handed Caetal a hip quiver packed with black-fletched quarrels. His eyes, when they met Caetal's, looked sunken and tired.

....

A few hours later, Bergrem and more than half of the gathered Eldwood Rangers launched in three skin boats out onto the shallow lake. Bergrem hugged Caetal in a rough embrace before he left, but as the boats pulled away, he never looked back. Caetal and Old Tom watched in silence from the shore until the thin fog swallowed the sight of them, and the croaking frogs drowned out the soft splashing of their paddles. Then Old Tom sighed and squeezed Caetal on the shoulder.

"Let's get to it, lad. There are a lot of preparations ta see to before we are able ta go home."

It took three more days before Caetal and Tom left the Muinaislinna and the company of those rangers who had stayed behind. Three days that dragged by as slowly as weeks to Caetal. Missing Dubby had become a mournful tirade of thoughts as morose as any divorce. In the deep darkness of that hillside labyrinth of stone, he slept through half of each day and didn't care. He missed his jackwolf, and until they were reunited, pining for Dubby became his sullen obsession. Not even the teasing of Old Tom and the other rangers could rouse him from his torpid lurking, and it finally got so bad that Tom forced him to go walking out in the swamp for most of the last day just to keep his messy melancholy from getting annoying.

The other men worked hard to prep a covered wagon and load it with whatever *supplies* were worth disguising in the secrecy of nailed wooden crates and water barrels. Caetal was not allowed to see any of it, of course. He was not yet truly of the Oak — he had not bled for the cause or taken his vows. On the third day of his ill humor, when he was busy slumping around kicking at rocks, Old Tom came downhill and showed him a handful of small green plants that he had never seen before. They looked like squat triangular succulents with broad, fat leaves. At the top of each grew a bulb that would blossom into a pale white flower only once a season, or so Tom said.

Tom told Caetal to take as much time as he needed (*a good, long time would be best*) and gather as much of it as he could find. The plant, which was called *sürra,* excreted a pale green pulp when cut or broken that numbed the hands. Caetal ignored it at first, heedlessly tearing up bundles of plants where they grew by the shore of the shallow lake. By nightfall, his hands were blistered and chapped, and they stung with a wretched burning that felt like he had squeezed a handful of stinging nettles.

He complained bitterly to Old Tom, who admitted (rather shamefacedly) that he had forgotten to warn Caetal about the caustic nature of those plants. He took the boy down to the spring and had him soak his hands in the cool running water, carefully rubbing them for a few minutes. Then he applied an oily salve, which brought immediate relief from the hot pain. Finally, he wrapped Caetal's hands in a cloth that he soaked in red wine vinegar from a cask in the larder. The old man and the boy sat and watched the sun set. To take Caetal's mind off of his pain, Old Tom decided to show him something to distract him.

"Watch lad, an' watch carefully. You think this plant hurts when you harvest it? Its sting is a minor inconvenience ta your bare skin, for, in this state, the plant is holding back. Like many young things, it does not know its own power."

While he spoke, Old Tom ground one of the plants underfoot. It made a pulpy green and white smear, like a smooshed bug, onto the stone floor of the entrance to the Muinaislinna. Caetal watched it carefully, but it did nothing else but look smashed. After a moment, he cocked his eyes up to Old Tom and shrugged.

"Didn't do anything. Just looks like a smashed flower. My hands hurt, old man."

Tom cackled and cracked his knuckles merrily. "Patience, boy! All is not as simple as it seems! Sometimes for something ta really come into its strength, it must first be ground underfoot. And of course, some things need a little outside encouragement."

And now he did a curious thing. As Caetal watched, Old Tom drew out his dagger and gently pricked the tip of his thumb with it. He knelt on the stone next to the plant smear and dripped a few drops of blood onto it. Where they hit the plant, there was a splashy sizzling sound, and the green paste roiled and heaved with red-tinged bubbles. Now an acrid smell wafted into Caetal's nose, causing him to cough and gag. Tom did as well, and both men got up quickly and left the area alone as the green pulp broiled and simmered with a thin, venomous hiss.

"W-w-why did it react like that?" Caetal scrubbed his aching hands against his pants nervously, imagining what would have happened to him if the cracks that had formed in his hands had split all the way down to the quick and the plant sap had gotten into his bloodstream.

"I don't know, honestly." Old Tom shrugged. "Something in tha plant is excited by blood. But what is even stranger is tha it only *really* reacts when also in contact with a stone. If you get it into your bloodstream, it will make you plenty sick, o' course. Enough of it can kill, or so I've been told. But when iron-rich blood and calcium stone is present, then look out! It will eat away at the stone in a few minutes like what would take flowing water a thousand years to hollow out. It eats until it's spent and satisfied. I don't know what your father has in mind, but before he left, he told me to gather lots of it. Let's wrap our hands good and crate it up tight, lad — I fancy you have no wish to handle it bare-handed again."

Later that night, bedded down under the stars on the stone gallery that ran the upper hillside, Caetal rolled over and asked: "W-why does sürra grow here? I've never seen it g-growing in any other part of the swamp. Is it a wuh.. a w-w... a lake plant?"

Old Tom's open eyes were thin slits in his dark face. He was quiet for a moment before answering. "Things grow where they are called ta grow by the gods. Each thing grows where it feels best or is needed most. Sürra isn't a water plant; it has no true natural environment that I know of. Sürra grows where blood is spilled. Lots of it. Where so much blood is spilled that tha ground drinks it down deeply, right down to the fungus an' tha roots and tha worms that move around under everything. I don't know wha' happened here, down in the swamp. I don't want ta know. But if you go diggin' around down there long enough, you'll find a lot more than a patch of sürra growing. You'd maybe find a lot more than you want ta find."

....

The White Crow

High above, I see everything. Old one, young one, rolling along with their wagon of secrets. Ox breathes hot life in plumes; poor beast does all the work as man sits tall on his cart, so proud of his brain. Man does not know what colors Ox is dreaming in; Man, who has thought himself out of balance with all other animals. The restless meddler, forever rearranging the world around him. He does not smell the stink of his own secrets, hidden so carefully in crates with false labels. In this shape, I can sense the cold iron as clearly as blood. I can sense the tension hammered into the layers of steel, that energy which comes from forcing something out of True.

I am Crow: we sense death coming better than most. We are the first to find the battlegrounds when the fighting is done. We feed on those that come there, so eager to die. It is our gift from Man. We guide those silly, eager boys into the Nightlands, and they make us the only offer that matters in exchange — themselves. Their flesh. It is a fair trade. It is our right.

I have seen this boy before. He drew the arrow on me, but the old one knew better. I should not have been so clumsy as to land near where the humans are hunting. The hunger can be terrible; shifting between shapes, weakness makes me stupid. The old one saved me; I must admit this is so. I do not like this. I do not like to owe them anything. But the code of Crow is as true as sky-above, and roots-grow-deep. Debts must be paid. So, I watch and wait for a moment to be free of them both. Debt repaid; balance restored.

Old ranger is tired. Boy is tired, shuffling along in his borrowed armor. Walking all night makes young paws heavy. Below me is a girl hiding in the ferns. The boy is not stupid; he must know she is there. I can see his eyes following her trail of prints in the soil. I see the flickering of his thoughts: judging her size, her care in concealment. He is too tired to flush her out, and that is a mistake. She is a woman alone on the road. She is as much of a threat as she wants to be. I can see her in colors he could never begin to imagine. I can see so much.

I follow them until the sun sets. I am too tired to fly further — Crow shape needs to feed. I cannot stay like this much longer. I will lose what I have become and forget what I have worked for so many years to learn.

My adopted girl-child runs on four paws in the woods tonight. I can feel her appetite down there in the dark. I will not get near her while she is hunting. She is so young; I cannot be sure she would know me in time to keep her jaws off my neck. She is still new. A star just beginning to burn: a danger to everything around it. I must fly home and leave the woods to her tonight. I will find the old ranger and the boy again. They will need me soon enough. Then debt will be done, and I will be rid of them.

The Boy from Far Away

"Those busted knuckles are your own fault, so stop sucking on them. If you had kept your waster up at Long Point instead of letting your damn elbow drop, you wouldn't be bleeding right now."

Tarquin winced, sucking winter air through his teeth and blinking wet pain. The sunlight was so bright against the snow. The cold made the purpling knuckles sting outrageously, and the snow glare blurred his eyes. He wiped them angrily against his dirty shirt and pulled himself back to his feet, using the chipped wooden sword for leverage. Across the clearing stood the man he had grown to hate and reluctantly admire more than anyone he had ever known. The pale man who owned him by right of law.

"Long-fucking-point, little pissant. That means tip up and elbows engaged, not tip trailing and elbows wherever the fuck feels good to you. If these blades were Erdin steel instead of oak, that sword would be on the ground with your severed hand still holding onto it. Now stance; now tip. Good enough. Defend against me."

The wooden swords came together with a clatter. The man circled the boy, pushing at his guard with lethal nonchalance. He struck at him with lazy pleasure and was pleased when only *most* of the blows were blocked. He was almost as pleased when they landed. Liam was not a man who minded teaching with pain. He didn't mind it one little bit.

....

It had not been long since Tarquin had come to Holm, but days meant nothing to him here. His far-away island had once felt so small, but now it seemed as big as memories of childhood freedom. Here his world was a dark copse of trees and a muddy landscape of snow. He almost never went into town. He almost never went more than a hundred paces from the squat wooden shack that was his new home. He slept in a loft with drying animal skins, and his dreams were sharpened with pain. Every morning, he awoke so stiff and aching that sometimes he was surprised to wake up at all.

Any moment of reverie brought the lash of the wooden sword. Any private moment, any hesitation or doubt. It was almost as though Liam could sense when Tarquin would grasp for a memory of his old life.

He would drift, for just an instant into ::*his mother's stories, his father's strong hands weaving patterns at the loom, sunlight sifting down the cliff and lighting up the ocean below*:: and WHACK went the wooden waster, across his cheek or arm or chest, and all was immediate and stinging again. It was a strange relief to not be allowed to remember.

Tarquin threw himself into the training. The hours of simple chores were harder — drawing water from the well, scrubbing pots, freshening the sawdust on the floor and cleaning out occasional messes from the goats when they came inside. These were things that left him alone with his thoughts for too long.

The house of Liam was a haunted house. It was a restless place, haunted by the living who tightened the air with unspoken tension. There were three of them there — Liam, Tarquin, and an older boy named Shandus, who came by infrequently and went on his way in a reticent silence, never speaking to Tarquin at all. Yet there lingered a sense of him observing from just around a corner, or listening behind closed doors. Only when Liam wasn't looking would Shandus dare to stare at Tarquin openly; a bitter tunneling look that bore right into him. When Shandus was around, Liam was in a brooding temper and the heavy quiet in the house creaked underfoot, occasionally broken by voices raised in cursing. From politics to religion to the consistency of the evening stew, there was nothing they seemed to agree on. Tarquin never saw affection shared between father and son, if Shandus was indeed a son of Liam. They certainly looked similar; dark hair and pale, with mouths like thin wounds. There was an empty gulf that separated them where a mother and wife might have once been, and that lack of her presence haunted the house most of all.

....

The winter winds that rattled the trees whined at night through cracks in the walls. The air inside was hot and smoky amongst the rafters and cold by the floor, and often Tarquin would lie awake in his stifling loft and listen to something wailing away off in the dark. Sometimes beasts would go bounding by outside in howling packs, and their keening cries were almost unbearable. One night they leapt against the side of the house in snarling waves, and Liam yanked Tarquin up out of sleep and the two of them stood by the bolted door with swords drawn — one of splintery wood and one of oiled steel.

They built up the fire for better light and sweated it out, watching the door shudder and imagining the things that scratched and growled outside under darkened windows. Away in the barn, they could hear the wood splintering and the panicked screaming of the goats. Then, after a gruesome while, a quiet descended that was almost louder than sound; a quiet punctured by Liam hurling the table over and swearing profusely.

They stood in martial readiness until dawn light crept between the trees and the night hunters slunk away. Out the window, they could clearly see the bloody furrows in the snow where the remains of the goats had been dragged off into the forest. When they finally went out and checked the barn, all that could be seen was a tangle of sodden straw and three severed hooves that had been shucked off like shoes.

At last, Liam stashed the steel sword back into a hidden hollow above the lintel and sent Tarquin to bed. After that night, Tarquin's chores were fewer, there was a lot less meat and milk on the menu, and sword practice became everything that either of them cared about.

....

The wooden waster tip bobbed sinuously in front of Tarquin's face like a snake turning to strike, and Tarquin snapped back to focus. He gripped his shabby training sword in sweaty hands and tried to anticipate the pale man. Cruelty is as predictable as anything if you get to know it well enough. After hundreds of welts and bruises, Tarquin had begun to intuit a pattern to the strikes. Nothing that his waking mind could make sense of yet, but sometimes his sword leapt to defend against a blow he hadn't even seen coming.

Fool's Guard to protect his knees ::*let the tip drop so low it makes little furrows in the snow*:: Ox Horns to arrest a charge ::*skewer the eyes so they can't see to strike you*:: Half Iron Gate to surprise a shield ::*only a fool forgets where their feet are.*::

They rested for lunch, and Tarquin boiled oats and cut in wrinkled slices of dried apples. Over a steaming bowl of slop, he summoned up the courage to ask Liam to let him handle the hidden steel sword. He had never seen one up close before, and the urge to hold its weight and marvel over it had grown into a boy's quiet obsession. Liam said nothing, just stared at Tarquin as he swallowed the last few spoonfuls of his bland winter pottage. Then, without a word, he rose from his seat and walked to the doorway.

He slid his hands up overhead, into the shadow above the wide carved lintel, and did something with his fingers that Tarquin couldn't see. The panel shifted, and Liam slid the wood back and brought forth a long object wrapped in leather. Before he handed it over to Tarquin, Liam retrieved his oak practice waster and laid it on the table between them. The subtle threat was more obvious than words. Tarquin nodded, and Liam handed him the sword.

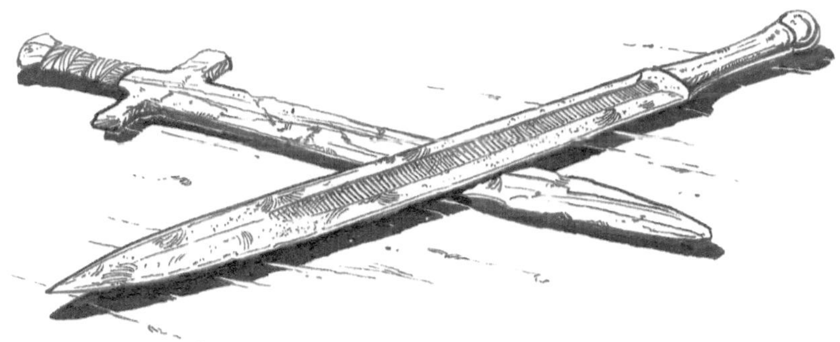

It was as heavy as Tarquin guessed it would be, for the wooden wasters were carved in weighted mimicry of steel. But he had not been prepared for the coldness of the steel blade. It seemed to drink the warmth from his hand as he ran his thumb carefully down the sharpened edge. The oiled blade shimmered in the firelight, and the edges of the sword were jagged and scarred. To a martial eye, it was a simple sword — steel hammered to six hand lengths and half a hand wide. It was deeply fullered, with a blade that widened towards the tip like a leaf. The bone handle was long enough for a two-handed grip, capped by a heavy steel ball as a pommel. There was no hand guard to speak of; nothing to protect the hands at all but the skill of the person who wielded it. The blade was a mottled shimmer of polished steel and darker pitted spots where the hammer had shaped it long ago.

"Hold the sword out before you. Feel the subtle shifts in balance as it moves through the air. It is an extension of you — the muscles of your arm, the length of your will." Liam spoke from somewhere behind Tarquin, and Tarquin did as he was told.

He could not take his eyes off of the sword. The firelight rippled up the blade hypnotically as Tarquin moved it slowly around him. Each stance he took felt familiar, and yet completely different, with the cold insistence of real steel in his hand. The wooden sword on the table seemed like a comforting toy in comparison.

"There is nothing like iron; nothing in all of creation. It is stronger than wood, or bone, or copper. It is less brittle than stone, and as cold as moving water. It can sharpen to a shaving edge and open a throat as easy as singing. And in human hands, it can be hammered into steel. The Erdin hoard the steel, and steel rules the world. That is why our island is so fucked, boy. That is why we are all the slaves of foreign men."

Tarquin glanced up at Liam at last, long enough to see the twisted anger in his smile... and the wooden sword in his hand.

"Iron is created in the burning body of a god on the day it dies — did you know that? Long ago, when a god was slain far away to the west, it was the Erdin that discovered where it fell. They dug the iron ore out of its corpse and forged death itself into weapons that scythe through our native copper like wheat. From their distant island they spread out and conquered whatever they wanted. When they landed here, they took our island of Eld for themselves. They were armored in steel and fought with steel, and there was nothing we could do to stop them.

"So we submitted to their rule, and they created the Iron Ban to horde all the steel for themselves. If you are not of Erdin blood, and caught with an iron tool in hand, you lose that hand. If it is a forged steel weapon, it is used against you to separate your head from your neck. That is why I must keep this sword hidden away from everyone, even Shandus: because I love my pretty head so much. If you ever tell anyone where this sword is hidden, you will not live to regret it."

Liam stepped forward and tugged the sword away from Tarquin so suddenly that his fingers bled where they had been gripping the blade a moment ago. Tarquin blinked as the mesmeric shine was pulled away, and the glittering view of steel was replaced by the dull planks of a wooden table once again. He shook himself and sucked on his bleeding fingers. The drops of blood welling up on his fingers reflected the firelight. Everything else around them was dark and drab, and suddenly the house seemed claustrophobic. For the first time, Tarquin hurried Liam back out to the practice yard to continue sparring. Liam, more quiet than usual, returned the sword to the hidden compartment and followed Tarquin outside.

....

On a day when the melting snow was dropping in wet slurries from the tall branches, a bear of a man and his large son came to visit. They were announced at the edge of the clearing by the glad barking of a very lanky dog. While Liam and the bear man ducked into the shack to drink and speak in private, the large boy approached Tarquin warily. The dog did not share his master's reluctance, however, and set to licking the cold sweat from Tarquin's bruised face with such a jolly will that it knocked him off his feet, and both boys started laughing.

The boys threw a stick for Dubby all afternoon, quickly learning those unspoken things they needed to know about one another to become friends. Each was headstrong and brash, and in their own way, each meant well. Such friendships begin easily between children, on a warming winter afternoon when there is nothing to worry over but amusing a tireless jackwolf.

When Bergrem left the house of Liam at last, twilight was gathering between the trees. Caetal waved goodbye to Tarquin and followed his father back into the woods. Liam strode over to where Tarquin waited, wooden sword already up in Plow and feet at heavy-ready. But the pale man waved him off, and Tarquin slowly lowered his stance.

"No more for today, boy. Best you heat up some snow and take a bath instead, and I'll have one too. Tomorrow, I am away to Bergrem's — their milking goat just had kids, and I've made a deal to collect one. We shall keep it inside with us, so the damn night-howlers don't get at it, and you are entirely responsible for its care."

"Can I name the goat?"

"I don't give a damn if you do or not, boy. It's your goat. We'll more than likely eat it by next winter anyway."

Tarquin nodded, but privately began to ruminate over the most elegant goat name he could imagine — something with real class. At first, he thought *Noquomis*, which was the most beautiful name he knew. Then a terrible ache forked up inside of him, and he shook his head hard to try and drive out the sudden crowding of ghosts. Lost in the moment, he almost missed the importance of what Liam said next.

"You, on the other hand, are going over to that damned abbey tomorrow, so put on whatever shirt is the cleanest. The priests of Cuthain are offering public schooling, and the rangers think it's time for us to learn what we can about them. So be polite, and keep your eyes open, and report back everything you find out. And I mean *everything*, pissant. I'm not sending you there to learn to read scripture or pray; don't waste your time on that nonsense. I'm sending you to learn about what the abbey is really there for.

"Nobody invests that much gold to just build a nice place to sit and think about their god. Churches are built for influence, or for wealth, or for power. Find out which of those it is. And if you fail me at this, then the sparring bruises I've welted you with so far are going to feel like a ruddy game we've been playing together. Keep secrets from me, or lie to me, and you will find out quickly enough what *real* pain feels like."

....

In my Own Words.

...Well, Talara Helped a Little

The rest of this story is hard to tell, because at the end of it, I cripple my best friend.

It has already been told, up to a point, and that's fine. But I need you to know how it happened for me. I don't know why that matters — I guess it is because I will carry the guilt of what happened to Melvinari for the rest of my days. And if I am the only one who knows the how and the why of where I tried to do right and where I failed... well, there is a lot more darkness inside than light, sometimes. The sun that sets inside our own chests creates the longest night there is. For some people, it never rises again. I don't want to be one of them: one of the lost. I have to tell somebody.

....

Life was simple enough for a while when Old Tom and I returned to Holm. I got my jackwolf back, and for a few days, Dubby and I were so busy playing together and making up for lost time that I didn't even notice that Old Tom had continued on without me, pulling that cart off to Dekainak with its hidden cargo inside.

I showed my mother the crossbow, of course, although I shouldn't have. She swore a blue streak and cuffed me about the ears, and hugged me, and cuffed me again, and hid the crossbow in the root cellar.

I found her crying about it later that afternoon, but I didn't know what to say then, and I still don't. I have never learned to be good with crying people, particularly when I can't understand what they are crying about. But I think she was scared and very angry with my father.

I will always remember sitting in the common room of our house with the afternoon light pouring in through the window, and roughly patting my mother's back as she sobbed against my shoulder. I felt so old then, to feel her leaning against me like that. I had often come crying to her from skinned knees and bee stings, but that was the first time our roles reversed. It made me feel a bit queasy, as though the floor of childhood was falling away beneath me, and all I could do was tumble down after it.

Out the window, patches of snow had melted and revealed brown smears of the winter ruin of our herb garden. As I held her, I stared out the window; looking at the sky, but not really seeing anything. Then something hopped and fluttered between the high branches of an old climbing oak. That impossible white crow was perched out there, watching me. It startled me so badly I almost jumped up, but I would have spilled my grieving mother onto the floor, and then what kind of son would I be? So, I sat and held her as she finished weeping for whatever secrets were troubling her, and I stole glances at the huge white crow that gazed right back at me.

....

I saw it a few times again over the next month — not often, but enough to start watching the high branches and to feel the rising prickle of goosebumps from my inflamed imagination.

A bit later on, my father returned from Kräke. Whatever had gone down there had gone well, for he was in a powerful humor and spent much of his time in the company of other rangers, planning the future. On the one hand, I wished to join with them and share their secrets... but on the other, I instinctively felt that the long days of childhood were slipping away faster than they were being replaced, and I was greedy for the company of my jackwolf and the freedom to run around kicking up dead leaves.

Dubby had surprised us all by finally figuring out how to be a hunting dog. He had learned to contain his excited yelping until the chase was on and no longer cleared a thousand yards of game in all directions by barking at every breeze. The first time he caught a rabbit in his jaws, he looked so genuinely surprised with himself that Melvin and I bust up laughing hard enough that we fell over. Dubby yelped excitedly with his mouth full of dead rabbit and shook it around so vigorously that there was very little left to do with it when we all calmed down but to bury the poor ragged thing.

Since then, I had taught him to let go of what he caught before the drool soaked it too badly and with only a minimum of excited shaking. So before too long, we were bringing home small game as fast as my mother could cook them. With my father so often away, I was doing my best to keep meat on the table during the lean winter months, and with Dubby's help, I was doing a fine job of it, too.

One afternoon, about a week after my father returned from Kräke, he surprised Melvin and me while we were immersed in an unusually complicated game of Ghost Mallet. *(I'd explain the rules, but they won't do you much good if you don't have access to a haunted wooden hammer).*

When I looked up at him, I knew in an instant that his good mood had soured. His face was hard and drawn. He gestured towards Melvin without looking at him.

"Your game is done now, boys. Go home, Melvinari. I must speak with my son alone."

Even a fool can taste copper in the air before lightning strikes, and Melvin was no fool. He gathered himself and departed without a word, only once looking back.

Melvin was barely through the bracken when my father pulled me to him by the nape of my shirt and growled, *"That boy is no longer a friend* of *yours.* Not anymore. He is the soft whelp of a coward who fattens his pouch with Erdin coin. You are forbidden to keep such company. Do you hear me, Caetal?"

I felt heat flush my face, and my legs were suddenly shaking. I could feel the anger coming off from my father in waves, but nothing he was saying made any sense to me.

I babbled, "But that is Melvin, father... j-just Melvin, don't you know him?"

"Of course I know him, boy! What manner of idiot question is that? He is Daedrim's skinny brat, and I tolerated him well enough for years, and now I'm done. *We're done,* do you hear me? They act like learne'd lords, living in that house of stone. They've grown wealthy by whelping on the iron tit. He weakens you, just as his father weakens this whole community. You look me in the face, boy, and you tell me you understand what I'm saying, or I will beat what sense into you I must. It is done; *it is over.* I will find you a more suitable friend — one who does not bow and scrape before the chapel door."

I had no answer to give, and that seemed to satisfy his fingers enough to loosen them from my throat. He lowered me slowly, and in that moment, the musky odor of bear rolling off of him was so pungent and strong that it made my eyes water. I had always been comforted by the honesty of that smell. It was his pride, and he wore it well. But now, the sour animal smell of anger made my throat itch.

I turned on my heel and walked to the edge of the wood, staring across the field in the direction that Melvin would have headed to go home. Behind me, I heard a twisting crunch of sinew and the dragging shuffle of my father's booted feet as he walked away through the crusts of thawing snow.

When the tears had finally dried on my hot cheeks enough to turn around, I saw that my father had twisted the head off of one of Dubby's dead rabbits and tossed the headless corpse back on the ground. A splatter trail of red droplets stained the path he had pushed through the underbrush. It looked like red berries had sprouted from the rabbit's exposed spine and were blooming in the cavity of Bergrem's footprints.

Now, what was that for?

....

I did not sleep well that night. I have never been one for restlessness; once the darkness behind my eyes drops around me, it drags me down with it as deep as sleeping goes. It is a point of constant ribbing amongst my father's friends, for nothing will stir me from sleep but a rough rousing of hands or considerable noise. It is unbecoming of a ranger to sleep like that, in the wild. It is unbecoming of a man and brings me shame that I was cursed with such heavy eyelids. I have also not often been one for dreaming. Melvin swears that everyone swims through the ether all night long, dreaming of other lives and places the waking mind discards. I think he cannot be right. Where I usually go when I sleep is as deeply underground as the Muinaislinna.

But that night, I twisted with sweat in my sleeping furs, tormented by visions of my island tipping sideways in the ocean like a capsizing boat. In this dream, my family slid helplessly down a tilting horizon of shattered trees, pierced by jagged branches as they fell. I clung to the creaking stump of a dead oak and watched them plummet into the ocean, impossibly far below. I clung there until the strength in my fingers failed, and when I fell, I was relieved to know I would not have to live in the world without them.

I awoke with my heart racing, still thick-headed with sleep. The morning stars lightened above the trees as my heart slowed, and before the sun was fully up, I left my house and went in search of Melvin.

....

He was not at the abbey, for the tap of hammers did not ring out in the cold morning air. I didn't have to wander close to the churchyard to see it was dark, so I passed it at a distance and continued on into the woods. It is not a short walk to the South Hill quarry from my home, and by the time I made it there, sunlight was stabbing through the longleaf trunks and the forest floor was steaming.

Winter shadows painted everything the light neglected. Moss grew over all of it. It felt so familiar then, so terribly similar to something...

My dream. It began like this. And then everything started to tilt, and the trees began to break.

I could hear the chitteries cease their singing as I walked beneath them, until the silence pressed in so closely that my own footfalls crackled ominously on the carpet of pine needles. I slowed and looked around me in sudden fear of seeing the white crow. And as I did, I stepped down on a fallen branch, and it snapped loudly beneath me. This is a great embarrassment to any ranger's son, and I froze where I stood. The rock quarry had just come into view through the trees, and I could smell the faint cooking char of the limestone kiln. Moments later, there was a flurry of hoof beats, and Melvin galloped nearby, astride his gray horse. His face looked flushed. He paid me no mind, it seemed, but raced away down the hill as though something dread was giving him chase.

I should have called out to him then. I know that now. I had walked so far to speak with him, after all, and skipped out on my damn breakfast to do so. But I thought perhaps it was me that he fled, and a flush of hurt went through me as I listened to the fading brattle of hoof beats leaving me behind. I stared after him until he was out of sight, whistling sourly to myself. Then I stood there a while longer and tried to figure out what to do next.

I wandered through the clearing towards the edge of the quarry. Here the exposed stone looked to me like a great beast had torn bites off the slope of the hill. I placed my cold hands on the warm sides of the cooling kiln and helped myself to the heel of a loaf of bread that Melvin had forgotten in his haste. It was not until I stepped to the edge of the clearing to relieve my bladder that I found the *Kaninhode* staked into the ground, and I knew why Melvin had run.

My stomach tightened to look at it, dismay shivering my skin like cold. I had never seen a Kaninhode before, but I knew it well enough from grim stories traded around the ranger's fires. It was a sigil reserved for the direst of warnings. *We are coming for you. The natural world rejects you, and we are coming to hunt you down. We will tear you apart piece by piece, and burn your bones to ash, so that on the salted patch of earth where you are buried, nothing living will grow to replace you.* A rabbit nailed to a post, opened but ungutted. An unfinished circle of woven wicker tacked up behind it representing the cycle of nature, broken and out of reach.

Like Melvin before me, I turned and fled the clearing.

....

Days passed, and I avoided speaking to my father. I couldn't bring myself to face that black stare and ask the question I did not want an answer to. The mood in our house quietly stretched with secrets that nobody knew how to share, and for the first time I could remember, my father and mother slept in different beds. During the daytime, we were all outdoors as often as possible, of course, but the nights together eating around a silent dinner table were hard.

The weather seemed to darken with Bergrem's darkening mood. Snow began to fall, and the midday sky was iron gray during those short winter days. Without Melvin, I had nobody left to play with but Dubby. One day my father asked me to accompany him to the house of Liam, and I met Tarquin for the first time. That was good. I liked him as soon as I heard him laughing — some people are like that, and Tarquin is one of them. He has a merry laugh. Also, he was nice to Dubby and didn't tease me at all about how thin and patchy he looks. You can tell a lot about a person by watching how they treat animals.

When my father and Liam parted ways, he seemed at last in a better mood, and instead of going home again, he turned us eastward onto a deer trail and led me into a stretch of the Eldwood that I hadn't explored before.

The evening was gathering in around us. Winter ruled the forest here; the vast trees were draped in cold silence. Brown sword ferns bowed below the white weight of snow, pretending to be dead. Normally, when the two of us are out together, it is our custom to walk in silence. It is better that way. But today, my father broke the quiet between us. He did not look at me as he strode ahead but spoke over his shoulder in a companionable way. I was glad to hear his thoughts and I drank them in greedily as I followed behind him, sharing footprints to disguise our tracks. He remarked on a set of badger's tracks; the hollow bulge of a crimson oak with a family of treeweets living in it; the shrunken carcass of a wildcat. At this, he stopped awhile, and we stared together, noting the leathery skin and the tunnels that scavengers had burrowed between the bones.

We came at last to a wide clearing, an hour after full dark was well upon us. For a while, we stood in the center of it and looked up at the vastness of the night sky and the glittering stars. No moons could yet be seen, and our breath fogged the air between us as we stared upward in silence. There was something here that I could not name. It was in the reverent shapes of the trees that all seemed to bow inwards towards the center of the clearing. My feet felt leaded as I shifted from foot to foot with cold, as though the very gravity of the spot was heightened.

At last, my father set to building a fire. Often when ranging, we would make do with a careful lean-to of well-banked logs, meant to warm, but not to light us overmuch, for the eyes of the world are drawn to firelight. But this time, he spent long minutes gathering and splitting the better part of a felled tree and stacked a chimney of wood that roared with hot light when the fire caught it. The heat forced us back a fair pace, and we stripped ourselves of our snow-sodden furs. The clearing throbbed with heat, pulling back the blanket of snow around us until it looked as though an early spring thaw had come to just this part of the wood.

As the snow melted and the ground became visible, I noticed a curious feature of the grove. A rock of unusual size had been hidden under a snowdrift behind us. As the fire's heat ate the snow, the stone seemed to lengthen before my eyes. It was as wide as the body of a cave bear, flattened along the top side and as long as forty strides. At one end of its length, the stone angled downward until it vanished into the soil — the buried length of it was lost from sight. At the other end, it branched into what seemed like twining roots. Its surface was bowled and etched by carvings that became ever more legible as the snow around them receded. For a melting moment, the pattern stood out in stark white against the brown stone. I could see now that the carving formed the shape of a great boar, as big as a house, with tusks as long as curving swords. I watched it in fascination until all traces of snow had steamed away, and the details were obscured by the leaping firelight.

When the flames were at equal height to his eyes, my father, at last, seemed satisfied and turned to look fully at me for the first time in days.

"Here is a special place, my son. Yonder lays a fallen oak of the ancient world, so long buried beneath the ground that it has petrified into stone. Upon its trunk is carved the likeness of Torc, sow-queen of boars, who shares her skin with Green Karnonou, who himself is father to the race of Fae. Here on this tree of stone is where children lie down to die, and rangers stand up reborn. Here is where the Fýrii taught themselves the value of sacrifice and where generations of the Order of the Oak have come to bleed and take their vows. Our people have defended the whole of this vast forest from the invader's axe for more than three hundred years."

He coughed for a moment, turning away from me. When his throat cleared, he wiped his eyes and looked at me in silence. The fire crackled and snapped, and our breath fogged the air. I knew he didn't expect me to speak, so I didn't. After a long minute, he spoke in a voice that was solemn and low.

"When the Erdin sailed forth from Erdo-Usk to claim our forest for their own, it was the men and women of the Oak that rode out to meet them and set torch to their ships as they sailed below the beam at Bajlkr-Bec. When they tried again, we gave such blood on the downs at Melrgraes in defense of our land that the wild grasses grow red there still. We have toppled every settlement they have ever hewn from our forest in vengeance for the slaughter they brought to Dekainak, and the ruin of that great city. At Ofan, and at Kräke, they tried to burn the Eldwood to the ground, and we repelled them.

"They have tried to settle the wilds of our country, and we have tricked them with our craft and driven them fleeing before us, with haunted tales of trolls and driftwisps hounding their heels. For more than three hundred years, the Erdin strove to wipe us out and scatter our memories, and always we have stood against them. We are here still.

"Someday soon, you will lay upon the trunk of this stone tree and speak the history of these events as I have now told them to you. Here, on this sacred table, the weakness of your youth will flow away as blood beneath you and be replaced by the strength of our people. You will be an Eldwood Ranger then, and I will be as proud of you as a father has ever been of his son."

"...This is w-where the rite takes place?"

"Yes, Caetal. When the time is right, this is where you will die and be reborn. I wanted you to see it for yourself."

The clearing danced with the light of our fire, and the stars turned above us. I could think of nothing else to say. He stared at me with his dark animal eyes for a long time, and I stared back at him. Then he nodded and turned away to tend the fire. I watched his back as he worked, where the scarified likeness of his guardian bear contracted as his muscles flexed. I could feel everything, all at once — everything that was living around me, and inside of me, and the place I was meant to hold in all of it. It was a profoundly peaceful feeling to know with such certainty that I was my father's son.

And all I had to do, to become myself, was to grow up to be him.

....

It was in that moment of peace, in the only moment I had ever known where I thought that all the pieces of my life finally fit into a shape, that I met the only girl I would ever fall in love with. I saw her; I saw what she really was, and all my sudden self-assurance softened underfoot like sand.

....

I did not see her before my father did; I saw his muscles stiffen as he raised his head from tending the fire and looked across the clearing. And I couldn't see the old man at all from where I stood, as the leaping glare of firelight blocked him from view. So when he suddenly spoke, I almost jumped out of my skin because I thought the bonfire was talking to us.

"Bergrem, son of Rahana and Owein, Brother of the Oak. Caetal, son of Nura and Bergrem. Another night you will be welcome here again, but now you must go. This place is needed tonight for rites that you are not meant to witness."

At the rippling edge of firelight, I could see them now. An old man, as brown as black walnut, with a beaking nose and ropes of white hair that twined like vines into his snowy beard. A girl, perhaps younger than me, crouched on the grounded branch of a reaching oak. Their image distorted in the swimming heat, but what I saw of them was enough to drop my fool mouth wide open. They were both shirtless, for starters, and if that's not enough to set a winter mouth to gaping, I don't know what is. He was clad in fitted breeches of downy pale skin and wore nothing else but a cloak of white feathers, each as large and sharply defined as a dagger. The skin of his chest hung loosely over corded muscle, across which was spread the scarified woad tattoo of some large bird with wings outspread. His fingers were long and branchy. I could not clearly see his eyes, but there was something familiar in their shining scrutiny.

But it was the girl, of course, that struck me slack-mouthed and sense-less. It was not her beauty that I first noticed, but her *otherness*. She was shirtless, as I have said, and the budding curves of her adolescence un-nerved me badly. She may even have been bare as a stitch to her toes, for what I could see of her, because all that she wore was a pelt of grayish fur that was so fitting and seamless that it might have grown from her skin. A large and fluffy tail was tucked out of sight behind her back, but around her head, a telltale halo of white fur was blooming like a secret. Her teeth were sharp, and her ears were black-tipped and cocked toward me with curious interest. Her hands and feet were gloved in socks of black fur. I stared at her, and her at me, in a moment that could never have been long enough. And even in that barest moment, I could see her changing. Now the tips of her ears rounded out, and the purplish-gray fur retreated. Her smile seemed suddenly more shy and less sharp, and a blush of pale brown skin was beginning at the fur on her belly. I could have stared at her face until the light of dawn painted the true color of her hair. But before I could even close my gaping mouth, my father tightened his grip on my arm painfully, and I knew there was more I hadn't seen.

There were people ringed all around the clearing now. I must call them *people*, but they might have been otherwise. I only saw them indis-tinctly, washed in the glare of firelight. I cannot describe them; I do not know if there are words that can. They were *shifting* before me. The very sight of them slid across my eyes like rain. *Flesh of woven roses; muscles of tangled vines. Something that leaks fluid and circles the grove on four feet. A man whose shoulder bones branch through his skin like antlers. A parliament of owls all perched together in fluttering mimicry of a human form. The torso of an old woman growing out of a donkey's back.*

All this I saw as my father pulled me roughly from the clearing, out of the fire's hot radiance and into the shocking cold of the woods. I heard the trees creaking as they swayed around us, and I saw the firelight behind us dim to bright slices as the trunks and branches seemed to shift together to block our view of the way back. Before us, the path opened up as we jogged towards home, our heads ringing from cold and exertion. When I looked back, a wall of trees had grown thickly together where we once tread between them. No more light was visible through them, although it still flickered in the high branches of the canopy.

But when we heard those voices lift in sudden singing, we broke into a run like something was after us. It was a sound I hope to never hear again. That sound rushed upwards and crashed, then lifted again, all the more wild and keening. It blended, although it should not have, for each separate voice was so different. Something stretched in the air around us and stirred in the earth underfoot. We tucked our heads and sprinted between the trees with the sounds of grinding stones and cracking branches coloring the forest behind us. We heard them faintly from a long way off when we stopped at last to rest, gasping and winded, my father coughing with exertion.

We heard their voices crescendo. Louder still was the silence when the singing stopped. The forest was suddenly drained of noises: unnaturally quiet.

We ran all the way home.

....

From the abbey, a ripple had spread. Something profane; something sacred spoken in violation; A Thief of Names uttering the True Name for stone. The Tyrii who listened to stones had felt it first, as they groaned and shifted below ground. Word spread quickly; a gathering was called. Something must be done to silence such blasphemy that stirred within that human hornet's nest, with its bars of dead iron buried inside the walls. Even at a distance, those forged iron bars could be felt. They buzzed with dark ambition. And so those that heeded the call had come together that night to do what must be done, to finish a fight the followers of the foreign god had started.

....

The Thing They Made

It could not be made without blood to bind it, and so they all gave what they could spare. Each bled themselves first, of course, for such evocation demands a binding price. Thereafter was the time for the offerings, and this was the part that was hardest for Rahyn to bear. Each of the Fýrii present had merged their fundamental essence to a source, and it was from that source that the sacrifice must be made.

Rahyn was too young to have been bound to a primary source yet; although she was a dryad's daughter, she had not yet begun to walk the path of her life's passions far enough to have fully encountered her own power. So when the moment came for her to sacrifice, Djaro told her to call forth the animals that travel low to the ground. She wept as she called them to her, one by one, and broke their necks. Each life that ended in her hands was an ecstasy of grief that tore through her, and she raised her trembling voice in singing as she ran the claw of her bone and copper karam knife under their limp bellies and bled them out upon the stone tree. A vole; a squirrel; a brown-throated trickwit; a pair of snow hares, as thin as winter grazing. A tiny mouse, which almost broke her heart as it crawled into her hand. She saw a fawn nosing towards her at the edge of the wood and desperately wished it away, but it would not go. She wept and cradled its head in her lap as Djaro looked on in approval, with tears sliding down the wrinkles of his stern face. Then she cut its neck open and held it tightly as it kicked and shivered.

The last to respond to her call was an aged beaver, waddling up from a thawing creek. He limped unsteadily on an old injury, dragging his tail behind him. This one crawled up onto her lap as willingly as someone relieved to die. But even so, the blood she spilled from him felt as precious as though it was her own blood, and she moaned as it stained the steaming stone trunk of the petrified tree. All the while, Djaro sang above her where she sat. His gravelly voice cawed and rippled amongst the highest branches, and sleeping birds awoke and flew to their deaths, dashing themselves bloody against the altar of the stone tree. Djaro knew the moment when they had given enough and taken enough in sacrifice, and he squeezed her shoulder with the strength of a claw on the branch. She gratefully ceased her calling. She was as bloodied as the altar, and the weight of so much death felt like a piece of the stone tree had rooted in her heart.

....

All that survives, eats. The living eat what they are able to and become a feast for others when they pass. If you or I stood side by side with each plant and insect and animal we have consumed to grow up into the person we are today, a great palace would fill to overflowing with the lives we have ended and blended into our own. But the creature that was beginning to form underfoot had to be fed all at once, for when it awoke, it would never eat again. For those that gathered to create it together, it was a staggering reminder of the death that life demands. But each was aware that they themselves had eaten that much and more in their time. And so, they fed the living earth that was encircled between them and gave thanks to those doomed plants and animals that gave everything.

....

All the wood was silent now, but for the chorus of grief rising from so many throats to honor such sacrifice. All creatures that were called came to the fire. Nothing could resist the Fýrii as they communed together, and nothing wanted to.

Some coaxed flowers out of the frozen soil just to bury them again. The rarest fungi were burnt and powdered and sprinkled over the consecrated earth. Feathers were plucked painfully and fed to the fire, and fur likewise scraped from flesh. The ancient likeness of the Great Boar carved upon the tree filled with offered blood until it shimmered in the firelight, and all who saw it felt certain that it shivered with movement, as though the sigil was leaping with remembered muscle. Looming just past the outer edge of the circle, the Stone Tree pulsed with energy like a beating heart, warming the air around it.

At the height of their singing, when all present had done what had been asked of them, there was a sonorous cracking sound, and the singing fell suddenly silent. A single chunk of one petrified root of the stone tree had sundered and fallen. With shaking hands, Djaro stepped forward and lifted it high for all to see. It was as big as the heart of an ox and so heavy that Djaro's thin muscles strained as he bore it aloft and lay it on the slick ground at the center of their circle. There, in a wet puddle of petals and herbs and blood, it sat. The Fýrii watched in silence as it sank into the wet earth, and when it was swallowed completely, they turned away and scattered from the clearing in ones and twos until only the elder remained by the fire.

The fire was fed and tended by the plodding old woman with the lower body of a gray donkey. She was a Kinnaras, her name was Atlata, and she was the last living of her kind. She was the most revered of the Fýrii, and it was her gift and her right to attend as a doula during the long hours before the Homsaöl was truly born.

....

For all that night and into the following day, the trees bent inward towards the center of the grove, and the sanctified soil drank of their offered sap until the earth and stones and roots therein coagulated into one mass. And this mass was rich with pulsing fungus and wreathed with worms, and as it hardened, it drew in on itself until there was a large mound that began to form in a widening crater. This mass was as heavy as the stones that are hidden underground, with a broad back and wide limbs tucked up beneath it. The bonfire that Bergrem had lit still burned on its forming shoulders.

Let the Monster in

We didn't tell my mother what we had seen out there in the wood. We probably didn't have to — she was cleverer than my father ever knew, and she had better hearing than either of us. Noise carries a long way, as everyone knows, but what carries even further is silence. Many there were in Holm who awoke that night to the sudden stillness in the forest, not even knowing what was wrong. By sunrise, my mother was out on the snow-laden porch, straining her ears for the sounds of birds calling in the trees. But there were none. The sunrise was a thin well of light that was quickly quenched by iron skies. All that could be heard throughout that morning was the soft pattering of snow that fell from heavy clouds drifting above the Eldwood like breath gathering at the tops of the trees.

....

The trees were drained by their work, as each gave what sap they could until they drooped. The animals were likewise silent, huddled in fearful awe beneath the bowed trees. Snow fell fitfully. But as the day drew on, a mass of clouds began streaming in from the north. The trees, weakened from so much loss, were drawing the rain down to renew them. Atlata watched the clouds amass throughout the long afternoon and carefully built the fire up to a roaring height to prepare for what was coming.

....

By noon, even the most oblivious of Holm's farmers had noticed the ominous quiet in the woods. Neither the chittering of squirrels nor the barking of foxes could be heard. There was no clatter of bucks rubbing antlers against the trees to help shed them, hares startling across the snow, or hunting dogs braying in their wake. The inconstant fall of snow would have muffled sounds anyway if there were any to hear. But for hours, the snowfall would cease, and the quiet in the forest remained. The silence stretched on as the morning overturned and the afternoon crept in, and nerves stretched with it.

It could be felt at the Welcome Holm tavern, where the thin new serving wench bustled about with a rag and refills, trying to keep conversations alive to dispel the heavy silence that hung between the rafters. Even the crackling of the fireplace seemed garish in the laden air. She was new to the small town and was, therefore, still a curiosity, yet she bantered with such easy grace that few of them noticed that she never answered questions about herself or her home. But she felt the pall of silence stronger than any of them, for she had built musical palaces in the air on foundations of sound. When she could uphold the poor cover of thin conversation no longer, she snuck out the kitchen door and into the cold tavern yard. Rising proudly on the hill above the town, the walls of the abbey gleamed a pale red under their dusting of snow.

The Rhymira girl from Dunmarsh stared up at the abbey thoughtfully, clutching the hem of her skirt in one hand and softly humming the wordless melody of an ancient intonation to ward off ill fortune.

....

The boy with his mother's eyes and his father's sharp features napped and read throughout the quiet day. Yesterday he had met the wizard Drinn and learned the True Name for stone as it was spoken out loud. He had felt the vibrations of that name spreading out in ripples that made the walls of the abbey shift and groan. Tomorrow his legs would be crushed by the sabotage of the arch he had worked so hard to build.

....

The boy from far away had awoken early, put on his finest shabby shirt, and been taken to the abbey to be schooled by the clerics of Cuthain. He had never been in a building so grand, and while his owner argued with the clerics about the cost of educational tithing, the far-away boy wandered through the cold stone hallways, touching everything with a careful hand. The silence did not bother him here; within these walls, it felt like reverence. He stood below the beautiful dome of the apse and stared up in artful awe. There were ocean waves carved in bas relief and the half-chiseled figure of a stern, bearded man astride the prow of a great ship. And far behind this man, there was the image of a tiny island, seeming to grow ever smaller as the boat moved proudly towards the center of view. The far-away boy did not notice the tears slipping slowly down his face as he stared at that vanishing island. But another boy did.

....

The pale Erdin boy was orphaned from birth: one of many unwanted children left on the chapel steps, and he knew a fellow orphan when he saw one. In the service of Cuthain, they were called 'ordanians' — those that were ordained into righteous service because they had nowhere else to go. They were the bastards of the faithful, born to the unfortunate and abandoned without parents to guide them. The ordanian noticed the tears on the face of the lonely boy who gazed up at the carvings that stretched across the curve of the apse. He mistook them, for a hopeful moment, as the tears of one so moved by devotion to their god. But as he looked closer, he saw that the fists of the weeping boy were clenched and shaking with rage.

....

Through the open arches of the arcade, the first soft tremor of thunder grumbled softly in the northern sky.

....

The foxgirl watched the sun set and felt the wind rising. From the tall branches of a fortress oak, she could close her eyes and feel untapped energy gathering in the air around her. The westlight was a smear of purple shadow where the sun had set. Last night, she had killed and bled for the good of her island home, and tonight the daylong summoning would be completed. In the distance, above the grove where the Stone Tree lay, a slowly turning vortex was forming. The clouds that formed it were as dark as dreaming. With the vortex came the rain. It looked like a river of individual drops flowing down the funneling corkscrew of clouds. The foxgirl hugged herself and shivered with excitement. Djaro had told her what signs to look for. Wind and Water had given their gifts, and now five of the six elements were present in the formation of the Homsaöl. Only one more to wait for, and she could sense it coming. She tipped her head back and howled her excitement into the rising wind.

....

And I, Cactal, son of Nura and Bergrem, was oblivious to all of this.

I was playing with Dubby, who was playing with a dead rabbit. Melvin says that being willfully ignorant of a problem is as bad as participating in it directly, but I'm not sure that's always true. Sometimes, life gets to be a little too much all at once, and it's just best to take a break from thinking about any of it. Jackwolf-dogs are great distractions. Dubby leapt and bounded and shook that rabbit to pieces, and I chased him all over, trying to steal it back from him. The unnatural quiet wore on throughout the day, and I didn't give a fiddler's fart about it. I willfully didn't care at all, and it felt great.

....

My father, however, did not share in my careless afternoon.

He ranged all through the woods around our house, tensely preoccupied. I had rarely seen him look so flushed and bestial, and I turned away to keep him carefully out of my line of sight. Twice I heard him coughing in a deep brattle. On the few times he passed where I was playing, he was nearly on all fours, sniffing the air and looking hard on the ground between the trees for something that had no name.

I think the silence in the woods had him badly spooked. It was uncomfortable to watch him suffer such disquiet over something so formless. It takes a lot of mental effort to ignore someone going through that, and by the time afternoon began to fade into iron twilight, I was pretty much worn out from trying so hard not to care. It had been an hour or two since I had seen him anyway, and when I couldn't put off the lengthening shadows any longer, I left the shreds of the rabbit behind, tied Dubby to his drooling post, and walked away from my yard. I briskly followed the trail that skirted Tanner's Creek, looping around the frozen pond until it led me out onto the Thegn's Road. Without the distraction of Dubby, I felt the quiet press down on me all at once.

My father was in the right, of course, to feel so ill at ease. I should have been helping him find whatever he was looking for. I felt a pang of guilt for ignoring him. After all, he and I were the only ones in Holm who knew what the source of the silence was, if not what it meant. The Rangers of Eldwood, though aligned with the Fýrii in principle, were, as a rule, spooked by them. We borrowed the use of their sacred groves on occasions that were significant enough to warrant such intrusion, but we sure as sunrise cleaned up after ourselves and left in a hurry when we saw them coming. None of them were human, after all.

The coming darkness was closing in, and although my mind was far away, my body followed the road towards Melvin's house. I could not have told you why I was going there — perhaps some unconscious whim to clear the air, or restless habit. Soft rolls of thunder were beginning to peal, and the northern sky was lit by forks of distant lightning. I knew my mother would be worrying now: at home with a storm drawing in and her family out in the gathering gloom. I imagined her stirring a hot stew alone in the kitchen, sweat and private tears stinging her eyes, trying her best to upkeep a home for a husband and son who were so often away. What loneliness; what unbearable loneliness she must endure, with nobody to speak her private worries to, when the only people who might listen are the very people who cause them.

I was brought up short with those thoughts, with my breath hitching up in my throat and such love and grief for my mother mingling inside me that I felt woozy holding all of it in at once. I could just see Melvin's house coming into view: a hulking stone cottage with firelight warming the windows. A drizzle had begun to fall, and a sudden lifting of wind drove the wet mist into my face. His house still looked a far way off in the darkness, and I suddenly felt bone tired. I resolved to turn back then after all, to hurry home and become a better son before one more awkward evening eating in silence drooped around the dinner table.

It was then, as I turned homeward, that I caught sight of my father. He was lumbering towards Melvin's house through the frozen wheat stalks of a fallow field. His head was bowed, and his feet kicked through the accumulated snow drifts. Something was clutched in his hand.

The rising wind carried the rattle of his coughing into my ears, and I felt a sudden fear twist inside of me. *Why is he coughing so much lately? Why haven't I asked him about it?* He had always seemed so powerful, so in control of the world around him. He was a force in my life as elemental as fire or water, and yet he was neither of those things. He was flesh and bone, and vulnerable to time. He grew older with every sunset. I stared at him as he trudged by in the dark and was amazed that he did not see me, for I made no move to conceal myself. Each moment now, the wind was rising, suddenly rising as though the quiet of the day was being overturned in a cresting wave of sound. The thunder no longer was distant now   it crashed down overhead. Lightning lit the trees in a confusion of glare and flooding shadow, and the wind sucked up around us. It felt like the sky was taking deeper and deeper breaths without ever letting them out again. The air seemed so suddenly thin that it made me light-headed. Rain began to patter down. It was warm, strangely warm. I blinked and shook it clear from my eyes, and in a moment's wet blindness, I lost sight of him. I cried his name out, once. But the thunder rolled, and he did not hear me.

....

The vortex of cloud sucked into the Homsaöl, and the wind howled in a voice that sounded like singing. The ribbon of raindrops descended with the wind, and into the Homsaöl the water absorbed, and the creature of earth and stone swole up like a tick as the expanding mud cocooned around it. In the center, Atlata's fire roared upward into a second cyclone that dragged heat into the clouds. The sound of thunder was deafening now, and Atlata had moved as far back from the fire as she dared. On her knees, battered by the wind and almost concussed by rolling waves of sound, Atlata prepared herself for the final moment of summoning. The daylong silence of the forest was broken at last, and animals who had spent the day huddled in reverence now fled to escape the fury of the storm, their instincts overwhelmed and their cries echoing through the trees. Atlata gathered the energy she could feel rising in the earth and began the chant to call the lighting up from the ground.

....

The dead grass in the fields swayed in clashing ripples, stirred by the tearing fingers of the wind. In the time it took my father to break from the trees and cross the fallow fields that abutted Melvin's house, the storm had worsened from distant to dangerous. It was sudden violence unlike anything I had ever seen, and the blinding flashes of light left an inky red blackness where my night vision once was, as though I was staring at the inside of my own closed eyelids. I became afraid. I could not see my father; I couldn't see anything but the rips of sudden light that split the fabric of night and made the world all the darker when they passed.

There was a roaring concussion of thunder that was so loud I almost dropped to my knees. Lightning struck the road behind me, just a few hundred feet away. There was a flare of something exploding into fire, and suddenly the patter of falling rain thickened to a warm downpour. It pounded against my skin, and a cold winter wind rushed in behind it. The fire on the road was quickly doused in the deluge, even as I ran towards it. When I got to the spot, I could see nothing left of what had been burning but smoking char. The sandy bank on each side of the road was a steaming ripple of blackened glass.

Then my father was there. He was suddenly beside me, gripping my shoulders and lifting me off the ground in a hug that bruised my ribs. The rain on his bear fur further soaked my sodden tunic, and over the jagged light and booming thunder, he was coughing and yelling something in my ears that I could barely understand.

"I know now why we were there in the grove last night, why we built that fire. ... We are the arm that holds the sword the Fýrii can swing! Something is awoken that Erdin steel cannot kill! We are meant to steal the slaver's iron and cast down their false gods. It is time; tonight is the start of it!"

His eyes were glassy and bright, and water dripped from his beard onto my face. His long hair hung unbraided in tangles down his back. Wet heat rolled off his body.

"It's our time, Caetal. Don't you understand, boy? Tonight, Karnonou will guide our hand by smashing a hole in the abbey wall, so our monster can grapple their god! You begin to be a man tonight; you must help me, Caetal! Come with me. I will show you what the rangers and I have been so busy preparing for!"

He dragged me with him down the road towards the abbey. Water ran in sheets across the ground, lit in fleeting moments by the pale light of the Ash Moon. He kept his arm wrapped around my shoulder and leaned heavily on me as we walked.

I could hear his harsh breathing more and more clearly as the rain began to soften and the thunder rolled on by, quieting as it crashed further and further away. The walk up the Thegn's Road less than a mile from Melvin's house, but by the time we neared the steepness of the uphill climb, my father was coughing so badly we had to stop. He sagged against me, and through the soaked layers of our clothing, I could feel the dull heat of fever radiating from him. Moonslight flooded the road briefly as a rain cloud passed overhead. In the wet light, he looked sallow and haggard, with eyes like sunken holes. His beard dripped with rain.

"Father... w-whatever it is you wuh... w... need to show me, it's not w-worth it. Not tonight. Ma is probably half mad with w-w-worry anyway and... I really think w-we should be g-getting you home."

He shook his head and drops of water flew. But when he tried to pull himself upright, his legs buckled. His fingers were gripping my tunic hard at the shoulder, and when his knees sank into the mud of the road, the neck of my shirt tore at the seam. He didn't let go, and neither did I let him, until both of us sank into a squat in the freezing mud. Rain drummed on our heads.

"Da... *please*. You always told me a good hunter knows when the prey is lost. Tonight is done. You are sick, and the storm is w-w... *winning*. In another hour, you might be lying on your back in the middle of the road. I can't carry you all the w-way home, and neither can Ma. Please, please: you have to let it g-go, just for tonight. Maybe in the morning, you'll feel better, and w... w-w... you and I can come back out then?"

He stared at me in stony silence. We had knelt in the dark shadow of the abbey walls, rising on the hilltop above us, and I could barely see him but for the reflection of light in his eyes. I could sense them searching my face. He began to speak; I'll never know what he meant to say because the coughing took him badly then. When he could breathe again without choking for air, he simply nodded to me, and I helped him stand and walked him slowly home. He leaned heavily on me then, body and spirit. It was the loneliest walk of my life.

....

At last we were home again, and there was mother. Her anger and relief swayed her between shouting and tears, but relief won out in the end, and we both got put to bed with soup and a scolding. I had never seen her flatten my father as she did; as weak as he was, she loomed over him and pinned him down in a dark and loving fury. I didn't get the earful of what she told him as she tucked him into bed and fed him soup, but I didn't have to. I couldn't understand how such love and resentment could live side by side in her heart. But then again, I didn't know the first thing about women, and I'd certainly never had to bear being married to my father. I rolled over and fell asleep with the rain pattering ever more lightly on the roof and the dark punctuated by coughing and fierce whispers.

....

I awoke twice that night, and I will spend the rest of my life wishing I hadn't. But perhaps none of it, or us, could have happened otherwise? I'm no philosopher, not by a long shot. But in some ways, this was the start of all of it, if there is truly a beginning to anything.

....

As I said, I was awoken twice. The first time was to my father looming over me, swaying unsteadily on his feet. His breathing rattled, and his breath stank. He leaned down close to my face and whispered:

"The sürra that you gathered is in a crate, beneath your bed. You must do what I can't. Open a hole in the abbey wall to let the monster in. ...I need you, son. We all need you."

Then he turned and walked unsteadily back to bed. I heard the bed frame creak as he lay back down onto it, and I heard my mother mumbling tired comforts in the dark. I closed my eyes and listened to the pounding of my heart until sleep stole over me again.

The second time I woke, I got up and carefully slid the crate out from under my bed. The moon had set outside, and I dressed in the dark in clumsy silence, braiding the long back of my hair as quickly as I could. Then I let myself out into the starlit cold of our yard with the crate in my arms, and jogged towards the abbey to do my father's will.

....

As the last stars faded from the blushing sky, I clambered over the garden wall of the abbey and set to work. All traces of the storm had passed in the night, and the morning was quietly creeping in. The wind had died, and the air was fragrant with moisture. One large candle had been lit in the abbey window against the darkness, but its light was ceremonial, and the predawn gloom that surrounded the churchyard seemed all the darker for it.

I moved with the quiet stealth of a ranger's son, keeping close to the long shadows that stretched from the walls. A glance around the compound quickly showed me where to breach a hole — a large archway that would soon be sealed by a heavy iron gate, which rested nearby. The arch was the newest construction, still shrouded in an oilskin curing cover. To my mind, this made it seem more vulnerable to sabotage. *A gate cannot hang in a broken arch.* The builder's scaffolding was still in place beneath it. It was only the work of a few moments to scramble up those wooden supports. Soon my outstretched hand touched the cold weight of the keystone.

I rested there for a moment. Dawnlight was just beginning to seep across the courtyard. I felt guilty, of course, for the damage I was about to do to Daedrim's masonry. For some reason, the idea of a rampaging forest monster smashing the abbey apart didn't really bother me so much as the reality that I was about to personally sabotage something Daedrim *(and Melvin too; but I mustn't think about that)* had built.

But it was a fleeting thought, because the one that came immediately after it was the image of this Erdin stronghold tumbled into ruin, and the heroic boy responsible for doing it. I imagined the booming crash of collapse and the joy on my father's face when I told him how I had brought the abbey down. In my mind, I could see him so clearly: laughing and hugging me, no longer coughing at all. I could imagine him in the spring, gathered around the fire with the Rangers of the Eldwood arrayed around him, telling proud tales of his son that I was meant to overhear. I would be nearby, blushing a bit, of course. And I would speak little of their praise, as he does, because I wouldn't need to speak. My achievement would be self-evident whenever anyone looked up at this high hill and saw the forest overgrowing the tumble of stones that was once the house of a conquering god.

And while I sat there grinning to myself, I took my belt knife and dug it into the palm of my hand. The pain welled, and so did blood. I wiped it onto the mortar that surrounded the keystone and all the stones just below it on the arch — everywhere I could reach from the top of the scaffolding. Then I ground the green sürra underfoot and, wrapping my hand carefully in the loose bottom of my tunic, smeared it onto the fresh blood. Immediately the air began to stink, and the mortar started to bubble.

I scampered down the scaffolding and quickly wiped the lower hem of my tunic in the wet grass. But I could still hear the sürra sizzling on the cloth, so I tore a strip of it off entirely and rubbed it roughly on the cobblestones below the scaffolding. My blood, mingled with sürra, left a purplish smear. I wadded up the torn cloth and stuffed it into my pocket as I stared at that smear. From where I was standing, the smear looked a bit like the crouching shape of a rabbit.

The terrible image of the Kaninhode crept to mind, with all its dire symbolism. I remembered how scared I had felt when I first saw it at the edge of the quarry. *Had that only been days ago? I have grown up so much since then. A boy's fears. Now here I am doing the work of a man, and the symbol is just a symbol, after all. Let me sign my work with my father's warning; then, he will truly be here with me in spirit.*

As dawn's light began to touch the tips of my boots, I knelt on the cold cobbles and arranged a ring of stones around the rabbit-looking smear. The rabbit of sacrifice, ringed by the broken circle. *Let these stones carry the message clearly: our island will not tolerate your god. We are coming for you. The natural world rejects you, and we are coming to hunt you down.*

Also, it made me feel like a righteous tough guy to sign my work. I was an artist of chaos, now: an instrument of sacred revenge. It lit me up good to feel like that. Let's not pretend otherwise.

Then I ran away, through the tall grasses that grew wild on the hillside, all the way to the cleared edge of the forest. There I spread my oilskin cloak out just under the cover of trees and sprawled down on it. And as the rising sun warmed the chill out of my bones, I fell asleep.

....

And the rest, you know. I awoke in the early afternoon, just in time to watch the stones collapse on Melvin, but not in time to warn him. And when that keystone fell, the man I thought I was becoming was crushed beneath it. I was a scared boy again, and I had destroyed the life of my best friend.

....

It is Alive

Not so very far away, in a clearing that had been buffeted by wind and blackened by lightning, a creature of living stone arose from a smoking crater. The Homsaöl raised its head until sunlight lit the blind hollows of its eyes. It was born knowing everything it needed to know about what it was and what it was meant for. Even from such a distance, the dead iron in the walls of the invasive god's house buzzed inside its head. Only destroying it entirely would cease that terrible hum and allow a return to the stillness of oblivion.

With the slow inevitability of the first moments of a landslide, the Homsaöl began to drag itself towards the distant abbey.

....

"There was a grinding shriek of stone dragged across iron.
A sudden bloom of sparks lit up the sight of the Homsaöl starkly, so that I saw
it quite clearly for the first time. Its eyes were a stinking smolder of burning
phosphorus. Its mouth was a widening pit fanged with jagged protrusions."

IRON
~ The Sixth Story ~

"*I**lium... sacrum... pubis... and the damned femur too. Incredible.***"** Heiro Manan muttered to himself as he probed the shattered pelvis with the pitiless fingers of an old surgeon.

Nearby, on the stretched hide of a second sickbed cot, the ordanian named Mathias groaned in unconscious sympathy. Heiro Manan glanced with concern at the young cleric. Almost three days had passed since the faulty arch came down on the boy who built it. When the capstone of the archway had fallen on the legs of the mason's unfortunate son, he should have died. The impact of such terrible weight overcomes all beneath it; when heavy stone collides with flesh and bone, bone loses. By the time Heiro Manan and the other priests rushed to the scene, there should have been nothing left to do but cover the crushed boy with earth where he lay and carve his epitaph into the stone that killed him.

But instead, the startled clerics found the granite slab that should have pinned the boy had exploded and scattered into steaming shards, and their own timid ordanian was collapsed unconscious by his side, with his hand encircling the back of the wounded boy's head. When the priests had labored to move the two boys into the infirmary for care, they could barely slide the mason's mangled son onto the medic cot in one piece. When they tried, both boys woke up as one and began to cry out in pain, their voices blending into one disconcerting scream. It was an unnatural sound, and the priests warded themselves against evil when they heard it. The two boys were laid side by side on cots, and never once did Mathias remove his grip from the back of Melvin's neck. They lay there still, pale and sweating with shared pain in the dim coolness of the infirmary, while the stained-glass window above them poured colored light across their faces.

Another boy — a large, brutish-looking lad who never yet made eye contact with Manan — had trailed in after them and sat nearby, hour after hour. He had stoutly refused to explain himself or to leave their side.

Heiro Manan was too old to care. He had no wish for noisy company, and the attentive quiet of the carpenter's hulking son did not vex him. After all, tears of grief are their own form of prayer if they are shed in Cuthain's house.

What did vex him, and continued to, were the bones regenerating beneath the damaged boy's skin. His fellow clerics would scarcely have believed him if he had told them the truth, and so he came back often to check for himself, just to be sure. Both boys lay on their sides; one was pale and pulped with bruises of the deepest purple red that covered a third of his body. The other was flushed and sweating with an unnatural fever. The fact that the mason's son had lived was an obvious miracle, of course: but did not Cuthain work such wonders as he crossed the sea and discovered these islands for his chosen people? The old cleric was steadfast in his faith that some were chosen to pass and others to linger, and that was the will of providence if nothing else was.

But the miracle that kept him coming back into the infirmary over and over again was not what his eyes could see, but only what the delicate touch of a surgeon's hand could tell. The impact of the stone had fallen squarely on the hips and the top of one leg. When they had dragged the screaming boy inside, his body had been mangled, the bones shattered into protruding splinters. Yet, within minutes the seeping blood had slowed, and by nightfall, the terrible splitting wounds had shut. Overnight, as the boys slept entangled in the submersed unconsciousness of two bodies fleeing together from terrible pain, the scattered chaos of bone shards had reordered themselves under his skin like a puzzle being solved. By morning, Melvin's hip began to resemble a hip again, and his legs were no longer a meaningless mess of flesh.

As the days passed, what began as a vigil became a spectacle. At first, it was only members of the clergy who clustered into gossiping gaggles, peering at the boys from a respectful distance and pestering Heiro Manan until he shooed them out quite forcefully, with some of the same temper that Cuthain was famous for in *His* crusading youth. But word of the miracle could not remain unspoken for long. Cuthain's priests have no spiritual qualms about frequenting taverns and, like anyone, tend to talk overmuch when they are deep in the cups.

Soon a few farmers found their way to the top of High Hill to make enquiries about the boy who should not have survived. On the third day after the accident, the doors of the infirmary were swept open, and a great wailing was heard. Heiro Manan left the room respectfully as Daedrim the mason fell to his knees at the foot of the sick bed and wept like the father he was over the broken body of his son. Caetal, the carpenter's silent boy, was suddenly nowhere to be seen, although Heiro Manan sensed him squatted like a beast somewhere out of sight. The behavior of children was never something Heiro Manan understood even when he was one, so he left the room to walk in the dead garden and think a while, while the sounds of heartbroken sobbing silenced the songbirds that nestled under the roof of the arcade.

....

In the long quiet of evening, while both moons shone like lanterns held at heavenly height, Mathias the ordanian opened his eyes. He slowly relaxed his hand from around the back of Melvin's neck. The muscles in that hand had cramped his fingers into claws, and it took a few minutes of gentle flexing before he could close the hand into a fist again. He lay there for a while in the moons-spattered darkness, watching the dull throb of pine coals in the fireplace and feeling the winter chill radiating out of the stone walls.

At last, when he felt the world slow on its spinning axis enough to stand, he arose from his cot. On shaking legs, he wobbled: half upright and barely conscious. But he could sense that the other boy slept on without him, free from the killing pain.

Carefully, Mathias made his way out of the dark room. The stone floor was frigid on his bare feet, and the breath of evening crept unhindered through the thin linen of his infirmary robe. But it felt incredible, because the feelings he felt were *his* again. The cloister lawn was slick and cold; the frozen ground crackled underfoot. With both moons suspended overhead, the world sparkled with a dusting of frost, and the vault of the sky glittered with stars.

Mathias lifted his head and breathed in as deeply as he could and knew for certain that he was no longer completely himself.

....

The Boy from Nowhere

The true circumstances of Mathias' arrival in the care of Cuthain is known by only one priest, and this is the story that he tells about it.

It begins in a small wooden crate, left on the worn steps of Cuthain's house in Ulfaang. It was autumn in that coastal town of plunging cliffs and howling drafts, but luckily the night was warm, the baby lay there for quiet hours, unnoticed. No moon had risen; the evening was pocked with startling starlight that reflected in the baby's mismatched eyes. When a priest came home at last from a solemn night of barbarous revels, he found the unfortunate child by stumbling onto the cradle crate in the dark. There was nothing to justify the baby but a note scrawled across the lid of the crate, which was propped up on the step nearby: *"Save him or bury him."*

This was not as rare an occurrence as one might wish for. Every year, babies are left on the steps of churches, for the world is full of mortal misfortunes. The young bearing young is never easy on anyone, and where could a desperate mother hand over a child she couldn't hope to keep? To the gods, to the wolves, or to the slavers. The choice was usually an obvious one.

But this child was different. Abandoned with no name, no well-wishes. Only a fitted lid so that the manger could be buried like a coffin if the church chose not to trouble itself with raising the child. The priest, who was called Fahru Manan and would one day hold status as heiro, was already getting well on in years and was certainly well deep in the drink that night. He scooped up the crate with no special care and, carrying it inside under one arm as one might hoist a grocer's basket, bore it into the chapel and placed it unceremoniously onto the lectern to consider it better by candlelight.

There he pondered a bleary while, swaying on his feet and basting the baby in beery breath until it began to squirm and cry. The child stank of neglect and lifted his thin arms pleadingly at Manan. Drunk though he was, his primitive paternity instincts finally overtook the fugue of his pickled mind, and he gathered a pulpit cloth and lifted the child up to change its soiled diaper. Holding it up in the candlelight above the manger's shadow, he sucked in his breath in wonder. For here, at last, did he discern the likely cause of the baby's abandonment. Although the newborn looked in every way like a healthy Erdin child (but for the neglect of enough feeding and care), it had a most unlucky face. The eyes of the child were startlingly mismatched. The left iris was as darkly green as sorrel leaves, but the right iris was a pale yellow, like gold with the shine drained out of it. The baby's head seemed overlarge on a thin neck, and it stared at Manan with almost cross-eyed consternation, like it was looking inside of him. Fahru Manan, plastered as he was, had the good sense to not drop the child, though the muscles of his arms spasmed in superstitious recoil.

....

It is known in Erdin culture that mismatched eyes are portentous. Not of evil, necessarily, but of a body born with a soul that straddles two worlds. Those with this rare affliction are usually smothered at birth to save them from a difficult and unnatural life. Of the few that survive to adulthood, most go mad. For who could set a steady course through life with each of both eyes seeing two different realities at once?

....

Carefully, Fahru Manan made to tuck the baby back into the crate. Yet, in the tangle of cloth that the child had rested on, his eyes caught sight of a folded piece of vellum. He tucked the baby under one arm and fished the folded scroll out to read it. Here he assumed to find the usual details of the child's name, instructions for care, or promises of legacy and financial support that would never materialize. What he found instead puzzled him then as greatly as it would puzzle Mathias throughout his young life. The ink was a rare red; the handwriting was fluid and bold. These were the words that were written therein.

They stole pieces of their parents and the slumbering dreams of the Fae.
Drank freezing cups of northern wind,
Carved up and ate the shimmering marvel of their own wings.
Immortal edacity; yet what was disgorged?
Bedlam, feathers, and a son.
All things should end for the sake of beginnings,
But not all things can.

....

The child that belonged to nobody did not die, of course. Manan sobered up throughout the night and brought the child to morning mass at sunrise. Here, after discussing what was best to be done for the boy, he handed him over to the authority of Heiro Baliol. It took only a few days, however, for that learned cleric to disavow himself of interest in the orphan's future and pass the boy off to Fahru Tomas. Tomas was a man of perpetually righteous fury and swore to teach the child such discipline in the service of Cuthain that his bones would nightly ache from it. But not until he was weaned to solid food, for no holy penance of hair shirt or lash can be imposed on a baby at the breast. So, Tomas grudgingly turned the orphan over to the church laundering woman named Emmuline. She was flowering with the milk of motherhood from her own firstborn and took on the role of wet-nurse for a modest sum of coppers. It was Emmuline who finally had the decency to name the child, whom she called Mathias to honor a woman named Mathia she had loved and lost to a swollen river in her youth.

....

When the boy was old enough to toddle about and eat solid food, his future was once again rewritten, as Fahru Tomas was struck to palsy by a sudden failure of the brain, caused by overexertion of passionate shouting at prayer and a fatty diet of duck eggs and clotted cream. Mathias was then shunted into the tutelage of Fahru Leon, who was rumored to be inappropriately overfond of young boys. Manan, meanwhile, had sobered up well enough and long enough to have been promoted to Heiro Manan, and exercised his first tenet of authority by reassigning Fahru Leon to a hermitage hut of piled stones far from the presence of children, and reluctantly took Mathias back under his own tutelage.

Shortly thereafter, the construction of the abbey at Holm received the approval it needed from Thegn Rory, and funding from the cathedral coffers at Portuan. A master mason and skilled carpenter local to Holm were selected, and building began in earnest. As soon as temporary staffing quarters were erected, Heiro Manan assigned himself and eleven other clerics of Cuthain to people this new parish. He chose from amongst the brothers at Ulfaang those who had shown a will to work hard or had demonstrated some artistry in the carving of wood or stone. He took the boy Mathias with them when they departed.

So, at the age of three, Mathias came to Holm and was raised to boyhood in wooden bunkers just down the hill from the slowly growing walls of the abbey. This is where his memories began, and the troublesome nuisance of his double sight.

....

A childhood spent alone on a windy hillside above a quiet farming village is its own sort of wonderment, only able to be imagined in a watercolor of moments: thoughtful, peaceful, and indescribably lonely. Mathias grew up apart from other children, for he was an ordanian with expectations placed upon him by the church. He was to be reverent, of course, and useful too, for the expense of raising a child that nobody wanted came directly out of coffers meant to support the poor. While other children might be free to play leaping games through the wild barley on sunny afternoons, he was at study, doing chores, or tending to the sprawling herb garden the clerics cultivated. He often saw Melvin and Caetal roaming around at the edge of the forest, beating the bracken with sticks or hanging from the trees like heathens; all the while hollering with laughter at their secret games of triumph and tragedy.

He would watch them from the little kitchen window with his hands in a soapy dish basin and imagine what it might be like to play with friends on a sunny afternoon. Sometimes he almost struck up the courage to go greet them, but they seemed so sure of each other that it made him unsure of himself. It did not look like a friendship that needed an awkward third. So he learned to dry herbs, and press cider apples, and cook with seasoning skill. In his free time, he practiced at the crofter's pipe, which is a double-headed flute with a droning thumb hole that makes a melancholy warbling like terns flying away at sunset. There was daily singing at vespers, and plenty of scribing work to do, and the study of medicinal healing and the history of Erdin culture and of Eld particularly, which was full of the glorious sorrow of war.

The worst of it was the headaches. Lightning clusters in his brain that would come on suddenly from a long way off. He knew that they had something to do with his eyes, and they were worse when he looked at things that moved by choice. Still things and rooted things, like trees and boulders and the columns of the abbey — those things were good to look at for as long as he liked, and he often did so, appreciating the littlest details. The real problem was the visual doubling of things that were animate and in motion. Plants were fine because it was only the rustling of wind coming from different directions at once; the leaves would blur around the edges a bit, but nothing distracting — it was actually sort of lovely. But people were hard to look at for long. They would often appear to double in his vision: one would go off one way and the other in another. Sometimes they were wearing different clothes, or one version would be shouting and the other quite still. He could not hear the words the other spoke, of course, just see the anger in their faces. It was hard to know who was standing in the room with him and who was as far away as distance goes. He didn't understand it, and the discrepancies gave him vertigo. So, he rarely made eye contact with anyone, tending to look somewhere off to the side and past them when they spoke to him. Nobody seemed to mind, for it was difficult for them as well. It was his eyes, of course; such unlucky eyes.

....

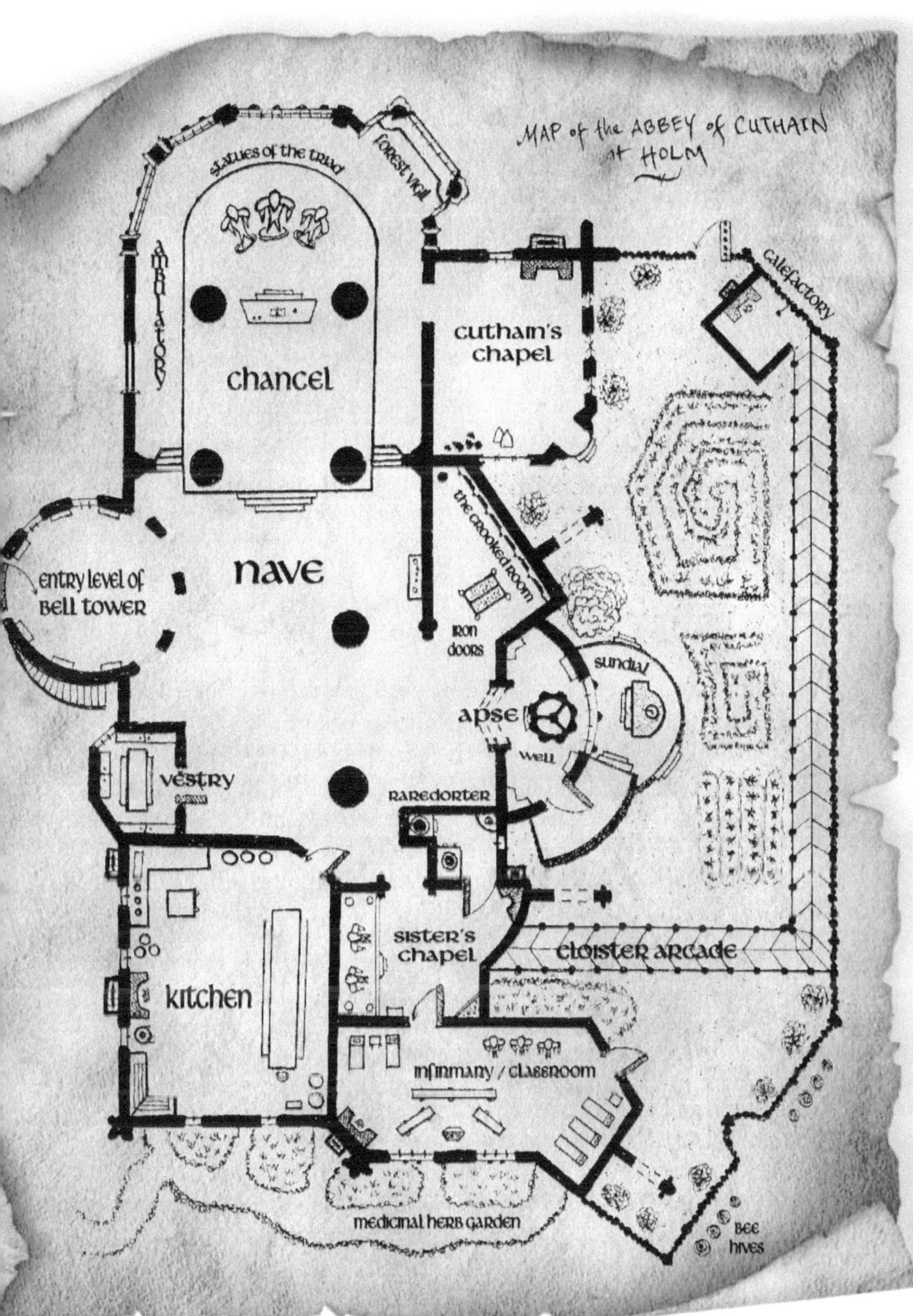
MAP of the ABBEY of CUTHAIN at HOLM
statues of the triad
forest vigil
calefactory
ambulator
chancel
cuthain's chapel
nave
the crooked room
entry level of bell tower
iron doors
apse
sundial
well
vestry
raredorter
sister's chapel
cloister arcade
kitchen
infirmary / classroom
medicinal herb garden
bee hives

The Abbey

Years passed, and the outline of the abbey grew slowly and inexorably into a building. Mathias was as proud of every stone of it as though he had arranged them each by hand. He would often walk the construction grounds and run his fingers along the stones and marvel at how seamlessly everything fit. It was not a big abbey, but to Mathias it was a wonder of effort.

A traveler approaching the abbey would follow the Thegn's Road all the way to the front door and have the looming edifice of the bell tower in sight the whole time. Where the road was meant to continue on from there was anyone's guess, for by all appearances it simply ended at the abbey, as though to imply: *here was so worthy a holy house that a pilgrim from Portuan would have come more than a hundred miles just to see it.* The front door was set at the base of the bell tower; an exterior staircase of narrow stone curved upwards out of sight towards the belfry. Here a single iron bell hung, adorned with a bronze etching of Cuthain's seeing eye. It gazed down across the valley below, winking in flashes when sunlight passed over it.

The front door itself was the cheery reddish purple of oiled daganwood, hewn and imported from some distant island. Above the door for all who looked — and could read in the Uisen language — there was writ: <u>Darkness and light are both alike to the blind, but warmth and cold are felt by everyone.</u> This was one of the nine tenets of faith for the followers of Cuthain, and Heiro Manan believed it to be the most appropriate for a welcoming front door — the other eight were rather more forceful.

Beyond that door, the abbey opened into a rounded tower base with six wooden benches inset into the walls, where the weary might remove their shoes before wandering further into the nave. The clerics of Cuthain were supposed to walk unshod by holy tradition, but on floors of winter stone, slippers were (guiltily) preferred. Mathias always went barefoot. It was, after all, a decree of his faith. So he obeyed it.

Flanking the entry tower was a little vestry. In it was a meeting table surrounded by three built-in wardrobes. The room had been constructed as a place for the faithful to conduct private business, but it was only ever used as a storehouse for sodden cloaks and muddy boots. The room was overcrowded with furnishings and smelled perpetually musty.

The nave was a simple one, so far as naves go. Cuthain is a blind god, and his clerics are not themselves well known for ostentatious ornamentation. That said, the two grand pillars supporting the center beam that crossed this lofted space were carved into an intricate scene of ocean voyaging. The curving arches that ornamented the stone walls were likewise carved in bas relief scenes of the rewarded faithful and the enactment of punishment for wicked men. Although Cuthain was blind, his religion was well-funded, and it never hurt to impress visitors. The nave was where the masses would one day gather in prayer, and it had been built for reverence and not for comfort. The large space was drafty and echoed underfoot.

To the east, a squat set of stairs ascended to an even more impressive chancel, upon which the initiated would sermonize the crowd below with four grand pillars to either side and statues of the Triad looming behind them. It would appear as though the Three True Gods were towering in artful support just over the shoulders of their priests — with Cuthain in the middle, of course — and that was as it should be.

A second smaller set of stairs descended three steps to an ambulatory that ringed the chancel from behind. This walkway allowed visitors and priests to stroll below those impressive windows of cut and leaded glass that lit the chancel from above with colorfully illuminated scenes of submission. Recessed into the eastern wall of the ambulatory was a carved stone seat about thirty feet long, with a large window running full length behind it. This window was different than the stained-glass windows inset into the wall above. The panes were not leaded, for one, but encased in a tracery of wrought iron. They were as clear as glass is made, and thicker than a finger. The space was known as the Forest Vigil and spoken of with as much careful reverence as any altar. It was inset in the wall behind the backs of the statues of the Triad on the raised chancel. The purpose of this seat was to watch the forest for trouble. It was understood that although God and the Goddesses are infinitely wise, they are also infinitely busy. The faithful must watch Their backs to protect Their churches from whatever lurks in the darkness of the forest.

The ambulatory ended at a construction site: a plain stone chapel where the grand fireplace would someday do its best to warm a space that was far too large for it. Because of the local carpenter's boycott that Bergrem arranged, the room was only partially constructed. One outer wall was complete, but for the empty archway where a door should hang.

That archway led to the cloister arcade outside and had been covered with a heavy oilcloth for more than a year. Pieces of carved but un-hung window arches were stacked in a pile, with one damaged one lying on a cracked sandstone tile where it had fallen from hanging height. The other walls of the chapel looked like the jagged teeth of a broken smile. The garden-facing walls had never been shorn up past the point where wooden joists would be needed to tie the structure of the room together. Green and white lichen stains colored one pillar and the edge of an outer wall. The room was curtained off from the chancel by cloth tarps. When it rained, the water fell unimpeded on the chapel floor, and the winds of winter brought drifting snow indoors*

....

*Talara note_: I hope all this description of the abbey is not overly dull. Mathias insisted upon it and considering that the abbey features very heavily in what happened next, it seems important for you to know your way around. Shortly following, there is a rampaging elemental, and much damage is done, so if you are the sort of reader that is just waiting for the destruction to begin: hang in there. It's coming._

If you grow restless in the meantime, just try to guess what parts of the abbey are going to get smashed and ruined — that should keep you amused for a while, you barbarian. Skip ahead if your attention span can't handle the architectural tour. I hope you don't, but I won't judge you if you do.

....

South of the nave and chancel were two of the more unusual features of the abbey. The first was a half-room that jutted at an odd angle from an otherwise straight wall. Inset into the ground in the center of the floor was a massive set of doors, which looked at a distance like a gleaming metal rug. The doors were solid iron, ten paces long and eight wide, and every inch of their surface was etched with visions of the afterlife. These stately doors were the most impressive in the chapel by far: they had cost a small fortune to cast and transport. Rarely was this portal to the underworld disturbed, for it took the cranking of a lift-wheel and two pulley chains mounted to the ceiling to hoist them open. Beneath those doors were a short flight of stairs that opened into a descending tunnel, which eventually made its way to a large cave system. Those caves formed the rooms of a natural crypt for the future generations of dead clerics and were part of the reason the abbey had been built on this spot. A small subterranean stream flooded some of the deeper grottos entirely. Mathias had explored the caves only perfunctorily, as he was a thin and superstitious boy, and found that a lot of time spent barefoot underground gave him chills.

The far wall of the Crooked Room (as it came to be called) was inset with empty alcoves. These were meant to house future tombs for high-ranking patrons in the expensive honors of death.

The second unusual feature was the apse. It was built that way so that any who entered the abbey might first set eyes on the apse before all else. It was a semicircular arched recess — half a room — and dovetailing the curve of the ceiling was a beautifully carved lintel portraying Cuthain as he sailed towards Eld. There were also ornate stained-glass windows patterned with scenes of sunset and sunrise. Two curved benches of stone sat below them.

But what was really meant to draw the eye was a grand well that occupied the center of the room. This was a feature found in each of Cuthain's holy houses and represented the journey over water and the endless pursuit of the intellect. The well was circular and built of stone, fifteen feet in diameter. Joined above the center of it were three arches of exquisitely carved stone, designed so that the twining knotwork carvings hollowed at each knotted center so that colored light from the stained glass passed through the stone arches in patterns of sacred geometry. Suspended below the meeting apex of those arches was a bucket of the finest hammered steel coated in beeswax polish. The well was deep, but water could be seen at the bottom. Into this well, all pilgrims were encouraged to drop their coins to seek the blessings of Cuthain. The "spirit" of the coin would pass through the water and be gathered by Cuthain himself in the lands beyond. The "body" of the coin, now presumably drained of its spiritual endowment, would be caught in a cunningly woven net out of sight just below the water line. This net of coins would be hauled up weekly to contribute to the financial maintenance of the abbey.

On the west end of the nave, a short passageway opened into a humble but well-appointed room with a curving southern wall, inset with a second fireplace. This room was the Sister's Chapel and was devoted to the worship of the twin goddesses that were always seen flanking Cuthain on both sides. The sisters were portrayed as nearly identical, for their nature was complimentary. The elder was called Embara, and her statue was carved of red stone, as the red moon was hers. She was the goddess of creation and was always portrayed with her hands clasped before her, where a secret seed was growing. Around her waist, a belt of braided chain was set, and a circle as red as blood was painted on her bare chest. The younger goddess was known as Hausa, and hers was dominion over death. She was the soul gatherer and the lady of hunting and war. Her countenance was sterner than her sister, but also sadder. Her statue was carved of pale stone to remind her disciples that the yellow moon was hers. She wore a necklace of heavy chain and an open shroud for a garment. A circle as white as bone was painted on her chest.

There were two stout wooden doors in this room: one to the kitchen, inset at the beginning of the abbey's only hallway, and one which opened into the infirmary. The doors were quite mismatched, as they had been harvested from other buildings after the carpenters had all quit the construction project. In fact, none of the wooden doors in the abbey had been built onsite — all had been salvaged from elsewhere. It was an embarrassment to the clerics, but what could they do?

The Sister's Chapel also had a small reredorter, which is just a fancy word that means bathroom. There was a basin for washing hands and two holes cut into stone seats with an empty cavern below them. The bathroom smelled of beeswax candles and incense smoke, and was always cold.

....

The kitchen was a cheery place that was dominated by a very long refectory table on one side; a stove, pantry, dish tub and baking counter on the other. Three small windows were set above the sink for light, and two more were inset near the top of an adjoining wall. There was a large but troublesome fireplace that vented poorly, so that the fire had to always be stoked quite robustly, or smoke would draft backwards and choke out the cook. Classes were often taught at the refectory table, where the smells of baking bread would properly madden young students. Here also, the clerics would gather twice daily to sup and share verses. The kitchen was the only part of the abbey that was already in very regular use, for it had politely been constructed first.

The least occupied part of the abbey had been the infirmary, up until Mathias and Melvin were housed there to recover. Before that time, it had only been used to try to prevent a fatal reaction to a bee sting, which had unfortunately failed. So, there was one grave in the new graveyard outside the abbey wall and perpetually empty cots in the infirmary. The infirmary also doubled as a temporary classroom, with a teacher's lectern near the fireplace and two rows of benches set up in the center. High windows of stained glass lit the large room.

Here were displayed another three statues of the Triad — although these were of moderate size and carved in a more impressionistic way — and an unusually thick door that opened towards the herb garden and wide expanse of lawn at the rear of the building, with the cloister arcade beyond. The lawn was used for sparring in fair weather or for games on those rare days when the clerics felt playful enough to toss horseshoes or play stickwicket. Apple trees had been grafted from the wild ones outside town, and they ringed the lawn like tiny sentries, for they were too young to bear fruit. The lawn was kept level by one fat sheep that the clerics had fondly named Greed.

....

Seen from the outside, Cuthain's abbey had a roof of slate tile, all but the lowest section that shelters the cloister arcade: that was sheeted with wimpled copper and fullered by channels to help shed rain.

The back door opened onto a raised stone porch, with stairs descending from there to a stone platform onto which a brass sundial was set. A bergamot tree grew in a place of honor nearby. It was stubbornly and reverently tended, as it was the only one of its kind to grow on the island outside of the Queen's Garden in Erdo-Usk. A few steps down from there led to the lawn and gardens, with the cloister arcade dividing one from the other. It was a covered walkway that surrounded the rose garden and vegetable patch and ran parallel to the eastern outer wall. Those outer walls were unusually thick and unusually tall. Empty alcove pedestals for future statues were inset into them. There were two gated entrances in the outer wall: one to the north, and one to the south-east. (At least, there were meant to be two, but the south-eastern gate was incomplete, and the collapse of the keystone arch would set that project back even further.) The final room of note was a small calefactory built under the arcade roof, where a cold cleric might warm their hands over a simple iron stove.

There were three stone buttresses arching down from the top of the garden-facing exterior wall. These seemed almost ornamental but for the concealed purpose of sluicing rain or snowmelt through cunning copper pipes that ringed the crenellations. These seasonal slurries were channeled away from the building into little streams that bloated with moss and ate away at the garden path. The building, not yet complete, was already under siege by the encroaching wilderness. Though the priests did their best to keep the larger vegetation hacked low, more simply grew up to replace it. Lichen crept defiantly across every joint of mortar, pushing with relentless intent between the grains of solid rock. In warmer months, little purple toadflax flowers bloomed brazenly at the base of the outer stair. Though the building was not yet finished, it already bore a pelt of vegetation with the awkward weathering look of a beard growing on the face of a young boy. Only the copper roofs of the cloister and the humble bell tower seemed un-weathered. They shone in green and blue swirls of oil and patina. To the eye, they seemed to ripple like the movement of the sea.

....

Here and there, outside the abbey walls, the stumps of once-massive fortress oaks dotted the hillside. They were each the size of a grand and empty stage, now crumbling under the soft decay of time. Where those trees had once shaded out the ground below with the dominance of their canopies, sunlight poured unimpeded over everything. The ground here grew thick with thorny gorse and bracken. Sword fern and seeding bramble surrounded the outer wall, pushing inward with the leaning force of a breaking wave, though it gathered speed so much more slowly. It was all the clerics could do to keep the growth from clearing the tops of the wall. In the few spots that had been successfully cleared, beehives hummed quietly in cold wooden boxes.

....

The Path of the Homsaöl

There was a road that led through the grove, and it had not been there for long. It was nothing like the meandering pathway of a deer, which slips between the trees so gently that it is often spotted only as a ribbon of bent fern fronds. It was a road as mindlessly straight as a knife wound. The road was jarring to behold, as though it had been made by two massive slabs of stone dragging side by side across a mile of understory — which it had. Deep furrows of muddy soil had been pushed up and compressed to either side, and small trees were broken and splintered beneath the great weight that had passed over them.

In one spot, the body of a coney was smashed across the lip of its collapsed burrow — both being pulverized to the point where they were almost unrecognizable as a creature that once ran under the sun and the home it made for itself. The timeless layer of decomposition on the forest floor was churned up in drifts, with the naked earth exposed beneath it. Only where the Homsaöl had intersected the base of a fortress oak or elder hickory did the destructive road veer from a straight course, and there were great gouges in the bark of these giant trees where the stone creature had striven against it in some unknowable fury. At the first point of circumference around the base of those trees, the path would continue onward, always towards the abbey, with a smear of crushed vegetation pasted grotesquely down the center of it.

The Homsaöl was not moving quickly. It did not need to. When the time came — when the place it was born to destroy was in sight, it would charge. But until then, it moved so slowly that lizards strolled across it, convinced that it was still. And yet it pushed the earth up before it in a relentless shuffling scar, and it never tired, and it never slept. The Homsaöl traveled with the rocking slowness of inevitability, and everything that could move got out of its way.

....

The Things They Learned

"The Erdin culture has *stewarded* the growth of our island of Eld from the primitive ancestral backwater it was only three hundred and thirty years ago to the relatively peaceful and lawful agrarian monarchy that it is... *today.*"

Fahru Nariman had a voice that stretched and retreated like a yawn, and he took so much time wandering through the drowsy oration of his history lessons that his students were likely to be lulled into a stupor of distracted daydreams. He rarely gestured or altered pitch when speaking, and had the disquieting habit of ending sentences with an unnecessary pause. He also made infrequent eye contact with his students, instead choosing to speak over his shoulder while staring out the window. His eyes were wet and bathwater gray. His tusking teeth had little gold caps on the ends of them.

"As you well know, the Erdin are regarded as '*the Children of Iron*' and are the undisputed Lords of the West. They rule the various islands of the Améan Ocean, and thus they govern over the '*Children of Water*' with the justice of the queen's... court. What you don't know is the *etymology* of the word Erdin... itself. Etymology is the study of the origins of words and their historical meaning, and the chosen of Cuthain are devoted students of philological... traditions. And of course, that includes the toponymy of the names of... places. The etymological root of Erdin means 'Firstborn of ERO,' which is, of course, the Creator of ...all. *He who was slain in betrayal will arise again in glory, for His body stands for all time as the Iron Tower, and His children still remember His name.*"

These last words were intoned solemnly, but with the detached after-thought of something that is often said but not truly thought about. The Father of History — as he was formally and reluctantly called by his bored students — paused for a ritual moment as his pupils dutifully mumbled the phrase back to him. Eight of the voices came from the two rows of uncomfortable benches where his motley class of farmer's children sat. The ninth child remained mostly silent in his infirmary bed at the rear of the room. He was propped up on pillows and watched the teacher's back with glittering eyes. It was only at the phrase "*for his body stands for all time as the Iron Tower*" that Melvinari joined in the muttered reply. But he spoke the words with an introspective softness, and his voice did not carry to the rest of the class.

"Etymology is an engaging field of linguistic study, to anyone who can boast of a... classical *education*. An understanding of the historical structure of a word helps to unlock the innate power of the spoken... language. Well, it is at least accurate to say that of the Queen's Tongue, the language of *Lùn-Una*. This, as you don't yet know, is the highest form of language known to all of... Homm."

At that, Melvinari snorted with such derision that even Fahru Nariman took notice. He swept his eyes from the window overlooking the garden and raised a disapproving eyebrow at the lean boy in the infirmary bed. Melvin met the aged cleric's stern gaze with a shrug of his shoulders. From the second row of benches, the indentured boy named Tarquin stifled a laugh that turned into a cough. Sitting next to him, Mathias shot him a glare that he intended to be withering but instead looked a bit confused and cross-eyed. This set Tarquin off even more, and he began to shake with the quiet wheezing of suppressed laughter. Mathias looked away and bit the corner of his lip with a frown. A cleric of Fahru Nariman's status should never be so disrespected!

All the while, as the other children shuffled awkwardly on their hard benches, the paralyzed mason's son and the Father of History stared each other down in silence. It was Fahru Nariman who broke the gaze at last, turning back towards the window and continuing on with his droning lesson as though nobody had interrupted him.

"As I was *saying*, Lùn-Una is a challengingly intricate and complex language. It is a language of metaphor and simile that has been artfully culled from the memory of the Immortal Language, which was used to ascribe the true nature of all things onto the tablet of... creation *itself*. Contained within the language are legendary layers of Erdin cultural record predating the settling of Eld, which are otherwise... rare. Most born of lower social status know very few words of Lùn-Una, for it has always been reserved for nobility, other members of the highest echelons of social strata... and we lucky clerics, who study it most diligently down to the smallest morpheme through the application of... etymology. Clerics that serve all three deities of the Trinity can speak it with varying levels of... fluency. But only *Cuthain's* clerics are trained in the necessary intricacies of writing the symbols down in their successive layers of... meaning. It is a rarified and *noble* task."

Here the self-proclaimed Father of History clenched his palms together just below the small of his back and stared out the window solemnly. Even Melvinari seemed impressed, for the room remained hushed until Fahru Nariman resumed.

"There is, *of course*, a second Erdin language that is widely spoken by laborers all over the island and across many others. The language is called Uisen, and it is a simple, almost brutal language that evokes little etymological interest in educated circles. And yet, it is a very practical language for the conduct of commerce. It contains directions, sums, a wide array of words for fishing, battle, farming and... business-"

Fahru Nariman coughed into his sleeve for a moment: the hacking brattle of a pipe smoker's lungs. Then he took a sip of cold tea from a ceramic mug on the shelf of his wooden lectern and continued.

"-Or simple emotional states. This language is spoken everywhere that is governed by the queen. The common language of Eld, which is known as 'Common,' was apparently originally a native dialect of Dekai, but has been broadly transformed by Uisen... terms. This, of course, is the language in which I am currently orating and the language through which your ears are hopefully gathering and retaining this... knowledge.

"Many toponyms, for example, that might be familiar to you on a map of our island are Uisen names that were installed during the original manifest of Erdesh colonization that brought... civilization to the island. *Fahru Dornen*: the peninsula called Father's Hand, which wraps protectively around *Ummu-Baya*: the Bay of the Mother. *Hälling Ghora*: the Dancing Mountains. *Kräke* is Uisen for Crow, and each is used interchangeably in Common; nearby is the aptly named Lake of Feathers: in the Uisen vernacular, *Loc Luma*. The list goes on: *Bjalkr-Bec* is a Uisen name so old that it translates into the simplistic term 'Beam-Over-Stream,' which is, ironically, meant to describe the magnificent architecture of the Great Bridge. Uisen does not have the word for such a bridge in it, and Common makes up for where Uisen... left off. But there is a certain brash poetry to be found there too; some might-"

The door to the infirmary — and the temporary classroom contained therein — creaked cautiously open. Standing in the doorway was a thin girl with dark hair and skin tones in a cinnamon range. Although she had similar coloration to a Dekai at first glance, there was something about her features that seemed enticingly foreign. The sharpness of her nose, her high cheekbones perhaps, or the unusual leaping thickness of her expressive eyebrows. In a classroom of gawking farm boys, she looked about as out of place as a deer swimming laps in the ocean. Talara's glance ran rapidly down the row of gawping faces, then she strode up to the startled cleric with a wrapped bundle in her arms. Before Fahru Nariman could utter a word, she quickly said:

"Greetings! You must be the Father of History? I am called Talara; I am recently in residence at the Welcome Holm and would like very much to stay there a while, but to do so, I must bow to the earnest wishes of Yrsa the Innkeep — you surely know her — who *insists* that my worth as a citizen of Our Queen's Empire would be greatly improved by any manner of proper education, for you see-"

(and here she drew a deep breath and prattled on rapidly before he could respond)

"-I am otherwise stranded in moral limbo as a godless heathen, whiling away my days in the baseness of my inelegant ignorance. And I know you might *naturally* have objections to allowing a girl into your learned program of studies, and this is only right that you, at first consideration, would-"

(as Fahru Nariman prepared to interject, she unwrapped the bundle in her arms and exposed a bottle of that infamous golden mead that Yrsa so prided herself on brewing. She handed it over to Fahru Nariman, who clutched at it immediately)

"-And as Yrsa believes so strongly in the need to have me educated to save myself from sin, she has offered you one bottle of Innkeeper's-"

(here, Fahru Nariman began to mumble a weak objection, so Talara rushed on)

"-One bottle of cask-conditioned Innkeeper's Private Reserve *every time* you let me sit in on your lesson and do my humble best to gain the benefit of what snippets of logic and moral reasoning I can glean from so learn'd a cleric as yourself. She entreats you therefore, as a would-be patron and grateful friend of the abbey, to do what is most charitable and right for an otherwise *hopeless* case such as myself."

Fahru Nariman stammered while his small class looked on agog. Then he glanced down at the bottle in his hands, and for one moment, the kids all saw a flash of genuine emotion on his face: greed for the mead that was almost lustful. Then it was gone, and he smiled a tight little benevolent smile and said:

"Although the traditional dictum of our order discourages such *intermingling*... it would be troublesome and unbecoming to deny such a provincial request from an important... friend like Yrsa. Please take a seat in the furthest back row and give my warm regards to the Innkeeper. ... Now, let us continue where I left off. Uisen makes its way even into the politics of the Common tongue, for is not *Portuan* the most direct way to describe the presence in that glad city of the thegn's sea throne?"

As instructed, Talara walked through the assembled boys to sit in the back of the second row. But while the Father of History began to drone on comfortably again behind her, she caught Mathias' glance and winked at him covertly, then rolled up her eyes and stuck out her tongue. Mathias blushed to the very tips of his toes. Nearby, Tarquin nudged him in the ribs and grinned. Mathias surprised himself by grinning back.

Tarquin leaned over towards her when he was sure Fahru Nariman was lost in a pontifying moment and whispered, *"My name's Tarquin. You're called Talara, right?"*

"Nope." She whispered back. *"I'm Mathias. Talara is the blond kid sitting next to you. Isn't she cute?"* Then she reached out and pinched Mathias' cheek.

Mathias giggled, then blushed and clapped his hand over his mouth. Tarquin snickered and poked Mathias again. Fahru Nariman glanced over his shoulder and frowned. But he could not place the origins of the giggle, so he continued on with his lecture. Mathias slumped down gratefully onto his bench with a sigh.

About a minute later, Talara leaned back towards Tarquin and whispered, *"Why do you have so many bruises on your face and arms?"*

"Because the guy who owns me keeps hitting me with a wooden sword."

"That's terrible!"

"My fault. I'm still learning how to block and parry. Well, mostly my fault, anyway. He's sort of a bad person. Sometimes he does it on purpose, just because he can."

Talara nodded somberly, remembering the cruel man she had seen buying Tarquin below her window. She wondered if she would ever tell him that she recognized him from Dunmarsh. *Probably not.* She thought to herself. *What good would it do to remind him of that night?*

Tarquin leaned over again, but before he could speak, Mathias put a finger to his lips and pointed at Fahru Nariman. Tarquin grimaced, but remained quiet. The lecture droned on.

A few minutes later, Talara leaned over to Tarquin again and whispered:

"Did you know that 'Tarquin' is actually a bad luck name? In Rhymi-ran, it means, like... a type of restlessness that leads to ill-fortune. Kind of like wanderlust, but more foolish."

Tarquin cocked an eyebrow, and whispered, *"Oh yeah? Is that really true?"*

Talara nodded mournfully and patted his hand. *"Truly true. So, you probably should change your name to something luckier. Maybe you wouldn't get so many bruises."*

Tarquin grinned and glanced over at Melvin. *"Well, since the names 'Talara' and 'Mathias' have already been claimed twice today, I guess I'll have to swap mine too. You can call me 'Melvin'. That guy in the bed is stuck being Tarquin now."*

Melvin at first appeared to not be listening. Then he leaned in quietly and whispered, *"Shit, I'm bad-luck-Tarquin now? That must be why both my legs got all busted up!"*

Talara and Tarquin barely managed to stifle their giggles, but once again, Mathias' mirth squeaked out from between his fingers. Fahru Nariman glanced in irritation at the boys on the front bench, who shrugged and pointed behind them. The cleric glared vaguely at the back of the classroom before turning back around to the lectern.

A minute of droning lecture continued until: *"Psst — Mathias."* Mathias and Talara both glanced over at Tarquin. *"No, sorry: I meant new-girl-Mathias,"* Tarquin whispered. Mathias held his finger to his lips and desperately tried to hush Tarquin, but he ignored him and kept on whispering, *"I've decided that I am going to have to become an exception-ally lucky person to compensate for my bad-luck name."*

"Great. That sounds like it's going to work out really well for you." Talara replied, winking.

"You guys, please shhh." Mathias whispered. But they ignored him.

"I hope so. What does the name 'Talara' mean?"

Talara leaned in and whispered grandly, *"Oh, it means: 'Gracious Queen of the Gullible Farm Boys.'"*

Tarquin grinned and poked Mathias in the shoulder. *"Look at how lovely your new name is! You just got elected queen!"*

Mathias squirmed. *"You guys, seriously, please don't get-"*

"MATHIAS." Fahru Nariman barked, punctuating the offending name with a whap of his pointing stick on the lectern. Mathias and Talara both startled in their seats. Melvin chuckled.

"I expect better of you, *ordanian*." Fahru Nariman huffed. "It is your duty to set an example of appropriate decorum for our newest ...student. Unless you like talking so *much* that you would rather come up here and teach the rest of this lesson?"

Pale and blushing in spots, Mathias scrunched down into his seat. "...n-n-no thank you, *fahru-* Father of History, sir. I'll... I promise I will do better."

"You'd better." Fahru Nariman replied sternly. Then he sighed and turned back to the lectern. For a moment he stood there with his hands folded in his sleeves, apparently lost in thought. Then he lifted up the innkeeper's bottle of mead that Talara had brought.

"Let us recess for lunch while you children take the time you apparently need to... compose yourselves into respectful students again. I should deliver this bottle to the kitchen... anyway. I'll return shortly."

Fahru Nariman tucked the bottle into the sleeve of his robe and strode out of the room without a backward glance.

Talara snickered. "I bet the kitchen never sees a drop of that mead."

Tarquin chortled. Mathias glared at him and slumped his head into his hands.

He would have liked to believe Fahru Nariman wasn't just leaving the classroom to go drink that mead, but he knew that he was. Mathias closed his eyes and felt the sting of unfairness at being publicly shamed for disrupting the lecture. Tears prickled in his eyes, and he felt very alone in the suddenly boisterous classroom.

Then a cool hand rested on the back of his hot neck. He glanced up in surprise. Above him stood Talara, who leaned in and murmured conspiratorially:

"Don't worry, Mathias. He'll come back smiling in a half hour, and the

lecture will be a few glasses of mead less boring. You did great."

Tarquin stepped over and patted his shoulder too. "Yeah, sorry we got you in trouble, kid. But you've got to admit: the afternoon just got a bit funnier, right?"

Mathias nodded slowly, admitting to himself that this was true. Then, almost shyly, he glanced over at Melvinari in his infirmary bed. Melvin was staring right at him, and when their eyes met, he smiled.

"I'm glad you shut that pompous windbag up for a few minutes, Mathias. I've never met a cleric who more thoroughly enjoys the sound of his own voice."

"Ya, me too! I was worried that lecture would never end — I was half asleep before Talara showed up, and Mathias suddenly became funny." Tarquin said gratefully, rummaging through Mathias' lunch sack. "Hey Melvin: do you want to join us outside for a bit? I'd like to feel some sunlight on my face before the rain comes back again."

Melvin considered for a moment. "That actually sounds great. Thank you." He replied, hoisting himself up on his elbows. "I haven't been outside at all since... you know. The accident. I'm afraid you'll have to carry me out there, though. Maybe you and Mathias can-"

"I'll carry you." Talara chimed in. "I'm stronger than Tarquin, anyway."

"No, you *aren't*." Tarquin snorted.

"I bet I am." Talara grinned. "I do an hour of strength and balance training every morning. I could walk from here all the way back down to the Welcome Holm in a handstand, if I wanted to."

"Bug shit. I bet you couldn't make it to the end of the garden like that."

"Watch me!" Talara turned and marched towards the door, with Tarquin following.

Melvin interrupted. "How about you two goons take turns impressing each other by picking me up and getting me outside instead?"

"Oh: right! Sorry Melvin, I forgot about-" Talara began.

"Me first!" Tarquin crowed, scooping up Melvin like a sack of potatoes and rushing out the door with him jostling over one shoulder. Tarquin and Melvin's laughter disappeared through the garden doorway.

Talara started after him, and then stopped at the door. She turned back to where Mathias was sitting.

"Aren't you coming? I brought food to share."

Mathias stood up slowly. "I probably shouldn't, I've got-"

"Besides," Talara interrupted "someone has to witness how much stronger I am than Tarquin."

"Well, Melvin is already-"

"Melvin is busy being carried. He is the competition, not the audience. We need you out there with us!"

"But... I-"

"Come on, Mathias." Talara said firmly, taking him by the arm and tugging him towards the door. "You rescued me from dying on the Wayward Road, and now you're stuck with me. By the way, in case you didn't know: you blush a lot. You're doing it now. It's probably the pale skin though, don't you think? I wonder if I blush as much as you do, but my dark skin hides it better?"

"*I... I'm pretty sure it was the fox that saved you.*" Mathias mumbled.

"What?"

"On the Wayward, I mean. I wouldn't have known you were there if I hadn't followed the fox into the old orchard. She was waiting by you. I think... she knew something was wrong, and was trying to get my attention."

Talara squeezed his arm. "Was it the fox that got me up onto the very unusually stinky donkey and took me to the Welcome Holm? Was it the fox that made sure I got fed, and traded all his honey away and then left the money he got for it in my tip hat so that I had a place to sleep out of the cold?"

"...No." Mathias said quietly.

Talara reached out and lifted his chin until she was looking into his mismatched eyes. She felt an involuntary shiver go up her spine, but gripped his arm all the harder for it.

"I truly believe that fox helped me get to the orchard — that she guided me there in a way that I am still trying to understand. But it was you that got me to Holm, and gave me the chance to prove myself to Yrsa. I am alive to enjoy myself today because of *you*. Thank you, Mathias. You are my very first friend that I've ever had."

Mathias smiled crookedly, and a single tear rolled down his cheek. He tried to wipe it away, but Talara was holding both his hands.

"You're my first friend too."

"It feels *good*, doesn't it?" Talara laughed and shook her head, releasing his hands to quickly wipe her own eyes. "To say it out loud, I mean. When something real is happening — something important. To acknowledge it."

"Yes, I suppose it does." Mathias exhaled a gust of breath, not knowing he had been holding it. He glanced around, grateful that the classroom had emptied. Feelings that he didn't have names for yet were stretching his insides in a light-headed way that felt as glad as prayer. He could hear the boys running around outside, whooping and tumbling in the grass.

"Now let's go outside and make some *more* friends! Want to befriend that lame boy and the jolly idiot?"

Mathias glanced at her in shock.

"I'm just *kidding*, cleric! ...Well, not about Melvin being lame — obviously his legs don't seem to be working so well right now, which is really sad. Those guys are fun, though — let's go join up with them before Tarquin eats your lunch. Do you like onions, by the way?"

"Yes."

"I've finally decided I do too. Took years."

"Well, they do have a pretty strong flavor."

"Like me!"

"Um... I guess so?"

They wandered toward the back door.

"Is Tarquin actually a bad luck name? Or were you just messing with him?"

"Totally."

"Wait: do you mean totally *true*? Or you were totally messing with him?"

"Totally."

And with that, she pulled Mathias by the arm through the rear door of the abbey and into the first friendships of his life. Warmed by the winter sunlight on his skin, and the reassuring feeling of her hand on his arm, the lonely weight of isolation finally began to fall away — a weight that he had been carrying unconsciously for all of his life.

....

There were other clerics to learn from and other lessons to sit through in the next few weeks, but no more sunlight to be seen. For more than a

month, the rain was almost constant. Creeks flooded, and fields turned
to shallow ponds.

Cuthain's clerics, still short on visitors in an unfinished abbey, were
happy to spend their afternoons educating the youth of Holm, and appreciated the supportive alms the parents might send. Those youth were
often much less happy to be receiving those lectures. But it beat house-
work and rainy farm chores, so they dutifully slogged up High Hill and
tried to open their minds to a "proper education." They would come in
wet and chattering, bearing whatever donation their parents might send
— a loaf of fresh bread, a jar of soft goat cheese, a few copper knockers,
and once or twice some other sundry that a parent cleaning house might
disguise as a gift. These they would place on the lectern shelf, and whatever cleric was guiding their education for that day would receive the pile
of trinkets with a nod or a frown. Fahru Nariman always made sure to be
present when Talara arrived, smiling at her indulgently and whisking the
bottle of mead away to his private chambers before another cleric had the
chance to claim it.

A great deal of their learning was not from the subjects being taught,
of course. They quickly discovered who amongst them was fidget-prone,
bathed irregularly, or stammered when questioned. They learned who
excelled at learning and who excelled at pretending to learn. They began
to segregate themselves into social groups with pecking orders and preferred seating arrangements. Talara and Mathias, therefore, continued to
find themselves on the back bench with Tarquin and near the infirmary
cot Melvin was trapped in. The four of them did not at first choose to sit
together because they thought they had anything particular in common
— it was the things that they did not have in common with the others that
quickly became obvious.

The front bench was reserved for the two sets of three boys who would
grow up to be exactly what was expected of them. Griffen, Balric and
Everett were the sons of grain farmers and would inherit their farms and
their father's ambitions and prejudices without a second thought. The
three of them bathed irregularly, told crude jokes, and spent half of their
learning time playing pranks on each other. The other three were Devin,
Hosten and another Everett. They were the children of the local butcher,
cordwainer, and cartwright, respectively. And although they were somewhat better dressed than the farmer's sons, they also had no illusions that
the majority of what they learned in their brief time at school would be

of little practical use to them. They were just better at pretending to pay attention and got in trouble less often than the other three.

It did not take the clerics long to realize that they should be addressing their instructive efforts towards the children in the back row, who seemed to be their smartest pupils. Yet what good would it do to educate an indentured thrall, a sullen cripple, and a flippant young bar wench? Their own ordanian was usually a model student, of course... although many of the clerics muttered that the children Mathias was spending time with were a disruptive influence. But the winter was slow, and the clerics were bored, so they shrugged their prejudices aside enough to teach these unusual children the things that they believed would be best for them to know.

·····································

They were taught about counting sums and practiced writing their own names. There were simple reading lessons that were very difficult for many of them. These were lessons that Talara excelled at, and Melvin slept through. They learned a very slanted history of famous battles. They were lectured intently on how good it was for all of them that the Erdin monarchy ruled the island. They learned a great deal about the triad of gods and goddesses known as the Trinity, and why Cuthain was considered by his clerics to be the most important of the three. There were also lessons that were genuinely enjoyable, and these helped deepen their interest in the wider world around them.

There were classes on singing in a group, and the abbey cook led them in a few enormously entertaining culinary courses, one of which ended in a raucous food fight with handfuls of bread dough. (Afterwards, they learned how tedious it is to carefully clean a large kitchen).

There were lessons on the growing and use of herbs. One day Fahru Stromo unrolled a large map of the entire island, and the children crowded around it and stared in wonder. He pointed out the various towns and mountains, and the geography of the four domains that split the island into uneven quarters. Most of them had never seen a map of the island before, and the experience was almost overwhelming. Following that, they were instructed to wander around the abbey with slate and chalk and try to draw an accurate floor plan of the building — which Mathias was unsurprisingly good at.

One night, when there was a break in the rain, they trooped out to the edge of High Hill to observe the hidden pictures that can be made by connecting the stars like dots. Fahru Ascofina, who was surely the most distracted and mellow of the senior clerics, took great care to point out many constellations for them and recited such wonderful stories to describe them all that even Talara was in awe.

The next day Talara announced she had just turned fourteen years old, and, to celebrate her day of life gift, that night they got to have a slumber party in the Sister's Chapel. Tarquin convinced everyone but Melvin to join him in a game where they bounced around in tightly wrapped bundles of their sleeping furs. The point of the game was to go crashing blindly into each other like colliding balls and then fall over into prepared piles of bedding. So they did that: dodging around each other, grunting with impact and whooping with laughter until they were all dizzy. From a distance, they looked like large blind padded worms, giggling and smacking into one another like giant animated pillows.

Melvin watched from his bed, trying his best to enjoy himself as an observer. Caetal was also present that night, as he sometimes was, and split his attention between bowling all the rest of them over onto the bedding pile (he was the biggest and strongest by a fair bit) and sitting quietly beside Melvin. Melvin had not spoken to him since the accident, so Caetal didn't try to make conversation. Just sitting side by side in silence was the best that either of them could manage.

Mathias laughed more than he ever had in his life, even though he got the breath knocked out of him a few times and Talara accidentally split his lip when she fell on him. He careened around blindly, cocooned in blankets and knocking kids over without a thought for his dignity or their feelings. It was a wonderful night; for a moment, he wondered if it was his first *perfect* night that he had ever experienced.

Yet later, as he sat there panting and recovering his breath from so much laughing, Mathias couldn't help but admit to himself that something was missing. He gazed out of the dark window at the even darker forest and shivered, feeling that same gentle tugging of invisible strings that he had felt the afternoon he found Talara laying behind the fox on the Wayward Road. It felt like forgetting a word that he ought to know, or reading a beautiful poem that was lacking the last line. *Something is out there. Something is coming to change us.*

The Things She Learned

Here is the child that no cleric of Cuthain would ever teach, not for all the mead in Holm. This is earlier; winter still, but spring is coming. Time means less to a shapeshifting crow and his foxgirl pupil than it does to the clerics of Cuthain, but the turning seasons mean more. So let us start a bit backwards in the past and catch up rapidly, so that everyone is sharing the same moment again.

....

Crow says: "It all begins underground, where the roots are growing out of sight of animals like you and I that occupy that space between soil and sky. Beneath our feet, time moves more slowly. The deeper you go, the slowered-down it gets. In the Underneath, everything is interconnected by the web of roots and fungus, all lit up with living purpose by pulses of energetic lightning that animates spirit like the contractions of a heart. The blending of that energy is the shared solace that other beings exist — that nothing in the world is truly alone. Like you and I sharing warmth shoulder to shoulder when the wind blows cold."

Crow is dressed in the brown flesh of his grandfather man-shape Djaro tonight, with loose skin and long ropes of white hair. He runs his fingers through his beard, unconsciously preening. By the light of a small fire, his words are steaming in the cold air. Rahyn watches him, and every time he looks away, she steals glances at the stars shining brightly overhead. There has been so much rain lately, it is exciting to see the stars again.

"Because time moves more slowly underground, the lightning crawls. Inside the deep lightning is the energy of life-insistence. But also, *language*; it carries tidings and gossip between the roots of everything that grows. Without this flow-exchange, this conversation, there would be no community of life at all."

"*The lightning crawls underground.*" Rahyn repeats softly. She imagines the forking spread of tree roots all aglow with hidden light and shivers excitedly.

"Plants enslaved by dreams of agriculture do not communicate in the same way as wild plants. They are stunted by the farmer's urge to control — uniformity is the antithesis of *community*. A room full of strangers that aren't given enough time to become friends: you understand? Even planted forests do not behave with the depth of interaction that natural forests do. It takes time, and fungus, to make a community. It is fungi that makes a *forest* possible. A single fungus can cover many miles over the course of centuries, turning an entire grove of mixed plants into one big community."

Rahyn wriggles and scratches at a flea. Djaro nods to himself; scratching what itches is always good. She asks: "Are you old?"

Djaro seems about to say something, then closes his mouth with a snap. He glares at the campfire, muttering. Then he swivels his neck in a rapid jerk; the vertebrae crackle. He sighs contentedly.

"Am I *old*? Compared to everything around us, I am new; I am a chick only recently hatched. But none of us hot-blooded beasts ever make it all the way to 'old' anyway. Old is just young with the blanket of time pulled up a bit closer to the chin."

Rahyn nods. "I hope I live to be as old as a tree. I want to see what everything on Eld looks like then."

Djaro gazes at her thoughtfully. "You just might. Who knows what Twilight runs in your veins? You might outlive me by countless seasons. Or you might kill me today by interrupting my lessons so many times that I finally die of it!"

"Well, I don't want to do *that*. Either of those things."

"Then may we both live as long as our curiosity demands. Where was I?"

Rahyn considered a moment. "Fungus helping other plants become a community."

"Well, hold on. Fungi are not quite *plants*, exactly... they are closer to animals than to plants. In some ways like an insect, and in others like a flower, but in most ways, like nothing else there is. They absorb their nutrients from other sources like we do — meaning they don't make food out of light like plants do. They are an ancient race that came here from elsewhere in the sky, riding on the back of pieces of falling stars."

"*Mushrooms rode down from the sky on the backs of shooting stars?*" Rahyn whispers to herself in wonder.

"To exist is to be in a relationship with *everything*: that's what I'm getting at here, Rahyn. We are able to exist only because we interact. Trees that live together have much longer lives than trees that are born far from the company of other trees. They nourish one another — even a cut stump can be kept alive to regrow again where love exists between trees.

They communicate that love underground through their roots, nursing the severed stump with nutrients for decades. Anyone with a brain can learn a lot from a love like that. Even foxes can learn." He snorts, shaking his head.

Rahyn grins. "Foxes know more than they let on."

Crow cackles. "Ha! Crows can fly circles around what a fox knows, and trees know things that crows can only guess at. It is the reason the Fýrii sought me out to join them in the first place: my connection to the Memories of Crow. All crows share information into a deep well of group memory — it is how we trade news and secrets and warn each other of danger. That collective memory is older than the coming of time to this world and full of fathomless layers of observations from uncounted ancestors of Crow. That said, it is also rife with an indescribable mess of gossip, heresy and outright lies.

"I plunge into Crow Memory carefully when I must, like a diver navigating dangerous undertows. Otherwise, I find myself learning about how unkempt some crow thought some other neighbor crow's nest looked like, and they both lived thousands of years ago. ...A real jumble of opinionated blather in there, actually. But a good place to go hunting for old stories!"

....

It is later. Spring has warmed the snow from the canopy. Rahyn and her mentor are high above the ground, sitting on the broad branch of a fortress oak. The branch is as thick as a road; a step over the edge is a deadly plunge to the forest floor far below. Djaro the Crow is still teaching — always teaching. He knows he is clever, and he likes to hear himself talk.

"Trees can smell and taste — just as acutely as foxgirls and old crows. They warn each other of the leaf-eaters that dwell in the high branches: this is why the animals that feed on leaves must always keep moving downwind from tree to tree, because a tree that feels its leaves being eaten releases a smell into the air that signals the other trees nearby to flush their leaves with distasteful and bitter flavors. See: I will show you. We can try it together."

Djaro picks a leaf for him and for Rahyn, and they chew on them thoughtfully. Then he has them touch their tongues to a few more leaves nearby the ones that they ate. Then they wait a while, because he says to do so. Sunlight dims to pale gray, and a gentle rain begins above the forest. Down here, at the lower branches, the water droplets are fat and full of space between them. Finally, he picks another set of leaves to chew. The taste has changed slightly: a numbing bitterness has crept in.

"With our mouths, we taste the leaves and note the changes between them. We have taken from the tree and, by doing so, have made the annoyance of our leaf-harming presence known to it. Each leaf is like a tiny mouth that the tree can use to taste the world. If we handle the leaf but do not pluck it from the branch, it tastes our hand to make sense of us. If we touch the leaves enough times and do not pick them, the tree will recognize us as a non-threat. Then we get to observe them in their relaxed state and listen to them breathing.

"But if you happened to be a leaf-chewing insect, and not a wide-eyed forest girl, the tree would defend itself against you. It would taste your saliva while you chewed holes in its leaves. It would know you as a threat. While you ate, it would perfume the air around you with scented signals concocted to attract the very predators that feast on whatever type of leaf-chewing insect you happen to be. *It knows you.* It remembers your species of insect. That species has chewed on it, and on its ancestors, for the countless passing of years. The memory of your kind has been transmuted through the slow lightning of shared thoughts in the mycelium web underground. It uses the wind to broadcast that predator-calling scent until those predators arrive, and before you know it: *CHOMP!*"

He snaps his arms down on Rahyn's face like big jaws, and it makes her giggle and squirm. It is hard to sit still for long. Usually, they walk or climb while talking; they are both restless by nature. Life is too exciting to remain in one spot for long.

"*CHOMP CHOMP!* You are a gypsy moth, and this tree just perfumed the wind to help a swooping cuckoo find you! Now you have become a snack. This is why the tree and the clever crow are friends: we use the tree for perches to nest in and branches to rest on, but we give back in return by helping eat the bugs that bite the leaves and burrow into the bark. A crow is a kind friend to have — eating is one of the many things we are so good at!"

Djaro tips his head back and laughs in gravelly gulps, strutting along the branch in a hopping shuffle. Even dressed in the brown old man-shape, he still acts like a crow. His moods are like the wind. They gust suddenly, and you can see the storms gathering from a long way off.

It is easy to understand these lessons, as easy as breathing, and I've learned them quickly. I was in the womb of a tree as it was becoming itself. Tree is a language my spirit is fluent in.

....

For all his chatter, most days pass in silence.

"Look." Crow says, and points at where the wind flutters the torn threads of a delicate spider's web. We watch it from different angles, while the sun moves across the sky. Each thread is lit up with a gossamer rainbow of shifting colors. A change of perspective changes the whole color palate. The spider rebuilds the web with artful diligence. I hold my face as close as I can until the web ripples in and out with my breath. Crow watches me. Crow suddenly eats the spider.

Now I am breathing on an empty web, with a crow beak-hole ripped into it. I wonder why the end of something and it's beginning often look so similar. The torn spider web flutters in the zephyr of my breath.

"Everything is a meal to someone," Crow mutters.

....

Now I will talk at you. Talara asks me to describe those days of time passing. How can I tell you about days? Are we meant to count each beating of our heart? I do not understand the need to do so. There are moments I could share, so many moments that I could mound them into a pile like leaves and you could jump into them. Crow points at everything and says, "Look: do you see? Look closer; look underneath; lay down and look up."

I have learned to hypnotize frogs by laying them across my hand and gently stroking their stomachs. Crow laughs: he thinks it's funny to see them like that. But he does not like that I won't let him eat the frog in my hand. The frog is trusting me to hold it, and I cannot reward such trust with treachery. Crow thinks my sentimentality is stupid, but I think he is just being cranky. Later, he seems to have forgotten he was angry about the frog and flies over excitedly to report that, after weeks of observation, he is now certain that bats always fly to the left of a cave mouth when they come fluttering out on their dusk-dim moth hunts. He demands I find out why they never fly to the right of the cave. I never manage to find out.

I still don't know.

"Look at the trail that a wandering mouse left in the fescue. It has stepped right over a sleeping snail. That snail can sleep for years at a time; can you imagine that? ...Look at the tiny flowers growing in the soil where you just walked.... Look, Rahyn — look here. The rabbits sometimes dance on nights when the moons are thin crescents in the sky — leaping and twisting in the air for the thrill of being able. They are a feast to fox and crow alike, yet they do not fear us tonight. Darkness has made them brave. ...Look: the blackberry thicket is a carnivore plant — look at where the fawn has feasted on berries, and the clumps of thorn-torn fur are whetted with blood. The clever vine creates berries to lure its prey into the thorns. The thorny thicket drinks the blood and makes that iron-rich blood into more berries. And if a trapped animal dies in the thorny thicket, the plant can feast on its body for a generation!"

I discover that I can coax the thorny bushes towards me with whispered promises of blood. They coil around the low branches of trees if I ask them to, so long as I leave a trail to follow in drops of blood. Here is my finger pricked and promises kept. I look where Crow points with a feathery wing. I learn what I can.

....

"Do you mind that I ask you so many questions?" I question.

Crow laughs. "Not nearly as much as it seems like I do. I would be very disappointed if you didn't. Each question is a perfect expression of interest in the mysteries of the world around you. It means you are so interested in being alive that you want to know more about it. That's good! Every animal should feel excited to learn. Questions are good. It's so-called *answers* that you must always try to be suspicious of. Whoever tells you they know exactly how something is or works is probably mixing a little bit of information with a whole lot of opinion. Everything is too spectacularly complicated to know even the smallest bit of completely."

"Except you, right?"

"Well, naturally except me. I know just about everything there is to know, foxgirl! I told you; the Memories of Crow are older than the beginning of time. That is why I was chosen to teach you the ways of the Fýrii: because I am so good at it! That way, if you continue to ask an endless series of perfect questions, and learn how to become as much an extension of the forest as each oak and fern and fluffy treeweet, then you may be selected to be the first of your kind to join the Fýrii."

"Will I get to have bones made of wood, or skin that can turn into a flutter of butterflies?"

Crow laughs. "Yes, and no. You will be very much the same. But also, more. ...Or entirely changed, it's hard to tell what you would become. Once you fill yourself up with the Green so much that it is a part of every tiny space inside you, you can become whatever part of it you wish to be. That is how I learned to be a Bone-Dancer. But more importantly than being able to turn into butterflies, you will be a part of the ancient guardianship of the health of the Eldwood. The Fýrii are only chosen from Fae-blooded, or those who have the timelessness of Twilight inside them. It is the greatest honor that a flea-bitten foxgirl could ever hope for, and you were lucky to be born into a chance to earn that honor!"

I do indeed feel lucky. It is nice to know exactly what your purpose is.

....

"Listen." We have begun a day in the dark of predawn. In the fox form, I can hear the trees gossiping through their roots, like a very low creaking that rolls through the ground, so faint and timbre-deep that only my whiskers can hear it. It is a language that my bones can almost understand, for wood and bone are close cousins. Flesh and earth are likewise related; blood and water, life-desire and sunlight. The canopy of leaves that shivers overhead is as surely the lungs of the island as any set of animal lungs: inhaling from the ground and breathing out clouds.

With my sensitive ears against the bark, I listen to the slow contractions in the xylem veins, as sweetened water is pushed upward towards the crown through arteries of hardening cork. All the forest breathes together, and I breathe with it. And when a tree goes silent, I can hear that too. Not in the quiet that is left when the attention to living is lost; it is the feasting of insects gnawing beneath the bark that can be heard by ears that are listening. I know I should not feel bad for the tree, but it is hard to say goodbye to such a lofty friend.

"*Listen. Listen to everything.*" He is silent and watchful, his black eyes sharp as volcanic glass. They seem out of place in the soft landscape of his grandfatherly face. I believe the crow's white feathers fit his spirit more truthfully — all angles and overlapping points. His feathers fluff when he is angry with me or excited by his own brilliance. Sometimes, when he is sleeping, I creep up to him in fox form and knock him off the branch he is roosting on with a swat of my paws. I cannot help myself; it is just too funny. He wakes up in a squawking tumble, as cranky as a winter badger, and tries his best to peck my head. Then he will fly off in a huff, and I might not see him for days. But while he is gone, I listen to the forest, like he said. I know he will ask me to tell him the story of what my ears have learned when he comes back.

I must always keep learning. Djaro says that animals who stop learning are going to stop living soon after. That is why I must occasionally topple him while he sleeps! I have learned how silly a surprised crow looks like when it is pushed off a branch, and he learns to sleep lightly around foxes.

....

It is later — it is almost now. We are in a storm, and I am a frightened fox tonight. The branches are creaking and snapping overhead; the canopy rocks and shudders. Trees that would be toppled in such wind lean heavily against each other, with branches intertwining, and now I understand why. The evening is lit by lightning and the tumble of echoing thunder. I am digging, frantically tunneling to get underground. But the crow-man scoops me up by the back legs, and I cannot help but bite him. I am no lap creature to be held like that. So, he grabs me by the ruff of my neck and says,

"Do not be afraid. The sky rages, but the trees will calm it soon. Do not be afraid, Syrahana-yerall-aneh. Be brave for Rahyn so that I might teach her something worth knowing."

The fox shape kicks and twists, but an undignified dangling by the ruff is enough to get the point across, and eventually, fur retreats from bare skin and I am Rahyn again. Djaro waits patiently through the transformation. Sheets of rain drift and recede around us.

When I am enough myself to wrap my arms around my knees, Djaro speaks. "Every creature sees things differently. Colors that are visible to the crow are not the same as what the fox can see. The human child who hugs her knees sees more colors than she will as an adult, and humans already choose to see so little. Poor old Djaro can see the shadows thickening under the leaves, but the grays and blues are blending together these days. Age steals colors from us."

The crow-man pauses and cocks his head to one side. His eyes screw up in concentration and he mumbles a question to himself. He scratches thoughtfully. "I feel like a snack. What were we talking about?"

"Colors?"

"Why were we talking about that?"

Djaro puffs his feather cloak up and preens at his rain-whetted mustache. Another flash of lightning flares somewhere away in the woods, and a splintering sound crackles into hearing behind it. Firelight pulses between the trees.

Djaro and I make our way towards the light at a leisurely pace, as the rain is falling steadily now. The lightning tree is hard to miss. It is a purple pine — a small one too, barely shoulder height to a fortress oak. The outer bark is lightly scorched, but the lightning strike has split one side of it wide open, and a fire is burning inside the wound. It is morbidly mesmerizing, watching the flames burn the heartwood from the inside out. Running upward from the flaming split is a forked scar of cambium, pink and pale, where the bark has been blasted away. I feel the heat on my face. Rain and my tears are beginning to mingle. Djaro, on the other hand, wanders around the base of the tree like a proud father, cawing and nodding and patting it with his gnarled hands. He seems unconcerned by the fire and uncaring that the tree is dying from it.

Something rises in me that I have not felt before. It is not as hot as anger, but it burns. I would later learn to think of it as a sense of "injustice," but at the time it felt like indigestion. While Djaro is distracted, I lay my head and hands on the pink lightning scar. The rain falls on my eyes, the fire splutters just above my head, and I'm speaking words I have borrowed from nowhere: words beyond meaning. They sound like water running through cork and are full of the pleading of a young heart. I feel that pleading spirit pouring through my hands and into the purple pine. Abruptly the squelching hiss of thwarted fire can be heard from inside the tree, and plumes of smoke roil out. The flames are being doused! Djaro stops cooing to himself and rushes over. By the last of the spluttering firelight, we can see that the hollowed gouge inside the tree now sparkles as brightly as the inside of a split geode. Thousands of droplets of watery sap have risen to the surface of the charred walls. The fire is snuffed as suddenly as it began. All that remains is the quiet hissing of thwarted heat, and my rush of pride at my accomplishment.

I turn to Djaro excitedly, expecting praise. What I receive instead is a slap across the face that knocks me off my feet. He is so angry that when he tries to yell at me, all that comes out is a guttural croaking sound. I lay on the ground where I fell. I can taste copper and my cheek is burning hot, like a secret fire has been lit under my skin.

I stare at him in hurt amazement. When he collects himself enough to speak, the transformation into a large white crow is already underway. His face is stretching around eyes like pale disks, and white feathers are blooming from his neck. But his voice still carries the very human taint of judgment.

"Wretched, stupid human! We do not interrupt the ritual of lightning. We must not meddle in such things! It is courageous to burn in the battle between soil and sky. Crow knows what stupid foxgirl does not. *Kreeach!* Humans meddle, always meddle — so much need to control things that should not be controlled. *Graaak*: do not be fox-stupid and human-stupid too, or there will be nothing left for me to teach you, and then you must go away to the Nameless Place, where humans go who know too little and yet too much. They will come for you, and take you away, and you will never return again in this life. And where will I be then? Alone, stupid fox: that's where. Alone and talking to myself! *Krake achakala craw!*"

He turns and strides off, his words failing into grackling caws, his shoulders hunched and diminishing in size as he goes. Then, still cawing with anger, he tumbles forward into a series of hops, launches onto wing, and flies above the rain and out of sight.

I watch him vanish behind the clouds, still rubbing the sting out of my throbbing cheek. But it is not the pain that troubles my mind or coils like a low warning in my guts.

"What is the Nameless Place?" I whisper aloud.

....

The Games We Played

Day after day, the rain continued to drench the valley of Holm. The snow that had blanketed the ground for months vanished, carried away into the river by slurries of dead leaves and displaced topsoil. The river Tanis swelled to just below the Orchard Bridge. At the highest point of the arch, a foolhardy child could lean way over the rail and almost touch the water rushing by. The river was ruddy with the stain of captured clay, and large branches bumped into small trees as all were swept away down towards the Trask and from there out to sea. Travel along the Wayward slowed to a trickle as the rain continued to flood out the lowest elevations of the road, and traditional roadside camping spots turned into a patchwork of small bogs.

In Holm, the damage to houses and fields was a growing cause for alarm. Most of the farm fields were now underwater. Basements had flooded out all over town, and overflowing outhouses were leaking night soil grotesquely. There was a fetid smell of decay that flavored the valley air during the few hours that the rain would let up.

At the Welcome Holm, Eorik the stableman had begun to sandbag the steps leading up to the front door, and Talara encouraged him to convince Yrsa to hire Tarquin and Caetal as strong young backs to help transfer all the keg barrels up to higher shelving and out of standing water.

The mood in the town was strained with anxiety. Only once before in living memory had the Tanis overflowed its banks, and when that last happened it had collapsed barns, damaged homes, and drowned many who could not swim. For if the river flooded, it would mean that Loc Enum itself was flooding and then the whole area would quickly end up under a few feet of flowing water. It had flooded at night the last time, and the rushing water had been a deadly surprise to the sleeping hamlet. Not again; this time, the town was determined to make a plan and work together to protect their homes from the pitiless deluge.

The next night was chosen for a town meeting, and the mayor's barn was selected to host it. Yrsa had argued that the Welcome Holm would be the more hospitable spot for a meeting, but the mayor wisely reasoned that with nerves as frayed as they already were, a few too many beers could bring the sour mood to a quick boil. Yrsa acquiesced. When the following night arrived, most of the adults in Holm carefully slogged their way toward the mayor's house for what was surely going to be a long night of passionate shouting amongst neighbors. Children were either shut in at home or excused from chores. A few were encouraged to head up to higher ground at the abbey, and the clerics agreed to keep them overnight until a plan to contain the swelling river could be discussed. The next few days would almost certainly include digging channels and filling sandbags, but for the night, it was best if the children stayed away and let the adults handle the important business of shouting at each other.

....

Liam had already been gone for four days on some clandestine business for the rangers, and left Tarquin in the care of the clerics as an uninvited house guest. Melvin was still unable to go home, though his grieving father checked up on him regularly and paid the clerics for his continued care. Talara had been excused from her duties at the tavern for the evening, and even Caetal was at the abbey that night. As always, his presence there was a secret carefully kept from his parents.

It had been easy to avoid their scrutiny lately, for his father Bergrem continued to suffer from the bronchial affliction that had confined him to bed for weeks. His coughing was painful even to listen to for long; his mother Nura would be at the meeting in Bergrem's place. Although she felt conflicted about leaving him alone, it was obvious from her thinning temper these days that she needed a break from playing full-time nurse-maid to her sick mate. Caetal was, therefore, only too glad to keep away from home.

Griffen, Hosten and Balric were also at the abbey that night. Griffen and Balric had been "encouraged" to help prepare the evening meal in the kitchen because they were caught kipping bread and honey from the larder. The cook told them crossly that they were volunteering to assist on the stew prep, or each would feel the sting of a rather large ladle on their backsides for their thieving. The boys wisely chose to chop veggies and stir the pot, which left only Hosten to join the other kids in playing a game that Mathias had devised for them to pass the time until dinner was ready.

The rest of the clerics had gone down the hill to attend the town meeting, as the abbey would be a likely gathering place if the floods got out of hand. Besides the cook, only Fahru Fren, who limped on a club foot and was too old to travel in the rain, had elected to stay behind and keep a vague eye on the children. In actuality, he retired to his chambers for the evening in the barracks down the hill and snored so loudly that he slept through all of what was to come.

....

At first, Rahyn had been deeply excited by the Homsaöl. It was immense, and powerful, and she herself had taken part in its supernatural birth. Yet, as it slowly ground its way through the forest, she felt a growing sense of unease. Daily she had spent time watching it from as close as she dared — perched on branches above it or gazing at it from behind a tree trunk. Although it moved with the slowness of melting ice, she was always aware of the secret thrumming of its petrified heart. The creature was purposeless but for a single objective, and all the forest around it was being damaged by its passing.

When she was first told of what the Fÿrii were gathering to create, she had imagined the Homsaöl would be like the Fae guardians of old stories. In those tales, a brave Fÿrii would summon the spirit of stone to protect themselves from attack or overthrow those that would wish to do the living world harm. But this creature seemed less like a defender and more like a monster every day. Rahyn could not help but wonder how attacking the abbey without warning was any different than attacking the forest without cause. She had never been one to dwell on the difference between justice and vengeance; both behaviors are irrelevant to the animals of the forest, and Rahyn was as close to one of them as a two-legged girl can get. Such unnatural thoughts were troublesome to her, and her dreams became branchy with doubts and the dark creaking of ill portent.

Without Djaro around to guide and lecture, her days filled with a type of uneasy listlessness that she had never known, and for the first time, a feeling of loneliness as well. When she was not tending to her grove or marking the slow progress of the Homsaöl, she often found herself just behind the garden wall of the abbey, peeking over the top to watch the clerics in secret.

She noticed children playing together in the yard when the rain did not drive them indoors. On the night they sat on the hillside stargazing and telling stories of the pictures they made, she was hidden nearby so that she could hear every word. The foxgirl perched behind a flowering wintersweet shrub, gazing up at the stars with the same curious wonder as the other children. She hadn't ever tried to make pictures out of stars, and now that she knew how, she could never unsee the constellations again.

Amongst the gathered children, she recognized the dark-haired girl she had saved on the Wayward Road. Sitting by her side was the blond boy that Rahyn (in the fox shape) had lured over towards the apple orchard so that the girl would be cared for by her own kind. But wasn't Rahyn her kind too? She forgot, sometimes, that she was mostly human. On that night, with her arms wrapped around her knees, she strained to hear their stories and strongly wished that she could sit nearby and be welcome amongst them.

As the path of the Homsaöl covered the last distance towards the abbey, Rahyn finally realized the full danger of what might happen. The creature had begun to move faster, and was now nearing the edge of the abbey clearing. Soon, all too soon, the building itself would come into view. And when that happened, the elemental that she had helped create would smash that stone house to ruin, with all those children inside.

Rahyn did not care one bit about the abbey itself. She had been raised to hate the sight of it, and so she did. If the Homsaöl were to tear it apart stone by stone, the forest would regrow all around it until the memory of the abbey was swallowed up forever in the endless green. But those children would die unless she warned them. She had to figure out a way to do so, and she was out of time. Night was falling, and rain was dripping through the forest canopy. In the highest window of the abbey, just coming into view, a candle flared into light. Rahyn felt the Homsaöl shudder once. Then a deep grumbling began, so low inside it that it was almost below the range of her hearing. A momentary panic of indecision tore through Rahyn. Then she felt the heat of the fox shape beginning to boil up inside of her on its own accord, and she turned towards the abbey and ran.

Sometimes she could not control the transformation into the fox form. Under too much stress or unexpected danger, she often found the shape rapidly overcoming her. When this happened, there was great pain in her stretching joints, and it was all she could do not to throw up or pass out from it. Sometimes the change even happened from vivid dreams while she slept, and she would wake up disoriented and running on four paws, miles from where she had laid down. This was such a time, in a jolt of stress and the slowing of a moment that felt like dreaming. The fur began to ripple up over her body. She fell to all fours on contracting limbs, crying out in a shrill bark of frustrated pain.

How would she warn the children now? The fox form made communication difficult, and after even just a few minutes, it was hard to recall human cares. She had waited too long to decide to help, and now, in the other body, she may not remember to bother. In the last moments before a girl became a fox, she looked back and saw the hulking monstrosity of the Homsaöl crouched at the edge of the forest. A pale ghostlight had begun burning in the empty hollows of its eyes.

....

"Now, please close your eyes."

Mathias paused from his instruction for a moment to blow out the flaming match from the prayer candle he had just lit in the tower window. He had to blow at it a few times before he got it extinguished. Caetal snickered.

"This game is one I've only ever played alone, and I know this place quite well, so the rest of you are going to have to be careful. Ok, actually, how about I keep my eyes open for safety, and I will make sure none of you walk straight into a wall or fall down the privy or something."

Tarquin made a falling noise with a splatting sound effect at the end of it; Caetal and Hosten laughed appreciatively. Talara glared at the three of them. She had been taught it was very rude to interrupt someone when they were telling a story or trying to explain a game. Mathias continued on as though he hadn't heard them.

"Ok, here's how the game is played. I have identified twelve primary smells that are most obvious when walking through the Abbey at this time of year. I also have privately made a list of another sixteen or so secondary smells, which are harder to guess but are also present if you really use your nose. You must keep your eyes closed the whole time you are wandering around, and really try your best not to cheat, or the game isn't any fun. In fact, if you are worried you might cheat compulsively, here are some strips of cloth to cover your eyes with. Melvin is going to be here — the infirmary is home base, by the way — and he will have a slate to write down all the smells you collect and tally up the total points you each earn."

Caetal grunted. "How do you earn points from smelling things? That's wuh... w... that's dumb."

Mathias blushed and stammered: "Well, I gave this a lot of thought.

The way I was going to suggest we can keep score is that each of the twelve primary smells are worth one point if you can identify them correctly. The sixteen secondary smells are worth two points because they are harder to identify. There is also a bonus smell which is worth a whole five points because you have to be a really brave sniffer to find it. These smells are all able to be collected from inside the abbey, so no going outside is needed. Oh, and don't wander into the kitchen at all; the cook is pretty mad right now, and he will probably whack you with a spoon. So just avoid that area entirely. If it's a kitchen smell, it's not on my list — those smells change too constantly to tally. Um... ya, I think that's it. The winner is whoever can collect the most smells between now and the ringing of the dinner bell. Does that sound good to everybody?"

The kids all nodded, and then started laughing because their eyes were closed, and nobody could see each other nodding. Caetal had privately decided that the 'smells for points' game was actually a pretty great idea and that, as a ranger's son, he was sure to win it. To prove he could not cheat even if he wanted to, he wrapped his eyes with a strip of cloth. Talara and Tarquin followed suit because nobody wanted to be accused of cheating, and each of them privately decided they were determined to win. Hosten also wrapped his eyes but was quite prepared to lift the bottom of the wrap a little if identifying smells by nose alone turned out to be too hard. He was eight years old and hadn't yet learned how self-defeating it is to cheat at games. He still believed that games had losers, and he didn't want to be one.

·····································

Melvin privately wished very much that he could go around collecting smells, and while the other kids were preparing themselves to play, he quietly turned his head away and shed a few frustrated tears, although he was careful to hide it. The tragedy of losing the use of his legs was so fresh for him that everything in his life was still muffled by shock. There he sat, day after day, with his back propped up against a pillow and his useless legs splayed out in front of him. They were as still as stones: deadened to the touch like the severed legs of a stranger.

All around him, life in the abbey turned on an endless rotation of motion, as set and predictable as the slow drifting of stars. Everyone moved freely; even the branches of the trees swayed when the wind danced through them. Not Melvin. Not anymore, not ever again. He felt like a human from the waist up and clay from his hips to his toes; a halfway petrified statue with a trapped soul beating its fists against the walls from the inside. It took all his daily strength not to scream in panic while the world ambled by unimpeded around him.

Sometimes he cried; he could not help it. His tears were a bitter heat that he did his best to keep to himself. It would not do to see the pity that came so easily to the other children's eyes. He did not want to be pitied by his own friends. He would rather have been left for dead beneath the crushing capstone.

....

With a blindfold over your eyes, time becomes slowed and stretched. Every dragging motion of your feet is a wary voyage into unknown darkness. The kids staggered around carefully, a leading foot probing ahead with the cautiousness of a field mouse expecting the sudden drop of a hawk. At first, they were clustered together where the game began, sniffing at the bedding, walls and statues of the infirmary. Tarquin got almost immediately too close to the fireplace, and Mathias pulled him back just in time to prevent most of his eyebrows from singeing right off of his grinning face. Then he made a blind beeline towards the bell tower and the Sister's Chapel, and Mathias lost sight of him because Caetal was moving with incautious speed and almost tumbled into the privy hole of the reredorter. Melvin and Mathias were doing their best not to laugh out loud, but the excited smother of their snickering set off all the children into a giggling fit at how foolish they knew they must look.

One by one, they wandered out of Melvin's sight, with Hosten being the last to go. The little boy blindly lifted the handle of the wrong door, and, missing the abbey entirely, exited out into the garden. Melvin watched him go, smirking to himself. *Already out of bounds. Hosten's game is lost.*

....

Unknowable minutes passed in slow quietude, as the three remaining children explored the abbey sightlessly. Without their ability to see what lay ahead, each of them quickly felt familiarity vanish, replaced by the creeping insecurity of the unknown. Sudden sounds startled. They often froze where they stood, blindly sniffing about in deep breaths as a hunting dog does before the prey is sighted. Tantalizing aromas wafted from the direction of the kitchen, which overshadowed smells that would have otherwise been clear.

Tarquin was quite hungry and was at first annoyed that the warm smells of simmering stew were so distracting. Then he hit on the idea of using the kitchen door as a compass by which to get a sense of direction. He found it easily by following the demands of his gurgling stomach and listening to the muffled griping of the cook. At the door, he laid his hands on the wooden planks and sniffed them deeply. *Oak.* That was a good smell. He had already made a mental note of the caustic smell of the fireplace and would later argue that besides the charred smell of the burning logs and the dusty gray smell of ashes, the fire itself had a vibrant smell too. Mathias and Melvin would disagree.

Tarquin had also collected the smell of Melvin's pillow, the acrid medicinal mix they used to bathe his useless legs, and that almost inde-scribable smell that rain makes when it is hiding in the stones of the walls. He wandered on through the nave and into the small vestry, no longer greatly impeded by sightless disorientation. The smell of beeswax was strong here, and he made a mental note to find out why after the game was over. He also discovered that oak and cedar smell quite different. He stuck his head into a cedar cloak closet and breathed in the scent of wet wool, and then recognized the funk of his own leather boots that he had tossed earlier onto the closet floor. He decided to count *leather* and *Tarquin foot stink* as two different smells and was pleased with himself for thinking to do so.

······································

Talara quickly discovered two things about herself. The first was that she had an unexpected fear of the dark. With the blindfold on, a half-re-membered dream of being submerged in dark water overcame her senses, and she wasted valuable minutes taking small steps on shaking legs. Then she felt a warm presence behind her, and a hand gently squeezed her shoulder. She felt the tickle of Mathias' breath against the hair around her ear, and he whispered, *"You are in the nave, and you are facing the archway of the apse. Just keep going."* Then he took her by the shoulder, moved her about an inch to the left, and steered her gently forward. The touch of his hand flooded her with warm relief of knowing that he was somewhere nearby; she was not alone in the darkness. The feeling of fear passed, and the map of the abbey that she had drawn a week ago bloomed in her head. She moved confidently forward under the lintel archway until her hands felt the carved stone edge of the prayer well.

The second thing she discovered about herself was that she really *was* good at this game. Her excellent memory, trained for years to recall vivid details, painted the room easily in her mind. She collected the cold smell of water coming up from the well, and the oiled iron from the bucket and chain hanging above it. She went on to identify the subtle green smell of the mosses and lichens growing inside the well, the oak smell of the sitting benches, and the aroma of the leaded glass windows behind them. She smiled to herself and began wandering towards the raised platform of the chancel, humming a snatch of an old traveler's tune.

·······································

Caetal recovered from almost tumbling into the toilet and, in doing so, noted the smells of night soil and the pine pitch incense being burned to mask it. Mathias led him by the elbow and released him into the nave, and after a quietly whispered warning not to fall into any more privy holes, Caetal heard him wander off and sensed himself to be alone in that large and echoing space. Enclosed by stone walls, without the shifting wind which carries smells so easily, Caetal suddenly realized he may not be as good at this game as he thought. The purple dark of hunting outdoors at dusk was nothing like the weighted blackness of cloth over his eyes. A vertigo of claustrophobia came over him, and he crouched on the floor like a beast for a moment to breathe through it. With his hands and knees touching the stones of the floor, his sense of internal balance returned, and he felt a bit better. He removed his shirt and his shoes and let the cold currents of air refresh him. By doing so, he noticed the drifting of a definite draft and shuffled forward in a loping crouch with one hand running along the edge of the wall.

He made it down the ambulatory stairs and followed the draft until it led him to the unfinished walls of Cuthain's chapel, where there was no ceiling and rain fell unimpeded onto the floor. Here he stood for a long while, enjoying the shock of water drops as they splattered against his bare chest and the cold of the flagstones underfoot. In this room, remembering what Melvin had told him over the years, he correctly identified that limestone mortar and granite smell differently, and imagined that the marble statues somewhere behind him in the hallway must have their own smell as well. Though the differences in smell of the types of stone were very subtle, it was also detectible, and so it ought to count towards his point total.

With the wind blowing in from the cloister gardens, he was also able to identify the smells of grass and soil easily, and the more exotic smells of those few plants that flower in the winter. The bright but slightly tangy odor of the fairy primrose blossoms; the indolic fragrance of winter jasmine; the spicy citrus of witch-hazel, which grew near the garden wall. The falling rain did little to diminish those smells from reaching Caetal's sensitive nose.

....

Out in the garden, Hosten was not doing well. He had been able to identify the wood smoke from various fireplaces and could smell the dirt and grass and rain, because he was standing right out in it. But after a few long minutes of wandering about aimlessly on the lawn, his boots were wet through to the toes, and he was beginning to shiver. Reasoning that it would do his health no good to wander through a downpour and get blindly poked with thorns besides, Hosten raised the edge of his blindfold and peeked around to make sure he was alone. He was standing in the garden, and on this moonless rainy night, it was almost as dark with the blindfold lifted. His shirt was tangled in a thorny briar, and he took painful care unsnagging himself. All around him, barren winter rose bushes clawed up from the ground like the grasping fingers of a dead giant that did not wish to stay buried. Rain drummed ceaselessly on his face and shoulders; water dripped into his eyes from his plastered hair. All else in the garden was silent.

Hosten shivered from more than cold and hurried to seek shelter under the roof of the cloister arcade. But there, the darkness was as deep as water. The yawning doorway of the calefactory looked like a hole that drained out of the world. Hosten knew there was a fireplace in there somewhere that could warm his hands if he was willing to build a fire. But he peered into the heavy gloom and could not see it. It was as though pieces of the room he knew had fallen away, and only a black void was left to mark what was missing. Rain brattled against the copper roof loudly in the gloom of this outdoor hallway. The sudden cawing of a crow tumbled around him as something large and white launched up from a nearby buttress perch and circled overhead. Hosten felt the leeching paralysis of fear creeping up from his numb toes to meet the chilled gooseflesh of his arms.

He knew that if he stayed out here too long, Mathias would come and find him. On the one hand, that was a comfort. On the other, Mathias would see what a baby he was — so afraid of the dark that he was hiding in plain sight with his eyes open and the game spoiled. He would be disqualified, and the older kids would think that he was too young to play with them. And so, he wavered there for long minutes, with hot shame prickling wetly behind his eyes. He felt unwilling to give up the game and unable to head back into the rain.

He had just made up his mind to run inside, regardless of the consequences, when there was a clattering of branches from the thicket outside the wall. Hosten skidded to a stop halfway across the lawn. Something long and lean scrabbled over the garden wall, landing amongst the primroses in an ungainly tangle. There it lay for a moment, writhing and moaning in what was obviously pain. The beast was a confusion of limbs and wet fur, and although it looked for the most part like an animal, it groaned like a frightened girl. And then that groan choked off into the braying whine of a fox in a trap, and Hosten felt the warmth of his fear leaking down his leg. The beast was looking right at him, and it raised a pleading hand.

What Hosten might have done next we will sadly never know. He felt then, in his bones, a dull vibration that pounded in a deep and growing rhythm. It was like a running earthquake, with each step pounding closer. It was closing in faster than a human could sprint. The ground was shaking all around him now and drops of water were flung off every swaying leaf so that for a few moments, the rain seemed to fall twice as hard. The changeling fox twisted upright and leapt towards him unsteadily. Then her legs buckled under her, and she collapsed again and lay still.

Hosten had one last moment to see the garden wall explode around the unfinished archway, collapsing forward in a roiling tumble as a massive creature charged through. Its eyes were pale pits that burned, and they swept over Hosten without ever seeing him. Then the monster of stone and earth, not even slowing in its charge, trampled the terror-stricken boy into the mud. He didn't have time to scream, and he did not get up again.

....

Caetal was the first of the children indoors to sense the incoming charge of the Homsaöl. Kneeling on the floor of the roofless chapel, he felt the ground shaking under his hands. The vibrations in the flagstones felt like the thundering hooves of a bull, but if that bull were as tall as a house and had the rolling weight of an avalanche. He sprang to his feet and tore the blindfold off his eyes just as the monster burst through the gap he had made in the outer wall, and although he could not see it, he knew in a moment what it was. *I'd forgotten. Oh gods, how could I forget what was coming?* He turned and ran into the chancel just as the booming shockwave of sound went rolling through that cavernous space.

A horrid memory of the archway he had sabotaged collapsing on Melvin ripped through his mind in a guilty panic, and he sprinted towards the infirmary.

Talara had not felt the approaching vibrations in the ground, but the sound of the collapsing garden arch was so loud where she stood on the raised dais of the chancel that she turned her head away as though slapped and clapped her hands to her ears.

The ringing in her head was for a moment more alarming than the source of the explosion; she treasured her hearing above all other senses. The sound of footsteps sprinted by, echoing crazily from the peak of the vaulted ceiling. She yanked her blindfold off and blinked around her in the gloom, and for a moment, all she saw was the dance of candlelight on the prayer table and the sound of her heart hammering against her ribs.

Then there was a second explosion, even louder than the first. She saw the oak door that led from Cuthain's unfinished chapel to the outer garden blown apart like kindling, and the outer wall collapse all around it. If there had been a ceiling in that space, it might have caved it and obscured the terrible view of what pulled itself through that hole in the wall. As it was, all she could make out was the monstrous size of the creature and the dead-moon glow of its eyes.

It was enough. Talara turned and leapt from the chancel, clearing the three descending stairs in one jump.

While the Homsaöl smashed its way through the outer wall, Tarquin was in the entry tower, sniffing the front door to see if he could honestly tell the difference between the smell of daganwood and the smell of oak. He had assumed he could not, but then he smelled the door and laid his hands against the sanded softness of its planks, and memories of his time playing in the daganwood grove on his tiny island came back to him in a tender rush. He stood that way for a long time, laying his head against the door, breathing in deeply through his nose and watching pictures of a vanished life playing out in his mind. Just before tears wet the cloth over his eyes, he heard the impact on the garden wall. He removed the blindfold in time to watch Caetal sprint towards the infirmary and marvel for a moment at what he could have done to cause such a racket.

Then a second explosion rocked the air, and Talara jumped off the chancel platform and also started running. Looking back, Tarquin was to wish that his young instincts had been sharp enough to flee without hesitation. But his was the sort of curiosity that demands to see a monster with his own eyes, not just hear tales about it later. So, when the towering elemental lumbered into sight, Tarquin was there to see it. He noted the churning roll of stones that served as its legs. He saw the living vines that crawled through its mass like flexing muscle and the grinding girth of its earthen arms.

With fists the size of barrels, it smashed through a stone pillar, and the glass of the vigil windows shattered and fell like glittering knives. The noise was an unbearable clamor amplified with redoubling echoes. Tarquin had seen enough. He covered his ears and came to his senses on running feet, tore across the abbey with his shirt fluttering, and slammed the door of the infirmary behind him. Only then, when the bolt was slid, did he turn around.

Melvin was across the room in bed, wide-eyed and pale. Caetal loomed protectively above him. His hands clenched and unclenched, and he stuttered incoherently. Talara was half hidden behind a statue with her ears covered tight. Hosten and Mathias were nowhere to be seen. The crashing of collapsing stone and breaking glass was barely muffled by the closed door. For a minute that felt unending, it was all they could do to listen in a flattened panic to the sounds of the building being torn apart around them. It was only when the ominous creaking in the roof beams began that they came to their senses enough to wonder what to do next.

....

Mathias, meanwhile, had gone looking for Hosten. He had checked every room a blindfolded eight-year-old might be. Now he was at the back door, exiting towards the garden, when he felt a fluttering vibration through the cold iron handle.

"That's odd." He whispered to himself and paused with his hand on the door. The vibrations increased perceptibly under his fingertips. He pulled the door inward; the night air rushed in, and then the loudest clapping of thunder that Mathias had ever heard. Mathias threw himself involuntarily against the door, and it slammed shut. He gathered his wits from a moment of shock, during which time Caetal ran right by him without even glancing his way. Then he yanked the door open again and let himself out into the dark.

There was no moon to be seen behind the smear of rainclouds, and no stars. The lawn was a carpet of midnight green that ended at the gray-black silhouette of garden walls. Mathias carefully took three descending steps onto the raised platform on which the sundial was set, and the bergamot tree grew. All the while, a thrashing clamor rolled through the brittle stalks of the winter rose garden, as though something enormous was tearing through them. These steps that Mathias took were very brave, for everything in him cried out against going towards that sound.

Whatever it was smashed into the outer wall of Cuthain's unfinished chapel. There was a momentary pause of diminished momentum, then the intruder forced its way through the gap it had made in the chapel wall. Guttering torchlight illuminated the back of a nightmare as the creature of earth and stone entered the chapel and began to destroy it. Rain muffled the cacophony of tearing wood and breaking glass. Mathias hid behind the sundial pillar. His thoughts were soupy with disbelief, and he stood there in statuesque shock, touching one fluttering hand to his mouth.

Then Hosten ran towards him up the stairs. His eyes were wide, and his muddy hands stretched out pleadingly in front of him. He cried out in silence.

....

Mathias had lived with double sight all his life. But he had never seen a ghost. In a shock of wrenching clarity, he knew that he was seeing one now. Somewhere, as close or as far away as two separate moments creating different outcomes, Hosten still lived. He ran towards Mathias now, with tears on his face and arms outstretched. In another place that should never have overlapped with this one, the boy had rolled away just enough; the crushing mass of the Homsaöl had charged right by him, gouging the ground nearby into a smear of mud. That Hosten had lain in the dirt on his belly until he saw that Mathias open the abbey door, then had run gratefully towards the crack of light.

Soundlessly sobbing, the image of Hosten leapt towards Mathias. Then he passed right through him, and the sight of him scattered between the falling rain.

Mathias knew with grim certainty that the body of Hosten was lying somewhere out on the expanse of dark lawn. An involuntary moan choked through him at the awful thought of it. Startlingly, he heard a replying moan somewhere near the arcade walkway.

Mathias' heart leapt in his throat for a moment as his fantasies grasped at the impossible thought that Hosten still lived. Then he heard the moan again and realized that it did not sound quite human.

He moved towards the noise in crouching readiness. The groaning animal did not move or call out again until Mathias almost stumbled on top of it. He could not make out clearly what it was in the rain-slashed gloom. The creature was about his size, sprawled in the wet grass. It had fur that was plastered thinly to an otherwise bare body.

In his double view, the creature appeared as two shifting beings, disorientingly rippling between pale skin and a dusky grayish pelt. The animal struggled to rise on all fours again. Outlined in the dim light spilling from the breach in the chapel wall, Mathias could now see the blooming musculature of human legs and the spread grasp of a five-fingered hand. The face was far from human, but so near to it as well that tears were rolling out of golden fox eyes, and the mouth snarled in a sobbing grimace.

The foxgirl fought for every human moment. She could feel her tongue tumbling against the roof of her mouth, trying to make words out of the insistent alarm of her thoughts. She had never held herself on the tipping point of transformation before. She had never struggled to remain unaltered; she hadn't known how. The fox had always stolen whatever time it needed from her in exchange for sharing the most intimate secrets of the forest that every animal knows.

Now each shaking breath was a painful tug between the feral immediacy of the fox, and the urgent agenda of the two-legged girl. Both bodies writhed and kicked for space inside of one skin. She saw a flutter of white wings and heard the piercing cry of a crow echoing sharply around her. A beak tore savagely at her shoulder, and she snarled and bit at it in a sudden fury.

Then a boy's shadow fell across them both, and with a kick and a cry, the white crow launched back into the air, grackling raucously. Rahyn had barely lifted her head to watch the circling crow when a sudden tingle of contact thrilled through her, and she froze in a surprise that the girl and fox shared. A hand had grasped her by the back of her neck. She held still for a moment in a shock of panic, but the hand did not squeeze. It held her firmly, and with the contact of human fingers, a sudden warm clarity seeped through the pain.

She opened her eyes. She was sprawled on her side with her head cradled in a boy's lap, and his hand was supporting her neck. He looked down at her in obvious concern that crinkled up with a touch of fear at the edges of his eyes. The grip of his hand made her feel strangely drowsy. And with that sudden warm stillness, the fox form began to retreat, burrowing down underneath her slowing heartbeat. She closed her eyes again and let herself go limp, listening to the rain and the booming thunder of the rampaging monster inside the abbey walls.

Then her eyes opened. They had shifted into dark green with a retreating ring of gold around the pupil, and Mathias could see humanity clarifying in her gaze.

"*I can help you-*" She whispered in a throaty growl, "*If you carry me inside. My legs are still remembering themselves.*"

....

The Company of Six

Beyond the oaken door, a storm of colliding stones was raging. Pillars collapsed under the tireless pounding of the Homsaöl's earthen fists. Many were ornamental, but a few were not. The wide beams in the roof overhead began to visibly bow. A crack like a climbing vine was creeping up the infirmary's western wall.

There were six of them together now in that stone cocoon, and five of them were staring at the sixth in harried wonder. Even with the abbey shaking all around them, they couldn't help but stare. The new girl squirmed beneath their collective gaze, her retreating pelt of fur showing more skin by the moment until Melvin coughed in his bed and muttered, *"For pity's sake, give her my blanket."* Then Tarquin did, and she drew it up over her head like a hooded cloak and wrapped herself in it. Bundled up in the woolen coverlet, the small girl looked twice again her size, with only her eyes and the tip of her nose peeking out at them shyly.

Mathias spoke first in the awkward lull of a quiet room surrounded by crashing noise. His voice was shaking. "Hosten is gone. Shouldn't we go outs-"

Then there was a resounding clamor from beyond the door, a rending boom of impact that was even louder than any of them had heard so far. The ground shook underfoot. Across the room, stained glass windows splintered in their leaded casing. Shards of sharp color fell to the floor, shattering and scattering dangerously. Mortar dust crept down the wall around them like fog; stones shifting that were never meant to be moved. The doorway that led to the garden warped so suddenly that the door it contained popped open like a cork, slamming against the outer wall. Fresh air and the smell of rain washed over them. The candles blew out, and the fire in the fireplace guttered and spat. All of this happened in the space of three seconds. Then there was an eerie silence in the abbey, but for the muffled screaming of the cook in the kitchen.

"One point for the smell of rain," Tarquin whispered hoarsely, licking his dry lips in the gloom. They all glanced at him incredulously. Except Melvin. He laughed a hitching laugh, long and loud. His laughter made about as much sense as anything else in that surreal silence, with the stone dust dancing madly around them.

Then, speaking at the same time, Rahyn mumbled from her blanket wrap: "*My name is Rahyn.*" while Melvin announced, "The roof of the nave has collapsed."

Then, again in the same moment, Talara took Rahyn's hand and formally proclaimed, "We are well met," while Mathias murmered, "*The monster is surely buried beneath the rubble.*"

Another long pause followed as everyone listened to the throbbing silence that replaced such terrible noise. At first: relief. The hammering of their hearts and hitching breath, and stillness beyond.

Then there was heard a creaking of shifting beams and lifting rubble, and Caetal muttered, "Not buried for long."

....

"*I can see a... I think that's a hand.*" Tarquin whispered to the others, his eye at the keyhole of the infirmary door.

He was quiet for a long moment and then muttered, "Never mind. It's too dark out there now; I honestly can't see much. The rain is falling indoors. The ceiling is all over the floor. There is a lot of dust in the air. ...I can hear movement, but I can't *see* anything." He withdrew from the keyhole and blinked, massaging the bridge of his nose until he sneezed once, loudly. Then he shrugged. "Pretty dark out there. But I don't think it's dead."

"*Why wouldn't it be dead?*" Talara whispered sharply. "It collapsed the roof right onto its own head. Nothing can survive that. Not even a monster."

"*It is no 'monster.' A monster is something unnatural. It was born of earth. It is the Homsaöl.*" Rahyn whispered so quietly that everyone strained to hear her, and in doing so, they could all clearly hear the rubble shifting beyond the infirmary door as the creature dug its way out of the wreckage.

Then there was a scuffle of scraping noises behind the kitchen wall and the sound of shouting.

"It is too a monster," Caetal said, and he flushed. "I know how it w-w-was made. Natural things don't need magic to be born."

Rahyn stared at him for a moment and then shook her head. "It was born of a storm. And everything that lives is magic." Then she sighed and pulled the blanket up tighter. "I should have come sooner. The boy that played in the grass is dead, and he might have lived. I'm sorry. I didn't know what to do in time to do it." She hung her head and scuffed one bare foot against the stone floor.

Mathias let out a soft little mewl of mourning, and Tarquin said, "Wait, what? The monster killed Hosten? I thought you said 'gone,' like: Hosten ran away home."

Mathias shook his head, and tears welled and scattered in the dusty air. "I said what I meant. Gone with Hausa across the Dark Sea, to meet his ancestors. ... It is my fault. I should never have let him play with us. He was too young to follow the rules, or to die. Now my spirit is heavy with what has been lost."

Mathias covered his eyes with his shirt sleeve, wheezing with grief. Talara patted him awkwardly, and Tarquin hugged him.

Melvin spoke from where he lay. "We will grieve for Hosten after we prevent ourselves from ending up like him. We must get out of here before the rest of the roof comes down, and we are all buried under it. Caetal: lift me up. Get me onto your back. You will have to carry me like that; I'm afraid there's nothing else for it. Let's head for the garden and, from there, out the hole in the wall."

Caetal was already scooping him up before he finished speaking. It was the first time Melvin had spoken to him directly since the accident, and Caetal took it as a good sign. Melvin had always been a wiry boy and had atrophied some muscle in his legs in the last few weeks. With his arms wrapped around Caetal's shoulders and his legs tucked underarm, he did not feel overly heavy. More like a backpack loaded with rocks and opinions.

They were almost at the door when Mathias spoke up, wiping his eyes. "We cannot leave the others. They are trapped inside the kitchen. We must help them, surely."

Tarquin nodded. "If that monster-"

"*It's not a monster.*" Rahyn muttered.

"Fine. If that monstrous not-monster gets into the Sister's Chapel, there are only two doors from there — unless it feels the need to use the toilet. One of those doors leads to us, and one goes into the kitchen. We can escape out the back door, but those guys in the kitchen are stoppered up like a cork in a bottle."

Caetal narrowed his eyes. "Horseshit. They can break a wuh... a w-window and crawl out."

Mathias shook his head. "The kitchen window is too small. Griffin might be able to squeeze through, but Balric and Cookie are too big. And the other windows are just as small and ten feet higher up."

Melvin sighed. "Damn. They were only installed to lighten the room — we never meant them to be wide enough to wiggle through. When a masonry budget constricts, it's always the windows that shrink first. *Kae kefe...* let me think a moment."

Talara paced the room in restless agitation. "Stay and help them? With what? That thing just collapsed a whole room on top of itself and didn't die. What are *we* supposed to do?" She pointed at Rahyn with an accusing finger. "Can it be banished or unmade?"

Rahyn thought for a moment, then shook her head. "I don't believe so. What is made with stone is made to last."

Talara threw her hands up. "Well apparently not this building!"

"It was not built to withstand a rampaging elemental, Talara." Melvin retorted frostily.

Rahyn glared disdainfully at Melvin. "*Yes, it was.* I can feel the dead iron buzzing in the walls. The clerics put it there to try and stop us. But the wall was split open so that the Homsaöl could get in."

"...Us? Who is *us*?" Mathias asked.

Rahyn flicked him a glance, and he could see the whites in her eyes quite clearly. The rims of gold had retreated but were not yet gone. She did not answer.

Melvin stared at her for a long moment. Caetal, holding him saddleback, shifted impatiently from foot to foot. He glanced longingly at the open garden doorway, from which the scent of the lawn still wafted enticingly.

"*Iron... the bars in the walls, set every three handspan apart,*" Melvin muttered, his eyes boring into Rahyn, who shrank back. "You say it had a purpose? It was meant to keep this creature out?"

Rahyn nodded. "It, and others like it. The fae will not touch iron willingly, and neither will their creations. It burns the spirit like cold burns skin. It is death."

Tarquin spoke up. "Iron can harm it? Truly?"

Rahyn shrugged. "If anything can. It will not touch iron willingly, as you would not touch a campfire."

Without warning, Tarquin strode over to the fireplace, grasped an iron poker, and ran from the room. There was a moment of quiet while the kids stared in shock at the now-open doorway. Then there was the unmistakable sound of metal smacking against something in quick succession, followed by a bellowing roar that was like the tumbling of rocks, and the rapidly gaining sound of running feet. Tarquin burst back into the room and slammed the door behind him.

"Okay, important update: iron doesn't seem to hurt the creature. It just makes it really mad." He panted, waving the fire poker like a clumsy sword. "I think we should reconsider fighting it."

Mathias and Melvinari looked at each other for a thoughtful moment, then Mathias said, "The Crooked Room. The iron doors lead underground."

At the same moment, as though speaking with one mind, Melvin said, "What cannot be killed can sometimes be caged."

....

The six children created a plan as quickly as they could. Every tense word exchanged was haunted by the alarming sounds of the Homsaöl digging itself out from the rubble. It is unnecessary to expound on each point and counterpoint made, for there were many ideas that were presented and discarded rapidly. Arguments began and were quelled in fierce whispers, and some damaging accusations were spoken like thorns that would draw blood later on when they were remembered. But for now, they did their best to be guided by haste and ignore their differences. In the end, a patchwork plan was stitched together.

In the meanwhile, Caetal and Talara made an attempt to sneak past the Homsaöl and free the cook and two other children from the kitchen. Their efforts proved disappointing, however, for the outward-swinging door to the kitchen was blocked by the partial collapse of the ceiling. A wide chasm of open sky was exposed overhead, and the falling rain made the ruin of the ground slick with sodden plaster. As they began the attempt to unblock the door, they saw behind them that the earthen creature had now freed itself to waist height. The thrashing malice of its struggle and the burning foxfire of the pits of its eyes at their backs while they worked was too much for their courage. They returned in a hurry to the council of their friends, achieving only a few shouted words of encouragement to those unfortunates trapped inside the kitchen.

....

The great iron doors that led to the catacomb caves belowground were at the hopeful center of their planning. If what Rahyn said was true, and the grand doors, now shut, could be opened... and further still, the Homsaöl could somehow be tricked into following the children down into the underground labyrinth of caves... well, then it could be trapped (hopefully) forever and left to wander like an earthen specter in that sprawling underworld. On this general plan, there was no disagreement, for no other reasonable option could be entertained. Left uncaged, the creature could bring the whole abbey down. Those trapped in the kitchen would be crushed, and though the children themselves might easily have wandered out to the garden and left the building to its tumbling fate, the best they could hope for from there is a great view on the top of the hill from which to watch the Homsaöl lumber down to Holm and do the same to the town below.

Rahyn had at first voiced the opinion that the creature would do no such thing, but all she got in reply was the doubtful stares of her new companions. Privately, she admitted to herself that she had no idea what would happen to the creature when the abbey was leveled and its purpose for being, likewise spent. Would it simply cease to move at all and stand thereafter as a grotesque statue surrounded by the rubble of the ruined abbey, until the work of rain and time had washed its muddy skin away? Years from now, would it remain as a pile of boulders with the plants that were once its living muscles growing all over it? Or would it carry on and, freed of the burden of imposed direction, continue rampaging elsewhere? Such a thought surely led to the flattening of the farming community that sprawled across the valley below, and to the bodies of many more children mashed face-down in the drowning mud. Rahyn shook her head of such grim thoughts and rejoined herself to their belief that the creature must be penned up for good. But how to get it through the iron doors at all?

....

"Now remember," Tarquin whispered, *"we have to make it mad. Hopping mad. If Mathias is right, the monster can move as fast as a daydream if it wants to, and that's what scares me."*

They were circled together in the infirmary for the last time, with all their foreheads pressed so close together they were almost touching. Each held a salvaged piece of iron in their hand, except Rahyn, who would not be coaxed to touch the iron at all. A motlier bunch of improvised iron weapons could not be imagined. Tarquin had the best of it with his fire-poker, and Caetal had to make do with the iron log tongs. Mathias had commandeered the heavy iron sundial from the garden platform, swinging it so awkwardly that Caetal snorted out loud and forced him to trade for the tongs, which he wielded thereafter. Talara had figured out how to remove half a hinge from the reredorter door (to her credit, she had ground one edge alarmingly sharp on a rock), and she now palmed it like a shank. Even Melvin was armed with his own iron bedpan, although he had no intention of using it.

Tarquin spoke earnestly. "Rahyn and I will engage the monster-"
"Homsaöl"
"*Monster.*" Caetal growled. Rahyn glared at him.
"-Right, *Homsaöl,* as planned. We'll try to get it mad, but not a full raging foamer. Just enough to hold its focus. Caetal, Melvin and Mathias will sneak into the Crooked Room and get the doors to the catacombs open. You guys will have to work double fast on those pull chains because if that creature charges, Rahyn and I have to retreat towards you with nowhere else to go. Talara, you head to the Pilgrim's Well in the apse and crank the water bucket and chain all the way down, so we have a way to climb back out of the caverns again. Remember, Talara: it is all counting on you! If the bucket and chain don't make it all the way down to the water, we can't get out. And if you aren't up here to close the iron doors behind the mo- the *Homsaöl* after it chases down after us into the dark, it will just come right back out again, and you might have to face it on your own. You got that? Everyone knows what to do?"

Talara nodded solemnly, and the others followed in turn. Tarquin looked around the circle of faces and saw the same paling fear that he felt in himself. But there was a grim excitement as well, reflected in the shine of their eyes.

Tarquin continued. "There are six of us now, and that's my lucky number. I hope that luck is something we can all share. If we want to survive tonight, we have to become something bigger and... something more *real* than we were before now. Something that means *us.*"
"A Company." Melvin said thoughtfully. "It is an old word that describes those who share bread, and friendship, and danger together."
"*The Company of Six,*" Talara whispered aloud, then smiled shyly at Tarquin. "Six is a lucky number amongst my people as well. It means

family, the heart of things. A hope of returning light. It is good to name aloud those things that matter most. Let us be true, together."

Mathias shivered and hugged himself, nodding. He said nothing but felt everything. It was a very big feeling.

The six of them stared openly at each other for a few slow breaths, and their shared regard spoke words they could never have articulated out loud. Eyes of mixed color, eyes of deep brown; eyes with the blue of water in them, and moss green, and pale gold. Then Tarquin grinned and booped Talara's nose; she growled and bit his finger, and then they were all laughing. They hugged each other around their shoulders in a grateful ring. It was a moment that none of them were to forget for the rest of their lives: the moment that they all began to fall in love with each other.

"For Hosten. No more children dead tonight. Stay alive." Tarquin said.

"For Hosten." They all replied, except Rahyn, who whispered, "*No more dead children.*"

Then the pounding of indomitable fists could be heard booming through the infirmary. The door bulged and splintered, and the Homsaöl was upon them at last.

....

The Iron Doors
~ The last part of the tale, wherein Mathias speaks for himself ~

A plan is a funny thing. We know it will never work out the way we first envision it should because we think of things through the limiting rails of connecting lines. Oh, we can imagine the twists in a road, to be sure, and think that because we can, we have the agency to predict the unexpected. But what we can never account for is the fact that our lives are not so much like a road at all, but rather like a marble that is shot out at random amongst countless other marbles, careening unexpectedly off of every other person, action, and opportunity that happens to have been rolling towards us. In the battle between Order and Chaos, the army of Order is a handful of good intentions with a bucket on its head, waving an ideological stick and pretending to ride a realism horse. The army of Chaos is every part of everything else, and it's trampling over everywhere, all at once.

Success, therefore, comes down to having the courage to put that bucket on your head, waving your hopeful stick, and doing the best you can against literally unimaginable odds.

....

When the Homsaöl shattered the infirmary door and wedged itself into the room up to the shoulder, we scattered and fled. There we were, united in a hopeful daydream, then there was a roar of noise and dust and the imposition of one huge grasping hand. I saw it close around Tarquin's leg, and he cried out in pain. It seemed for an awful moment that his leg would be torn right off at the thigh. Then he shoved against the creature mightily; there was a rending of cloth, and the woolen breeches ripped clean off at the thin fabric of one knee. In the brief second I saw him clearly, he was hobbling towards the far corner of the room, brandishing his fire-poker with one pant leg half-gone and blood smeared all over his calf. Then he shouted "RUN, MATHIAS!" and I ran.

I burst out the garden door and careened headlong into Caetal, who had Melvin slung across his back. We tangled and fell into a heap, and Caetal swore mightily and shoved me off, cradling Melvin as we all toppled roughly into the sundial pillar. Cold stone bit hotly into my hands and shoulder, and then we were gaining our feet in a hurry. I shouted something like *"this way!"* and sprinted across the rain-slick lawn, forgetting for the moment how hard it was for Caetal to keep pace with me, burdened as he was with Melvin riding saddleback. In the darkness, I almost tripped on something and leapt clear over it without giving it thought. It was only when I heard Caetal stumble and cry out that I remembered, with a flush of profound shame, that it was Hosten's body.

We passed through the gap where the chapel wall had been sundered and into the hollow of what was once my beloved abbey. The gutted interior of the building was nightmare dark; all light had been snuffed when the roof caved in. How long we might have picked senselessly through this tumbled wasteland, I cannot speak to, but Melvin would have none of it. We spent a handful of precious minutes searching what remained of the walls for an unspoiled oil torch. Finding one still in serviceable use, we wasted yet more time with the clumsy fumbling of Caetal's flint and tinder.

All the while, the terrible scrabble of the Homsaöl trying to force the rest of its body past the narrow infirmary door could be heard echoing through that dead holy house. It sounded like a gargantuan rat gnawing through the wall, and it set my teeth to a frightful chattering. I was grateful not to be the one trying to light the torch, for my hands would surely have shaken so badly I might have dropped the flint and lost it amongst the stone shards. Finally, light leapt across the walls, and we raised our arms to shield our eyes from the flaring brightness.

"Take comfort," Melvin whispered hoarsely, *"the Homsaöl would not be going through such effort to breach that wall if our friends weren't tormenting it with iron on the other side. They still live, I'm sure of it."*

I nodded and held the relief of that thought close to my heart as we began our cautious foray into the ruin. By the flight of the crow, our journey should have been the work of simple steps. It was only the best part of a hundred feet from the open chapel wall to the Crooked Room, with the raised dais of the chancel between.

And yet, the way was so completely remade by the landscape of ruin that it was like traversing a series of treacherous canyons. On either side of us rose jagged peaks of fallen beams, splintered at the ends. Wall arches and pillars lay in half-toppled piles, looking all the ghastlier for their ornate beauty. Wreckage on the floor shifted dangerously underfoot; every step was a sliding balance of caution. Here and there, jagged nails bloomed like thorns beneath our bare feet.

On the chancel, the Triad had all fallen statues. Embara was buried, and the statue of Cuthain was crushed into pieces on the dais, with his severed head and part of one shoulder staring up at us from where it had tumbled onto the ambulatory floor. I only saw it for a moment as the torchlight passed over the statue's empty eyes. A feeling of terrible dread sluiced through me, numbing my heart and erupting gooseflesh on my arms. I rubbed them absently as we walked, trying to calm myself and banish the ill omen from taking hold of my heart.

Caetal stopped midway to abandon the sundial he held and swapped it for a length of broken beam with multiple iron nails driven through it at crossed angles. He hefted it and nodded grimly. Melvin had already dropped the bedpan in our first tumble and clung to Caetal's shoulders with both hands.

All the while, we slunk as quietly as thieves. Or so we hoped, for we did not wish to alert the creature to our presence. When we at last arrived at the Crooked Room, we stopped as one, and stared for a while in dismay. Here too, the roof had partially fallen in, and although the way to the iron doors set in the floor was mostly freed of obstruction, the heavy chains to crank open that ponderous portal — once hanging by pulleys from reinforced ceiling beams — were now strewn in useless piles on the rubble.

Each door had to weigh the better part of a hundred stone. There was no way the three of us could lift even one of them on our own.

"W-w-well... *shit.*" Caetal muttered.

I couldn't have phrased it any better.

....

Five minutes later, Melvin and I sat alone by the doors inset in the floor. Caetal had, of course, already attempted to pry them up and open, using increasingly large beams for leverage. The failure was forgone, and all his labors achieved was shortening his already stunted rope of patience. So, when Melvin sarcastically commented that perhaps he could look for yet another useless beam, Caetal had told him where to shove that idea and lumbered off into the nave to go assist the others in pestering the Homsaöl.

Since much of our plan had expired untimely, we found ourselves in the late-stage difficulty of casting about for another plan, though we knew already that none would do. Simply put, the doors *had* to be opened. All our hopes depended on luring the creature underground before we were cut down, one by one.

Without the distraction of Caetal stomping around and swearing, we found ourselves in a quiet moment that the eye of the storm allows. All around us was the muffled pounding of chaos, but we two sat leaning back on back, and had a think together.

Since the accident that first brought Melvin into my life, we had often caught ourselves sharing overlapping moments. I could sometimes feel the atmosphere of his thoughts overlapping mine, and I believed he felt the same. I had given him something of myself when I dove into the deep well of his pain as he lay dying under that stone. And I had surely taken something from him as both of us kicked upward towards the light, helping each other swim up out of his mind. We had rarely been alone since then and never talked about what we knew we shared. We had somehow become two neighbors living on each side of a thin, conjoined wall. The kind of neighbors that could hear all the private sounds that are normally kept hidden.

Now we sat very still, without talking. The sands of time were tumbling through the narrow of the hourglass, and we needed to generate the kind of plan that leaned way out on the thin branch that some call magic, and others, a miracle. So, I peered into his thoughts on purpose, as I had not done since I held him dying in my hands. I could feel Melvin doing the same to me, combing through hidden parts of the person I am that I will never see for myself. It was like having someone peering at all my organs while they were still inside my body. Not an emotionally comfortable experience, I can tell you.

Our backs began to stick together with mingled sweat. I took a steadying breath and closed my eyes again, and with a heartfelt prayer to Cuthain, dove ever deeper into the colorful darkness of Melvinari. Just when I felt like I could hold my spiritual breath no longer, I sensed the incredible murmur of vibration that sounded something like *EBEN*. It was wrapped like a banner around his bones.

I opened my eyes, squinting dully in the bright glare of torchlight.

"I believe you can push these doors up and open from below," I said,

and my breath was hitching like I had run the length of the hillside.

"I think you can help me do it." He replied.

....

We sat side by side, directly facing the iron doors inset in the floor. He could not stand, of course, and I did not trust myself to bear his weight. I could sense the breadth of Melvin's nervousness. He had never attempted to grasp the attention of stone on purpose, and the last time he had used the power at all, the word had been ripped from his throat in the grip of utmost need. It is one thing to be saved by a burst of prodigious speed when pursued by danger and quite another to summon that same speed without it. But the bellowing of the Homsaöl was a testament to its gathering rage, and every wasted minute diminished the possibility of our survival. In short, we had to get this right the first time.

I placed my hand on the back of Melvin's neck and felt the warm flow of connection between us. Closing my eyes, I imagined pouring the faith of my support into him. I then sifted my thoughts into two intentions. The first thought was as easy for me as breathing. It was of Cuthain, as I always imagined him. Lordly, inside of the light. Cuthain the Just, who has the wisdom to weigh the worth of something as delicate as hope. The father who truly cared for me. The father who stayed. I asked him to guide me now.

The other thought was for Melvin. I could feel the immortal sound of *EBEN* rushing to crowd the blood from his veins and fill his heart up with the sharp purpose of power. I could sense how big the word was: so much larger than his body, as wide as the curvature of the world. I hoped I could help him contain and soften it, for the breath of a moment, so it would not split the walls asunder as it tore from his chest. I held his neck, and I murmured, as quietly as I dared: *Just a whisper will do. Just one little whisper. Call the stone towards you. Say it so quietly that the ground needs to lean in, just to hear you better.*"

I'm not sure if those words were my own, although I was convinced of their truth as I spoke them aloud. Either way, I felt the sweat bead on Melvin's neck beneath my hand, and he nodded. Then he parted his lips the tiniest bit, and a susurration of the sound of *EBEN* rippled out of him between clenched teeth.

To say it rippled is the best way I can describe it. I did not hear the word with my ears; I felt it sluice through my body. The flagstones between where we were seated and the door in the floor lifted and settled in a spreading ripple like water lilies on the surface of a pond. Melvin did not let the word spring forth in one leap — he drew the sound of it out, stretching it across the air like a hum. For the barest moment, my heart ceased in my chest. The doors lay still before us, looking like an iron-colored painting on the floor.

For a shameful moment, my faith fluttered, and I sullied my purpose by believing that what we hoped to do was impossible. Then tears of lightning flared like an afterimage behind the lids of my eyes. I shut them, blinking back my own tears. With my eyes closed, I could hear the groaning of the metal as it was lifted from below.

I was afraid to look at first. Afraid that my sliver of doubt would pop the magic like a soap bubble. It was the long wait of ten heartbeats before I dared to open my eyes again. When I did, I beheld the wonder I had hoped for. The doors were almost fully open now. What was lifting them from below was the miracle of six stalagmites of stone, growing up from the tunnel like fingers. Even as I watched, those mighty doors — which were each four feet wide and the better part of ten long and as thick as an inch of cast iron — lifted as gently and quietly as ever they had.

Just shy of lifting the doors fully open, Melvin's breath ran out. His face was ruddy with exertion; a vein throbbed on his forehead, and he shut his eyes as though sleep might overtake him. I lost my grip on his neck, and he slumped over sideways. I, too, felt like I had swum the width of the river through a heavy current. So, I lay back with my head on the seat of a broken bench, panting with the victory of our efforts. It was, of course, a short-lived moment.

....

Thinking back later on what happened next, I can only assume that the ripple of energy that rolled the flagstones like a zephyr passing over water spread out in all directions, not just towards the door. Because suddenly, the harassed bellows of the iron-tormented Homsaöl morphed into one prolonged bugling roar that shook us out of our stupor. I scrambled to my feet and did my best to drag Melvin up with me. We could hear Caetal yelping as he sprinted barefoot towards us across the rubble. Three times he stumbled, no doubt punctured cruelly by broken glass or nails, but he kept on at great speed towards us, as though the Wild Hunt itself rode behind him.

He burst into the bright edge of our torchlight and did not pause even a moment, but scooped up Melvin across his back and ran for the tunnel that sloped downward into the dark behind the open iron doors. I grabbed up the torch and followed. Only seconds behind, the Homsaöl thrashed towards us at great speed through the ruins.

We leapt down the stairs, two at a time, dodging easily between the stone stalagmites that propped the open door. The tunnel began where the stairs ended, descending in a curve out of sight. The leaping flame of our torchlight at a run made everything seem to slide and dance crazily. For a moment, we paused, looking back to see if the creature would be baited. Our torchlight ceased at the tunnel doorway, illuminating the stalagmites like teeth with the dim view of the abbey segmented between them.

Then into view, the Homsaöl rocked on its stubby legs. There its charge was arrested by the presence of the iron doors, as we feared it might be. It was easily as wide as the portal or wider, and to fit down the tunnel at all it would have to make scraping contact with the doors on both sides. As a lodestone is repelled by the magnetism of another lodestone, so too did it seem unable to cross the iron threshold of those doors. It swung its head in blind anger like a bull, and the sockets of its eyes burned with fierce white phosphorus. We heard the distant shouting of our other friends in the room behind it. But the beast would not be moved a step further. It crouched at the tunnel entrance in hostile stillness.

It would wait if it had to. It could. Time meant nothing to the Homsaöl — it could wait. Elemental patience that would outlast life, until our bones dissolved into calcium and the cave remade us into more stalagmites. We had been foiled by the very iron we aspired to trap it with and were now in a subterranean cell, staring back up at our jailor through the stone bars.

Or so I thought. But Melvin would prove to be less easily thwarted than I, though his ingenuity nearly got us killed. He narrowed his eyes at the creature. Then he inhaled deeply and spat out the name *EBEN* as sharply as a thrown knife. The Homsaöl's chest cracked, and a rock the size of a shield split from just below its arm and tumbled to the floor. The bellow the creature emitted into that tunnel was the loudest yet — so loud that the walls shook with it. There was a sparkling flash of pain, and my eardrums burst. I didn't know what had befallen me until warm liquid started dripping out of my ears, and the noise in the tunnel suddenly softened to a buzzing hum.

The creature surged forward reactively as it roared, smashing through the thin stalagmites like they were barely there. In doing so, the heavy doors pressed down upon it from above, and I was grateful I could no longer hear the highest notes of the trumpeting of its pain, though I could feel the shock of it chattering through my teeth. As the closing doors pressed down upon the Homsaöl, it was pushed forward into the tunnel by the folding pressure of their great weight.

A burning torch that was hurled from behind it clattered across its shoulder and fell uselessly to the floor. Likely thrown by Tarquin; for a moment I heard him shouting, but the sound was wetly muffled by the liquid in my ears. There was a grinding shriek of stone dragged across iron. A sudden bloom of sparks lit up the sight of the Homsaöl starkly, so that I saw it quite clearly for the first time. Its eyes were a stinking smolder of burning phosphorus. Its mouth was a widening pit fanged with jagged protrusions. My bladder almost loosened as it bellowed again, rumbling towards me with arms outstretched.

Then, with a whooshing of dust that nearly doused both torches, the doors clanged shut again with Talara, Rahyn and Tarquin on the other side.

We three were trapped underground with the monster.

....

At a dead run, on level ground, the Homsaöl would have had us. It tumbled towards us faster than running, like stones rolling downhill at a speed greater than human muscle could match. By the end of that first curved hallway, we could feel the terrible tremors of impact gaining behind us, and I knew we would be ground beneath it. Exhaustion slowed me, and I admit that if Caetal was not running just at my heels, I would have given up and fallen underfoot. I was sedated by the relief that we had succeeded — that though we were to die down here, we had saved a part of the abbey and perhaps the whole town. Barefoot, I stumbled painfully on a ridge in the stone floor. Caetal wheezed with exertion, carrying the weight of two. Melvin looked half-dead from expended effort already; he jounced around saddleback with the ungainly slump of one who was nearing unconsciousness. Each moment of that final sprint, the creature loomed taller and taller at our heels. And that, in the end, was the only thing that saved us.

Just ahead, the leaping torchlight painted the form of an archway. We had made it to the crypt. Here would rest entombed the bodies of future generations of clerics who had lived and died in Cuthain's calling. At present, it was naught but a large empty room with a dozen or so carved sarcophagi recesses. Multiple passages branched off from here. Thankfully, the archway to the crypt was a bit narrower than the long passageway we had just sprinted down. The momentum of the elemental was checked. It did not take the Homsaöl long to compress itself down enough to grind through into the crypt, but those brief moments of relief were enough to allow us to catch a measure of our breath and get a better grip on our instincts. From this point forward, I knew there were only natural passageways. These would be shaped by the casual design of time and water, not by the structured intention of masons. There would be places where the passage narrowed even further. We'd have to find them to stay alive.

....

It chilled my heart to watch the way that the Homsaöl squeezed through that door. Earth and living vines are, to some degree, more malleable than flesh. The Homsaöl could therefore compress itself to fit through almost any entranceway. But it was not a quick transformation, and we used that to our advantage. At each narrowing juncture, the creature would be forced to stop and reimagine its own proportions. Then we could rest for a moment or wander further on to investigate.

Tunnels meandered in all directions, sloping upwards and spiraling off, sometimes plunging without warning into absolute blackness underfoot. After a long while, we could no longer hear the scratching of the Homsaöl at all but for a grinding reverberation felt in the ground. I strained with ruptured eardrums to listen for the Homsaöl, and the fear of knowing that the creature could be much closer behind us than what we could hear began to sap my nerves. And all the time, I strained above all to hear the sound of an escape bucket splashing down into water. But there was nothing. Just vibrations in the ground behind us and the hollow humming in my ears.

....

We had chosen the wrong tunnel, perhaps many times over. We had descended so much deeper into the hill that we were surely a long way from the abbey. The light of the torch was dim and throbbing now; the slightest breeze shuddered it. Ahead was a cave with a diminishing ceiling; a carpet of pale draping mosses grew so low in there that it almost brushed our faces. Caetal was much cheered by the moss, for he reasoned that where moss grows, water flows. Melvin was all for carrying on in search of the source of the water, but another forty steps into the cave, and our wavering light fractured into the darkened mouths of five different tunnels. The entrance to each was softened by moss and crusty with lichen. Any of them, or none of them, could lead to the underground lake. And even if they did, the chance that we would be able to follow it back to wherever the bucket was dipped was as slim as the last of our light. An awful feeling of the weight of all that stone around us made my heart stammer. The air felt stale and thin. We stared in frustration at the five tunnels.

There is nothing worse than hopelessness. It takes all and gives nothing in return. Fear at least lends the speed of flight and the strength of desperation. I felt the hopelessness in my legs first before I let it gain ground in my heart. I was kneeling now, no longer moving forward. I couldn't remember why, or how long I'd been squatting there. Caetal was nearby, slumped against the wall, with his face turned away. Melvin lay on the ground with his eyes closed. In silence, we watched the dull blue flicker of the torch flame and silently counted the moments until we would never see light again. I prayed, of course. It was all I could think to do. Yet, I felt in my heart that nobody was listening. We were lost.

....

But of course, we were not as alone as we imagined. The three of us were but half of six, and while we were getting lost in the tunnels, our friends had been doing everything they could to find us. Talara would later recount the harrowing details of their descent down into the midnight-dark lake in a well bucket, then a blundering search that led them straight to the Homsaöl — whose scrabbling noises they had mistaken for ours. But the creature seemed entirely oblivious to them in its pursuit of Melvin, Caetal and I. They watched from a wary distance as the elemental continued burrowing ever deeper into narrowing caverns.

This proved to be a stroke of good fortune, for by following the Homsaöl, they were being led ever closer to us. Without suffering the prolonged fear that had quickened our flight, they were more able to maintain the faculty of good sense.

Talara had "borrowed" a wedge of chalk from Fahru Nariman's lectern before she, Tarquin and Rahyn had descended the chain into the well. Once they had reached the water, they swam to the edge of the subterranean lake. *(Talara had dog paddled admirably, for she did not yet know how to swim).* Once again on land, she had taken the chalk and marked an arrow on the wall of every cave they had followed the Homsaöl through. Finally, they came to a room where the creature had considered a moment before continuing on, and in that brief consideration, the three of them had slipped past it and ran on ahead. The tunnels interwove alarmingly. Their progress began to be slowed by Tarquin, who was limping with increasing tenderness on his wounded leg. Rahyn at last had brought them to a stop and willed herself into the transmutation of the fox form. Swift on four legs, she continued forward in pursuit alone.

So, it was just as the last of my dimming hope was failing that I espied the fox as it bounded towards me from a low tunnel. I cried aloud with relief at the sight of it. Only hours before, I would have counted this shape-shifting fae amongst the boldest foes of Cuthain and his church. Now I wrapped my arms around her, buried my face in the wild scent of her fur, and wept like the child I still was.

....

Our journey up from underground was laborious and slow. But we were alive, and we were together, and that was all the miracle I could have hoped for. Our torch failed, and theirs did likewise not long after. The final part of the return trip to the surface was a slow shuffle of the blind leading each other, with Caetal in the rear and me up front, holding to the soft plume of Rahyn's fox tail. It was she who led us, by scent, to the edge of the midnight lake and from there, into the water. We did not encounter the Homsaöl again, although the grinding sound of its tunneling echoed ominously in the blackness all around us.

Rahyn swam out with Tarquin first, guiding him to the submerged bucket at the end of the well chain. Once he was safely clinging on, he wrapped his legs around the chain and provided a crude light for the rest of us to follow by striking his flint repeatedly overhead. Those that could swim helped those that could not, and so in slow pairs, we paddled out to the chain. I was the last to go, floating for a long while on my back in the cold water.

In telling it, I suppose it was strange of me to float in the cold blackness of the lake, and not simply wait on the dry shore for my turn to cross. And yet, the brisk water numbed my aching ears, and with my eyes open, I watched the small bursts of light from the striking flint dance like ghostly fireflies across the cave ceiling. It was as peaceful as falling backwards into arms you know are waiting to catch you. I was weightless, the future was limitless, and I was, impossibly, still alive.

....

While Caetal and Talara were busy cranking the chain up the liftwheel with Melvin riding up in the bucket from below, Tarquin wandered over to me with his hands in his pockets, whistling unconvincingly. Trusting in the rattling chain to conceal his query, he leaned in close and asked, "What was the bonus smell? From the game — the one that was worth five whole points? I know it seems a silly time to ask, but..." he shrugged. "I think it would drive me crazy not to know."

I shook my head in bemusement. I'm sure I will never quite understand Tarquin's mind. His fascination with secrets is like his imagination: some galloping thing even he can hardly keep a saddle on.

"The bonus smell was the scent of the catacomb tunnels. I never expected anyone to bother getting those doors open to smell it. I guess, in the end, we all won the extra points for that experience."

Tarquin nodded solemnly to himself. "I like that." He swiveled on his heel and seemed about to walk away. Then he turned back with a sly grin on his face, punched me in the shoulder companionably and declared: "I KNEW it was the catacombs smell! It just had to be!"

Whistling, he strolled back to the well to assist with getting Melvin out of the bucket.

....

While my friends worked together to clear the rubble that blocked the kitchen door, I circled my weary way up the eighty-two steps to the tower belfry. The downpour and darkness had broken into masses of leaking clouds with slices of red moonslight pushing through. It was half ten of eve by the drip of the water clock when I raised my hand to the pull-rope and began ringing the iron bell: thirteen peals to signal trouble to the folks of Holm. The somber gonging rolled across the valley below. Standing so close to that ringing bell, I was grateful that my eardrums had already burst.

I hoped that the sound would carry above the downpour, all the way to the mayor's barn, between the slats of those wooden walls and disrupt the boisterous arguments of worried adults. If the boom of the collapsing roof and the roaring elemental had gone unnoticed, I wouldn't be holding my breath. But you never know how something might turn out until you try it.

So, I rang the bell with solemn duty, filling each strike of the iron clapper with my prayers. At the bell's first tolling, a large white crow launched into the air from the tower roof. It circled once around the belfry in silence, staring down at me. *The same bird that was attacking Rahyn in the garden, surely — the largest I have ever seen.* Then I tolled the bell again as hard as I could, my hands shaking with sudden anger, and the crow veered off towards the west. I watched it go until it was a speck of white against dark clouds, chasing it as far away as I could with the ringing of Cuthain's bell booming out behind it.

When the last echoes of the bell had rolled away, I finally heard the sound of flowing water. Any fool with working eardrums would have noticed it already. I stepped to the edge of the bell tower and leaned over the iron railing, gazing down towards the valley floor below. A profound sense of disorientation seized my senses — the valley was crawling away from me! A wet mass of mud and broken trees seemed to be flowing away to the east, towards the sea. The demarcation lines of rock walls that divided the valley into farmsteads had all vanished, overborne by the restless churning of a sudden lake with pieces of tiny houses jutting out of it like islets. While we were underground, Loc Enum had flooded its banks and claimed the valley of Holm.

....

The End of the Path

There is no wind that blows underground. No showers of rain fall beneath the earth. Sunshine will never light the honeycomb of tunnels that intersect below the abbey built on High Hill.

Time moves slowly in the deep. Years pass in their countless thousands as calcite-heavy water forms stalactite cones that drip from the ceiling like melted wax. Above ground, the turning of seasons flicker rapidly by in comparison, overarched by spinning revolutions of the sun.

In the world above, the cycle of seasons would have slowly worn the Homsaöl away. Wind would have tumbled against it; rain would have dissolved its earthen skin. Frost would swell and recede inside of it, slowly cracking its stones apart stratum by stratum. But here, underground, there were none of these things to assist in unmaking it. Only the heavy grating of itself against the ground as the Homsaöl lumbered ponderously through corridors of stone. It was searching for the abbey it was born to destroy, with those forged iron bars that hummed the dirge of death inside its walls. It was searching for the boy who had diminished it with a single painful word. But it could not sense them anywhere.

The Homsaöl arrived, after the longest while, at the edge of a lake. Here the creature paused on the shore and could go no further. Across the water, a stone's throw away, an iron chain descended like a single trailing vine, growing down the hole of a well. At the end of this chain, there was a bucket. It knew, inherently, that it could not cross a lake such as this, or it would be unmade by the scattering drift of the current. Yet the Homsaöl could feel the hateful iron from the shore and the last traces of the painful immortal word that the boy had spat at him before he climbed that chain and vanished.

It will end them; that is certain. As certain as the dull thumping that rolls up from so much deeper below: a rhythm so slow that an hour passes between each beat. The hidden heart of the Terrasque. It is the only sound that matters, down there in the dark.

So, the Homsaöl crouched at the shore of the midnight lake and waited patiently. Pale lizards crawled across it every now and then, but nothing else moved in the stillness of the deep.

....

Now the chain is dull with dust. The iron bucket drifts half underwater, listless and still. Blind fish swim through the rusted holes that time has eaten away.

The Homsaöl is still there, crouched by the shore of the midnight lake; waiting to finish what it began, what it was made for. It dreams of smashing the rest of the iron bars hidden inside the abbey walls. It waits for the children who harmed it to return.

It waits there still.

....

PART 2
Cards of Fate

We were all of us drawn towards a common center, like metal tugged by a lodestone — the force which some call destiny, and others shrug off as happenstance. After Rahyn led us into the caverns below the abbey and safely out again; after we had been brave enough, and stupid enough to believe that we could trap a monster together, and were proven right... that's when the adventures really began.

We had become "us" just as suddenly as the rest of the world had become "them." Rahyn was the last one to enter into our Company of Six, and the invisible door of welcome closed behind her. I believe that is how most groups are formed — like a game that doesn't really begin until all the players are seated around the same table. What we did not know yet is that Fate had already stacked the deck we were playing with. One by one, as though compelled, we began to draw the cards.

A Progress Report

Weeks of rain can dampen everything but good news. And so it was with some appreciable excitement that Thegn Rory received a long-awaited report from Captain Dané.

She did not deliver the report in person this time. It had been written onto a small scroll of parchment with letters crowded in cramped penmanship, squeezing large tidings into insufficient space. Rory broke the wax seal with the imprint of a helmet with a single central eye on it, unrolled the diminutive scroll, and read it by candlelight.

Thegn Rory,
Flooding very bad here — hope this message gets through. Water almost to the base of the outer bailey wall. Yet warming weather brings changing fortunes.
After months of waiting, we have captured a troll. It tore apart three of my soldiers before we were able to cage it. Have not seen evidence of any others, although it seems prudent to assume they are out there. Began experiments on how to dispatch it. Wounds regenerate: forge-heated steel slows the process, and it is wary of fire. When the time comes we will burn it to ashes, but before we do, I shall learn what I can from controlled mutilation. If there is another way to kill it, I will find out. Perhaps your scheme to recover Drôle and complete the Thegn's Road might work after all.
Fera Dané
Captain, Her Majesty's Iron Guard

....

"You're godsdamned right it will." Rory muttered to himself, rolling the little scroll back up between his fingers. "The road is just the beginning. But you will not live to see how it ends, dear captain. And neither will our queen."

Then he held the small scroll in the candle flame until it burned to char, and left it laying on the table for someone to clean up. Pulling his finest fur-trimmed cloak up around his shoulders, he ducked out through the tent doorway, whistling to himself as the rain fell all around him.

....

The Fool

"The plan they came up with was terrible,
and that is what made it so magnificent."

THE FOOL

~ The First Card ~

In happier times, the six children might have become local celebrities, for news travels quickly in small towns. By noon of the next day, half the town knew that a monster of living earth and stone had smashed the abbey, and that six unusual children had managed to trap it in the caves below. By the following day, most of the village inhabitants had been forced to flee the rising waters to High Hill, gazing for themselves in shock at the ruin of Cuthain's holy house, and sharing amongst themselves the story of how it was brought low. But there were no praises for the children that might have saved their town, for looking down upon the churning lake that had swallowed all the land below, it was hard to imagine what had been spared, to be saved.

....

The flood killed twenty-two residents of Holm. As luck would have it, most of the adults were crowded into the mayor's hillside barn when Loc Enum overflowed and swamped the valley. On paper, when the record of that flood would be recorded and filed at Portuan in the annals of the Domain of Fýrii, it would be positively noted that the death count was down from the previous flood in that area. *Of course, the population of the valley had dwindled somewhat in the last fifty years, so per capita numbers inflated the comparison total somewhat grimly, but: all told, a better flood.*

And yet, the dead were entirely children and elderly. Those that had been left behind at home to keep them safe. Wisely, no census-taker ever stopped in at what remained of the houses of grieving parents and cheerfully announced that it was a "better flood than last time." There are not words to convey the sorrow of those parents, who swam or waded as fast as they could back to their homes and families, only to find doors that had once held their children safely behind them torn away, and a river that shouldn't exist flowing through their houses. The richer farmers, whose dwellings were built on hillsides with views, found most of their children safe in attics or straddling roof beams, wet and scared but unharmed. Here, as always, the burden of loss was almost entirely borne by the poor.

....

Terrible days passed. The rushing current slowed to meandering, and the valley became a brown lake full of broken things. Bodies of humans and animals started to be recovered from where they had snagged at the edges of the forest or had been deposited on high ground as the water slowly receded. I shall not burden you overmuch with the miasma of wet rotting smells, and the hitching sounds of weeping that carried so clearly across the waterlogged valley. A flood does not just sweep people and their objects away. It swamps the unconscious assurance of dry ground itself. *The earth underfoot, and the sky up above.* It seems so immutable, until your house goes floating by you. For all the topsoil it left, the flood took something from the valley that time did not replace.

Many of the hillside houses remained, of course. Families that had dwelt in Holm for generations had slowly drifted further uphill, for the valley flooded at least every hundred years. Melvin's father had built on a rise that did not flood past a few inches, and Caetal's house was on a low forested peak. Rahyn did not live in the valley at all, and Mathias dwelt above it. The Welcome Holm tavern was elevated by five stone steps, each sandbagged so thoroughly that only the cellar flooded, so that Talara's bed had to be moved to the attic.

Tarquin was the only one of the six of them to have his dwelling flooded out, for although it was a ways from town, the house of Liam was built in the sloping bowl of a partially cleared grove. Now it was a pond with a hovel squatted in the center of it. Having no basement or lift of any kind, the common room and lower bedrooms flooded up to the height of the fireplace mantel. The structure was spared the danger of rushing currents, as the basin of the forest floor simply filled up like a bowl of soup, and then drained itself out a few days later. Liam's bed and personal effects were ruined, and so were those of Shandus — at least, all those things that were lower than shoulder height.

Neither father nor son were there to see it happen, as each was gone from Holm when the flooding began. Only Tarquin returned to the house while it was underwater, and he alone cried out to see it, thrashing through the water into the darkness of the creaking house. There was only one thing that the flood had taken from Tarquin; he knew right away that it had gone out an open window, and felt the loss of it profoundly. But it was not a thing at all: it was a young goat.

A search of the house did not recover her body. Nor did hours spent combing the woods, calling her name. Finally, when hope of ever seeing her silly face and hearing her bugling bah again had almost subsided, Tarquin found traces of hoofed prints pocking a muddy slope. They led straight into the forest, heading vaguely north. He followed them until they came to a hillock of tumbled stones with large ferns growing in clusters all about them, and there he lost the trail.

"*I must get help.*" Tarquin muttered to himself. He often narrated his life out loud — it made him feel more excited about living it. "I don't know the forest well enough to track her, and every moment that passes is a moment closer to her getting gobbled up. I must gather up the Company: though they be weary, we must press on. Shamsala needs us! We are her only hope!"

....

It could rightly be said that our adventuring ambitions began with the quest to find my lost goat, Shamsala. Not a very dramatic start to such a dangerous career, but it is often little successes that rouse the appetite for greater ones.

She was not a very impressive goat — a bit gassy and ill-tempered, (likely from being so often gassy), but she was mine to take care of. And in those days, I didn't own anything more than my wooden wuster, and the clothes I was wearing when I was brought to Eld in chains.

So the flood that caused her sudden loss was enough to provoke much foolishness in my attempts to get her back, and almost cost us all quite dearly in the end.

The Quest to Save Shamsala

It was not as difficult to get everyone on board with the Quest to Save Shamsala as one might have imagined. The initial difficulty was in getting everyone to agree on the title for the quest. Talara insisted on "The Quest to Save Shamsala." It appealed to her sense of oratory style, and Tarquin liked it too. Melvin at first suggested "The Quest for the Burgled Billy" until Mathias pointed out that the goat hadn't been stolen, and was a girl goat besides. Caetal wanted to call it "The Quest to Find Tarquin's Stupid Goat" but everyone else was polite enough to ignore him. Although by the end of the troubles we went through, popular opinion agreed that Caetal's quest name was the most apt.

....

None of us had recovered from the aftershocks of trauma that the Homsaöl and the collapse of the abbey had caused, let alone the persistent nagging fear that the monster was not trapped underground after all. All of us (except apparently Rahyn) suffered nightmares of the elemental bursting up out of the caves to finish what it had started. I believe Melvin had the worst of those nightmares, for he woke us up on occasion even years later, bathed in sweat and crying out the secret name of the Homsaöl.

The point is, we were all pretty rattled, and being around the horrifyingly adult task of parents fishing bloated bodies of their children out of the floodwaters was nothing that any of us wanted to experience. And there was still Hosten on our minds — always Hosten. The smashed thing that used to be our youngest friend.

The morning after the abbey fell, when the clerics and parents finally arrived through the flood waters, they found us standing in a circle around what was left of Hosten's body. We had tried at first to bury him, but even Mathias did not yet know the proper rites to speak over his body to send him to the Returning Place. So we had covered him with earth and piled a cairn of stones above him, right there on the lawn. No parent should have to see what we saw of his body. It is better for them to only imagine what had become of their youngest son, and barely even that.

"He was struck down by the monster, and we honored him and covered him with stones." Mathias said, and all of us wept together. He could not have said it better.

....

A more proper funeral for Hosten was requested, but with so much death in the valley and the abbey itself in ruins, the clerics refused all but the simplest rites until they could get word to their order in Portuan and make plans for what to do next. The funeral was delayed for a month, and even Mathias was encouraged to make himself scarce for a while. So on a cold morning, three days after Holm flooded and the morning after Tarquin pleaded with them for help, the six friends gathered at the house of Liam where the tracks began, and set out to find Shamsala. Privately, most of them believed she was already dead. But the thought of taking a walk in the woods together was cheering, and nobody had anything particular to go home to.

They brought snacks, and a few small weapons. Caetal wanted to bring Dubby, of course, but Tarquin said the jackwolf would most likely frighten Shamsala away. Caetal argued, but eventually admitted that Dubby had not been trained to track goats, which might become troublesome. Then he wanted to bring his heavy crossbow, but he was afraid of losing his few bolts. So instead, he only brought his belt hatchet and a sulky attitude. Mathias brought his symbol of Cuthain's eye, which he wore beneath his shirt in case he got teased about it. He also brought a bottle of mead he had found unbroken in the kitchen. He kept this a secret, because he felt guilty having taken it without asking, and he knew they were too young to be drinking it anyway. It remained unopened for the quest, but it made him feel very adulty to have it in his backpack.

The day warmed up as they walked.

....

"Everyone doing this whole 'rushing out on the battlefield to die' thing has got it all wrong." Tarquin stated, as the five children (with the sixth strapped in saddleback) walked slowly through the forest, all in a line.

Each had a backpack packed with some valuables, and some nonsense. Except for Rahyn — she carried nothing but a small copper knife. Caetal was in the lead, carefully following Shamsala's hoof tracks. Tarquin walked just behind him, carrying Melvin saddleback.

"The real point of the battle isn't to kill the guy across from you. That guy is probably some Bartholomew who grows cabbages and hosts the local trade blanket back home. A conscript to the army, know what I mean? The real point is to kill the queen or lord or whoever gathered up that army in the first place."

Talara nodded, just behind him. "You have to disrupt the attacking government, and that means taking out leaders."

"Right." Tarquin continued. "So here's what I'm on about: if I was told to rush out and get myself hacked up, I'd want to play a different game, because who wants to be the dead guy? Not me, and I'll bet not Bartholomew. Instead of that, I'd get my hands on the smallest crossbow I could find, and then I would go take a privy break when everyone else in the army is lining up for the charge, so that I end up in the back row. From there I'd watch to see what happens, and wait until someone on my side gets a near-fatal injury, but not fully dead-dead. Then I'd run right over and throw myself down nearby and pretend to be corpsified."

Melvin snorted, and shifted his arms around Tarquin's shoulders, trying to hold up some of his own thin weight. "Why would anyone believe that you had actually been killed? You're just laying there with a loaded crossbow, looking alive."

Tarquin's face screwed up in a moment's concentration, and he hoisted Melvin up further on his back. He was panting from exertion; they were climbing a low hill now.

"You're right. I'm going to have to go over to the wounded guy and borrow a few handfuls of his blood. '*Sorry guy*' I'd say, '*this is for the best.*' ...He probably wouldn't mind loaning me some, because what does he need all that blood for anymore? He's already dying. So I would smear it all over myself, then go lay down a little ways off from him, and then-"

Caetal interrupted from up front, where he was bent over, studying the ground. "How far away? Sixty feet?"

"No, closer than that. About twenty feet. Then-"

"W-why that close?"

"You'll find out, if you stop interrupting."

"Fine. I was just trying to picture it clearly in my head. Twenty feet between you and the almost-dead Bartholomew. G-go on. But hold on, I need a moment, the tracks are confusing. I think she was w-w-wuh. wandering in circles here for a w-while. She must have been grazing. Put Melvin down."

Tarquin took a breath, and slowly lowered Melvin off his back and on to a rock, being careful to lean him up against a tree. The others paused to rest, passing around dried apples and bits of hard cheese. They had been hiking through the forest for about an hour now, and though sunlight danced through the leaves overhead, the ground was still quite soggy. They sat on mossy boulders and feasted on their simple fare.

Tarquin continued:

"Ok, so I'm still laying there, soaked in that wounded guy's blood and maybe a little of his guts or whatever. Meanwhile, the battle rages. If our side wins: great! I get back up again, and none the worse for it but a bloody tunic. If our side loses, this is where the real game plays out. So, the victorious queen wants to tour the battlefield and appreciate all the trouble she's caused to people like Bartholomew, who by now arc scattered around in pieces all over the place. Eventually the queen strolls near enough to where I am laying, surrounded by her knights and thegns and whatnot. Everyone is laughing wickedly about all the slaughtering they just did. But after they pass by me, I sit halfway up and loose my quarrel into the back of the queen's neck, and then toss the crossbow over onto the dying guy. The queen falls dead off her horse, now everyone is shouting — *'betrayer! Assassin!'* And they are all looking around wildly for the crossbowman. *'Who did it? Who killed the queen?'* And there he is laying on thc ground with the murder weapon at hand: mortally wounded already, just waiting for some avenging nobleman to finish him off."

Tarquin took a deep breath, and smiled smugly. "So: I've toppled the monarchy *and* helped a wounded guy get properly killed, as they obviously head over to whcrc hc is and stab him a bunch of times until he's good and dead."

"Ah, I g-get it." Caetal nodded. He had found the track again, but paused to sit down and eat dried apricots. "That's w-why you w-w-w... needed to be so close to the dying guy. So you could throw thc crossbow over on top of him."

"Yep. Plus, I bet having a crossbow land on him would rouse him up a bit too — make him look livelier for a few moments. Even a dying guy is going to react to having a crossbow flung at him."

Melvin nodded from where he was propped up. He was staring at a ladybug that crawled slowly up his leg. "A more plausible threat if he seems lively."

"Yes. Pausible — just so."

"*What if they stab you too?*" Talara enquired, around a mouthful of bread.

"What? Why would they do that? I'm just another dead guy laying on the ground with all the other obviously dead guys. We're all perfectly deceased: nothing out of the ordinary here."

"Well, now they know they can't take a chance, because there are any number of supposedly dead guys in the area, and look: one of them just knocked off their queen. Time to get stabby on everybody, just in case. Got to make sure those corpses aren't faking."

"I — um..."

"Also," Mathias interjected, "why did the queen remove her helmet?"

"Pardon?"

"Well, you said that you would shoot her in the neck. What if her helmet and gorget is still on, and her neck is protected? Are you supposed to take a shot anyway? Because if your shot pings off and goes wild, the whole plan is a flop."

"What's a *gorget*?" Rahyn asked. She had gathered a bowl full of wild red clover, chickweed and wanderer's lettuce, and, having crumbled up her hard cheese, now sprinkled it on top. She scooped small handfuls of it into her mouth.

"It's... neck armor. I think." Mathias replied, grimacing as he watched her eat salad with her hands. She didn't notice.

"Oh. 'Gorget' is a nice word. It sounds really full and round, but slightly spiky."

Tarquin flushed. Without noticing, he squeezed a handful of cheese until it mooshed between his fingers. "Look, she obviously took her helmet off to have a good laugh about her victory with her thegns. Plus, it's hot out, and she's just been fighting, so it's time to take her helmet off."

Caetal groaned. "W-when did it get hot? W-w-what if it's raining, clotpole?"

"It isn't raining, fart-breath. It's hot and sunny in this story. Who wants to fight a war in the rain?"

"It happens all the time."

"...Really? That's dumb. Everyone should just go home if it's raining and wait to fight on a nice sunny day. Dying in the rain and mud? No thank you, army-captain-sir." Tarquin stood up, brushing crumbs of cheese off his hands and onto his pants. "Go find yourself a different Tarquin. War is dumb enough without being soaked through. Rainy war is too dumb to be real."

"Not rain, though. Rain is perfect just as it is." Rahyn said, smiling to herself. The others stared at her doubtfully.

"Ya, but we've sure had too damn much of it lately. Now come on brave adventurers, let's keep questing for my stupid goat."

"Aha!" Caetal crowed. "I knew you w-would come around to my quest title!"

....

At the mercy of those faint hoof-tracks, the children were forced to amble at a leisurely, somewhat boring pace. So they whittled sticks into staves, dangled from low-hanging branches, and rooted around for freaky-looking mushrooms. When the trail crossed stretches of clear ground, they were able to pick up the pace to an almost normal walking speed, as the goat tracks became so obvious that "even Mathias could follow them." This was pointed out, rather rudely, by Caetal. Then followed an earnest discussion of who had spent the least amount of time in a forest environment. It was a toss-up between Talara and Mathias, but Caetal thought Talara was the better-looking of the two, so Mathias got stuck being teased about it from then on.

All told, they had not gone more than three miles from where they had begun, having spent about three hours doing it, when they emerged at the edge of an unexpected river. Even Caetal, who had ranged all over these parts, was surprised to see it. The river would be quite a bit thinner by summertime, but now it had widened far beyond its bed into a slowly drifting swamp with a fast current hurrying down the center. There are many rivers in that part of the forest, all pouring in and out of Loc Enum, or Xor Uru, or one of the uncounted tributaries of the southern-flowing Trask. So many rivers, in fact, that they have never been individually labeled or mapped, and all bore the collective name of *Bec-Dorni* — which means, in the Uisen language, "Streams-like-fingers."

This stream indeed seemed like one of those fingers. *"Perhaps the middle one?"* Talara was heard muttering. For there, in clear view and on the other side of it, was Shamsala. She was grazing by the river's edge, as contented as any goat might be who was born on the far side of this wide waterway. The children looked at her, and then in silence glanced up and down the wide and flowing highway that stretched between themselves and their quarry. The river was the better part of two hundred feet across, with a churning set of rapids dancing around submerged logs.

Tarquin cupped his hands and bellowed: "SHAMSALA!" across the water, and the goat perked up her head and maaaed at him, wagging her stumpy little tail. Then Tarquin maaaed back, and a bleating exchange followed, with Tarquin trotting up and down the bank maaaing soothingly, and Shamsala doing likewise on the other side. Even Caetal admitted it was pretty cute.

When he returned to the group, Talara asked what was on everyone's mind: "How in the moons did she swim across this? She's got tiny, useless, flappy little hooves!"

"Actually, goats are very good at swimming." Tarquin replied, panting slightly. "True story: sometimes they even swim in the ocean between islands. That's how my Grandda said goats got to Aethys. They must have swum over from another island — maybe even Eld."

"W-wow!" Said Caetal, who had no idea how far apart those two islands were. But it sounded impressive.

Melvin rolled his eyes. "The important question isn't how she got over there, it's how we get her back. None of us can safely make that swim."

Both Caetal and Tarquin said, "I could!" at the same time, and then glared at each other competitively. Each was already stripping off his shirt when Talara pointed at the swift flow at the river's center and said "Don't be thick. There are hidden rocks and trees all under that water. You'd both be bashed into biscuits, and we'd have to fish your stupid bodies out miles downstream. Stop being such boys." She winked at Rahyn, who wasn't looking, and missed it.

"I could swim across." Rahyn said. Everyone looked at her. She turned a little pink, and ducked her eyes from their stares. "I mean... the fox could do it. I know she could. Foxes are almost as good swimmers as goats, when they want to be. I could go get her."

Tarquin beamed. "That's a great idea! Thank you Rahyn! Okay, go ahead and turn into a fox."

Rahyn squirmed. "I... It doesn't just happen when I think about it. I have to... it takes some special... I'll go try. But nobody peek while I'm changing, ok? It can get... hard to watch." She glanced at Mathias sympathetically, and he looked away and blushed. Then she hurried off into the forest and disappeared from view.

The other kids exchanged glances. After a few moments, Melvin whispered *"look, I don't want to state the obvious, but even if she can figure out how to change into a fox, how is she going to get Shamsala back across to this side? A river this wide could be hundreds of miles long, and it's not like a goat is going to follow a fox back over across the river out of natural instinct. We need to come up with a different plan."*

Mathias, carefully moving a pinecone one inch to the left, said: "We could build a raft?"

Caetal snorted. "Out of w-what, ordanian? W-wuh: *we* don't have any rope or tools. Don't be *valea*."

Mathias blushed. The pinecone rolled over too far. Mathias returned it to where he wanted it, then looked up and saw everyone staring at him. He blushed even deeper.

"Well... we can walk back and get some. Tools, I mean. And rope."

Talara perked up. "Yes, I like this idea! I didn't pack for an overnight anyway, I need to pick up some blankets and... probably food? If we are planning on staying out here. How fun! You guys, I've never actually been camping in the woods before!" She frowned, suddenly. "At least, not on purpose, anyway. And not with friends."

"How far could you shoot an arrow?" Tarquin interjected, tapping Caetal's arm.

Caetal glanced across the river at the trees on the other side.

"Are you asking if I could shoot an arrow that far? ...Ya, I could. It w-w-wh.. I'd have to do an arc shot with a heavy-pull bow, maybe like a longbow or my crossbow. But I could make the shot. W-why? You change your mind about eating Shamsala?" Talara punched his arm, and he grinned wickedly.

"No, donkey-socks. I was thinking about a rope and pulley. Maybe when Rahyn gets across the river, we could shoot her over a rope, she could tie it off to a tree, aaaaand... we could lash Shamsala to the rope and guide her back across like that? I mean... I'd honestly rather build a raft, because it would be more fun —" Tarquin squeezed Mathias' knee, who smiled gratefully "— but I think a rope pulley might be a lot faster than-"

"Not happening. We would need at least four hundred feet of rope, plus ideally a proper pulley on both sides to make that work." Melvin interrupted, gesturing with his hands. "There is *no way* an arrow could fly that far dragging a long rope behind it."

"Well, not if it's some heavy hawser rope, but I bet if the rope was thin, I could shoot an arrow that far." Caetal spoke up.

Melvin looked at him like his rear end was growing out of his shoulders. Talara started laughing. Tarquin, trying to imagine himself making that shot and not picturing success, said nothing.

"Oh yeah? What do you want to bet? I've got a Silver Spriggan on it that your arrow doesn't make it halfway across that river, regardless of how thin your rope is." Melvin glared smugly at Caetal, who flushed. A silver was a lot of coppers, after all.

"You're on, rich kid." Caetal sneered, sourly. "I'll trek back to Holm w-with w-w- whoever's needing supplies and go get a longbow and rope. Let's meet back here in a few hours."

"Great!" Talara said, standing up and brushing dirt off her breeches. "Mathias and I will come too: won't you Mathias? That way we can get packed for a campout, and pick up some of those raft-making supplies that I'm sure we will need when this pissing contest is over. You coming, Tarquin?"

"No, I better stay here to keep an eye on Melvin and Shamsala."

"*I don't need a nursemaid to tend me, Tarquin!*" Melvin snarled. "Don't lump me in with the livestock! I'm sure I will be just fine sitting here; it doesn't take two of us to watch your damn goat. Go on, help Caetal find the world's thinnest rope. He'll need it."

Tarquin stammered something unintelligible, then nodded. As the others filed off back the way they had come, he quietly doubled back and touched Melvin's shoulder. Melvin shrugged him off.

"I'm sorry, Mel. I didn't mean... are you sure you don't want the company?"

"I'll be fine. I'm always fine. Don't trouble yourself. Besides, Rahyn is somewhere nearby. She'll look out for me." Melvin said softly, folding his arms across his chest. He leaned back against a log, with his feet splaying out towards the river. Across the water, Shamsala grazed on cattails.

"...As you say. We'll be back before it gets dark. If Shamsala tries to wander, make bleating noises at her." Tarquin turned and jogged off to catch up with his less grouchy friends.

....

Melvin sat and watched the rolling water. He watched the goat forage and marked the sinking progress of the sun. Dragonflies darted in and out of the rushes, as big as his fist and as colorful as crystals. He watched those too. But all he felt, besides a cramp in his back from leaning against the log, was the hot spread of shame at the way he had treated his friends. He never should have made such an expensive bet with Caetal. He knew a silver piece was a lot for the woodcutter's son. And he was as certain as momentum, drag and parabolas that an arrow with a rope lashed to it could never clear that river. It seemed... *unkind* to fleece his illiterate friend over something that had to be learned in books, or from actual failure. Melvin had an unfair advantage, and he had exploited it.

"*Gods dammit.*" He muttered to himself, wiping his eyes.

At that moment, a large fox came loping out the forest. It had dusky purple-gray fur and bright amber eyes. The vixen did not so much as glance his way, but leapt into the river upstream of Melvin. Paddling hard against the current, the fox drifted a few hundred feet downstream as it swam. Once passed the most treacherous part of the current, she paused midstream on a partially submerged log. There she took a quick break, stretched, and shook the water out of her ears.

Shamsala had her back to the stream and her head in some skunk cabbage, and had not yet noticed the approaching fox. But Melvin saw the fox's head perk up as it gazed upon the swaying backside of the grazing goat. The fox slipped back into the river, now swimming almost lazily, with her tail drifted out behind her. Melvin watched in fascination, his heart racing and his mind daydreaming about shape-shifting magic. The fox gained the shallows a hundred feet downriver, and, still keeping her eyes on Shamsala, shook the water out of her fur. She began to pad towards Shamsala, closing the distance quickly between them. Then, to Melvin's mounting concern, he saw her lower herself into a hunting crouch, and, as quick as a purple streak, went launching at the unsuspecting goat.

"RAHYN, NO! RUN SHAMSALA!!" Melvin shouted. But it was too late.

Shamsala was not the smartest goat, but neither was she a fool. Though raised in captivity, she knew the smell of fox and winded the sudden rush of approaching danger just in time.

She jumped a foot in the air and spun, taking the impact on the back of her body instead of her neck. The vixen bit down hard into Shamsala's thigh, and scrabbled with her claws to gain a hold on the goat's back.

Shamsala bolted forward into the water, screaming wretchedly and dragging the fox in behind her. Both animals toppled through the shallows, then submerged underwater.

A tense minute passed. Melvin tried instinctively and uselessly to push himself up to his feet to better see the thrashing tangle of the two animals. Then Shamsala burst up out of the water, bawling with pain and sprinting downriver along the shore. Blood was leaking from multiple wounds on her hindquarters.

The vixen tried to pursue for about fifty feet, then stopped. Her back arched and she shuddered a few times, then stretched her mouth open wide and vomited up river water. For a while she sat grooming herself, ignoring Shamsala entirely as the wounded goat bounded out of sight around a bend, and was lost from view in the bracken.

"RAHYN! COME BACK!" Melvin called out, hopefully. Then he cupped his hands and called out again.

The fox glanced at him, sneezed, then wandered off into the forest.

"Double dammit. And triple dammit too." Melvin said, sliding back down against the log.

For the thousandth time, he wished with every desperate fiber of his body that he could walk again. Even a wobbling stumble would suffice, or crawling on his hands and knees. Yet he could do nothing but wait for his friends to return. The afternoon stretched on towards twilight; the nasal chittering of the treeweets calling to each other in the high branches felt like mockery to his darkening thoughts. The sounds of the forest seemed to close in all around him: stranding him in his own silence, reminding him of how alone he truly felt.

....

The Magus and the Mason

Daedrim stumbled through the ruin of the abbey alone. He was trying to get drunk for the first time since his wedding night, so many years ago.

Carefully he stepped through the ruin of his labors, each foot treacherously sliding across the debris. The piles of shattered wood and stone were lit by afternoon light: they sparkled jaggedly from a hundred hues of broken glass. Heiro Manan and most of the clergy had departed to Portuan to confer with the Heirogoth and the Elder Council. Farhu Fren, who had slept through the rampaging monster, had been dismissed in disgrace and awaited the return to Ulfaang when the roads were passable again. Only a few members of the town militia were stationed at the abbey now. Three were posted "on duty" outside, but they were just farmers who wanted an excuse to distract themselves from their own fallow fields and ruined crops. So they drank, and muttered bitterly to each other, and let the mason wander the halls unsupervised.

Scattered fragments of ornate carvings littered the ground. Daedrim stepped over the broken statue of one of the Triad laying on the floor. As he walked on the prostrate torso he ground the heel of his foot against the curve of the stone back, above where the heart would be. *So many wasted years of my life, and all the stone shaping that my son will ever do. Now it lays in piles on the floor where drunken militiamen can pee on it at night. Nothing that matters ever lasts.* Daedrim kicked the severed head of the god he had just trampled on into one corner, and although it hurt his foot, he felt a little better. Then the head rolled to a stop facing him, and he saw the eyeless stare of Hausa the Soul-Gatherer. A cold flutter went down his spine. *Bad luck to kick the Dark Sister.* He took another swig from his mead bottle, but it didn't make him feel any drunker. Just heavy. *Better get outside into fresher air. Pay some respects to the dead boys.*

....

A half hour later found him leaning against the sundial pillar just outside the back door. He felt unwilling to move. No amount of mental self-coaxing could convince him to step onto the back lawn. Also, he was out of mead and nowhere near as drunk as he had hoped to be. So, he leaned against the pillar, letting the late-day sunlight warm him, and stared over at the hole in the wall that the monster made when it broke through, and the capstone of the (now collapsed) archway that almost killed his son. Grass was growing up tall around the stone pieces, which still lay where they had fallen all those weeks ago. The rest of the lawn was trimmed and level. *One direction leads to little Hosten's grave, and the other to the spot where my son should have died. How can I be expected to set foot on that lawn again?*

No footfalls announced the arrival of Drinn the magus. And yet suddenly he was there, just a few feet from Daedrim's elbow. Drinn looked as pale and plain as ever, but for the auburn hair, and his improbable green eyes. He smiled politely, and tipped his head in the faintest bow. Daedrim snorted, and looked away. He was just tipsy enough not to be impressed by the sudden appearance of the magus, and was in no mood to share the afternoon with such supernatural company: the sort who appeared and disappeared without warning, as though an introvert like Daedrim wouldn't mind the intrusion.

"Good afternoon, mason."

"Is it?"

"Ah. I see."

Drinn paused, then tried again. "Where is Melvinari? Is he at home?"

"He is not. He has refused to return home since the accident. He still needs help in ways that make him feel uncomfortably helpless. He insists that the clerics are better suited to the task."

Drinn nodded. "He prefers that Cuthain's Chosen empty his bedpan, and not his own father. That is understandable."

Daedrim smiled tightly. "My son has never been over-fond of the clergy anyway. I think he enjoys having them clean up after him."

Drinn chuckled. "I was thinking the same thing, but I didn't want to be the one to say it out loud. Good for him. But has he... does he retain awareness of... how extensive is his paralysis?"

Daedrim stared at the magus, frowning uncomfortably. "Are you asking if Melvinari is incontinent? No, thankfully he is not. The keystone crushed his thighs, not his spine. And yet, though the bones appear to have healed enough to bear weight, his body cannot seem to remember the use of his legs. Something must have been damaged that time has not been able to repair."

"Indeed. That is a relief."

"For him?"

"For everyone involved, I'd imagine. A relief to not change linens out a few times a day, and for him, to not be sitting in soiled clothes."

"…I suppose so."

There passed an awkward moment of silence between the two men. Each coughed, and readjusted where their feet were planted on the stone platform. One wished he had remembered to bring his pipe, and the other resented the emptiness of his mead bottle.

"Well: obviously Melvin is no longer in the care of the clergy — no place left to tend to him, and I've seen no clerics around to bother." Drinn gestured broadly to the abbey ruin, and Daedrim frowned. "So where is he?"

"Elsewhere. His friends have taken him with them into the forest to go camping and look for a missing goat. It will do him good to spend time in the woods with companions for a while; perhaps get the chance to feel like the boy he was for a few fleeting hours again."

"Ah: indeed. I hope he finds joy of it."

The aroma of the blooming bergamot tree permeated the air with a forceful floridness.

Finally Daedrim, sounding a bit cross and seeing that Drinn was not inclined to leave, said:

"You did not come here to talk to Melvin, did you? Let us speak plainly; I feel a headache coming on, and I have no wish to linger here overlong."

Drinn looked at Daedrim with a predatory gaze. "Nor do I. Very well then — plainly spoken, I am here to remind you of the promise you made to me. Build me my tower, mason. In winter I told you of the project, and we came to accord: the offer was made and shook on. Now it is spring, and the time for building is here. I will pay you twice the thegn's offering, as I said I would. You are the only one I trust to chisel precise symbols: it must be you, and no other. You understand the truth of stone — an artisan's talent, wasted on repairing a broken church."

Daedrim sighed. "I would not take the thegn's coin again, or rebuild his ruined church. This abbey is cursed. It cost Melvinari the man he could have grown into. It cost my son his life, if such a thing is measured in opportunities. My apologies, magus, but I am done with stone. I wanted to build something that could survive beyond the petty races of Humanus; something to outlast all our senseless machinations. But I cannot forgive myself for failing to safely instruct my trade to my son. It was my failure as a mentor that allowed that arch to fall on him. My pride in my teaching let him work unsupervised."

Drinn began to retort, but Daedrim interrupted him. "No, don't say anything. I know well what my failures are." He clenched his fists in anger, beating them against his own thighs unconsciously. "If I had been there with him, instead of on that bloody road on an errand to please the thegn and earn more of his wretched coin, I would have supervised Melvin in removing the scaffold. I would surely have seen the signs of porous mortar, or stress cracks."

Daedrim's voice started shivering, like the wind was blowing through him. "I would have... he never should have *guessed* about such things, and I thought I was so careful — you must *know* to be a mason, you cannot afford to guess, because so much depends on getting everything right. You can't just *guess,* do you understand?"

Tears welled and fell, and he wiped them away impatiently. His knuckles were heavy and gray, like the stones he carved, yet his hands shook with tiny tremors, and his skin looked as papery as drying leaves.

Damn the mead, I never should have drunk mead. It always makes me maudlin.

Drinn watched him with eyes that glittered in an otherwise placid face — yet when he spoke, his voice sounded warm and in earnest. Daedrim had turned away from him, and therefore could not see the hungry shining of his eyes.

"I understand, and I sympathize. The artistry of magic demands no less. The fate of a careless magus is the same as that of a tumbling keystone, or the unlucky boy pinned beneath it. Yet magic is the most powerful force on Homm, and those who learn to wield it hold advantage over all around them, as the herdsmen has advantage over his flock. You say that you are done with stone, but I cannot believe you, for I see in the lines of your future that you have one last great masonry project left inside you. Also: there is a tower ruin already present at the site for you to rebuild from. That should save you considerable time."

Daedrim said nothing for a while, taking the time he needed to collect himself. Drinn waited patiently. Eventually Daedrim shifted back around towards him and replied.

"Not necessarily. Repairing a ruin might complicate the project more than beginning the build from an architectural sketch."

"Whyever for? A stable base to build up from lessens labor and reduces the effort of importing building materials."

Daedrim nodded. "On the one hand, yes: it is often easier to repair than to build from scratch. On the other, there is always a *reason* a building was ruined. Sometimes it is the violent luck of warfare, or general neglect."

"Or a Homsaöl."

"A what?"

"A monster of earth and stone. Like the one that destroyed the abbey."

"...Yes, I suppose. What I'm getting at here is: sometimes a ruin is created by a fundamental flaw in design. A tower built on an overly shallow foundation, say. Perhaps soft soil or clay where bedrock was needed. A freestanding tower is more of a marvel than it seems, and often extends deeper underground to support itself than a glance can guess."

Drinn nodded. "Comfort yourself with knowledge: the old tower is a ruin made not through architectural folly or neglect, but through magic. Actually, I suppose one could call it 'neglect,' but of the sort that is made by an overly heedless magus neglecting to protect themselves from the harm of their own ambitions."

Daedrim eyed him with disdain. "*Ah.* I am not predilected towards building on the sites of old curses or magical misfortunes. No thank you, good afternoon."

Drinn smiled tightly, a hint of condescension in his eyes. "Have no fear of the ghosts of toppled walls and scattered rubble. It is the surrounding lake that is properly haunted. I didn't expect a learned man such as yourself to spook so easily."

Daedrim frowned. "I do not consider caution towards the supernatural to be a character failing. As you can see from the ruin we are standing next to: I have become recently accosted by the reality that such forces *do* exist and must therefore begin to be wary of them."

Drinn laughed. "Well and wisely spoken! I appreciate your caution, and can assure you — as someone who knows the supernatural well — that your concern is unnecessary."

"So you claim."

Drinn's tight smile reformed. "Trust me: it would be unwise to refuse my offer. The rebuilding of this tower is the opportunity that will take your skill to its absolute zenith — a project that, when completed, shall fund your retirement from brute labor until the end of your days. Under kinder circumstances, I would hope *that* in itself would be enough reward to entice you. But hear me now, Daedrim, son of Alvis, for a magus does not make the same offer twice. If you agree to my request, and undertake the building of this tower, I will provide you with something far greater than wealth. I will take your son Melvinari as my apprentice while you are building, and teach him what knowledge I have of the invisible world. If the gifts I see in him ripen as I believe they could, then when the tower is complete, he shall come to live inside it in safety and in rare opportunity. There, and only there, might he learn to evoke the power he needs to regain the use of his legs."

Daedrim stared at him sternly. His tongue made a little clicking sound against the roof of his mouth, but he didn't reply. Drinn continued:

"Before you answer, I would caution you to restrain from speaking prejudice against a magus, for I will not suffer it unprovoked. I know that fear of magic taints the minds of provincial thinking, so I would expect no less from you. Melvinari will not be instructed in unscrupulous or unraveling arts, I give you my word on it. Your son shall never be turned against kindness, or common sense, while in my care."

Daedrim snorted. "My son already has more common sense then both of us, for we repeat mistakes that he hasn't had the foolishness to attempt. I hold little prejudice against the use of magic — it is the magicians themselves that I distrust, just as much as I would distrust *anyone* who compares the rest of us to beasts, and imagines themselves our herdsman. And yet, I have no answer to give you. I cannot speak for Melvinari, and the decision should be his."

Drinn was silent for a moment, and stared past Daedrim at the small pile of stones that was Hosten's cairn. The afternoon sunlight slanted so that each stone cast its own shadow. When he spoke again, his voice was soft.

"Mason, you know as well as I that Melvinari will do absolutely anything to walk again. For if he does not, he will always be a burden to the only people who love him, and that would be intolerable to someone like him. There is nothing in this world that will stop him from seeking to master the use of magic, once he deduces that it is his only chance to feel special again. He has been obsessing about it even now, I promise you; he has manipulated the True Name for stone, and now he wonders about the Names for his own bones. He will be my apprentice, whether or not you allow him to be — there is no choice in the matter for either of us: none at all. You may choose to grow old and die with grief, and I might continue to flee what pursues me, and spend what remains of my life alone. But Melvin will seek out the magical arts with all that is trapped inside of him. It is his fate."

Now it was Daedrim who stared in silence at the boy's cairn, and the shadows of the stones lengthened as he thought. Drinn did not move, or speak. The magus and the mason stood nearly shoulder to shoulder.

At last, Daedrim slowly nodded his head. His finger tapped the iron sundial three times, then he spoke.

"Fated or not, he is almost a grown man, and he must answer your offer himself, for that is what growing up means. As for me, I do not wish to spend my twilight years lamenting the knowledge that I was offered a chance to help my son, and did not take it. I will therefore accept the construction of your tower as my last masonry project, and likewise accept your coin with as much dignity as a grieving fool of a father can muster. But know this, oh magus, for a master mason does not repeat himself twice: *I am building this tower for my son, and for his future.* To me, it is yours only in name. If what you say is true, and magic might be useful enough to help Melvinari walk again, then I am your mason. Show me the place and name your terms. I shall pack and we can leave within the hour."

Drinn smiled tightly. "I shall show you the place, but you do not have to pack. We can leave immediately." Cupping one hand behind Daedrim's neck, he placed the thumb of the other in the center of his forehead. Then the magus spoke two words. The first sounded like a gale blowing between creaking branches; the second one vibrated as a thrown rock does when rebounding across the surface of a frozen pond. Their skin sighed, and the air around them folded inside-out. Then the two men evaporated.

....

The Quest Continues

The sun was sinking behind the hills when the Company of Six regathered at last by the river's edge. The returning children, having walked nine miles there, back and there again — let alone the difficulty of gathering supplies in town by wading through waist-high water — were thoroughly spent. Their moods went from tired to depressed as Melvin related to them what Rahyn's fox shape had done and how she had vanished in the forest thereafter. He tried to keep Shamsala's injuries from being the climax of the story, but there wasn't any decent way to tell it otherwise. Tarquin excused himself and went to sit alone by the river, and the other three who could do so began to set up camp before dark came on. The first hours of their first campout passed glumly. Nobody commented on the heavy bow Caetal brought and left by the river or the coil of thin rope that was so long it had filled a whole backpack to overflowing. Caetal and Melvin carefully avoided each other's gaze. Caetal built a fire, Mathias managed Melvin, Melvin managed dinner, and Talara went and sat as close as she dared to Tarquin.

She still did not know how to feel about Tarquin. On the one hand, he was the easiest of all of her new friends to connect with. He was jovial, irreverent, and was always one grin away from goofing off. But in sudden moments, she would see a private flicker of shame or grief burn across his smile like a flashfire. She would think: *you were the boy that I followed when I had nowhere else to go. You led me to Holm.* In such a young friendship, she had not found a moment to say out loud the question that was in her heart. *Did you recognize me too? That I was the girl in the upstairs window, who knows that you used to be free?*

But she, who had so many stories crowding up the room inside her head, could think of no way to begin that story of connection that starts with: *you don't know it, but we were already special to each other before we ever met.* So instead, she perched herself at the far end of the same short log he was sitting on and tried to pretend she couldn't see the tears on his cheeks as he stared at the darkening forest across the river. After a while, she found the courage to rest a pinky finger on top of one of his, and he smiled wearily at her. It was the best they could do.

"I hope she's okay." Tarquin sniffed.
"Rahyn?"
"Shamsala. I hope Rahyn got indigestion from chewing on my goat.

I hope she's somewhere feeling awful and farty and miserable. ...Unless she's not the fox anymore. Then I hope she's not alone out there in the dark woods. But I do hope she feels bad for what she did. ...Unless the fox took over completely, and she didn't know she was doing it. Then I guess I hope she doesn't find out. ...Until she does, and then I hope she still feels bad, but not miserable. Dammit, I just really, really hope they are both ok."

"Me too."

"Thanks for sitting here with me." The tips of their pinkies brushed together: once, twice.

"You're welcome. I mainly came over here to avoid having to help cook dinner. You just happened to be already sitting on the log I wanted to sit on, so: lucky for you."

"I had that feeling."

She reached over and poked his ribs until he laughed and slapped her hand away. Then she took his hand and pulled him up off the log.

"Come on, oh Mighty Quest Leader. Quit moping. Let's go eat that good smell."

"I probably do deserve a snack after all that hard moping I've been doing." Tarquin mumbled wryly, blushing a little.

"Ya, self-pity really works up an appetite."

Talara walked Tarquin back to the warmth of the campfire, and though they didn't hold hands, they both wondered if they could have.

....

The children slept poorly. At first, they had arranged their sleeping furs and blankets around the fire but were awoken in the deep evening by falling dampness that couldn't decide if it was a mist or drizzle. Caetal was the only one who had brought an oilcloth tarp, so he got up while everyone else was complaining and used part of the long rope to string up a simple tent between two low branches. Then everyone had to crowd into a moistened pile in the center of the tent, which was great for warmth but not fantastic for breathing.

The next few hours were fitful with the shifting of bodies rolling towards or away from the center of the pile, and by dawn Caetal (who had a fear of being smothered in his sleep) returned to the fire and did the best he could to fall back asleep wrapped up in his damp cloak. After a half hour of grumbling and rolling around, he gave up on sleep and contented himself with building the fire back up and boiling dried dandelion tea in the cooking pot.

He was blowing steam off his cup when he saw Melvin squirm out of the pile of sleepers. He dragged himself forward on his elbows until he had cleared the tent far enough to begin looking around for a place to drain his bladder. Caetal set his tea on a log, and approached warily.

"Need help?"

Melvin sighed. "I guess. I haven't figured out a way to do this yet that doesn't involve embarrassing assistance."

"I bet there's a w-way." Caetal lifted Melvin under the arms and walked him a distance from the tent. At least, Caetal walked, and Melvin was hopped forward like a marionette, with his legs slightly dragging. They moved a distance from the campfire to a place where the ground sloped downhill towards the river.

"I bet you get tired of needing help all the time, huh? That w-w-w ... I bet that gets frustrating."

Melvin, sighing, began to loosen the tie on his breeches. "It's indescribable how much I hate it. The fact that I need you to hold me upright so that I can do something so trivial as peeing feels like a punch to the gut — which, if I'm being honest, I'm not sure I could feel anymore."

Caetal nodded. Instead of standing with Melvin, he slowly lowered him to the ground at the edge of a low slope. Then he disentangled their arms and faced Melvin towards the river.

"You don't need me to help you pee, Mel. All you need is a downhill slope. I'll go make you a cup of tea." And he walked away towards the fire.

Melvin craned his head up over his shoulder from where he lay, until Caetal was out of sight. Then he adjusted his breeches and sighed contentedly while a satisfying arc of nightwater went streaming away downhill from where he lay. *Caetal is right. I didn't need the help after all. I just need a downhill slope!* Melvin smiled widely, took a deep and gratifying breath of morning air, tied his breeches up, and dragged himself back to the campfire on his forearms, where Caetal was waiting with a steaming cup of tea.

....

"It's not g-going to w-w-work, is it?" Caetal asked quietly, between sips.

Melvin stared into his cup. "It's pretty much impossible. You ought to try, of course. But quite likely that rope is going to get used tying logs up into a raft."

Caetal sighed forlornly. "Ya, I figured. I don't have many memories of you being w-w-wrong about stuff like this. ...I couldn't find enough rope anyway. I may not even have enough to stretch across the river at all, and it sure isn't as thin as I'd like. Tarquin said w-wuh: we could use hemp twine and still satisfy the bet-"

"Not hardly. Twine is different than rope; that's why it has its own name. But the twine likely wouldn't work either."

"Either way, w-we didn't have even a hundred feet of twine, although I brought that too, just to see if it works." Caetal glumly poked at the fire, stirring the embers. "Do you think my heavy crossbow w-w-w... might have been a better choice? I'm not supposed to be carrying it around because of the Iron Ban, but... oh man, Mel: that thing has crazy kick! I propped up a big pumpkin against that dirt mound in my backyard, and fired off a bolt at it from the crossbow. I'm not kidding: it went right through that pumpkin like it w-wasn't even there! Buried itself in the frozen hillside halfway up the fletching!"

"Oh *wow!*"

"I love that crossbow! Maybe it w-w-would have a better chance at-"

"I don't think the bolt would be able to properly lay in the flight groove with a rope tied around it."

"But maybe it could be... like, maybe the rope could tie from the top? So, then the bolt w-would still be able to-"

"Honestly, the bolt would probably skitter off or shatter if the rope got in the way when the string fired off."

"But w-w-what if I got a really, *really* thin rope?"

"Look, Caetal: the point I'm trying to get at is that I should never have made that bet with you. I know you don't have a silver to lose, firstly."

Here, Caetal began to protest, but Melvin held up his hand to shush him.

"And secondly, a bet between friends is something that should only be made when the odds are fair. I'd bet my legs..." Melvin broke off, laughing. "Nevermind, I can't bet those. I'd bet my arms that your arrow won't clear that river dragging a rope behind it. I'm so sure of myself that, if I were wrong, I would be willing to risk being an armless, legless human potato. And it's not because your bow isn't heavy enough, and it's not because you aren't a good archer. It's because the arrow is light, and the rope is long, and every inch of it makes the arrow's flight increasingly more difficult. Do you understand?"

"Ya, I think so. It was a dumb bet to take. I just g-g-got mad."

"Then let's forget it. Keep your silver to buy some longer twine for next time. But I still want to see how far the arrow can go, just for a laugh."

Melvin grinned, and Caetal smiled too. Then his face screwed up and he spat shreds of roasted dandelion root into the fire. He started coughing like he'd got something up in the down pipe and pointed weakly across the river.

"Mel: *(cough cough)* don't look suddenly, *(cough cough)* but I think Rahyn is back. And she doesn't have a *(cough)* stitch of clothing on."

Across the river, a shape could be seen peering out of the ferns. It was somewhere between girl and fox, but tan skin was rapidly overtaking pewter-colored fur. Melvin waved, and they both glanced and tried not to glance, and then did it once more. Then each of the boys turned away, busying themselves with washing out cups and poking at the fire in a very obvious, not-looking kind of way. Caetal went and woke the others up.

....

By the time the sleepy adventurers were all clustered at the river's edge, Rahyn was almost entirely human-looking again. She stood there with her head bowed, not meeting anyone's eyes. Her foot fidgeted nervously with the back of her other leg, and she shivered a bit from the cold of the morning. But otherwise, she stood there, naked and oblivious to the shuffling discomfort of her friends on the other side of the river. Finally, Tarquin cupped his hands and called across to her.

"IS SHAMSALA ALRIGHT?"

Rahyn looked positively miserable. She nodded her head yes, then no. Then she shouted back: "SHE IS ALIVE. BUT SHE NEEDS HELP. SHE WON'T LET ME NEAR HER."

"*I'll bet she godsdamn won't let you near her,*" Tarquin muttered. "*You probably reek of fox smell.*" But out loud, he only yelled back: "WE WILL FIGURE OUT HOW TO GET ACROSS TO YOU. STAY THERE. ...AND MAYBE THINK ABOUT PUTTING YOUR CLOTHES BACK ON?"

Rahyn shook her head. "THEY ARE ON YOUR SIDE OF THE RIVER."

"PERHAPS THIS WAS NOT THE BEST PLAN!" Talara shouted, giggling.

Rahyn shot her a look, but didn't reply. She retreated back up into the cover of the ferns.

....

Before the log raft construction began in earnest (as it was now obvious that Mathias' plan was the only one that might work), the children attended to the pressing necessities of the morning. For an adult, this would include making breakfast or folding up the tent. For young adventurers, this meant a handful of trail mix and the public settling of a bet. Mathias carefully lashed the thin rope to the furthest end of the arrow, near the fletching. Tarquin coiled the neatest pile of rope he could, so that it wouldn't tangle. Talara retrieved her shawm from her backpack and played a merry rope-coiling tune, improvising a song about how brave the arrow was to fly so far. Soon enough, everyone was laughing, except for Caetal.

At last, when all was prepared, he stepped forward and hefted the bow. With proper diligence, he wrapped his braided hair around his neck like a scarf. To the string he set the arrow, careful of the rope trailing behind him. Talara swelled the piping music of the shawm dramatically. He pulled the longbow back mightily and true, lifted his aim towards the heavens, and fired.

The arrow launched and soared off into the sky...

...and plummeted, almost immediately, into the water. There it drifted with the rope snaking out behind it. It had not traveled the better part of thirty feet. Talara started laughing, and the music farted out disparagingly.

Caetal flushed and glared at Tarquin. "Rope g-got tangled, Log-Noggin. Stretch it further out. Not a coiled pile."

Tarquin saluted smartly. "Right away, Dubby-Pile, sir!" Then he turned to Mathias and bellowed into his ear: "STRETCH THE ROPE OUT FURTHER, SOLDIER!!"

Mathias jumped and grabbed up the end of the rope. Fishing the arrow out of the river, he walked slowly backwards into the woods, straightening the rope all the way out into a reasonably straight line. It trailed over ferns and twined a bit between trees, but it was as straight as he could get it. When he returned, Tarquin nodded, satisfied. Then he clicked his heels and turned back to Caetal and bellowed: "READY FOR ANOTHER SHOT, CAPTAIN DUBBY-PILE!"

Talara swelled the music dramatically again. Caetal, noticeably sweating, lifted the longbow again, tugging the arrow back as far as sinew allowed. Then, with a whir and a snap, the arrow launched.

This time it made it about a quarter of the way across the river before it splashed down. There it drifted, with the children howling laughter on the shore. Even Rahyn was giggling from the other side of the river, and she cupped her hands and called out:

"PERHAPS THAT WAS ALSO NOT THE BEST PLAN?"

Which, of course, set off such a round of hollering that it had them rolling on the ground with tears streaming from laughing eyes: none amongst them louder than Caetal and Melvin.

The arrow drifted listlessly, nibbled upon by a curious fish.

....

Eventually, they got down to the serious business of building a raft. They were fortunate, as Caetal had built one before and knew how. They were even more fortunate that the movement of flood waters had toppled a few smaller trees near the river's edge, saving them the effort of felling. (Had they tried, of course, Rahyn would have strongly objected.)

Mathias unpacked a hand saw and a hatchet. Caetal had brought two more hatchets besides his own, having already privately resigned himself to Mathias' raft-building plan before he had gone back to get the long-bow and rope. One by one, the children located the appropriate trees: four small poplars and a stunted cottonwood. As the morning stretched, they hacked the limbs off and took turns with the larger saw, cutting the trees into lengths that were roughly "two Tarquins and a Talara" long, with a pair of logs a bit thinner and longer than the rest. They then rolled them together down to the water's edge and lined them up in a row so that Melvin and Mathias could notch out one side of each end evenly. When completed, four of the logs were floated out onto the water, where

Caetal, Talara and Tarquin worked together to lash them into a large buoyant frame with the long archery rope. One by one, the floater logs were dragged out into the water and placed side by side, then tied together beneath the frame.

The afternoon was not yet long when the raft was completed. There it proudly floated, with Caetal's oilcloth tented in the center. Caetal cut three long poles to serve as oars, and one by one, the good swimmers helped the timider swimmers aboard.*

....

*It ought to be noted that I, Talara, who could not swim in the slightest, demonstrated remarkable courage in scrambling onboard at all. My years of playing amongst the wooden piers had apparently served me well.

....

With Rahyn keeping a trotting pace on the opposite shore, the children poled themselves out into the river and quickly found out how hard it is to paddle a log raft with any real skill or direction when one does not have the proper paddle. Eventually, realizing that the raft would not reach her shore any time soon, Rahyn dove in and swam out to meet them midway. There she retrieved her clothes, and the six of them were on their watery way downriver, tugged along briskly by the flowing current.

At Rahyn's insistence, they let the river carry the raft for the better part of two miles. The wooden poles were wretched for paddling, but they were quite handy for deflecting the raft off rocks and submerged logs. With the river tugging and the raft randomly rotating, the children bobbed along through the first sets of rapids as merrily as they might. The weight of all six of them on board (and their somewhat slapdash craftsmanship) made the raft ride low enough in the water that everyone got boot-moist and soggy-rumped from spray. But oh: that joy of floating on a raft built together by friends!

Soon enough, however, Rahyn beckoned them insistently towards the shore. They tried again to paddle with the ungainly poles, but most of their efforts were a churning comedy of spray.

"*There!* See where the river forks? We must now follow it towards the east!" Rahyn called from the front of the boat. "Shamsala's trail goes into the forest by the big dogwood up ahead. Paddle harder!" She frantically gestured with her hands.

"It's no good!" Tarquin grunted, poling clumsily. "It's like trying to climb a ladder with most of the rungs missing. We have to get into the water and flutter-kick with our feet. Yes, get in: Caetal, Mathias — get in! I'll go too. Rahyn and Talara: take the poles. No, Rahyn — stay where you're at, be careful not to tip the raft too much. Mathias: hand the pole to Rahyn. Talara: come over here and grab mine."

"How do I...?" Mathias began, but Tarquin interrupted him.

"Just grab the edge and kick with your feet! It's no good waiting for instructions; we'll miss the fork and end up going the wrong way! No, don't stop to take off your pants. Oh, by the Triad — you're getting soaked one way or the other! Come with me, and here we go!"

Tarquin grabbed Mathias and leapt off the raft and into the water with a shout, and Caetal dove in behind them. Rahyn, ignoring instructions and the pole entirely, dove in off her side. All four of the kids grabbed the raft at the edges and began churning the water with the effort of their fluttering legs. Talara and Melvin poled as best they could, and it was not long before the taller amongst them felt the soft muck of the shallows underfoot, and the boat bumped to rest on the bank amongst a wide blush of cattails.

They dragged themselves onto shore and flopped down to catch their breath. They were soaked from their labors and muddied to the hips. But before they were comfortably rested, Rahyn was already tugging at them to find Shamsala's tracks. Caetal groaned, swore, and got up to join her. The two of them wandered out of sight back up the riverbank, moving in almost a crouch as they each scanned the ground.

They were gone for long enough that Talara and Tarquin were able to lash the raft up, disembark Melvin and all their gear, and Mathias had managed to slip out of sight and change into dry clothes when the four of them were surprised by the sound of bare feet running in soft river clay. A moment later, Rahyn burst through the bracken, wild-eyed and panting.

"Shamsala's tracks have vanished!"

"You couldn't find them?" Talara asked.

"No, we found and followed them... into the woods for a ways.... Then, beneath a lovely hazelnut tree... the tracks simply stopped. Shamsala was... lifted off the ground, somehow! Caetal is there still, trying to find a new trail... But we must hurry! Something has taken her — something large enough to carry her!" Rahyn managed to get out between gulping breaths.

Tarquin was already dashing off as she finished speaking. "Where, Rahyn?! Where? Show me the trail. Come on, hurry!"

He ran ahead about fifty paces and then swore and doubled back. He grabbed up his forgotten backpack while the others were shouldering theirs.

"Mathias; Talara. Can you carry Melvin between you? Get your arms up under his shoulders together; that's the way. Rahyn, hurry! Run ahead; we'll follow!"

Nimble as a faun, Rahyn bounded ahead along the riverbank, then veered into the forest with Tarquin right behind her. The other three huffed along as best they could, Melvin bumping back and forth between them. Rahyn leapt fallen logs and ducked between the spreading fronds of giant sword ferns while Tarquin hacked at them with his wooden waster. His heart was racing in his chest, and his ears were pounding with pressure by the time they slowed to a stop again. Although Caetal was not in sight, Rahyn suddenly clapped her hand over Tarquin's mouth and pressed him back under the ferns so that they bungled into the other three children coming up behind them. Everyone ended up in a tangled pile on the moss, with Rahyn shushing for silence.

There they lay, the sounds of the forest chittering around them. Long minutes passed. Melvin, stretching his arm out overhead, pointed at the cut end of a dangling rope that was slung over a low branch. Then he walked his fingers across Mathias' leg like a four-legged animal and, with his other hand, pantomimed a noose trap going off, and the animal being swooped up and dangled. Talara nodded and was about to whisper something when the soft padding of hurrying footfalls could be heard from the trail up ahead. The children huddled down even lower, scarcely daring to breathe.

Then a low, warbling whistle was sounded from nearby, and Rahyn sat up and winded the same note back, cupping her mouth with her hand and fluttering her fingers to do so. Caetal stalked towards them and squatted down on his heels.

"G-g-good news and bad news." He whispered. *"Bad first: there are at least five Orlŭks bivouacked up ahead. Could be more. They're camped in*

a little glen between two low hills; there's a bit of a stream running through it. Pretty nice camping spot actually. There's a bear-sized cave entrance into one of the hillsides: I couldn't get a good view, so I don't know w-what's in-side. They're gathering w-w-wood for a fire near the cave entrance. They got w-weapons, and they have Shamsala. She's tied to one of the trees. They're probably g-gonna roast her once the coals get hot enough."

"What the heck is the good news?" Tarquin hissed. *"That all sounds like a bunch of really godsdamn bad news!"*

Caetal patted his hand. *"W-well, obviously, the g-good news is Shamsala is still alive, and she hasn't been eaten up yet."*

"Well, then let's go get her back!" Tarquin whispered hoarsely, rocking onto his heels and brandishing his wooden sword. Talara grabbed his ankle before he could stand up.

"Hold on, ochoya-ber! We can't just walk over and demand her back, now can we? And were you planning on fighting all of them? Because if so, I'm going back to the boat. No offense to Shamsala, but I am not trading my life for a goat today."

Tarquin looked at her sternly and whispered, *"What does 'ochoya-ber' mean? Because I'm guessing it means something rude."*

Talara snickered quietly. *"It is a Rhymiran insult — a really old one. It basically translates to 'bag of useless lumps.' Or... like: ill-formed marbles, made by an idiot."*

Tarquin looked impressed and squatted back down. *"That's a good insult, I'm going to try to remember that one. Okay: oooookay. Think-think-think: think of a plan. Go Tarquin-brain, go."*

Mathias said quietly: *"We do not need to kill them, do we? I don't feel... it doesn't seem right. Even if we could. I've never killed something so... person-like before."*

Rahyn nodded. *"They are animals trying to eat another animal that they caught. We must not waste their lives for doing what is natural."*

Tarquin flushed. *"Shamsala wouldn't be about to be Orlŭk food if you hadn't tried to eat her in the first place. It was the fox that drove her into their damn trap."*

"Then do not turn my shame into everyone's," Rahyn replied softly. *"There has to be a better way than wasting life."* Tarquin growled; Rahyn reached over, timidly, and squeezed his hand. *"I'm sorry for what Syrahana-yerall-aneh did. She is fond of the taste of goat. I should have remembered that, and I'm sorry she hurt her."*

Tarquin looked away and wiped his eyes. Then he shook his head and whispered:

"*It's no good. If we can't kill them, and we can't ask for her back, then what do we do? She's a goner without us. I love that goat, you guys. I can't lose her too.*"

Talara smiled ruefully. "*Do not give up on her yet. We must trick them. We have to do something so scary that they run in terror. Or tell a story so funny they collapse into laughter! Or perhaps confuse them to the point where they forget about her entirely. There must to be a way to jape them and steal her back. Take heart: we are smart enough and desperate enough to try something ridiculous.*"

Melvin pointed over their heads. A little way off, a thin plume of smoke was rising between the trees.

"*Whatever the plan will be, we better think of it quickly. They've got their fire lit. Shamsala does not have long to live.*"

••

The Quest Gets Out of Hand

The plan they came up with was terrible, and that was what made it so magnificent. It was a desperate, stupid plan. But they were too young to know better, and there is a particular magic in that kind of foolishness. It is luck, intuition and brave fumbling that keep adventurous children alive long enough to grow up. They say that the Immortal called Luck is a fickle mistress for adults, but I believe that she has a soft spot for children and tends to give them an occasional pass and a couple of do-overs.

....

Here was the plan that Tarquin suggested: they were all to work together to create a convincing illusion that the cave mouth and surrounding hillside would morph into the semblance of an angry elemental goat god who was manifesting, enraged, to punish the Orlŭks for trying to eat Shamsala. That was his plan. The rest of the kids were so impressed by the audacity of the plan that they didn't bother taking the time to think of a better one.

After a few minutes of frenzied input, the recording of which would be too crowded and overlapping to bother to describe, (most of them got excited about the role they would play, and they all started talking at once until Mathias sternly reminded them that they had to be quiet, for Cuthain's sake), the children headed quietly up the trail in ones and twos. They each collected what was needed from their supplies and exchanged what hugs and hopeful wishes they had a moment to share.

Mathias, who had been left behind as the "getaway guy," gathered up their various backpacks and bedrolls into a pile and then began to strap them in layers facing frontwards and backwards onto his own shoulders. He then wrapped what remained around his waist, until he was as round as a beadberry; top-heavy and tottering with their combined weight. Five backpacks are a lot to carry for one smallish boy; he could barely see above the top of them. Then he waddled over to the appointed low-hanging fern, leaned his now ponderous weight on a fallen log, and nervously waited for his cue to run.

....

Carrying Melvin saddleback, Caetal led the children cautiously up the back side of a steep hill. Budding foliage was dense and verdant all around them; the chill gloom of early evening was just drawing in. For Caetal, who was used to stalking with animal quiet, his friends sounded like wayward cows forcing their way through a briar patch. Rahyn thought so too and made herself scarce skirting the base of the hill towards the far side of the camp. They saw no sign of a posted guard. The four children crested the hilltop on their bellies, crawling along on knees and elbows until they could peek down on the scene below.

Caetal had described the scene adequately, but he had missed two details that now impressed themselves upon the children. The first was how lovely the glen itself was. The "pretty nice camping spot" was a thin and densely forested vale, barely longer than a hollow between hillsides. Squat oaks, burled and dark, straddled a rushing creek that tumbled down a descending set of shallow falls into rocky pools. Sunset made a patchwork of ruddy watercolor between the branches, and where it touched the ground, a thick layer of moss and fallen leaves were illuminated. A rolling hum of frog songs droned from the shallows of the creek bed.

From where they lay on their bellies, the cave could not be seen. Caetal pointed downhill and below them and made a sign with his fingers. As they scootched forward for a better look, the second startling detail came into view. That detail was the *reality* of the actual Orlŭks themselves: the size and shape of them, their living, breathing, dangerous immediacy. They were big — as big as Caetal, and heavier set. The boar-men wore brain-tanned leather in overlapping layers that resembled armored aprons. A multicolored patchwork of various fabrics could be seen underneath. All were barefoot. Even from a distance, they smelled sharply pungent, and the language they spoke to each other brayed and growled.

A campfire burned in a shallow pit at the base of the hill, and four of the boar-men sprawled around it in various states of repose. Besides Caetal, none of the children had seen an Orlŭk up close. Their stooped and brutal bestiality was startling, for though they looked almost human, they moved with the heavy lope of an animal that can run at great speed on four legs.

At first, the children did not see Shamsala, and despaired that they had arrived too late. Then Melvin pointed excitedly towards a stand of trees, about sixty feet from the fire. Even from a distance, she looked miserable. She was sprawled as though asleep, with her head flopped over onto her shoulder and a rope tying her to a tree by a lead line around her neck. Her fur was matted with blood and mud and all manner of burring leaves. From a distance it seemed like she was already dead, until they heard her give a plaintive little bleating maaa. It was that small, pitiful sound that brought the whole scene into sudden focus. The reality of what they were about to attempt and what might happen if they failed at it almost unnerved them all right there. It is one thing to make heroic rescue plans and quite another to look upon the faces of creatures that would be glad to kill and eat you and very well might do so in the next few minutes. But they knew that Rahyn would soon begin her part of the plan, and they had no means to warn her off if their nerves failed them. That meant she would be at the mercy of the Orlŭks alone.

Tarquin touched them each on the arm, then hurried away downhill towards Shamsala. His role in the plan was to sneak over and cut her free during the distracting appearance of the angry goat god. He was then to lead her back to the boat, where Mathias would be waiting with the rope unmoored. If all went well, each of the others would arrive at a run shortly thereafter, they would escape downstream all together, and everyone would pretty much live happily ever after.

Oh, for the naivety of youth!

....

Here is what actually went down.

Let us begin with Rahyn, who slipped between the shadows of the trees as quiet as a foxgirl, focusing in her mind's eye on a shape that Melvin had drawn for her in the dirt. It was a scramble for her to get into position, for her route went wide around the back of the hill that the rest of the children had climbed. Doubling back from there, she crept her way downstream toward the Orlŭk camp.

She followed the creek, hopping rock to rock midstream in the twilit gloom until she neared the tree where Shamsala was tied. She had no illusions of getting any closer: she would have liked to rescue the goat, of course, but even at this distance, the faintest of fox smells still lingered on her, and she saw Shamsala's head come up and look around. The goat began to make low, whickering sounds in the back of her throat, rising to her feet and peering out into the dusky woods. So there, Rahyn was forced to stop. She was much further from the light of the fire than she had hoped. Her part of the plan was meant to be large and dramatic: a disturbing and symbolic gesture. But if she was so far from the firelight, would they see it at all?

She would have to do the best she could from the water's edge. So, she reached inside herself and invited the fox to begin sharing space with her body, until she felt her fangs sharpen and the bloom of soft fur spreading across her belly. Then she bit down hard into the pad of her own thumb. Blood welled from two puncture points, and when it began to trickle, she dug her hands into the soil of the creek bed. A curious kudzu twirled up around her finger first. Then a raspberry vine forced its way up to sample her wound like a snake susses the air with its tongue.

"There will be blood tonight, rich with nutrients." Her heart whispered to them. *"Grow in that direction: I will show you. Grow as if the seasons were rapidly spinning, and you were always full of sunlight. Forget the limits of time. Grow to the edge of imagination."*
She visualized the tree that Shamsala was lashed to and the shape she wished the vines to become. *"I call to you: caneberry, ghostburr, night-berry. Brambles thick and humble — I call to the sumac, and to the ivy. Dream yourself tall and interwoven, like a rising moon caught in a trellis of branches."*

Rahyn had dwelt in the womb of a blooming dryad and been carried by love and magic across the threshold of timelessness beneath the Stone Tree. She was born speaking the Green Language as well as any rooting native, and the added offer of blood is very persuasive. And so, whispering like a thousand buried secrets tunneling up into the moonlight, all the vines in the area began to slither their way overland and underground towards the tree that Shamsala was lashed to.

As exhausted and dispirited as Shamsala felt, she sensed the supernatural movement of the plants underfoot, with all of them suddenly coming towards her. She began to shriek loudly. When the nearest Orlŭk looked up in surprise at the squalling racket, he saw her wailing and bucking, flopping around at the end of her leash like a hairy, screaming fish. Grumbling to himself, the Orlŭk drew a long boning knife and got up from his warm seat by the fire.

A sliced throat is quieter. He thought to himself.

....

Or, at least, that was a pretty good guess as to what he had in mind. Who knows what Orlŭks say to themselves in their own heads? Yet, when he approached the tree to unleash the troublesome creature from the obvious burden of her life, he began to hear the rustling susurrations that she was hearing. The frogs had fallen strangely silent, their croaking overtaken with creaking whispers travelling across the ground and into the branches of the tree. The boar-man looked up, ears cocked and brow furling.

Through the foliage, the red moon could be seen. It hung like a staring eye, as clear to view as though he was gazing at it in an empty field. For where the canopy of branch, leaf and twig should have otherwise obscured it, all had been bent into the shape of a great and growing wreath. Tendrils of climbing vines, many layers deep, were wrapping themselves around the trunk of the tree. They spiraled up into a massive ring, so densely interwoven *and still moving* that the sight of it was like watching a hundred green tentacles that were each a hundred feet long, all bursting forth from the earth and coiling around each other in pulsing, creeping waves of growth that *hummed as they grew.* That eerie humming was countless tiny thorns all rubbing against each other like creaking crickets.

The Orlŭk at the base of the tree began to yelp in mounting fear, for those supernatural vines had wrapped themselves around his legs as he stood staring up at the moon and were now lifting him into the air. They crawled up the fabric of his breeches and went burrowing down the sleeves of his shirt. Upwards he was borne aloft, with his legs kicking and his fearful yelps deepened into screaming as the vines unsheathed the deadly bloom of their freshly sprouting thorns.

....

Meanwhile and a little beforehand, Talara and Caetal crept down the hillside towards the mouth of the cave and their role in the plan. They had left Melvin hidden up at the top, out of sight from the campfire. With a hatchet in one hand and a big skunk cabbage leaf in the other, Caetal took the lead. Talara carried her shawm tucked under her arm and parted the underbrush with a thin copper knife that she held out in front of her. Both were tense with fearful excitement, for their part to play in the deception was a dangerous juggle of timing and opportunity. They snuck as close as they dared to the edge of the cave. The campfire was but a stone's throw from the cave mouth, and all that lay beyond the trees they hid behind was exposed by firelight. It would be a dash across lit and open ground to reach the cave, and between them and there were the Orlŭks. So they waited, tense and sweating, for Rahyn to begin the game.

....

Elsewhere, Tarquin was also creeping through the underbrush. He kept his eyes fixed on Shamsala and moved forward in a shuffling crouch with the blade of his copper dagger clenched longways between his teeth. He did not actually need to carry the dagger that way, but he had heard that pirates did that when crawling into the rigging of a ship, and he had always imagined it might make him look pretty tough in a 'no prisoners left alive' kind of way. So the whole time he was sneaking up to rescue Shamsala, his mouth tasted like metal, and he was drooling a little. He was also humming a sailor's tune to himself so softly that he didn't even notice he was doing it. But having his dagger between his teeth did leave his hands free, which turned out to be helpful when the fifth Orlŭk, who had been missing from the campfire, stepped out from behind a tree and clamped his hands around Tarquin's neck.

....

At the top of the hill, Melvin closed his eyes and did his best to stifle worried thoughts of the fate likely befalling his friends. What he was about to attempt was far beyond his sense of his own skill and utterly, alarmingly nonsensical. Having barely touched on the knowledge of stone and with no magical control or proven artistry to speak of, Tarquin expected him to be able to recreate an entire hillside.

"Tarquin *hoped*, not *expected*. And I told him he was *muli* to assume I could! It's not my fault if this fails! *Skabde muli!*" He swore quietly to himself. His palms felt as clammy as a handful of clams, and he knew that if he could feel his knees, they'd be knocking. But he took a deep breath anyway and laid his moistened palms on the cold grass. He closed his eyes and breathed in deeply: once, twice. On the third steadying breath, he fell backwards into himself. In the darkness inside, a light that was not light began to glow.

"*EBEN*." He whispered. The bedrock beneath the hillside shifted. Then he opened his jaw, lengthened his throat, and repeated the word again. It came thrumming out of him, and he held the sound steady as long as he could and, at the same time, tried to summon to mind the image that Tarquin had requested.

All around him, the ground began to roll outwards like a ripple. Then he heard a scream.

....

As safely far away as he was, Mathias could not ignore the screaming.

Though it sounded almost inhuman, how could he be sure? He couldn't abandon his friends to torture! So he ran towards the campground at a frantic waddle, with the bulk of backpacks swaying so ponderously that he could barely keep from toppling over. Each step felt like he was trying to sprint with a Melvin on his back and another on his chest. But the screaming only grew louder, so he ran straight towards it.

....

By the campfire, the three Orlŭks jumped to their feet and snatched up their weapons: two spears and a brutal-looking club. Fire-blind as they were, they stood tensed and blinking, peering into the gloom towards where the goat was tied up, trying to locate the source of the increasingly frantic screeching. Talara, seizing her moment, began to make her way swiftly and quietly towards the cave, at one point passing breathlessly only a few feet behind them. Caetal followed, stepping ranger quiet and danger careful. This was a terrible moment for the two of them, as they were brightly lit and easily in spearing range. But the Orlŭks moved away towards the source of the screaming and took no notice of them.

They held their breath until they were well inside the cave and hidden from view behind a jut of stone. That was when they felt the first tremor from the rocks above.

"Now or never!" Talara whispered fiercely and nudged Caetal hard in the ribs. He rolled the skunk cabbage leaf into a funnel and held it to his lips. Talara slid her two small copper castanets up onto her knuckles and raised the shawm to play, nervously licking her lips.

Then the shaking in the walls got much worse. It was not like a normal earthquake at all. The entire cave seemed to *bubble.* The ceiling rolled; the walls bulged alarmingly. A shower of dirt and pebbles began to patter down like rain. The earthen floor beneath them bobbed in waves like a ship at sea. From down the receding throat of the tunnel, a crackling boom of tumbled rocks sounded, and suddenly Caetal reared up and bellowed through his skunk leaf mouth trumpet in the deepest voice he could manage:

"RATAK ECK-GŬNTA MAKTURADA!! NOK TÁ ADARA KA'AT! RUET, VALEA ET NOKI VAT TERAGA! ORLU ADARA-TZOR!"

Caetal, who had a tenuous grasp of the Orlŭk language, was pretty sure he had just shouted: "HEAR ME, PIG-SON FILTH! YOU TOOK MY GOAT-CHILD! RUN, FOOLS, OR YOU PERISH! I AM THE GOAT GOD!"

But what he actually yelled was much closer to: "HOLD STILL, PIG-GONAD WASTELIFE! YOU WHO GOAT SUNRISE! RUN, STUPID-WHO-LINGERS, OR NAP! WE AM THE GOAT-BEYOND!"

Orlŭk language does not translate well even if you know how to speak it fluently, which Caetal did not. Talara punctuated his speech with a ghastly shrieking warble from her shawm, played with decadent dissonance, while clattering her copper castanets against the rock walls. The effect was closer to 'jarring' than 'chilling', but they did the best they could with the moment they had.

Meanwhile, the roiling and shaking of the cave worsened all around them.

....

Choking with shock (and with actual choking), Tarquin was hoisted into the air by his neck and found himself dangling face to face with his first Orlŭk. The knife fell from his mouth in a sucking gasp for air. Through the sudden tunneling star-lit darkness of his vision, he saw the puffy grayish skin, tusked teeth, and small dark eyes that glittered with what might be amusement. The smell of the boar-man as it breathed on him was like rancid pig fat, and he heard the creature muttering something which sounded like grunting and cracking walnut shells.

Tarquin assumed the phrase was some version of "Well, what have we here?" But since his air was running out, his neck hurt enormously, and he didn't have much time to live, he reacted without bothering to translate further. Tarquin threw out his hands, slid them underneath the armored apron, and twist-pinched the absolute adrenaline-fueled fury out of the Orlŭk's nipples. The creature howled in pain, digging its claws further into Tarquin's neck. So, he swung both feet forward and double-kicked the beast in the groin. The Orlŭk dropped to his knees and released Tarquin, and they both rolled over onto the moss and groaned miserably. Neither one was in a hurry to get back up, so they lay there together for a while and marveled at how painful pain can be.

Then Mathias ran right by and did not see either of them, blinded as he was by backpacks and ferns and the dense dark of evening. Tarquin tried to call out, but all he could manage was a feeble croaking sound. Mathias was heading towards Shamsala, whose bawling now mingled discordantly with the increasingly frantic screaming of the vine-hoisted Orlŭk.

....

Let's take a moment to appreciate the scene from the point of view of the other three Orlŭks. After all, they were the intended audience for the disturbing and bewildering performance that was taking place all around them.

Halfway to their screaming companion, they were brought up short by the noises emitting from the cave. Now they swiveled their heads back and forth in mounting alarm. In front was an abomination: a tree swelling with a thickening braid of snake-like vines that had lifted one of their fellows into the sky and was now apparently drinking his blood, for drops of it were pattering all over the ground underneath him. His armor was rent; his clothing ragged, with viscera-like vines pushing forth through them.

What chilled their hearts even further was the grim symbolism that became apparent when viewed from below the tree: the woven circle of vines, with the Orlŭk taking the place of the sacrificial rabbit. The *Kaninhode* was a dire warning as old as their memory of the island. The dangling Orlŭk moaned pitifully. With the red moon shining behind him and his blood sprinkling down, it was a bladder-draining sight. The dinner goat who had been tied to the tree was now nowhere to be seen; only a severed leash remained. The sudden silent lack of her was even more chilling than her screaming had been.

"The tree must have eaten her first." One Orlŭk squealed to another. They clutched their weapons limply and sweatily, making signs to ward themselves against evil as they stumbled back towards their campfire. But the weirdness only worsened from there.

Before their eyes, the cave hillside shivered like pudding. It broiled, and it roiled, with rocks pushing up through the dirt then tumbling over and vanishing again like carrots floating to the surface of a simmering stew. The leaping firelight made the effect even more vertiginous, with shadows stretching and retreating across the heaving ground. The shape of the hillside began to morph, growing angular and snouted. Horn-nubbin boulders bulged to either side of the crest, with two hollows retreating away between them, tunneling inward. They almost resembled the eye-sockets of a ram's skull, and for a moment, the Orlŭks fancied that's what they were looking at. Then there was a bellow of sound from the cave entrance, and a dusty wind pushed up from underground. It carried a cacophony of disturbing words, with a warbling screech and clatter wrapped all around them: a deep voice shouting about a life wasted watching goat sunrises, pig gonads called forth from the goat beyond, and the pressing need to flee or lay down and nap!

Meanwhile, the animal skull face that the hillside was forming into began to deflate grotesquely. The goat daydream became a nightmare of sagging soil and gibbous rocky protrusions. Cold air belched from the cave mouth, and from within, the shrieking of sound began to intermingle with actual shrieking. The ground shuddered fitfully underfoot as displaced topsoil rolled off the hillside like wax.

....

The undergrowth tore vengefully at Mathias as he blundered through it, dragging Shamsala behind him by the leash he had cut. He could barely see what was before him, so dark had the night become, and with bouncing backpacks crowded closely around his eyes. Behind him was the howling of the Orlŭks and the very real danger of discovery. So, he ran towards what he guessed was the river and would have kept right on running if he had not tripped and sprawled over something that groaned.

Whatever it was grabbed at him painfully until Shamsala stepped on its arm. Then there was a struggle. Mathias thrashed and shoved; he felt Shamsala's weight roll over him and the sharpness of her kicking hooves. One of the backpacks tore and spilled, and his nose was full of the stink of Orlŭk. Then he heard three dense thunking sounds. The creature he was tangled with stopped struggling. Mathias felt a hand grasp his arm, and he was pulled upright onto his feet. By the pale firelight visible between tree trunks, Mathias recognized Tarquin. He had his wooden sword in one hand and Shamsala's leash in the other.

"Don't worry, I bonked that Orlŭk on the head a couple times. I'm pretty sure he's napping now. Good job freeing Shamsala!" He whispered hoarsely, rubbing his throat.

"Glad to... be helpful." Panted Mathias.

"No time for tea; follow me!" Tarquin turned around and ran ahead, with Shamsala bounding next to him, maaaing joyfully. Mathias did his best to keep up, wishing that Tarquin had taken at least one of the backpacks.

They heard the river before they found it, and soon enough, the ripple of red moonlight on water could be seen between the spreading bracken. They fumbled their way down towards the shore, pushing through the cold rattling wetness of spikerush and pickerelweed until their boots were soaked by the shallows, but they could not find their raft. Up and downstream they searched — their feet being sucked at by the muddy shoreline and becoming ever more alarmed at their raftlessness.

....

The three Orlŭks, convinced beyond doubt that this part of the world was obviously ending, fled into the forest, braying like frightened hounds. Behind them, the bubbling hillside slowed to a simmer of settling stones and topsoil. At last, all was still.

Talara and Caetal, who had almost been crushed under a partial collapse of the cave tunnel, crawled out into the night air, coughing and wiping dust out of their eyes. The campsite seemed abandoned, and the night had strangely quieted. Even the Orlŭk in the tree wasn't wailing anymore, having passed out from fear and blood loss. The vines had ceased their supernatural growth, with him still splayed fifteen feet above the ground like a fly in a web.

"W-w-well," Caetal coughed, "I think we did ok."

Talara patted him on the shoulder. "We were great. Legends shall be told of this for years to come: haunted stories that the Boar Women tell to their quaking piglets to scare them to sleep at night!"

Caetal laughed. "Damn right! W-w-wrathful is the G-goat G-god: w-ware to those who anger him!"

"Or her: I'm pretty sure it was a goddess."

"How could it have been a *her*? I w-was speaking in a really deep, obviously manly voice."

"I don't think gods have genders unless they want to, and I'm convinced the Goat Goddess prefers to be a female. Anyone with sense and a choice would choose to be female."

"W-why is that?"

"It's a pleasure thing. I'll tell you when you're older."

"W-whatever," Caetal muttered uncomfortably. "Let's g-get up there and carry Melvin down. W-we g-g-gotta make it to the raft before Mathias leaves without us."

"Don't bother." Melvin's voice groaned weakly from the top of the hill above them. "I'm so exhausted I feel like my skin is clay and my bones are stone. Just leave me here to die a hero's death, or at least to pass out and sleep a really long, heroic time."

Caetal snorted. "Big baby. He rolls a few stones around w-w-with magic, and now he's too lazy to use his legs and w-walk to the boat."

"I heard that, *kefe-muli*. Come pick me up so I can weakly smack you." Melvin grumbled.

....

Finally, Mathias pointed excitedly at something floating ahead, and they thrashed towards it, kicking up spray. Moonlight painted the edges of a round coracle of woven wicker, lashed to a tree by a rope, with three paddles stowed against a rowing bench.

"*Orlŭk boat?*" Mathias whispered.

"*Gotta be,*" Tarquin whispered back. "*Gives me an idea, though. Hold Shamsala.*" He handed the leash to Mathias. Then he went over to the tree and unwound the mooring rope. Wading into the river, he pushed the boat out into the water until it was floating deep enough to scramble up into. Then he paddled away from shore, disappearing from view into night's swallowing dark. Only ripples of moonslight the oar strokes made could be seen from shore. Mathias heard a splash, and about a minute later, Tarquin swam back. The boat drifted on without him.

"I swam out far enough to see the raft: it's downriver, but not by much. And there are torches coming this way through the forest, so we really, very much should leave now."

"What?!" Mathias croaked. "The Orlŭks?"

"Of course, fiddlewits! We didn't bring any torches, so it wouldn't be any of us." Tarquin scooped up a couple backpacks, steering Mathias into the cover of cattails. The growling sounds of the Orlŭks could now be heard nearby.

"But won't they be mad about you pushing their boat out into the current?" Mathias whispered as they ran.

"Gosh, I sure hope so!" Tarquin chuckled, whacking at the cane grasses with his waster to clear a path. "Otherwise, what's the point?"

Mathias groaned. Shamsala farted companionably.

....

From two directions, the children hurried back towards the raft. There they found Rahyn waiting anxiously, with the line untied and a pole in hand. Tarquin helped Mathias heave the backpacks on board. They tried to lead Shamsala onto the floating logs, but she began to fuss so loudly that Tarquin had to haul her forcibly onboard, and even then, she wouldn't stop bawling until Tarquin held her in his lap and kept his arms wrapped around her. He was happy enough to do this anyway, and when Caetal and Talara arrived carrying Melvin, the adventurers shoved off from shore and let the flow of the river take them.

...and not a minute too soon, for torch lights swirled in the forest, and the grackling squeal of voices calling to each other could be heard.

"That sounds like a damn few more than five Orlŭks," Talara muttered. Caetal nodded grimly and began to string his longbow.

....

The current bore them onward at a pace that could be felt but not often seen, for ruddy moonlight painted the water in occasional patches between the trees, and all else was pitched in shadow. The yellow moon had not yet risen, and all about them was the chuckle of dark water over hidden rocks.

They dared not light a lantern, relying instead on Rahyn to keep them from rebounding off anything sharp. She did her best with a long pole extended out into the water, for she had the keenest night vision amongst them. Even with Rahyn spotting, they regularly bumped across submerged impediments, and for the first half hour, the raft was spun and jostled about like a giant's toy. For Melvin, who could not kick his legs to save himself, and for Talara, who did not really know how to swim, it was a terrible experience that they did their best to be quiet about. For the rest of them, the relief that they seemed to have outrun pursuit overwhelmed their fear of dark water.

After a while, the trees thinned somewhat from the river's edge, and the yellow moon rose as fat and full as a pumpkin in the eastern sky. At such a dawning angle, the light of that moon lanced across the water in pale ribbons between the sable trees.

Soon enough, the current slowed to a wandering crawl, and the raft was no longer revolving. Caetal relieved Rahyn at the pole, and Tarquin felt certain that luck had prevailed over caution and insisted on lighting the candle in their lantern. Circled up around that tiny warming flame, they all laughed as Mathias told them about Tarquin loosing the Orlŭks' coracle into the river and laughed even harder when Tarquin told them about wrenching the boar-man's nipples and kicking him in the nads.

Everyone petted Shamsala a lot, who bleated with pleasure and did her best to lick every finger that came into tongue range, except for Rahyn's. Nobody had seen how close to (or far from) Melvin's magic had succeeded in creating the likeness of a giant goat face, but they all just assumed it had looked great, and praised him heartily for the part he played. As to Rahyn's grim artistry, not much was mentioned. It still creeped most of them out that she could enchant thorny vines with her own blood, so it was only Melvin who congratulated her for it. She ducked her head and nodded thanks, but mostly kept her eyes on the river behind them.

....

Evening darkened into night. The river exhaled mist that clung to the surface of the water in clammy patches they drifted through. Bullfrogs sawed in the shallows, interrupted only by the splashes of diving night-fishers. Overhead, branches creaked and leaping things rustled. An owl hooted. Dampened by fog and drained from their adventures, most of the children curled up together under the wedge tent that Caetal had strung up with his tarp. Only Tarquin and Rahyn remained awake: she sitting at the back of the raft, and he up front with Shamsala in his lap. When the goat had fallen asleep enough for him to scootch his legs out from under her, Tarquin got to his feet and stretched and then wandered over to sit with Rahyn. She glanced at him, but he could not see the details of her face well, as he had left the lantern at the front of the raft to light the way forward. Only the shine of her eyes could be clearly seen, which were green and amber and reflected light like an animal's eyes. He sat to her side so that his shadow diminished the shining of her pupils.

For a time they did not speak. Dark water flowing slowly all around them, and Tarquin dipped his fingers into it. After a while, he said softly:

"She's going to be okay, you know. The scratches you made are deep, but they seem clean enough, and the wounds are dried and healing."

"I know. I would have tended to her otherwise. I still intend to, when the sky lightens, and we come to shore."

"Thank you. That's a kindness. She's a good girl. I mean... she's a nice goat, you know? I don't want... I want you two to get along. If you tend to her, maybe she won't be afraid of you anymore. She's not very smart — I think she will forget about it soon enough."

"Forget about what?"

"That you can change. That the fox and you are one person."

"But we aren't, you know. We are different."

"How is that... possible? I can't think of a better way to phrase it. How can two things share the same body? There are times when you... are kinda furry or seem partway between a girl and a fox."

"Syrahana-yerall-aneh is a vixen. So, I am always a girl, in fox-form or otherwise."

"You know what I mean, Rahyn. What I'm asking is: sometimes you are one thing, and sometimes another. But sometimes, you are also somewhere in between, and at those times, it seems like you cannot be entirely her, or entirely you, but a bit of both. Does that make sense?"

Rahyn cocked her head. "Not... really. What are you asking?"

Tarquin sighed. "If you and Syraha-yera-ahanawhatever-"

"- Syrahana-yerall-aneh."

"Yes, her: if you and she are as different as you say, how are you also sometimes the same? If you handed me a stone and said, 'this is a stone,' and then handed me a berry and said, 'this is a berry,' I would nod and say, 'yes, I can see that.' But sometimes, you are a berry-stone. And when I see you as a berry-stone, and you pretend that the berry and the stone aren't one thing, and then you go ahead and hurt my goat, I get mad. I don't want to be mad at you, but I need to be sure that I can trust you not to hurt her again. Do you understand?"

Rahyn was quiet for so long that Tarquin thought his question had gotten too convoluted, and she hadn't followed it through to the sensical root. Then he glimpsed a tear falling from her cheek that caught the moonlight before it joined the river. A hot flush of shame dropped from his throat to his belly, and he hugged her tightly.

"I'm sorry Rahyn... I'm so sorry. I didn't mean to make you feel like anything less than a person that I am proud to be friends with. You helped to save Shamsala from being eaten tonight, and it means a lot to me. Thank you."

He hugged her, and her hair filled his nose with her wild scent. It was... *green.* It was the warm smell of green drinking up sunlight. He couldn't think of any other way to imagine it. She clutched the hand of the arm he held around her, and he felt her sagging against him. Her small body shook with weeping, though she made almost no sound. She burrowed her face up against his neck, and he felt the cold wetness of her nose. They sat like that for a time that was not nearly long enough, and yet so long that his arms ached from hugging her tightly. At last, he felt her shift, and he released her.

"I don't know how to answer you, or how to thank you for being yourself. I will do my best. Syrahana-yerall-aneh comes to claim me when I am in need of her or when she decides that I am. She is older than me and stronger than me, and she takes what opportunities she can to run on all fours as she used to, before she died giving birth to me."

"Ok... I don't think I exactly understand any of that, but I'm glad to hear about it anyway."

Rahyn laughed. Out of all of Tarquin's friends, she laughed the least often, and he was always the gladdest to be there when she did. Her laughter was something that leapt out of her suddenly and vanished just as quickly. It was a lovely, awkward, leaping laugh.

"I will try to tell it in a different way, then. When the vixen takes my place, I become... almost asleep inside her. Like I believe she dwells when she is in me: that halfway state between awake and asleep. The things she does when she is fully awake are like... perhaps how you feel when you are dreaming. Sometimes I can feel myself sharing choices with her. Influencing the dream. But other times, I cannot move my will through her, for she rises up before me in her strength and takes charge like a mother fox would with a wayward kit. In those times I remember nothing at all when I wake up into myself, the way a dream slips away at dawn, no matter how hard you try to grasp at the memory of it."

"Is that what happened when she attacked Shamsala? You were lost inside her?"

Rahyn turned her face away. Her shoulders hunched.

"Not... exactly. I wish I could make you feel better by saying I had no knowledge of what was happening. But that is untrue. It is more real to say that I was swept up in the carnivore's calling, as I have so often been. To hunt what runs, to taste the heat of blood and know the gratitude that what was once their life will now flow into me and allow me to live with their strength inside of me... it is a powerful feeling. I remember swimming halfway across the river, and my intentions were fixed on Shamsala. Then Syrahana-yerall-aneh saw her for what she is: a grass-eater with her back turned, unaware of how sneaky a hunting fox can be, and she woke up entirely and took control. In that moment, I forgot why I was seeking the goat and thought only, '*ah: this is it. This must be the reason, and it is good.*' And I relaxed and let myself be still."

Tarquin did not reply, but he nodded slowly. His gaze was far away, across the water. Rahyn squeezed his hand and continued.

"I cannot ever promise that I will not behave as a fox when I have become one. It is against the pattern of things. I would not ever ask you to not be you, and I hope you would never ask me to stop being me. It is the only thing I can never learn to do."

Tarquin nodded again, his look far away, staring upriver. Rahyn waited for him to speak, but the silence stretched on.

"Tarquin. Do you hear me?"
"Uh huh."
"...Are we well?"
"I don't think so. Is that moonslight on the water behind us? The yellow moon rising?"

Rahyn turned and peered into the misty night. She was silent for a moment, then sighed.

"No. There are three lights, and none of them are moonslight. We are being hunted."
"Hells and horrors... I'll wake the others," Tarquin stammered, then whispered: "*oh Gods: please don't let me get my friends killed tonight.*"

Rahyn scooted to the front of the raft and snuffed the candle between her fingers. In the dark, Tarquin heard her whisper back:

"If we are killed tonight, you are not responsible. We all chose to be here. You cannot ask them to be other than themselves, either."

....

By the time everyone was more or less awake and readied, the danger was clearly visible. Three torches made orange patches in the fog upriver, and the speed that they approached the raft was the speed of pursuit with oars. The children huddled, bleary and shivering, and considered their few options.

It was obvious that outrunning them was impossible — a coracle with oars moves at speeds that a drifting pole raft could never match. There was not even time to get to shore, although the urge to try was strong, until Talara pointed out there may be boar-men keeping pace in the woods, unseen and unnumbered. So, they must fight midriver. They had one bow, five arrows and no other ranged weapons to speak of unless one of them hurled a hatchet, which Caetal begged them not to do.

"Perhaps they won't see us with the lantern doused? Maybe we can follow the fog, and they will row on by us?" Mathias whispered, his voice shaking.

"No," Rahyn whispered back. *"They hunt at night, by sight and by smell. They have seen us already, or they would not be so bold to light torches. They may even be able to smell us from here."*

"Why are they coming after us at all? We did them no harm: it was the Goat Goddess who frightened them off." Talara asked quietly.

Rahyn shrugged. *"We have stolen their food. They are in pursuit to try and get it back. I'd do the same."*

"They might also be mad that Tarquin untied one of their boats and sent it drifting off downstream," Mathias suggested, fidgeting with the placement of the tent rope. Tarquin glared at him, and was about to say something when Caetal interrupted:

"Anyone w-who can needs to take shelter in the tent. A loosely draped tarp is better at slowing arrows than it seems."

Tarquin nodded. "Yes, and pile all the backpacks around you. Perhaps they can shield you a little too. Caetal and I will do what we can to stop them, or die trying."

Caetal stared at him blankly. "You don't have range, Tarq. W-w-what are you g-going to do? Throw insults at them?"

"And who says you get to die out here with us cowering inside the tent?" Talara interjected. "If you two lackwits get yourselves killed, what's to stop them from boarding the raft and just spearing us? We fight together."

Melvin spoke up. "I have no strength left in me for magic, but if it comes to a boarding party, I will stab their feet and slice their knees." He clutched his dagger threateningly from where he lay in the tent.

Mathias twisted his hands together in his lap, then nodded grimly and whispered. *"I will fight too, with my hands, if I must."*

Tarquin patted his shoulder. "It's more important that you hold onto Shamsala and keep her from getting too scared."

Mathias nodded, looking somewhat relieved. "I'll guard her with my life. But what do we do now, Tarquin?"

They all looked at him, and he looked back at each of them. Then he sighed deeply, ran his hands through his hair, and in a tight voice, he said:

"When they are in arching range, light the lantern, and shine it in their eyes. Let us see them clearly and let them think we aren't afraid. It may blind them enough to reduce the accuracy of their shots. Caetal, try to take out one or two right then, if you can. Concentrate your fire on one boat at a time so there are less boats to keep track of. Talara, Mathias and Melvin: take shelter, but if they board, fight like your life depends on it. Rahyn: you are the best swimmer amongst us, bring your knife and come with me. My mother was one of the finest divers on our island, and she taught me how to hold my breath for a long time. I hope it helps now."

And with that, he shed his boots and slipped off the raft as quietly as he could, with Rahyn right behind him.

Talara moved the lantern aft, and Caetal kneeled and readied an arrow on the string. Mathias led Shamsala into the tent, and hunkered down next to her. As Talara headed past Caetal into the tent, she stopped and kissed him on the cheek.

"So much for not trying not to kill Orlŭks." She whispered into his ear.

Caetal snorted. "It's kill or be killed now. Even Mathias can't argue with that. Time to earn my blue. Can you help tattoo the w-woad after-wards? Ripple of circles on my shoulder. Hard for me to reach."

"If we live through the night, I'll help tattoo an entire Orlŭk army on you, if you like."

"Just the ripples are fine. I've got five arrows, so let's hope for five ripples. Take cover, and ready the lantern."

....

The lantern they had was a fine one indeed; a bullseye of hammered brass, with a convex lens of glass on one side of it, and a mirror hidden inside. Lens and mirror together focused the light into a single, amplified beam, much brighter than a small flame's radiance could have otherwise been. The bullseye belonged to Caetal's father, although after this night he was never to get the lantern back again. The lantern's clear lens could be switched out for one of green or red glass, depending on the night's intended use, but neither of those lenses had been brought. It had a thick candle inside with a very fat wick, and when all was shut tight, could be swung around with some carelessness and still remain lit. Talara held the lantern grimly, and waited for the signal from Caetal.

The coracles pulled ever closer by oar, until such a distance where the figures in each boat could be seen. There were three Orlŭks overcrowded into two of the coracles, and two in the third. All had spears at hand, and each boat had a standing archer bearing a compact bow, short and thick. At the back of each raft, a small torch burned in a metal sconce. The boats were swift. Caetal grunted again and shifted nervously from one knee to another. The sounds of the Orlŭk oars could be heard splashing the water.

> *"Eight of them,"* Caetal muttered. *"Twice my count of arrows."*
> Talara glanced at him. "Twice five does not equal eight."
> Caetal shrugged. "More or less."
> "Less. Make them count, Caetal."
> "I'm not g-great at counting, but I'm pretty g-g-good at shooting."

....

Not long now. Inside the tent, Melvin coughed, and Shamsala bleated at him reproachfully. As though signaled by the sound, two of the Orlŭk archers loosed their arrows towards the raft in high arcing shots. One splashed down about twenty feet shy of them, and the other fared no better. Caetal grinned to himself. *Still out of range. You need bigger bows, lads.* Then he hefted the longbow high, pulled back to his cheek, sighted and loosed. The furthest rear archer dropped to his knees, gurgling and clutching at the arrow that had sprouted in his neck. The other Orlŭk in that boat scrambled to retrieve the dropped bow.

"Light it, Talara!" Caetal called out, nocking another arrow.

Talara rapidly struck flint against a fire-iron, driving a small shower of sparks into a tinderbox full of charcloth, and blowing on it carefully. Guided by the leaping light of the sparks, the third archer loosed his arrow at her. This one splashed down right in front of the raft, about three feet from where she was crouched. By the care of her breath, a tiny flame caught in the charcloth. Lighting a flamestick with it, Talara touched it to the lantern wick. Then she snapped the bullseye lens closed and swung it around with her hand over the lens. She waited until she could see the two standing archers nocked and drawing again. Then she moved her hand out of the way and aimed the light beam directly into their eyes. The Orlŭk's eyes glowed like green fire, as did the eyes of all the Orlŭks when the light was shining on them. They let out growls, and those that could threw their hands up to shade their sight.

Caetal immediately loosed his second arrow into the chest of an Orlŭk holding a paddle, who sagged against the side of the boat. The overloaded coracle dipped towards that side, off-balancing the archer, who fired wildly and then fell forward into the wounded rower. Although the third Orlŭk in the boat leaned back to try to compensate, the lower lip of the boat dipped below the water and the boat capsized, spilling the survivors overboard. The two unwounded Orlŭks scrambled to cling to the inverted bowl of the whicker boat, the archer paddling with one hand and trying to hold her bow above the water with the other.

Then bubbles churned up from below where the Orlŭks were clinging. Rahyn and Tarquin surfaced nearby and stabbed them from behind with knives. They aimed to harm, not to kill, as neither of the children felt up to the Reaper's calling. Once in the leg — once in the arm — then they dragged the Orlŭks back down with them into the dark water, where they thrashed and bled. The archer swam towards shore with her blood making a trail in the water behind her. The other one dragged himself back up onto the belly of the capsized boat and lay there groaning. Rahyn and Tarquin dove again, swimming underwater towards another boat.

Talara swiveled the light of the lantern and trained it on the last standing archer, and not a moment too soon. The glare-blinded bowman shot, and though he could not see clearly, his aim was nearly true. The arrow thunked into the wooden logs of the raft, a scant few inches below Caetal's raised knee. He whistled sourly at it.

"Close call! But I don't w-want your arrow, thank you anyway. Let me return it to you." He yanked the arrow out of the wood, slid it to the string, pulled back quickly, and fired.

The Orlŭk archer got his arrow back.

....

Seemingly undaunted by their losses, the two remaining coracles closed distance as fast as oars could row. The boats split up and moved to flank the raft, rightly judging that the troublesome glare could only follow one of them at a time. Talara did her best to swing the bullseye back and forth, but now the Orlŭk archers were both in range, and each time she blinded one, the other had the chance to fire. Talara was forced to leap behind the backpack pile, as one arrow went skeeting over the leather of her boot and ripping a bloody gouge across her leg that stung like crazy. Her tumbling rocked the raft: the lantern toppled, and the light extinguished.

In the sudden dark, Talara heard Mathias fumbling for the flint and tinder. Every few moments, the oilskin tent would billow with the impact of arrows striking against it. As often as not, there was a ripping sound — the arrow hissing as it passed through, twice burying into the backpacks that were piled up all around them. One hit Mathias' backpack with a shattering sound, and the stuffy gloom of the tent was suddenly drenched with the heady smell of honey alcohol. Mathias struggled to relight the lantern. The shower of flinted sparks onto the tinder lit the faces of three fearful humans and one oddly unworried goat in sudden flashes of light. An arrow deflected off the tent near Mathias's head, and they heard Caetal swearing as he leapt to his feet and tried to retrieve the arrow before it rolled between the logs and was lost in the water.

Caetal stuck his head into the tent and shouted: "Prepare to be boarded!"

"Where? Port or Starboard?!" Melvin cried, scooting himself towards the back of the tent.

"W-what? I dunno Mel, I'm not a *skabde* sailor! W-which side is Starbo-AGH, KEFE! OH, KAE VALEA KEFE!" Caetal dropped his bow and tumbled forward into the tent with an arrow clenched in hand. For a moment they thought he was holding onto it tightly. Then he doubled over in agony, rolling onto his side with one fist clenching the wrist of the other. The arrow had punctured straight through the palm of his right hand, between the third and fourth knuckle. Blood leaked down his arm and soaking into the cuff of his shirt sleeve. He moaned painfully, cursing and thrashing away from Mathias when he reached out to try and help him.

"Orlŭks on both godsdamned sides." Caetal growled between clenched teeth. Shamsala licked his bloodied hand, and he groaned.

Then they heard the grassy whump of a coracle thumping against their raft and felt the log platform sway beneath the boarding weight of uninvited company.

There was a light far up ahead: a strange light — a blue flame so pale that it was almost white, shining close to the ground like a fallen star. Tarquin and Rahyn could see the tiny glow of it downriver, every time they surfaced for breath. They were hard at work stabbing at the underside of one of the boats and dodging the spear that snaked down at them repeatedly through the water. They had already made some sizable gashes through the stretched horse hide that covered the tightly woven reeds, and the growl of the Orlŭk was becoming higher-pitched, as its boat began to fill with river water. One more poke, and Rahyn kicked herself off back towards the raft.

Tarquin tried to catch the Orlŭk spear as it took another stab at him, but only managed to cut his hands on it when the spear was withdrawn. So, he took a deep breath, and dove down into the cold blackness, praying to Cuthain that he wouldn't catch that spear in the ribs. But their sabotage to the coracle was sufficient, because no spear was thrown. When Tarquin came up for air, he was just a few feet from their log raft again, and able to look back and appreciate his handiwork. The Orlŭk on the sinking coracle was abandoning ship and started swimming back upriver.

Tarquin laughed uproariously at the sight of his victory, accidentally breathing in a big mouthful of river water. He coughed hard, spraying water from his lungs and slapping his arms blindly against the surface of the river. Still trying to clear his lungs, he felt his hand brush against the side of the log raft and pulled himself up towards it. He opened his eyes just in time to see a familiar-looking Orlŭk looming above him on the log raft, with one hand wrapped around Rahyn's neck, who was twisting and growling in his grasp. Then Tarquin saw the swift incoming of the bare foot of that familiar Orlŭk kick him in the face. He toppled backwards and sunk underwater.

"That will teach you for striking my gonads." The Orlŭk sneered in the Orlŭk tongue at the bubbling spot where Tarquin had submerged.

Although a more direct translation would be: *"My wounded gonads send their wrathful regards."*

....

While the first Orlŭk was busy choking Rahyn and kicking Tarquin in the face, the second boar-man was circling quietly around towards the back of the tent. He could hear the rapid hitch of the children breathing and smell the acrid sweetness of their fear. There was a smear of blood at the front tent flap, from the human he had shot in the hand, and the Orlŭk carefully stepped over the large, discarded bow that the young human had dropped. *I'll be taking that with me soon enough.* The Orlŭk thought to himself. *But first to quiet the squealing Manlets.*

The Orlŭk positioned himself by the back tent flap, where the smell of fear and goat was most pungent. He raised his spear above his head. Then there was a blur of motion, and Melvin's hand whipped out from the base of the tent, stabbing the dagger it clutched deep into the tendon at the back of his ankle. The Orlŭk howled, collapsing heavily onto the log deck. The raft tipped and rocked, bowling the children over into each other inside the tent. Caetal yelled with pain, Talara with surprise, and on the far side, the Orlŭk choking Rahyn swayed backwards against the sloping tent wall, toppling into the canvas right on top of Shamsala, who flipped out.

....

Rahyn felt the clawed grip on her neck loosen for just a moment as Shamsala bucked beneath them. It was the opportunity she needed to grab two of the Orlŭk's fingers and pry them backward far enough to gasp in a breath of air. The change into the fox shape had already begun, and she lunged herself forward on top of the sprawled Orlŭk and sunk her sharpening teeth into the creature's throat, clamping down as hard as she could on his windpipe. The Orlŭk, who outweighed her considerably, started thrashing beneath her, and rolled himself over until the full weight of him pinned her down. She felt his awful bulk pressing the air out of her lungs, but she would not let go of his neck. Instead, she wrapped her fingers into the greasy crest of his hair, and yanked his head further back to get a deeper grip on his throat. She heard the clicking gurgle of his panic, as he tried to drive his knee into the side of her ribs. Her mouth filled up with the choking warmth of the boar-man's blood.

....

The second Orlŭk, (who was named *Lahkruk*, by the way, which translates to the Orlŭk equivalent of *Larry*), lay for a moment on the log deck and considered his sudden misfortune. He had not wanted to go on this ridiculous trip downriver in the first place. His boar-man-boss had gotten kicked in the downstairs bits, and Orlŭk Larry had been pretty much forced into paddling the vengeance boat on behalf of his boss' wounded pride. Now here he was — miles from his home on a cold night — and he had just gotten shanked in the ankle by a nasty human child. He would probably be limping for the rest of his life. *Although,* (he reflected after rolling over and observing the struggle going on nearby) *at least I don't have a wildling girl chomping on my windpipe. It is good to keep bad things in perspective.*

Just then, a small blond boy with a rather large head rolled out from under the flattened tent canvas, and charged at him, shrieking desperately. Lahkruk threw his arms up to protect his face, and the terrible child hurled itself down on top of him, and bit poor Orlŭk Larry savagely on the thumb. Lahkruk howled, and the boy howled around a mouthful of thumb, and pummeled the Orlŭk with an unskilled flurry of fists. Then a dark-skinned girl rose up above them both with a knife clutched in her hand and weird grin on her face, and Orlŭk Larry knew that it was past time to bail on this floating nightmare. He headbutted the blond kid, who reeled backwards, releasing his hurtful grip on Larry's thumb. Then before the girl could start stabbing him full of holes, he rolled sideways off the raft into the cold river, and began swimming towards shore, churning the water feebly with his one working foot and his throbbing, painful hand.

Human children are awful, Orlŭk Larry thought to himself. Then, as if summoned by his own fear, he saw another one swimming right towards him through the dark water. This boy-child was leaking blood out of his nose and had a crazy look in his eyes. Lahkruk/Larry shrieked and paddled away from the pursuit of this terrible child. He swam in a raw and painful panic, and only when he finally reached the shore did he dare to look back.

Behind him, the river was quiet; the child had vanished as though he had never been there at all. But then, midstream, Orlŭk Larry saw the boy emerge from the water, pulling himself back up onto his wretched raft. He saw the child help the other children roll the body of his Orlŭk boss into the river with a somber splash. Then they stood there all together, staring at him across the water. Even the goat was there, and it maaaed malevolently. By the light of their relit lantern, Orlŭk Larry could see the flat and devilish darkness of their eyes. A creeping fear shivered down his spine. *They know where I live.* Lahkruk thought to himself. *They will come for me when I am sleeping. I must move away — far away, where the Manlets cannot find me!*

Orlŭk Larry hobbled off, determined to avoid human children for the rest of his life.

....

"Boy Mathias, I really think you scared the spirit out of that boar-man!" Tarquin croaked, laughing around his fingers while he pinched the septum of his nose to stop the nosebleed.

Mathias blushed with pride and shrugged. "Well, I did bite him pretty dang hard."

....

Onward the current swept them; one log raft, one empty drifting coracle, and one capsized coracle with a wounded Orlŭk clutching the top of it. Now the banks of the river were closing in on both sides as the water slowed and the channel deepened. Ahead there shone that pinpoint of pale blue light, seeming brighter all the time as they drifted towards it, yet still somehow retreating away in front of them. The size of it grew no larger in their sight, but they knew with some innate certainty that they were gaining on it.

Indeed, so focused upon that otherworldly light had they become that they barely noticed the moonslight on the open water in front of them until they emerged from under the vaulted canopy of branches and saw the starlit sky opening before them. The edges of the river veered away on both sides, and the boats drifted onto the expanse of a wide lake, with shores that were so distant to one another that in the dark of night, they could only be sensed, not seen. All around them was the rolling of shallow waves, lit on opposing sides by the light of two crescent moons and stirred to rocking by fitful gusts of wind.

Near the center of the lake was the silhouette of a small islet: a blot of shadows amongst the ripples of moonslight. On this islet was the source of the mysterious blue-white light, illuminating a rounded section of broken walls looming behind it in a ruin so jagged that it looked like a tower that some Colossus had bitten the top floors off of. As they drew nearer to the islet — for the tide carried them straight towards it — they could see that the light was a single blue flame suspended in a silver lantern. The lantern hung from a wrought-iron lantern post, stuck into the ground, and on either side of that lantern post were erected two tents. Sitting between the tents was a table with papers strewn across it, over which two seated figures were hunched at study.

....

Daedrim rubbed his eyes wearily, grateful that the nausea of traveling by magic had finally faded. He and Drinn had been debating the details of an architectural sketch for most of the evening. Try as he might, Daedrim could not find substantial flaws in the tower design, and that had annoyed him fundamentally, so that he found himself criticizing petty particulars of masonic minutiae, until Drinn had forcefully encouraged him to shut up and join him in downing a large dram of whisky.

Now Daedrim leaned back in his chair, tasting the heat of the liquor on his tongue and enjoying the fog it raised in his mind. Helping himself to a second tip of the snifter, he let the moonslight rolling across the water lull his mind into the silly fantasy that he saw his son sitting with his friends and a goat on a floating raft that was drifting right towards them. Then his whisky-addled mind, apparently fixated on further phantasmagoria, invented the vision of tentacular horrors rising up from the surface of the lake behind them. It was a most unlikely apparition.

"Drinn, I believe I am seeing visions. I should never have let you talk me into drinking whisky. I haven't the constitution for it, apparently."

Drinn glanced up at him from the architectural print. Then his focus sharpened on the lake behind him.

"Skabde kae!" He exclaimed and forcefully arose, knocking his chair over in haste. Before Daedrim's marveling gaze, the magus sprinted to the shore of the lake and fell to his knees, submerging his hands until his cupped palms filled with water. Then he threw his arms backwards, flinging the water overhead and behind. A noise sighed out of him: a wetly pouring intonation that saturated the air with the sound of *NAUNE.*

The log raft, as well as the six children and one goat that were huddling on it, were suddenly lifted from the surface of the lake in a rushing plume of water that rose to the height of a rearing wyrm and then deposited them in a soaking tumble a hundred feet from the water's edge. In the movement of one passing moment, they had gone from floating on the lake to picking themselves dazedly up, rubbing beach sand out of hair and eyes, and coughing it up in lungfuls. Their raft lay nearby in a tangle of torn ropes, loose logs, and scattered backpacks.

"Was that truly necessary?" Daedrim called out irritably, trying to untangle his dazed son Melvin from the pile of his companions. "The mooring dock is just down the beach! Now you have ruined their raft."

Then he turned to his son. "HOW? And WHY? These are words that are coming strongly to mind as I see you here, barely believing that you exist on this islet at all but as a folly of drink-addled visions! Why in the name of learning are you here?! How did you get here?"

Drinn said, "By magic." And at the same time, Melvin muttered: "*By raft.*"

Daedrim just stared, his mouth opening and closing like a fish.

Then Talara, who had gracefully rolled away from the boat's impact on the sand and quickly recovered her wits, pointed out across the moonlit surface of the lake and said:

"Where did the wounded Orlŭk on his overturned boat go? He was just behind us on the water — I was keeping his boat in sight the whole time, and now I don't see it anywhere."

It was true. Though seven sets of eyes scanned the water, there was not the faintest trace to be seen of the boar-man, nor the overturned boat that bore him. Only large circles of ripples, already vanishing from sight in the gentle lapping of waves.

Drinn broke the peering silence, speaking with the confidence of a slightly drunk magician.

"The Orlŭk is gone: no doubt claimed by the unfortunate somewhat dead magus that haunts the lake. I would, therefore, not advise further nighttime sailing. For some reason, unnatural entities become restless under moonslight. It is a phenomenon that defies the contradiction of logic."

"We can't sail anywhere: you just broke our boat," Tarquin grumbled, petting Shamsala.

"Irrelevant." The magus replied, waving a dismissive hand.

"*Hardly.*" Talara muttered.

Then Drinn gazed down on Melvin, where he lay propped up on his elbows in the sand.

"So, young Melvin: the whim of fortune has summoned you to the edge of this lake, towards the light of my ensorcelled lantern, and the piece of fallen star trapped within. Personally, I'd look such things in the face and call them *fate*, but I'm the sort of superstitious fool that believes the universe notices individuals amongst the teeming multitude and takes an interest in the unfolding stories of their lives. Are you also that sort of fool? Your father would like me to ask you formally."

Melvin squinted up at him. "Drinn, what are you saying? Please re-phrase the question in a way that doesn't make you sound crazy. We had a very long and difficult night so far, and I have a sinking feeling it isn't done yet."

Daedrim laughed, suddenly and abruptly. Melvin looked over at him and smiled. He had rarely heard his father laugh, and he enjoyed the sound of it. Glancing back, he saw Drinn trying to hide his own smile behind an upraised hand. Melvin felt a sudden shifting inside of him then: the pull of celestial forces, unknown but not unknowable.

Drinn squatted, and peered intently into Melvin's eyes. The boy and the magus stared at each other for a long moment and might have kept at it for a while longer if Shamsala hadn't wandered over and nudged her way between them, intent on getting a mouthful of Drinn's hair. The magus pushed her impatiently off and said:

"Melvinari Selgaunt, son of Daedrim and Abella: how would you like to begin your training as my apprentice?"

Melvin nodded. "Of course. You knew I'd say yes, or you wouldn't bother asking. But I've given this some thought, and I have conditions: I want weekends and festival days off from training, so I can visit my father and my friends. And I'm not going to call you 'Master,' and you're not going to talk down at me like I'm a child because I'm at least as clever as you are. It's straight talk between us and time off when I want it, or no deal."

It was the first of only three times that Melvin was ever to see Drinn look completely surprised. His mouth gaped open, as shocked as a farcical puppet, and he stammered indignantly.

Daedrim took one look at his face and began laughing again, so raucously this time that he started coughing on his own mirth, until Talara had to pound on his back.

••••••••••••••••••••••••••••••••

A Closing Moment

At the center of the vine woven Kaninhode, the suspended Orlŭk finally woke up. He had been pierced by a hundred small thorns and was weak with blood loss. His clothes were shredded to a shabby cloth suggestion, and his armor fared no better. But the thorny vines that had once constricted him hungrily now just held him aloft with his feet awkwardly dangling. He looked down. He was about fifteen feet above the ground. Behind and above, the red moon shone redly. The smoldering remains of the campfire were deserted. It was cold. A nearby nighthawk chirruped at him, sounding slightly hostile. The bullfrogs croaked, and the creek burbled. He cleared his throat.

"Uh... hello? Guys? Where the heck is everyone? Can someone help me get down?"

The Orlŭk said, in his Orlŭk language. Although it more accurately translates as... well, honestly, the translation is close enough.

....

Tidings and Torture

Not so very far away, and just as ruddled by the bruising light of that waxing red gibbous moon, another creature hung suspended above the riverbank.

From the ground below, the large wooden cage seemed to contain no more than a discarded tangle of limbs: so lanky and entwined as to appear like a pile of branches gathered around a central stump. Only a closer inspection, dangerously close, would reveal the rubbery sheen of amphibian flesh. Under red moonlight, the skin looked as blackly purple as an old clot, but the occasional flare of passing torchlight revealed it to be a darkly mottled green. Holding such a torch, and at a careful distance, Fera Dané could not help but stare in admiration at the caged creature. *Even its blood is green.* She mused to herself, watching it drip steadily into the river. *As green as an algae bloom. I wonder if this creature also bloomed up out of the mud like algae, or an overgrown skunk cabbage? It certainly smells similar.* She wrinkled her nose in disgust.

Still musing, she dipped the head of her long-handled spear into the sluggish current of the river shallows, stirring it around to wash the troll blood off of it. By the time the blade was clean the jagged wound on the troll's flank was already sealing itself back up. The pattering blood slowed to a dribble that ceased entirely, until only the wet shushing of the river could be heard once more. Then a passing breeze swiveled the cage at the joint of its hanging chain. The iron chain squeaked, the thick tree branch it hung from creaked, and from within the cage, a throaty chuckle could be heard. Fera Dané frowned, peering at the dark presence between the thick cage bars. The reflection of the torchlight glimmered wetly in its eyes.

"Laugh all you want, river-man. We both know how this will end." Fera Dané said.

The Drôle known as a *troll* chuckled again, clicking and burbling to itself. It did that often, particularly while Fera Dané or one of her soldiers were cutting on it. Sometimes she imagined that the muddled mouthfuls of clacks and squelches might be some primitive troll language; the oft-wounded creature may be attempting to communicate. After weeks of studied torture, Fera Dané was grudgingly willing to admit to herself that the mind of the troll was nowhere near as bestial as she had first imagined.

Although it had amphibian skin and the folded lankiness of a frog, it had been running mostly upright when they first caught it. And a somewhat crocodilian countenance did not diminish the shine of cunning in the dark undertow of its eyes.

Casually she raised her torch overhead until the flames licked at the creature's skin. The troll gave a satisfying hiss, clumsily scrambling up and backwards until it was clinging to the upper interior of the cage like a spider. There it perched and glowered. In the glare of torchlight, the diminished state of the captured troll was much more obvious. Weeks of surgical mutilations cauterized by white-hot iron had turned the green skin into a patchwork of pale scars. One leg had been removed at the knee, and all of the toes on the other foot. One arm had been removed down to the elbow. On the left hand, only a thumb remained.

Its face, however, was unmarred by blade or burning. A few weeks back, a drunken soldier had tried to cut off its nose when he tired of the croaking warble of its singing. The troll had bitten that soldier's arm halfway through and torn the rest of it off from the shoulder. It ate the soldier's arm while he bled out on the ground. Now nobody got near its face.

"I could set this cage on fire, you know." Captain Dané quietly spoke up to the troll. "That would cook you like a carrot, and good riddance. Your kind shouldn't exist at all. You are an *infestation*, no different than lice. And your regeneration isn't worth a damn if your whole body is burning. Nothing survives fire — not even you."

As she had a few times before, she wished the troll could understand her. But it only stared at her darkly, muttering to itself. The small throat pouch beneath its chin flexed and bulged.

"We've learned everything we need to know about you. We've learned how to cut pieces off and make sure they don't grow back. How to exterminate you and your whole kind. Thank you for sharing this knowledge with us. Perhaps you would like to be released from this cage for good? I can arrange an end for you."

Lately, alone at night, she had caught herself taking a stroll across the river to come talk to the troll. It was poor company, and it stank, but it always seemed to pay close attention to everything she said. *It's nice to talk to someone who is really listening.* She thought to herself, then shook her head grimly. *Don't think like this, Fera. It's not a 'someone' — it's a 'something.' Better to just kill the poor nasty thing and be done with it.*

She glanced at it again, almost furtively. The troll stared at her; the light of the red moon reflected like pale fire in its eyes. It began to flex and strain, swinging the cage back and forth until the branch creaked and the chain rattled in a steady rhythm. Then it started to mutter to itself — shushing and hissing, grunting and grumbling — and all the while watching her closely. For a moment, it seemed like some strange form of singing. Then Fera shook her head and shivered, pulling her cloak closer together against the cold dampness of the midnight river.

Not tonight, though. I'm too tired to kill it tonight. Lieutenant Darrow can come back out and finish the job in the morning. Let the slaughter of this abomination be someone else's bother.

....

She turned on her heel and walked back towards the distant warmth of the barracks. Behind her, she heard the troll's croaking song swell to a crescendo, but she did her best to ignore it, listening instead to the sound of her feet crunching across the small stones of the riverbank. She walked up over a low bluff and pushed her way through ferns until she reached the abandoned section of the Thegn's Road which led past the unfinished ruins of Revis Keep — known in modern times as Drôle.

Her breath steamed as she walked; the river exhaled mist all around her. A quarter mile ahead and across the water, the ruins of the unfinished castle seemed as vaporous as a phantasm. Only the two torches that lit the yawning arch of the raised portcullis looked real. The night began to hum with croaking frogs and the sinuous burring rattle of giant dragonflies. *Night hunters, all of them. Everything that is awake past midnight is looking for a meal. What in the hells am I doing out here, night after night? I really must be cracking up.* She increased her stride, unconsciously resting her hand on the hilt of her sheathed sword where it bumped reassuringly against her hip.

As she neared the bridge that spanned the river to the castle, she was surprised to see a light coming towards her in the dark. One torch held overhead; the sound of trotting hooves clattering wetly on the stones of the road. She drew her blade and withdrew towards the edge of the forest until she felt the comfort of a tree trunk at her back. A tense minute passed while the stranger approached. Fera cursed herself for the bright torch she was holding like a flickering target. Finally, she recognized the red and silver tabard of the court at Portuan, and gratefully sheathed her sword. By the time the messenger drew up next to her, her heartbeat had almost slowed to normal. The woman on horseback saluted, and retrieved a scroll case from within the bundle of her cloak and riding furs.

"Your pardon if I startled you, Captain. I carry a message from our thegn that could not wait until morning. Your men at the castle told me where to look for you out here."

"I was not startled, but I am glad you found me. It is dark and the air is thick with vapor on this side of the river."

"It is dark everywhere, Captain. I'm grateful you had a torch in hand or I would have ridden right by you in this *skabde* fog."

"Hand over the message, soldier. Hold your torch up so I can read it."

"Yes Captain."

....

Captain Dané,

Your troll experiments better have achieved the results I need, because you are out of time. I was just informed that my godsdamn new abbey I have been paying to construct on High Hill got wrecked by some kind of stone monster. One which, by the further godsdamn way, may still be at large.

You and your soldiers are now assigned to clean-up duty. Leave half of your number to hold Drôle and protect that stretch of road. Take the other half and march to Holm immediately. Establish a presence of force at High Hill and begin to empty the abbey of rubble. Conscript locals to assist you by any means necessary. I will send reinforcements to meet you at the Orchard Bridge.

Rory, Great Thegn of Southern Fýrii

....

At the unfinished castle called Drôle, soldiers were hurried from sleep and spent the last hours of night saddling horses, polishing armor, and preparing to march at sunrise. Those who had been chosen to depart for Holm considered themselves lucky to be leaving the haunted winter they had just spent in that miserable ruin behind them. Those that remained grumbled to themselves and did their best to sleep through the clatter of their departing companions. At least the order had finally been given to put that troll to the mercy of the pyre. Four good soldiers had already died capturing and torturing that cursed creature. Better to be done with it. Perhaps the rest of their duty at Drôle could be spent fishing and playing dice. A chance to relax while the captain was away.

....

Evening wore on, and the mist arose from the river until the sight of the red moon was obscured within it. Alone in its cage, the dying Drôle rocked on what was left of its haunches and sang a song of sacrifice to itself. The words it sung were new, but the song itself was as old as the memory of that river; a story of little deaths, and what comes afterwards.

Then it sank serrated teeth into its own flesh and bit off its last remaining thumb. The pain was terrible, as it always was. But the thumb would regrow over time; the soldiers might never know what had gone missing. Without its feet in the river it was born in, the regeneration process would take quite a while. Each week that had passed in that hanging cage slowed the process down further. Someday soon it would stop all together, and the Drôle would dry up and die like any river plant stranded too long out of water.

The Drôle held up the severed thumb and said a blessing over it. Then, before the bleeding had stopped, the river-man threw it out of the cage and into the shallows with a bloody splash. It sunk down into the water until it came to rest, half buried in mud.

....

In the cage overhead, the Drôle's bloody knuckle slowly began to regenerate a new thumb.

Below the surface of the water, cradled like a seed in good river mud, the severed thumb began to grow a new Drôle quite a bit faster.

....

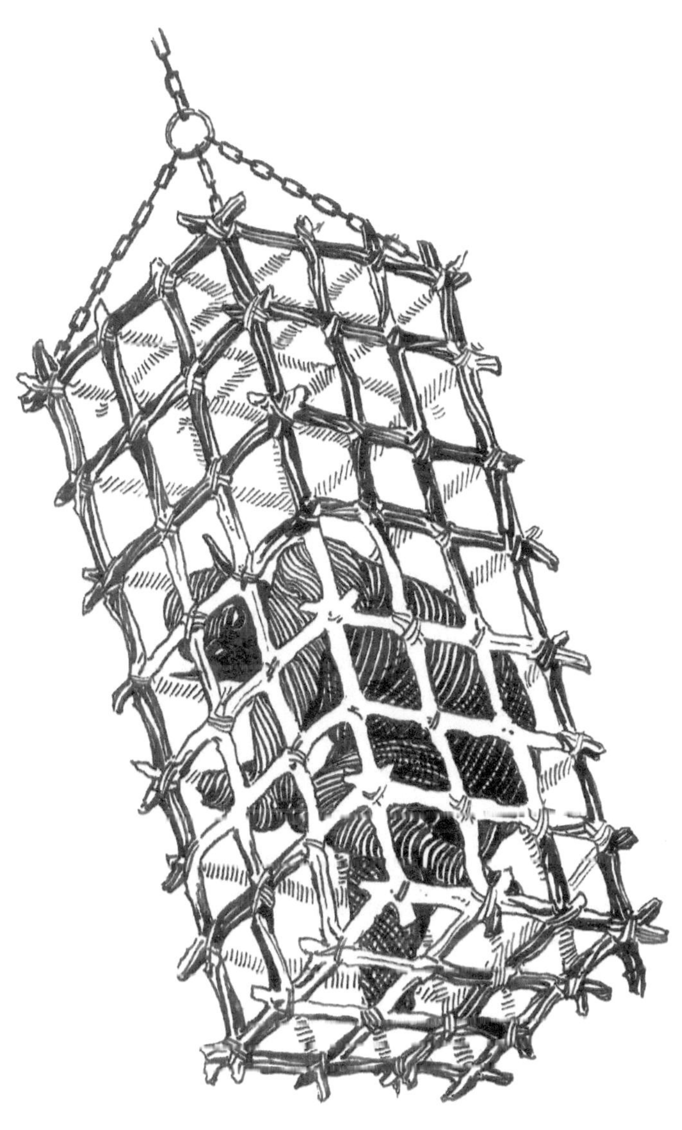

Last Song of the Riverman

I shall die in the air, as dry as bones scraped clean by sunlight
I burn again tonight
To please you.
I do not know why you are angry, torch-bearer
I do not know you; I have not learned your name.

Are you alive, or dead? Or are you caught between?
You hold fire in your hand like a plucked flower
and encase your living body in dead iron.
You reek of fear, how can you stand
To be yourself, like this?

You will not find
What you have already lost
If you don't know you lost it.
It is late. Let me free. We can both heal
In the soft flow of the river.

Or perish, as I must perish to please you.
Tonight, I see you as you must be seen;
Joints, spine, meat worth wasting
All mushy to the eye
All throw-away mushy.

I shall be reborn, but you must not be allowed;
You who eat the whole earth and are never filled,
You who drink from the hearts of strangers.
Why do you choose to take so much from me?
You have become umbra, obscuring all meaning.

Our end is coming, my last companion
And for just one moment everything makes sense:
rain jumping off of rocks,
snow drifting out of empty air:
each transformed to make room for them both.

And so, I sing our death song; paean pours from my throat.
Let us cease; let us listen; let us be transformed.
Let us listen; let us be transformed.
Let us be transformed.

The Hierophants

"We do not fight for rewards or for glory. We fight for vengeance against those who have taken what was ours."

The HIEROPHANTS
~ The Second Card ~

On an afternoon that turned out unlike any other, the White Crow returned.

....

It had been five days since Melvin accepted Drinn's offer of apprenticeship and four since the other children were dispersed by magic to their various homes. Rahyn, who had no wish to travel by being evaporated through spaces that did not exist in the familiar world, had been paddled to the shore of the lake by rowboat and trotted upstream from there in fox form.

She had made her way back towards the cave, her heart heavy with the unfamiliar human feeling of guilt for having left the Orlŭk she had captured with vines strung up for so long. But when she returned to that vale, she found the boar-man had apparently freed himself many hours prior by chewing through the vines that bound him and climbing down from the tree. The scent of him was faint and fading: the Orlŭk campsite had been likewise abandoned.

Having nowhere pressing to go towards or away from, and liking the tranquility of the hilly hollow besides, Rahyn set about to empty the cave of soil and rock that Melvin's magic had shook loose and tidy up the mess of bones and debris that the fleeing Orlŭks had left around their campfire. The spring weather warmed unexpectedly for a few days, and the little valley steamed in the warm afternoons and thickened with fog by nightfall. It was through this spring steam that the crow appeared, landing ungracefully on the ground nearby as Rahyn was rolling a particularly heavy rock away from the cave mouth and towards the stream. The crow watched her quietly for a few minutes, cleaning his feathers and grumbling to himself. Rahyn, with her heart perched between relief and an unexpected sense of foreboding, politely ignored him until his feathers were well sorted, and he had shifted into the man-shape.

As afternoon shadows began to lengthen, Djaro squatted and built a small pit fire, helping himself without asking to a few fish that Rahyn had dragged up from the creek earlier that day. With the perfume of roasting fish wafting enticingly amongst the twilit trees, Djaro finally beckoned Rahyn over to come perch on a rock beside him. They sat that way together, nursing an awkward silence, and ate the roasted fish. Only after the bones were buried did Djaro finally speak. His voice was strained; it quivered with fatigue, as though it had been years instead of weeks since they had last spoken together.

"I have been out of sight longer than I have been gone, but even so, I was summoned to report to the Fýrii, and I traveled quite far to answer that summons. I have a lot to tell you, and I ask you now to hear me through the telling of it as well as you can, without your usual fidgets and interruptions. Can you sit still and listen carefully?"
Rahyn nodded carefully. "I can. I have missed your teachings."

Djaro smiled at her suddenly, and she was surprised to see tears sparkling at the edges of his eyes. They vanished into the maze of wrinkles.

"I have missed teaching you too, foxgirl, more than you know. It was difficult to be away, hard to watch you make your choices and not be allowed to stop you. Harder still acknowledging to myself how much you are growing into the human you have always been. I have never asked you not to become all of yourself, but I hoped..."

He trailed off and looked away.

"That I would not?" Rahyn murmured.
Djaro sighed. "I suppose. As foolish as wishing winter snow would warm into summer rain without the passing time in between. Forgive me for all that I have tried to keep from you."

Rahyn wanted to ask a thousand questions about what he meant, but he had requested that she not interrupt him, so she bit her tongue and simply shifted back and forth a few times on her rock.

Djaro cleared his throat. "I want to start by telling you a story, one I have not told you before. It is a long-ago story of the Immortals and the choices that led to your human ancestors. The consequences of their actions — the Immortals and your ancestors — continue to shape the future of Eld. Your future in particular, for oaths were taken back then that still must be honored now. Parts of this story have been passed down since before the beginning of time itself. It is important that you share that honor and burden as well, so that you might pass the story on to others one day."

Rahyn wiggled a little despite herself. "A story, hurrah! It is your stories I have missed most of all!"

Djaro cocked his head and smiled wryly. The campfire sizzled and spat.

....

"You have heard already of the two Giants, who were the foreparents of the energies of creation on our Homm. Their excitement in one another had awoken the world around them to the possibility of life. They had birthed the moons and the first monster. But their elemental explorations were far from finished. Their pleasure inspired the Celestial planet itself to begin to experiment with these new combinations of energy. This caused a slow spread of plant and animal life across the surface of Homm, particularly in the oceans.

"Because the sky was now governed by the pull of two moons, the ocean waters began to rise and fall between them. These tides, reaching ever towards the pull of the moons, continuously mixed the waters and drew up the rich elements for life from the deep. Many diverse creatures blossomed in this oceanic olio. The whole of Homm became a canvas on which inspiration could be sketched and animated with vibration and purpose. Salamanders of fire were birthed from the deepest molten drifts. Winged reptiles took to the skies, and birds eventually followed — probably crows first, I would imagine, for we are a proud and long-lived people!"

Rahyn smiled, and Djaro stroked his beard fondly.

"As I was saying: the first land animals crept from the waters — timidly, to start with, but emboldening over time as legs strengthened and gills became redundant. Adaptation became the artistry of evolution: each creature adjusting to its environment and the environment subtly reshaping to welcome it. The Hum of Creation had become a planet-wide song in which trillions of individual notes blended harmoniously."

"I love this!" Rahyn said, her eyes shining.

"It is the most important story of all, foxgirl. What is there not to love? The story of life itself: the question to which each of our lives is the same answer, repeated over and over again."

....

"*During this period of growth and experimentation,*" Djaro continued, "six more Immortal children were born to the Giants. Each of these second generation of beings were infused with the energy of the continuing evolution of life on the planet. These children, and their children that followed, were to shape much of what became of the future of our world. There were three daughters born, staggered by three sons. The names they were given then were not the names they bore in later years, nor was the shape of the skin they were born in the same as the skin they later wore. But I will tell you of them as best I can.

"The firstborn was a daughter, and at first, her parents feared she would be another Terrasque. She, like it, was scaled and bony and sharp of tooth and claw. But when she opened her eyes, they were beautiful slits of amber, and her natural rage was checked by the glimmer of obvious intellect. She stretched, unfurling leathery wings scaled with shimmering night-blue iridescence. Her breath was the warm flame of her father, and the air was hers to command. She was named Dragon and was to be the matriarch of that great race."

"*Dragons. Yes.*" Rahyn whispered, wiggling.

"The second was a winged son, and he was the first to wear the skin that would later be mistaken as the shape of Man. Obrin was the name he gave himself. He was restless and secretive, a wanderer who travelled constantly. Those who looked on him admired him, almost instinctively, but his skin tingled with buried lightning, and his eyes were as cold as the sea. He sired only once: an immortal son that would never grow up. He was named Hobin but he would come to be known as the Trickster thereafter. Obrin and Hobin were the first to discover the doors between worlds."

"He discovered the way into the Twilight Lands?"

"This was before the Twilight Lands even existed, for Obrin was born into a world that did not yet know time. *Hush* child; let me continue."

Rahyn clapped her hand across her mouth.

"The third born was another son. He was called Karnonou, and took much after his mother. His was a body of living earth; he had a pelt of plants that grew like fur, and skin of soft mottled green. Great antlers sprouted from his head, and his nature was sensual and wild. With his mother's help, he cultivated vast forests across the surface of the world and, in his time, was to progenerate the most prolific and unique race on Homm, known collectively as the Fae. It is from this race that the Fýrii are chosen, and it is the touch of Karnonou that chooses them from amongst their kindred. You know well of Karnonou already, of course, for he is Lord of the Wild, and you were born with some of his spirit inside you."

Rahyn nodded, still covering her mouth.

"The fourth was a daughter, as fair to look on as could ever be borne, for she never looked the same way twice. To everyone who viewed her, her beauty was perfectly extraordinary. But she had a heart of ice, and her hands were tipped in bloody claws. She was called Fate, and her influence would shape the rise and fall of nations yet to come.

"The fifth: another daughter. She was a lucky girl named Rhea; the fortunate counterpart to her older sister Fate. Like her lunar siblings who came so long before her, she was born with the shining sphere of her heart held in her hands. It flitted and shone with a prismatic playfulness. When she released it, (which she was at first afraid to do), it rose into the heavens with leaping joy, and has drifted and wandered above the planet ever since. Folks who are lost or wandering have followed that star towards unknown ends, as she is said to favor those who take their destiny into their own hands."

"*Luck*," Rahyn whispered into her hand, as quiet as a prayer.

"The last of that generation of Immortals born was a handsome boy of frail health. He was unique among his siblings, born without the ability to shift in aspect. He would grow wise in time, but not before he lost his mind, and betrayed his own kind. He had dark skin with dust-pale freckles and auburn hair and was the patriarch of a troubled race known as *Humanus*. His name was Lëth.

"There is much to tell about Lëth's story: his struggles to create humans in his own image, his loneliness, and his madness. It is the success of his failures and longevity of their survival — that is the point of what I need to tell you about tonight, Rahyn. So, we will not focus on Lëth the Immortal, and what became of him in the end — although it really is quite an engaging tale, and it includes the story of how *time* actually came to Holm — but I will continue on towards the races of Humanus on our island, and why that matters to us tonight."

....

"*Now the children of giants made children of their own, in an age-less cycle of inspiration.* All was Now — all had always been Now, for the Song of Creation and Destruction cantillated on in the world before time, mounting in pitch and growing ever more complex. There was inspiration, and action, and consequence. There was interest in Self, and curiosity of Other. Everything changed and shifted, and everything decayed and renewed. This was the balance the Celestials had instilled from the moment of their energetic genesis. There had never been a need for anything else.

"Now the forests were vast tapestries that grew in layered ripples, recycling themselves elegantly. The Fae became varied and numerous, and their progenitor Karnonou watched over them in the green. Now dragons were lords of the sky. The experimentation of the Giants and Immortals had given life to all manner of strange and beautiful beasts. The rich hum of Homm took over from there. Uncountable generations of evolution became so complexly playful that almost no two creatures ever looked similar. To describe them as individuals would be beyond imagining, but their forms took shape in mimicry of plants and earth and elements. Feathers that glowed like fire; scales like armored fruits; wild grass fur as soft as bee pollen; bones formed of roots and driftwood.

"And above it all, orbiting in the sky: two moons, a red one and a pale one. The hearts of Ember and of Ash. From Ember flowed the energy of creation, and to Ash was drawn up the energy that had been spent. In this perpetual 'Now,' it was not yet thought of as the drifting move-ment of souls, but it someday would be. The yellow moon would become known as the realm of rest for the dead. The red moon was the promise of reincarnation."

Djaro paused in his story for a moment, glancing at Rahyn as though expecting her to interrupt. She was staring into the fire, lost on the story bridge of long ago. Djaro smiled to himself and continued.

"Of course, there was destruction too, as there must be. Sometimes flights of fancy failed, and new shapes for trees and beasts tore themselves apart. Sometimes shifts in environment and climate created storms that toppled fragile ecosystems. On rare occasions, the Terrasque chewed through the mountains where it laired and laid waste horizon to horizon. Its roar was louder than the booming of thunder, and it could be heard even on Eld from far across the sea. When the Terrasque awoke, all the children of the Giants withdrew, for there was nothing in creation that could check its feral brutality. They would wait until it had smashed, rended, and eaten whatever it wanted of the world, and returned to sleep again under the mountains. Then the other Immortals would do their best to rebuild and repopulate.

"The Terrasque was searching for its heart, of course: always searching for it. Yet nobody could remember where the heart was buried, because there was no such thing as memory. For to create a memory, you must have time. Only time demands that something comes *before* and something *after*. Time alone insists that we learn from our mistakes, for it is our understanding of our own mortality that makes us aware of how much we want to survive. Yet the Immortals were grateful that the heart was never found, for they had a strong sense that it would mean the end of all the world if it was. The Terrasque, wide awake and in the full knowledge of its purpose that the heart would surely bring it, would eat the world until there was nothing left but an iron center, and *that* it would gnaw on slowly like an apple core until nothing of creation remained alive on Homm but the Terrasque itself, floating forever alone in space where the Celestial of Homm once was, with the two moons orbiting around it... until it ate them too.

"But we now live in the Age of Time, and there are memories of the ancient world that have been passed down as legends. One of these is about the lost heart of the Terrasque, and where it is hidden."

Rahyn interjected. "I have heard of this part of the story from you before. You said that Eld itself is formed around that heart. Is that legend, or is there truth in this?"

Djaro shrugged. "It is said to be so, by the descendants of the race of Mŭrian — I have heard it from Hel'hannah themself. Their memory, and the memories of the other Mŭrians, go back almost as far as the memories of Crow. The precise location of the heart has never been known   or perhaps known by someone, but guarded carefully. Many have believed that it is from this hidden heart that the violence that has always haunted the history of this island is sourced. To dwell above the buried heart of an immortal monster must be the cause of some calamity, surely?"

It was Rahyn's turn to shrug, mostly because she did not know what the word 'calamity' meant, and for some reason, she did not want to find out.

"What does the lost heart of the Terrasque have to do with your worry for my future?"

Djaro took her shoulders in hand and gazed grimly down at her.

"A lot. Yet it is your blooming humanity that worries me more."

....

"*Another generation of Immortals followed the six that I just told you about:* this you must know, Rahyn, for it will be important to the shape of things to come. The one that matters to your story is how Karnonou made Mab. It is an extraordinary difficulty for an Immortal to reproduce itself. It is not like the elemental recombination of the Giants, and it is not like the pleasurable heat of coupling. To create something so powerful as themselves required a drawing out of their own essential essence. A *sacrifice* is a simple way to say it, and what was cut off from themselves didn't ever grow back. So, for each of the Children of the Giants that chose to create another Immortal to expand their number, they lost something in return."

....

"*Karnonou was beloved of his Giantess mother and had worked with her tirelessly to cultivate the race of Fae.* But he felt himself wearying of all of their fawning and attention. Whenever the Lord of the Wild walked amongst them through the forest, they did him reverence as a living god. He, in response, grew ever more distant to their needs. It was the quiet singing of growing things that held his heart.

"The Fae were created in a world without time, and so their nature was one of ceaseless probing and exploration. Karnonou wished for a queen amongst them, to guide and protect their interests, and to give him the respite from their demands that he longed for. So he tore out his voice and his most secret desires for glory, and fed them to Torc, the greatest matriarch of the race of elder boars. The sow swallowed Karnonou's voice and his desires, and when they expanded inside her, the hoary hide ruptured and out from her steaming corpse arose a queenly maiden, dripping with gore. She had skin as green as shadows underwater, and ropes of hair that crawled with living moss. Karnonou's desires glowed through her skin in sacred toroids and nautilus spirals that burned like brands of fire. She was called Mab, and she would rule the Fae thereafter. Karnonou lost the power of speech, but he wore Torc's empty skin upon his shoulders in tribute to the sow's sacrifice and gained the honor of shifting shape into the great boar."

"It is the likeness of Torc that is carved into the petrified tree, isn't it?"

"The very same. It is known that Karnonou carved it into the tree himself to do her honor."

....

"*We have spoken of Giants and their Immortal offspring*, and a view of creation that is world-wide. Let us return the focus now to our island.

"If it is true that the island formed itself around the iron heart of the Terrasque, then it began as a very barren place indeed. Yet eventually plants and people populated this landscape of iron and rock. Reaching back into the Memory of Crow I know that for much of the island's history, there were no people at all on Eld: at least, of course, I mean '*no two-legged beings that imagine themselves superior to other beings.*' Yet eventually, the first of them arrived on the island. They were the Mŭrian. But they did not arrive by boat — they were born here.

"The Mŭrian are Mab's only children. While the celestial energy of her creation still crawled like living fire under her skin, while it smoldered so hotly that everything she touched either bloomed or burned, Karnonou wrapped himself in Torc's protective hide, and lay with her in passion that they shared together for one ageless evening. Thereafter, she declared herself queen of the Fae, as he had intended, and they were rarely to see each other again. But she swelled with life from the union of their coupling until she birthed a litter of eight children. These children would grow to be the first of the Mŭrian. They were born here on Eld, and here they lived and had children of their own amongst themselves until, after countless cycles in a world before time, there were a few hundred of them. The span of their lives were without limits, for they were the endlessly living children of two Immortals."

"Aren't the Mŭrian without gender? How did they have children?"

Djaro shrugged. "Generally, yes — although there are exceptions. They also might have both genders, or none, or the body of one gender and the spirit of another. They may take on a gender long enough to procreate. I don't know, I've never been invited to share a bed with one. But they figured it out somehow, because there are certainly more than eight of them on the island now, and there used to be hundreds. ...Where was I?"

"You were talking about mating Mŭrians."

Djaro snorted. "I certainly was *not*."

....

"As I said before, all of this took place in a world before time. Then the time came when time came, and it washed across the world like a drowning wave. The island began to change around them, though they themselves seemed immune to time.

"They noticed it first in the food that they ate, for they had always favored the eggs of the rarest birds to eat, and the most unusual mushrooms, and took pleasure in gathering up as many as they wished. But now sometimes things that were plucked did not grow back again in the same spot. Now the eggs that were stolen from rare birds diminished their population, and fewer of them would be seen again. They realized that everything was finite, even though they were not. Scarcity was a bitter lesson; a lesson that was sharpened dramatically by the coming of humans to the island."

"These were my ancestors?" Rahyn asked.

"Not yet. These were the Orlŭks."

"Orlŭks are *human*?" Rahyn felt something drop in her belly. Her throat constricted.

"They are. They are an older species than all the rest, in fact. When Lëth first began to experiment with creating Humanus, he was trying to create a creature who shared his secret burden of the knowledge of time. The first attempts failed — the earliest humans went mad and died from the knowledge of their own mortality. Eventually he figured out ways to ease that burden, but in the meantime, there were a few generations of humans that survived but did not recover fully from the trauma of their knowledge of time. The Orlŭks are their descendants."

....

"The arrival of Orlŭks to Eld did not disrupt the ecology of the island. The Orlŭks had fled the mainland for reasons that are still unknown to me, and when they arrived here, they settled into communities that kept mostly to themselves. To my knowledge, Orlŭks and Mŭrians coexisted separately. Crows believe Orlŭks sense the inherent agelessness of the Mŭrians, and carefully avoid them. There is knowledge of some cautious interaction over time, but no memory on either side of bloodshed between their two races."

"Perhaps they are repelled from each other, like opposing sides of a lodestone?"

Djaro glanced at Rahyn thoughtfully. "Because of the burden of the knowledge of time? Hmm... perhaps. That is an interesting possibility, fox-girl. Another possibility is that the Orlŭks adapted to their environment without disrupting it. By doing so, they became the important distinction between something that is *naturalized* and something *invasive*. Plants behave in the same way when they begin to grow somewhere they did not originate from. If they suppress and colonize the local plants around them, they are considered invasive, and disrupt the environment dramatically. If they adapt and share space with other plants that existed before they got there, they are welcomed into the community of the forest. If only humans were as willing to learn to adapt and share space, then the history of the island would not be the bloody tapestry of conflict that it is!"

....

"*There was another race of humanity, however, that arrived on the island many thousands of years later and behaved quite differently.* Recall that we are now talking about the world after time had been loosed upon it. Mab was long gone from the island by that point — trapped in Twilight when the world was twinned by time. So too were the Giants gone: one dead, and one sleeping until the end of days. It was the time when the Immortals and their games of empire ruled the surface of Homm. Your ancestors were one of the eight surviving races of Humanus: the Dekai. The People of Water. Born with a wish to explore the oceans and a talent for the building and sailing of skin boats, the Dekai fled in vast numbers from the continent, and over the course of a thousand years, peopled all the known islands of the Améan Ocean. But it was here on Eld where they truly flourished and claimed all the resources of the island by right of dominion."

"But there were already people here. Did they not know that?"

Djaro grimaced and spat. "They knew. Of course, they knew. The races of Humanus fantasize about the mastery of time and of empire, and they take whatever they want to achieve those fantasies. It is as fundamental to their nature as thorns are to briars. As individuals, they can learn to think differently. But in groups..."

Djaro trailed off, and poked the fire with a stick, turning and prodding the smoldering branches until the flames brightened. Rahyn stared into the hot light, her head pounding. The word *invasive* stretched through her aching mind like strangling vines.

"What... happened when my ancestors arrived?"

"When the Dekai first arrived in their skin boats, the Mŭrian were curious and made them welcome. The Dekai were then, as they still are, a quick and clever people — easy in love, easy to anger. Some Dekai and Mŭrian even intermingled, and if their children survived, they were counted amongst the strongest and strangest of both races. But soon the Dekai began to claim vast areas of land for themselves, and they bred so quickly — in the way of other short-lived animals — that their population exploded. The rivers became overfished, and the rare birds were exterminated, and the most fragile mushrooms picked to extinction.

"The Mŭrian chose at last to defend their territory, and the Dekai retaliated with what became the first war the island had ever known. This led to the destruction of more than half of the Mŭrian, and the burning of most of the original Dekai settlements. The Mŭrian became desperate and marshaled the Fýrii to animate earth and stone to fight beside them. The Dekai were driven back to the sea by a legion of Homsaöls, who slaughtered the Water People in great numbers. Legends are still told of it on both sides.

"During this last battle, a wise leader amongst the Mŭrian named Sha'anna was taken captive in battle by a Dekai chieftain who was called Nanko, and though she was his prisoner, they formed an unlikely respect for one another. For three days-"

"Wait: she, not they? Sha'anna was one of the Mŭrians that identified as female?"

"Yes. That is what is known. As I was saying, for three days there was a lull in the fighting while these two walked the shoreline and gazed first-hand upon the terrible cost of their war. The ruin of the coastal towns, the disruption of harvest, the disturbance to animal life. The shallows were red with blood and everywhere the slain and wounded washed in and out with the tide. The sky was loud with cries of their pain and darkened to gloaming by the wings of a million crows. Our memory of that day has never faded.

"Sha'anna was able to demonstrate to Nanko that his people were unwittingly stripping the island of its resources, and that even if they won this war, they would lose everything in the end. She showed him that unless they learned to sustain and adapt, the Dekai would perish and starve, and all the life of the island would go with them.

"Nanko was ashamed, and begged Sha'anna to teach him how to restore that which was almost extinguished. So, she spent many years sharing with him the secrets of life itself, and when at last the Green shone like light inside his heart, so that she knew that he had changed from the baseness of his human ways for good, she blessed him as the guardian of his wayward people, and named him the first *derŭ-weid*: the human that knows the True Names for the trees.

"Nanko and Sha'anna remained fast friends all the days of his life, and when he died, the Mŭrians and the family-clans of Dekai gathered together and buried him with the honors of a hero who had gained the wisdom needed to stop a war. Sha'anna herself sang his funeral rites, and her continuing friendship towards his people even after his death brought great honor to his memory. The walled city of Dekainak was eventually built around the fabled spot where he was buried.

"But before he died, there was an oath that Sha'anna made him swear to with the last of his breath and the heat of his blood: that the Dekai who were his people would be bound to the fate of the health of Eld, and that there would always be a derŭweid to protect the wild places of the island from the harm of human ambitions. Further, that the derŭweid would make it the goal of their life to seek the source of violence that grows on this island like a cancer: the buried heart of the Terrasque."

....

"Nanko agreed and named a young girl in his village as his successor, for she had shown great love for the Eldwood and was young enough to train, but old enough to bear the burden of such heavy responsibility. So Sha'anna took the young human out of our world, to a secret Nameless Place far out to sea, and trained her. And her successor, when she died. And so, it has continued for thousands of years. It is the greatest honor you humans can hope for, but it is also a terrible burden to undertake the role of derŭweid, and it is a burden that must be borne alone, for there is only ever one Derŭweid of Eld."

Rahyn muttered bitterly: "Then eventually the Erdin came to the island, and all the bloodshed started all over again. The derŭweids haven't been very helpful in stopping that, have they? Erdin burned and salted huge swaths of the forest, and where were the Fýrii and the derŭweid then?"

Djaro sucked in his breath and let it out sharply. "Fighting, foolish fox. They have been *fighting*; for more than three hundred years, the fight has never ended for the guardians of the Eldwood, even though the rest of the island believes they are living in times of peace. It is more than the land that the Dekai are fighting for: they are desperately holding on to the very last scraps of their own Story, the character and memories of their culture, which the first Erdin conquerors were so successful at wiping out. And another war is growing out of sight, like a blight just beginning to corrupt the leaves of the lowest branches. Thegn Rory's road building project is the source of it. You humans may not know the smell of death before the corpses start to rot all around you, but crows can feel violence coming from a long way off."

Unable to contain herself, Rahyn blurted out: "I know you are Fýrii, but are you not also human? You keep saying 'you humans' as though you are not one yourself."

Djaro looked hard at her, frowning. "There have never been Fýrii who were also human. Not once. I hung my hopes on you being the first, because of the unusual circumstances of your parentage and birth, yet... We will speak more on this later. But no, foxgirl. I am not human. I am a skin-shifting crow that has learned to wear the seeming of a man. I walk on tall legs under the trees and have taught myself to talk in the languages of Humanus: I have taken my pleasures in this skin disguise — particu- larly the drinking of stout beer, which I've grown quite fond of! I have enjoyed, above all else, donning the man-skin to be your Grandfather Djaro, and teach you all the things you have managed to learn from me. It was my duty to care for you: a burden that I am grateful to have borne. But much is changing inside you, though you may not know that yet. My time as your guardian is almost done."

"*No*," Rahyn whispered. She felt dizzy from the sudden heat bloom- ing in her chest.

"The Fýrii have withdrawn their support for your training. Your human insistence on interfering with what should otherwise be left to the will of Karnonou has led them to believe you are unsuitable to join the Fýrii. You have been recommended instead to the training of the derŭweid, as I feared your humanity would eventually lead you. When the current derŭweid decides, you shall be sent for, and taken to the Nameless Place to begin your training. And I am afraid, so very afraid that I will never see you again."

"No," Rahyn said louder. "*No*. I will not be taken away from you;

they shall not take me. I am fast, and I can hide! I will never become the derŭweid! I refuse!" Rahyn's voice began to hitch, and she hid her face in sudden shame.

"It is not a choice, little one. It is the will of your fate, and the cost of your ancestry. You shall be summoned, and when you are, you must answer it. There is no other way."

Djaro leaned forward stiffly, reaching out shaking hands to wipe a tear that was trickling down the bridge of Rahyn's nose. She hugged her knees to her chest, burying her head into her folded arms.

"Have you returned just to leave me again so soon? Don't you care for me anymore?" She sniffed from the space between her elbows.

"Of course, I care for you! It is not I who am leaving, granddaughter. The Fýrii know you betrayed them by helping the human children cage the Homsaöl in caverns below the hill. The abbey is damaged, but not destroyed, and even now the clerics return to reclaim it with the support of the thegn's soldiers to back them. You were to be one of *us*, Child of Twilight, and now you have chosen the enemy instead."

"It wasn't like that!" Rahyn sobbed out between her arms. "There are friends among them; they are good and kind! Caetal is of the Eldwood Rangers; Tarquin and Talara are not even from this island at all, so they aren't part of any ancient grudge-wars. And... and-"

"And the mason's son, who *built* the cursed abbey in the first place, and now dabbles with stolen True Names that can twist and distort the natural world." Djaro snapped, rising from his seat in anger. "And the ordanian boy, who is being groomed to burn the forest and salt the very ground it grew from! The next generation of Cuthain's crusaders, and their terrible road of progress!"

"I couldn't just let the Homsaöl kill them, Djaro! They are children; *we* are children!" Rahyn shouted angrily, also rising to her feet. "We did not cause ancestral wars; we were not born to hate the same things you hate! We have the right to make up our own minds about each other!"

"You are too young to know how wrong you are. You have no idea how deeply this conflict extends."

"You and the Fýrii may see them as enemies, but all your anger does is *teach* them to become the enemies you imagine they are. You say you know so much, but you have never learned this! *You have never learned!* And now you tell me I must leave you, and them, to be alone in some nameless place across the sea to pay for the crimes of my distant ancestors, and train there, so I can spend the rest of my life searching for some cursed heart that nobody has ever found?! I won't do it! I WON'T DO IT; DO YOU HEAR ME?! I WILL NOT BE UPROOTED TO WITHER AND DIE BECAUSE I FAILED SOME TEST I DIDN'T EVEN KNOW YOU WERE JUDGING ME ON!"

She was shouting at Djaro, shouting and beating her fists against the frailty of his chest until he swooped her into his arms and hugged her so tightly she could barely breathe. The struggles of anger turned into heaving hiccups, and all they could do was cling to each other, feeling the familiar edges of their life together slipping away all around them.

"Shhhhh... don't cry, please don't cry. You must... you must go, I'm so sorry Rahyn... it is the touch of Fate: it is Her claws." Djaro whispered, hugging her and petting her hair.

"I know that saving them was the right thing to do. I *know* it with all that I am: all that matters inside me, all that makes me matter to myself." Rahyn sobbed against the feathered cloak around his thin shoulders. "Please do not tell me I am wrong to have done it, for then you are telling me that it is *wrong to be myself.* And there is nothing worse that you could say to me; nothing else has ever hurt so badly to hear."

Djaro shook his head and wept into the trembling softness of her hair. "I cannot know the future that your choices will create. Forgive me, my fox child. I am afraid of what will happen next, and fear makes the heart unwise. *Forgive me, please forgive me!"*

....

They wept like that for a long while, holding each other close as the stars came into view above them; one by one, and then in their glittering thousands. They wept until their eyes were as dry as their hearts now felt, and the quiet space that was growing between them seemed as vast and silent as the night sky.

....

The Bear is Waking

On a morning too much like other mornings had lately been, Bergrem woke up choking on his own phlegm.

As usual, he awoke damp with sweat and tangled in his blankets. Since the last days of winter, when his sickness had begun, sleep had become an elusive uncertainty. When it came, it could last for most of a day, and he was often faced with nocturnal terrors: the kind of fever-dreams that an old ranger earned from a life spent prowling through the deep Green. More than a month ago, his wife had made herself a bed in the common room of the house, where she would be less likely to get caught up in his thrashing dreams or wake to the hacking brattle of his coughing.

Rolling over, he spit a mouthful of phlegm into the clay crock that had stood by his bedside for weeks. Then he lay there panting, allowing the shade of his nightmares to steam out of him with each shallow breath.

It's not real. I'm not certain this bedroom is real either, but this is better than where I just came from. I dare not imagine I'm still dreaming. Bergrem reminded himself, as he so often did now. *This is real, I must believe it. I can call out to Nura, and she will hear me from where she rests across the wall. She is not dead, here. I did not kill her or eat her. I never could have.*

Bergrem slowed his wheezing breath as best he could and listened intently to the quiet in the house. Something had awoken him from his nightmares, and it was not the familiar drowning feeling of his lungs filling with liquid. He could hear the slight scuffling of a mouse gnawing its way through the floorboards, and the skitter of its feet as it fled. And suddenly there it was again: a sort of *thwump swuzzle WUMP* sound, from outside. Bergrem, of course, did not think of it as a *swuzzly* sound at all, but how else could his mind have described the sparkling-static-ripping-thwomp of air magically folding itself inside-out?

Dubby began to bark and whine from where he was tied to the long leash behind the house. Bergrem slowly swung his legs out into a sitting position, feeling the coldness of the floor underfoot and the pressure of his bladder complaining to be drained. He arose on shaking legs and swayed there for a minute in the grip of vertigo. He listened hard. Now he could hear the labored hammering of his own heart, and Nura yawning in her bed... and also the gagging ululations of multiple children vomiting all at the same time out on his front lawn.

....

By the time Bergrem wrapped himself in a robe, retrieved his dagger and made his way on swaying legs to the front door, the worst of the gagging was over. So, what he saw when he opened the door was a bit less disturbing: just his son and a few of his friends in various states of collapse and disorientation around regurgitated piles of what must have been breakfast. Above them, the air itself was purpled like a bruise, which faded rapidly into a faintly oily-looking scar of void, and then vanished. Caetal waved at his father weakly with a bandaged hand from where he was sprawled.

Had this been a few months ago — before Bergrem's body wasted into muscular gauntness from disease, and his mind had begun to twist from sleeplessness and perpetual nightmares — he might have been fundamentally shaken by what his eyes insisted he saw floating in the air above his son. Few living people ever see Voidlight, after all. But now Bergrem simply rejected the idea of it, and instead stared in glowering silence as the other children recovered from their disorientation. A familiar-looking boy helped a girl and a smaller, pale boy to their feet, and after furtive apologies aimed at Bergrem but meant for Caetal about leaving their digestive messes on the lawn, they departed on shaking feet down the path towards Holm. Caetal was the last to stand upright after his friends had gone, and he still looked a bit green around the gills.

"Son, who was that boy?"
"W-w-which boy, father?"
"You know damn well which boy. The Erdin kid with the weird eyes."
Caetal made a face. "Oh him. He's the cleric's ordanian. Just some kid from the abbey that hangs around my friends and I sometimes."

Bergrem frowned at him. His face had already been intimidating before he got sick: the dark piercing eyes, heavy brow, and thick black beard had since been gauntly accentuated by the progression of his malady. Now his eyes appeared to bulge in tight and sallow skin.

Bergrem stared after the small blonde boy until he was out of sight. Then he looked back and Caetal, who blurted out:

"I've been keeping an eye on him, father: pretending to be his friend. He is the only ordanian of Cuthain in the valley, and the clerics w-w-wuhill return from Portuan soon with news, and soldiers. I figured it might be helpful to us if we learned w-what I can from him."

Bergrem continued to stare at Caetal searchingly, as though looking for lies in the lines of his face. Whatever he did not find seemed to please him, however, for he smiled with tight lips and said: "That was well thought, son. Boys gossip more freely than men, and a child of the abbey overhears much that is not bothered to be hid. Promote the appearance of friendship for as long as the Erdin boy believes it and keep me appraised if you learn something worthwhile."

"Of course, father. It's g-good to see you upright again! You look w-w-"

Bergrem snorted. "Well? Don't ever lie to me, boy. I look like I'm dying. But I'm not. I've had a lot of time to think, Caetal. A lot of time to really get to the heart of things. I'm not as strong as I was, but I am still *sure*. It's important to be strong in your mind too. To be sure of things, son. It makes it easier to know what to do; how to proceed."

Caetal nodded. He was still queasy from the effects of the traveling spell, and his bones felt tired. He didn't know what his father was talking about but was pretty sure that if he kept nodding and agreeing, eventually Bergrem would let him come inside and lay down. He was also anxious to tend to Dubby, who could hear his favorite boy from behind the house and was whining plaintively.

"You have been too long on your feet, father. W-we should g-go inside and lay down."

Bergrem waved him off. "Time enough for that, boy. Been laying on my back all spring; I sweat when the sun comes out, and it stings my bedsores. I need to be moving. I'm not sure I ever want to sleep again, in fact. It's no longer good for my constitution."

Caetal nodded his head back and forth but didn't disagree out loud. From inside the house, he heard his mother beginning to stir. He hoped rather strongly that she would come outside soon and interrupt them.

Bergrem pointed at Caetal's hand. "You hurt yourself?"

Caetal nodded. "Caught an arrow the hard way. Hurt a lot. Still hurts."

"That happens sometimes. I need to ask for your help one more time, son."

Caetal frowned, disappointed that his father didn't care enough to ask for more details about his wounded hand. "W-w-what's on your mind, sir?"

"I've been too long away from the rangers. They know I've been sick, but now I need them to see that I'm getting better. The pack will lose faith in me if I am gone too long, and then where will I be? What will be left of me then?"

"Ah. True." Caetal affirmed, not knowing what to say, but wanting to sound supportive.

"But I am still quite weak, son. Weaker than I can let any of them see. This is no *sickness*. It is a curse. I am sure of that. Otherwise, why have you not caught it, or your mother? You have both lived within the poisoned vapors of my contagion. And yet you suffer not at all, neither of you. It is only I who am afflicted."

"Father-"

"So, who would have cursed me, Caetal? Who would my enemy be? Ask yourself this, my son: who is the one person who would stand to gain from draining my life away?"

Caetal's breath hitched in his throat. Thoughts of Daedrim, and his grief over Melvin's shattered legs leapt unbidden to his mind. But he shook them off. Then Melvin himself drifted through his thoughts.

"Who would have the power to cast such a spell or the resources to find someone who can? Think about it carefully, son. I hope you begin to see what I have known for weeks. I hope you are smart enough to see the truth that is right before you."

Caetal's head swam, suddenly crowded with images of the deep rage that Melvin must be feeling; power distorted by the terrible burden of helplessness.

But then a new face appeared in Caetal's imagination: a slender face with amber eyes, its other features obscured by layers of colored cloth.

"... *Hel'hannah?*" Caetal wondered aloud.

"Hel'hannah." Bergrem exhaled, leaning heavily against the door-frame. His eyes were bright with satisfaction. "The Warden of the Eldwood Rangers. *Our skabde quiene* Warden themselves, draining my life away with fae blight and fell sorcery! They think they know what it takes to kill a bear. But they will learn soon enough how hungry hiberna-tion can make me."

Bergrem pounded his fist against Caetal's shoulder. "And now my cub is almost grown and grows stronger every day! You will help me, boy: they will not expect to be hunted by two bears at once! Nothing survives in the Green that is so hunted!"

Caetal grinned, feeling pride swell inside him. "How can w-w-we know for certain Hel'hannah is behind your curse? W-what could w-w... we do to prove it?"

"That is the great trick, my son. There is no clear way to root out wyrdcraft, but to destroy the witch who uses it."

Caetal's stomach dropped. "Father, no. You cannot murder them. It is forbidden."

Bergrem glared at Caetal, then muttered: "*By whom?* Who forbids it, I wonder."

Bergrem said no more for a while. He stood there, swaying in the doorway, lost in thought and blocking Caetal's way into his home. Then he said:

"It was not my intention to kill them: your chastisement is unwarranted. They don't need to be killed to be destroyed. We may yet cut their power out from under them, root and stem, by revealing their treachery before the council of rangers. Popular opinion is already turning against them. Hel'hannah has ruled for far too many years, and the rangers grow tired of generations of deference to their inhuman agenda. It is time for my son and I to step forward and do what nobody else has the courage to do."

"*...Just us?*" Caetal swallowed.

"Yes, justice. But we will need support. I will speak with Old Tom first; I trust him with my life, and he's well enough respected amongst the other rangers. He can rally supporters for our cause. In less than two month's time, the full strength of the Eldwood Rangers will gather in solemnity at Dekainak to pay homage to the Wheel Moon: that night when the smaller Ember moon nearly eclipses the Ash moon, both in their fullness, and the Wheel of Fate is formed in the sky. On that night, and that night alone, the gateway to the Dead Moon swings open, and reincarnation of human souls becomes possible for those that came untimely to the cold desert of death.

"You know this already, but what you don't know is what the Rangers of Eldwood do to celebrate it: twelve hours of the observance of rites before the sacred *bonefire,* and the following evening there will be a planning council for the upcoming year. It is then that we shall confront Hel'hannah openly and overthrow their wardenship. The Authority of

Holly will pass to me, and likely then to you, when I die. With Dekai once again in charge of the Eldwood, we will finally be positioned to shake the oppression of iron from our island and drive the Erdin back into the ocean to drown: them and their unholy triad of pretender gods!"

Caetal's heart leapt to see the color returning to his father's cheeks again, and the strength he still projected. He had not realized how much he missed the clarity of his father's vision. *He is sick, but he is my father still!* He thought, and clasped Bergrem in a grateful embrace.

"Woah, careful there lad! I'm full of nightwater!"

Caetal laughed and wiped his eyes. "G-go pee then, sir. I w-will give mother my love and say hi to Dubby to shut him up. Then I think I need to lay down for a bit and rest."

"As do I, son. But don't sleep the whole morning away. We have a ways to travel before nightfall, and I am as weak afoot as an old man these days. I must saddle up and rouse Old Tom. We need him for the ceremony tonight."

Caetal gaped. "Tonight? But the Wheel Rites are not for many days! W-why must w-w-we leave today? I just g-got home from camping with my friends!"

Bergrem smiled secretively. "It is not to the ruins of Dekainak that we go a-walking today." Then he clasped his son by both shoulders. "It is no boy that I need by my side when we face Hel'hannah before the council. It is a man grown enough to do what needs to be done. And only a sworn ranger earns the right to speak before the council. It is time for you to become the person you are meant to be. You must be bound to the trunk of the Stone Tree and speak the history of the battles of our people. You will be bled and sanctified in the honors of the rangers; honors befitting my only son."

Caetal was stunned into silence. He had not expected this ordeal; he had not anticipated or studied for-

"-But father! I don't know the histories by heart yet! I didn't expect to earn my cloak for at least another year! How w-w-will I-"

Bergrem growled and waved off his concerns. "You do not need to remember the histories perfectly. It is a formality of peace that must be set aside in these warring times. I shall speak the histories for you, and all you need do is repeat what I have spoken aloud."

Caetal hung his head and stammered: "I don't... feel ready to be a

man, father."

Bergrem squeezed his shoulders tightly. "Neither did I, when my time came. But the problems of the world do not need us to be ready for them to handle them anyway. That's what *responsibility* means, son. It means the courage to respond to your own fate and the will and ability to do so. The necessary burden of responsibility begins when you are old enough to accept that it has already begun."

Caetal nodded mutely, his eyes wet and his stomach twisting inside him. Stepping carefully past Bergrem, he was almost down the hall when he turned and said: "I thought for sure you were dying, father. I'm... really g-g-guh: it pleases me that you are feeling better."

"I am still dying. I weaken every day, until Hel'hannah's wyrdcraft is undone. But I swear to you boy, I shall live to see it happen. Now go kiss your mother and get some rest. I will hasten to gather Old Tom and return to rouse you when it is time to depart."

....

Ember was already a crescent on the horizon when the three of them reached the Glade of the Stone Tree, and the crescent of Ash had followed behind it by the time the horses were tied and the bonfire was stacked and lit. The night was cold and clear, those thin slices of the two moons made the stars appear all the brighter in the dark sky.

While Bergrem prepared the fire, Old Tom lay his cloak down next to the petrified tree where the carving of the great boar Torc could best be seen. Then he dug into his worn leather satchel until he located a small, stoppered jar. Inside it was powder, blood-red and rarely made. This he set on his cloak, and next to it an arm-length reed pipe with a small scoop on one end and a carved mouthpiece on the other. Lastly, and reverently, he set down a black ceramic urn that was corked and sealed with wax, and a thin copper dagger with a long bone handle and a razor's edge. Then he sat himself down cross-legged and gestured Caetal over to sit beside him.

"This is a proud day for your father an' I, lad!" He began. "Though it be a bit earlier than I would have reckoned you was ready, I guess times are what they are, an' there ain't much for waiting any longer. Bergrem is goin' ta lead you through your initiation, and I'm heading inward to find the spirit of tha animal that will guide you into manhood and protect you with guidance throughout your life. You have already proven yourself man enough to hunt Orlŭks — and defend your friends agains' them too, if your story of the last few days is the truth."

"I told you true when I told it to you, g-g-gramps. Every w-word." Caetal replied, softly.

Old Tom smiled. "I believe you, and that arrow wound in your hand will remind ya of your duties to your friends for tha rest of your life. A ranger is tha protector of those who depen' on him, first and foremost. Whatever else you manage to accomplish in the time you have under tha trees, always remember your duty to tha family you were born into, and tha family you choose for yo'self. And when you arise a man from your time tied to the Stone Tree, that family will now include tha other rangers of your pack, the Order of the Oak. We stay together, pack-strong, an' we look out for tha Eldwood. You understand? That is our purpose. That's what we are meant for."

"I understand."

"Good. Very good."

Old Tom patted Caetal's cheek fondly. "I love you, lad. Glad to tell ya that I'm proud of who you are, and that's my truth. Now here's the start of it: watch, an' help. Hand me the charn."

"The w-what?"

"The red powder, lad. Good. Now hold the blowpipe out in front of ya, with the mouthpiece pointed your direction."

Caetal did as instructed, and Old Tom carefully unstoppered the cork of the little glass jar and even more carefully poured a tiny pile of the charn powder onto the shallow scoop at his end of the blowpipe. Then he turned his head away and cleared out his nose with lots of loud honking into a handkerchief. Turning his head back to Caetal, he directed:

"All right lad: it begins. Your father has readied tha fire, an' your bindings are prepared at tha Stone Tree. Now take a breath, an' blow one small puff through tha pipe when I tell ya so."

Old Tom positioned the end of the blowpipe with the little scoop of charn against his nostril. Then he said "*Now -*" and again: "*Now.*"

Into each nostril, he inhaled some of the charn as Caetal exhaled into the other end of the pipe until the scoop was emptied, and he was wiping his nose and muttering to himself. Old Tom's face began to tremble with what looked like pain, and he seemed as though he was about to sneeze.

Then his hands went slack in his lap, and his eyes rolled up into his head until only the whites were showing. There he sat, immobilized by the blooming of a vision. Caetal stared in awe, watching the vision trance come on until he heard from behind him:

"It is time, son. Remove your jacket and shirt and come lay face-down upon the length of the Stone Tree. I shall bind you to the tree, and together we will speak the history of our people, as I have spoken it to you once before."

From where he was sitting, Old Tom began to hum deep in his throat, a droning ululation that was deeper and wilder than Caetal had ever heard before. It coiled and rocked inside him, twisting and leaping out of Old Tom's open mouth in tones that barely sounded possible –- as though something else was singing through him from a long way off. His eyes were white, and his breath plumed before him in the chill air.

....

I lay on my stomach upon the Stone Tree, with my arms stretched above my head, hands pressed together. My chest is bare, and the stone bark is so cold against my ribs that my breath aches. If not for the heat of the bonfire stack nearby, I would be shaking with the cold already. Now one side of my body feels numb, and the other side prickles with heat.

With my face pressed against the stone, my view is entirely full of the carving of Torc the sow-queen, matriarch of boars. They are as deep as my finger to the second knuckle, and almost as wide; a pale green moss is growing inside them. From so close, they are a confusion of intersecting lines whose meaning I could never have guessed without stepping back and seeing the whole picture. I suddenly realize how true to life this thought is: how much it applies to everything. I am afraid to lose myself and become something else, yet I am excited too. I have made plenty of mistakes as a boy, but none yet as a man. It is a chance to be remade, and those kinds of chances are rare. It was a boy who crushed his best friend's legs by accident: a boy that I no longer have to be.

... .

My father has lashed my hands together. My legs are likewise lashed. He says it's to help me with the pain. I don't know how it could. He stands above me and to my side. I hear him speak the histories in words, his voice is low and raw. After every sentence he speaks, I repeat the sentence back to him as accurately as I can. Meanwhile, Old Tom continues his throat singing, stopping only to join in speaking the vows of the order. Those we say all together: three voices strong with power. I know the words to the vow already. I have known it since I was young.

"When the Erdin sailed forth from Erdo-Usk to claim our forest for their own, it was the rangers of the Order of the Oak that rode out to meet them and set torch to their ships as they sailed below the beam at Bajlkr-Bec."

"WE AROSE TO JOIN OUR SEPARATE PURPOSE TO ONE GREAT STRENGTH. WE HAVE BECOME MANY BRANCHES OF THE SAME OAK."

"When they tried again, we gave such blood on the downs at Melrgraes in defense of our land that the wild grasses grow red there still."

"WE DO NOT DIE, FOR THE MANY ARE NOW ONE. WE JOIN OUR SEPARATE LIVES TO ONE LIFE."

"We have toppled every settlement the Erdin have ever hewn from our forest, in vengeance for the slaughter they brought to Dekainak, and the ruin of that great city."

"WE DO NOT FIGHT FOR REWARDS OR FOR GLORY. WE FIGHT FOR VENGEANCE AGAINST THOSE WHO HAVE TAKEN WHAT WAS OURS."

"They tried to settle the wilds of our country, and we have tricked them with our craft and driven them fleeing before us, with haunted tales of trolls and driftwisps hounding their heels."

"THEY FEAR WHAT THEY WILL NEVER UNDERSTAND. WE DO NOT FEAR THE WILDS THAT ARE OUR HOME."

"At Ofan, and at Kräke, they sought to burn the Eldwood to the ground, and we repelled them, though many of the Order were slain."

"THE OAK THAT IS BURNT IN SUMMER IS REBORN AGAIN IN SPRING."

"For more than three hundred years, the Erdin strove to wipe us out and scatter our memories, and always we have stood against them. We are here still."

"ALWAYS WILL THE ORDER OF OAK STAND IN DEFENSE OF THE ELDWOOD. I AM THE ONE WHO NOW PLEDGES MY LIFE TO THE MANY. I AM GONE. WE ARE HERE STILL."

Then the throat singing ceases. Old Tom rises from where he sits, with arms outstretched. My father stands right above me now, so close to my face that his steaming breath fills up my vision of the sky. It is my turn to speak alone.

"I pledge my allegiance to the Order of the Oak. I shall defend the Eldwood, and the memories of my ancestors and their sacrifices, w-w-wuh ...w-with the effort of each breath, until my very last. I will carry in my blood the ashes of those ancestors w-who have g-gone before me. I w-will accept their strength into my body through a talisman of scars. Let my g-g-guide come to kill me and let me be reborn."

And then the need for talking is done. I am a Ranger of the Oak in soul now. Only the sacrifice of boyhood remains to finish the pledge. A child must die on the Stone Tree, so that a man may live. I shut my eyes tight, knowing the pain that is coming.

••••••••••••••••••••••••••••••••••••••

The throat singing begins again, my father's voice now deepening the chant of Old Tom's. I feel my father reach up under my head, and he pushes a thick strap of leather between my teeth. I bite down hard on it. I am ashamed to feel a child's tears forming at the corners of my eyes. The first cut is the worst, but it is only the beginning — there will be many. As the droning chant continues, Old Tom makes diagonal cuts across the center of my back, angled to be shallow and wide. With the length of each cut completed, my father reaches into the black ceramic jar and pulls out a pinch of the mixed ashes of my ranger ancestors who have fought and died in defense of the Eldwood. These he packs into the fresh wounds to empower me with their strength, and to form a proper scar. It hurts so badly that were it not for the leather strap in my mouth I would be screaming until my throat is as bloody as my back.

There is a shape beginning to form on my skin in vivisected lines. It is the image of an animal that will guide me throughout my adulthood. Old Tom has seen it approaching the Stone Tree in his vision and now he is cutting its likeness into the skin between my shoulder blades. Blood is trickling down both sides of my ribs now; I can feel it crawling across my skin like ants. It is cold on the dark side of my body and hot in the firelight. But no fire burns so badly as the skin above my spine.

I feel drunk for the first time, reeling with the enormity of this hurt. I have never known what pain can feel like when there is so much. It rolls over me like water; I am drowning in it and floating above it at the same time. The muscles in my arms and legs are shaking. I can see the moss in the carving of Torc drinking up the blood that is seeping down into so many curves and swooping lines. As I bleed out, Torc must surely be awakened to my suffering. The great sow will carry the child that I was away to the pale moon, where the desert of death stretches on forever under the cold scattering of starlight. There he shall play in a place where he can always look down again on the world below.

....

I have never felt so relaxed and so tired. So far away that it barely matters, I can hear that the chanting has stopped and been replaced with the unlikely sound of an argument taking place. I try to listen, but the closer I get to the words that are being spoken in anger above me, the more my body returns to the pain. I can feel the stubborn thrumming of my heart, though it stutters a little. I am grateful to have a heart. Not everything does.

My father's words make sense in my ears at last:

"—Because he is my son, that is why! What nonsense is this? Even his name carries the bear spirit inside it."

"Jus' because a bear appeared as *your* guide when you lay down upon tha tree, does na' mean it is meant for Caetal to follow in every step you take. I saw what I saw, Bergrem."

"The *haietlik* is not even a real animal, you old fool! And it is sisiutl at that: double-headed! Why don't you just carve a big lightning bolt as well, and we can write a faerie story in blood about the return of the fabled lightning serpent while my son dies from your nonsense on the Stone Tree!"

"*I saw what I saw.* It is not your place ta overturn *everything* in creation that displeases ya, Oweinson! Ya already rushed yer way through tha histories: tha boy didn't know them by half, and now he may never feel tha need to know, and that's something yer impatience has taken from him-"

"Watch yourself, Tom," Bergrem growled. "I am still weak, but strong enough to remind you how to hold your tongue."

"And you would say that ta a friend such as I? A friend that has looked after your son like an uncle — yes, an' you too, while ya lay there as sick as death wi' nobody but tha few of us to mind ya? Shame on your pride, Bergrem Oweinson! Your father had more sense than you are showing, at half your age!"

Bergrem's voice paused, considering. When he spoke again, it was in a more respectful tone.

"...Fairly said. I am in your debt for the care you have shown my family."

Tom snorted. "It is not debt, but lasting friendship, that you are stuck owing me for."

"But really Tom: is it not possible you have witnessed the vision wrong? If it was no bear that came to guide my son, why then I shall be all the bear he needs to guide him. But... are you sure it was a haietlik, and not an ordinary serpent that you saw?"

"As clear as I am sure that tha ground is below and tha sky overhead. Tha haietlik came slithering out from tha roots of tha petrified tree. It curled around tha boy an' stared down upon him with both heads considering, and when I stretched my hand to shoo it off, it reared an' hissed at me, and lightning come forkin' out of its mouths where it ought to have tongues. It is a haietlik that has chosen the boy, an' there will be no other guide beside it. I would'na endanger the life of the lad by cutting a lie into his back an' spillin' tha child's blood for nothin'. You know me better than that Bergrem, though in your anger you chose ta forget it."

Bergrem grunted. "So be it. But what can it mean to have a myth as a guide and no proper animal spirit to speak of?"

I heard Old Tom reply just as the swimming darkness in my head pulled me down into the unconsciousness of blood loss.

"Who knows? Perhaps it means he himself will end up keepin' company with myths someday or become one himself. Or perhaps tha haietlik is not gone from tha world after all, and we are lucky enough to see it return in the scars on his back. Who can know those things tha' are not meant for knowing? As ya said, Bergrem, wisely but not well: I am only an old fool, after all. Wha' do I know?"

··

The Welcome Holm

For those who are of an age to while away an afternoon playing games and sipping suds at a proper tavern, you will surely have realized by now that there are few finer things that aging provides. Yet anyone who has gone into a variety of public houses — or even stood in the open door of one — will quickly identify that there are striking differences between them. Some of those differences can be easily observed or smelt. Some of them need to be *felt*, and that feeling is as real and as indescribable as any of the other dubious miracles of adulthood.

Firstly: distinctions must be drawn between a bar, a tavern, and a pub. Any self-respecting patron of the Imbibmentary Arts should be able to recognize the difference between such establishments on sight, if not at a distance, by reputation or general character.

A *bar* can be any bunker of brick, wood or wattle and daub that is licensed to pour booze and willing to tolerate sinners. A bar exists for one purpose only, and that purpose is as obvious as the clientele that each bar draws; a place for like-minded people to get absolutely snookered amongst their own kind. Bars that survive into their later years tend to grow some manner of soul over time, but almost never do they overcome the limitations of their patrons. Bars remain quite popular in every known city and timeline, and certainly have their uses for clandestine business for rogues, or general drunken rousey amongst the skulkers and ne'er-do-wells that frequent such establishments. A bar does not, by definition, serve actual food. If it does, you probably shouldn't eat it.

A *tavern* is often an older and more respectable watering hole, although the etymology of the word "tavern" originally indicated a place for imbibing established in a wooden shed — as many original taverns, in fact, were. And some of those taverns still survive, hundreds of years later. They have been patched and re-furbished, re-roofed and re-conditioned over the many years of their lives. Yet they remain. Because there is often something indescribably *alive* about a tavern: something scrubbed into countless layers of oil on the old timber floors or baked by pipe smoke into the walls. A tavern also serves decent food, and that puts it in a more civilized category than your average bar; although, admittedly, the distinction is often blurred when a brawl breaks out and the first stool is thrown.

A *pub* is a fondly lazy shortening of the term *public house,* and a good pub will be as similar to a bad bar as a horse is to a horsefly. As the name indicates, a well-established public house will feel like a comfortable lounge, kitchen and living room all rolled into one space: a home in which to relax away from home. There will likely be food worth paying for, and drinks good enough to savor on the way down. There will often be a fireplace warming the space when the outside air is chilly, and games to play at sturdy tables. It can be as quiet as a library or as rowdy as a troupe of bards, but nobody should ever expect a fight to break out at a pub — at least, not a physical one.

Intellectuals with a will to swap opinions tend to gather at their local pub, for where else can a person get slowly basted while debating passionately before a tipsy audience? It is the time-honored proving ground where the witty and the wanting wage skirmishes of opinions until the evening's last drop is drunk, or until the beleaguered proprietor removes them forcibly. A pub might also have rooms to let for weary travelers spending the night, and a proper stable for horses besides. Some of the older taverns can also boast such features, but they are uncommon.

....

The Welcome Holm was a tavern by name, but one of those rare taverns that survived the first hundred years of its rowdy youth and mellowed gracefully into a pub of true distinction. The building itself was now one hundred and sixty-eight years old. Well, at least parts of it were. The topmost layer of thatched roof was replaced every thirty or forty years, as a damp climate demanded, although the majority of the innermost thatch layers were as old as the building itself. The kitchen had twice been gutted and repaired from fires — expanded a bit each time, for the original kitchen had been quite cramped. There was a stable and yard on one side, a modest orchard of pears, apples and black walnuts growing behind it, and a low hill on the other side with three wooden privies built at the top. Here, just below them, is where the crossroads met.

The building itself was the height of three stories above ground, and at least one story below. The subterranean level had two stone-tiled bathing chambers with copper basin tubs. These rooms were the pride of Yrsa the Innkeep, for clever pipes that ran behind the upstairs fireplaces and down through the wall brought heated water on its way from the well into these baths, and they even drained away through pipes that emptied near the orchard out back. It was the finest bathing opportunity a traveler could have between Portuan and Dàrû, and Yrsa made sure every passing traveler knew about it. The rest of the lowest floor was the booze cellar and was locked from access behind a sturdy door. There were rumors of other secret rooms below-ground, but Yrsa discouraged such gossip as idle imaginings.

The upper floor of the building was divided into ten rooms — nine bedrooms to rent, and one sitting room with a staircase that led upstairs to the private rooms of Yrsa, Eorik, and now Talara, who were the only staff that lived onsite. Those rooms were squat and wide attic spaces that sloped heavily on one side where the thatch roof of the ceiling met the floor. They had no windows, and smelled like a hayloft in warm weather, and a wet hayloft the rest of the time.

....

The ground floor was almost entirely a common room, with a bar running along the north wall and a kitchen hidden away behind it. There was a large bell-shaped bread oven in the kitchen, and a bell-shaped cook named Noran who tended it. The common room was warmed by two stone fireplaces: one on the west wall between the front windows, and one on the southern wall. Following the walls and abutting the fireplaces on both sides were wooden booths: heavy tables and benches attached to the wall, so they could never be upended and hurled in a brawl. In the center of the room were two long common tables flanked by benches that could hold twenty people on each side with room for the elbows. These tables each had three large candle-basins with beeswax candles as wide and tall as a farmer's forearm. They were lit during the dinner hours, and burned as long as the kitchen was serving the evening meal.

The tables were all built of wide planks from a long-ago shipwreck salvage and were polished by so many layers of beeswax that the wood was satin-soft to the touch. The taproom smelled like summer, tinged with the sweet decay of barley and malt that had made its way between the floorboards after so many years of spilled beers. The floor was lightly dusted with wood shavings. Scents of honey, pine-smoke and baking bread mixed with the pipe tobacco that wreathed the common tables like a gentle fog around the farmers that gathered daily to dice and spread gossip. The walls, originally whitewashed, had been stained by smoke in lightening layers from ceiling to floor: browned like old parchment around the roof beams, yellowing into white near the knees, and then browning again with dust at the trim boards.

There was a locked cabinet on one wall that held a wide variety of carved pipes that generations of tavern owners had collected. These magnificent pipes were ostensibly for sale but were so enjoyably arranged that it was almost a disappointment when one sold. There were long wizardly pipes, and squat mushroomed pipes; clay pipes carved into the likeness of mermaids and dragon-turtles and grasping krakens whose clever tentacles held the smoking bowl. There were simple pipes that had once belonged to complicated people, and complicated pipes that simple people had never appreciated properly. A fool in motley on his back with his feet upright as the stem; a rearing bear holding a beehive; a one-legged crow with his head cocked to the side and a knowing look from eyes inset with amber. In the weeks that she had worked as a bar wench at the Welcome Holm, Talara had taken the time to dust and polish them all, holding each one in artful wonder. Yrsa encouraged special care for beautiful things and never minded when Talara snuck over to the cabinet for another peek.

Next to this cabinet was a long shelf lined with twelve large glass jars, each filled to various volume with a variety of pipe tobaccos. Yrsa sold them by the pinch or by the pouch, and whenever a lid was lifted the air nearby would become fragranced with earthy perfumes: plum and loam, pepper and tar, cavendish sweetened with cherry mash; flavors of smoky oaky tartness that evoked the imaginings of far-away places. Yrsa herself was an avid pipe-smoker and, in her time as innkeeper, had set up a network of trade with passing peddlers who would bring her sacks of tobacco from all over Eld and even from across the sea.

....

"It is often the solution, not the problem, that becomes the real problem," Yrsa said, eyeing her new protégé Talara across the bar.

"This is true in almost everything: love, politics, and of course, in managing a tavern. I could give you relationship examples of that bit of worldly wisdom that might make you blush and political examples that ought to fill your waking thoughts with anger at the inherent injustice of rule. However, since I am not trying to redden your cheeks or politicize you, let's focus on how that statement applies to tending bar."

"Perhaps just one *tiny* little romantic example to start with? Something from your past?" Talara queried.

Yrsa snorted. "I shouldn't have listed love as an example. My fault; too tempting a topic. Alright, let's see... my original problem was that dating any of my regular patrons was a terrible idea, and falling for a traveler was even worse. Did that once, and once was too many times. I don't like being off-balance, particularly around men, because they always try to take advantage of it. So, my solution to that problem was to stop letting myself fall in love with anyone at all. Now my problem is that I no longer remember what romance even looks like, which scares me to think about, and that fear itself becomes the new problem. One supposed solution became two new problems: fear of falling in love and fear that I no longer can. See what I mean?"

Talara reached out and squeezed Yrsa's hand across the bar.

"*Wow.* That was a really depressing example. Thank you."

Yrsa swatted her with a bar rag. "Such cheek! You wouldn't understand; you are too young to make the kind of mistakes I have. You have years of your own stupid romantic decisions still ahead of you."

"I guess it's good to have so much to look forward to," Talara muttered, fiddling with a saltshaker.

"There's always something to look forward to. Like today: we have the incoming lunch crowd to look forward to. Hop to it."

She wet the rag and tossed it to Talara, who made her way over to the long tables and started wiping them down. The woman and the girl worked together without speaking further: one absorbed in future fantasies, the other avoiding thoughts of the past.

....

Through careful questions plied casually, Talara had learned what she could about Yrsa during the first week she worked for her. Some of the locals had been frequenting the Welcome Holm since before Yrsa owned the place, and they shared memories of her as a young woman. Apparently, she had indeed once been in love, although nobody Talara spoke to could remember anything about who that person was except that they had been a traveler, and they did not stay in Holm long. Some of the older locals remembered a pregnancy that had begun and ended, but nobody could recall why.

Yrsa was a very private person, even at a younger age, and the years between then and now had blurred the recollection of a rounding belly and a lost child. Talara would not have given those fading memories much consideration at all but for an inexplicable wistfulness that Talara sensed in Yrsa's glances when she believed Talara was looking elsewhere. Talara prided herself in reading the concealed emotions that other people's faces could not always hide. But something in Yrsa was buried as deep as desires go, and what traces that secret longing left on her face could only be seen in flickers that softened her eyes but hardened the corners of her mouth. Yet, she was always polite to Talara and seemed even to genuinely care for her.

It was the kindness that was the most confusing. There had never been an adult that treated her the way Yrsa did. Talara was an obvious benefit to the Welcome Holm; as a young bard, she was just as popular in Holm as she had been in Dunmarsh, and she had a natural gift for the kind of playful chatter and attention to detail that is the secret to tending a good bar. So she could understand why Yrsa would have offered her a job and an unused room in the attic to stay in — although even that was an obvious kindness. The feeling that Talara found so confusing was the respectful way in which Yrsa spoke to her and the fondness that her otherwise gruff demeanor could not always hide. Talara's mother had gazed at her fondly from time to time, of course, and had often told her how much she loved her. But those looks had always been crowded at the edges by other emotions as well: hunger for what Talara still had that she herself had lost. They were the looks that a fading flower might give to a blooming one, if flowers ever exchanged those sorts of feelings.

So Talara watched her closely, over those weeks that she had worked at the Welcome Holm, out of the corner of her eye. Yrsa, it seemed, was doing the same thing. They were the only two women currently working at the tavern, and they circled each other throughout each day in a carefully friendly manner with the precision of two soldiers from opposing sides trying to decide whether to duel or drink a toast to unexpected peace. Besides, Yrsa was an Erdin, descendant of a race of conquerors and slavers. She had power over Talara: as her boss, as her landlord, and as an Erdin. So Talara worked diligently, spoke cheerfully, played music whenever it was asked of her, and kept the taproom as polished as a pearl.

....

The day finally came when all the floodwaters had receded to puddles, and the valley returned to a seeming of itself again; grassy hills and farmland, now covered with drifts of red river clay. Everything still squelched underfoot, of course, so that only the roads were worth traversing: the fields were bogs that a person might sink into above the boot lip. Yet sunlight was everywhere, baking moisture out of the ground and the hopelessness of winter out of heavy hearts. And on that day, emerging from the mist evaporating off the Thegn's Road, a company of his soldiers marched into the village: an Iron Guard on horseback leading it and an Inquisitor of Cuthain trailing behind. What villagers who dared ceased in their labors to gaze upon the glittering parade. Talara and Yrsa gawked from the tavern doorstep.

It is known to any who must live their lives under the constant threat of organized violence that not all soldiers are created equal. Some are no more impressive than the underfed peasants they were before they were armed and aimed, and some are made dangerous by the benefit of coordinated costuming and good training. But these soldiers of the thegn were something else entirely.

They marched with almost mechanized precision, feet clattering against the steaming stones of the Thegn's Road like the brattle of drums. Sunlight dazzled off overlapping layers of banded armor plating and chain, framed by a slate gray cloak bisected with a single crimson stripe from the right shoulder to the bottom hem. Helmets crested with bristles of boar. The soldiers' faces were hidden behind visors cast into the seeming of a metal mask — features as formless and vacant as molded clay, with empty cavities for eyes. They all looked the same, as they were meant to: as uniform in height and bearing as automatons.

Excepting that she rode on horseback, only the mask of the Iron Guard made her distinctive from the other soldiers. From the slope of the forehead to the upper lip, the steel mask was the depiction of a woman's face: the Queen, in fact, though nobody present would have recognized her likeness. From the mouth down, there descended strips of steel which narrowed to points just below the chin, like a beard of fangs. One riveted iron band overlapped the center of the spikes, where the mouth would be. The helmet of the Iron Guard was crested with steel-tipped bones sharpened like porcupine quills.

The Iron Guard marched the soldiers up the Thegn's Road toward High Hill, ignoring equally the scattered waving and fearful muttering from the villagers they passed. Each soldier was wearing more steel than most of the citizens of Holm had ever seen in one place in their lives. The masked soldiers must have all been pure-blooded Erdin, for no descendant of Dekai would have been permitted to adorn themselves with steel armor. The Iron Ban, the oldest and first of Erdin laws, forbade it. Caught so armored, a Dekai risked not only their own lives but the lives of their family.

When the soldiers passed from sight behind the rise of the hill, with only the faint clatter of their footfalls still dimly echoing, the farmers dispersed at last. Many of them returned to their homes and slid the bolt across their doors, and those were the wiser ones. The rest decided to drink.

....

By dusk, High Hill had sprouted a bloom of canvas army tents, and torches could be seen burning inside the ruined abbey. By nightfall, the villagers and their opinions crowded the taproom of the Welcome Holm. Talara did her best to navigate amongst the gossiping throngs with a loaded tray carefully balanced across one arm. She listened eagerly to everything she overheard, for most of the patrons ignored the thin serving wench who flitted among them, refilling drinks and plucking coins from distracted fingers.

The air was thick with pipe smoke, and the nervous heat and swelling noise of so many people debating and speculating made Talara feel queasy so that she longed for fresh air and the quiet of empty places. Even retreating to her room would barely muffle the racket, and Yrsa might be tempted to box her ears if Talara left her alone to manage the capacity crowd.

Theories about why such a force of soldiers had arrived varied from table to table, but from the snatches that Talara could stitch together, it seemed like the majority opinion favored the belief that Thegn Rory had heard about the monster caught in the caves below the abbey, and wanted to be sure it was safely trapped for good. *Perhaps he even intended to seek the creature underground and destroy it properly!* If so, there would be work for the villagers: supplies needed, assistants hired. It would be helpful to be working for coin again. The flood had left many a family in daily growing need.

However, unpopular minority opinions kept the crowd uneasy. There was concern that the soldiers had arrived for a less wholesome purpose. Nobody could agree on what the purpose was, but each person who voiced their fears aloud was countered by someone else who was equally declarative. Some were sure that the soldiers were here for loot and to enslave thralls. Some were convinced that the abbey was a part of a secret military plot and, like a hornet's nest, had been punctured and was now buzzing. A few speculated that a war was beginning somewhere, although nobody really believed that a community like Holm was the place where it would start. More than likely, the soldiers were only encamping there for a short while, long enough to feast on the already diminished food stores of the valley before marching on towards their true objective. It was obviously a show of Thegn Rory's strength, but for what purpose? Who was the intended audience of such a show?

The debates continued into the still hours that followed midnight, well past when the doors were normally shuttered. Finally, when it was all Talara could do to keep her leaden feet from dragging and her tired eyes open, Yrsa helped the stragglers gather up their sodden wits and future headaches and gently shoved the last of them out into the night, barring the door behind them. The two exhausted women glanced around the soiled taproom, noting all the spills and sticky table rings, quietly breathing in the smoky draft of the embers dying in the fireplace. Then, without a word wasted between them, they both decided to leave the whole mess of it unwiped and unswept and head straight up to their beds.

Yrsa began blowing out the last of the candles, and Talara said goodnight and managed to drag herself all the way up to the landing of the second floor when she heard an armored fist rapping against the tavern door. Her heart jumped into her throat, and instinct backed her up against the shadow of the far wall, away from view up the staircase.

The door rattled again: five brisk knocks. Talara heard the tired shuffle of Yrsa's feet and the sound of the locking bar being lifted. Then a moment of sudden silence where voices explaining themselves should have spoken. There followed the sound of multiple heavy booted feet clumping into the common room and the squeak of the door being closed behind them. The bar slid back into its locking cradle with a thunk.

Talara strained to hear over the sound of her own heart pounding. When a single set of footsteps approached the stairs, she backed herself quickly into an empty bedroom and crouched down in the dark behind the doorway. Through the open crack of the bedroom door, Talara saw Yrsa mount the staircase landing and stand there, shining a lantern down the hallway towards the attic rooms where she and Talara slept. There she waited for a moment, listening intently. Talara was convinced her own shallow breathing sounded like the whine of a boiling kettle, and the excited hammering of her heart could surely be heard at a distance. But after a few searching moments, Yrsa descended the staircase again with her lantern in hand, and the hallway of guest rooms darkened around Talara.

With her heart slowing until the sound of it was no longer rushed in her ears, Talara could hear muffled conversation coming up from the taproom. By carefully wriggling down the hallway on her belly, she got herself as near to the staircase as she dared, and from over the topmost stair she could see a thin slice of view of the room below.

Gathered around the furthest table from her were three soldiers, each holding a mug of ale. Yrsa was sitting at the table across from them, and standing above those seated was a robed figure with its back towards Talara. There were two sheets of vellum in front of Yrsa, and she seemed to be reading over them with some care. The soldiers did not talk, but glanced around and drank in stolid silence. What dialogue there was took place only between the robed figure and Yrsa, who seemed to be asking questions or, perhaps, answering them. The conversation was so carefully contained between those two — voices pitched almost at a whisper — that Talara could make out none of what was said. But she could see Yrsa's face by the shine of her lantern on the table, and there was a grim countenance upon her that seemed to grow darker as the conversation progressed.

Finally, she made a slashing movement with the palm of her hand. The robed figure brought forth a quill pen and a dipper of ink, and Yrsa took it from them and made her mark upon both sheets of vellum. That done, the figure produced a drawstring pouch that was heavy with coins. It settled clinkingly onto the table where it was set down in front of Yrsa, who withdrew it quickly from sight.

As though cued, the soldiers arose and headed towards the door. The robed figure rolled up the vellum parchments, sliding each into separate metal scroll cases and capping them. Yrsa bid the four figures to the door, and by the time Talara heard the locking bar drop behind them, she had already made her way tiptoeing back to the attic stair and was convincingly abed when Yrsa passed by on the way to her own bedroom a few minutes later. Soon enough, she could hear Yrsa settle onto her woolen mattress with a sigh and, not long after, the sawing of her snores. But it was a restless while before sleep quieted the questions in Talara's mind.

What did Yrsa trade that was valuable enough for such a heavy coin pouch? What could she have signed that was worth recording on vellum and storing in steel scroll cases?

And the most uncomfortable question of all: *is Yrsa a spy?*

Before she was able to drift off to sleep, Talara had to allow herself to make up her mind. So she chose the only two things she had witnessed that she felt any certainty about and changed them from questions in her thoughts into statements. And that certainty allowed sleep to steal her away at last.

Yrsa is in collaboration with Thegn Rory and his soldiers. Yrsa took their bribe.

....

Secret Keys for Hidden Doors

Some truths cannot be told directly — they must only be hinted at. They are the sort of truths that stable-seeming empires are precariously balanced on. Very few people are trusted with such knowledge, and a great many people die to make sure it is kept that way.

In Erdo Usk, on that island within an island that had been the political heart of Eld for more than three hundred years, there lived such a woman: one who had stolen keys to doors that opened onto secrets of slaughter. From these hidden rooms she gained knowledge that made her valuable to the kind of people that kill for secrets. This woman, talented though she was at gathering such information, was even more talented at keeping herself alive. She cultivated a vibrant presence that allowed her to be something for everyone and, in doing so, made her life more valuable than her death. So they traded her more keys in exchange for those secrets that she chose to share.

She was the sort of person who seemed to have a knack for being in the wrong place at the right time, and soon she had collected enough keys to need an expansive ring of informants to help consolidate them. Over time, she amassed many of the kinds of influential friends that you keep at arm's length, and courted a few who made her fairly (if discretely) rich. At least, wealthy to the degree that a brown-skinned woman was tolerated to get within the courtly labyrinth of the pale and predatory.

She had advanced a long way from her tragic origins (the story of which changed for every person she told it to). There were none still living who knew her true name, and only a few who had ever seen the entirety of her face, for she wore a beaded veil that obscured her mouth and chin at all times when in public. One of those few who was familiar with her face was the Queen of Eld, who knew much about deception herself, and to whom this woman had now sworn allegiance. For the queen had the greatest collection of information and opportunity keys to be found anywhere on Eld. And Cea (which is the name this woman had decided to be called) had ambitions to collect each and every one of them.

What the queen intended through such an alliance was one of the secrets that Cea had not yet managed to collect. So she made herself relevant enough to Her Majesty to begin to have access to some of the most important keys of all: secrets of power and of state. Secrets of restless things that were buried alive. Secrets of the story of culture that the Erdin had stolen from the Dekai long ago.

Yet, like so many people who collect such dangerous keys, she finally got her hands on an unexpectedly personal one. And, by doing so, accidentally opened the entirely wrong door.

But we shall learn more about that, as she does, in time.

The Empress

"I know many things that are my right to know / I know the names of rivers that flow hidden underground / I know the names of enemies unborn / I know the names of all who live to serve me."

The Empress
~ The Third Card ~

Tan Njal was a thin man, as thin as a whippet. His clothes were tailored loosely to his gaunt frame, for he was also a sweaty man. This gave him the unfortunate appearance of swimming in the excess fabric of borrowed clothes so that the lavish cloth looked somewhat gaudy on him, as hand-me-downs sometimes do. His beaked nose, bushy downturned eyebrows and gentle blue eyes set deep in pale skin gave him the perpetual countenance of someone who has just heard sad news and isn't yet ready to discuss it.

Today he was in a hurry, for he was on his way to deliver a message directly to the queen. He had stuffed his loose doublet with layers of scarves to absorb his sweat. It would never do to stand before the Queen of Eld with perspiration making a wet patchwork of his doublet, after all. He intended to discreetly leave the dampened scarves beneath a rosebush and retrieve them later. It seemed a good enough plan to a nervous man.

....

He hastened in a near canter under the bright midday sun. The gravel path crunched beneath his feet. All around him arose the rearing beauty of the rose garden, fragrant and bristling. Now, in the month of New-green, most of the flowers were still tight in their buds, although here and there, a patch of color flamed boldly amongst the twining thorns. Their scent was already cloying the air. Tan Njal sneezed loudly into the billow of his sleeve.

He hurried past the iron guardhouses that dotted the garden like bee-hives. He hurried past the silent gardeners who tended the vast landscape of the gardens. These he found of particular interest — though he dared not make eye contact with any of them, stealing only furtive side-eye glances as he passed.

The "gardeners" were warriors, all: trained from the day their cearta was announced by the Triad clerics. That fateful day in their youth, they had learned from the clerics of their gods that their highest ambition would be to protect the queen and tend to her garden. Those gardeners worked in the midday heat in armor of steel and leather and slept by night in the wrought iron beehives. They would live each day of their lives in this garden, and when they died, their bodies would be mulched and their bones ground into powder for fertilizer — even in death, they would still nourish the roses. It was considered a great honor to be placed here by the will of the gods, so close to the queen and in view of the ziggurat. Just as Tan Njal had himself been honored to learn in his cearta that he was destined to serve the ruling elite of Erdo Usk as a messenger. One of the few messengers who was privileged to learn to speak the language of Lùn-Una. It was the greatest honor of Tan Njal's life to be conversationally fluent in the queen's speech. He practiced the use of it daily, in private.

....

It took Tan Njal the better part of an hour to walk through the rose garden on the straightest road. This was the main avenue that bypassed the meandering paths under the blooming bergamot trees and alongside tiny, cultivated creeks: paths that ended at leafy bowers trailing honeysuckle vines. He ignored the various gazebos offering bench seats and cooling shade for his hot face. He mopped the sweat off his brow with a scarf instead and hastened on towards the dazzling light of the ziggurat that was rising in view ahead.

Crunch crunch crunch crunch went the sound of the gravel underfoot. Weeks of winter rains had ceased a few days ago; now, the damp heat of spring dissolved all but the most entrenched puddles. Water glittered in sculpted channels under the shade of trees, but none for Tan Njal to whet his dry throat with, although he entertained the ludicrous fantasy of getting down on his hands and knees and lapping at a puddle. *How will I speak gracefully with a dry mouth?* He wondered. Then he practiced wondering that same thought in his head but through the complex metaphor of the language of Lùn-Una. *My mouth is barren as though the sun shone between my teeth / what words may arise / from the dry tunnel of my throat?*

All too soon, and not soon enough, he arrived at the Queen's Bridge. A few paces before the bridge, the garden ended suddenly. About a a third of a mile further ahead, the glass and steel ziggurat was so radiant with the sunlight splintering off it that he could not look at it directly. Only the gray smudge of smoke that rose from the eternal flame burning at its peak was comfortable to look at without squinting, and so he switched back and forth between looking at that and staring at the flapping motion of his feet.

In front of him, the Queen's Bridge loomed. It was a marvel of metal: steel beams, woven steel cable — not a bit of stone or wood to be seen. A delicate arch of a bridge, engraved in bas relief with blooming flowers, spanning over a moat that surrounded the entire half-mile stone plateau on which the ziggurat was centered. The bridge was wide enough for four to walk abreast with room to spare, and yet Tan Njal felt trepidation as he gazed upon it. For uncomfortable minutes he stared at it and willed his feet to carry him forward. He did not know why he felt such fear. He had crossed this bridge four times before — well, two round-trips, really — and each time experienced the mysterious dread that made his bowels feel loose and his muscles shaky.

To calm himself, he stared at what details lay before him. The moat extended to either side in a great circle as far as the eye could see. It was not a terribly deep moat: a wide stone channel, perhaps fifty strides across and eight feet deep, in which a river of crude oil sluggishly flowed. The air around it reeked of bitumen fumes, and breathing was difficult. This was the main defense of the ziggurat, and it was an impressive one. The river of oil seeped up from underground, and if a torch were to be dropped upon it, a wall of fire would burn indefinitely until hidden sluice gates were activated to cut off the flow of oil. That fire would engulf the metal bridge and heat it until it was red hot, making passage across impossible.

Mounted on the four corners of the bridge were four skulls. The skulls had been coated in steel and accented with gold at the teeth and eyes. One of these skulls belonged to the previous king of Erdo Usk. In his day, that king — who was called Eomen, and fancied himself "Eomen the Tyrant" — had hung many bodies by cage or gibbet on both sides of the bridge and let them yellow in the sun. It was a grim reminder of his ruling grip over the island. When Queen Thyra came to her throne as a young woman, she did so by killing Eomen in a duel under the lawful dictum of cearta. Her inaugural edict as ruler was to do away with the ghastly gibbets. Instead, she had Eomen mulched, and his body became the first of many to feed the young roses planted in the royal garden to celebrate the beginning of her reign. She ordered that his skull would be coated in steel and mounted to the bridge as a permanent feature. It was meant to warn future assassins to reconsider and not end up likewise. Three times during her rule, that warning was not heeded. Three more steel-dipped skulls had joined the late King Eomen, gilded and mounted. It had been many years since the last assassination attempt.

Tan Njal closed his eyes and forced himself across the bridge. He could hear the hollow tapping of his feet on the metal planks. His sweaty scarves clung to his chest like leeches. Beyond the moat, the clumping of his footsteps dulled, and he opened his eyes. Now he beheld nothing before him but the empty plateau of fitted stone that extended all around the ziggurat, like a wide dinner plate with a peaked delicacy mounded at the center. The stones beneath his feet were a dusky pinkish-orange and slotted together with skillful precision. They formed a road that ran straight to the front door of the ziggurat, which could still scarcely be seen in the distance but as some pyramidal shape that shone with brilliant light. The path he walked on was as wide as the bridge had been, and all the ground around it was flat gray cobblestones.

It was an empty vista. The green ring of the surrounding garden was still visible, like the sea seen at a distance on a very wide beach. The contrast between that lush space and this desolate landscape dampened Tan Njal's spirits. Listlessly, he laid his three moistened scarves on the edge of the path and felt lighter without them. In a few minutes, he had walked far enough to where he drew up near the base of the ziggurat and came to stand at the edge of its shadow. Here, at last, he took a moment's rest to admire the beautiful structure without the blinding glare obscuring it.

....

The ziggurat had three equal sides that rose to a peak just over a hundred feet in height, and at each of the three corners the structure was supported by massive steel beams. Between those beams, the walls were interlocking blocks of glass. Each beam was enlivened by carved artistry celebrating the worship of one of the three divine authorities of the Triad. The two beams that flanked the wall facing the road were devoted to the Twin Goddesses — the red moon of Embara, and the pale moon of Hausa. Scenes of planting, fertility and helpful industry climbed up Embara's beam, and Hausa's was carved with images of war, hunting, and fishing the bounty of the sea. The third steel beam, set at the rear of the ziggurat, would surely display the worship of Cuthain through sailing, medicine and literacy. Tan Njal had never seen that side, but he hoped to someday.

At the apex of the pyramidal shape, the ziggurat was crowned with an iron cap, upon which a steel spike extended another fifteen feet in the air. This spike was wimpled and twisted slightly, thick at its base and thinning at the top. The spike was hollow and must have been fed by cunning pipes hidden under the steel corner beams, for from its peak, a perpetual flame arose in a spiraling gyre, and oily black smoke leaked into the sky all around it. That flame had burned day and night since the ziggurat was built, reminding all those that beheld it of ERO, the Father of Fire and Air, who is the creator of the gods and of his chosen people, the Erdin — and whose body is the Iron Tower that rises to the edge of the sky on a far-away shore.

"He who was slain in betrayal will arise again in glory, for His body stands for all time as the Iron Tower, and His children still remember His name." Tan Njal whispered to himself, staring up at the incredible flame. Unconsciously, he ran three fingers down his chest, across his heart.

Then there was the subtle clearing of a throat, and he turned in surprise to see a thin young woman standing nearby. She must have come around the building as he loitered there, gazing at the peak with his neck craned back, like any gawping tourist. Tan Njal cleared his dry throat a few times and smoothed the rumples of his baggy doublet in embarrassment. The young woman was dressed in layers of pale-yellow robes that crossed and belted in the center at hip level. The lower half of her face was veiled by a mask of delicate black beads; what could be seen of her features was Dekai-dark skin and pale green eyes. She handed him a glass of cold water rimmed with a slice of bergamot and gestured him towards the intimidating ingenuity of the steel front doors. They opened quietly inward from inside, and he walked through them into the warm light of the ziggurat interior, with the woman trailing right behind him.

....

Seen from within, the ziggurat was even more stunning to behold. In daylight, as Tan Njal was seeing it, the interior of the pyramid was so brightly lit that his eyes took a moment to adjust to the scintillations of colored light. This light came from everywhere. The three walls were made of stacked blocks of glass; viewed up close, their true artistry was revealed.

Each glass block had been poured over intricate panels of cast iron, which were suspended in the center of them. When assembled as they were into a wall, the iron panels formed into a swirling geometry of patterns. These patterns were designed to hide the appearance of their seams so that even though hundreds of individual blocks must have made up each wall, it appeared (particularly from the inside) as though each wall was one massive unbroken sheet of steel incased in glass, with only the faintest lines of demarcation between them. The colors of the glass likewise intermingled, from swirls of orange and tan to pale blue and whitish gray: a sunrise full of drifting clouds. The glass contained thousands of tiny bubbles trapped within it.

The room was not just lit by sunlight. At the base of each of the three massive steel beams was placed an iron cauldron about five feet in diameter. Fire danced above the cauldron rim. More cauldron torches, half-round, were inset into the iron beams every fifteen feet, rising towards the peak of the pyramid and diminishing in size as they climbed to further emphasize the height of the space. The beams were themselves cast in a rippling ocean motif that reflected the light from their cauldrons in undulated patterns. The air at the top of the pyramid was hazy with a perpetual layer of smoke, through which the uppermost sextet of torches looked like fireballs seen through smog. Although there must have been hidden vents to allow air and smoke to escape, they seemed to work imperfectly.

The interior edges of the pyramid were lined with armored figures standing at attention. The first time he had been in the ziggurat, Tan Njal had assumed, as many did, that the place was full of guards. So fine was the armor, and so cleverly posed were the figures, that it was only on his second visit that he realized that they must be statues. None had shifted even to breathe, and in the warm air of the ziggurat, they would have stifled in that heavy armor. The armor itself appeared to be chiseled out of a midnight gray stone. There were at least a hundred of these statues, and they made the space feel crowded, and the air felt strangely dense around them. There were apparently no living guards in the ziggurat. Whether that was a cunning threat or an outrageous bluff, Tan Njal could only guess. Privately, he believed that the statues were ensorcelled and would animate to defend the queen against any attacker. But that was not the kind of childish fancy that a gentleman would speculate on out loud, so Tan Njal pushed the thought quickly out of mind. Magic of any kind gave him the creeping heebies.

....

The queen's messenger was walked forward by the silent pressure of the robed woman keeping pace a few steps behind him. He was led past the armored statues — an oddly tight squeeze by the two flanking the front door — and into the center of the room. Here was the most striking feature yet to be seen: an item of such sublime and simple beauty that it made the rest of the ziggurat appear gaudy in comparison. The Agate Throne. But it was not a throne at all, in the traditional sense of the word. It was a shrine, the size of a modest dwelling, with pillows sitting on top of the roof.

The shrine was cut from a single fire agate hauled up from the deepest caves of the earth: the most massive ever found on the island, as big as a boulder. It had been chiseled and hollowed into a windowless room with a kneeling bench and altar for faithful reflection so long ago that no tale of island memory existed before it, even amongst the Mŭrian. The shrine was known as "the Heart of Eld" and very much looked the part. The exterior of the shrine was polished to a sheen by thousands of years of oil and care; swirling eddies of deepest gamboge and garnet, rusty orange descending into rich layers of reddish brown that shone as wetly as muscle through the gloss.

Inside the shrine, it was rumored that the walls were rough-hewn simplicity, cave-like in contrast to the exterior so that a person at prayer would know that they were sitting inside the natural heart of the stone. Few living had seen the shrine's interior, however, for it was blocked from view by layered curtains of copper beads. Only the queen and her attendants were allowed inside, for there is where she rested between visitations of court.

Until eight generations ago, this shrine was located hundreds of miles away, on the far eastern edge of the island. Before it was called the Agate Throne and served as a seat for conquerors, it was a place of worship dedicated to Karnonou, lord of boars and of the Eldwood, and was the pride of the city of Dekainak. That city was grown from living trees and long served as a stronghold for the Fýrii and their faithful. It is now a somber ruin, burnt and buried by a siege that lasted for almost forty years.

When the city fell to the Erdin at last, the Heart of Eld was absconded and taken by ship back to Erdo Usk, so that future generations of rulers could sit in dominion upon the greatest treasure of their ancestor's conquest. What remained of Dekainak was obliterated by fire. The forest around it was likewise scorched for miles; the ground itself was then scraped down to hard clay and rock and doused with salt and ash. What the Erdin had worked so hard to kill, they meant to stay dead.

....

His head awhirl with the mesmerizing shimmer of the throne and the grim reminder of how it got there, Tan Njal barely had the sense to kneel in reverence before his Iron Queen as she stepped from between the beaded curtains. He felt the treacherous dampening of dignity as his ungrateful armpits immediately moistened. With his eyes on the ruddy marble of the floor, he heard the soft whisper of her steps as she ascended a hidden staircase to the top of the shrine. For long moments, the room was only filled with the uncomfortable hammering of his heart — which sounded to his ears like the frenzied pounding of a wet drum — and the quiet shuffling of Her Majesty as she seated herself upon her dais of pillows above him. Then there was heard a metallic clunk as she laid the jeweled Sword of Rule unsheathed on the stone before her. He knew the time had come to rise to his feet and deliver the message he had come so far to say. His tongue whetted the desert of his thin, dry lips with what moisture prolific sweating had left him, and he spoke in the ceremonious musicality of Lùn-Una.

"Pride flows where blood once wandered / I stand before you // lifted yet humbled / I was born into the service of your reign // which only my death shall sunder." Tan Njal's voice cracked anxiously, and the silent attendant in the yellow robes handed him another glass of water, which he greedily gulped.

He wished his heart would slow and his thoughts would quicken. The queen waited in silence as he drank, but for the tapping of one long white fingernail against her naked sword. Cross-legged she sat, in layers of quilted robes, and though he stood upright before her, his eyes were barely at height with her ankles. Her feet were bare.

His throat gratefully whetted, Tan Njal began again. "Honors bloom like roses in your vast garden-"

"You live in the light of my service / all is known. You croon like a peacock // better to quack like a duck." The queen replied tersely. "Tan Njal must speak in straight lines / I am not so young that time overlooks me // the sun is sinking on my day."

Her reprimand shrunk Tan Njal visibly, although he felt a warming thrill that she had remembered his name, and before he could stop himself from speaking foolishly, he blurted:

"My name on your lips // such honor to name the stones beneath your feet!"

The queen chuckled dryly and sweat moistened his socks. He bumbled onward: "I spoke with clumsy swinging // a woodpecker knocking against an empty branch. / I am surprised to hear my own name voiced / from the red mouth."

He dared a look at the lower half of her face, although he would not dream of meeting her eyes. Her mouth was indeed red, as was the entirety of her chin, and two stripes painted upwards in bars that must intersect her eyes. The rest of her face was the thick white of ceruse paint. She frowned slightly as he spoke, and he saw the flash of golden scrimshaw on her tusking canines. He could see the makeup on her cheeks crackle, and the lines of age it was meant to hide showed through like seams in folded paper.

The queen spoke. "I know many things that are my right to know / I know the names of rivers that flow hidden underground / I know the names of enemies unborn / I know the names of all who live to serve me. Uncoil your purpose and lay it before me // I am too long awake."

Tan Njal swallowed and bobbed his head. "Service is life."

Then he leaned back until he was able to see at least to the height of her shoulders — noting, as he did, the sparkling sword on her lap. It was to the sword that he continued addressing his report.

"The message follows: news from the east // in the lands of Fýrii. A town so small // barely worth mention / Holm it is called // but a pause on the Wayward-"

"Holm is known to me." The queen interrupted. "A place of barley and hops / the Orchard Bridge crosses the Tanis / farmers birthing farmers in countless generations. It is noteworthy // everything is. Speak further."

Her long fingernails tapped rhythmically on the sword, and Tan Njal could see the tiny diamonds that rimmed their edges like drops of water.

"Apologies / knowledge of the island is thin to me // your palace is my world."

The queen nodded approvingly. "All is as it was made to be / continue your report. I will forbear further interruption / an arrow disrupted in flight is an arrow lost."

Tan Njal dipped his head again gratefully and continued. "The message follows further: an abbey therein // a house of Cuthain / was tumbled into ruin // by the efforts of a monster."

The fingernails ceased tapping.

"The monster was a child of stone and animate earth // powerful enough to topple walls."

"Bled of Fae / I am wondering?" The queen interupted.

"Seeming would say. The forest is ocean-wide // as thick as waking nightmares / the abbey was a boat that floats on dangerous waters. This is belief your nephew upholds // he is the thegn of mighty Portuan / and counts his years wisely."

The queen snorted and, to Tan Njal's horror, interrupted his carefully delivered Lùn-Una with the guttural brutality of the other Erdin language called Uisen. It is the language of warriors and common laborers, and Tan Njal was surprised the queen knew how to speak it at all. *But of course, she knows so many things. Why wouldn't she?*

"Piss on that. The thegn is a pompous gasbag. He is as shameless as a common whore, yet has far less sense than one. If we were not related, I would have chummed him for fishing bait in his youth. I knew he was worthless even then."

To have tumbled from the hypnotic lilting symbolism of Lùn-Una into the guttural growls of Uisen was like watching an egret soar majestically into a pile of sharp rocks. In her royal mouth, the words sounded like gravel and crunching eggshells. Tan Njal was so startled by the sudden transition that he committed a solecism and made eye contact with the queen.

It was only the flutter of a moment, but it was untoward. He saw deep-set eyes of the palest blue, as sharp as shards of ice against the stark white landscape of her face paint. Crow's feet grasped deeply at their corners. Her forehead was furrowed from years of concern that no white mask of ceruse could hide. He saw that red painted stripes intersected her eyes and disappeared into pale gray hair that crested her head in a tight braid and was shaved low to the scalp on both sides. She wore a vertical steel diadem that ringed her face like a sunburst. And when he glanced at her, she winked at him boldly and laughed in a deep throaty chortle that seemed as out of place as her crude words.

"Shocked senseless, Tan Njal? Sorry to disappoint you. I could have wasted many flowery minutes describing how little I think of my nephew in the silken runaround of Lùn-Una, but the language lacks a palate of truly scathing slurs."

Tan Njal nodded in quiet acquiescence, too embarrassed to speak. Hearing her talk in Uisen was as shockingly uncomfortable as it would have been to hear her fart loudly.

"Now: You were saying that a Faeress stone creature, likely a Homsaöl, smashed up Cuthain's holy house in Holm and that my idiot thegn has an interest in reporting that to me? Why, I wonder, would my nephew send a messenger so far to keep me informed of such provincial concerns? I'm guessing he has encouraged you to press me for a handout."

"I am sure your thegn carries wishes of your pleasure // like the doves of morning that fill the sky with singing-"

"Cut that shit out, Tan Njal. I want the rest of my report in the Common tongue. How dare you reply to me in Lùn-Una when I have spoken to you in Uisen! Do you desire to put your words above mine? I should have you mulched and fed to my garden for your insolence."

....

It was at this point in the conversation that Tan Njal fainted dead away on the floor. He later remembered it as the most embarrassing moment of his entire life.

....

He awoke to a splash of cold water in the face, with the sloping walls of the ziggurat swimming into view. He was convinced for a moment that he was surely in some strange nightmare, for everything drifted as though underwater. And most disturbing of all, he imagined the Iron Queen was looming right above him, holding his ankles. His legs were sprawled wide with his feet straddled on either side of her hips, and the attending woman in the yellow robe kneeled beside him with an empty water glass in hand. The black beads of her face mask swirled in his blurry vision like flies.

"By the Triad, Tan Njal — I was *jesting!* I didn't take you to be the fainting type. You must consider eating a diet that is higher in fiber: more bran, more beans. Bran is good for fainters. Now get up off my royal floor."

Tan Njal struggled to get up, but vertigo intensified, and his stomach lurched up towards his throat. He got no further than his elbows.

"I'm afraid that I might vomit if I attempted it, your Highness. Everything is spinning... I am beyond embarrassed, your Excellency. At this moment, I would prefer that you weren't jesting about having me mulched."

The queen chuckled, dismissing his embarrassment with a flick of her fingers. She gestured to her attendant, who arose immediately and took over holding Tan Njal's legs. Then she disappeared briefly through the copper curtain into the secret interior of the Agate Throne and returned with two heavy pillows. She dropped one onto the ground near where Tan Njal sprawled, roughly lifting his head to stuff the other one under his neck. The look of surprise on his face must have been entertaining, because she burst out laughing again for a long minute, barely regaining her composure by the time she had settled cross-legged on the floor pillow.

Having his queen casually sitting nearby him on the floor of her own throne room was so deeply unsettling for Tan Njal, so fundamentally impossible to his thinking, that he decided it must surely be a dream. He was probably already dead somewhere in the real world and being mulched up to feed the roses. So, he chose to relax into the absurdity of his own afterlife, and it's a good thing that he did. The rest of his report went much more smoothly.

Once settled, the queen spoke. "Refreshed enough to continue?"

Tan Njal nodded.

"Good. Let us try again. The abbey is destroyed, and my nephew wants me to know about it. Why?"

Tan Njal, still believing himself dreaming, didn't think twice about looking her full in the face and speaking plainly. "Apparently not completely destroyed. The roof and one wall only: the monster did not entirely succeed in its task."

"Indeed?"

"Quite so. The abbey of Cuthain in Holm was built to serve as an outpost of Thegn Rory's authority in that area. As I'm sure you remember, his grandfather — your uncle — attempted in his lifetime, to complete a road that extended between Portuan and the fortress of Ofan by way of Drôle, thusly consolidating his base of power in the south and avoiding the long travel and expensive tolls levied for passage over the great bridge at Bjalkr-Bec. It was the goal of your uncle Eckhart, when he was thegn, to continue the construction of this road from two directions easterly towards Atlaga from the Wayward, eventually bridging the river Trask, and westerly from Holm to try to reclaim his grandfather's infested fortress of Drôle. That goal was never realized in his lifetime, (may his spirit find peace in the land beyond sight), although he did extend the road by three miles: across the river Tanis, and through the town of Holm, to the crest of High Hill."

"All this is known to me, Tan Njal. You were not sent here to remind me of the deleterious labors of my dead uncle. Tell me about my nephew. I have guessed that he plans to follow in his father's failed footsteps?"

Tan Njal nodded solemnly, which is hard to do with a pillow wedged under your neck.

"Your nephew the thegn does indeed intend to complete the labors of his grandfather. Rory may very well be all that you think of him, but he is also cunning. It is a blow to the pride of Portuan that the Thegn's Road has never gotten further than Holm. For more than a hundred years, the thegns of that great city have promised to bring the dangerous wilds of the Eldwood to heel and push their road through to the interior of the island. They have met with generations of failure. The forest has rapidly overgrown their efforts, and Portuan, for all its self-proclaimed grandeur, remains the poorest of Your Majesty's major cities — as does the entire thegndom of Southern Fýrii. Your nephew no longer wishes to sit idly in the long shadow of your uncle's failed vision. ...Am I speaking too immodestly?"

"No. You are speaking with the clarity I have always wished of my servants. Modesty and flattery are the enemies of communication, and I am too old to be aroused by decorum. Go on, Tan Njal. You have come a long way on a hot day, and it suits me to sit with you on the cooling stone floor. Have a temal. Speak your mind."

Here the queen gestured to her attendant, and the robed woman left the room to prepare a platter of snacks. While she was gone, Tan Njal continued. It was so strange for him to lay there with his head almost in the queen's lap. He took the time to stare up at her face and noticed that she had three earrings of bone and gold, and a thin scar that ran up her neck and onto one cheek.

"All that I know of Thegn Rory, I have learned through the network of your servants, so I cannot speak to his character but through the biased lens of gossip. I have not myself been to Portuan — as I said earlier, I have never left Your Majesty's island home and would consider myself lucky if I never do. However, the message I bear for you about the thegn was brought to my attention by a runner who serves an informant of yours who works for the Heironeth of Cuthain's abbey in Portuan that the thegn frequents. So I must confess — it is not a message directly from the thegn. It is only tidings of his intent. My informant contact overheard the thegn and heironeth planning, and I was instructed to make you aware of the course of events as they have unfolded so far."

The queen nodded and said nothing. A plate of chilled temal was set before her, and she gestured that Tan Njal should join her in eating it. He propped himself up on his elbows, noted with satisfaction that the room was no longer spinning, and ate a few of the leaf-wrapped delicacies. They were far too spicy for his palate. He began to sweat again.

While the queen ate, he continued.

"As I said, the abbey at Holm was apparently built as a staging point to rally conversion in the area and begin the necessary clearing of the forest to connect Holm and the ruined stronghold of Drôle. What your nephew intends to do to retake that ruin and route it of trolls, I have no idea. But for the last two seasons, he has made efforts to marshal a standing army of conscripts and mercenaries, and I would guess that a full-scale assault is his goal."

The queen nodded approvingly. "Good. Let him waste his ambitions on trolls and the dreams of dead men. And if he does manage to stumble into success, then all the better — the empire invested considerable resources building that old castle, and it would be a boon to refurbish it.

I predict that would be the moment that my dear nephew reaches out to me for money... unless he first comes crying with an outstretched bill for the golden cost of so many soldier's funerals."

"Quite likely so."

"So, the abbey was wrecked by a monster, and his plans were dashed already?"

"No, Your Majesty. On the contrary, your informant told me that the thegn is in high spirits and that plans continue ahead of schedule. He is using the partial destruction of the abbey as an excuse to move his strategy forward and has sent a regiment of soldiers to Holm. The town will soon be commandeered for military occupation under the guise of an edict of imposed safety. Even now, his agents are fomenting local anger over the destruction of the church to enlist the formation of a militia. They will be the first sent into the forest and will be the expendable wave of any military offensive on Drôle. ...After the flooding subsides, of course. I forgot to mention the flooding. The Tanis apparently has overflowed its banks, and Loc Enum besides. The ruined abbey is now a peninsula in a shallow lake."

"A shame. And yet lucky for my dear nephew: the loss of crops and livestock turns farmers into mercenaries as quickly as hunger demands. Farmers have big families. Lots of mouths to feed, and nothing dry to feed them with. How did the monster die?"

"Pardon, Your Eminence?"

"The Homsaöl tore into the abbey as you said, and then it, too, was destroyed? Otherwise, there would be little remaining of the town, and nobody left alive to report the tale. Legends describe the Homsaöl as nearly unstoppable until its true purpose is spent. And yet you said the majority of the abbey still stands. So, I ask again: how was the monster vanquished?"

Tan Njal smiled wryly and propped himself up on both elbows. "Even a dark tale sometimes contains humorous wonders. The monster was evidently lured underground and trapped in a vast system of caverns. And this daring entrapment was undertaken by a group of children! They must have been quite resourceful indeed, for only one of them perished in the attempt."

"Children? Brave sons and daughters of those hungry farmers?"

Tan Njal shrugged apologetically. "I'm not sure whose children they were, My Queen. All I gleaned is that there are six of them, and one is an ordanian of the abbey: a special child blessed by Cuthain with a rare gift of healing. The heiro of the abbey apparently raised and tutored the boy himself. The other children must have been his peers."

"How old?"

Tan Njal blinked and cocked his head. "Er... younger than adults, but old enough for some schooling. The ordanian has not yet gained the purpose of cearta or formalized his clerical vows. So, I'd guess... twelve winters? Thirteen?"

"Interesting. *Very interesting.* Impressive to accomplish such a feat at so tender an age."

"Likely just lucky. Children are simple-headed. But I suspect a rock monster is even more gullible." Tan Njal chuckled.

"Perhaps *you* were a simple child, Tan Njal. I was not. The seed has far more potential than the tree, for it can grow into any shape that it can imagine, and has not yet been stunted by the limitations of the world. Never underestimate youth. Empires are toppled by the young."

Tan Njal blushed and perspired.

"As you say, Your Eminence. Please forgive my lack of vision."

"Of course. You were not raised to be imaginative, only dutiful. It is not your fault."

The queen was silent for a long moment, chewing thoughtfully on her temal.

"I have underestimated my nephew's grasp of ambition. I do not like underestimating anyone, Tan Njal. A queen rules only for as long as she can outthink her vassals, for there is always someone waiting to profit from my mistakes. I imagine that the life of a servant is much easier — or at least more straightforward. But then again, I cannot afford to underestimate even you, can I?" She patted his head fondly, like a pet. Then she stood up and walked abruptly over to the Agate Throne, reaching her hand up to retrieve the Sword of Rule where she had left it.

Turning away from Tan Njal, Her Majesty moved through a series of thrusts and strikes that were as fluid as dancing. She handled the sword with a half-century of practiced grace. Tan Njal watched her in fascinated silence, propped up on his elbows. *Magical statues or not, this is why she has survived three assassination attempts. It is not just luck that makes a queen.* When next she turned back to him, she was shining with sweat, and her eyes were hardened.

"So be it. My nephew shall have my support, and if you do your job well and carry my instructions in absolute secret, he will be taken by surprise that I have not only heard of his plans but am actually on his side for once. This will keep him off balance in case his ambitions get out of hand.

"When the floodwaters recede, I will send an additional phalanx of soldiers to the area for the attempted retaking of Drôle. I will also offer a public reward of ten thousand gold fauns to the person or persons who successfully empty that stronghold of trolls. That should incentivize local support — even the rangers will be fighting on our side for once! In the meantime, I want one canvas tent sent to the area for each displaced family in Holm. Have the local militia set up a proper refugee camp on High Hill. And as those shelters are being erected, encourage a public crier to read proclamations of the benevolence of Cuthain and his humble accomplice, their Queen at Erdo Usk."

The queen chuckled to herself. "Gratitude towards the church will encourage religious conversion. Get the whole community working together to clean up the ruined abbey and prepare it for reconstruction efforts."

"Of course, Your Majesty. It shall be-"

"But how will I stay informed of the progress in these efforts? I will need someone stationed in Holm; someone loyal, and willing to send regular reports. Someone unthreatening and unremarkable, who is able to blend in and disguise their purpose as an informant. My nephew and his military imposition will turn Holm into a seething mess of resistance planning if he is not careful. And if that happens, I want to know who the leaders are immediately, so we can deal with them before it gets out of hand."

"Yes, Majesty. But to whom-"

Before Tan Njal could finish his query, the queen raised a finger for silence. In the quiet that followed, she strode across the room to where her masked serving woman in the yellow robes was stationed. The two of them conversed in hushed tones for a few minutes, while Tan Njal strained to eavesdrop, carefully standing back up on his feet again as the vertigo finally subsided. But the only thing he clearly heard was the veiled woman's laughter. At a gesture, the maidservant removed a long matchstick from a pouch on her waist, lit it from the flame of a nearby candle, and handed it to the queen. Her Majesty turned and handed it to Tan Njal.

"Hold this. *Do not drop it.*" She commanded.

Tan Njal stared in consternation at the long matchstick he now held. He watched the flame slowly eat the oiled wood; he watched consumed sections of the match fall away onto the polished floor. In stillness and in silence, the queen and the veiled woman stared at him expectantly. Sweat began to slick his palms. The flame had eaten down the length of the match until only a tiny bit remained. Soon his skin would begin to burn.

This is a test, of course. Tan Njal thought to himself, licking his moist upper lip and trying to steady the treasonous tremoring of his hand. *I must hold the match and bear the pain. I dare not fail.*

The flame licked the tip of his finger and thumb, and pain ripped through his mind. Unable to stop himself, Tan Njal exhaled rapidly and blew the flame out. There was a small puff of smoke, and the sudden loud rushing of blood in his ears as he stared in horror at the tiny blackened stick he clutched.

I am the coward that I always worried I might be. Tan Njal hung his head, and felt his eyes moisten treacherously. For a long moment, silence mingled with the smoky air. Then Tan Njal held out the burnt matchstick dejectedly, no longer daring to meet his sovereign's gaze.

"I'm sorry, my Queen. I have failed you."

"Do not assume what I do not tell you to assume. I told you not to *drop* the match. I did not instruct you not to protect yourself. That choice was yours to make."

Tan Njal glanced up. He wiped the sleeve of his robe across his blurring eyes.

"I have let fools burn themselves unnecessarily to demonstrate their determination to cull my favor. I have likewise witnessed those who consider themselves quite brave drop the match when the flame sears their fingers. You did as I would have done: protected yourself from harm, while still achieving your objective. You did well."

While the queen was talking, the veiled woman departed from sight. She returned with a lap board, writing utensils and a small roll of parchment. These she handed to the queen, who scrawled a missive on the parchment. Then it was handed back to the veiled woman, who rolled it up into a case of bone, tying that off at both ends with a waxed ribbon.

"If it pleases your majesty, I was just wondering-"

"Tan Njal: the letter contained in this scroll case must be delivered to the heiro in charge of the abbey at Holm. Not his replacement or his assistant: he alone. Please instruct him that it is a private matter of personal interest to me. There will be a second sealed letter that will also need to be handed directly to Captain Dané of the Iron Guard clarifying the edicts I have instructed you towards. You shall be my agent in this action, of course. It is time to prove yourself useful to your queen."

Without thinking, Tan Njal earnestly spoke in Lùn-Una:
"I live inside my service to you // nothing else is pleasure but the weight of your command."

"Such pleasure in righteous service is only for your knowing / trust is like a spear that must be first thrown to be earned // like my spear I will throw you a great distance above my enemies // they will not see you landing in Holm / my faith in you is only just beginning to bloom // as are my roses here in Newgreen // you also must blossom or die in the bud // far from your home."

Tan Njal's eyes had grown wider and wider during the queen's reply until he looked as shocked as a sleeping barn owl awoken by sudden thunder.

He stammered, in the Common tongue: "Are you... are you saying you want me to *leave* your palace island? To travel all the way across Eld... through the deep woods ... to Holm? And stay there? *Live there?* You want ME to be responsible for executing your plans?"

The queen shrugged. "Sure, why not? It will be good for you, Tan Njal, to see the outside world. But you will have to depart alone. The plans you enact on my behalf are far too sensitive to trust to the gossip of men sharing drink and campfire stories."

The world began to spin again. Tan Njal felt the blood draining back out of his face.

"Don't worry, Tan Njal. I will give you written instructions, so you don't forget anything important, and even a sword of your own to carry. And I'll send that retinue of soldiers when summer comes, so if you get into trouble, just wait a few months for rescue! I'm sure the adventure will be quite exhilarating — in fact, I envy you. It's a beautiful time of year to travel." And she clapped him on the shoulder.

....

For the second time in the same day, Tan Njal passed out on the floor of the queen's throne room. His last waking thought was that he must remember to retrieve his sweaty scarves from where he had left them on the path to the ziggurat. The last thing he heard before his unconscious head bounced against the floor was the sound of his beloved queen laughing at him.

....

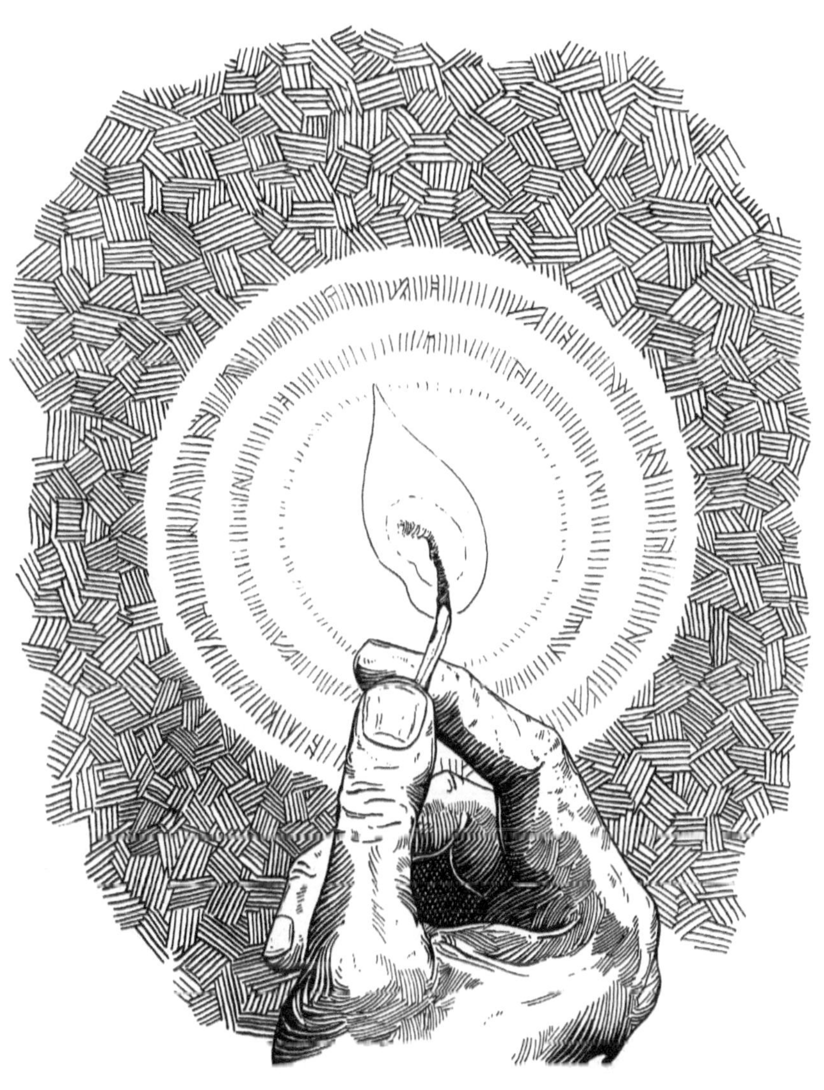

~ The Magician ~

"There are Words that comfort the mind like a mother's touch; Words that overcome reason to banish fear; Words that paralyze all senses. Words that kill."

The Magician
~ The Last Card ~

Melvin leaned against a log with his legs splayed out in front of him. He was staring at the stillness of his bare toes. He could still remember what flexing his feet felt like, and so he imagined each toe illuminated by energy. In his daydream, magic obeyed him as its rightful master, and the enchanted toes wiggled with new life like fat worms coming up from underground after a long winter. But his daydreams were the churning rapids of fantasy bound up in the cold clay channel of reality. As hard as he stared, not a single wiggle of life could he will into those treacherous toes. They were as distantly dormant as tragedy had made them. He sighed, and looked away.

All around him, the wild grasses of the lakeshore flexed beneath the dragging comb of a spring zephyr. Interspersed along the rocky shoreline were branchy patches of Eldic calluna, just starting to bud. In the fullness of bloom, they would purple into crimson flowers that would contrast beautifully amongst the yellow flowers of the spiny gorse shrubs that clustered up everywhere that wild berry bushes had not already claimed. Behind him was the dark green edge of the forest, but he could not see it from where he sat. As Drinn had intended, his view was dominated by the rippling vastness of the lake, and the ruined tower that squatted on the small island at its center.

My future home, if I am sure I want it. Melvin mused to himself. Sunlight reflected off the surface of the lake like light splintering on a broken mirror. Melvin squinted in the glare. His eyes watered as he stared across the dappled surface light at the ruinous ground story of the tower. It poked up from the soil like a broken molar protruding from a dirty old jaw.

Melvin watched the figure of his father from a distance, about a mile away across the water, setting up scaffolding against the tower base. *From here, with so much space between us, he looks so small.* Melvin watched him work and wished that he wasn't there. *This is between me and Drinn, father. You do not belong here.*

Melvin sighed. His immobile body felt as heavy as stone. A guilty feeling wormed around inside him, and he shook his head irritably. *Obviously, I didn't mean that logically. After all, the tower can't rebuild itself.* But the irritation remained, staining his appreciation of the view before him. So he glanced down at his feet again, and watched a fly crawl across his toes.

"At least I can't feel how much that tickles," Melvin muttered, smiling to himself. "Got to appreciate the little things."

....

A week had passed after Melvin's acceptance of Drinn's apprenticeship. It was a strange time for Melvin: half of it comfortably spent with friends that were beginning to feel like family, and half spent with his father, who was, for reasons that Melvin could not explain, beginning to feel like a stranger.

Daedrim and he had been magically apparated back to their house in Holm to await the summons of the magus. It amused Melvin that his father had gotten sick from the vertigo of travel, but Melvin had not. *At least, not sick enough to vomit in front of him, and that's what mattered.*

Sitting in what already felt like his former bedroom, Melvin marveled at how little time it takes to outgrow your own life, if you are determined to do so. He had spent a day in that room gathering what little clothing and supplies he cared to bring with him. Against the objections of his father, he had done so by dragging himself across his bedroom floor, doing his best to heave himself up chairs and clamber hand over hand up the frustratingly tall frame of his bed. Since the accident, his arms had grown wiry with new muscle at the same rate that the muscles of his legs continued to atrophy.

Tucked into bed that night, he stared at the ceramic bottles full of coal ash on his bedroom shelves and the little piles of clinker that he had horded, and chuckled to himself wryly. *A child's ambitions fit so easily onto shelves. Just a pile of junk, really. Why did I hold onto this stuff for so long?*

But the next morning he slipped one of the more dynamic pieces of clinker into his duffle bag just in case, and a few of the nicer ceramic bottles. *I will wash the ashes out of them when I get the time. Perhaps the bottles will prove useful in storing actual spell components.*

The rest of that week had passed awkwardly — at least, the time spent at home. During those long hours, his father doted on him with the bumbling insistence of someone caring for the infirm who has no practice at it. In fact, for most of Melvin's memory, his father had barely paid much heed to his son at all, except as a reading companion and someone to share food with. The majority of his attention had been instructive, or work-related, or the brief mustering of some tidbit of local gossip. Now Daedrim fawned on Melvin in an irritatingly present manner. His tea cup was refilled before Melvin had time to drain it; snacks materialized on small plates left near at hand. On the first night home, he even stammered through an offer to help Melvin bathe, although he looked relieved when the offer was brusquely refused.

Melvin found himself spending as much time as he could away from home in the company of his friends, or with the door of his room closed between them. He dreaded treading through forced dinner conversations. The only commonality that felt comfortable to share was plans for the future. In one week, they had discussed construction plans for the tower so thoroughly that Melvin could have told you the future dimensions of each room with his eyes closed.

....

"I'm worried Yrsa is a spy. Am I working for a spy? I sort of hope so. Spying seems like an exciting profession, don't you think? Actually, I would honestly make a pretty good spy. My mother trained me how to lie. Not in a sideways way, like 'I was raised with the role model of my mother deceiving others, and so I could not help but become a deceiver.' I mean, she actually spent a considerable amount of time teaching me how to do it in a skilled way. It was like attending a Fahru Nariman history lecture, but a lot less boring. And the teacher was slapping my face all the time. My mother — not Fahru Nariman. I would have liked to see him try." Talara clenched her fists. "I'd have busted his ribs if that silly cleric ever slapped me the way my mother used to."

It was a warm day, one of those spring days where the weather can't seem to make up its mind about what the plan is. Tufts of rain-gray clouds trundled about in vaguely threatening masses through an otherwise bright sky. The resultant heat was moist and sticky, with odd little gusts of cold air whooshing by at random. The air smelled like fading petrichor *(that word that does nothing to describe the vibrant smell of earth soaked in fresh rain)* as well as the gently amphibious smell of algae blooms warming on sun-heated river rocks.

....

Melvin interjected. "Talara — you lost the point of this story a couple of breaths ago. What are you actually trying to say?"

"Did Fahru Nariman slap your face?" Mathias gasped. His pale cheeks flushed.

"What? No, you lackwits: I'm worried that Yrsa isn't just the innkeep that she seems to be. I'm trying to share with you my concern that she might be an agent for the thegn, or for the Iron Guard."

"Too many tangents." Melvin muttered. Shamsala maaed in agreement, thoughtfully chewing on Melvin's hair. Melvin pushed her away.

The children (and goat and dog) were flopped out under those trees which grew near the cave that they had scared the Orlŭks away from. Since then, they had felt compelled to return whenever they could, particularly now that Rahyn had cleaned the site up and adopted it as her home. There was something enchanting about that oak dappled glen that had drawn them all back to it. Branches festooned with bearded lichen; clusters of pale mushrooms that caught the last light of sunset and glowed for an hour thereafter; the creek and its tumble of descending waterfalls; rocky pools whose crescent shores were matted in mosses that had been growing undisturbed since time first washed over Eld. Even the shadows were green beneath the squat river oaks. The whole place hummed like a secret that they were excited to share amongst themselves.

Mathias nodded. "Yah, you could have just said that bit and not wandered us off into the weeds. You got me all flustered about Fahru Nariman."

Talara stuck out her tongue. "I forget you ignorant *moros* don't have the attention span for a decent story. Fine. What am I supposed to do about Yrsa? What do we do?"

"Well, for starters, how do you know for sure she's a spy?" Tarquin piped up. "I met her a few times and she sure doesn't seem like one. She seems completely and utterly like a regular tavern-tender."

Talara whacked his head. "Well of course she does, dingus! A good spy never *acts* like a spy — they act like they are anyone else."

Tarquin ducked out of swatting range, and went to sit with Shamsala. "Well, that tallies. I'm convinced. What do you think, Mel? Secret double-life for Yrsa: yea or nay?"

Melvin grunted. "I refuse to have an opinion on this. Ask Mathias."

Mathias shrugged.

....

They had lashed together a replacement raft to ford the river, improving upon their original design by enlarging the deck for pets, adding a steering rudder, and not building in a hurry. Caetal whittled them a few proper paddles, making it much easier to control their orientation in the current, and thusly to cross the river without being swept too far downstream.

Perhaps it was that the cave was miles of travel from Holm that also enticed them; a few hours trek that allowed some distance from the pressure of work, home, and the invisible weight of the expectations of their elders. Also, every time they looked at the strangely formed hill that Melvin had magicked into the vague resemblance of a goat head with a yawning mouth, it cracked them up good. In honor of those efforts, they had formally named the cave "Adara-Tzor-Eae," which Caetal confidently assured them meant "Goat-God-Hill," but actually meant "Goat-Beyond-Lumps." Privately, Rahyn thought of the place simply as *The Den* — and that, of course, is the name that stuck.

....

"Well... dammit, it feels important! I have to live with this woman, you know? I work with her almost every day. How am I supposed to... I don't know. Maybe I'm being paranoid."

Tarquin shrugged, petting Shamsala. Dubby wandered by, whining quietly to himself and sniffing trees. "Does it matter? Who would she be spying on, anyway? It's hard to imagine who would care what farmers are gossiping about at the end of the work day. *'Be warned my wicked comrades: I hear Farmer Jenkins had an unusually red harvest of rutabagas this year! We better send news to the queen! Bring forth a quill, and your fastest raven!'*"

Talara glared. "Fine. Whatever. I just.... I saw her talking to some soldiers late at night a few days ago. She signed some official-looking parchment and they gave her a bag of coins. The conversation seemed important. I've been wondering what it was about, that's all. It's been weighing on me what Yrsa was up to."

"Well, why don't you ask her?" Rahyn said.

"Don't be simple."

Rahyn blinked, cocking her head. "Why not?"

"Oh nevermind, all of you. Just forget it."

Tarquin patted her shoulder. "I tell you what: why don't you ask Yrsa if she needs a hand keeping up with the tavern crowd? I'd be glad to work there with you, and that way I can also secretly help you keep an eye on her. Maybe you're right, and something is going on that shouldn't be. Two brains are better than one when it comes to sorting out riddles!"

Talara grinned. "Yes, even if that second brain is yours."

"Don't be a fartmouth."

"Wouldn't the money you earn just get taken away by Liam anyway?" Talara asked. There followed an awkward silence that was just long enough to make her feel how much she'd stuck her foot in it. Talara blushed. Mathias coughed uncomfortably.

Tarquin shrugged elaborately. "I dunno. I guess so. I forget sometimes for a few minutes that I'm a slave now. Thanks for the reminder."

"I didn't... I'm sorry, Tarq. That was rude of me."

Tarquin grinned, but his eyes were wet. "I'm just teasing you. Of course he would take all the money I earn. But maybe he could use some of it to buy me a new shirt. Plus, I bet Yrsa would feed me lunch sometimes if I worked hard enough, and whatever she's cooking has got to be better than what Liam makes. He's a pretty great swordsman, but he cooks about as well as a blind guy riding a donkey backwards through an herb garden."

Melvin laughed. "What the heck does that even mean? Is the blind guy trying to cook while he's on the donkey's back?"

"Is he g-gathering herbs too? Is that w-w-why he's in the garden?"

"Maybe he can gather the herbs by smell?" Rahyn reasoned.

"It means whatever you moon goons want it to mean. Plus, I honestly just need a good excuse to get out of the house. Staying home is boring me senseless, and I want to avoid being around Liam's son Shandus. There is something wrong with that kid's head, I'm telling you."

Caetal nodded sagely. "Foaming-dog-sick, but inside his head. You can see it in his eyes."

"Well, his dad is the same way. I think that's why he turned out like that. Liam is a bit crazy too."

"—But not *Shandus* crazy."

"Not hardly. One time I woke up in the middle of the night and Shandus was sitting next to my bed, just watching me sleep. And he had this... *bad look* on his face. Like he was trying to decide whether to eat me after he killed me, or just kill me. You know what I mean?"

Rahyn nodded. "A predator."

"Yes! Exactly like that. A predator look. I kept my eyes closed and pretended to still be asleep, but I think he could tell I was faking it. He stood up and went to bed after a while, but I lay awake for the rest of the night. Liam isn't like that. He is a mean bastard, but he doesn't treat me like a future meal. His son is well on his way to supplanting him as Holm's craziest citizen."

"Well, that's horrifying." Talara shuddered and stood up, stretching her arms above her head. She began to climb a squat tree nearby, hooking her knees over the lowest branch until she was dangling upside down. "Of course, I'll try to get you a job, Tarq. I can't make any promises, but it's worth a try."

"Thank you, Tee-lar."

Talara stuck her tongue out and grinned from where she was dangling. Her hair pooled around her face like a brown cloud. "You're welcome. Sorry I reminded you about, um... your thrall... slavery stuff."

Tarquin smiled thinly and raised his wrist, tapping the fingers of his other hand against the leather and iron thrall's cuff he was lawfully bound to always wear. He didn't reply; he didn't have to.

....

The croaking of the frogs could be heard in a rising harmony, and for a while they all quieted down to listen to them, grinning at each other when particularly loud ones disrupted the chorus.

Caetal, whose back was hurting badly from his ranger's rite on the Stone Tree, took his shirt off and tried to lay with his hot back against a cool rock. But the skin was too tender, so he rolled over. Dubby trotted over and made a nuisance of himself, whining and licking at the wounds until Caetal swore at him and sent him away. Mathias dug a wound salve out of his backpack and offered it to him, and Caetal grudgingly agreed. Carefully, he daubed the salve across the scarring red lines that formed into the picture of a two headed snake. Frowning, Mathias traced the lightning pattern that forked from its mouth. The skin was puckered and raw. Caetal winced, and his breath hissed between his teeth.

"Do you guys... Do you wonder if we are *supposed* to outgrow our own parents? That it might be something that we can't help but do, regardless of how much we don't want to?" Melvin enquired broadly from where he was laying on his back, watching a drifting cloud. The thought had been on his mind for days.

There was a general silence after Melvin's question, while each of them pondered the nuances of their own situation. Tarquin, who did not enjoy thinking about his parents, got up and wandered towards the creek, out of sight enough to pretend to pee, but within hearing range of other people's answers. Orphan that he was, Mathias also remained silent. It was Caetal who spoke up first from where he lay face-down. His voice was muffled because he was speaking into his own crossed arms. The children had to lean in to hear him.

"I don't think that w-w-we *outgrow* them, so much as... huh. Maybe it's more that they expect so much from us, because they raised us to be like them, and- ouch, g-godsdammit, Mathias, that hurts! Talara, can you rub this stuff in? The Erdin kid is back there scraping my flesh off."

"Sorry." Mathias mumbled, blushing. "I'm trying to be careful. The skin on your back is really enflamed; some of it is infected. I bet it hurts pretty badly, huh?"

"Damn right it does." Caetal growled.

"Believe me, you don't want me on salve-rubbing duty." Talara interjected from the tree branch she was dangling on. "My fingertips are all callused from playing rebec every night. Yrsa has me barding hard these days when I'm not serving drinks: working double shifts to keep up with the crowds. You are in better hands with Mathias."

"Fine. Whatever. Just be more careful, alright? It stings like w-wasps are nesting under my skin." Caetal grumbled, shifting around on his stomach until the leaf-dappled sunlight no longer felt like it was cooking the tender skin on his back.

"I'll continue to try my best." Mathias replied. Melvin glanced over and frowned, privately wishing that Caetal wasn't always so... Caetally.

Rahyn scootched over and dipped her fingers into the salve jar, quietly joining Mathias in applying it. "Finish your thought, Caetal."

"Oh, right. It's... w-w-well, I'm trying to say that sometimes w-we don't live up to all those expectations, even if they'd like us to. It's like... my father is a *lot*, you know? Melvin knows. He has a lot of big ideas of w-wuh... *what* is best for everyone — my mom and I, the entire island. Especially me. Sometimes I don't know how to even begin to be the person he expects me to be. Sometimes I can't, or shouldn't. I care for him though, you know? He isn't ...w-w...wrong. He just might not be *right*, either." Caetal muttered into his crossed arms. There was a moment of silence, then he said: "It's easier between my mom and I. Always been easier. It doesn't feel like she expects me to be anything but *me*."

Talara groaned. "That must be nice. My mother was impossible to please."

"Was? Has she passed back into the circle?" Rahyn asked.

"I honestly don't know if she's dead, if that's what you meant." Talara replied, tightly. She dropped down from her branch and sat against the tree trunk, tucking her legs up under her.

"You don't talk about her very much?" Mathias asked, caution turning a statement into a question.

"Oh, I do. All the time. I talk about her constantly, inside my own head; you just can't hear it. I talk, she talks back: she's always talking, always commenting on whether what I'm doing is *worthwhile*. It's like an argument that I'm stuck repeating with her over and over again. It's *loud* in my head, children. You should be glad you don't have to spend time inside my mind."

Melvin arched an eyebrow and grunted. "Noted. How would you answer that same question then?"

"Depends on how you asked it."

"I'm asking it like this: do you think we can't help outgrowing our parents?"

"You originally said *supposed* to outgrow."

"Don't be a puckerditch."

"Don't dongle up your own question then! Which question is it?"

Melvin folded his arms. "Whichever one leads you to quit stalling and answer it."

Talara covered her mouth dramatically and exhaled in a slow whistle between her fingers. Her friends stared at her expectantly, waiting for her to continue. She shrugged self-consciously, halfway crossing her arms and then letting them drop back to her side again.

"Alright, fine. Let's see: I never knew who my father was, but my mother assured me many times that he was a worthless waste of skin, so I guess I've outgrown him already. As for my mother... I'm not sure I will ever outgrow her, and I'll certainly never be able to grow up to become the person she was trying to raise me to be. The Rhymir, my people, are scattered and vanished; some of history's losers in the games of empire. I've never met another Rhymira, besides my mother. I doubt there are any others on this whole island. In fact, I'm not even sure they ever existed at all."

"*They were real.*" Tarquin said softly from where he stood at the edge of the grove. "I've heard stories of them all my life. They were called the 'Daughters of Joy' once. The greatest singers, performers, and storytellers were trained in old Rhymir for thousands of years. I wanted to be one so badly when I was young."

Caetal snickered. "You w-wanted to be a bardic w-w- ...g-girl when you were young?"

Tarquin blushed, looking down at his feet. "I wanted to be great at creating something *worthwhile* — something beautiful. It didn't matter to me that they were all women and I wasn't. I didn't think about that. It's obvious now, of course, but... I don't know. I just imagined being able to sing or play an instrument like that; music that charms the birds out of the trees, or the ability to tell someone a story that blooms inside their heart and fills them up with emotions that are so big and important that there aren't even words to describe them. You know what I mean?"

Talara reached out a hand towards Tarquin. Blushing self-consciously, he walked over and stood beside her. Shamsala trotted after him. Talara gently pushed Shamsala's seeking head away and took both his hands.

"Thank you, Tarquin. There is nothing silly about you wanting to be Rhymira when you were young. So did I. It is a great relief to find out that you have heard of my people. I think I have always been afraid, deep down inside, that my mother had made the whole thing up — all of it — to make herself seem important."

Tarquin squeezed her hands. "She didn't have to make anything up to be important. She was your mother, that's important enough. What was she like?"

Talara paled visibly, and released his hands. She stepped back, fumbled with a pouch on her belt as though looking for something. Then she pushed up the bracelets on her wrists and sighed.

"Hard to describe her, really. At her best, she was an incredible singer, a gifted musician, and a storehouse of old tales and stories that vanished with her the night she left me behind. She was also a very selfish person who used her talents carelessly and was a complete idiot about men. She loved me in a way that made me feel special, and smothered. I... it's so hard-"

Her voice hitched, and she glanced away, blinking rapidly and wiping her sleeve across her eyes. Tarquin reached out to touch her shoulder, but she shrugged him off.

"It is... a very difficult feeling... to be expected to uphold a legacy of something that is already so diminished, and was once so great. And to learn about it from someone who was exactly the same way. Diminished and lost. I feel like a person who can speak just a few words of the most beautiful language in the world, and the only other person who could speak that same language is *gone*. So, yes: to answer your damn question, Melvin — I don't know if outgrowing our own parents is even possible. I already hoped I had, but apparently, I was wrong. The only thing I can do is try not to *become* her, because she was a *mess*. She probably still is, wherever she ended up."

Talara brusquely wiped her eyes with her sleeve once more. The boys shuffled and looked away politely while she composed herself, but Rahyn stood up and padded over, leaning forward until their foreheads were touching.

"A language isn't dead until nobody remembers what it sounds like." She murmured. "Tell us the stories that mattered to your people. We will help you keep them alive."

....

And that, of course, is when I really started crying.

One minute, you are hanging around enjoying the bragging of the bullfrogs on a warm spring day, and the next minute, a dam bursts. One godsdamn question too many; one moment of unexpected kindness that you discover, too late, is the loose seam that unravels the whole shirt of self-control. All of a sudden, your heart is a heaving boat on a troubled sea, and if it wasn't for the love of good friends, you'd be capsized and drowning. Rahyn held me while I came apart, and the boys circled around us and held us both together. As Tarquin had said, the most important things don't have words to describe them.

I suppose that would have been a good time for me to have told them more about her, and about the swamp she raised me in. It would have felt so good, just then; so on cue. That was the moment, and I was crying so hard that I missed it. It was years before I began to tell the story of my life again, and it only ever came out in small, hard pieces that I wrapped honeyed lies around so that they would go down sweeter. I don't know why I'm like that. There are few things more useless than lying to your best friends. They usually find out anyway, and the hurt from that kind of deception does not heal cleanly.

....

There were more stories that came out that day — a great deal more. As the afternoon faded and the stars brightened, we learned how little we had really known about each other. I was the first to cry that afternoon, but not the last, nor the worst wounded by it.

Children are rarely polite, but they are far too often shy. This is because they feel so much. We are born with huge feelings inside tiny bodies, and though we grow into bigger bodies, our feelings stay about the same size, and often diminish into something far more garish and useless: pride; ambition. But when you are a child, you ARE what you feel — all the rest of it, what adults call "personality," is what we are all making up as we go along. One moment we were kind to each other; the next we were cruel. Childhood is a tangle of magnificent joys and plunging sorrows all wrapped up in restlessness and longing that gets you as far as it can each day until exhaustion claims you.

But there are moments that are larger and clearer, and most of us remember a few of them for the rest of our lives. That day, we learned that we wanted to share as much as we could. We each felt time dragging at us; I'm sure that was part of it. Melvin was eager to leave his childhood behind — not to leave us, necessarily, but where he was going was not an easy place for us to follow, even for a visit. Caetal had bled for the rangers; he already wore a man's cares in boy's clothing, you could see it in his eyes. I was busy with tavern work, Tarquin was owned and therefore loaned to us on borrowed time. Mathias belonged to Cuthain, and Cuthain belonged to the Erdin empire. And Rahyn was to be taken across the sea someday soon, maybe never to return.

None of us knew that stuff. Not yet. But we finally found the courage to ask, and to answer. Caetal admitted to fears about his father's failing health, and the obvious strain it was placing on his mother. Mathias shared what he knew about how he ended up on the steps of Cuthain's church as a baby, and did what he could to describe the lonely life of a child that could see two worlds at once through cursed eyes. We learned about the Twilight Lands, and how a skin shifting old crow came to raise Rahyn from birth; how much she longed to return to that timeless land and seek out the mother who let her only daughter live without her in a world she had left behind. We found out that Tarquin had not been born a slave, but was instead an orphan of murder, taken from his island and everything he knew. I had guessed at part of that, of course, for I was watching from the window above when he was first sold. It was a tragic, wrenching story, and we could tell he was reliving the awful details of it as he shared it with us. Afterwards we held him close as he wept like he would die from the grief of it.

They were lonely stories, bruising and raw. Yet also lovely, in the way that a broken heart that is trying to mend can be. We had not known, until then, that so many of us were orphans in one way or another. A version of those stories we shared that day is what makes up the first half of this book. It is my honor to record them as they were shared with me by my first friends.

I told them as much as I could bear, as I said. But it was years before I had the courage to write my own chapter into this book. Though my chapter falls in the middle of the other stories, it was written last, for I found it very difficult to speak some truths even to myself. I learned, by writing it, that I was sometimes a selfish and ungrateful daughter. That my mother, for all of her failings, did as every decent parent does: prepares their child to survive long enough to outlive them.

....

An important story that did not get shared at all that day was the sequence of events that led to the loss of Melvin's legs. Caetal did not admit to it, and Melvin did not elaborate on the hunch that was growing just out of sight like a cancer inside of him. Perhaps if he had, much that soured later between them might have been avoided, and the clarity of perspective could have been the beginning of forgiveness. But if Caetal had admitted to his sabotage, he would have also implicated his father. Regardless of his failings, the old bear was still the hero of his cub.

And as for Melvin: I remember him on that long-ago afternoon better than any of the rest of them. It was his silence that I remember best. The rest of us were caught up in a storm of stories and the relief of sharing answers to questions that, at last, someone had bothered to ask. But he was like the rock on which the water of our emotions dashed and turned to mist. He was calm, and polite; a good listener, a solid companion. He comforted, he consoled, and yet he kept his own thoughts as close to his chest as any gambler concerned about protecting a winning hand.

We were there, all together — for better or for worse, increasingly tangled up in each other's lives. Yet he was somewhere else, dreaming how to climb the ladder of his own destiny without the use of his legs. He was miles away, sitting alone by a lake. He was already gone.

....

The Boy Who Sits Alone

Melvin's first formal day of training in the magical arts had begun, appropriately, at dawn. Drinn rowed them both across the lake, from the island to the mainland, while the sunrise cracked the edge of the evening sky and cold drafts of early morning wind churned the water into white-caps. Drinn was quiet as he swung the paddles in their oarlocks, only muttering softly to himself from time to time. During the whole ride, Melvin stared down into the swaying blackness of the lake, expecting all the time to be capsized by the broiling spirit that apparently haunted the water. He clutched at the rowboat rail in barely contained panic, imagining himself overturned into the cold darkness and dragged below by the weight of his useless legs. His knuckles were white and aching by the time the boat beached at the shore.

Drinn hoisted Melvin up onto one shoulder, and dragged him in an ungainly half-carry a few hundred feet uphill from the waterline. There he was flopped down with his back resting against a stout log of sun-bleached driftwood. Drinn carefully positioned him so that the island with the tower ruin was in view.

Then, as the sky began to truly lighten, Drinn squatted down next to Melvin. The magus and the boy stared at each other for a few searching moments until Drinn spoke.

"I have never had an apprentice, and I never wanted one. It has al-ways seemed like a trivial and disruptive vanity to waste time and effort on teaching. What is the value for me of retreading my own steps back to the beginning; the rote memorization and trifling discoveries that are the foundations of aptitude. I have worked so long to distance myself from those frustrations — I could not comprehend why many magi bothered to expend time and money on the nonsensical nurturing of the next gen-eration. After all, we mages did not pursue our power out of a sense of altruism. Ours is an entirely selfish goal, and don't ever believe a word that whispers otherwise.

"However: my perspective on teaching has altered somewhat with age. The shifting circumstances of my magical pursuits have — shall we say — *broadened* my understanding of the value of an apprentice. It is important to have someone with which to share the deal of fate; to spread the load out a bit, as it were. To be a magus is a dangerous profession, after all. And it is my duty, therefore, to speak plainly about what the study of the magical arts will entail, and provide you with one last chance to refuse my offer."

Melvin cocked his head and frowned. "I had made up my mind before you ever asked me. I will train with you, and become a magus."

Drinn smiled thinly. "You are still a boy, Melvinari. You have no idea what that means; what terrible risks are involved, body and soul.

"A magus is a person who risks all to steal directly from the gods. It is the True Names of things that are the prize; a chance to peek over the shoulder of the Play of Creation and read from the script directly. It gives us the ability to write new chapters of reality itself, and if we live long enough to become exceptionally clever at it, to re-write what has already been written.

"Most magi do not live that long, however, because they do not prioritize their own survival over the opportunity to explore the powers they have stolen. They forget, in moments of transcendent foolishness, the most important lesson of the magus: that you stole what you are playing with from someone who wants it back. And that 'someone' is something we call a *god*: an Immortal of incredible power and an unending grudge towards those who would dare such blasphemy as we dare. Against such a foe, there are only frail defensive tricks we must practice daily, *hourly*, to disguise ourselves and preserve our longevity. And when those tricks fail, we run, and hope we are fast enough to outrun the servants of those gods.

"So: before I let you begin training, I want you to sit here alone for a day and think about the implications of what that really means. At sunset tonight, I will return to ask for an answer to this question: do you understand that a magus is just a thief of True Names? Those very words that the Immortals created to define form from formlessness. There is no glorious nobility in what we will be striving for, but instead, the most loathsome and deplorable talents of burglary."

Melvin folded his arms across his chest, but his voice was trembling. "This extra day to think about it is unnecessary. I've been thinking about it for months. I have already decided."

"Don't be a godsdamn fool, Melvinari. You will do as I tell you and take the time to really *understand* what use of magic entails — not just fantasize about it — or I'll send you home right now. I will be training you to be a thief, plain and simple. A burglar who steals words that are more precious than gemstones, and risks a lot worse than death to do it. You will never be loved or honored for this: you will be shunned, as a leper is shunned. You'll be cast out of the company of all lesser men, and forfeit any mercies the gods may have otherwise bestowed on you. You will be despised, fundamentally, *by the world itself.* And to remind you of all that, while you are under my tutelage, I shall not call you 'magus' or 'apprentice'. I shall call you Thief, and you will call me *Kinnari*, which translates roughly into 'one who steals shadows.' You are Thief, and I am Kinnari, or Kinnari-Drinn if you are feeling particularly gracious. Do you understand?"

Melvin was silent for a long moment, staring out past Drinn across the water. The rhythm of his father hammering scaffolding together could barely be heard from the shore, like the distant clattering of some woodpecker.

"Yes, Kinnari-Drinn."

"No, you don't understand. You can't. But you have until sunset to try and grasp the least of it. Do not waste that time fantasizing about future magical successes. There will be some, and they will feel better than anything has a right to feel. Instead ponder the terrible price of failure. Think about that poor *skabde-valea* magus who once owned that tower out there, and now haunts this lake. Think about never being able to properly *die.*"

Drinn spat, and wiped his mouth on his sleeve. Then he dropped a full waterskin next to Melvin, and turned to walk away.

"Drinn, wait! What about food? I have not eaten yet today."

"It is Kinnari-Drinn, you insufferable idiot."

Melvin frowned. "No, it isn't. It is Kinnari only if I continue to choose to train with you after the sun has set. Until then I will call you whatever I want to. Now what about food?"

Drinn looked back over his shoulder at Melvin, and his sneer turned into a chuckle.

"What a piece of work you are, child! Alright then. I'm glad you were paying attention. And to answer your question: you don't get food today. Your insignificant hunger from fasting for one day will remind you of the fathomless hunger the cursed magus who haunts this lake feels, and will always feel, until she is lucky enough to dissolve into nothingness on that distant day when every drop of the entire lake dries up. So, sit here for a while and think about *that* while you bear the burden of some rumblies in your tummy."

Drinn smiled down at Melvin for a moment; a truculent smile that was smeared with loathing.

"Get used to fasting, child. Mages have to do it quite often. There are in-between places where we must go out-of-body; places where the spirit rejects the physical. Vomiting up your food might kill you if you breathe it back in while your body is still unconscious. Why do you think I gave you such a heavy coat to wear? I am thin beneath my clothing, as you will be. We magi get cold easily."

Drinn patted Melvin on the head.
"See you at sunset."
Then he walked back to the boat and rowed away.

....

Melvin tried all day to ponder his future in an appropriately serious way.

He organized the projected years of his life into the acts of a play and performed various versions of it before the critical audience in his mind. To be fair to the exercise that Drinn had insisted on, he started out by imagining a life where he didn't seek out magical training.

In the opening act, he was very young. He decided the first twelve years ought to be thought of as one act, because he had spent all that time just learning how to become the Melvin that he currently was. Melvin did not consider himself to be a particularly sentimental person, so he skipped rapidly through this first act and labeled it "childhood." That portion of his life obviously ended when his legs were crushed. Looking back on it from where he sat on the shore of that lake, it felt like it had happened to someone else, a long time ago.

Act two. A young man with a keen intellect and lifelong access to book learning has plenty of opportunities, even with his disability. Perhaps he could journey to Dárû and work as a transcriber in the Glass Library, making copies of moldering tomes before age and bookworms made a meal of them. He could do accounting for a thegn; manage a thriving mercantile from the back room; or become an architectural mason like his father. (Melvin watched his father working for a minute, and then shuddered.) Well, perhaps he could *teach* masonry? Anyway, there were sure to be plenty of jobs for a smart young man with a good education.

Act three brought up uncomfortable questions that he did not have answers for. Marriage? Children of his own? Would anyone want to marry a person that needed constant attendant care? Melvin had wasted very little time in his life pondering the indescribable pull of attraction, and where he fit into a world that seemed obsessed with coupling. He skipped over this third act even more quickly than act one, with the judgmental audience in his mind all the while muttering and taking notes. *I'm sure there will be… someone in the future. They will likely be beautiful and very devoted, and won't care about something as trivial as working legs. Not worth putting too much thought into something so far out of my control. Moving on.*

But without act three sketched out clearly in his mind, act four became fuzzy. He could imagine himself well-to-do in the distant future; gray-bearded and wealthy in a house of stone somewhere near enough to the ocean where he could hear the distant shooshing of the surf from an open window. He imagined walls of books, a comfortable chair, and a goblet of wine perched nearby atop a fashionable side table. And servants. *Well, at least one servant anyway.* He strained to see himself contented by a life well lived: one in which the questions of his heart had found satisfying answers through diligent work and overcoming the daily limitations of his paralysis. But what questions are more worth asking than those which comprise the strands of the skein of reality? *What answers could I possibly find that are worth more to me than the secrets that even gods wish to keep hidden?*

In the fifth act, Melvin was dead. In his imagination, he died alone and his servants made off with the silver spoons and the bed linens before his body had the chance to stiffen. None of his friends attended his funeral, because he had forgotten to imagine them into the play of his life.

How could I have forgotten them? Was the thought of a life of business that alluring? Why didn't they show up in my imagination at all?

....

Melvin stretched his stiff shoulders and sighed. The sun had drifted to empyreal crown: nearly noon. His stomach gurgled, so he drank as much water as he could to fill up the empty space inside of him.

What about my friends? Think it through. Where will they be in my future? He tried to picture them there by his side, but the effort stalled out under the reproving critique of his imagination. *Would Rahyn care to wander the sterile enormity of the Glass Library? Would Caetal sit quietly through a mercantile business meeting — would anyone have considered letting someone who looks like him through the front door in the first place? Perhaps I could get Tarquin a job working at one of my future rock quarries, but it would bore him senseless. And then he would become my employee, not my friend. He would hate it, and I would hate it.*

Melvin could imagine an older version of Talara playing music for him while he sipped wine in his finely furnished house, but it was just as easy to imagine a faceless trio of hired performers somewhere in the background where he could more easily ignore them while he was reading. *And Mathias...* he was the easiest to imagine in any of those scenarios, for he had a cautious but able mind that could be marshaled towards the diligence and frugality of business. But his silly obsession with his religion would likely always remain as the dominant focus in his life, and Melvin would be double-damned before he would willingly step into one of Cuthain's churches ever again.

Again and again, he tried to fit the image of his friends as they were now — young and playful, goofy and uncommonly wise — into his vision of that future. But every time he tried to age them in his mind and warp them into shapes that would fit like puzzle pieces into the holes of his theoretical adulthood, the picture fell apart. Melvin yawned and shrugged to himself. *Oh well. I guess I am not meant to know them for that long. I am told the friendships of childhood rarely last into maturity anyway.*

But although that thought hardened in his mind, something softer inside his heart cried out sadly. He remembered that it was his father who had told him that phrase. His father, who even now worked alone on a small island, building a tower at the insistence of a magus. Forever in service as a simple laborer to the designs of more worldly men. His father: who preferred to horde the accumulated fortune of his knowledge in the introverted vault of his mind. *His father who had no friends, and therefore did not know what he was missing out on.*

Melvin's breath hitched in his throat. *I don't know what my future as a magus might hold, or how long I might live to experience it. But I do know that I am different than my father. My ambitions begin where his have ended.*

The sun swept slowly across the sky. Beneath it, Melvin surrendered into the many-hued imagination of his life with magic at his command. Now it was easy to see his place amongst his friends, for he knew where it was already. *I am their magus: the Miraculous (or maybe Marvelous? Magnanimous?) Melvinari! We shall travel the whole world together and do whatever we wish. My magic will tease open the opportunities of adventure! If we are lost inside a labyrinth, I shall create a door. If we are drifting in the doldrums of open water, I shall beckon a wind into the sails. Those that threaten to harm us will burn for it. They will never think of me as a burden, crippled under the fallen stone of fate. Through magical mastery I will regain the use of my legs. I shall become the most powerful of us all.*

The long hours of the afternoon passed quickly, overrun by the galloping chariot of his daydreams. Drinn's warnings were gladly forgotten.

....

"Have you decided?"

"Yes."

"This work is incredibly dangerous. Very few magi live to old age. Most of them die horribly."

"I understand."

"While you are under my instruction, I will do my best to keep you from accidentally killing yourself, but my best very well may not be good enough. There is a reasonably high chance you might not even survive long enough to become a real magus. Many perish during their apprenticeship."

"I get that."

Drinn arched his eyebrows and stared down at Melvin. Sunset bloodied the air all around them. Melvin stared back up at him.

"You are sure? Last chance."

Melvin nodded slowly. "I should have died beneath that keystone, but I didn't. My magic saved me. I owe my life to it."

"It was mostly the ordanian boy who saved you, not your magic. Perhaps you should join the clergy instead?"

Melvin grimaced. "Look, are we doing this or what? My back is cramped from leaning against this *valea* log all day. I want to be a godsdamn magus, and I don't care what it costs me. Help me up, Great

Supreme Master Kinnari-Drinn. My butt has gone numb."

....

Slippery Slopes

That first night, and for many thereafter, they slept in a tent on a flat stretch of ground between the rise of two grassy hummocks.

It was surprisingly austere accommodations that Drinn must have set up in advance: a tent, a ring of campfire stones with a pot, bucket and kettle, and a wooden table with two squat benches.

Although Melvin felt mentally drained from his ponderous day, his body hummed with excitement. Neither moon had risen yet in the night sky, and the last purple of sunset was already pocked with stars. As they flared into view one by one, the electrical shivering in his muscles seemed to clarify in such a manner that Melvin felt himself bobbing like a boat tugged within the pull of invisible currents. He sat in the open doorflap of the tent and gazed at the sky in wonder, painting constellations in his mind and swaying at the waist like a charmed snake.

"Quit wobbling like that and lay down; how are you already getting on my nerves? You need sleep, and I need even more of it. *Go to bed.*" Drinn grumbled from under his blankets on the other side of the tent. "The morning will only come more slowly if you stay up waiting for it."

Melvin sighed, and pulled the tent flap closed. His view of the stars was snuffed, but he could still sense them crawling across the sky in their glittering multitudes, tugging the world along behind them. The night was quiet in a way that loudened the thudding of his own heart. There ought to be crickets whirring, beasts prowling about, or the muddy tumult of frogs boasting of their own virility. But all he could hear was the stuttering wind and the sound-beyond-sound of singing stars in the vault of night.

Melvin mashed his backpack down into a serviceable pillow and tried to relax. But the minutes dragged into hours while he flopped side to side, shivering from ground chill and sighing with frustration. The smell of old canvas made the tent stuffy. Drinn wheezed as he breathed, sleeping on his back with his arms draped awkwardly across his face. His snores were punctuated with sudden gasps as the night wore on, and he thrashed uneasily in the grip of dreams. Well past the midnight hour, what thin sleep Melvin got was punctured by lances of Drinn's snoring, and when dawn finally bloomed, he blinked at its offending light and felt slighted by the rest that had eluded him.

Before Drinn had the chance to wake up, Melvin heaved himself outside and drag-crawled his stiff body through the dewy grass. By the time he crested one of the low mounds and positioned himself to pee, the front of his clothing was damp and his elbows were clammy. He shivered and grumbled to himself, then sighed with relief as the steaming stream arced away downhill.

From the top of the mound he lay on, he could see the land stretching away towards the lake in a grouping of hummocks. Morning mist flowed around the base of them, so that the long mounds resembled a cluster of squat islands in a drifting sea. Some bristled with gorse; some bloomed with heather. Wild grasses claimed all the other land that could be seen down to the rocky shoreline. It was an enchanting sight when observed at a glance. Yet there was something off-putting about the mounds too: the loneliness of something abandoned. Melvin's draining bladder sharpened his perception. The impression of even rows could now be seen.

Melvin squirmed back downhill, and was almost stepped on by Drinn as he came yawning out of the tent.

"What manner of place is this, Kinnari? There is *something* here. I thought it was the stars last night, but... well, I guess it might have also been that. I barely slept at all; the blankets were warm enough, but my bones felt cold all night."

Melvin rolled onto his back and looked up at Drinn from the ground. The magus blinked and rubbed his eyes elaborately before he answered.

"Impressive instincts, Thief. You're right to feel uneasy. A battle took place here some while ago. Actually, it's likely more accurate to describe it as a slaughter. Soldiers were slain in their predictable thousands. Such carnage cannot be easily burnt or individually buried. It is likely that the survivors dug shallow pits and stacked what remained of the corpses like logs, one hundred in a line and three rows deep. That is what usually happens. Then dirt would have been piled up on top of them so that the survivors could try to move on with their lives and forget what happened here."

"That's terrible!"

Drinn glanced at Melvin impassively. "Lots of things are terrible, but burying the dead is just polite. Trying to forget why they died is much worse. So now we are left camping amongst unnatural hills in orderly rows, and no record anywhere of who died here, or why. Are you old enough for black tea? I drink loads of it. Let's have some."

"*Barrow mounds. Of course, that bone-deep cold should have been obvious.*" Melvin muttered to himself. Then he glared up at Drinn.

"Why did we *camp* here? You knew these were barrow mounds — why in the hells would we pitch a tent in the middle of them? No wonder I slept so badly!"

Drinn shrugged. "They block the wind. Don't be superstitious; you didn't sleep well because your pillow is a lumpy backpack. I'm off to fetch water; a few cups of strong tea are essential for my morning constitution. Get a fire going."

And he strode off with a bucket.

....

Two pungent cups of tea and a breakfast of buttered bread and kippers were created and consumed before Melvin was allowed to broach the subject further.

"Kinnari-Drinn: might I ask a few clarifying questions?"

Drinn smiled to himself wryly, leaning his arms on the picnic table and wiping herring grease off his mouth. "A formal request that falsely implies deference to my function as your teacher: how very proper of you! Go ahead and ask your questions. Lasting learning is entirely comprised of good questions and the sense to apply the answers successfully."

"Firstly, why did you pick this cursed place to build your tower?"

"I'm not going to answer that question."

Melvin folded his arms. "Great follow up to your speech about the importance of asking good questions. Very helpful."

Drinn snorted. "Alright, fine. Let me clarify: what I meant is I'm not going to answer that question *honestly*. If you want me to lie to you, I'm happy to make up excuses about rebuilding a perfectly good shattered tower base, or making use of an existing well. The only true part of the answer you will get out of me is that I enjoy the isolation. I don't like people very much."

"I've gathered that. Okay, my second question is: who were the soldiers buried in those barrow mounds fighting for? And why did they come here? There is nothing anywhere around here but the-"

"-Ruined tower that was not always a ruin. You already know why they came here, because it's obvious. To destroy the magus who lived in that tower."

"Who sent them?"

Drinn shrugged and glanced away. "A king, perhaps. Or a thegn. I honestly don't know; as I said, that information has not been recorded anywhere I have thought to search for it, and that, in itself, is unusual. You would think the death of thousands of soldiers would end up on *somebody's* tax records, but nobody local has claimed responsibility. So, all I can say for sure about who sent the soldiers here to die is that it was someone who was afraid of the magus, and had the resources needed to turn that fear into slaughter."

Melvin swallowed, nodding carefully. "And they... succeeded?"

Drinn gestured vaguely around at the grassy mounds. "None of *these* guys succeeded. They died. A whole lot of people died. Only the survivors succeeded, and even that *success* is debatable."

Drinn paused for a moment with a look of concern on his face. Then he grimaced and spat out a wad of wet tea leaves.

"There is a hole in my steeping pouch that I have been meaning to repair. Have you noticed how easy it is to put off the little things?"

"Yes, Kinnari. Please continue."

"Alright. *'There was once a powerful woman who lived in that tower, and now her body has been destroyed and the tower has fallen.'* That's the beginning and end of what I'm sure I know about it. I suppose while this magus lived, she had the ability to travel elsewhere and make trouble if she wanted, but she likely rarely did. Most magi stay inside their towers as much as they can. It is the safest place to be, and there are plenty of things more dangerous than an army that hunt mages."

"There are?"

"Of course. I already warned you about that yesterday, Thief. Don't be thick."

Melvin glowered.

"As I was saying: by destroying her, they transmuted a mobile but unlikely threat into an actively hostile one that is still haunting the water to this day. Did you notice that *nothing* lives in this lake now? No fish, no amphibians, no otter or beaver or turtles. Not even migrating birds will rest here. Anything that washes down the river is eaten up. When night falls, the water itself begins to feed. That is why the lake is now named Xör Uru."

"*The Hungry Deep.*" Melvin whispered to himself, and shuddered.

"More like '*depth*', but translations are often dodgy. It didn't always have such a foreboding name, though. ...Well, actually, the old name was even worse. Once th- *ach, hold on.*"

Drinn spat out more little bits of tea leaf.

"They always get so acrid when they steep too long, have you noticed? Tastes like a scalding mouthful of moist dandelion root. I wish we had some honey."

Melvin just stared at him, until the quiet got awkward. Drinn coughed once, picked a few more stray leaves out of his teeth, and continued.

"Look: all I have been able to find out about the bodies in these barrow mounds is that they gathered at Drôle before marching here, and that a good number of them drowned trying to take the tower by boat. This was back when Drôle was still called the Revis Keep, mind you: I think the troll infestation happened shortly thereafter, because most of the soldiers didn't survive to return to their posts. I'd bet that's when the trolls saw the opportunity to sack an emptied keep and took it."

"But they still managed to kill the magus and raze her tower down to its foundations."

Drinn snorted. "Not in the least. A magus as powerful as she was had little to fear from swords or pikes. The tower fell because she shattered it. I don't know why or how, but her protective spells were set off. It was likely the resulting blast that destroyed her body too."

"I still don't understand why you brought us here to train. This place gives me the creeps. Why don't we train on the island? And don't tell me that it's just to get somewhere out of the wind, because that is a screech of fiddle-squawk."

Drinn chuckled and poked their dwindling campfire with a stick. He sipped at his cooling tea before bothering to reply.

"Fair enough. We came here to reflect on yesterday's important lesson. Do you recall what that was?"

Melvin stared at the fire for a moment.

"That a magus is always in great danger simply because they are a magus."

"Exactly. They are a danger to themselves, and a danger to those around them." Drinn gestured towards the barrow mounds. "These mounds are a reminder of the importance of why someone adept in the magical arts keeps a low profile, for otherwise death will be drawn to you as inexorably as iron is to a lodestone. The gods despise us, the races of Humanus fear us, and even the simplest animals learn to be wary, for they can sense more subtle disturbances than a human can."

Melvin nodded mutely, gazing into the pale campfire flames.

"These mounds are a lesson: *anonymity is the first defense of a magus*. As tempting as it is to flaunt yourself and the power of your craft, you must always remember that the eyes of the world are watching. It is no accident that a Homsaöl tore that abbey apart. The use of magic is surely what brought it there."

Melvin's gaze snapped up to Drinn. "Are you insinuating it was *my fault* for what happened? That saving myself from being crushed under that rock led to Hosten getting killed?"

"The resonance of magic ripples out far from its source, like sound traveling through water. There are those that are trained to 'listen' for that resonance; enemies to magi who respond to what they perceive as threats to the natural world. The abbey was the source of that resonance, and so, likely, the abbey was targeted. An undisciplined use of magic bangs loudly against the strings, that's all I'm saying. Whether you take on that child's death as your fault or not is entirely up to you."

"*It wasn't my fault.*" Melvin blurted out, scrubbing his eyes against his sleeve.

"I literally don't care either way." Drinn replied.

"Well, I do. It's important to me."

Drinn smiled dryly. "We shall see how long that endearing concern lasts."

....

Words Unspoken

"Magic is a conversation held between the magus and the universe. This conversation, like any, is centered around a *motivation* nestled inside a cocoon of specialized vibrations that we call *Words*. The hidden motivation behind this conversation might be to increase knowledge or spread disinformation. It could be to alter perception, or force change. Perhaps it is a conversation of loneliness for connection. There are Words that drain all will away, or enflame in someone such passionate ire that they would be inclined towards violence against the next person they see. There are Words that comfort the mind like a mother's touch. There are Words that overcome reason to banish fear. There are Words that paralyze all senses. Words that kill."

"You can kill someone with a single Word?" Melvin asked, in awe.

"Yes. Killing is very easy."

"How?"

Drinn smiled grimly. "I knew you would ask me that. Why do the young have such morbid curiosity? I was the same way when I was your age."

Melvin shrugged. "*I'm just curious,*" he muttered.

"Of course. What are some ways that I could kill you? Well, for starters I could convince your blood that it is boiling away into steam, or shrink your bones to the size they were when you were first born. I could cripple your heart with longing, stop your breath with sudden fear, or say those terrible Words I know that would cause the underside of your skin to long with such ardor for the feeling of sunlight that your flesh would burst and invert itself."

"You know all those True Names?" Melvin piped up, his voice cracking in the highest register.

Drinn cracked his knuckles and smiled. "Most of them, and many more. You will never know what I do and do not know, because that is part of the secret that keeps me safe from you."

Melvin stared, and said nothing. His hands felt clammy, and he wiped them on his shirt.

"But there are more important Words than those. Words that draw night crawlers up out of the soil to bait a fishing hook. Words that purify water, mend cloth, and inspire helpful dreams. Those are the sort of Words that I will be teaching you to begin with."

"How is it more helpful to summon a worm than to be able to convince someone to turn inside out and explode?"

Drinn chuckled. "Because we get hungry a few times each day, but very rarely have to explode people. If you find that you are exploding people so regularly that it becomes more useful than fishing, I promise you: wrong life path. And likely well on your way to ending up partially dissolved and haunting a lake, like that poor cursed woman. What you call 'reality' does not take kindly to magi enacting such violent fantasies."

"What do you mean, Kinnari? I thought a magus could do whatever they want."

"Well... yes and no." Drinn sighed. "The more fluent you are in your understanding of the language of creation, the more complex conversations between you and the universe can become. An evolving vocabulary expands communication, at least up to a point. But in conversation, it is not just what you are able to say that matters. It is also *how* you say it, and why, and who or what you are trying to convince. The more extreme your proposal is, the more it is likely to fail."

"So, like... if I enchant someone lonely into falling in love with me, it works easily because he was already wishing for love?"

Drinn arched an eyebrow.

"...Or she. He or she: them. You know what I mean."

"Yes. That is an easy example. The closer the suggestion is to what the heart is already secretly longing for, the less resistance there will be. It's like being a merchant that is always trying to sell something to everyone who passes his stall. An apple vends itself to a hungry mouth, but if you try to convince a man that his dead and buried wife needs new jewelry, you are in for a very hard sell."

Melvin laughed. "Noted."

"And this is not just convincing people that I am talking about here. A magus can be in communication with *everything*, so long as they understand the hidden meanings of the Word that describes it. Your familiarity with stone is the reason that you are able to speak its True Name in a way that excites it enough to answer. Years of working with stone allowed you to delve into the nuances of its fundamental nature. Your hands were intimate with its contours; your mind was aware of the slow flow hidden inside of what appears to be an unmoving solid mass. When we are ignorant of something, our instinct is to disregard it. That is how something like war becomes possible. It is only terrible ignorance that allows a person to look at someone who is so inherently similar to themselves and imagine they are different enough to become an enemy.

"Did you know there are no True Names that describe different appearances amongst the same grouping of things? For instance, there is no Word that segregates between basalt and granite, or granite and obsidian. There are only Names for differences that separate types of things so completely that the *things themselves* understand how different they are. Animals are the same way. There is only one True Name that describes the animal family that includes the weasel, ferret, the martin and the stoat. Though they seem to be different types of animals, in the beginning, when they were first Named, they were the same. Only time, distance and temperament have altered them from one another.

"Humans are the same: exactly the same. We pretend we are segregated from each other by how much sun we are exposed to while growing up, or what part of which island of rock we have evolved on. But the truth is that none of that matters in the slightest. Our differences are only as deep as the stories we tell ourselves. There is just one True Name for the peoples known as Humanus: Orlŭk or Erdin; Rhymira; Dekai — all the same. One Word. Ramini; Dyleet; the Seth... even the Delvin and Gree: one Word. Children of the sea, or stone, or iron. Children of fire, children of mist. The Broken People. The Forgotten People: one True Name. All the same people, according to the Immortal that first named them."

"What about the Mŭrian? I noticed they didn't get mentioned in your list."

"The Mŭrian are... different. They are the only children of Mab, and their True Name is still hidden from me. I'm not sure it is known amongst the race of Humanus at all."

"Ah. Maybe they don't have one?"

"Of course they do."

"Do I?"

"...Yes. Sort of. Each individual has their own True Name in a way, and even casual knowledge of that name grants an extraordinary amount of power over the person it belongs to. But it is not an Immortal Name, per se — more like the summary of secrets that are held inside the heart. A name that is grown over time as an accounting for the effort of each life. Do you understand?"

"I'm not sure."

"It's a lot to take in. I can see that from the look on your face."

Melvin shook his head. "Actually, I was just stifling a yawn."

Drinn rolled his eyes.

"How do I know what my own True Name is?"

"You will know when you find it. One way or another, someone will call you by that name, and you will feel inside of yourself how wonderful and dangerous it is to be *known* like that. Or you will grow old and die without ever having it spoken aloud, and the lack of hearing it will hollow you out. I honestly don't know which is worse. But I've spent most of my life avoiding attachments to people, as you likely will too. For a magus, your True Name is something that must be guarded like the most precious treasure. It is the secret inside your own story — far more personal than a key is to a lock, but almost as easy to steal for someone who knows how to look for it."

....

As the morning dwindled towards afternoon, the wind picked up. All around them, the wild grasses leaned and trembled. Little white-capped waves crawled across the surface of the lake. A cold breeze moaned between the barrow mounds with such insistence that Drinn and Melvin retreated into their tent. There they sat and tried to talk over the sound of the canvas tent walls lufting and the wind-rattled ropes.

"Before you wandered onto a tangent, you were talking about the True Name for stone." Melvin enquired. "I think you were attempting to make a point that I missed. Can you try again?"

Drinn had spent the better part of a few minutes struggling to boil some water for tea, but had given up when the wind whipped the flames of their little campfire dangerously close to the tent walls. Grumbling, Drinn drank the tepid water. Little bits of unboiled tea leaves could be seen hidden between his teeth as he spoke.

"Yes, I was indeed making a point: one that I felt rather succinctly connected the complexity of human folly to the simplicity of stone. As I said, for all of our presumed differences, there is only one Word that describes *humans*. Yet there are *two* True Names for stone, because they have fundamental differences between them. One names a type of stone that was once the liquid blood of the planet itself. Cooled and hardened, or hot and flowing; it knows what it is, and where it came from. The other is the name that describes a stone formed from compressed layers of silt, dead plants, pulverized animal skeletons, and incredible pressure. This type of stone is like a book in which the history of immense time can be read. Both of those two True Names for stone contain great reverence for that difference, although to the untrained ear, they sound like the same wor-."

"You are saying there is another True Name for stone besides *EBE-*"

Drinn reached out and backhanded Melvin across the mouth. Melvin cried out in pain, reeling backwards and holding his face. Drinn glared.

"Listen, you little *kae kefe*, and understand: you never, *ever* say the True Names out loud, unless you absolutely have to! Not without protective measures in place. Don't be a damn fool, child: there are ears everywhere."

"Well why the *skabde muli* didn't you start out by saying THAT in the first place, you giant walking shit?! How about: 'Hey kid, before I waste your whole morning ranting about how dumb humanity can be, I should mention first that in this magic training class we aren't ever going to be able to <u>actually</u> say any magic words?' Dammit, Drinn, that *hurt!*" Melvin's eyes reddened with unshed tears, and he sucked painfully on his lower lip.

Drinn leaned back on his heels, and clicked his tongue thoughtfully. He closed his eyes and didn't respond.

"And what in the hells did you mean by *'there are ears everywhere'*? We are alone on the shore of an empty lake. You said so yourself: this place is cursed and abandoned. There aren't even turtles or frogs or... whatever the hell else, because the lake gets hungry and *eats* them, right? So who would be listening out here?"

Drinn opened his eyes and frowned. "I think we need to start over and try this in a different way."

Then he stretched his mouth open wide. His jaw trembled like the muzzle of a cat when it is watching a dancing moth, and a thin warbling cry crept plaintively out of his open throat. Behind that sound was a Word, but darkness rushed all around it and the sound of the Word was lost. Blackness swirled across Melvin like a curtain drawn suddenly, and he felt no more.

....

Melvin Shares a Dream

He is gone. And I am alone.

{ No. You are not alone. Focus. }

He is gone. I am not alone, *and the dead are rising.*

*{ Is this real? Or am I unconscious, surrounded
by a circle of cut pine branches? }*

*The dead are here. This is what we are facing.
This is what the training is for.*

{ Focus. Doesn't matter if this is real or not: energy is real on both sides of Dream. That's what counts. Focus on your senses. Where are we? The story just finished; now the battle is coming. Just as Drinn wanted. I feel… an unnatural cold pushing up from underground.   }

{   I can hear...   }

∞∞∞∞∞∞∞∞∞∞∞∞∞∞∞∞∞∞∞∞

I can hear the brambles crackling; of course I do. I don't need to look for them in the dark; I know their shapes well enough without light to see them by. They are the dead soldiers Talara's scary story was about. We have camped amongst their barrow mounds, guaranteeing that we are surrounded and outnumbered. We did that on purpose.

No: Drinn did that to us on purpose.

I don't know how much of Talara's story is true and how much she made up. I guess it doesn't matter after all. Were the dead summoned to us by their own story being told? I should have warned her about the skabde barrow mounds. Godsdamn me for the idiot I must be.

My head pounds as I cradle it between my knees, the pulsing pressure of my own blood disrupting my thoughts. My Kinnari is dead — devoured by the lake, and his protections are broken. We may be trapped in Mathias' mind forever now. We could die and be dragged down into a dream of earth. Drinn, you valea muli! You haven't taught me yet how to get out of a dream once I am stuck inside it!

Focus, Melvin. Head up and look around. Focus. Remember what you are here for. Use your magic to keep your friends alive.

∞∞∞∞∞∞∞∞∞∞∞∞∞∞∞∞∞∞∞∞∞

The Shamblemen are tunneling up out of their burial mounds like maggots wriggling free from a carcass. At first, I try to explode them the same way I blew up the imaginary rocks with such ease on the patchwork mountainside of my own dreamscape. But here in Mathias' dream, my imaginary magic is as useful as imagining it won't really hurt if those un-dead soldiers get their hands on me. So I lean into what I already know, and whisper the True Name for stone. The sound of EBEN cracks a fissure open underfoot that a Shambleman shambles right into, sinking up to the knees. A good start! I fold the Word shut in my mouth with a sound like folding paper, and the ground closes up again around its skeletal legs.

At first the undead is pinned, and I begin to turn away in satisfaction. Then I see it dig sharp finger bones into the soil and wrench itself apart at the torso. It begins dragging its remaining upper half towards me. Not good. I believe I have the power to swallow them all back into the earth, but not the power to keep them there. I need to come up with something better, quickly. But there is only one other Word that I know; a Word that Drinn instructed me to never say out loud, unless I was here, in Dream. The True Name for Change.

∞∞∞∞∞∞∞∞∞∞∞∞∞∞∞∞∞∞∞∞∞

I have never spoken to fire before. It does not listen easily; it is reckless and full of hunger. Unlike stone or water, it does not long to remember where it came from. Fire wishes for nothing but to spread and transmute everything it touches into heat and light. It is creation that consumes; al ways hungry — always wanting. Yet promises can be offered as long as they are promptly kept, for fire knows its life is as short as opportunity and kindling. I raise my arms and make the only offering I have; I offer air, and plenty of it. I speak aloud the Word for change — that Word which might convince the fire that, for a minute, it can ride on the back of the wind.

The campfire lifts up from the ground with a rush of delight. A small tornado of fire spirals towards the sky. It is an incredible sight.

There are no descriptions for what bending a twisting inferno of fiery wind with only your own will is like, as nothing I can say will come close to exalting it. It is a painful ecstasy of exchange — like bargaining for wings by selling your own heart. The enormity of speaking in the Immortal language empties the air from my lungs until my heart feels like a wet rope lashing against my ribs. As the dead men stumble towards me, I roll the cyclone of fire onto them and they are lapped up by that coiling tongue of flame.

{   PLEASE WAKE UP   }

Who was calling out? My attention snaps back to the moment. There was a voice, calling from a long way off. A large fox with lavender fur darts across the edge of firelight and disappears between the trees. There are others here; yes. I was so focused on my magic, I forgot about them.

{   help us   }

Across the clearing, my friends battle the revenants for me. Mathias and Caetal fight back-to-back; Caetal crushes one with a flaming log that is as big as his leg. I think he is grinning, but it might be a grimace. Mathias is also brandishing a burning branch. Yet even through the shimmering air I can tell that something is wrong with his arm; his face is sweat-soaked and wracked with pain. Talara races by with Caetal's huge crossbow slung across her shoulder and a dead man on her heels. Tarquin and Rahyn are nowhere to be seen, but I can hear Tarquin swearing as he is dragged down-hill towards the lake. Then the rush and roar of the fire becomes so loud I can barely hear anything else anymore.

{   help   }

That voice again, but this time so faint that it's easy to ignore.

And yet, from far off — a sound that shouldn't be there. It shivers through me, disrupting my concentration. A ululating cry rippling across the clearing, low and old; a Word that agitates the grasses around us. The slithering clatter of blackberry vines can be heard crawling all over each other, chittering madly when the thorns snag. They stretch towards us, pouring over the mossy boulders. I cannot move from where I am sitting; my godsdamn legs don't work here. I am as immobile as any plant should be; how is it fair that I sit still while the vines advance? The dead live again, here; plants wander towards me, animated by the haunting sound that cried out from the empty darkness of this starless night. When everything that should stay still is moving, who is left to be punished with rooted pa-ralysis? Only me.

A branch constricts around my leg, its thorny tendrils tear at my skin. And when I look down, it is no plant at all but the upper half of a leering corpse with vines bursting through its mouth and eyes; fingers half-digested into time-sharpened claws. The Shambleman whose legs I trapped in the earth. Those bone claws bury themselves up to the first knuckle in my leg. I do not feel it, of course — but it's easy to imagine how much it would hurt. I scream; I can't help it. Concentration shatters; magic scatters.

The fire goes out.

∞ ∞ ∞ ∞ ∞ ∞ ∞ ∞ ∞ ∞ ∞ ∞ ∞ ∞ ∞ ∞ ∞

We Are Awake?

The morning had aged into afternoon; the wind picked up. All around the two of them, wild grasses bent and shook. The breeze that bowed the grasses also wrinkled the water on the lake, until everything looked like it was crawling. Tendrils of chill mist poured between the hill mounds, dampening everything. Drinn and Melvin retreated into their tent. There they sat and tried to hear one another over the sound of the canvas tent walls flapping.

"Before you wandered onto a tangent, you were talking about the True Name for stone." Melvin enquired.

Drinn stared searchingly at him.

"*I think you were...*" Melvin trailed off. He stared at his hands where they were sitting in his lap. His fingers flexed and uncurled as though he was moving them. His cheeks were hot. They felt like they ought to be stinging, but it didn't seem important. "I, uh... believe you were attempting to create a teachable example that I missed. Can you try again?"

There was a teacup in Drinn's hands now. He sipped from it.

"Yes, I suppose I must have been. To be honest, most magicians never create a single useful thing in their lifetimes. Although the public may see us drawing a flame out of empty air, we didn't actually *create* the flame. We just reminded the various gasses in the air about their own inherent combustion potential. Put simply: we *excited it.* See how the air itself seeks us out now, as we discuss it."

As Drinn spoke, mist was pouring through the tent flap. Within moments, the two of them seemed to be submerged in a puddle of chilly fog, so that only Drinn's torso could be seen. The tips of his mouth wandered across his jaw, but his eyes seemed thoughtful.

Melvin blinked rapidly. He was supposed to say something now: a question that connected to *before.* But the only thing he could think of was the word ROCK carved in large stone letters. He imagined the letters falling into a heap, then rapidly growing moss.

"What about a rock that started out as the word for *rock*, but was changed into another word? ...You know: by magic."

Drinn sighed out of his fuzzy, wiggly face. "I think you aren't ready for this."

Melvin tried to frown. "I'm not sure what you mean by 'not ready' — you're the one who looks weird. Your face is wandering all over the place, not mine. Have you always had a mouth for eyebrows?"

"You're probably right." Drinn said through the thicket of his teeth. "I wasn't prepared enough for this either. I got distracted and forgot about the topic of stone entirely. Let's call this one a practice round."

Blackness again.

∞∞∞∞∞∞∞∞∞∞∞∞∞∞∞∞∞∞∞∞∞

There was a wind outside that chased all the mist indoors. Fog lay all over the ground like a rug, but nobody seemed to mind. Drinn had a fire going in a large bowl that the swirling vapor rug was being very polite around. There was a tea kettle bobbing on the flames like a drifting boat.

"Tea?" Drinn asked, out of his very normal face.
"Yes, please." Melvin replied. "Thank you Xôr-Drinn."
Drinn paled with shock. "How did you know that name?"

Melvin didn't know what his own face looked like, but he assumed it was less surprised looking than Drinn's.

Melvin spoke carefully: "I don't know what you are asking, Kinnari. Is this guessing game part of the magic training?"

Drinn chuckled dismissively, but his eyes were cold and searching. He had a plain face, no doubt about that: strangely plain. *But the eyes are wrong, Melvin thought to himself. I should never forget that this mist likely flowed out of his eyes. It's good not to be too trusting with someone who can do that.*

"There was a question you were asking me, Melvin. Can you remember what it was? Something about stone; something you were curious about."
Melvin blinked twice. "...What... oh. What about a rock that started out as one type of rock, but was changed into another type by heat and force? Does that have its own True Name?"
Drinn nodded appreciatively. "A very good question! How does my face look?"
Melvin considered for a moment, taking his tea cup in his hand and sniffing at it. The tea smelled like nothing.

"Your face?"
"Yes."

They were both seated cross-legged; mist flowed over their legs like water, as though they were sitting in a bath of liquid air. The sky was also an enormous tent, but Drinn's face looked reassuringly unremarkable.

"Your face looks like it suits you."
"Great!" Drinn said, rubbing his hands together. "Glad that's sorted! The answer to your question is no, but also yes; a single Word that you will use as a magus more than any other. I'm going to write it out for you once, but I don't want you to repeat it quite yet, even in your own mind. Just let it drift by you; a leaf borne aloft on the wind of recall, one amongst many. A part of it will remain with you, of course. But in the art of thieving Words, such as I am beginning to attempt to teach you, a True Name must first be glanced at very casually from the side of your eye. It is only a reflection in the mirror of your interest. The Word cannot know that you intend to catch ahold of it. Do you understand, Thief?"

Melvin shrugged.

"This word is summarized — or more accurately bastardized — in our language as the word *change*. Contained in the True Name for change are elements of risk and reward that motivate all of conscious life towards the radical act of evolution. It describes the streak of inventive madness that transforms a flower into a fruit and compels an otherwise contented caterpillar to spin a cocoon, where it will digest itself into liquid and re-imagine itself as something that flies. And why does it do this? Why does *anything* risk obliterating everything it is, and ever has been, to become something new and unexplored?"

Drinn raised his hands to the canvas sky in a wide gesture that seemed to welcome in all of the weirdness of creation. Then he leaned in closer and whispered:
"Look closely at the wall of the tent."

Melvin looked. There was something there: a Word. For a moment it was painted by tendrils of fog; another moment it was stitched into lines of canvas thread. *LËTH.* Then it vanished again, and Melvin was staring at a rippling shadow.

"Yes: you saw it. The True Name that describes a powerful ambition to reinvent for the sake of reinvention. Because life itself is restless, and death seems so unbearably still. It is the most dangerous of the stolen Words, and the Word that humanity still pays the highest price to handle. Even here in this tent, I hum it softly and insincerely in the back of my throat, but I dare not intone it aloud with any depth of intention, for I do not wish to be overheard speaking the name of the Immortal responsible for the creation of all the races of Humanus."

Melvin nodded mutely. The Word *LËTH* reared up inside his mind, but he did his best to trample over it with a crude line from the song *Blow-Tarry-Blow* that Talara had taught him:

Yet how could she marry / a thing that's so hairy / when all that she wanted / was a taste of his-

"Wait, hold on: back up a moment. I thought caterpillars turned into butterflies so they could mate? That doesn't sound like some great mysterious guiding force to me." Melvin asked.

Drinn dropped his arms and exhaled for a moment, visually deflating. Then he sighed.

"Yes, that too, of course. Almost everything in the natural world is obsessed with reproducing itself. It is a predictable and somewhat tedious subtext to just about any story. But that is a lesson we will discuss more when you are, uh — a bit older."

"Or not at all. The mating urges of insects is not a topic I'm keen to explore." Melvin imagined himself blushing, and it annoyed him.

"Nor I in teaching about it." Drinn muttered, sounding relieved. "In fact, I think we strayed too far off topic, let's reset and try this one again."

"No, no thank you," Melvin said quickly. "I appreciated what you said. Whatever is going on here-"

(Melvin gestured broadly around at the improbably enormous / totally reasonable tent)

"-is fine with me. Really. Let's continue "

{ the alternative is jarring sudden darkness,
and conflicting fragments of memory }

"-with the lesson. Tell me more about anything. I don't mind if it jumps around — you are doing a fine job, Kinnari. I'm a hard pupil to teach. I don't expect you to be perfect at it."

Drinn smiled, looking a bit sheepish. "Alright then. Let us proceed, if you are ready."

It was one of the only times that Melvin was to ever see him look like that, and he knew it was something scarcity made precious. So Melvin tucked the memory into his tea cup and drank it down warm.

∞∞∞∞∞∞∞∞∞∞∞∞∞∞∞∞∞∞∞∞∞∞

Wind rattles the tent. Nothing smells like anything. There is mist everywhere below the waist, and Melvin ignores his crossed legs, because sensing they aren't real makes him sad. *WHAT IS REAL?* Sits up in his mind, begging for the treat of attention. Melvin ignores it. Drinn is talking again, speaking carefully out of a very ordinary face.

"Let us take a moment to clarify what I mean when I am teaching you about the use of magic. 'Magic' is a word that we magi use to describe the purposeful manipulation of energetic forces. Many of those forces are *exterior* to our perception of ourselves — meaning, of course, outside of what we call 'our body.' And yet, our bodies are like our world itself in miniature, just like any child resembles its parent. Protective skin layer over productive core, heated blood, energetic field, blisters and blemishes: the list goes on and on. All of it animated and alive because of the existence of energy and water. And surrounding everything — vast amounts of empty space. We are like the planet and the whole sky too, but flipped inside out; the empty space is inside of us."

Melvin looked at him thoughtfully. "Do you mean, like... loneliness?"

Drinn began a reply, then stopped. He clucked his tongue against his teeth and closed his eyes for a moment. "Hm. I'm not sure I have an answer for that, but it is an interesting thought. No, I meant that the body is made up of a vast array of tiny parts, and there is a lot of empty space between them. Imagine it like you are a creature made out of animated grains of sand, but that the space between each grain is almost unthinkably vast. You would never know it to look at yourself, of course, but our limited perception of ourselves is part of what we magi struggle to overcome.

"The first time I learned to evaporate with magic, it was entirely because the magi who taught me insisted that I accept the insane idea that my body is made almost entirely out of empty space miraculously attracted to itself *energetically*. Just like an *idea*; do you get what I'm saying? I didn't believe my Kinnari for a long time either. I couldn't; it was too strange of a thought. But one night I got drunk enough to accept almost anything might be possible, and before I knew it, I folded inside out and was wandering through Void. It was terrifying. It still is, every time."

"Who taught you to do magic?"

"Nobody 'does' magic. Magic does them."

Melvin waited for an answer to the question, but it was not forthcoming.

"So: yes. Where was I? Oh yes: the Void. Fundamentally, your body is exactly as void of matter as is the sky, as I said. You are, literally, a tiny universe that tells the visual story of a solid mass of living, breathing matter. A perceptual illusion — a reflection of the underlying intelligence of structure that some part of the unknowingly magnificent energy field of life took an interest in. I used to think that things were separate from one-another: each one itself, and not another thing. That a unique finger-print of carbon and energy somehow *clarified* a being from its surround-ings. I imagined the walls of selfhood as impermeable. I know better now.

"The recipe for life is insanely complex. Like anything 'magical' it is very difficult to describe in a way that makes any rational sense, because the more encompassing the description of a living organism becomes, the more fundamentally unbelievable it ought to be."

Melvin nodded slowly, his gaze following the drifting fog. Drinn glanced at him warily, but continued.

"I know I'm repeating myself a bit, but I find that simple metaphors and some repetition help large concepts become more digestible. So here is another one: imagine your body is one unimaginably long road, but all of the cobblestones are constantly being taken out and replaced. From one day to the next, it *looks* like the same road, but, in fact, is constantly changing. Those tiny little cobblestones that make up 'you' are being snatched away all the time, but are rapidly replaced by others. The inher-ent intelligence of your body is what enables the shape of you to remain in a recognizable pattern year after year. As the years pass and the story of your body changes, you might gain or lose some features like hair, fat, mobility — even the color of your eyes and skin will change. But it is still, incredibly, you. The idea of physical form is nature's most persistent fantasy.

"That said, for the sake of magical work, I have found that it helps to simplify the perception of the self into something more solid. I don't know about you, but thinking about all that empty space in my own body tends to give me the creeping heebies."

"Not me. I don't mind thinking about it. *I could drift around weightless inside the wind.*" Melvin mumbled, his eyes still following the drifting mist. Drinn didn't seem to hear him, so he spoke up louder.

"Kinnari: could you teach me the True Name for wind?"

Drinn shook his head. "I don't know it. It is very difficult to find the True Name for something that is always changing unpredictably. It may have one True Name or many — I've never found any. In fact, I've only ever met one man who knew the Name of the wind, and it was a long time ago in a different land. But I was a different person back then too."

"Younger?"

"That as well." Drinn sighed. He seemed about to stand up, then changed his mind and shifted his legs into a new position.

"Let's get to the point. Wind is empty, yet full. So are you. Only a fundamental knowledge of all the empty space inside of you allows you to walk through the dreams of others, and is half of the state of mind necessary for evaporative travel across long distances."

"You are going to teach me to walk through dreams?!" Melvin gasped excitedly, snapping his focus back.

Drinn blinked, looking vaguely confused. "Yes of course. I have to. Didn't I mention this already? The majority of all of your magical training will be done inside your mind while you are sleeping. You will join me in a prepared dreamscape, and there I shall teach you how to engage in what we magi call *liminal lucidity*. Within a dream, we will be able to discuss True Names more safely, without the waking world eavesdropping. Until my tower is built and we can shelter inside the protective wards I will place on it, dream-walking is the least dangerous way for you to train."

"Least dangerous?"

Drinn glanced away. "Well, yes. Nothing comes without some risk in life, particularly for a magus. Within the dr-"

"We are still in danger inside a dream?" Melvin interrupted.

"Of course." Drinn stared pointedly at Melvin. "The realms of Dream are vast, but the Immortals roam freely through them. Their servants do likewise. But within my dreamscape, or a shared one, the reverberations of discussing True Names at least won't be overheard by the Fýrii or any other self-appointed meddlers on Eld."

"I'm... not sure I want to ask what dangers a dream can contain. I'm guessing nightmares are the least of it."

"Yes and no. In a certain sense more 'no' than 'yes', because actually almost all the danger in Dream is nightmares, the same way that almost all the danger in sailing comes from the ocean itself. But there are other types of danger traveling through Dream. Sudden storms, or places of terrible emptiness, so bleakly still that they can starve your mind into madness, like a ship becalmed on a windless ocean long enough that all the sailors onboard it starve. There are nightmares that are burrowing worms that eat their way between worlds, infecting your waking thoughts. Living nightmares that serve those powers that rule in Dream; Immortals, Ethereal Specters, that sort of thing. But I probably shouldn't be telling you most of this. It's best for you to learn for yourself what can be avoided, and what must be defended against. And of course: when to flee. That is the most important lesson of all."

Melvin shivered once, like a horse shaking off flies. For a while he said nothing, staring at his crossed legs.

"Dammit. We are inside a dream already, aren't we? I was hoping this was real — that I was really sitting like this; that I could sit cross-legged again. I hate remembering that I can't."

"Very perceptive. I would have thought the sky-high tent ceiling would have given it away sooner."

Melvin shrugged self-consciously. "For some reason I just accepted it."

Drinn smiled. "Dreams are like that."

"So, what... you knocked me unconscious? Because I certainly don't remember going to sleep."

"Almost nobody remembers falling asleep once they are inside of their own dream."

"I'm pretty sure it was late morning when we entered this tent in the real world, and I've never been much of an afternoon napper."

"*But was it late morning though?*" Drinn smiled smugly, folding his arms across his chest.

Melvin looked carefully around himself for the first time. His eyes followed the tent ropes that snaked all the way up to vast arc of the canvas sky. The stars were star-shaped holes punched through the canvas. There was a dull red light shining from somewhere behind them. Out the flap of the tent door, the barrow mounds rolled away from view, bobbing slowly like swells in the ocean. The drifting mist covered everything else he could see.

"Drinn, come on: tell me the truth. Did you hit me over the head or something? Am I, like... laying on an altar somewhere, all stretched out and bleeding? Because this is *not* my dream, I can feel it. I think if it was, I would have noticed it sooner. I don't dream like this. I mostly dream in words and colors. Sometimes feelings. We are in *your* dream, aren't we?"

Drinn sighed. "Dammit Melvin. You are making a difficult thing harder. Ok fine: I knocked you out with magic. And yes, your body is lying on an altar-like camping table. I won't have a proper altar until the tower gets furnished, so I'm working with what I've got."

Melvin chortled. "An *'altar-like camping table'*? Hahaha!"

Drinn frowned. "And yes, you are in *my* dream. Your father couldn't pay me enough to go wandering around through the dreamscape of a thirteen-year-old! I have some idea what is down there in that swamp of puberty. I'm sure we'd encounter all kinds of embarrassments."

Melvin folded his arms and glared. "Oh ya? Like what? There's nothing wrong with my dreams."

Drinn raised an eyebrow and shrugged. "Hmm. Well then: apparently another thing to discuss when you are a bit older."

∞∞∞∞∞∞∞∞∞∞∞∞∞∞∞∞∞∞∞∞

Melvin awoke amongst a scattering of bread crumbs and kipper smear. His face felt tender, and his back was cramping from hours lying flat on wooden planks. He rolled over and irritably brushed some freshly clipped pine boughs off the table that seemed to be encircling him. From a half-seated position, he could see a few other spell-casting implements arranged nearby: a silver chalice; a mirror of blackened glass; a golden coin with a hole drilled through the center of it. The sun was bright on his skin, but his shirt was clammy with sweat.

He rolled to the other side, and was unsurprised to see Drinn blowing steam off a tea cup. A more alarming sight was a dagger that rested on the oak table planks in front of him. The blade was polished copper, and twisted back and forth towards the tip like the body of a snake.

"My head hurts, Drinn."

"It's *Kinnari-Drinn* to you, Thief."

"Is that knife there to finish me off?"

"I cut those tree boughs with it, and also bread. I'm going to try not to stab you until my tower is done. Want breakfast?"

"Sure. I still can't believe you knocked me out and left me on a picnicking table. That's cold, Kinnari. Even for you."

Drinn chuckled. "Tonight, you can have a blanket."

....

Tarquin in the Dream

We heard them coming before we saw them, but not soon enough. How could we have known what we were hearing, and what it meant? The wet furrowing of earth under bone fingers. The muted clanking of rusted metal dragged up from underground. Rain-rotted leaves overturned in pulpy sheets, sliding off the rising red earth pushed up from below. The crackling sound of undergrowth was suddenly all around us. I should have smelled their decay before the fire lit the shape of their shambling bones, but I couldn't seem to smell anything.

{ *I should be able to smell.* }

They are everywhere; clawing up out of those low mounds. Barrow mounds. Beneath where the berries grew, beneath the carpet of wildflowers.

They are closing in on all sides, and we can hear the awful, mossy grinding they make: bones rubbing bones with nothing gentle between them. And inside of that sound: a keening wail like wind blowing through shattered rock. Whatever terrible will is holding them together causes their teeth to grind ceaselessly; their eyes burn with black fire. Something flutters and thrums inside the empty cavity of their ribs. They drag themselves against us in a tangle of disparate motion, swinging broken swords with graceless, jarring force. They are terrifying, but as hollowed out as gutted candles: as if the dead men's shadows are trapped inside them, tugging on the strings of marionettes built of their own bones.

I wish that I could say that I was the first to notice them, but I wasn't even close. I suspect Rahyn felt them coming before any of us; she is gone, I know not where, yet I am keenly aware of the lack of her. Melvin is slumped by the fire, his head cradled in shock between his knees. He mumbles words to himself that sound like prayer, but the air is popping and crackling around him. Caetal rises to his feet with a burning log hefted in his hands, and his back to the blinding firelight. Someone is running — was that Talara? Her cloak is in a pile on her sleeping roll, with her shawm laid across it. Mathias stands up slowly, staring at something that stirs in the lake behind us. He clutches the iron symbol of Cuthain in his hand so hard his knuckles whiten. I can hear him praying, but the words seem uncertain. They flutter slowly out of him in an oddly unhurried way. Time is elastic now.

**{ *How do I know this? Is there anything else*
to compare time to except itself? }**

The drawing-in moment fills like a bladder stretching, until the insistence of it, the impeding weight of it, pushes every other distraction out of its way. The moment stretches out until it ruptures, then all other moments that were crowded out come rushing back into the space it filled so fast that I barely notice them passing.

I rise to my feet with my wooden sword in hand. I wish I could have imagined something better to brandish, but I can't seem to. I can see fearful disbelief on the faces of my friends — these people I am beginning to love so much there has become little room in my heart for anything else — and I can't help but wonder if that is all I am good for. I have big dreams, and I love my friends dearly, but I'm worried I'm making everything else up as I go. The wooden sword feels as flimsy as a twig in my hand, so I reach for my dagger. But when I draw it from the sheath on my belt, the blade is also carved of wood. I know then, for certain, that I will never be any good at killing. Not even in a dream.

But the moments before the fight have stretched as far as they can. Then they burst, and the undead are everywhere.

∞∞∞∞∞∞∞∞∞∞∞∞∞∞∞∞∞∞∞∞

The Shamblemen heave themselves into me; a tangle of rusty blades and crusty bones. I think I block one, maybe more — I'm stabbing out so quickly I can't tell. My wooden sword and dagger clatter across metal, and when they hit bone it's as useless as trying to saw tree branches with a buttering knife. Something freezing grabs my throat, and I fling my arm into a rib cage and push back hard. My wooden waster is torn from my hand, and all I know, all I have room left to be, is a frantic wrenching of my living muscles against cold bones. I do not mean to leave the light of the fire behind, but I am suddenly running, dragging a few of the Shamblemen along with me. I tear at them as they tear at me — I have no idea how many I'm fighting at once; in the darkness, they are a puzzle of branching bones that I am dragging down towards the lake.

They are wrapped around me now, squeezing my living breath out through my lungs, as numbing cold clenches at my guts. I thrash and roll over, slipping in the rain-soft earth until I skid to a stop near the edge of the lake. There is a sudden roar of crackling light uphill behind me; our simple campfire spirals up into a tornado of flame. Wavering light splinters across every ripple in the water, and I can see the old boat dock clearly now, and the pale tower that looms on the island at the center of the lake.

Back at the campfire, someone is screaming. I begin to panic —

{ I should have protected them / I should have died defending them / I never should have left / What am I doing here? }

— and for a moment everything tilts, and I recall myself.

∞∞∞∞∞∞∞∞∞∞∞∞∞∞∞∞∞∞∞∞∞

{ I wonder if the rest of them remember they are in Dream? It doesn't matter if this is some magical nightmare or not, because my gut tells me we can all still die in here, and I trust my gut more than I trust Drinn. His eyes are too bright to belong to that empty face of his. If he is still in here, there are more monsters inside this dream than are attacking me right now. ...Whoops! I'm in the middle of a fight! Silly Tarquin, pay attention before you get yourself }

—killed. I manage to pry one of the dead Shamblemen loose and trample him underfoot, and something sharp cuts my leg badly enough to send me spinning. My feet are pounding across the soft rot of the wooden dock with only one undead soldier still holding onto me. Abruptly, a second figure rises up to my left out of the high grass at the shoreline. Then I hear the snap and thrum of a crossbow firing, and the dead man slams against me. A hot pain leaps inside my lungs, and I am suddenly connected chest to chest to the thrashing corpse by a shaft of wood that has pierced us both. My feet slip out from under me, and the Shambleman and I fall together into the lake.

{ Oh crap. Was that Drinn? Maybe he overheard me thinking rude things about him... Can he do that in here? That's not good. ...Shit, I got distracted again. I think I'm beginning to drown. It feels just as terrible as I can imagine it feeling. Entirely the same — }

Black water closes over both of us.

∞∞∞∞∞∞∞∞∞∞∞∞∞∞∞∞∞∞∞∞∞

The Patchwork Mountain

"The realm of Dream is an unimaginably vast and ever-changing landscape, and godsdamn tricky to describe. Already I have misled you in the attempt. For, of course, it is not *unimaginably* anything — every wisp and thread of it has been imagined by someone, or how else could it have gotten there? And to describe the realm as *a landscape* is also misleading, for although much of it is clothed in a terrestrial guise and masked by the pretense of horizon, it is more accurate to think of it as something which stretches out fluidly in all conceivable directions. Like an enormous tapestry, where each thread is the landscape of an individual dreamer — a ragged tapestry with constant revision, as threads are yanked out and replaced. And it is a tapestry that fills every inch of the sky, ground, and deep realms beneath."

"Wow!" Melvin breathed.

"Well, actually it's more like a blanket of patches, with edges overlapping. Each patch is the temporary worldscape of a dreamer, do you get what I'm saying? But they all interconnect. ...Also, the blanket isn't much of a blanket, because it is not flat at all — I don't want to give you that sort of impression."

"Wha-"

"But a blanket made of fluid: a bulbous, patchy, water-blanket. ...Like cloth seaweed that changes if you look at it too closely, of course, as though it is somehow actually *self-aware*... Dammit, this is a bad metaphor for Dream."

Drinn sighed, and rubbed his hands through his hair in irritation. Melvin smirked contentedly. He lay on the canvas tent floor, belly down with his elbows on the ground and his fists propped up under his chin. The tent was warm and muggy.

"*How does one describe something that is always changing both shape and character?*" Drinn muttered, frowning. "I suppose it makes the most sense to encourage you to imagine it however you want."

Melvin harumphed. "The image of a sky-high mountain of abandoned wet laundry came to my mind, but I'm pretty sure that isn't what you were intending to describe."

"Yes, but the laundry is all loosely sewn together, and keeps tumbling down all over itself in landslides. That's not a bad analogy, actually." Drinn admitted.

"I wish Tarquin were here. He has a great imagination. I bet he could come up with something better than a mountain of wet laundry."

"Well, perhaps we could bring him here and ask him how he would describe it?"

Melvin frowned. "Really?"

"We can circle back around to that idea in a bit. But first, let's return to my patchwork quilt idea, and reimagine it as your laundry mountain. But entirely made up of one enormous patchwork quilt. Let us both focus on that image together. Close your eyes now — yes, right now, Melvin — and picture this place as I describe it to you, down to the smallest details you can imagine. The clearer it is in your mind, the more secure it will be for both of us."

Melvin opened one eye. "Secure? What do you mean?"

"Just shut up for a moment and do what I tell you to do. Not everything can be explained with words. In fact, most of everything can't. Close your eyes. *Both* of them."

Melvin muttered coarsely, and closed his eyes again. Now he could see the red darkness and the tracery of veins on the inside of his eyelids.

"Okay — go ahead, Kinnari. Tell me what to see."

"We are standing on a mountain-"

"Where? At the top?"

"Nowhere near the top. We are on the lower side of the mountain, barely out of the foothills. We are standing on a path that we have been climbing to reach this far. We have stopped here to catch our breath. Below us, stretching out as far as we can imagine—

....

—is the sea. The wind carries the sounds of seabirds; they are soaring amongst a drift of pale clouds. Looking back downhill from this vantage point, the mountain tapers down into foothills that erode into dunes, and those dunes flatten out to a shoreline. The path we stand on is a thin shelf carved into the side of the mountain. We have come here to seek knowledge that is hidden at the mountain's peak, and have been traveling all day. Our packs rest nearby. Yet this is no normal mountain that we are climbing, and no normal expanse of ocean that stretches out before us. It is a patchwork quilt; all of it. This patchwork mountain is a metaphor for the unimaginably expansive interlacing patchwork of the ethereal arenas of individual dreamers. Picture it now, as I describe it to you. For the sake of consistency

between us, let us decide that the patches have some aesthetic sensibility to them — which is often not the case in Dream. Therefore, the patchwork of the mountain is assembled of stony gray fabrics and earth tones, with here and there a tasteful scattering of embroidered flowers. The patchwork of the dunes are a bit more tartan; shades of tan broken up by patterns of green and splashes of yellow that suggest plants are growing. The sea itself—

∞ ∞ ∞ ∞ ∞ ∞ ∞ ∞ ∞ ∞ ∞ ∞ ∞ ∞ ∞ ∞ ∞ ∞ ∞

—undulated in a pastiche patchwork of blues and greens that tumbled into combers of braided silvery ribbon upon the shoreline. Melvin stood on the path with an upraised hand shading his eyes against the glare of an imagined sun, gazing around in wonderment. Behind him, Drinn was seated on a gray lace doily, boulder-big and squatted on the trail. He was wheezing a little, having decided beforehand that he was out of breath from hiking all day. Melvin had forgotten about that prompt, so he felt fine.

For a while the magus and the boy stared out at the landscape of motley cloth, feeling wealthy with pleasure, and saying nothing. The wind tickled at Melvin's hair. He longed for the smell of the ocean, but was disappointed to realize that he couldn't smell anything at all. The place was entirely quiet but for the shushing of the same cloth and ribbon wave rolling over and over again upon the shore (Melvin could not think of any other way to imagine it), the distant cries of sea birds, and the repetition of Drinn's panting.

"I think you would have caught your breath by now. *It's been a while.*" Melvin eventually muttered.

"I suppose so." Drinn admitted, stopping immediately. "I was distracted by the view. We did well, imagining this place together. I was just reminding myself that you are the first person I have shared a dream with in a long time."

Melvin nodded. "You too, for me, but that doesn't count for much. So, this place is inside your head?"

"In yours, actually. I implanted the suggestion; your mind filled in the rest. My patchwork ocean would have had the waves on a rolling rotation that tucked back under themselves after they splashed. Your single repetitive wave is a bit puerile."

Melvin frowned. "I really dislike that word. And this is the first time I've imagined a cloth ocean, so don't be an ass about it — I can fix the waves later. Why are we here? What happens next? What's the point of all this? Are we supposed to climb higher or go down to the shore?"

"If you like." Drinn folded his arms. "Do whatever you want. Go explore. But I've decided I'm still tired from the hike, so I'll stay here."

"How can you be tired from pretending to take a hike you didn't actually take?"

"It's your incessant questions I'm tired of. Go away and play somewhere for a while so I can pretend to nap, will you?"

"Snack on a turd, Kinnari."

Drinn suddenly had a hat, and he pulled the brim of it down over his eyes dismissively and leaned back against the doily boulder with a contented sigh.

"Careful what you imagine here, kid. Stay close to the mountain — I don't want you wandering off the map and slipping into someone else's dream."

∞∞∞∞∞∞∞∞∞∞∞∞∞∞∞∞∞∞∞∞

The best thing for Melvin about hiking up the patchwork mountain was hiking up the patchwork mountain. The incredible enjoyment of using his legs again made every step a skip. Although the path was a trampled gray wool that was as soft as sand underfoot Melvin trotted along it merrily, dragging his feet through the dense wool in exaggerated bounding steps. The winding path steepened as he walked, often only a few precipitous feet wide and boarded on the ocean side with a cliff that plunged away steeper with each step he took. Melvin never ran out of breath, because he refused to imagine himself getting winded. Soon the circling shorebirds were far below him, and the view of the ocean was obscured by passing clouds.

After a while, Melvin stopped to pretend to rest. It seemed as though he was at least a mile above the foothills. The curve of the tartan ocean was dazzling. Shoreline stretched away in both directions as far as sight could tell, with that one single wave flopping and withdrawing from the beach over and over again. Melvin grimaced. It looked even weirder from up here. *I'll do better next time.* He thought to himself. *How else was I supposed to imagine a cloth ocean would tumble into waves? Cloth can't disintegrate and wash away. Only water can do that.*

But he was apparently wrong. For beneath his gaze, the cloth wave sizzled and spread out, foaming and churning like water. The blue dye in the tartan cloth leaked out across the pale tan patches of beach in staining veins. What remained of the wave disintegrated into fragments that were quickly absorbed by the ground. Now the cloth combers were truly rolling in, with each new set churning and degenerating across the tan shore until the length of it became a brackish blackish-teal.

Melvin did not care for the look of it — there was something macabre about the wet smear of disintegrating cloth that seemed almost gory. He shivered, pulling his gaze away from the surf. In doing so, he noticed that from this height, he could see the shape and shadow of some structure further down the shore. It was partially hidden from view by the patchwork dunes. What could be seen looked like the topmost story of a broken tower. Running towards it from between the low foothills was the black ribbon of an old road, bleached to a gray dapple by the idea of sunlight.

∞∞∞∞∞∞∞∞∞∞∞∞∞∞∞∞∞∞∞

"Kinnari, what is that ruined tower?"

"I don't know. This is all in your head, remember? I am only a tourist here. Why don't you tell me what that tower is?"

The magus and the boy stood together with their feet half sunk in the soft burlap of the shore and gazed at the tower from a distance. The thought nearly occurred to Melvin to wonder how they got there from the mountain, but it was a disruptive query that never finished forming. The cloth sky was mottled with dyes the color of sunset, and bisected by lines of cotton clouds that ran in all directions like the fragments of a smashed mirror. The shushing of the ocean sounded like a warning.

Melvin refused to look at it: he did not care to witness up close that slick bruise of dyes where the surf bisected the shore. Instead, he focused on the ruinous tower rising up a ways ahead *like a broken molar protruding from a dirty old jaw.* Melvin unconsciously ran the tip of his tongue across the inside of his front teeth. He did not notice that Drinn had walked on ahead of him until he had to jog unsteadily across the burlap to catch up.

The tower was familiar: Melvin admitted to himself that he already knew that. Transported to this place and distorted by his imagination, the humble ruin of the dead mage's tower that he had stared at for days across the lake now stretched up above him to an unlikely height. Roosting sea birds cawed down at them mockingly. From the broken summit, a fist-sized stone crumbled off the carapace of its outer wall and cratered into the soft burlap ground a long moment later with a dramatic *whump*.

"It is likely the importance of the tower in your mind that makes it so tall here in Dream." Drinn called out over his shoulder. Tossed about on a passing breeze, his voice sounded hollow and far off. He stood with his hands on his hips, neck craned back far enough to see the top. Wind tugged at his coat. The empty windows of the tower stared blackly down at them.

"But... why is it here? And why is it the only thing that isn't part of the patchwork blanket? It feels like it-"

"Like it isn't a part of the same dream? It's not. It's what we magi call an *Indelible*. Something drawn onto the story of your subconscious that is not easily able to be erased. These Indelibles are occasionally encountered in your own patch of Dream: someone you were close to and lost touch with; a house you grew up in that burnt to the ground long ago and was rebuilt in your head. Sometimes there are violent aftershocks of a bad fight that reverberate over and over again here as your dreaming mind struggles to rewrite what actually happened. Your personal dreamscape is like one big organism made up of semi-cohesive smaller organisms — in this case, the individual dreams. It's just like a *body*, do you understand? And these Indelible structures are tumors that grow in hidden places between those dreams."

Melvin stared in awe at the tower. The double doors inset at the ground floor were partially broken: one door closed, the other had splintered and now hung slackly on one twisted hinge. The wind made the leaning door sway; the rusty hinge groaned; the darkness beyond beckoned.

"Are we supposed to... *should we go inside?*" Melvin muttered, feeling his palms sweat.

"Not for all the tea in Hälling!" Drinn said, cheerfully. "Who could guess what kind of ambitious horrors you have stuffed in there! I know for a fact that you have never been inside that tower in real life: none of us have. Your father only works on the structure from the outside; it doesn't take a magus to sense how haunted the tower interior still is. It might be much worse here in Dream. I shudder to imagine the revenants that wander in the dark places of your young mind."

Melvin licked his dry lips. "Me too. Let's get away from here. From higher up the mountain, I saw there was a road running nearby. I want to go take a look."

"*Ah yes.*" Drinn murmured. "The Wayward Road."

"Really? I created that here too? I wasn't even thinking about it when you described the place."

"No. You did not recreate the Wayward here. It was here long before either of us were born. I believe it might have always been here. It is the road between dreams, and it is very dangerous."

∞∞∞∞∞∞∞∞∞∞∞∞∞∞∞∞∞∞∞∞∞∞

Melvin and Drinn stood beside the Wayward Road and stared at it. There were no markers or signs that indicated it was, indeed, the Wayward. But Melvin had walked the Wayward for as long as the memory of his life — at least the stretch of it that traveled through Holm — and he was as familiar with its worn and pitted cobblestones as anyone who keeps the same daily routine can be. Here, in his dream, the Wayward looked like it was made out of an old black sheet worn out to dusty gray, with a cobblestone pattern stained onto it. But it didn't *really* look like that. Stare at it close enough, and the illusion wore away in little spots where the cobblestones were also missing. Here in Melvin's dream, the mountain might insist it was made of scraps of cloth, but the Wayward *knew* it was actually an ancient, dusty road, and pasted on the illusion of cloth with the minimal effort needed to play along. It was like watching a parent indulge in a quick game of harry n' hide with the children. *Let's get this over with, kids. I have grownup things to do.*

Neither of them spoke for a while. Above and around the Wayward, the *air* was completely still. Within a few feet of the road, the stuttering wind died away and the sound of calling sea birds snuffed out quite suddenly. Melvin found himself imagining the sound of his own heartbeat, just to hear anything at all. He was relieved when Drinn cleared his throat to speak. With his voice pitched to just above a whisper, he pointed at the road and said:

"The first response that the realm of Dream has towards an Indelible structure is to attack it and try to remove it — pushing it as far towards the edges of the dreamer's patch that it can. That is why buildings such as the tower end up in the wastelands of the dreamscape, so to speak. Areas of desert, or the edge of the ocean. Thick forests. Plains of shattered rock where nothing else can grow. Often this works, and the majority of those

things and places that haunt us in our youth are gratefully forgotten by the onset of maturity. But a true Indelible will not fade away. Very slowly, it will begin to decompose as everything created within time must. Yet the shell of it will remain; a gathering place for those creatures and things that prefer to dwell in abandoned places, hidden away out of sight. As I said earlier: a tumor, in all but name."

"And the Wayward Road is an Indelible too?" Melvin whispered back.

"Perhaps. But whose? I have never learned whether the road exists permanently because so many people on this island dream of it all at once, or whether it was imagined into existence by some Immortal, and has never been forgotten since. Furthermore, whether travel is possible between this road through Dream and the Wayward in the waking world, I am likewise curious. For years, I have searched for answers to these questions. I remain unsatisfied."

"Indelible <u>and</u> mysterious." Melvin muttered importantly.

"Indeed."

Drinn tugged at Melvin's sleeve, pulling him further back away from the Wayward Road until they were standing at such a distance that they could hear the comforting shoosh of the ocean and the grackle of sea birds again. Then he continued in a more normal tone of voice.

"Usually an Indelible 'tumor' is benign, and it settles into a spurious lump of emotional memory that the body of your dreams learns to adapt to the presence of. Some old wagon left to decompose on the side of a trail that your dreaming self no longer wanders? Fine, not a problem for anyone. Just another derelict piece of scenery in a vast landscape; a little out of place, but who cares? Benign. Irrelevant. However, some tumors grow and spread into healthy parts of your dreams. Then you begin to see it everywhere, and those things that are hidden inside it become an obsession that can damage you and all the dreamscape around you.

"We call these 'nightmares'. Yet most of those nightmares are just as harmless as any dream. They distract and bedevil the waking mind, but for a short enough while that their poisons have little effect on the worlds outside of Dream. This is very important to understand for any magus training in this place: most of what seems like danger in here are just phantasms. Driftwhisps of daydreams going rotten from a bit of dinner-time indigestion. Do not waste your fears on them; they are nothing more than startling illusions. It's those *other* nightmares that are the problem: the ones you have to fight, or flee from."

"And those are all the dangerous ones you mentioned the other day? Worms that burrow between worlds and servants of Immortals and that sort of scary?"

"Yes. Although I'd much prefer if we return to the waking world before discussing such things further. In fact, that's a lesson for another time. I don't want to frighten you off prematurely before I've had a chance to teach you anything worthwhile."

Melvin shook his head. "Nothing you can say will scare me away from this place. I can *walk* here, Kinnari! I could run up that whole mountain if I wanted to!"

Drinn stroked his chin, hiding his smile behind his hand.

"You can do a lot more than run up that mountain. You could fly over it, or run right through it! In your own patch of Dream, you can learn to do just about anything. It is your little world to make and manage; to explore whatever the light of imagination touches. As long as you are careful about where the boundaries end, there is little harm you can do yourself here. It's very difficult to die inside your own dream. Not impossible, however..."

Drinn trailed off, and glanced back at the Wayward Road. Melvin followed it with his eyes as well, to where it disappeared from sight amongst the low hills.

"...I can follow the Wayward right out of my own dream, can't I? Is that the danger of being on the road?"

"Yes." Drinn sighed. "And other travelers can follow the road here to you. There are no real boundaries that I know of in Dream. No walls strong enough to keep an enemy out. With enough training in liminal lucidity — meaning conscious presence inside of this place, and other in-between places like it — you can gain a great deal of mastery over your own dreamscape. You will become safer in here than anywhere else in Dream, and likely anywhere in the waking world besides. That is why we come here to learn and to practice. But the problem with training in here is that you are almost *too* safe. Any threats we can invent for you to practice on in your own patch of dreamscape, you will find that with a minimal amount of training, you can overcome them easily. They are only phantasms in your own mind, after all."

"So, I must go somewhere else to learn anything important?"

"In essence: yes. As I said before, everything is woven together, so there is almost nowhere you can't go inside Dream. And the temptation to go exploring can be terrible, particularly for a young apprentice thief who gets the basics of liminal lucidity training down and thinks that means they are ready to tackle something harder."

"You want me to train inside *your* dreamscape."

Drinn smiled thinly. "No. Training in my dreams is too dangerous for both of us. And before you barrage me with questions about that — as I can see you are preparing to do — just know that I have no answers to offer on that subject. You will never be welcomed deeper into my dream-scape than our own little tent between the barrow mounds. We shall have to find another dreamer for you to practice in. Someone who has more good sense than imagination; we don't want to overwhelm you on your first try, after all! The more predictable the battleground, the better. Perhaps... someone you already have a strong bond with, that would be willing to take a minor risk to help you truly begin your magical training."

"I... I'm not..."

Drinn's eyes were bright green, as bright as spring leaves. He smiled warmly.

"I *know* that you have a few friends that you have grown quite close to lately. I bet there would be one or two amongst them who would be curious enough and brave enough to want to help you become the person *you are meant to be.* Are you sure there isn't someone you can think of who you can ask such a small favor from?"

∞∞∞∞∞∞∞∞∞∞∞∞∞∞∞∞∞∞

Caetal in the Dream

See: this is why you don't tell ghost stories around a Solstice fire. I warned them; I fucking warned them. This is also why you shouldn't trust wizards. Because just when you need them, they die. And where the godsdamn hell did my crossbow go?!

∞∞∞∞∞∞∞∞∞∞∞∞∞∞∞∞∞∞∞∞

When the dead come bursting out of the ground, what can I do but pick up a flaming log and beat them with it? It's not like my crossbow will do a godsdamn thing anyway. Against a Shambleman? No thank you.

I stay close to Melvin, and close to the fire, and I beat them with that log until their heads cave in and their bodies are ruined. One of them grabs Mathias and almost tears his arm out of the socket, and I beat that one too.

The log I'm holding is splintered, and the burning edge is spluttering. It seems to be working though, because we haven't been killed yet.

Tarquin is gone, and Talara is too; I don't know where, I can't leave the fire to find them.

{   ***Please wake up***   }

Rahyn? I can hear your voice in the dark somehow, but I sense that you are as far away as distance goes. Now the ground crawls underfoot. Please keep away from this terrible place.

Please save us, if you can.

∞∞∞∞∞∞∞∞∞∞∞∞∞∞∞∞∞∞∞∞

My hands are slick and cramped; my swinging shoulder is killing me. The fire is a hot hurricane that dries my sweat and makes the air swim hypnotically. We are all underwater; we are all drowning together in this roaring heat. But still they come limping into the firelight. How can there be so many? Are the barrow mounds so crowded with corpses, packed head to foot in cursed disgrace? Mathias is flailing behind me, almost back-to-back. I can feel his panic, and I don't like it. It will slow him down when it burns out. And that is when they will have him — probably me too.

Then Melvin screams, and the fire is suddenly snuffed. In the dark, everything is slithering towards us. I clutch the fear-slick log, brandishing it in front of me, and wait for our end to come. What else can I do? An animal knows when its running is done.

∞∞∞∞∞∞∞∞∞∞∞∞∞∞∞∞∞∞

What Friends Are For

Most of the next day, Melvin's body spent cocooned in magically induced slumber while his dreaming mind enjoyed bounding all over the patchwork mountainside, lifting rocks in the air with his mind, and blowing them up. He played with the imaginary wind by blowing cotton clouds around, as swiftly and accurately as shooting giant marbles in the sky. He tried tunneling into the patchwork mountain, but quickly tired of it when he delved into a layer where the cloth seemed wet and rubbery, and the sound of digging into it was like the slap of a meat slab onto a countertop. He also tried flying, but had little luck doing it. He managed to convince his mind that he could take increasingly large leaps, but over and over again his momentum overwhelmed him until he tumbled to the ground in a breathless pile.

Overall, it was great fun, but Drinn was right: learning to harness imaginary magic skills by attacking rocks quickly became boring. The whole process felt hollow, like a child's game of pretend. There was nothing in his dream that could challenge him by fighting back.

....

So, just before twilight on the day following the following day, the other five members of the Company of Six drifted to shore at the edge of that haunted lake called Xör Uru. Night was nearing, so Drinn did not risk wading out into the shallows to help draw them in. Instead, Caetal threw him a rope and he towed the raft in as close to shore as young legs could manage in a jump. Tarquin tied the mooring rope, and Rahyn and Mathias unloaded backpacks, an oilskin sack full of dead fish, and all their camping gear onto the old wooden dock.

Drinn chatted at them companionably as he walked them uphill to where Melvin and he were camping. He apologized for the somewhat startling nature of the magical message they had each received the previous day, although only a few of the children felt inclined to accept the apology. The magical summons had materialized to each of them in the form of a disembodied voice inside a large bubble that burst out of whatever liquid was closest to each of the children at the time. Talara had been mortified at work whilst carrying a beer over to a customer that suddenly exploded out all over him and started commanding her to come visit. Caetal had been scared literally shitless when a voice began to bellow up out of his privy while he was sitting on it. He was also feeling particularly sour that in the message, Drinn had forbidden bringing any pets. So now poor Dubby and Shamsala were tied up at home, and it would be years before Caetal felt comfortable in his own outhouse again. So he glared at Drinn's back as they walked, muttering darkly to himself. For the rest of them, having been personally summoned to a campout by a mysterious magus was enough of a thrill to let bygones be.

After greeting Melvin and stowing their gear in the tent, Drinn encouraged the company to head further uphill towards the edge of where the forest began and gather fallen branches for enough firewood to last the night. Meanwhile, Drinn opened up a bottle of wine for himself and started enjoying it.

Melvin, who seemed unusually withdrawn, quietly busied himself with frying up a large pan of the fish that Rahyn and Caetal had caught and gutted on their way downriver. It was an uphill hike to the edge of the forest, and a few roundtrips with armloads full of firewood had the children strongly wishing that the forest had grown down much closer to the lakeshore. On the third roundtrip, just as the last of the daylight was failing, Caetal noted the presence of a few extremely decayed stumps clustered at the base of one of the mound hills. Once they had been spotted, the children looked around more carefully beneath the clusters of berry bushes that grew there in thick patches. There were ancient stumps hidden under each of them, crumbling with decay.

"The forest used to grow right down to the lake." Rahyn said. "It was all cut down, many years ago. These bushes only grow in disturbed areas where all the canopy has been destroyed, and the ground is baked by sudden sunlight. Yet I see no trace of fire or fallen logs from a wind storm. What manner of monster would eat a whole forest so quickly?"

"War." Mathias replied. "Our ancestral monster."

"Maybe *your* ancestors." Caetal muttered.

Tarquin pointed down towards their tent, between the orderly rows of long hills. "Do you suppose those might be burial mounds? There sure are a lot of them."

Talara stared out across the lake, to where the shattered tower hunched like a carrion bird.

"You guys — I think I've heard of this place before," she murmured.

....

The campfire popped and spat; red sparks floated overhead like burning fireflies. Stuffed to the gills with fish, berries and goat cheese, the children sprawled around the fire and chatted companionably. If not for the presence of Drinn — who was now on his second bottle of wine, and had become verbose in the telling of random and disparate anecdotes about his life — the children would have felt quite comfortable. But it is hard to be young and trying to relax around your peers with one drunk adult hanging about. Eventually other conversations surrendered into silence until only Drinn's voice could be heard above the crackle of the campfire. Finally, Talara (bard that she was, and grouchy about losing her audience of friends to a dumb old wizard) interrupted Drinn's latest tale about a hazing prank he pulled in his days at mage academy and said:

"Not to sound rude, but nobody cares to hear more about people you used to know. Why did you summon us out here, Drinn? You said in your damn beer-bubble message that it was something important for Melvin's training. Well, we're all here. And the only thing that seems different about Melvin is that he is a lot quieter than he was a week ago. So maybe let him explain for himself why we're here?"

Then she turned expectantly towards Melvin, who just stared back at her and didn't say anything. Finally, when the silence got awkward, Tarquin flicked his shoulder and said "Mel. What's going on? How can we help?"

Melvin cleared his throat, glancing at his Kinnari. Drinn nodded subtly.

"Well, uh... yeah. So: okay. Thank you all for coming out here." Then he started coughing, and scootched sideways until he got out of the draft of the campfire smoke. He wiped his eyes, and cleared his throat again. Drinn snickered, and drank.

"Alright. Well: there is, obviously, a lot to training as a magus that I can't tell you about. I swore an oath not to, and that's just that."

The children glanced at each other uneasily. Caetal spit into the fire. Melvin frowned and fidgeted with his shirt.

"But I will, of course, simplify and tell you what I can. Basically: um... doing magic is like finding a big pile of beautiful treasure, and deciding to take some for yourself. Unfortunately, that treasure is guarded by a dragon. Actually, a few dragons. But they are gods. And so, if a magus gets that treasure, they have to run far away, and spend the rest of their life hiding from those dragons, or they will get speared and cooked like a fish fry. And if we say the stolen words out loud, it causes lots of trouble. Because certain people are always listening, and they get very mad when the words are spoken out loud."

Melvin licked his lips and glanced furtively over at Drinn, who nodded approvingly.

"So, obviously you probably shouldn't have gotten me to morph that hill into a goat god: that was wrong."

"Wrong," Tarquin replied, grinning. "That was awesome."

"Wait: *what*?" Drinn exclaimed, sloshing his wine.

"Nevermind that." Melvin waved him off. "It's not important. What *is* important to know is that in order to safely practice magic, I have to do it while dreaming. While *inside* a dream, actually. Specifically, one of yours. ...Hopefully inside Mathias."

"Wait: *what*?" Mathias exclaimed, sloshing his water.

"Look — I've been turning this over in my head all day. I first thought Tarquin and his imagination would have been the best choice to host us in his dream. But then I remembered the story of how he got to Eld, and it made me a bit nervous to go wandering around in there. No offense, Tarq."

Tarquin shrugged. "Your loss, my dreams are — wait: what?" Tarquin exclaimed, reaching over and sloshing Mathias' water. "Did I hear *us*? Did you mean to say *us*?"

Caetal spat again. "Nope."

Melvin glared at him and hurried on. "Please. I need help on this. Mathias is the right choice to try this out, I'm sure of it. Caetal's mind is way too jungly, Talara's is dangerously full of tales of a thousand tragedies, I can't properly train in my *own* dream, and as for Rahyn..."

Melvin looked across the fire at Rahyn. She stared back at him thoughtfully out of eyes that reflected light like the eyes of a wild animal.

"I'm sorry Rahyn, but I just don't feel like I'm ready to see the inside of your dreams. I might lose us in there."

Tarquin rolled up onto his knees and put his hands on his hips. "See, now you've circled back to this very important *us* word. So why don't you put your cards out on the table so we can look at them clearly? You say you need to train *inside a dream* — which sounds like great fun to me personally — but your use of the word u̲s̲ seems to infer that you intend to take us in there with you. Is that true?"

"Yes."

"Into Mathias' dream specifically?

"...Yes. Hopefully."

"Because you can't say magic words out loud in the physical world anymore, or a bunch of dragon-gods will come and eat you."

Drinn belched. "Yep, that's the meat of it. ...Yuck. Fishy."

"With red wine and goat cheese." Talara muttered, waving the offending odor away. She scooted over towards Rahyn.

Tarquin glanced at Drinn, then back at Melvin. He shrugged.

"Ok. That clears it up nicely for me. When do we do this? Tonight?"

"Wait. Wait: wait." Mathias stood up hurriedly, brushing the dirt off his bum. "How do I... you can't just go into... all of you *inside* my mind? It's difficult enough already with-" He glanced at Melvin guiltily, then he pivoted and hurried over to another spot across the fire. But it was too close to Drinn for comfort, so he edged slowly back to where he had started, mumbling protests all the while. "I don't... I mean, I hear *why* you want it to be me, I get that part. It's just a *lot*... How am I... well, for starters, how am I supposed to get inside a dream in my own head?"

Melvin raised an eyebrow. "Mathias, you will already be inside there, remember? It's your own dream. Haven't you ever showed up in your own dream before?"

"Well, ok: yes. That makes sense. But how are the rest of you getting in there? Are we going to be magically shrunk or evaporated? Because I threw up a l̲o̲t̲ from that last time, and I really don't want to experience *that* again. No thank you. I'm just not ready." Mathias crossed his arms and tried to look stern.

Melvin began to reassure him, but Drinn stood up rather suddenly, knocking over his empty wine bottle. He held out his arms for silence.

"Friends-"

"You aren't our friend." Caetal growled. "W-we barely know you."

Drinn smiled tightly. "Friends of Melvinari: hear me. Training to be wielded by magic is the only possible avenue by which Melvin can regain the use of his legs. There is no other road he can walk anymore. It is the path of a magus for Melvin or a life crippled by the loss of his mobility.

And he cannot continue in his training without your help."

Drinn paused and peered at them solemnly. The campfire crackled. The children remained silent, so he pressed on.

"All he is asking of you is that when you go to sleep tonight, that you will gather together inside the realm of Dream, and join him in a training exercise that Mathias will be hosting in his unconscious mind. That's it! And when you wake up, you will all have the same interesting story to remember together, as though you had all the thrills of a harrowing adventure with almost none of the dangers. It will be like playing characters in a harmless imagination game! So please: do the right thing. Reach inside yourselves and find the courage and compassion to be a good friend to Melvin. Can you all do that for me? Would you do it for him?"

Another silence followed. Melvin looked down at his lap, his eyes stinging with embarrassment. *Why did that sound right, but feel so wrong?*

"W-w-well... shit. *Godsdammit.*" Caetal muttered. "How do w-we do this thing? Just lay down and g-go to sleep?"

Drinn's smile was sloppy with satisfaction.

•••••••••••••••••••••••••••••••••••••

A Dream of Mathias

{ I was the only one facing the lake when Talara's story ended, I know that now. I was the only one that saw what happened to Drinn. }

∞∞∞∞∞∞∞∞∞∞∞∞∞∞∞∞∞∞∞∞∞∞∞∞

In the heavy silence that follows the telling of a somber tale, Talara quietly excused herself to tend to the business of a full bladder. Everyone seemed reticent, sprawled around the fire in thoughtful silence.

∞∞∞∞∞∞∞∞∞∞∞∞∞∞∞∞∞∞∞∞∞∞

I felt my gaze drawn towards the dark lapping of waves on the lake. There was something deeply unsettling about the story she had shared with us; something beyond the disquieting fear that the tale was meant to invoke. It made my skin prickle with more than cold, so I wrap my arms around my knees and idly watch Drinn in his boat as he rows towards us across the water from the tower island. I can hear the faint clunking of the paddles in the oarlocks. His silver lantern hangs at the boat's prow, bobbing with the rocking strokes of the oars. The blue flame burning inside it makes him look pallid and ghostly. He hunches his shoulders as he rows towards the dock at the base of our hill. He must have been cold without his coat on, for there it sits in a dark pile of wool across the fire from me. It strikes me in that moment that I have never seen him take that jacket off. I only have that moment to wonder why.

**{ As he was, with his back turned towards shore,
I never saw the look on his face when he disappeared
below the water. I'm glad of that still. }**

∞∞∞∞∞∞∞∞∞∞∞∞∞∞∞∞∞∞∞∞∞∞∞

It happens almost without a sound. Something rises up out of the black depths of the lake and folds entirely over him. It is a snake; a wave; the mouth of a cave. It is like none of those things at all. It boils up like blood gushing from a wound in the lake itself: a tangle of snarling teeth that swallows him whole. The boat is capsized and pulled underwater.

One moment he was there, and the next he is not. The blue lantern sinks down into the dark, glimmering unnaturally all the while. I rise to my feet, staring and gasping for breath.

On the island, across the water, a rippling curtain of light sloughs off of the tower roof and pours down the stone walls. It looks like shimmering oil, charring the stones as it flows across them as though infernal with heat. When this curtain of oily light reaches the ground, it scatters into drifting motes of dim iridescence.

I glance at Melvin, and I can see in the flush of his cheeks that he knows what I know. Even in here—

{ **—Inside my head, this is all living in here. What sort of a person am I, to dream these horrors into life? Am I bent inside? Even in here—** }

—it must have broadcast to him from the force of my shock. He slumps and cradles his head in his hands, as I cradle the medallion of the iron eye of Cuthain in mine.

∞∞∞∞∞∞∞∞∞∞∞∞∞∞∞∞∞∞∞∞∞

It is not what was there that I notice first, but what is suddenly gone. Between the march of moments, the wind ceases blowing, and the air becomes thick and still. When the wind stops, I suddenly forget how to inhale. The breathlessness of death creeps all around us like a fog. Even the flames of our campfire recoil and diminish in view, as though starving for air.

Then the edge of fire-sight flickers across the shuffling motion of animate bones, and waves of rotted Shamblemen begin to break against us. Strangely, I find that am not surprised to see them. The wretched spell that had drowned them alive in the earth and then held them there must have broken when that strange light poured off the tower, the moment that Drinn was swallowed by the lake. Now the dead are clawing up from under the blooming lupines.

∞∞∞∞∞∞∞∞∞∞∞∞∞∞∞∞∞∞∞∞

The fire roars behind us, and overhead. It is a giant snake of flame, rearing and striking, and we have become the clutch of eggs that it guards. From where he is sprawled on the ground, Melvin guides it as best he can. I have never seen him do such magic before; it is terrifying to be so close to it. Every time the flames pass nearby, I can feel my hair crisp and the moisture cook out of my skin.

Talara never returned to the fire, and Tarquin has been dragged downhill towards the lake, fighting as he goes. Rahyn is gone; I did not see her go. That said, I cannot recall if she was here at all. Once again, it is Melvin, Caetal and I left alone: we who were trapped underground together with that earthen monster whose name I can never recall. It was Rahyn, and the fox that shares her body, who saved us from wandering forever in the dark. I cannot hope for such luck again.

∞ ∞ ∞ ∞ ∞ ∞ ∞ ∞ ∞ ∞ ∞ ∞ ∞ ∞ ∞ ∞ ∞ ∞ ∞

The fire is blinding; the roar of hot wind nearly deafens us. By Cuthain's blessing, I am back-to-back with Caetal now. He hefts a burning log over-head, swinging it with deadly force. A chaos of sundered limbs and broken skulls scatters before him. I grab my own burning branch from the whirling base of the fire, and try for a while to fight like he does, swinging and whack-ing at the Shamblemen with it. But I am afraid, deadly afraid: my arms betray their shaking. The branch I wield is swatting, not striking, and the best that I can claim for my efforts is that the undead in front of me are held at bay by my fearful thrashing.

∞ ∞ ∞ ∞ ∞ ∞ ∞ ∞ ∞ ∞ ∞ ∞ ∞ ∞ ∞ ∞ ∞ ∞ ∞

Long minutes pass, and adrenaline is fading. My arms are leaden. My swinging branch is perceptibly slowing down, dragging as often as not across the ground in front of me; the clumsy menacing of an unwieldy broom. It is no longer even on fire.

The dead surge forward, trampling my branch underfoot. One of them grips my shoulder. The decay of time has shriveled living fingers into bony claws that pierce into my flesh. Shock stiffens me; sudden frostbite in my blood. All I can do is stare into those empty cavities which used to be eyes, and marvel at how gray and fragile flesh becomes after death. As drab as dry leaves, thinly scattered over a yellow skull.

Somewhere far away, someone that resembles me is struggling to escape the grip of the Shambleman. Time slows. Fear deadens, and my struggles cease. With the cold has come perspective, and now I can see that what is standing in front of me is not a 'what' at all. It was a person, once. Now it is an animated ruin, like the wind twitching a decayed cocoon that had once held a trapped butterfly.

Drifting in the void of that cold contact, my double sight returns to me unexpectedly. With one eye I can see the hollowed gray ruin of cheeks with cheekbones poking through. But the other eye sees a living face: an Erdin woman, a warrior, who once walked under a younger sun and wore her white-gold hair tied back in a thick braid. I can see her freckles, and the flush of life in her cheeks. The apparition of blue eyes stare into mine, but what subtleties of expression she might have once shared if she were still alive are lost on me. Her gaze is as piercing as I imagine a mother's might be, but her eyes pull me down like an undertow. I cannot bear to look at them for long; not while winter is inside of me, reaching towards my heart. I drag my gaze down her neck instead, and suddenly I can see what it was that killed her.

A netting of rusted chainmail drapes like a shroud on her shoulder blades // her chainmail hauberk is polished and bright. Both views at once, of course, but in both views, I can see a gash of missing links, rent and rimmed with red. In her last living moments, and now in death, her other arm is pressed over the wound that stole her life away. The view of what lies beneath that wound is hidden to one eye by the musculature of her shield arm. The other eye sees right through the fleshless bones, to the place where an iron spearhead is lodged. What is left of the shaft has decomposed, for the hollow socket can be seen. In my split vision, the spearhead is faintly illuminated. This glow is a dull red. It is so faintly seen that I cannot call it "light" at all. It is more like if a shadow could glow. It is deadlight.

{   But that isn't how the story goes, is it? Talara said they drowned in the mud, all of them, together. This isn't the story that Talara told inside my head. There is someone changing it from the outside; someone burrowing into my dream, I can feel it! }

Her bony claw grips even harder, and the deadening cold is sharpened by pain. My head clears enough to look up into her eyes again. In the vision of what was, where her eyes are still blue and still exist on her face, I can see an expression finally blooming. Pleading. I have seen her now; we are no longer strangers. I have become somebody that knows who she was, and how she died. And why she cannot rest in death the way that others do. Iron ore, smelted into steel, then pounded and forged into a weapon for murder. The energy of the blacksmith's hammer blows trapped inside of it in folded tension layers. She was invaded by iron, and died from it, and lay in cold clay awake underground, with that dead metal humming inside her, glowing dully with red shadows that only eyes like mine can see.

{ The medallion of Cuthain begins to heat up against my skin, and I can hear the sound of a hammer ringing against a forge, and a voice

speaking behind it; one that has always been speaking behind it. My chest fills up with a great gulp of air, and my heart is overfull of all the knowing a moment can hold. I am bidden; I am being instructed! }

In the grip of sudden knowledge, I reach my hand inside of her, between the shattered lattice of her ribs, and yank the spearhead out. Her hand on my shoulder relaxes, and following that there is a sighing noise that I can hear even above the whirling roar of the campfire vortex. She collapses against me then, scattering at my feet like an armload of dropped sticks. For a moment, I can do nothing but stare in pitying grief at the mess of dusty bones that once had a name, and died fighting for something she was told to believe in.

Then another Shamble(woman?) reared up behind her to take her place, and I step backwards in panic and almost trip over Caetal's feet. He turns around quickly, and smashes its head apart with multiple swings from a spluttering club of burning firewood. Then he bends down and picks up another flaming log, and hands it to me.

"Here. Make yourself useful." He growls, before turning away.

So, I do. I do what I can. I beat a few apart, but more come up behind them. It seems without end. My other arm is still deadened with cold, and hangs uselessly at my side. All around us, the undead are closing in. They approach with an awful shambling shuffle, like marionettes in a lethal puppet show. Each of them has a piece of smelted iron burning inside of them somewhere, shining through the thin webbing of their skin in a dim red deadlight. Arrowheads — axe heads — broken sword blades — rusting daggers. They are carrying steel, clothed in steel armor. I look around in exhausted awe. Before my eyes, the night is dimly lit by deadlights, like the slow flight of summer fireflies.

Then Melvin screams, and the campfire suddenly dies.

Now I can see nothing else but those shadow-red deadlights. They are everywhere. And they are all moving towards us in the dark.

∞∞∞∞∞∞∞∞∞∞∞∞∞∞∞∞∞∞∞∞

The Story That Should Not Have Been True

Drinn began to carve fresh cut branches out of a pile of pine boughs that he had apparently already prepared nearby.

"Perhaps the young bard — what's your name again? Talesa?"

"Talara."

"Yes, that. Perhaps you would be gracious enough to tell us a tale to set the tone of the dream? For the magic to work, we need to make a circle around our fire out of freshly cut pine boughs, and then unify all of our focus into one story. Something with a bit of conflict: we need a few challenges to practice on, after all!" He winked at Talara, who looked away.

"We are going to fight monsters inside Mathias' dream?" Rahyn quietly asked.

"I will." Melvin replied. "With practice spells. Hopefully the five of you can help a bit too. I spent all yesterday bounding down the side of a patchwork mountain and blowing up rocks with my mind. It was wonderful fun, you guys! Not truly magic use, of course — just stuff Drinn taught me how to make up on the spot. He said I have to be able to imagine I can do it first before I will ever be able to."

"And what about me?" Mathias asked, trying to keep the trembling out of his voice. "How do I host everyone inside-"

"*Shh*, don't trouble yourself with the details." Drinn patted him on the head. "You wouldn't understand those details anyway. Just have faith that everything will turn out fine."

"*Faith?*"

Drinn reached out and flicked the amulet of Cuthain hanging around Mathias' neck. Mathias blushed angrily and tucked it away beneath his shirt.

Tarquin held up his hand. "I'll help! I don't mind fighting things that can't really hurt me."

"Count me in too." Caetal said. Then he glared at Drinn. "They definitely can't hurt us in there, right?"

"Of course not! It's just a training dream. Now help me circle the area with some pine boughs. Then everyone just lay down and listen to the story, and I'll summon up the rest of the magicky stuff. Hey: did anyone bring a knife? I don't remember where mine wandered off to."

"Aren't you a little drunk to be spellcasting?" Talara pointedly asked.

"Nonsense! Mullered... *mulled* wine is still wine, even though it's been hotted up."

"...Wait: *what*?" Talara exclaimed. And although she wasn't holding a drink, if she had been, she'd have sloshed it.

....

Five of them lay in a circle with their feet facing the campfire and their heads pointed towards the dark of night. At first, Talara tried to lay down with them, but found it too difficult to summon the proper gravitas for storytelling while lying on her back, so she propped herself up against a pile of backpacks. Around the future dreamers Drinn arranged a circle of freshly cut branches, then sat on the table nearby. From there, he proceeded to dictate the rules of the game they had found themselves drawn into playing. The patter of his voice was a hypnotic purr that intoxication gently slurred.

"Alright, you very special children: for this to work, you must begin by concentrating on unifying your minds into one vision. Do not let your focus wander towards individual reveries, or you may find yourselves flung out into some uncharted dream and lost for the duration of the exercise. Mathias has agreed to host this dream, and so it will be inside his sleeping mind that you must gather. To make this as easy as possible for those of you who have never purposefully entered a dream before, I want you to look carefully around you. Commit to memory the location of each hillock in relation to the fire; take note of height and dimension, the presence of bushes growing up their slopes. The view from where you are lying, imagined amongst six minds as though by one mind, is the canvas on which the dream will be painted. Everyone got it so far?"

Various grunts and mumbles indicated compliance.

"I hope so; that was the easy part. Now, let's make some changes, because Dream will confound and bewilder reality as playfully and ruthelas... *ruthlessly* as a cat stalking a mouse. The more you envision the boundaries of your dream before you enter into it, the better off you will be. Particularly in a mind like Mathias'."

Mathias glared. "What do you mean by that?"

Drinn chuckled. "It means that the flow of your thoughts is confined by the channels of clerical thinking; those boundaries of zealotry are stronger than jail bars. I am, therefore, trusting your limited vision to help protect your friends from wandering off into the wilds of Dream."

Mathias, who had been strictly raised to not mouth off to his elders, pursed his lips tightly together and said nothing. He stared up at the starlit sky.

Tarquin reached over and squeezed his hand and whispered, *"I don't know if there was a compliment buried in that pile of scat or not, but I do know I trust you to keep us safe inside your mind more than anyone else here."*

Mathias smiled gratefully, but Tarquin's reassurance did not diminish the metallic taste beginning to bloom in his mouth. Blinking the wetness out of his eyes, he tried to refocus on what the magus was saying.

"What I'm trying to convey as simplistically as possible is that Dream will mess with you, particularly your sense of situational continuity. So, lets alter a few features on purpose, so that It has less to play around with once you are on the inside. Can anyone think of details they would like to change that they want to see manifest inside Mathias' dream? If so, say them out loud now so that all of you can imagine them together. Then close your eyes and begin it."

"I want to see the forest that was once here. As though all the trees were never chopped down." Rahyn said, closing her eyes.

"I w-w-w... I'd like Dubby in there with me." Caetal said.

"What is a dubby?"

"My jackwolf."

"You will regret that request if you try to imagine him in there with you, I promise." Drinn replied, wiping his mouth. "No pets allowed for a reason. They are impulsive, difficult to predict, and get lost or die easily inside of Dream. You cannot imagine him all the same at the same time; he will become insubstantial and scatter. Choose something else."

"W-well then, at least I'm g-going to bring my damn crossbow in there." Caetal muttered sourly.

"Where is it? Tell everyone where it's at, so they can all imagine it the same."

"It's over by the edge of the firelight, leaning up against one of Rahyn's trees."

"Great! That's basic enough. Now close your eyes and picture it. Who's next?"

"My wooden sword, too. And my dagger." Tarquin piped up.

"Right. *Blah blah blah:* everyone's personal stuff will be in there. It's scattered all around the campfire in exactly the same locations it is right now. I don't have the patience to help you picture every little thing."

Melvin quietly spoke up, "The tower will be in there too, won't it? At the center of the lake."

Drinn rubbed his hands together. "*It will now.* I'm frankly a bit curious to see it manifest outside of your patchwork dreamscape. Very curious indeed."

"Well, in Mathias' dream, it will still be standing. As it was when the magus who built it was alive."

Drinn eyed him warily. "An interesting choice, to lean into the presence of your Indelible Tower. Why choose that?"

Melvin shrugged from where he lay. "Why not? It gives us something interesting to focus on. And we may need somewhere to retreat to, depending on how-"

"*No!* Definitely not. You shall not retreat to the tower, do you understand?"

"Why?"

"Well, because… because I say so. The point of this training is to deal with what happens to you in there, *as you are now*. No help from me, and no retreat to the tower. So when you get into Dream, imagine me out of it. I have more important things to do in there than hang around watching you kids play at fighting."

Melvin rolled over and looked at him. "What do you mean, 'imagine you out?' Like… dead?"

"Well, that's a little maudlin, but I don't honestly care how you imagine me gone. I leave that up to you."

"*Dead it is.*" Caetal chuckled, very quietly to himself. Drinn continued talking.

"I'll still be alive somewhere in Dream anyway, working out of sight. But you cannot rely on the idea that I can assist you during this test — any of you. And your legs won't work in there either, Thief. You must practice casting magic from the ground, because that is how it will be out here in the waking world. Is everyone listening? Pay attention, this is important: Melvinari can't walk."

"Yes, obviously. *Thanks for the update.*" Talara muttered. Tarquin snickered.

"Fine, Kinnari. Whatever. Have it your way." Melvin grumbled, closing his eyes. "Crippled in a dream now too. How fun."

"It's all for your own good, you know. Try not to sound so ungramt-ful. ...Ungrateful." Drinn retorted, finishing off the wine remaining in his cup in two large gulps. "Okay then: anyone else? Any other baubles or bits of furniture you want to drag along into the dream? Or are-"

"Horses. I want to ride a horse." Talara interjected.

"Fine. There are some horses; I'm sure that will turn out well. Imagine them tied up nearby. Now: everyone close your eyes. It's time."

And they did.

....

For a while, silence stretched peacefully all around them. They could hear the crackling fire and the steady chorus of their own breathing. Wood smoke fragranced the air, and the smell of the cooling soil remembering the last of the vanished sunlight.

Then Rahyn spoke up, "I'm not sure I am going to be able to fall asleep. Sometimes-"

"Of course you will fall asleep. My magic will put you to sleep." Drinn interjected from where he sat nearby. "Now: Talesa-"

"*Talara.*"

"Sure, fine. Tell*ussa* that story. Make up something a bit scary: some-thing that takes place here, in this exact spot, underneath the spreading canopy of that quiet girl's imagined trees."

"I didn't imagine them. They used to be here."

"Fine: historical trees. *Ta-la-ra*: tell a tale about a time when the trees were still growing here. Tell us why they all got cut down. And when the moment is right, the dream shall carry you all away."

"Can I open my eyes now?" Talara asked.

"No. A true bard could tell this story with their eyes closed."

"*You don't know a damn about what a true bard could do.*" Talara muttered. But she kept her eyes closed, and began the story anyway.

....

"*Once, not so very long ago, the vast lake that is now called Xör Uru was known by a different name.*

"I tell you this to begin with, for it is understood amongst the wise that at the beginning of all creation the Immortals determined that the soul of each thing should be Named in such a way that honors its truest nature. As the smallest acorn contains within it all the purpose of a giant oak, so too is the story of an entire lake hidden within each drop of its water.

"In days that were younger than these, the lake was called Drôleduyan. Like many of the words that predate our modern tongue, the meaning of the name does not translate gracefully. The nearest elucidation is 'Cradle of the Living Green,' but we must settle for the cruder translation of 'Troll Cradle.'

"In those days, the lake was indeed a cradle for life. The sky teemed with birds; the water with fishes and eels, and the shadow-gray seals that could once be found this far inland. The great Eldwood grew all around it, right down to the shore. Yet, no creature living there thrived so well as the Drôle. They were the children of the lake itself, sired by the severed roots of animate plants and gestated within a womb of mud. They feasted on the bounty of the lake and lived there in peace for countless generations.

"Unfortunately, it is the cruelty of Fate that all that is bountiful in life will be coveted by those that lack. So it was that a nobleman overheard the gossip of a local fisherman, who spoke of a mysterious lake surrounded by a grove of red birch and pale pine, where the fish were so plentiful that they leapt above the surface of the water every sunrise in such numbers that they looked like raindrops rebounding off an enormous puddle.

"This nobleman was the recently declared thegn of Southern Fýrii; the youngest — and only surviving — son of Revis the Elder, who died of the same pox that previous winter that had carried off his other two sons. He was therefore called Revis the Younger, and was barely a man grown when he inherited the Iron Spear, untested in love or battle. His ignorance of the former was to become the cause of the latter, for he was quickly ensorcelled by the affections of a scheming magus, who enflamed his heart into the folly of young ardor through her diabolical enchantments."

....

Talara opened one eye and glanced over toward Melvin guiltily.

"Sorry about the magician-bashing tone. This is just how the story is told."

Melvin nodded, keeping his eyes closed. "No offense taken. Lots of people are afraid of the power of magi."

"Yes, and probably afraid of powerful women, too: you'll find out the one in this story gets a rather short stick in the end. It just goes to show you-"

Drinn interrupted from the picnic table, "Can you get on with the story? This is trying to be a spell, not a tavern tale. You aren't supposed to interject every disruptive comment that comes to mind."

"…Fine. We'll discuss this more later."

"And you *are* making this story up, right? This isn't a tale you heard from someone?"

"Of course I'm making this up!" Talara lied.

....

"Alright, let's see… where was I? …Ah yes: the plans of the magus.

"Wait, okay. There is an important detail I forgot to mention at the beginning: the reason the magus was manipulating the young thegn into falling in love with her was because she wanted him to build her a tower, and she didn't want to pay construction costs or any taxes on it or whatnot. So, when Revis overhead about the beautiful lake from the fisherman, he was like: '*Oh, this sounds like the perfect spot! I'll build her a tower there, and then she will finally have sex with me!*'"

"Not a bad plan, actually." Drinn murmured to himself.

"Yeah, the other magus thought so too." Talara reproachfully replied. "What a surprise."

....

"So: besotted with the enchanted beauty of his sudden paramour, and wishing to impress her so he could eventually undress her, Revis gathered a contingent of carpenters, woodcutters, masons, architects, draftsmen, la-borers and soldiers, and forcibly entreated the fisherman to show them the way to the hidden lake.

"Days passed as they picked their way through the dense green of the Eldwood, following their unwilling guide to the edge of the great lake Drôleduyan. When at last they beheld it, with the glorious light of a midsummer afternoon resplendent upon the water, Revis and the magus both knew immediately what a treasure they had discovered. For her, the sight of the lush island at the lake's center was the prize, for surely no fortress on Eld could boast of such grand and protective solitude. For Revis, it was the timber that he desired. Never had he seen such a valuable grove, for even in those days the red birch were beginning to grow rare and the pale pine had all but vanished, as both were coveted by carpenter and shipwright alike for their strength and straight grain. When Revis gazed on the grove that afternoon, he saw all the wood he would need to build her a tower, a castle or two for himself, and a hefty export to the timber-poor thegndoms of the west.

"Those haughty thegns of Strönd and Norlünd will pay handsomely for such a harvest. Revis thought to himself. *Then I can become the richest thegn of Fýrii in generations. With this beautiful woman on my arm and an army at my back, I will be the envy of all who live.*

"That night, she completed the spell and made him hers. They were married the next day, in a ceremony that felt very rushed, even to the thegn. The only witnesses present were those carpenters and laborers who were ordered to take the afternoon off."

....

Behind the canter of Talara's tale, the children could now hear a humming sound beginning to emanate from Drinn's throat. It sounded like an enormous bee buzzing a long way off, with all of the dip and rise of the pollinator's drone as it lifts and descends, flower to flower. The air seemed to soften and warm around them. They began to feel the gentle pressure of their own closed eyelids. One by one, yawns could be heard around the campfire. Talara struggled to stay alert.

....

"Industry began in earnest. Trees were bucked to length and carted away as fast as they could be felled. Near the water's edge, the red birch growing there were hewn into pilings and driven deep into the river mud to support a dock where supply ships could be moored. Those ships made twice-daily trips out to the little island loaded with stone and timber.

"Meanwhile, a new quarry was dug out near Holm to provide the masons working on the tower with the stones they would require-"

"Oh neat, guys — that's me an' my father's quarry now. Well... we rent. Future me... rock stuff." Melvin whispered blearily, just before the magical sleep claimed him.

Talara yawned deeply and pinched herself in the arm. Then she continued on.

"As well as the ...*yawn...* considerable number of stones needed for the road building project that Revis' father had first dreamed up before he died, and the toll fortress that the surviving Revis intended to build on it.

"For three years, the work continued as fast as funding would allow. Then one day-"

"But what... about the trolls?" Tarquin mumbled, yawning deeply in the middle of it. Then he wriggled like a dog shaking off water, and yawned again. "Didn't they attack anyone during those three years? I heard trolls are ...*yawn*... really scary. Scary bad."

The humming of Drinn's magic rose in pitch, as though annoyed by the questions of the children. The air thickened with the cloying smell of pressed flowers. Caetal began snoring.

Talara complained, "Drinn, they are ...*yawn*... starting to fall asleep. What's the point of telling a story nobody will be awake to hear the end of?"

"They can still hear you." Drinn muttered glottally, somehow managing to speak while rolling a hum around in the back of his throat. *"In fact, they can hear you even better now that the veil of waking distraction has been pulled back. Your story has begun to sink into their unprotected minds like a knife. So shut up, and get on with it."*

"How am I supposed to-" Talara began retorting, but Drinn hissed at her. The air around her head suddenly shrank and crackled alarmingly, so she scrunched her eyes closed again and continued hurriedly on with the tale.

....

"No, the 'trolls' did not attack during that time. Rarely had the Drôle of that lake encountered humans, and they had no idea what to expect from them. The ...*yawn*... character of their lives were measured by the movement of deep waters and the rotation of the sun. They saw that the trees were being felled upon the shore, but so what? Humanus are not the only industrial species, after all. A beaver fells trees; a bird gathers twigs, and otters make use of whatever they can get their paws on. The Drôle themselves are not the sort of creatures to use tools, although they are smart enough to do so if the need arises. They also do not seek to alter the landscape around them, preferring to dwell in natural grottos when they can find them. But when they cannot, they will dig burrows into clay and dwell along the water's edge. So, they understand the need to alter

the landscape to make a home. And the lake was immense — miles of shoreline where the trees remained undisturbed. *...yawn...* Why bother getting upset over the loss of one grove? If these strange beings needed to clear a wide space around themselves to thrive, who were the Drôle to interfere?

"Even so, their natural curiosity compelled them to observe the humans from a distance. They could often be seen around twilight, underwater to the neck *...yawn...* with only their eyes above water. It was an eerie sight to see drifting packs of them with the fading light of the sunset shining in their amphibious eyes. But they never got any closer. The dead smell of iron tools and armor repelled them."

....

Now Tarquin's snores blended with Caetal's. Mathias' eyes watered from heavy yawning. Resolutely, he clutched the symbol of Cuthain where it was hidden under his shirt and worried what his god might think about ordanians that allowed magi to ensorcell them. But his sleepy grip slackened around the edge of the steel amulet as the story continued.

....

"Yet, there was one human amongst the deathly-smelling crowd who fascinated the Drôle enough to risk contact. She was the only one who seemed to take an interest in the lake itself.

"While the trees fell and the laborers labored, the magus explored the vast expanse of the Green Cradle. By canoe and by day, through all the months of the year, she traversed the lake alone. *...yawn...* Sometimes she paddled herself, and sometimes a current of water was compelled to carry her small boat wherever she wished it to go. By the end of the first year, she knew every... inlet and tributary stream well enough to map them in her mind. By the end of the second year, she could have sailed the *...yawn...* whole lake in the dark with no light to guide her. But she never did — always retreating to the shore when the sun set. Night after night she sat, safely distanced from the water's edge, watching the moons rise and counting the pairs of shining eyes that watched her back. Occasionally, the Drôle called out to her in their guttural language, entreating that she take a risk and join them for an evening swim. For two years, she never responded.

"Then one day, she did."

...............................∞∞

Talara's jaw ached from yawning. Her head swam warmly in the flowering air. She blinked her closed eyes rapidly, trying to keep the fragile soap bubble of the story from popping in her mind. She could hear Rahyn softly breathing somewhere to her left, and to the right, the thin whine of Mathias' lungs as he gulped in the last waking lungfuls of breath before the magical sleep stole him away into Dream. Drinn's droning hum bored through her thoughts like a beetle.

...............................∞∞∞∞

"I cannot tell you exactly what transpired between the magus and the Drôle to inspire them to cooperate with her. Whether the enchantment that ensorcelled the Drôle was of a magical nature or ...*yawn*... or whether they were naturally enthralled by the first human that ever bothered to learn enough of their language to communicate, there are none living that can say. What we *do* know is that by the time the tower was completed, the magus had managed to acquire the greatest secret that the Drôle possessed: the True Name of the lake itself.

"As I said, whether that powerful Word had been offered trustingly or surrendered under enchantment's subtle tortures is unknown. All we can ...*yawn*... be sure of is that the day the tower was finished and the magus locked herself inside it, she was seen to be carrying only one thing with her as she crossed the threshold and shut the door behind her. Tucked under her arm was a large tablet made of baked clay. Carved into the tablet's surface was a single rune that dripped moisture and sighed with the wind's own breath.

"The door to the tower shut on a hot afternoon in the month of Zephyrlûn. After three days passed, the thegn began knocking at the door. For three weeks, he slept ...*yawn*... in a tent pressed up against the tower wall, waking up at all hours of the night to wail and curse her name beneath the open window high above him, begging her most piteously to restore the love he was sure they shared. Confounded and undone by the lack of her charms, he tore at himself in tantrums that shredded clothing and dignity alike, until his young beard was patchy and bloodied and his eyes were as raw as his voice. Finally, the captain of the guard had the good sense to beat him unconscious and carry him back to Portuan. There he wintered, and recovered, and brooded."

"At spring's first blush, in the month of Mistral, Revis returned to Drôleduyan at the head of an army. They set up camp near the pier, preparing ...yawn... to besiege her through the rainy season and starve her out.

"The days were damp and the nights were freezing. Often the fog was so dense that the lake looked like a stain on an endless sheet of white, and nothing else seemed left of the world but shifting vapors. At those times, the soldiers stared uneasily into the mist and privately despaired that they had come to such a place near the border of the Twilight Lands. Perhaps reality as they knew it was leaking away forever into the fog.

"Yet, there were clear days as well during that ...*yawn*... long wet spring; clear enough to see the tower across the water and observe its stillness. The magus that dwelled there was never seen, though a candle burned steadily in the open upper window as though someone had just set it down and forgotten about it.

"So, Revis ordered the last of the trees in that grove to be felled, hewn, and turned into ships of war that could ferry all his soldiers to the island. For although Revis owned a few longboats already, he was not foolish enough to believe that anything less than his greatest fighting strength had a hope against the magus. His love had soured into the sort of hateful madness that waking up from years of enchanted charms can cause. He did not give one thought to the scores of trees that fell to his axes, no more than ...*yawn*... he lamented the fate that awaited those soldiers.

"Instead, as every thegn who ruled before him had also done, he paced and plotted while less fortunate men labored through those freezing months to satisfy his will."

..........................∞∞∞∞∞∞∞∞∞∞∞

Half asleep, but proudly struggling against the darkness to finish the tale, Talara paused a moment and listened to the quieting night. She felt a warm pressure against her eyes, and dared not open them. No waking sounds could be heard at all anymore, not even the humming of Drinn's spell. All she could hear was the stuttering chorus of sleepers breathing, and the dragging drone of snores. Over in the direction where Rahyn slept, Talara heard the rustling of a body rolling over restlessly, and the crackling of dry leaves.

What is that quiet whimpering sound? Talara yawned deeply and struggled to make sense of her drifting thoughts. *The wind is whimpering.*

But she could feel her memory of how the story finished beginning to thin and disperse from her tired mind, so she cleared her throat and continued on towards the end of the tale. Her words sounded cottony and far away in her own ears, like someone else was telling the story on the other side of the dreaming wall.

····················∞∞∞∞∞∞∞∞∞∞∞∞∞

"*Finally, on a beautiful day in late spring, the soldiers boarded their longboats and prepared themselves for victory.* By now, months without seeing a sign of resistance from the magus had emboldened Revis and his soldiers alike. *…yawn…* The cold miseries of early spring were a memory that sunlight made scarce. They felt the warmth on their skin and the excitement for battle arose within them. The moment came when the boats all shoved off from their moorings, and the soldiers began the easy journey towards the small island. There was a fresh breeze blowing behind them and less than a mile of open water to cross.

"Yet, for the best of their efforts, they could not make headway toward the island. Though they rowed with the wind behind them, hidden currents bore them off course. The boats slowly spun in listless circles like leaves caught in whirlpools. Soldiers at their long oars rowed in mounting frenzy, shouting impotent challenges at the unruffled vastness of the sky. But *…yawn…* their efforts only scattered them across the lake until each boat drifted alone. One by one, the ships blundered back against the shore that they had launched from. Some damage was done to those vessels that bumped into the dock or beached themselves against rocks, but nothing serious. It was their prides that were damaged worse, for although their training and armor made them soldiers, many there were amongst them who considered themselves very competent sailors as well. No ballads would *…yawn…* ever be written to extol the honors of an army defeated by gentle breezes and hidden currents. The lake had made fools of them all.

"And that, of course, was not a slight that could be borne. The soldiers grumbled and muttered amongst themselves as they moored their ships at dock again and returned to their camps. Their moods were as sour as old milk, and an early evening fog rolling in off the water did nothing to revive them. Around their fires they clustered and drank and planned *…yawn…* and cursed and… drank. By nightfall, their wits were adequately pickled with spirits so that they were able to celebrate themselves again; the lucky survivors of water witchery. After all, was it not their skill as boatmen that overcame devious currents meant to topple and drown them?

"And none there were amongst them so drunk as Thegn Revis himself. Tumbled between boasting and spite, with his captains cheering him on, Revis devised a plan. He ordered his drunken army back into their longboats, insisting that a magus must *…yawn…* sleep deeply after hours spent in wicked sorcery. He bade each captain lash their boats together with thick hawsers, that they might not be scattered by currents again. He forbade the lighting of lamps at prow or stern, so that the mist would conceal them, pointing their way towards the island by the single glow of the candle that burned in the high window of the tower. This light could be seen haunting the foggy air with a spectral glow from a long way off. It was an ominous and unnatural sight, but it further emboldened the … *yawn…* drunken soldiers in their righteous efforts to snuff out the blue flame of heathen sorcery."

"*'You should have slit her throat at the altar, my thegn.'* The captain of the guard muttered overboldly as he watched the last of the… big ropes stretched between the waiting ships. Supplies and munitions were being loaded as quietly as drunken excited soldiers could load them.

"Revis dismissed the comment with a flick of his fingers. 'Would that I had. But there is still time. I shall… wrap my hands around her throat and throttle out the last of her loving lies until she is purpled and slain. Let us find out what honesty remains in a corpse when all deception has been choked out of it.'"

"That is something *…yawn…* I would like to see." The captain nodded grimly, scratching at the stubble on his neck.

"Bid all your soldiers to make ready; you'll see it tonight." Revis shrugged his heavy cloak over his shoulders. "I will board the lead longboat with you and sail to the island myself. Pass along the word to leave the campfires burning. Their lights will tell the story of… the fog will— … *yawn…*"

..........∞∞∞∞∞∞∞∞∞∞∞∞∞∞∞∞

"*Well, anyway… you know what he meant,*" Talara muttered, her voice sounding thick and slumberous. Her head lolled loosely on her neck. "The campfires were a distraction to make the magus think they were… still onshore, just in case she wasn't… you know… actually asleep and was paying attention to Revis. And his army."

......∞∞∞∞∞∞∞∞∞∞∞∞∞∞∞∞∞∞∞∞

"So: ...so. Yes. Off they... sailed again, steering through the ink-dark water toward the distant whisplight of the lit tower. ...Lit candle in the tower window. They were otherwise as blind as newborn kittens in that fog, which... pooled around their sight so densely that each *...yawn...* woman and man aboard could barely see each other's faces, though they were side by side. The boats scuttled ungracefully across the midnight water, lashed and bumping together with their thick... those thick ropes. So that the center boats were bound into a useless drifting struggle like flies in a spider's web, and... only the outer boats *...yawn...* could paddle on their open side. All... the-"

...∞∞∞∞∞∞∞∞∞∞∞∞∞∞∞∞∞∞∞∞∞∞

Talara murmured and sighed. Her head tipped forward, and she fell asleep. There was a moment of swimming vertigo; the feeling of dropping slowly from a great height. The pressure on her eyelids vanished, and she felt herself take a deep breath of air, although she sensed she didn't need to.

She opened her eyes to find herself sitting cross-legged around the same campfire. Across the swimming firelight she saw her friends were sprawled in various states of attentive relaxation. Talara smiled to herself and closed her eyes again, searching for the gossamer thread that led back to her memory of how the tale ended.

∞∞∞∞∞∞∞∞∞∞∞∞∞∞∞∞∞∞∞∞∞∞∞

"All voices were hushed into silence, so that the only sounds that could be heard were the uneven splashing of oars, the ominous creaking of ships bumping into each other, and the quiet cursing of their captains. The drunken bravado that had carried them back onto the water drained away into the fog as sight of the shore they had launched from was swallowed in vapor. Only the fading flutter-light of their abandoned campfires could be seen, and the single steady blue candle flame floating ahead and above them. Though they were buffeted by invisible currents, the tangle of ships pressed onward towards that light.

"It was Thegn Revis himself who first sensed the presence of the Drôle.

"From where he stood at the bow of the lead ship, he could not see them, for there was no light to reflect in their shining eyes. Yet he could hear them burbling and chuckling all around him; could feel the subtle vibration of many hands grasping the underbelly of the ship from below. The lead boats began to rock against each other; the hawser ropes twisted and tugged; the sound of gnawing could be heard on all sides. Revis called to his soldiers to draw bow and fire upon them, but what arrows were loosed splashed harmlessly into the lake.

"Within minutes, the hawsers that bound Revis' longship to those that followed it were chewed through and dropped into the water with a report of splashes. Then a steady tugging movement began below the water line; many webbed feet churning underwater all at once, and Revis' boat was pulled forward from the rest at a speed that paddling could not match. A sudden current arose against that tangle of ships and pushed it back towards the shore and the distant throbbing of light from their abandoned campfires. Suddenly alone in the fog, and with the curses of his captains fading out of hearing as they were drifted away, Revis and his crew found themselves smoothly tugged the remaining distance to the island, and pulled into dock. Having little choice, he called for the mooring rope to be secured.

"The captain of the guard, no longer concerned with stealth, yelled to his crew to light their torches and hold them overhead. The flare of that sudden firelight was reflected in a thousand pairs of froglike eyes and stuttered into sight a tangling litheness of hundreds of Drôle, crowding the beach around the tower like a rookery of wet seals drying themselves on the rocks. It was a sobering sight.

"When the soldiers stepped onto the dock at last, as they knew they must, the Drôle flowed in around and behind them like a tide, leaving only the way towards the tower clear. Revis and the soldiers were herded forward, many of them shuddering and holding their noses. The crowd of Drôle smelled rankly amphibious: a fleshy dampness like wet snake sheddings in curdled pond algae. To the Drôle, the men reeked of dead iron and the fermented exhalations of alcohol, now sweating fearfully through all their pores. When the Drôle had herded the soldiers to the tower door, they withdrew to the water's edge and warily watched from there.

"The moment that Revis had obsessed over for months finally came to pass, for when he craned his neck and looked up, he saw the figure of his lust and torment silhouetted in the open window above him. The blue candle sat on the windowsill before her, and in her hands, she clutched the clay tablet on which the True Name of the lake was writ. Thin rivulets of water dripped down her arms. Her face was impassive — as smooth and untroubled as a mirror. To Revis, whose heart still constricted around the buried shards of enchantment, her beauty was a wound that had never healed. He sneered, and spat, and looked away.

"*We have come here to end you, Witch.*' He called out, staring at the stone wall in front of him that he had paid to build. The frustration of that alone was almost enough to give him courage to look at her again.

"'But you cannot.' She replied, in a consoling voice. 'So, you should go.'

"'Why did you separate my ship and drive the others back if you did not want to see me again? Why did you bring me here?'

"'I did not. My Drôle did.'

"'At your command. You wanted to see me. Admit that this is so.'

"The magus frowned slightly and stared over his head towards the beach, not bothering to reply. The breeze carried the distant calls for order from the ship captains and their crews across the water. There was a moment of awkward silence while Revis' soldiers shuffled and jingled in their armor. The captain of the guard glanced at his thegn expectantly."

"'Apparently my Drôle wanted you here. There is nothing I require of you any longer. Take your soldiers and depart.'

"'You are my wife. *Mine.* You belong to me — you and this damn tower. Both mine.'

"'You know that isn't true. I can no more be yours than a snail can claim the tree it climbs. You are too small and fragile to own someone like me.'

"The captain of the guard drew his sword. 'Watch your tone, Witch. This is your thegn, not some thrall.'

"'He is a boy playing at manhood: you all are. Go home. You will not find your worth here adrift on my lake. Only death.'

"A collective hissing arose from the Drôle, and the dark mass of them constricted inward, narrowing the distance between themselves and the tower. The soldiers growled; torchlight shimmered on drawn blades. Slowed by caution, the Drôle continued to slink slowly forward. The air soured with their creeping smell. Revis spat again, and glared up at the candle that shone on the window sill."

"'You are a Fýrii whore who thinks it is human. I curse the day we first spoke, for I cannot get the taste of you out of my mouth. My army will besiege you here on this tiny island, day and night, until all your waking moments are spent in waste and mourning, as mine are. Your tower is a witch's cage that I have caught you in.'

"'You have no army.' She replied, clutching the clay tablet to her breast. The water running down her arms from the rune on the tablet overflowed the window ledge and began to drip down the stone wall. 'My lake is full of boastful children struggling to keep their toy boats in line. They have almost managed it, you know; I can see them from here, lining up those toy boats in tidy rows. Would you like to see? I shall dispel the mist for you.'

"And she did. The mist withdrew from the surface of the lake as quickly as though a vast set of lungs inhaled it all. Now Revis and his soldiers could see the ships of their fellows untangling their hawser ropes and lining up in rows again — pressed back against the shore as though they had never sailed that night. The soldiers muttered in superstitious wonder, and made signs to ward themselves against fae and evil.

"'You see? Fragile boats full of fragile children that will never again leave shore.'

"Thegn Revis grimaced. 'They do not need to. You are cut off from help or supplies. We can starve you out.'

"The magus smiled indulgently. 'You can try. The whole of this lake and all of its bounty are mine now. The Drôle will provide me with anything I will need. And they will die to protect me, if I ask them to.'

"As one, the Drôle hissed again, drawing inward like a noose around the tower and the cluster of soldiers. The sound of their anger was wet and steamy. Now the soldiers could see the glint of claws on flexing hands and bared teeth reflected in the firelight; the lanky height of these creatures that so rarely stood upright. Clearing their throats and glancing nervously back towards the boat, the soldiers shrank against each other. Revis did not seem to notice, or to care. He stepped further towards the tower door, and said:

"'We can wait for years. You will grow weary of cress and fish while we feast on venison and wine.'

"'It shall never be so. Go home, boy. You cannot understand me, and so I will spare you harm. My waters will carry you safely to shore again; go home.'

"'I am no godsdamn boy! I am a man grown, and will be the most powerful thegn in Eld! With you by my side, we could—'

"'I will never again suffer another moment of your company. I have no further use for you. Leave from here, or my Drôle will tear your soldiers apart.'

"The magus turned to step away from the window. And that is when Revis shot her."

∞∞∞∞∞∞∞∞∞∞∞∞∞∞∞∞∞∞∞

"He had not intended to shoot her. Or at least that is how the story is told.

"He had almost forgotten about the black crossbow he had been clutching beneath his cloak, for when he gazed again upon her face, he knew in his heart that he had already been defeated by her years ago; that the memory of this failed confrontation would haunt him like a ghost for years to come. There were no words that existed in his language for how broken apart he was for the lack of her, and how much he hated her for that. After all, he had amassed an entire army and cut down a small forest just to see her again. And isn't that love?

"Her dismissal slammed into him as it had been aimed to do. But it was when she began to turn her back on him, and he knew for certain that he would never see her again and she would not care in the slightest about it, that he yanked his cloak aside and his finger pulled the trigger.

"The crossbow was not carefully aimed, but it was fired at short range. As the magus turned at the open window, the bolt pierced through her wrist and slammed into her belly, shattering the clay tablet she carried in her arms. She sagged against the window frame in shock.

"Then a terrible screaming was heard."

∞∞∞∞∞∞∞∞∞∞∞∞∞∞∞∞∞∞∞

"Such a story is always told by those who survived it. Likely one of the soldiers, or perhaps the captain of the guard himself, who was amongst the fortunate few who lived to remember that night.

"What is said of the screaming that followed ELD is that it might have been the worst noise that was ever heard by mortal ears. It was the collective scream of the Drôle, hundreds of voices lifted in a cacophony of anguish and rage as they charged forward to defend their home. It was the banshee scream of the magus as she stared at the bloody water rushing out of her wound and the shards of the tablet that was crumbling in her arms. But most awful of all was the scream of Revis, who had dreamed of nothing but revenge against the only person he had ever loved for so long, and had never imagined how awful the moment would be when it finally happened. The spell she had laid upon him when they met had been utter and unending, so that he felt the pain of every inch of that crossbow bolt as though it had pierced his own body. He knew with sudden certainty how similar she and he were: empty and wounded and howling. And through the wailing collective scream, her words thundered over their heads like a breaking storm.

"'YOU DARE?! OH, WHAT YOU DARE!'

"Then she raised the largest shard of the tablet overhead like a knife, and stabbed it into the empty air. Water began to pour all around her, rushing out of the open window like a waterfall. The mortar between the stones of the tower bulged and sweated.

"The soldiers, knowing that their end was coming, held their swords aloft and prepared to die. The Drôle rushed over them like a wave and tumbled them to the sand. Some of the soldiers hacked and cleaved as they fell, and those that did died for it. A few were trampled underfoot by many webbed feet and did not move again. But it was towards the tower that the Drôle were rushing, and within moments the beach that had been swarming with angry Drôle was emptied.

"Noting that their ship now floated unguarded at the dock, the surviving soldiers fled towards it, with the captain of the guard cursing them all for cowards as he ran beside them. He dragged Revis along with him, who was stunned with shock and babbling nonsense.

"'WHERE IS YOUR ARMY NOW, REVIS? I AM DRÔLEDUYAN. I WILL SUFFER THEM NO LONGER.'

"The stones of the tower began to tremor under pressure as its interior flooded. Around the wounded magus, water gushed out the window with geyser force. The blue flamed candle was swept away in the deluge and lost from sight. At ground level, the front door creaked and groaned as water sprayed out around the edges of it. What magics had held it closed flared and failed. The double doors wrenched open with such force that their iron hinges tore like paper. Stampeding Drôle were swept back into the lake by that sudden gushing river, although some were able to reach the tower base and began to climb.

"'THEY COULD NOT SAIL ABOVE ME, SO LET THEM DROWN BENEATH ME. WATCH, GREAT THEGN, AND SUFFER.'

"Then the wounded magus at the center of the geysering window raised her arms above her head with her palms flat. She cried out a Word that gulped the air out of the sky. A crushing wave of pressure washed across the fleeing soldiers, flattening them against the deck of their ship. The ship itself rolled hard against the dock, and would have tipped completely over if all the water beneath it had not rushed away as it suddenly did. The body of the lake concaved from the island outward and reared up into one massive swell of water that flowed at great speed towards the far shore.

"There was precious little time for Revis' army to react. Some dove overboard from their ships and drowned in their armor. But most simply stood dumfounded as the still surface of the lake suddenly lifted the ready-line rows of their entire band of longboats on the back of that massive swell and swept them hundreds of feet upland, washing away all their tents and campfires in one great rush, and depositing their ships with the soldiers aboard into the mud amongst the stumps of the trees that had been felled to build them.

"Then there was a terrible moment of hope that befell the doomed soldiers. For if the great swell of water had behaved like a normal tidal wave, the ships would have been scattered and tumbled. But the swell that lifted those ships deposited them safely into the mud in the same rows they had been floating in, and then soaked away into the ground. Dazed but triumphant, the soldiers laughed and called out to each other, as they stood on the decks of their ships and stared around themselves in wonder. With the fog blown away, the light of both moons shone down on them and they could see the empty landscape of cut trees and trampled mud that their horses and industry had made. Yet at least they were safe on shore again.

"Or so it seemed. But the mud had become like quicksand; thick as porridge, deep as rising groundwater. The ships settled into it as low as they might on a tide, and continued to sink. The soldiers held their torches high and gazed down upon the mud in consternation, and beheld a horrible sight.

"The roots of the severed tree trunks all around them began to wriggle and rise. They swarmed up through the mud like rearing sea snakes; blindly seeking towards the ships. At first it was the thinner roots that broke the surface of the quickening mud, and these the soldiers hacked at as they began to wrap themselves around the ships. Then it was the thick old roots that had dove deep into the soil when they were feeding a living tree. These were as dense as brawny arms which grasped at ships and soldiers alike, and were difficult to cut and too wet to burn. Soon the sound of screaming began, as the ships began to be dragged underground by the dense tangle of the strangling roots. Muddy clay flowed over the gunwale and flooded the hulls of the ships, which only sped up their sinking.

"Many there were amongst the soldiers who chopped their way free of grasping roots and leapt over the sides of their ships to flee. They were the first to drown in the mud; their bodies were sucked down with their hands thrashing in the air above them. Yet there were equally many who simply stood and stared, and watched in awful melancholy as the ships they had built and sailed sank into the churning brown clay. Their last breaths were lungfuls of loam; their final view was of those dead tree stumps silhouetted against the sky all around them, whose vengeful webbing of roots wound around their dying bodies like funeral wraps.

"When the last of the trapped bubbles burbled up from underground, what was left was the barren landscape of a new swamp. In time, when the groundwaters receded and the soil settled and dried again, all that would remain as a reminder of the sunken ships and their doomed crews were long raised earthen mounds in unnaturally orderly rows."

∞∞∞∞∞∞∞∞∞∞∞∞∞∞∞∞∞∞∞∞

Talara glanced across the campfire at her friends. They sat in various states of listening tenseness — all but Rahyn, who must have wandered off. Talara nodded in satisfaction at the properly fearful glint in their eyes, as the story she was wrapping up made its indelible mark on their imaginations. All around them, the trees of the forest creaked in a well-timed sway of wind.

Perfect.

∞∞∞∞∞∞∞∞∞∞∞∞∞∞∞∞∞∞∞∞

"And what of the survivors who lived to tell the tale?" Talara murmured in a throaty whisper.

"As I said, there were few. Revis and his ship of soldiers paddled away from that cursed island as fast as fear could carry them. They headed up one of the tributary rivers, towards the shelter of the nearly finished stone keep that had also been under construction while the tower was being built. That luckless keep was fated to be overrun by the Drôle that soon followed after them, and would, in time, become known as the ruined keep of Drôle.

"Only Revis looked back at the island as they sailed away; he was the only one who beheld the unfortune fate of the magus. For when those Drôle who managed to climb the tower reached her where she stood in the open window, they did not help her as she had commanded them to do. Instead, they wrenched the shards of the shattered tablet from her arms and, grasping her limbs in many strong hands, tore her body to pieces. Upon the moment of her death, the upper stories of the tower ruptured and split.

"Those Drôle, and the pieces of her body, were swept into the lake on a bloodied flood of water that released from the tower with the force of a bursting dam. Within moments, the tower had become a ruin, and all the topsoil and vegetation on the island around it had been swept away by those sudden floodwaters and vanished beneath the surface of the lake. The lake claimed her body, but her spirit survived to claim the lake.

"Her vengeful spirit forced the Drôle to flee upriver from the lake that had birthed them, never again to return. Their descendants still live in that river, and that mage-haunted lake of Drôleduyan came to be known by the dread name that it bears to this day:

"Xör Uru. *The Hungry Deep.*"

∞∞∞∞∞∞∞∞∞∞∞∞∞∞∞∞∞∞∞

The tale finally finished, Talara uncrossed her legs and leaned backwards on her elbows, deciding she had a crink in her back, and taking a moment to stretch it. There was a respectful silence from around the fire, as each of them considered the story from the vantage of their own perspective.

"*Wow.*" Tarquin muttered. "Those poor soldiers."

"Yeah. It didn't turn out well for them. But that was the point of the tale. One of those cautionary ones. They always end tragically." Talara replied.

Mathias nodded knowingly, and shivered. "A moral too. A pretty grim one."

"Don't trust mages?" Tarquin queried. "Or thegns, or people who cut down all the trees. Actually, everyone in that story acted like an ass — the trolls were the best behaved. So maybe the moral is: '*don't act like a puckerditch or you might get killed by the very trees you cut down.*'"

"I don't think that was-"

"And you made that story up?" Melvin asked, staring at Talara with traces of undisguised admiration.

"Well, not *exactly*. It's a retelling of a story I heard from my mother years ago."

"But... didn't Drinn specifically instruct you to... I have this feeling you weren't supposed to retell a true story?"

Talara gestured towards the distant rowboat that Drinn was paddling out on the lake. The wind creaked through the branches.

"It's not like he stuck around to hear the ending anyway. What does it matter if the story is real or made up?"

Melvin frowned, struggling to recall why it seemed important. "I think it might matter a lot."

Talara shrugged elaborately. "I don't give a fiddler's fart what Drinn said. What harm could it possibly do? It's an old story — probably mostly made up anyway."

Melvin glanced at Mathias, who was staring intently out at the lake. Caetal decided the campfire smoke was blowing his way, and he ought to cough.

"W-w-where's Rahyn gone?" Caetal coughed, glancing around. "And w-where are we?"

The dry leaves on the ground began to rustle all around them, as though a wind was blowing.

Talara shrugged and stood up. "Excuse me, comrades: I probably ought to pee."

∞∞∞∞∞∞∞∞∞∞∞∞∞∞∞∞∞∞∞

Talara Escapes the Dream

If you want to know what bad luck feels like, try having a dead guy grab your leg while you are squatting in the dark to take a pee. I'm so mad I don't even manage to get properly scared until I have my breeches pulled back up and whirl around to punch a pervert in the face, and end up putting my fist into the reeking hole where a lower jaw should be. Then I yelp, of course, while pieces of the creature's jaw collapse around my fist. If I had not already drained my water, I might have wet myself right there. But I don't; in fact, I feel like I still have to pee. But how is that possible—

{ And that is when I remember that I am inside Mathias' dream. Ironically, my full bladder ended up saving our lives. But we will get to that shortly. }

The sudden realization of being in a dream saves me from a coward's drenching, but when the other shadows under the trees suddenly lunge at me, I run. Real or not, the undead are terrifying.

∞∞∞∞∞∞∞∞∞∞∞∞∞∞∞∞∞∞∞∞∞

I've never known anything as panic-inducing as having to sprint full tilt through the dark of night in an overgrown forest. I stumble over every snaking root and burst through an acre of clawing shrubbery, all in moon-dappled darkness. I run until my breath wheezes and my throat feels charred, and then suddenly remember I'm not really breathing. Yet, the fear seems very real, and I catch myself doubting my memory of being asleep on the ground in another world than this.

I thrash through the godsdamn trees that shouldn't even be here. I think I'm making as much noise as a human can possibly make who is not yet actively screaming. It's one thing to imagine all the horrors that could creep out at you in the night — like spiders, because I'm covered in webbing now and I hate it — and quite another to know what they are, and that they really are coming for you. After a solid minute of blind panic, I recover my wits and circle back towards the fire, to the far edge of the clearing where Caetal's crossbow lays on the pile of discarded saddle bags. He thinks the world of that thing, but for me just winding the cocking mechanism back is a ridiculous strain. But I need a weapon.

{ Oh wait a minute: the horses; we have horses

in here! We can escape on horses! }

I swivel my head around hopefully, scanning the trees for an escape horse. They must have been tied up nearby — I can see their broken tethers hanging from the lowest branches. Out in the woods I can hear them screaming. It sounds almost human. It is a horrible sound.

{ I'm so sorry, dream horses! This is my fault, I brought you into this! }

As I grab the crossbow and heave it across my shoulder, the air explodes into hot light and our happy little campfire spirals skyward like a vortex. I am flattened against the trees by the roiling heat. Now the ruins of a one-armed man is shambling my way, dragging a rusted axe through the brown blanket of autumn leaves, and I'm running again. The trees thin in front of me and I veer away from the fire at a dead sprint. I think I can see the boys fighting with a skeletal host, but the light of the vortex is blinding and the shadows leap and intertwine. The damn crossbow bangs painfully into my shoulder, the cocking stirrup whacking rhythmically against my spine as I run. I don't know how anyone ever uses one of these things. I've always longed to fire it, however, and tonight is the night to try.

I run almost to the edge of the beach before throwing myself down into the tall cattails. The ground is spongy and wet beneath me. Laying on my side, I slide my foot into the stirrup and wedge the tiller back against my belly. Now I am soggy with ground water, and I hope all the spiders still clinging to me are drowning. I can hear something thrashing towards me through the dark as my shaking hands crank the crannequin back until the string is loaded taut, just like Caetal showed me. Into the flight groove I slide the only bolt, and I chase it with a prayer. I can't help but wonder how such a slow and cumbersome thing is ever used in war — a sweaty minute I just spent loading it could have sent me to an early grave. I imagine the creature outlined in moonlight just as the red moon appears from behind a cloud. This is my moment.

I rise, brace the tiller against my shoulder, and fire. I hit the creature just as he nears the dock. When the trigger goes off and the bolt launches, the tiller kicks back against me so hard my eyes tear up and my vision blurs. And when it clears, I realize that I just shot Tarquin.

I mean, I shot the dead man that was on top of him too... but even so.

I hate this crossbow.

∞∞∞∞∞∞∞∞∞∞∞∞∞∞∞∞∞∞∞∞∞∞∞

He drops like he's been, literally, shot. He is pinned to the dead(er) corpse; in the red moonlight I can see the arrow tore straight through the creature's ribcage and went into Tarquin's chest. Tarquin groans, and the two of them topple off the dock and into the lake. I drop the stupid crossbow, giving it a scolding kick. Then of course I'm running, and of course I'm going to leap in and save him. Nonetheless, just as I brace myself to dive into the water, two things happen at once. First, I remember I can't swim. Second, within that tottering moment, the bright fire that has been lighting up the night from the hilltop is suddenly snuffed out. In the dark, my confident dive devolves into a gasping plunge, and I hit the water like a thrashing idiot.

It is cold, and it is black as jet underwater. In moments, I can't tell what is up and where the bottom is, and I'm kicking myself end over end with my hair tangling up in a cloud around my face. My heart is racing, and my feet are useless and heavy in the water. Years ago, my mother tried to teach me to memorize long stanzas of poetry by floating me in a bathtub at night with the windows all covered up. She said that, by drifting in a lightless place, I would be able to expand mental effort and recall the ancient stories with more ease. To her dismay, I think I am the only girl in the world who can't float. A half hour later the floor of my room was soaking wet from my thrashing, my mother had stormed off, and I hadn't learned a thing. For some reason, as I begin to drown, I can't help but think about my mother. I guess life is like that sometimes.

Then I sense blood in the water that's flowing into my mouth, and something down below me launches up from the bottom of the lake in a cloud of mud. I feel a cold (yet living) hand brush against mine, then clasp it hard. I kick, and so does he, and together we yank each other up into the chilly night air, which is amazing to breathe in again as soon as I finish all of the vomiting that I'm suddenly doing. I encircle my arms around the algae-slick pillar of the dock and regurgitate lake water all over the drifting marsh weeds. Tarquin wraps his arms around me, and it feels like a great comfort, but I think he is just trying not to go unconscious. So as soon as I can move again, I slither my leg up onto the wooden planks and pull us both far enough out of the water for him to drag himself onto the dock. Then we lay there on the dock all tangled up together. I press the palm of my hand hard against the hole in his chest, and we watch the stars come out as his blood seeps slowly between my fingers.

∞∞∞∞∞∞∞∞∞..................

{ I don't know how long I would have laid there like that, lost in the terror of the dream. Tarquin's lifeblood was ebbing away as I held him, and my body started shaking with strangely dry sobs. I felt so defeated, and so tired. From far away, I heard a voice calling out for help. The Shamblemen were almost on top of us again; dry cattails rattled as they stumbled toward us through the marshy shore grasses. It was no use trying to run; there wasn't anywhere to go. I could feel it happening; could feel myself relaxing into hopelessness and staring up at the stars, just petting Tarquin's hair with my bloody hands and whispering soothing nonsense at him. I even considered closing my eyes to prepare myself for the final darkness that comes at the end.

And that is when I realized I still had to pee. Because I never truly had. Because somewhere else, in some place that was actually real, my living body was lying on the cooling ground with a full bladder. And no amount of trying to pee in this dream will relieve one drop of that feeling, because I am a ghost here, and real somewhere else, and I really... really... }

∞∞∞∞∞∞......................

...have to pee. Talara sat up with a gasp, her vision swimming and her bladder cramping. She clambered halfway to her feet before dizzying waves of vertigo washed over her. The air all around her hummed with noise, and the ground slithered with shadows. With eyes too filmy to see clearly, Talara lurched towards the edge of the firelight, tripping over a sleeping friend and collapsing onto them in the semi-dark. Whoever it was groaned, but didn't wake up. Mumbling bleary apologies, Talara got back to her feet and stumbled out of the glare of firelight, tugged her breeches down, and settled into a grateful squat. She sighed with a stream of satisfaction, rubbing at her filmy eyes and feeling drugged and woozy. She stood, tugging her breeches back up.

Then two awful things happened at the same time.

∞∞........................

The first awful thing was that her eyes began to sting where she had been rubbing them. When she glanced at her hands to wonder why, she saw that they were smeared with blood.

The second even more awful thing was a skeletal hand that grasped her from behind. Freezing pain knifed through her shoulder.

This time, Talara screamed.

....

A Nightmare for Rahyn

Rahyn couldn't sleep.

It's not that she didn't try; it was that she was rarely able to. The spirit of Syrahana-yerall-aneh was the most active inside her around the liminal hours of sunset and sunrise when the veil between the spirit and the flesh is thinnest. Those twilit hours and the evening between them were the best hunting time for foxes and owls and other predators who could see well in the dark, and often when Rahyn lay down to rest, her body was borrowed and transformed into the fox.

There were times when Rahyn awoke from the deepest sleep and felt as though she had been running all night long. The days that followed those sorts of evenings were often spent napping. Too many restless nights in a row caused Rahyn a sense of drifting through her own life; awake inside herself far less often than she was dreaming, which only served to deepen her suspicion that time did not pass for her the way it did for other people.

Yet on that night, with the drone of Drinn's spell buzzing in her ears, she experienced something that she could not ever remember having experienced before: Syrahana-yerall-aneh — who had no knowledge of the spellcraft of magi, or resistance to it whatsoever — fell asleep so utterly inside of her that no sense of her watchful presence could be felt at all. It was the strangest feeling of sudden emptiness, as chilling and supernatural as a total eclipse, and for a moment Rahyn panicked. As Talara's story mumbled into sleeping silence, Rahyn lay there with sweat blooming on her palms and her heart stammering, nuzzling around inside her own mind for any presence of Syrahana-yerall-aneh.

She felt nothing. A spirit that sleeps does not breath or sigh, nor roll over and scratch at fleas. It is entirely still, as the living never are. So Rahyn lay there for a minute in that magically sodden silence with tears rolling down her face and felt lonelier and more abandoned than she had ever felt before in her life.

Then she heard the crackling of dead brambles being pushed aside, and felt the dragging tremors of many creatures digging up through the ground. Abruptly she sat up, gazing around herself and straining to listen for the source of movement. But it came from everywhere, all around her.

A smell of animate decay tinged with metal and a bitterness that burns as sharply as bitumen filled the air. The stink of undeath. Her gaze flickered rapidly across her friends, drugged by magic and asleep all around the campfire. Once more, she reached into the darkness behind her mind and called out in desperation for that feral mother-fox who had always been there to protect her, even when Rahyn didn't want her to. Yet there was nothing left inside her but herself.

With a low growl rolling in her throat, Rahyn sprang up into a crouch. She bounded over to where Drinn slept, sprawled awkwardly across the wooden table as though passed out drunk. She grabbed his shoulders and shook him roughly.

"PLEASE WAKE UP!" She yelled, her voice beginning to jitter with panic. *"HELP US!"* But though she shook him thoroughly, he lay there as pale and waxen as one who is dead. His clothes were soaking wet and his head lolled on his neck, as though he were drifting underwater.

"Help." She murmured, glancing around helplessly at the bodies of her friends. Mathias groaned in his sleep, rolling over and clutching his arm against his chest. Caetal sweated and thrashed. A thick trickle of blood drooled out of Tarquin's open mouth. Rahyn went over and kneeled beside him, carefully prying his eyelids open with two fingers. His pupils were rolled so far back that only white was visible. Tears leaked steadily out of the corners of his eyes.

....

The sounds of creaking bones and clinking armor could now be heard. The smell of rotten anger ripened alarmingly.

Rahyn yanked the claw-shaped copper karam from her belt sheath and sliced it rapidly across the palms of her hand, yelping twice in pain. Then she fell to her knees and dug her shaking fingers deep into the soft soil, closing her eyes and trying to clear her mind of everything but the Green.

"There will be bone tonight, rich with nutrients." Her heart whispered aloud, though it hammered fearfully against her chest. *"Taste of my blood and know my need. Source from me. The ungrieved dead are restless; they do not belong aboveground — they have already spent all the time the sky has given them. Catch them with your tendrils and net them in your roots.*

Digest their bones and recycle their nutrients. Grow as if the seasons were rapidly spinning, and you were always full of sunlight. Forget the limits of time. Grow to the edge of imagination."

She began to hum; a keening wail that branched up out of her open mouth with such force that it scraped her throat raw. She sensed her friends stirring uneasily in their sleep. Radiating out from Rahyn, a network of living tendrils began to emerge from underground. This carpet of blackberry and caneberry vines flexed itself forward in spurts of growth, crawling blindly across the soil, seeking to feast on the phosphorus and calcium of old bones. For those revenants that still lay buried underground, the contracting net of vines was quite effective; weaving itself between ribs and pushing through sockets, scratching and serrating, beginning the long work of turning bone into soil.

But there were many more revenants who had clawed themselves fully out of the barrow mounds. Most of them ignored those grasping vines or tore right through them, for they were far less dense and numerous aboveground. These Shamblemen began to close in hungrily around the warm bodies that sat or slept besides the campfire. Rahyn could hear them coming, and knew for certain that she would not be able to stop them all. She glanced down at her karam — that beautiful blade which had been the first gift that Djaro the Crow had ever given her. Its handle was wolf bone that had been shaped by fýrii magic to grow organically around the tang of the curved copper blade, so that metal and bone fused into one deadly purpose. She felt the weight of it in her hands, as heavy as hopelessness. Unconsciously, she tilted the blade towards her stomach.

Grandfather Crow: please find a way to visit my mother, where she stands alone in that good mud by the Twilight River. Please tell her that even the little I know about her made me proud to be her daughter. Tell her that Syrahana-yerall-aneh did everything she could to be the mother I needed all these years. Tell her that I lived well, because of the three of you, and the sacrifices you each made for me. I wish it didn't have to end like this. But if it must, then I am ready.

She began to hum an old song; one that she had heard her mother sing on the day she was born, so long ago that there was no memory of the moment at all, except the glad vibrations and the strands of sorrows that life is woven from. It was that song that every daughter finally learns when it is time to say goodbye. She squeezed her eyes tightly shut. Her hands tightened around the karam handle.

Then she heard Talara scream, and she opened her eyes again in surprise.

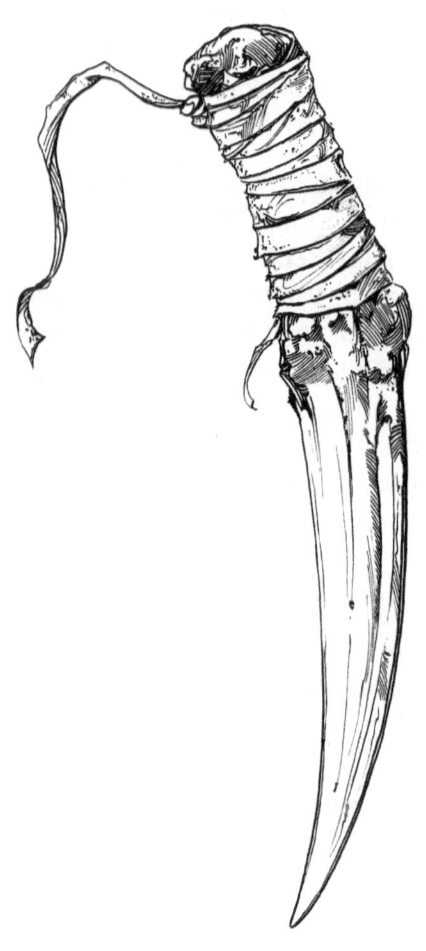

The Dreaming Dead

It no longer mattered whether we were awake or asleep. The veil between dreaming and awake is already as thin as daydreams, and now that veil had been torn by the claws of magic and the honesty of a story that was not supposed to be true. I, who share my body with a fox's restless spirit and live in such a state that wanders between dwalm and waking, knew immediately that Dream and Reality were bleeding into each other as though both were wounded.

The clearing between the barrow mounds had become haunted by trees; spectral, insubstantial, but stirred into rustling by a wind that felt real. They gathered in the dark all around us like smoke. The autumn-dry smell of their leaves faded and swelled as our belief in them wavered — or perhaps our presence had no bearing on them at all, and it was the memories of those old stumps that we were smelling. Maybe they were only real to me because I wanted them to be. I still don't know what Talara was seeing. I didn't have time to ask.

I tackled the first of the Shamblemen that grabbed her, tearing its boney claws out of her shoulder as rapidly as I could and kicking its body to pieces. Like a tick, it is best to pluck the undead off of living skin before they begin to energetically feed. This one had Talara by the shoulder long enough to leave red welts on a patch of skin that started to turn a pale gray, and I could see from the shock on her face how much it hurt. But she grasped up the rusty sword that the Shambleman dropped when I kicked its knees out from under it, and leapt into the fight beside me. It was the first time either of us had ever fought like that — back-to-back, keeping the fire between the revenants and us, and keeping ourselves between them and our sleeping friends. And all the while, as we hacked and swore, dodging between those thin moments that divide luck and death, the haunting forest flickered in and out of existence all around us.

....

I lashed out with my copper claw-bladed karam, and she with that rusty old sword. Bones splintered; papery flesh was punctured and torn, and my arms and legs and neck burned with cold where bone fingers had torn through cloth. They were blessedly slower than the living with a weapon in hand, for it is the vitality of blood and muscle that allows for speed. But the revenants had all been soldiers, once. Fighting instincts animated them as surely as the memories of the lives they had lost. Talara and I had not yet trained to sustain and survive in combat such as this, which drags on and on. We are both agile and quick on our feet, and both of us were defending sleeping friends who could not defend themselves, so we moved with the speed of desperation. But the living tire. The dead do not.

I cannot tell you how long we fought, except to say that it was so long that nothing else remained inside me but gasping determination. I was so worn out that even my fear had been consumed by the fire of survival. Talara and I now leaned against each other, sticky with our own sweat and blood and gasping encouragements to each other that we no longer felt were true.

Piles of shattered bones and rusted weapons were scattered around us in heaps, laying amongst the desiccated memory of leaves that had fallen beneath those ghostly trees. But there were more warriors shambling towards us; so many more. We were two, and they were what remained of an army. We needed help. Shouting and shaking had not woken our friends. We had to try something else.

"Wish we had those damn horses." Talara gasped, sagging against me. I felt the muscles in her back flexing as she swung her sword, and I heard her swear when it missed.

"*What horses?*" I panted, stabbing out. My karam caught on a bony forearm and was almost wrenched from my hand.

"Nevermind. Dream horses. They died already anyway."

"I'm sorry." I replied, not knowing what else to say. It was silly to mourn for imaginary horses, but I felt myself doing it anyway. Riding away from this nightmare sounded wonderful just then. But our friends would die if we fled, and that wasn't an option.

"We need to... hang on-" Talara said, and I thought she had finished her thought, for she stopped talking for a moment and began hacking vigorously at something that bumped into me from behind. I felt my feet slipping on dry leaves, and almost fell to my knees before I reminded myself they weren't really there.

"*We will hang on.*" I muttered, not really believing myself. But then Talara pushed me sideways, and we skipped together out of the way while a Shambleman teetered past us and stumbled into the campfire.

"Sorry, I was interrupted." Talara panted, grinning grimly. "What I meant to say was 'we need to wake the godsdamned wizard who got us into this mess.'"

"I already tried. He can't be woken. I think he might have drowned."

"Dammit, really? *What an asshole.*" Talara grumbled. She blocked the arc of a down-sweeping sword.

"Kick the knees out." I reminded, demonstrating. The revenant fell, still writhing.

"Thanks."

Together, we kicked the animated bones apart. Afterwards, as we dodged two more that lunged in towards us by leaping across the campfire, I felt her hand squeeze my arm reassuringly, and it suddenly struck me how grateful I was that she was here with me. *I hope we survive this. I don't understand why I'm so shy around her. I want to be a better friend.*

Tears begin to leak out of my eyes, and this strange feeling of giddiness came over me — likely some close cousin to hopelessness, but I'd never felt anything like it before. Everything seemed so *funny* just then. I turned in a wide circle, taking in the swarming undead, and the increasing danger we were all in. I started to shudder, tittering with suppressed laughter. Then Talara was shaking me, and my focus snapped back to the present moment.

"Rahyn! I've got an idea. Let's try to wake Mathias! He was the host for the dream. If he wakes up, the spell might break and tumble them all out of it. *Come on*!" She said, grabbing my hand and dragging me towards where he slept.

"What if-" My thought was interrupted as a legless skeleton on the ground whose knees I had kicked out earlier reached up with a rusty dirk clutched in hand and stabbed me in the boot. I felt the tip of the blade saw against my shinbone and yelped in pain, dropping to one knee. Talara whirled around and pounced on it, falling on the ribcage with her knees tucked up beneath her. The spine snapped; ribs scattered like ninepins. We helped each other up, dizzy and shaking with adrenaline.

"*What were you... about to say?*" She panted, uselessly brushing dirt off my knee. I could feel the blood oozing down my shin and making my sock squishy. Then she groaned.

"Dammit: hold that thought." She lunged over to where Tarquin lay, hacking at the skull of a revenant that was just starting to chew on him. I grabbed the corpse by the legs and dragged it further off. I could feel it squirming; the palms of my hands burned cold from where I grasped it. I shuddered and dropped the corpse quickly, turning around just in time to watch Talara boot the severed skull off into the woods.

"Alright, continue." She said, tucking a flyaway strand of hair behind her ear.

"I was just thinking: what if waking Mathias strands the rest of them in Dream? What if their bodies wake up, but their spirits are like drifting boats unmoored from a dock?"

Talara paled. She glanced at Mathias warily, chewing unconsciously on her fingernails. Then she glared at her hand and spat.

"Gross. My hands taste like old dead people. I'm such a *moros*; I can't *believe* I just put my finger in my mouth! Please remind me, when this is over, to stop chewing my fingernails."

Then she started laughing, and so did I. It seemed like the right thing to do just then. We sagged against each other with exhaustion and laughed so hard that we both got the hiccups. All the while, the Shamble-men closed in around us like the restless audience in a dangerous play. One of them stepped into a gopher hole and their leg got stuck and tore right off, and that *really* sent us into hysterics. I think we could have easily laughed ourselves to death right there, floating away from sense on the merry waters of absurdity. But then one of them swung a spear at Talara's head, and I tackled her to avoid it, and we both fell on top of Mathias. He woke up groaning feebly, his eyes as wide as saucers and the wind obviously knocked out of him.

Talara was so excited to see him awake that she grabbed his face and kissed him hard enough to split his lip with her teeth. I have never seen him look so surprised.

"Wake up, ordanian! We are up to our eyeballs in a steaming pile!" She said, petting his hair fondly.

"*My first kiss.*" He wheezed, wiping blood off his lip.

....

It did not take long to bring Mathias up to speed, as the undead threat was pretty obvious. He was dizzy and even more pale than usual, and his mismatched eyes kept swimming in and out of focus as he tried to align himself back into the present moment. He winced painfully when we tried to move him, and cradled one arm with the other. We did not have the time to let him recover, of course, so while he was struggling to get to his feet, we tumbled around the campfire smashing into Shamblemen and roughly rousing more friends. With Mathias awake, the spell seemed to be dissolving.

Caetal awoke growling and struggling when I clambered onto him. When he recognized me, he sighed gratefully and squeezed me in such a bear hug that I could scarcely breathe. His smile fluttered warmly through me, and I suddenly didn't know what to do with my hands, so I put one on his face. Then I leapt up and stabbed a Shamblemen, pushing it backwards into the fire, which roared up lustily. That's when Caetal noticed the undead. His smile died.

Talara took particular care in waking Tarquin, who had bled out badly from a wound on his chest that wavered in and out of existence in the same way that the trees were. Although his eyes fluttered open when we shook him, he remained unresponsive, and it was obvious that he was barely conscious.

In an unusually commanding wheeze, Mathias directed me to drag Tarquin over to where he was sitting, and while Talara and Caetal did the best they could to keep the revenants off of us, I placed Tarquin with his back leaning against Mathias. The young cleric put his hand on Tarquin's neck and prepared to slip into a healing trance. But before he did, he gestured me over.

"Cuthain sent me a vision while I was dreaming," he quietly whispered. I knelt with my ear closer. He was still struggling to regain his breath from having the wind knocked out of him. *"Although it was Talara's story that awoke them, it is the iron they wield that is the source of undeath. Take the iron away from them, and they will die for good."*

"How... are you sure it was Cuthain?"

Mathias smiled serenely. *"I am sure."* He whispered. Then his voice strengthened. "He is the Lord of the Forge, after all. Iron was his first gift to the world."

"A terrible gift." I muttered under my breath. But he had closed his eyes, and he didn't seem to hear me.

I hesitated for a moment, my thoughts churning. I did not care for Cuthain, who is a god of industry and the extractive knowledge that supports it. In his name, the Erdin had cut great swaths of the forest and blighted all of Eld with their repressive dreams of civilization. However, I could not deny that what Mathias said made sense to my heart. Iron is a metal that is formed inside a Celestial on the day that they die. It is death itself; the heavy stillness of ending. And when heated and folded, hammered and compressed; violently cooled by quenching, then sharpened into blades that are meant to share that death with everyone else... there is a malevolent restlessness that haunts a piece of hammered steel that the Fae can feel even at a considerable distance. Personally, I rarely touched iron if I could avoid it; it felt like holding an angry wasp in hand that had just decided where to sting. Perhaps the humming iron and the memory of a life they had lost was enough to call a restless spirit back from the Nightlands. And since we could not un-tell Talara's story...

The next Shambleman that came towards me, instead of kicking out its knees, I waited until it swung at me with the axe it held. Ducking beneath the swinging arc, I dodged in closer and tugged the axe handle out of its boney hands. The revenant seemed for a moment to pause; staring at me with empty eye sockets, head cocked as though in confusion. Using my karam, I reached up and cut through the rotten leather straps that kept the breastplate encased to the body. More rapid cuts followed. With each piece of armor that fell to the ground, the skeleton beneath it relaxed and began to slide apart. A few slices later, and there was a pile of rusted steel and a pile of bones that lay as still as bones should lie.

I glanced over at Mathias, grinning triumphantly. But he had fallen into the trance of healing, and didn't see it.

....

Meanwhile, Talara marched over to where Drinn was sprawled on the table and dragged him onto the ground. His head lolled as though his neck was broken. Water leaked out of his mouth. He didn't wake up when he flopped onto his back on the ground, so Talara swung her foot back and kicked him hard in the ground cherries. He jolted awake, spasming and disgorging lungfuls of lake water.

"BLAUUGH ... *You could have just shaken my shoulder!*"
"There were dead people trying to eat you and you didn't wake up! Shaking you wouldn't have done it!"
"Well did you even *try?*" Drinn asked, clutching himself miserably and groaning.

Talara smiled thinly. "No. Your dream game made a big mess, fancy wizard. Wake up and help us deal with this."

"By the gods and all their cruelties; I'd forgotten how much that hurts." Drinn grunted feebly, curling up in a ball on the ground.

Talara stormed almost six paces away before whirling back around and shouting:

"AND YOU'RE WELCOME FOR SAVING YOU FROM BEING DROWNED BY THAT GODSDAMNED DREAM. YES, THANK YOU TALARA!"

Then she marched straight over to Melvin and slapped him as hard as she could across the face. He woke up, gasping and blinking painfully.

"AND *THAT'S* FOR TRUSTING THAT MAGICAL IDIOT IN THE FIRST PLACE AND RISKING ALL OUR LIVES!" She yelled, grabbing the nape of his shirt and dragging him up into a sitting position.

"DAMN YOU — I ALMOST KILLED TARQUIN WITH A STUPID CROSSBOW! HE STILL MIGHT DIE, AND IT'S ALL YOUR FAULT!"

Then she sagged against Melvin's chest and burst into tears.

....

Once Drinn recovered enough to stand up and regain his wits, the battle ended quickly. I was able to convince him of the truth about the restless iron that Mathias had told me — at least, after I demonstrated the proof. Then Drinn raised both hands above his head and spoke a word that I was careful not to listen to, for the very sound of it made the iron in my blood draw eagerly towards him like a lodestone. I almost passed out from the feeling of it, and felt the effects of that Word for hours thereafter. All the pieces of iron or steel within the reach of sound leapt towards Drinn as though yanked by invisible ropes, dragging the rapidly expiring corpses along with them. It became our job to cut through leather bindings that did not snap on their own, and quickly separate out the disenchanted bones from those that were still animated by contact with the metal.

All of us could now clearly see the midnight-red glow of that oily light which leaked out of the old weapons and armor; the glow that Mathias called deadlight. It faded as the spell faded, but I doubt any of us forgot the sight of it for the rest of our lives. Some things are not meant to be seen by mortal eyes.

For a brief minute, the clearing became blessedly silent again. The ghostly trees slowly faded from view; the last of them were chased away by the eventual light of dawn. Everyone took some time to calm their breathing and check their wounds. Not one of us had made it through the night unscathed; there were scars that a few of us still carry. Talara's shoulder bears the pale claw marks of that revenant — particularly striking against her dark red skin. My shin has a thin puckered scar that time seems to have no interest in healing.

Then the arguments began. Talara ripped into Drinn, and Drinn into her. Each blamed the other entirely for what happened, and claimed no fault for themselves. Eventually, it took Caetal bellowing at them to shut them both up.

Personally, I wandered away from the fire for most of it. Who is at "fault" and who is "not" isn't something I was raised to care about. Things happen. We do our best to react and stay alive. That is all that is real; the rest seems to be something that people debate in order to protect themselves from feeling involved. But we all made the choices that brought us to that evening.

Mostly, I thought about Syrahana-yerall-aneh. The lack of her inside of me made me feel like an abandoned nest. I had hoped that she would return to me when the dream collapsed, and I waited all that night for her to come trotting home from whatever hunt that vast realm provided for her. I could not stop probing around inside my spirit with the morbid curiosity that a child feels when tonguing the hole in their jaw where a lost tooth once was. It hurt, over and over again, to feel the loss of her. But there was a strange excitement too — that entirely new feeling of being all alone in my own head. It felt like stretching out across a bed that was so much wider than I expected it to be. It was freeing, and deeply lonely. I did not weep again, although the empty space inside me throbbed like a wound. I didn't know that love could feel like that when the loss of it was so sudden.

At last, it became apparent that the healing work that Mathias was doing would save Tarquin's life. It was well past the deep of night when Mathias and Tarquin both fell asleep together. Once they did, the rest of the camp quieted into exhausted snoring. When I finally slept, I curled up as close to Talara as she could stand. My sleep was deep and dreamless.

I was the last to wake up, and the sun had crested the horizon by the time I did. My friends shuffled around the campsite all around me, gathering up their things in awkward silence. I lay there for as long as I could and watched the sun steam moisture out of my cloak. Finally, Caetal came over and shook me gently. It was time to say goodbyes.

....

While Drinn and Caetal sorted through the old weapons and armor to see if there was anything worth keeping, (including Caetal's crossbow, which seemed to have gone missing), the rest of us took what time we had left with Melvin. We all instinctively knew it would be a while before we saw him again; I'm sure some of them wondered if we ever would. Personally, I had no doubts. There are some things you just *know*. So, I forgot to say goodbye until it was almost too late.

Talara was the first to try to make amends with Melvin, but it didn't go well. She stepped towards him where he was sitting perched on the picnic table. He leaned back away from her, frowning and touching the tender red mark on his face where she had slapped him the night before. He would not meet her eyes.

Talara cleared her throat. "I'm sorry about last night. I shouldn't have hit you. But I didn't know what else to do." Melvin snorted, and rolled his eyes.

Talara fidgeted with her hair. There was a moment of silence.

"I should have tried something else first; some other way to wake you. I just felt so mad, and… I guess I didn't know any better, it was how I was raised. My mother-"

"That wasn't your mother that hit me. That was *you*. Whatever she did to you does not excuse you doing it to me."

And he stiffly turned away, blinking his eyes and staring towards the sunrise. After a moment, Talara walked away and went down to the shore to sit on the raft alone.

....

Caetal was the next to approach Melvin, with just about as much success.

"...And now my damn crossbow is missing too! Can you believe that? I told you so, Mel — I told you all this mucking around in dreams is a bad idea. I told you."
"No, you didn't. Go away, Caetal. Go home."

Caetal paused, considering his options. He chose the wrong one.

"W-w-worst campout, ever. Right?" He chuckled, elbowing Melvin, who flinched and scooted further away.
"*Go,* Caetal. Get away from me."
"Now, hold on-"
"You should all just go, please. I'm no good to any of you like this."

Caetal shrugged his shoulders, and jammed his hands into the pockets of his cloak. Then he shrugged again, and turned slowly on his heels and strode off. On the way down to the raft, he gathered up an armload of rusty weapons and took them with him, muttering all the time about crossbows that just vanish into thin air, and the ingratitude of wizards.

....

Mathias, who had watched both of these exchanges, approached Melvin cautiously. He walked around the picnic table and waited until Melvin looked up. Then he came toward him slowly with one hand held out in front of him; a gesture that beckoned friendship, like the sort that is used for greeting a skittish cat. Melvin sighed, and allowed Mathias to take one of his hands.

They spoke quietly together. But I have good ears, so I heard everything.

Melvin began. "How did it turn out like this? I didn't mean-"
"I understand. I can feel how guilty you feel. You aren't the problem, Melvin. What worries me is how guilty Drinn does *not* feel. Please be cautious."
"I know. But I need him. It's my only way out." He gestured to his paralyzed legs, and Mathias nodded. "I have to keep trying. But not like this. I can't endanger the rest of you any more than I already have. One night of involving you guys almost got everyone killed. I couldn't live with the guilt; it's too much to risk."

"We each have the right to our own risks, Mel. Maybe they could go, and I could-"

"You would be miserable here. Drinn would make sure of that. He doesn't like people very much."

Mathias grimaced. "The feeling is mutual."

"I'll come visit when I can, alright?" Melvin patted Mathias' hand.

"Please do. I'll keep trying to think of other options for your… for you in the meantime. I have heard there are very talented healers amongst the clergy in Norlünd. Perhaps you-"

"Don't bother. And don't you dare mention Cuthain; I can feel you thinking about it. There is no place for me in your faith, Mathias. There never will be."

Mathias blushed, and dropped Melvin's hand. "You can't know that. You aren't-"

"I am. And I do. There are some things you just *know*, Mathias."

I shivered, hearing my own thoughts reflected back at me. The boys glanced at me across the space of the clearing as though catching wind of my eavesdropping. Mathias stepped away from Melvin, gathered up his backpack, (and Tarquin's, who was still too weak to carry his own pack, and Caetal's, who had just forgotten his), and shuffled down towards the raft, waddling slightly under the weight of too many backpacks. Only Tarquin and I remained with Melvin in the clearing between the barrow mounds. Tarquin had been sitting quietly with his back against the still-warm circle of campfire stones. His breath steamed in the clammy air of morning. He nodded at me, silently asking for my support to stand him up and help him over to Melvin. I did so.

Together, the two of us sat on the picnic table besides Melvin. We didn't say anything for what felt like a long time. Instead, we stared out over the lake, watching the wind wrinkle the water into ripples. We gazed at the island in the center; at the ruined tower on the island. We listened to the wind as it shushed through the wild grasses. None of us were eager to move, or to speak. Goodbye is a hard word to say out loud.

Eventually, Tarquin cleared his throat. We both turned towards him expectantly. When he spoke, his voice sounded tired. His eyes were clear and thoughtful.

"I can't help but think of Hosten, in this moment. I can feel the wind on my face, and the sun warming the cold out of me. All around us are scattered the bones of people who lived and died a long time ago, because of choices they got to make. Hosten didn't live long enough to choose to die for anything. We almost didn't live long enough either."

Tarquin glanced over, his gaze searching Melvin's face. Melvin stared out at the lake. His mouth tightened, and he said nothing. Tarquin sighed.

"All I'm trying to say is be careful. We'll miss you, Melvin. Remember: no more dead kids, okay? Stay alive."

"I don't think we *are* children anymore." Melvin replied quietly.

Tarquin sighed again, looking down at his hands. His own dried blood coated the edges of his fingernails.

"You're probably right. I suppose there is a moment when childhood ends. But I'm not sure I'll know for sure when-"

"Like this. It ends in moments like this, when we accidently almost get our friends killed." Melvin patted Tarquin's hand. "It doesn't end that way for everyone, but this is how it ends for us."

Tarquin slowly nodded, no doubt remembering how terrible he had felt that night on the raft when he realized he might accidentally get his friends killed trying to rescue Shamsala. I sat perfectly still beside them, barely daring to breathe. I thought of my own childhood, and realized I had never thought of myself as a child, although I must have once, and must have once been.

"Some things you just know." I whispered aloud. Tarquin glanced at me, and squeezed my hand. There were tears in his eyes.

"I love you guys. I really do. I don't know how else to say that. I'll miss you, Melvin. I'll miss *this*: the Company of Six. All of us together."

But what I think he meant he would miss is our childhood. I didn't ask him to clarify. I guess I didn't need to.

"I love you too." I murmured, so quietly. But they heard. Melvin nodded, and blinked rapidly. He wiped his sleeve across his eyes.

"You guys should go. The others are waiting for you. Tell them goodbye for me, okay?"

"Alright." Tarquin said, trying to stand up. I helped him, slinging his arm over my shoulder to support him.

"Except Caetal," Melvin continued, wiping his eyes again and grinning. "Tell him I said to eat a big, juicy fart pie. Remember to tell him I said it was a juicy one too; not a dry pie."

I grimaced, imagining what a fart pie might taste like. Tarquin chuckled.

"I'll make sure to tell him. Good luck with your training."

Then I draped Tarquin's arm across my shoulders, and walked him slowly down to the raft.

I got him onboard, and Caetal made ready to cast us off from the dock. Then I remembered what I had almost forgotten to do, asked my friends to wait a few more minutes, and scampered back up the hillside. Along the way, I foraged around for a few handfuls of wild herbs and flowers near the campsite. In doing so, I managed to overhear Drinn returning to where Melvin still sat on the picnic table, and the brief conversation they had. I remained quiet, out of sight behind a barrow mound, so that I could hear them talk. Most humans think eavesdropping is rude. But animals know that carefully listening to the world around you is the only way to survive long enough to learn something.

....

"So: that went well!" Drinn said. "I like your friends — especially Talara, she has a lot of pluck."

I heard a silky shuffling sound that I can assume was him rubbing his hands together. I thought at first that he was being sarcastic, (I am only now learning about sarcasm, and I'm still not very good at it), but his voice sounded sincere. There was a pause from Melvin.

"Drinn, how did that *possibly* go well? We almost got those friends you apparently like so much killed. I'd say that went very poorly."

"Nonsense! Perhaps their part of it went poorly, but you and I succeeded spectacularly."

Melvin paused. I watched a butterfly try to land on the bouquet of flowers in my hand. It was a type of butterfly I had never seen before: wings that were an almost translucent blue, with little brown spots. Blue fur or feather coloration is very rare for animals or insects to have. I became so absorbed in the butterfly that I almost missed the rest of the conversation entirely.

"...We did?"

"Of course! You turned a campfire into a burning tornado by using the Word for *change*: very clever! I might not have even thought of that myself! Your longing to know the True Name for wind was expressed in a creative way that worked just as you intended it to. I would call that a success worthy of my apprentice."

"Thank you, Kinnari." Melvin said, sounding relieved.

Crouched behind the barrow mound in a patch of eldic peppermint, I felt a wave of pity for Melvin. You could hear in his voice how worn out he was — guilt is the heaviest burden I know of. I'm sure the praise he had just received felt like a glass of cold water to a thirsty throat.

"As for me, my success was even more noteworthy," Drinn continued, "for three reasons. The first is the accidental gift that Talara gave us. That story was surely as close to the true history of what happened at this lake as anyone knows. Years of fruitlessly searching for that information on my own were just paid off by a young bard who didn't know better. That story was as rare as silk, and she just handed it over for free!"

Melvin grunted, but didn't reply.

"The second success was potentially even more valuable. While you children were playing, I rowed as quickly as I could out to your Indelible Tower. And I went *inside*, Melvin! I saw the interior of the tower, as it surely was when it still stood!"

"How is that possible? I thought you were drowning in the lake."

"Well... a bit of both, actually. I saw part of the tower interior before water flooded out of the upper level and swept me off the island. Then I ran to the boat, and almost made it back to shore before she got me."

"So, even in Dream, the dead mage haunts Drôleduyan?"

"Apparently so. Mathias must have allowed her in there. True stories are powerful conduits for energy. Talara's story was the channel she needed to flow through."

The magus and his apprentice were quiet for long enough that I had to shift the posture of my crouch to take pressure off my knees. Then Melvin spoke up again.

"You said three successes. What was the third?"

"Ah yes. The third was the dream itself. Mathias created an unusually vivid landscape. I was surprised, in truth; I took him for being a rather bland and uncreative child."

"He is neither." Melvin said, with some heat in his voice.

"Well, either way, that dream he created was something I have only heard of, and never seen before — one that is so entangled with reality that it punches holes through both. I was particularly struck by the lasting presence of those dream trees in our world. And the implications of that are enormous, Melvin: do you understand? A dream like that could follow the Wayward Road all the way to where it begins. Perhaps even further. If we-"

....

I wish I could have listened to them a while longer but, unfortunately, the blue butterfly chose that moment to land on the tip of my nose with its tickly little feet. I sneezed. And so, of course, I quickly stood up and walked around the barrow mound and into sight. Drinn frowned, nodded politely, then made himself scarce.

Melvin stared at me uncomfortably as I walked up to where he was sitting. I suddenly felt quite shy, and realized that this was the first time we had ever been alone together. Not knowing what else to do, I thrust the bundle of herbs and flowers I had picked for him into his hands.

"Here: peppermint, arnica and lavender. I picked them. They're for you."

"Uh... thanks." He held the bouquet of flowers as gingerly as though it was a dead fish. Both of us stared at the flowers intently, as an awkward pause bloomed.

"So, um... why did you pick me flowers? I thought you guys had left already."

"Oh! Right, sorry: you should grind the mint and flowers into a paste, and smear it on your face where Talara slapped you. It will reduce the swelling."

"Ah. I'm not going to bother with that. The swelling will be gone soon. Thanks anyway."

He set the flower bundle down next to him. I didn't know what to do with my hands, so I clasped them together in front of me. He cleared his throat.

"You should probably go back to the raft. They're waiting for you."

"...I suppose so."

I sighed, and turned away. Sometimes things don't turn out at all how we imagined them.

....

I had walked halfway around the barrow mound when I heard Melvin calling me back. I returned to the table where he was sitting. He held the bouquet of flowers, and had clumsily started tearing them apart, trying to mash them together in his hand. He looked up at me with his cheeks faintly blushing.

"I changed my mind. Can you help me with this?"
"I'd be glad to."

I began to crush the flowers up in my hand, rolling them against my palm and mashing them together with twisting motions. Melvin watched in silence, until I blurted out:
"I am worried that Syrahana-yerall-aneh is gone. Since last night, I cannot feel her at all inside me anymore."
"The fox?"
"Yes. I fear she was lost in Mathias' dream. Drinn warned us that animals should not go into Dream if we wish to see them again. ...What if she-"
"I'll look for her. I promise." Melvin squeezed my shoulder. "I bet a fox could last a long time in Dream. Remember, she doesn't have to eat or sleep in there. All she has to do is hide and survive."

I slowly nodded, but couldn't reply; the fear of never feeling her soul curled up around mine again was unbearable. Yet, Melvin's words were a great comfort to me. I nodded again, mashing the flowers and mint into a poultice between two rocks.

"Yes. *Please look for her.*" I managed, before my voice cracked.
"I promise I will. Every night."

A few minutes later, I finished smearing the brownish poultice onto the bruised part of his face. He stared at me the whole time I was applying it, searching with his eyes for something in mine. I'm not sure what he found, but as I tenderly applied the last of the poultice, I saw that he had begun to cry. I gathered him into my arms and hugged him while he sobbed against my shoulder more quietly than I have ever heard anyone cry before. I would not have known he was crying at all, except for the way his shoulders shook.

"I'm sorry Rahyn — I'm so sorry. It's my fault that the fox is gone. All of it is my fault." He mumbled into my shoulder, shuddering with grief. His body felt thin under Drinn's heavy blue coat. I patted his back, and made noises in my throat like the sound that a treeweet makes to calm itself when it is frightened. It seemed to help, for he soon quieted.

Finally, I kissed his forehead, which felt warm and sweaty from crying, and extracted myself from our embrace. He snuffled a bit, and looked down at his hands.

"It feels like everything good is ending." He whispered.

A soft breeze blew across the lake. It carried with it the smells of spring — life waking up again from a long sleep; smells that not even the lifeless waters of Drôleduyan could diminish. The breeze was cooling on Melvin's hot cheeks, and he closed his eyes and breathed it in deeply.

"What seems like the ending is often just the beginning." I replied, not knowing what else there was left to say that mattered.

Then I turned and walked downhill and away from him through the mint and blooming lavender, towards the raft where the other members of the Company of Six were waiting for me.

....

EPILOGUE
A Burning Heart

The Derŭweid of Eld stood on an outcropping of rock that protruded from the mouth of a low tunnel and gazed down from a great height upon the hidden heart of the Terrasque. As they glared at the heart, they counted passing seconds. They did this by reciting the names of sixty trees at a steady pace. Every minute, they scratched another line with chalk onto the piece of slate they held in their hands.

"Ash... Rowen... Larch... Poplar... Pine..."
Another minute, another scratch of the chalk.

They had never ventured closer to that awful heart than the high-above ledge; rarely had they beheld the heart at all but to satisfy the once-yearly duty of inherited protocol, for it was a physically and emotionally daunting experience. The air in the enormous cavern that surrounded the heart shimmered with heat, and was so suffused by the stench of scorched iron that every breath felt like gulping bloody vapor.

....

Once a year, on the first day of Floodfollow, the derŭweid returned to this cavern to repeat the same ritual. The heart of the Terrasque had beat once an hour for the entirety of recorded time. The slow regularity of this heartbeat may as well have been the gruesome clock of civilization: so long as it remained steady, it meant that half a world away, the Terrasque still slept in its lair beneath the mountains. The lives of everyone depended on that sleep remaining unbroken.

But in all the history of humanity, from the rise of the Ten Nations to the modern day, the creature had never awoken. The knowledge that it existed at all had faded long ago into myth. Only the current Derŭweid of Eld, and those that had come before, knew for certain that it still lived. That they had long ago discovered the location of the heart was the greatest secret of their order. For thousands of years, a derŭweid had come here once every year to count all the passing seconds that filled up the hour between two heartbeats. To observe, and to be reassured by, the predictable cadence of the monster's heart.

"Willow... Alder... Birch... Chestnut... Oak..." The derŭweid murmured, scratching another chalk line.

....

The heart of the Terrasque was as large as a leviathan. It was iron ore spanned by branching arteries of fire. Those fiery stria lit the room redly; a dim light that bruised the darkness of the cavern rather than banishing it. Melting magma and flowing water had warped the cavernous cocoon that surrounded the heart over countless years into undulations of mounds bisected by channels. From above, the cavern floor resembled a gray skin cavity stretched over ribs, or the tight coiling of viscera that the throb of firelit veins shuddered the sight of into something flexing and fleshy.

All around the vast cavity there grew an inward-reaching thicket of stalactites and stalagmites; they pierced the heart in many places like stone thorns the size of giant redwoods, and had grown in such proliferation around and below the living organ that they had lifted it entirely off the cave floor. Now it hung suspended at the center of them, looking at once like something that had either been repeatedly stabbed, or some fat spider that dwelt in waiting at the center of a radial stone web.

"Impossible stalactites growing sideways out of the wall, and dead iron that lives forever. Why not?" The derŭweid thickly muttered and spat. *"Even the Green Laws have no sway over the Monster's Heart."*

There that heart sat, glistening wetly: the only living iron in all of creation.

....

The derŭweid shifted their weight from foot to foot and gritted their teeth against the malevolent aura of the heart. It radiated a rage that was prehistoric: undiminished by time, as compelling as magnetism.

It would not take long for us to imagine that no other feeling existed. The derŭweid mused to themself. *We could wrap ourselves in the heat of this rage and forget everything else. We wonder how many others have found this heart by accident, and dashed themselves to death against it in an anger more powerful than lust?* The derŭweid shivered and hugged themself, desperately digging through their memories for anything green. A picture of the first time they had climbed to the highest branches of a fortress oak that grew near their family home came to mind, and they clung to the dizzying height of that memory as gratefully as a child might cling to their mother's skirts during a lightning storm.

"*Hazel... Hawthorne... Aspen... Juniper... Beech. No, wait: did we say that one already? Birch. It was Birch. Damn, it doesn't matter. A curse on this stupidly complex counting!*"

They tipped their head back, tugging at their long braid in frustration.

We drifted off-time for a moment. Can't do that again. We'll just mark it down as one minute.

Frustrated, the derŭweid glanced at their slate board and sighed. The caustic air degenerated that sigh into a cough, and they wiped their arm across their mouth in disgust. Their spit tasted like metal.

This anger isn't real, and it isn't ours. It's the godsdamned heart. Can't let it get to us; only twelve more minutes to go.

"*One potato, two potatoes, three potatoes, four.*" They muttered.

Fifty-six potatoes later, they made another mark on the slate.

....

Before a storm breaks, the air pressure changes. Some describe it as an electrical feeling; some just feel the warm stillness descending and know instinctively that the thunder is right behind it. The slow beat of the Terrasque's heart was just like that. The derŭweid always *felt* it happen before they actually heard it, because the air in the cave would wobble like a drunkard taking a steadying step. Sudden static would raise the hairs on their arms. A warm pressure that could be felt in their eardrums would roll outwards from the heart as ventricles clenched and valves opened. The heart would contract as slowly as a stretching cat while the air in the chamber roiled and compressed. Then sound would follow it: a booming sluice of resonance so wet and deep that the soles of the feet and sinuses tingled. Then, the heart would relax once again. The air in the cave would settle into stuffy acrid stillness, and the ritual of counting would begin or end there.

Normally.

But on that day, as the second heartbeat finally began, there was another sound that proceeded it — a drizzle of sizzling patter that the derŭweid had never heard before. In fact, to the best of their knowledge, no derŭweid had *ever* heard it before in thousands of years of counting heartbeats.

The pressure in the room dropped as the heart began to contract. The sizzling sound became more pronounced, and the derŭweid leaned out over the edge of the ledge as a shiver of static passed through them, straining to see the details of the heart. But at this distance, nothing seemed out of the ordinary. Except—

Except the count was off. The heart beat early. The derŭweid scanned the slate board with their eyes; first carefully, then frantically, as desperate words like *impossible* scattered across their thoughts like clods of hurled earth. *Fifty-seven minutes between heartbeats. Fifty-eight if we're being generous about the few moments we stopped counting.* The sweat dripping between the curves of their chest felt as filmy as lye rubbed across dry skin. *No way that was sixty.* The sizzling patter was easier to hear now as the throb of the heartbeat faded away. The air sighed, and the heat shimmered, and the spattering sound was all that could be heard now, echoing hollowly in that vast stone chamber like rain striking a barrel.

We need to see what is causing that sound. We must.

Carefully, the derŭweid squatted, swung both legs over the edge of the ledge, and began to descend down the cave wall.

....

Up close, the heart looked different. *Older* and *larger* were obvious descriptions. As was *fundamentally terrifying*, the way that something can only truly terrify when the mind knows what the eyes are looking at, and cannot understand how that thing can exist at all.

The metal was *alive* in every way that metal could not be. It shivered and flexed in tiny ripples like the flank of a horse that a horsefly is tormenting. The tiny veins that covered it were as thick as human arms and burned steadily with a flame that was *meaty* in a way that fire should never be. From up close, the stalagmites and stalactites that pierced it in a hundred places no longer looked like they had grown into it, but rather that they had sprouted out from it; primordial feeding tubes that were latched securely onto the walls of the cave like suckling lips.

Standing beneath it, the heat was brutal. Yet the fire that burned the hotter was that which could be felt within. The derŭweid writhed in the scalding grip of unnatural rage, shaking in spasms of such tortures that only the mind can devise. Through the red haze that narrowed their vision into darkening tunnels, the derŭweid cast their gaze frantically across the ground for the origin of the dripping noise. They found it.

Droplets of something molten that glowed like lava and scalded like acid were dripping out of one of the enormous valves of the heart. The ground hissed and crackled. Whisps of acrid smoke began to drift up into the chamber.

"Oh, *fuck*." The derŭweid murmured, hugging themself. "That can't be good."

Acknowledgements

Though he likely may never read this book all the way through, let alone the acknowledgements section here at the very end, I would like to thank Jeff Lane for teaching me D&D when we were in 6th grade, and creating the original stories that these characters found themselves the main characters of. Melvin and Rahyn were his creations, and he was my companion in story and personality development for the Company of Six for almost thirty years. Much of the dynamics between the characters are owed to the dynamics we enjoyed and endured in our own friendship.

For Caetal and Talara I thank Shai Ben-Ari, who put them onto character sheets and then moved to Israel and left them for Jeff and I to raise. Further acknowledgement for character interactions go to Jason Hemp, Max Livingstone and Dave Waugh, who joined us in playing some of those long-ago adventures.

So much gratitude to Luke Eidenschink, (the enormously talented pen n' ink artist that did the chapter artwork), to Hiru Walisadeera for the epic map, Kurt Matson for character and cover art design and AJ Kyle Valdueza for the final cover art!

Additional well-earned thanks to David Diethelm at Eco-Justice Press | Goblin Press, who battled by my side for months to comb through and correct an outrageous series of technical glitches and ghosts in the machine that delayed the publication of this book for more than a year. I have learned so many lessons from writing this book, and one of them is to never write a book on an ancient laptop running Windows 97 in the year 2024.

I'd like to thank a few folks who were beta readers of the various draft incarnations for the stories that became this book: Laura Lynch-Miller, who tirelessly edited pages with a mother's thoughtful care. My father, David Peyerwold, who doesn't ever read fantasy but made a kindly exception to help me edit this one. Nokomis "Knockers" Baze, who declared herself the head of the Eld Fan Club and for whom a character is named.

Jen "Hyacinth" Tang was extremely supportive throughout years of draft revisions. Casey Jackson, who also shared in the old adventures and gave me excellent feedback on plot structure. Mercel "Puck" Chambers, who has been a grand story companion and once lovingly stranded me at a remote motel in Phoenix for five days to force me to get some damn writing done. Katrina Vahedi took time out of her busy cheese empire to help me strengthen the voices of my female characters.

Thanks to Li LeBlanc for some truly enlightening workshopping sessions.

Thanks to Thea Abbatoy, who was my final reader of the book, and provided kindly notes and dignity-saving copy edits just before publication. Astrid Lindstrom, who coached me through the important concept that yes: I really did need a cohesive plot! Jeff Behrends, Noah McLain and Azoulas Yurashunas have been — and continue to be — excellent world-building muses. Alyssa Myers did technical edits for the majority of the book — enough to truly help me understand how careless my use of commas has always been. For all the misplaced commas that remain, please forgive me. At this point in time, I'm just going to claim it's a style choice.

Also, thanks should go to my housemates, past and present: Chris Patterson, Alden Packard, Keenan Varley and Theresa "Gopher" Swanson for putting up with rambling narrative descriptions, pen n' ink drawings all over the wall, and those weird Eld coffee cups I keep creating.

To those folks who read parts of this book while it was in rough draft and offered kindly critique or supportive enthusiasm, and whose names have been forgotten here: either forgive me, or text me and complain about it. You will make it into the next book, I promise!

Appendices
Eld Map: Location Meaning

Aldr: An ancient place / a lifetime old

Alitururaii: A ruin that flooding has claimed

Amain: Easy taking / conquest

Améan Ocean: Joy in chaos

Ameru: Whale

Arbino Loc: Tumbling lake

Atlaga: To attack from a ship

Bec-Dorni: Streams-like-fingers

Bjalkr-Bec: Beam-over-stream (a bridge)

Brandr: Rocky spur

Bren: To burn / land of silver fir

Bruar: Bride

Búr: Little pig shed

Darasu: To be pushed away

Dárû: Fuel-trees / land of dark pines

Dekainak: House of Dekai

Drôle: Troll (a place of Trolls)

Dunmarsh: Sinking water

Ea: The house of water

Elva-Eru: River path

Elva-Ghora: A river of mountains

Elvaurhu: The flowing road

Embarni: To impregnate a woman

Erdo-Usk: Chief seat of the Erdin

Exerbec: Thousand Streams

Fahru Dornen: Father's hand

Feigr: Doomed

Forrad: Management / law of rule

Frami: Advancement / luck / fame

Fyriheimr: House of drifting spirits

Fýrii: Drifting Fae-fire / willow-o-whisp

Gamáru: To finish / to end

Gelaghora: Mountain kings

Ghent: Victory of fire / victory by fire

Hälling: To dance

Hälling Ghora: Dancing mountains

Haust: To pull harvest

Havoce-Baya: Ocean-bay

Hiraeth: Homesickness for a home that never was, or that you cannot return to

Holm: Flat fertile valley that was once a lake

Hösta Urhu: Way port / flowing road

Hraeddr: Afraid / to cause fear

Huerfa: To go missing; to disappear

Hurasu: Gold / to mine for gold

Hvóll: Round hill

Hylli: Allegiance of loyalty

<u>Illska</u>: Cruelty

<u>Illsbaya</u>: Cruel bay / bad landing

<u>Imbaru</u>: Fog

<u>Immeru</u>: Sheep

<u>Karmu</u>: Wasteland

<u>Kishar</u>: Foremost of the firm lands

<u>Kräke</u>: Crow

<u>Lamishii</u>: Island-like-breast

<u>Loc Enum</u>: Lake of the eye

<u>Loc Erú</u>: Copper lake

<u>Loc Hura</u>: Lake of gold

<u>Loc Illi</u>: Dark lake

<u>Loc Luma</u>: Lake of feathers

<u>Loc Tara</u>: Lake of tears

<u>Loc Tor</u>: Strong lake

<u>Malku</u>: Prince / counselor

<u>Mávar</u>: Sea birds

<u>Mclrgraes</u>: Dune grasses

<u>Menntr</u>: Accomplished, well bred

<u>Meru</u>: A rare fish

<u>Mordu</u>: Sun baked / dried up

<u>Morran Baya</u>: Sunrise bay

<u>Myrk-Faelin</u>: Afraid of old mysteries hidden in the dark

<u>Nanshe</u>: Goddess of fish

<u>Naudigr</u>: Against one's will

<u>Norlünd</u>: North-land

Ofan: Above

Ot-Berina: Head of virtue / virtuous

Peliana: House of Pelos (the North Wind)

Portuan: Sea-throne

Raatu-Dorni: Grasping fingers

Ryma: To stash / to stow away

Saoirse: To live free

Scatrishii: Scattered islands

Shoals: Shallow water (dangerous sailing)

Sildur: Stone bridge

Skati: Leader / ruler

Souan-Ghora: Mountain of tombs

Stadr: Abode, dwelling place

Strönd: Shoreline (good landing)

Tapahu-Ghora: Pouring mountain

Tashka: Treasure worth guarding

Thalasea: Alter-house of Thalasa

Thern: Legendary beast

Tor: Stronghold

Trask: Intestines

Trask Mar: Mouth that empties intestines

Uisce: Wave

Ula: Intimidating height

Ulfaang: Deep winter waves

Ummu-Baya: Mother-bay

Una: Queen

Ura: Heap of hill stones

Verdvar: To be on one's guard

Wolden: Hollow hill country

Xörghora: Mountain that eats

Xörn: A dead place / an unwinnable game

Xör Uru: Hungry depth

Zikia: Life where earth and water meet

Naughty words

(Do not read this list if the use of colorful language offends you)

Ai kae = eat shit
Bukioo = rectum
Kae = shit
Kefe = fuck
Moros = moron
Muli = butt
Puckerditch = butt crack
Quean = disreputable prostitute. Apparently, there are some linguists who insist that the title of queen actually basically means prostitute for the entire country. But that is quite rude, so I hope they are wrong.
Skabde = miserable
Swyve = to copulate with
Valea = stupid

Calendar of Eld

The Ramini Calendar has been broadly adopted across most cultures, as it has been determined to be beneficial to trade and commerce to standardize such things as days of the week and months. Before this calendar, each culture had come up with wildly varying versions of recording the passage of time. The days of the week are a motley of adopted contributions from various cultures; the tristurn were named after the climate patterns in the lands the Ramini once occupied.

Days of the week

Andír Toil Tend Festus Fastus Harriday Merriday Still

A week is called a 'turn' because of the phases of the moon. There are eight days in a week, three weeks in a "tristurn" (meaning *three-turn*) forming the twenty-four days of the Homm standard month, and thirteen tristurn in a year.

The names of the tristurn are as follows:

Tristurn (Months) of Homm

SPRING	SUMMER	AUTUMN	WINTER
Mantling	Tempest	Zephyrlûn	Frostgate
Newgreen	Midsummer	Gladharvest	Winternöcht
Floodfollow	Calefacht	Gloaming	Portaldark
			Charn

JORDAN MACKAY lives in a forest in Oregon, keeping good company with a whole horde of magnificent Goblins. This book took far too long to write, because he struggles with managing his limited free time and taming the wild, yowling kitten of his attention span.

Children of Eld is his first novel, and is intended to be the opening book of the *Heart of Eld* series. If you enjoyed this book, please feel free to reach out with encouragement or suggestions!

headlesstower@hotmail.com

9 781945 432644